EX LIBRIS

_____

_____

_____

Romance Treasury

THE ROMANCE TREASURY
ASSOCIATION

NEW YORK · TORONTO · LONDON

These stories were originally published as follows:

TO JOURNEY TOGETHER
Copyright © 1970, 1956 by Mary Burchell
First published in London by Mills & Boon Limited in 1956

I AND MY HEART
Copyright © 1970, 1967 by Joyce Dingwell
First published in London by Mills & Boon Limited in 1967

WINDY NIGHT, RAINY MORROW
Copyright © 1972 by Ivy Ferrari.
First published in London by Mills & Boon Limited in 1972

ROMANCE TREASURY is published by
The Romance Treasury Association, Stratford, Ontario, Canada.

Editorial Board: A. W. Boon, Judith Burgess, Ruth Palmour and Janet Humphreys

Dust Jacket Art by Don Besco
Story Illustrations by Muriel Wood
Book Design by Harold Boyd
Printed by Richardson, Bond & Wright Ltd., Owen Sound, Ont.

ISBN 0-919860-15-X

Printed in Canada

CONTENTS

TO JOURNEY TOGETHER

To Journey Together

Mary Burchell

Austria — Italy — Switzerland: Elinor had typed these exciting names many times in her work at the travel agency. Never had she expected to see any of them.

To be chosen as secretary-companion to Sir Daniel and Lady Connelton on a business and holiday trip filled her with great excitement, especially when she learned that the Connelton's nephew, Kenneth Brownlow, was also going.

Her happiness was somewhat dampened, however, when she inadvertently overheard a conversation between Lady Connelton and Kenneth. So much so, that when she met him later she introduced herself as: "the nice, quiet little girl who is going to bore you for the next couple of months!"

CHAPTER ONE

GLADYS SMITH, who was certainly the prettiest and most enterprising of the half-dozen girls in the office of Connelton Tours Limited, twiddled the fingers of her left hand and complacently watched the light glinting on the diamond that had so recently been placed there.

"And to think," she remarked to her admiring colleagues, "that none of it would ever have happened if I hadn't altered my name just a little and gone on that cruise!"

"Oh, I don't know that I'd say *that*," objected Sally Pascoe, the senior shorthand-typist, who preferred to be called a secretary. "I believe your fate will find you wherever you are."

"Mine wouldn't have found me in an English seaside resort," retorted Miss Smith, which was rather unkind of her and showed that she was getting a bit above herself in the excitement of her engagement, because everyone knew that Sally Pascoe went every year to Clacton for her holiday and, as a matter of fact, appeared to have a wonderful time there.

"There's quite as much drama and romance in a seaside town as on a boat," Miss Pascoe asserted, bridling slightly. "And I'm sure there are ten engagements made on land for every one at sea."

No one felt able to dispute these arbitrary statistics, so there was a short silence, until Elinor Shearn said tactfully, "I think Gladys's engagement is thrilling wherever it started. I'd never have had the nerve to do what she did, but it certainly seems to have turned out well."

Gladys Smith laughed, her usual good-humor completely restored, because she thought it really *had* been rather clever of her to book one of the firm's cruises for herself, in the name of Miss G. Dereham-Smith. And, if she had recklessly spent the whole of her Aunt Miriam's small legacy in fitting herself out lavishly for the occasion, who could now say that the extravagance had not been justified, since on that cruise she had met the rich and eligible Bernard Holman, to whom she was now engaged?

"It will be your turn next," she said kindly to Elinor, though without conviction, and then turned back to her work. For such a remark was merely a piece of good nature and not a statement of opinion when made to anyone as quiet and self-effacing as Elinor Shearn. She was a nice kid, Gladys Smith considered, with her big gray eyes and that pretty, shy smile, but she definitely lacked what Gladys characterized to herself as "oomph."

In this opinion Elinor would without rancor have concurred. She knew that if—inconceivably—she had ever brought herself to go off on a cruise like Gladys, no brilliant Bernard Holman would have crossed her path. Or, even if he had, she would have been too shy and uncertain to have known what to make of him.

Not that she was without her dreams. Sometimes when she typed what were known as the "itinerary sheets" of clients who were to spend their holidays in magical-sounding places, she thought she could visualize the scenes down to their smallest detail: the sparkle of sunlight on the snow in winter sports centers, the heart-searching blue of Mediterranean waters, the fairy-tale quality of ruined castles clinging to cliffs above the Rhine. She could almost see herself there.

But there was never anyone else there with her. Her imagination stopped short, or else her shyness and inexperience curbed it, at the idea of peopling the scene with any disturbing, unpredictable strangers.

Product, as she was, of a large, uninhibited, cheerful family, Elinor was curiously quiet and withdrawn in temperament. She loved her family and was exceedingly happy at home, but even there she preferred the role of observer, adviser and—on occasion—comforter, rather than that of the central figure in any situation.

Occasionally this worried her busy, but loving and observant mother, who said once to her husband, "I don't know quite what to do about Elinor."

"What should you do about her?" inquired Elinor's father with cheerful obtuseness. "She isn't sickening for something, is she?" He looked at his wife blankly.

"No, of course not. I should know what to do if she were. But she's so quiet and shy, and sometimes I think—"

"A good thing too," Mr. Shearn interrupted with emphasis. "If they were all like Deborah—" Deborah being his lastborn and of an energy, self-confidence and loquacity proper to her twelve years—"this place would be a madhouse."

"Yes, yes," agreed his wife soothingly, aware that Deborah was passing through a stage very hard to defend in one sentence. "But Elinor is twenty-one, you know. Three years older than Anne, who is already enjoying quite a lot of social life. Elinor should be going out to dances and tennis parties, and bringing home her boy friends."

Mr. Shearn thought otherwise, however.

"Haven't we enough with our own brood?" he wanted to know. "Not to mention that superior and disagreeable young woman Edward brought home the other evening. If he had no more sense at twenty-three than to pick her for a friend, I am thankful Elinor is twenty-one and content to stay at home. What induced him to bring the girl here anyway?"

"I suggested that he should."

"*You* did? Was that necessary?"

"Yes, dear, of course," Mrs. Shearn said. "It was only in his home circle that he was likely to see how unreal and pretentious she was. He thought her glamorous and knowledgeable outside, but he didn't really like the way she snubbed Elinor, you know, nor the way she looked at you when you asked if *Murder in the Cathedral* was a thriller."

"Dear me, did she 'look at me'?" Mr. Shearn showed mild interest. "Isn't it a thriller, then?"

"No. But that doesn't matter. We were talking about Elinor. I wish the child were not so shy."

"Nonsense. Be thankful she has good manners and a proper regard for other people's likes and dislikes. None of your other children suffers from shyness, anyway."

"That's true," murmured Mrs. Shearn, and wisely let

the subject lapse. For she knew that when fathers begin to refer to their offspring as "your children" it is best to retreat for the moment.

It was certainly true that none of the other young Shearns was shy. Edward might make an occasional error of judgment in his girl friends, but he was a pleasant, sensible, likable fellow, who was already doing well in one of the City banks.

Next to him in family order came Elinor, and then the eighteen-year-old Anne, who, after a long and insufferable period of being stagestruck, had now developed into a remarkably efficient assistant in the model department of a West End store.

Between Anne and the vociferous Deborah, who brought up the tail of the family, came Henry—regarded variously as a genius or a pest, according to the success or failure of the scientific experiments to which he was much addicted.

He had already blown the scullery window into the next-door garden (along with most of his own eyebrows) on one never-to-be-forgotten Saturday afternoon. But, on the other hand, he was undoubtedly the star of the school laboratory, and, as everyone knows, one cannot have a genius in one's midst without sacrificing some minor conveniences of living.

In these typical British-family surroundings Elinor played a quiet but vital role. To her went Edward for sympathy and understanding in his affairs of the heart, Anne for assistance in altering the occasional model she was able to buy from stock, Henry for consolation when great plans foundered on cruelly minor details, and Deborah for almost anything from help with irregular French verbs to a kindly ear into which to pour eloquent complaints about the extraordinary lack of understanding to be found in all teachers, but particularly in Deborah's math teacher of the moment.

"You always have *time* for people," Deborah said, having unburdened herself of a long and boring tale about herself and Miss Cox and square roots, on the evening after Gladys Smith's engagement announcement.

"Well, I remember I used to feel badly about square

roots sometimes," Elinor replied kindly, as she tacked lace on the hem of a petticoat, ready for applique work.

"That's awfully pretty." Deborah leaned over and breathed down the back of her sister's neck. "Is it for you or Anne?"

"For me, I think. But Anne did admire it—and I haven't got anything for her birthday yet, of course."

"You keep it for yourself," Deborah advised. "Anne's got plenty of glamorous undies and you haven't. Why, the only glamorous *dress* you have is that smoky-blue, pleated chiffon thing. You could wear that petticoat under that. It'd look awfully glamorous."

"I'll see," said Elinor, who knew from maddening repetition that glamorous was the word of the moment in Deborah's class. "I haven't really any special occasion for wearing either."

"You never know. Things *happen*," Deborah declared. "And then you want to look glamorous."

Elinor laughed. But then she sighed a little, because in her heart she thought that perhaps she was not the kind of person to whom things happened.

When she thought how pleasant it was sitting by the fire sewing, however, she felt ungrateful. And presently Anne came in and gave a most entertaining account of the film she had just seen, and a lively description of what had happened at her work that day.

"By the way—" she turned to Elinor—"your boss's wife came in for a couple of dresses. She's pretty nice, isn't she?"

"I didn't know Mr. Prynne was married," exclaimed Elinor, reflecting that the general manager looked a dried-up, confirmed bachelor, if ever there was one.

"I don't mean *his* wife—if he has one. I mean Lady Connelton," Anne explained. "She's Sir Daniel's wife, isn't she?"

"Oh—of course. I hadn't thought of him. We hardly ever see him, you know. He's been ill for ages, but I believe he is getting better now."

"Yes, he is." Anne seemed well informed. "He's reached the recuperation stage, Lady Connelton said, and they're going away to Europe. What fun! And it's still almost the middle of winter!" And she sighed enviously.

"I don't expect they'll be having fun, exactly." Elinor said. "He has been very ill indeed." But she decided that she must ask Miss Pascoe in the morning if she knew where Sir Daniel and Lady Connelton were going for the recuperation trip.

The following morning, however, she was late for the office, having been delayed by fog, and as soon as she arrived Miss Pascoe said rather accusingly, "You'd better hurry. Mr. Prynne wants to see you."

"Mr. Prynne!" Elinor was startled. Mr. Prynne hardly ever dealt personally with the junior members of the staff, preferring to do so by remote control, through Miss Pascoe. "Because I'm late, do you mean?"

"No. Though I don't expect he'll be too pleased about that," added Miss Pascoe, on principle.

Elinor went along to Mr. Prynne's office with considerable inner trepidation. She could not recall any real error in her recent work, but he might, of course, just have discovered something. Nervously she tapped on the glass panel marked "Private," and, in answer to Mr. Prynne's sharp, "Come in," entered.

An unexpectedly agreeable-looking Mr. Prynne looked up and said, "Come and sit down, Miss Shearn. I have something I want to discuss with you."

Secretly much astonished at being elevated to discussion level with Mr. Prynne, Elinor sat down and looked politely attentive.

"As you know—" Mr. Prynne leaned back in his chair and regarded Elinor with the slightly benign air he usually reserved for very important clients—"Sir Daniel has been ill for some time, and, although I am happy to say he has now largely recovered, his doctor has advised a long holiday abroad. So he and Lady Connelton propose to go first to Austria and then, a little later in the year, on to Italy."

He paused, while Elinor continued to look attentive and secretly wondered what all this had to do with her.

"While he is abroad Sir Daniel will be doing a certain amount of work, partly in connection with an amalgamation which—Well, well—" Mr. Prynne cleared his throat and seemed to think he had almost committed an indiscretion—"you will hear about that later. He will also take the opportunity of making some of those personal contacts by which, as you know, we set so much store." Mr. Prynne was now speaking rather as though he were dictating a brochure. "Unfortunately his personal secretary has had to leave suddenly, owing to family trouble, and the office has been asked to supply someone in her place. I have decided, Miss Shearn, that you would be the right person."

"*I*, Mr. Prynne?" Elinor looked—indeed felt—as though something had hit her. "But why me? Almost any of the others—" she began agitatedly. But Mr. Prynne interrupted her firmly.

"I have considered the matter very carefully. You are efficient in your work and very conscientious, which will suit Sir Daniel. The same could be said of several of your colleagues, I am aware. But you are also quiet and unobtrusive in manner, and that should suit Lady Connelton, whose companion you will, of necessity, more or less be."

"I—I'm very grateful, Mr. Prynne, that you should think so well of me," Elinor stammered. "But I'm not at all sure that I should be the right person. You see—"

"You must allow me to be the best judge of that," Mr. Prynne stated firmly. "There is no family or private reason, I take it, why you should not go?"

"Oh—oh, no," admitted Elinor, who could imagine the family's jubilant reception of the idea.

"Tell your people at home about it tonight," Mr. Prynne said, "and see me tomorrow morning first thing. You will be leaving in about a week's time, so we have to hurry things."

With a little nod he indicated that the interview was over, and, getting to her feet, Elinor somehow made her way toward the door. Then, as she reached it, some of the incredible magic of what had been said suddenly burst upon her like sunlight.

"Mr. Prynne—" she turned to face him again— "where did you say we should be going?"

"To the Tyrol first. You'll go through Holland and

down the Rhine, I expect, and stay one night in Munich. Then on to Ehrwald. You'll probably still get some winter sports there, and there is a good resident clinic in case Sir Daniel still requires attention."

"And—and didn't you say something about Italy later?"

"Yes. Florence, I think, and Rome, of course."

"Of course," murmured Elinor dazedly and groped her way out into the everyday world again.

It was the longest day she had ever known, for she could not bring herself to tell the other girls until the whole thing was confirmed. She could hardly believe in it herself, so why should they? But, released at last, she sped home, intoxicated by the unfamiliar sensation of being the center of a major event.

"Mother, Mother!" She burst into the house with an almost noisy impetuosity entirely foreign to her. "Mother, I'm going to Europe with Sir Daniel and Lady Connelton! For I don't know how many weeks. Down the Rhine—and then to Austria—and Italy! Winter sports—Rome in the spring! Oh, I can't believe it!"

"*What's* that, darling?" Her mother came out of the kitchen with a mixing-spoon in her hand and a look of incredulity on her face. "What's this about going to Europe?"

Elinor said it all again, while Deborah hung over the banisters with her ears on stalks, to use her own expressive phrase.

"But how wonderful, dear!" Mrs. Shearn delightedly kissed her flushed eldest daughter, while Deborah cried triumphantly, "I *told* you you'd need that petticoat!"

"I'll need more than a petticoat," Elinor declared with a laugh.

"You ought to have something in black velvet and terribly *slinky*," Deborah cried. "There's nothing so glamorous as *slinky* black velvet. Adventuresses always wear black velvet. And hats with ospreys," she added, in a final flight of imaginary *haute couture*.

"But I'm not an adventuress," Elinor pointed out.

"No," Deborah agreed regretfully. "But it's very glamorous to look like one, don't you think?"

Elinor said she did not. And then the others started coming in, and each in turn was told the astounding news. Anne thought it was a pity she was not taking in Paris, and Deborah said, rather irrelevantly, "Why not Cairo?"

Mr. Shearn asked if they taught any geography at all at Deborah's school and how she supposed one could go to the Tyrol via Cairo.

"I didn't think so," Deborah explained with dignity. "I just thought—why not Cairo?"

As this appeared to be a repetition that was getting them nowhere, Elinor hastily changed the subject to the question of her outfit, and everyone proceeded to make enjoyable suggestions. Deborah became very shrill again on the subject of black velvet, but the two really constructive suggestions came from Anne and Mr. Shearn.

Anne said, "Get a long lunch-hour if you can and come to the shop. I'll see what I can do for you."

And Mr. Shearn said, "You're the one who has never cost me a penny since you first started to earn your own living, Elinor. You can count on me for twenty pounds toward the wardrobe."

"Daddy!" Greatly moved, both by the tribute and the offer, Elinor went round the table to hug and kiss her father. "Everyone's being so marvellous about it. I just don't know what to say!"

The topic had been discussed from all its fascinating angles before the family retired to bed that night, and the next morning Elinor went to tell Mr. Prynne that she had full parental approval and was now ready to make the final arrangements.

"Well, I suppose you'll need to do some shopping," Mr. Prynne said, with unusual understanding. "And then there's your passport to get—unless you already have one?"

Elinor said she had not, and was immediately despatched to have her photograph taken and to complete the other formalities.

At this point she confessed to the other girls what was taking her out at this odd hour of the morning, and immediately found herself the center of interest.

"How *very* strange that Mr. Prynne should pick a junior," Miss Pascoe said tartly. "What could he have been thinking of?"

"I suppose he thought I could be spared more easily than a senior," Elinor said peaceably, thus salving Miss Pascoe's vanity though not appeasing her envy.

The others, however, were wholeheartedly congratulatory, for Elinor was popular in a quiet way.

"I'm just delighted," declared Gladys Smith, generous in the comforting knowledge of her own happiness. "It's what you need, dear, to bring you out of yourself. Why, I shouldn't wonder if *you* come home engaged.

Elinor smiled and slightly shook her head. But there was no denying that the future had suddenly blossomed with the most strange and enchanting possibilities.

Released from her office duties for most of the day, Elinor made all the arrangements for her passport and then went along to the store where Anne worked. Here, under her young sister's able guidance, she was gradually provided with a wardrobe which, if it did not rival that of Gladys Smith in chic and magnificence, at least provided for most contingencies in a very charming and decorative way.

Anne would have urged her to even further extravagances, but Elinor refused to lose her head.

"I'm only going as a secretary, when all's said and done," she pointed out realistically.

"And companion," Anne reminded her. "And, from the little I saw of her, I'd say Lady Connelton will be a very nice person to be companion to."

Elinor was not sorry to have this reassurance. She knew Sir Daniel as nothing more than a dignified and slightly alarming presence in the office, and the thought that his wife was less intimidating was a relief.

This relief was intensified when, during the next day at the office, she was called to the telephone and a pleasant voice said, "Miss Shearn, this is Lady Connelton speaking. Mr. Prynne tells me you are going to accompany us next week and be a great help, I am sure, to my husband. I think it would be nice if you came along to tea and we got to know each other, don't you?"

"Thank you very much. I should like to." Shy though she was, Elinor was too happy to sound anything but friendly.

"Shall we say half-past four tomorrow, then? I suppose you can have permission to leave the office about four?"

"I expect so. In the circumstances," Elinor added rather gravely, which made Lady Connelton laugh. And then, because she felt she simply must say something about the delight and wonder of the trip, Elinor ran on, "And, Lady Connelton, I . . . I want to say how thrilled and excited . . . I mean, I know I am really coming to do work rather than have a holiday . . . but it's the most wonderful thing that ever happened. I can't really believe it even now. It . . . it's like something one makes up, only it never happens. I mean—"

She broke off, suddenly aware that she must sound incoherent and naïve, and not at all like a cool, efficient secretary who could be trusted to keep her head in unusual circumstances.

Lady Connelton seemed to understand, however. She said, "My dear child, I'm glad you find it all so exciting. I like people who enjoy themselves. Have you been abroad much before?"

"Never."

"Never? Oh, then we *are* going to have a nice time together," the older woman declared. And on this promising note the conversation ended.

As Elinor set out from the office the following afternoon, she tried to keep her spirits from bouncing too dangerously high.

"There are bound to be a few snags," she reminded herself. "I mustn't be put out if things are not *quite* as I hope."

The Conneltons lived in a big, old-fashioned but handsome house near Regent's Park, and the maid who admitted Elinor was quiet and elderly.

"My lady is expecting you," she said in a friendly tone as she took Elinor's coat and then led the way into a pleasant firelit room. "I'll tell her you are here."

Left alone, Elinor glanced round with interest. The furniture, she knew, was good and what used to be called solid, there were one or two attractive and perfectly understandable pictures on the walls, and there were several bowls of flowers, well, but not too professionally, arranged. Altogether a room she liked on sight and in which she felt very much at home.

A little diffidently Elinor sat down, but she came to her feet again almost immediately as the sound of quick footsteps announced the arrival of Lady Connelton, and a moment later a very well groomed, gray-haired woman came into the room.

"Good afternoon, Miss Shearn. How nice of you to find time to come along." She spoke as though Elinor were doing her a personal favor in leaving the office early. "Do sit down and we'll have some tea."

Elinor sat down and regarded her hostess shyly, taking in the fact that she was a pleasant, forceful type of woman in her late fifties, and that there was a humorous lift to the corners of her mouth, which augured well for the future months together.

As she poured out tea, Lady Connelton discoursed at some length on the arrangements for the trip.

"Mr. Prynne worked it all out personally, partly to suit us and partly, I am sure, to suit the affairs of the firm," she stated with a laugh. "With Ehrwald as a center, Ken can go easily to most of the Austrian, Italian and south German holiday resorts, and to the music festival cities. Really, it was very well chosen."

Elinor agreed politely, supposing that "Ken" was her special name for Sir Daniel. But she could not help thinking it sounded an energetic program for an elderly man convalescing.

"Shall I be travelling to these places, too?" she inquired.

"Oh, no, my dear. You'll stay with my husband and me in Ehrwald. Unless, of course, you want to make any special arrangements of your own at any time."

"By no means!" cried Elinor, somewhat put out. "I am more than delighted to do whatever Sir Daniel needs all the time we are away. I'm afraid we were talking at cross purposes. I don't quite understand who . . . who 'Ken' is."

"My nephew, Kenneth Brownlow. Didn't Mr. Prynne

tell you he was coming with us? He's going into the firm
later in the year. So my husband thought it would be a
good opportunity for him to learn something of the
foreign side of the business now. It will save him doing a
lot of work himself and be good experience for Ken."

"Oh, yes. I see."

"Kenneth is my younger brother's boy," Lady
Connelton went on, as though Elinor would naturally like
to know the general family set-up. "There he is over
there." She indicated a photograph standing on a side
table. "Now tell me something about your family. Have
you any brothers and sisters?"

Elinor gave a brief, affectionate and surprisingly
amusing description of her family, and, while she talked,
she glanced from time to time at the strong, good-looking
profile of the man in the photograph.

He looked remarkably attractive. About twenty-seven,
she guessed. He was not smiling in the photograph, but
one had the impression that when he did smile it was a
quick, flashing sort of smile that reached his eyes.

Altogether a person one would like to know. It was
nice to think he was to be in the party.

Just before Elinor left, Sir Daniel himself came in, and
somehow in his own house and in the company of his
wife, he was not nearly as frightening as he had appeared
at the office. Indeed, Elinor was so sorry to see him
looking much more spare and gray than she had ever seen
him before that she insensibly addressed him with a
kindly concern that was almost daughterly. And, to her
immense surprise, when she was leaving, he said, "Well,
my dear, I hope you will enjoy this trip as much as you
seem to think you will. There won't be a great deal of
work most of the time, but my wife will be glad of your
company."

Elinor expressed her thanks and pleasure once more,
and then went out into the foggy night, feeling as though
the sun shone and the birds sang. Really, it was amazing
how nice and easy some people became if you just treated
them as you would your own family!

They were to leave London on Tuesday evening and
cross by the night boat to the Hook of Holland. Over the

weekend Elinor completed all her preparations and on Monday Mr. Prynne checked over with her all the tickets. Then, putting one set into a travelling wallet, he handed this to her and said, "Here are all your tickets. Put your passport with them. Now I want you to take the other three sets to Sir Daniel. You know the house? You have been there before?"

"Yes, Mr. Prynne."

"Very well. It's nearly four o'clock now, so there's no need to come back this afternoon. And tomorrow—" Mr. Prynne rubbed his chin reflectively, then he gave a wintry smile—"come in tomorrow morning, Miss Shearn, but we won't be too strict about your time of leaving."

Elinor thanked him with a smile and a little later set off for the Conneltons' house.

A small, rather rakish-looking sports car was standing outside the house. The sort of car, Elinor supposed, which might well belong to a favorite nephew.

It might not be Kenneth Brownlow's car, of course, but Elinor felt that familiar sense of shyness and reserve stealing over her as she mounted the steps and knocked on the bright brass knocker.

"I'm not sure that her ladyship's in," the pleasant elderly maid said as she admitted her. "If you'll wait here, I'll find out."

She ushered Elinor into a room she had not seen before. It was one of those double rooms so often seen in old-fashioned houses, and, although the maid had evidently not noticed the fact, Lady Connelton was obviously in the back room, since, almost before the door of the front room had closed behind the maid, Elinor heard her speak to someone.

"I can't agree, my dear," she was saying. "Rosemary would have been no use whatever to your uncle. I never believed much in her business-training course."

"I was thinking as much of the companion side of the duties," Elinor heard a rather abrupt but pleasantly pitched man's voice reply. "I should have thought Rosemary would have fitted that part of the program considerably better than some unknown girl from Uncle Dan's office."

"Not at all. The companion is for me, not you, you know! Though I don't think anyone could do other than the nice, quiet little girl Mr. Prynne has chosen for me."

"Oh, Aunt Millicent!"

Elinor found herself going scarlet at the tone of amused disgust and protest in which this exclamation was uttered.

"And what do you mean by that, exactly?" Lady Connelton asked crisply.

"I was just thinking what an unutterable bore any nice, quiet little girl can be if one has to have her around all the time," the other voice replied carelessly.

Elinor didn't hear what Lady Connelton said in reply. She was only aware of a wave of humiliation sweeping her and carrying away all the happiness and confidence of the last few days.

She heard retreating footsteps and a door closing and, in the knowledge that she was alone at last, she almost burst into tears. But remembering that presently the maid would surely find Lady Connelton, wherever she had gone, and bring her, Elinor somehow managed to retain her composure.

She determined not to think of what that horrible nephew of the Conneltons had said. She would keep her mind on something else, fix her attention on something. Anything.

The next room, she realized vaguely, must be something in the nature of a library. Subdued lamplight shone on well-filled bookshelves. And because books always had a fascination for her she tiptoed instinctively toward the archway dividing the two rooms. She would look at the backs of the books, make herself read the titles, make herself forget what she had heard.

"Hello!"

A voice made her nearly jump out of her skin. Flashing round to look at the other side of the library, she saw the original of the photograph Lady Connelton had shown her. He was standing by one of the bookshelves, his finger keeping a place in the book he had been studying.

Elinor stared at him in silence, her eyes widening and darkening.

"Come on in," he said good-humoredly. "No one's

going to bite your head off. And who are you anyway?"

It would be difficult to say what made Elinor behave in a manner contrary to anything she had ever done or said in her life before. But she was excited and indignant, and above all for the last few days she had been living completely outside her usual routine. She looked straight at the half-smiling man with the book.

"I'm the nice, quiet little girl who is going to bore you for the next few months," she said.

If a mouse had hurried out of its hole and given him a smart bite on the ankle, Kenneth Brownlow could not have looked more astonished.

"You don't say!" He came across and stood looking down at her with twinkling eyes. "Well, you know, you don't strike me as a quiet little girl at all. I'm not sure that you even strike me as nice," he added amusedly. "You look at the moment as though you'd stick a knife into me as soon as blink."

"Oh!" She immediately blinked her long lashes. "I'm sorry."

"No, don't start apologizing. That will quite spoil the effect of your wonderful entry. Besides, I suppose it's up to me to do the apologizing. I'm sorry if you overheard my remark. It was rather silly, now I come to think of it, and I don't think I'd have made it if I hadn't been rather ... fed up."

"I know. Because of my coming," she said, before she could stop herself.

"No. Not really that."

"Because Rosemary was not coming?" she suggested, again rather impulsively.

"Oh—you heard that, too, did you?" He laughed, a little vexedly, she thought. And then Lady Connelton came hurrying into the room, before they could say anything else.

"My dear, I'm so sorry! I've heard that you've been waiting quite a long time. I didn't know you were here. Drummond thought I hadn't come in yet. Oh, have you and Ken introduced yourselves?"

"More or less, Aunt Millicent," Kenneth Brownlow said, and Elinor noticed that irrepressible flash of amusement again, which crossed his handsome face.

She handed over the tickets to Lady Connelton, carefully explaining the points that Mr. Prynne had told her to emphasize. And then, though Lady Connelton kindly pressed her to stay to tea, she made her excuses and prepared to take her leave.

"It's my last evening at home," she explained. "The family will be disappointed if I'm not home in good time."

"Yes, of course," Lady Connelton said.

"May I assist by running you home in my car?" Kenneth Brownlow suggested.

"Oh, no, thank you!" Elinor assured him hastily. "It isn't necessary at all."

"But it will save a lot of time," Lady Connelton pointed out practically. "You had better let him take you, my dear. That is, if you don't mind travelling in his horrid little open car."

"I don't mind a bit," Elinor said with a slight smile. "I thought it looked a very nice car—if it's the one outside."

"Come along, then," Kenneth Brownlow said with a laugh. "We are bound to be friends if you defend my car against Aunt Millicent."

He lightly kissed his aunt—presumably to show there was no real ill-feeling—and then escorted Elinor to the car.

It certainly was rather open for winter travel, but her companion supplied her with rugs and told her to wrap up well. Elinor obeyed, wondering how she was going to think of enough entertaining conversation to occupy the journey from Regent's Park to Wimbledon.

Her companion spoke, however, before she could say anything.

"What gave my aunt the idea that you were a quiet, unassuming little thing?" he asked.

Somewhat startled, Elinor gave this very personal question some thought.

"I suppose," she said honestly, "that's really what I am."

"Now, you don't expect me to believe that. Not after your opening remarks to me, do you?"

"Oh—that wasn't a bit the way I usually speak," she explained hastily. "I suppose I was really very angry with you."

For some reason or other this seemed to amuse him a good deal. But, before she could ask him why, he inquired about the other members of the family. And, surprised that he seemed interested in the subject, she found herself telling him about them in detail.

To her further surprise, she found that they were home before she had had time to feel shy or stumble over any awkward gaps in the conversation.

"Will you come in?" she asked rather timidly. "My parents will be very pleased to see you."

But he smiled and shook his head.

"Not this time, thank you. I'm sure they want you to themselves this evening. I'll see you at the station tomorrow evening."

And, raising his hand in a gesture of farewell, he drove off, leaving Elinor wondering how she felt about his addition to the party.

The next day was like no other day she could remember. She went to the office in the morning, but no one seemed to expect her to do any work, which was just as well, since she felt so strung up and excited that it was difficult to concentrate on anything but her own affairs.

Then soon after lunch she was allowed to go home, accompanied by the good wishes of all her colleagues.

The quiet afternoon with her mother soon slipped away, and it seemed no time before all the others were coming in and preparing to say goodbye to her. And, at this point Elinor began to feel a ridiculously large lump in her throat. It would be so long until she saw them again! She could not imagine her home without her. Still less, for some panic-stricken moments, could she imagine herself without her home. She wondered now why she had ever agreed to go. With people she hardly knew—in foreign lands—and strangers everywhere. She must have been crazy!

When the taxi arrived to take her to Liverpool Street, she had a childish desire to run away and hide herself. But Deborah recalled her to her senses with brutal realism.

"Hurry up, hurry up! The taxi's standing out there ticking up money like anything."

So Elinor hugged and kissed everyone, except Edward who was accompanying her to the station, promised all over again to write often, thanked Anne once more for her help and her father for his generosity over the check, and ran out to the taxi with tears in her eyes.

Deborah pursued her to the gate, shouting final instructions about foreign stamps.

"It doesn't matter if you send lots of duplicates," she shrieked, as the driver started up the taxi. "I can always swop."

"All right. I promise, I promise," Elinor called back, her composure somewhat restored by the clamor.

And then the taxi started with a jerk, and Edward, slumping down in the seat beside her, said, "If any of us ever sets out for Australia, Deborah will deafen the neighborhood."

During the drive he told Elinor all about how he felt that perhaps he had not read his friend, Inez, quite right. She never seemed now to want to know what anyone else thought about anything—only to display (with even slightly boring repetition) what she new.

"Of course, she's a lovely girl and has a wonderful brain. But she's—tiring, if you know what I mean."

Elinor, who had been bored to exhaustion by the self-advertising Inez during her one visit, said she knew exactly what Edward meant and that, while no doubt Inez was very clever and well read, there were perhaps other qualities more endearing in people one wanted to know intimately.

"Yes, that's it. I thought you'd see my point," said Edward, who had taken much longer to see this particular point than all the rest of his exasperated family. But the talk about Inez did serve to steady Elinor and take her thoughts off the wrench of parting.

Liverpool Street station looked rather grim and murky when they arrived there, but to Elinor the whole place was irradiated by the sign that said, "Boat Train. Harwich—Hoek van Holland."

This was IT! The train that was to take her to strange

places as yet unknown—out on the Great Adventure.

The Conneltons were already there, Sir Daniel sitting quietly in his corner seat, and Kenneth and his aunt attending to the disposal of the last of the luggage.

Elinor thought she had never seen anything more fascinating than the tables with their shining white linen, their pretty individual lamps, and the cutlery already set out for dinner. It was almost like the opening scene of a perfectly wonderful play—her play.

Introductions were made, Edward and Kenneth Brownlow exchanged a word or two, and then Lady Connelton, satisfied that all the luggage was conveniently disposed of, turned to Edward.

"We are so glad to have your sister with us," she said. "Please tell your mother that we will take good care of her."

Then she and her nephew got into the train, leaving Elinor to have the last few minutes with her brother.

The minutes dragged as they always do between people who have already said everything there is to say at least twice. Then the porters went along shouting the final warning to board the train, and everything sprang into rapid and exciting life. Kisses were exchanged, last messages called from windows. Elinor found herself leaning from the corridor window as the train, with great breathless puffs, began to move.

Edward walked alongside for a few seconds, waving, but very soon the pace became too fast. The distance between them was lengthening, the links with home were stretching—stretching—snapping. She could no longer see Edward as an individual figure, only as part of a waving crowd.

The platform slid away, heads and waving hands were drawn in, windows were raised, people sought their seats once more. The journey had begun.

"Well, we're off!" Lady Connelton smiled at Elinor as she rejoined them.

Elinor managed to smile back quite gaily and not to think too much of the family as the train gathered speed.

CHAPTER TWO

ELINOR, who had so often typed details of train times and general information about journeys for others, knew that the run to the coast took only about an hour and a half, and she was not surprised that, almost as soon as they had finished their leisurely dinner and their evening newspapers, Sir Daniel took out his watch and said, "We shall be in in about five minutes. There are the harbor lights now."

She gazed eagerly from the windows, and through the dark of the late winter evening she saw lines of distant lights strung out at intervals, and once, where they clustered together to give concentrated light, the outlines of a two-funnelled steamer.

Everything was new and thrilling. Even though everyone else shivered when they stepped out of the cosy warmth of the train into the dank chill of Harwich station, Elinor hardly noticed the cold.

The quick passage through the Customs was a novelty rather than a nuisance, and when an official said, "There's your boarding card," and thrust a card into her hand, she looked at it as though it were a ticket to Fairyland.

It was only a short distance from the Customs shed to the boat, but Elinor stumbled twice, because she could not look where she was going—only at the big white ship that loomed ahead.

"Careful." It was Kenneth Brownlow who suddenly took her by the arm. "There are always chains and cables and goodness knows what lying about here."

"I . . . I'm all right, thank you," she assured him. But he kept his hand lightly round her arm until they reached the foot of the gangway that led on to the ship.

As Elinor stepped on board she became aware of an immense degree of efficiency and cleanliness all round her. The paint could hardly have been whiter, or the brass brighter, or the directions more explicit.

In no time she was being ushered into her small, bright

cabin by a brisk stewardess, who checked her ticket, told her when she would be called in the morning, and even, as though she were a child, added firmly, "I expect you'll want to go right to bed. It's a short night."

But Elinor—also responding like a child—had no intention of being hustled off early to bed when there were other, more interesting matters afoot. First she examined her cabin, delighting in her brass-bound porthole, the little light over one corner of her bunk in case she wanted to read, the washbasin, which really supplied hot water from the tap that said it would, and all the other neat amenities.

Then, having tested all these, she went along to her employers' cabin, to see if Lady Connelton required her for anything.

But Lady Connelton seemed to be more of the stewardess's way of thinking.

"No, thank you, dear. We shall go straight to bed and get what sleep we can. They'll be waking us about five-thirty, I suppose. But if you want to have a look round, you'll find Ken somewhere about. I'm sure he will look after you and show you anything you want to see."

Elinor thanked her and said good night. But she decided to avoid Kenneth Brownlow. She could not quite forget what he had said about "nice, quiet little things being boring if one had to see too much of them." On one thing she was determined; he should not have an opportunity of being bored with her.

It was easy enough to find her way on deck, and, with several other people, she stood at the rail, watching the last of the freight being lowered into the hold. It was a fascinating sight, the cranes lifting the great bales of merchandise, the cars and the heavy luggage, swinging them high overhead and then lowering them far down into the bowels of the ship.

Brilliant lights shone on the scene, illuminating it like a stage set, and the shouted directions and the rattle of chains running over winches added their exciting overtones. Elinor became completely unaware of who was coming and going around her, and she started quite violently when an already familiar voice said beside her:

"I thought you had gone to bed."

"Oh—oh, no. I felt I couldn't go while there was still anything to see. This is my first sea voyage."

"Is that so?" Something almost like indulgence sounded in his voice for a moment. "Well, there isn't much left to put on board now. We should be leaving in a few minutes. Do you want to come and have a drink with me?" Then, as though a rather unfamiliar idea struck him, he added, "Tea or coffee or anything?"

"No, thank you." She wished she knew how to leave him, gracefully and promptly.

"Are you afraid it will keep you awake?"

"Oh, no! Nothing ever keeps me awake. Not even excitement."

At that moment there was a final outburst of shouting followed by the rumble of something very heavy being pushed across the far end of the deck, and a sort of shudder running through the boat that announced that they were moving.

"We're off!" Elinor ran to the side and watched, fascinated, as the narrow channel of water between them and the shore began perceptibly to widen.

He came and joined her there, a little to her surprise, and stood there beside her as she watched the dark shores of England slip away into the night.

She turned away at last and walked along the deck with him. Then, just as they stepped indoors, a steward came up to her companion.

"You're the gentleman from one-eight-three, aren't you?" he said. "Mr. Brownlow?"

"Yes."

"Telegram for you, sir."

Elinor was not actually looking at him as he slit open the envelope and read the telegram. But she heard his exclamation of surprise.

She glanced at him then. "Is anything wrong?" she asked.

"Wrong? Oh no. No, of course not."

At that moment someone swung open the door leading on deck, and a strong draft snatched the paper from Kenneth Brownlow's hand.

It fluttered past Elinor and dropped a yard or two away. Quite naturally she started forward and seized it before it could blow right away. She had no intention of reading it, but as she stooped to pick it up the few printed words were clearly visible.

"Bon voyage," it said. "See you in Ehrwald perhaps. Rosemary."

Elinor returned the telegram to Kenneth Brownlow, who thanked her without comment. Then they bade each other good night and went to their cabins.

Kenneth Brownlow's private affairs were, of course, no business of Elinor's, but later, as she lay in her narrow but comfortable bunk, she thought for several minutes about him and the problematical Rosemary. Then she gave it up and settled down to sleep to the soothing slap-slap of the waves against the side of the ship.

"Five-thirty, madam! Here's your tea."

Elinor sat up and rubbed her eyes, wondering where she was. Then she remembered. On board ship, in her own little cabin! And they must have crossed the North Sea during the night.

"You'll need to hurry," the stewardess told her. "You're taking the Rhinegold Express, aren't you?"

"Yes," Elinor said. And when the stewardess had gone out of the cabin, she repeated softly to herself, "The Rhinegold Express." Because it was such a beautiful, romantic name for a train—the Rhinegold Express.

She rose and washed and dressed quickly, noticing through her porthole window that it was still quite dark. Indeed there was even a star or two overhead. Then she speedily repacked her nightbag, and went out to see if the others were ready.

The door of the Conneltons' cabin stood open, and Lady Connelton called across to her, "Good morning, my dear. Though it still seems like the middle of the night, really. Are you ready?"

"Oh, yes, Lady Connelton. Did you sleep well?"

"So-so. I shall sleep a great deal more on the train. No need to ask how you slept. You look as fresh as the dawn. The real dawn, I mean. Not this horrid sort of half-night."

Elinor didn't really think anything was horrid at the moment, but she smiled sympathetically. And then Kenneth appeared, followed by two porters who—with a few guttural words to each other, which Elinor took to be Dutch—shouldered immense quantities of luggage between them, and it was time to go ashore.

Landing cards were surrendered, and they stepped off the boat into the cold, fresh air of the morning. It was impossible not to yawn and shiver a little, but, in Elinor's case at least, the shiver was partly one of excitement.

Under the last few twinkling stars that were giving way to the first steely light of dawn, they walked to the Customs shed. On all sides were notices in foreign languages and a great babel of what seemed to Elinor many different tongues. But she was intrigued to realize that *Ingang* over one door was near enough to the Scottish "gang in" to mean quite obviously "entrance."

Uitgang, by the same process of reasoning, must surely be "exit." Elinor began to feel mistress of the situation!

Once more the Customs formalities were speedy, and less than a quarter of an hour after leaving the ship, they were installed in the palatially large and comfortable compartment in which they were to travel across Holland and Germany to Munich.

"It's surely much more exciting travelling this way than by air!" Elinor exclaimed, as she looked from the great wide windows on to the platform, where early-morning traders were already pushing barrows up and down from which one could buy papers and periodicals in several languages, steaming hot coffee in cardboard tumblers, or rolls, or fruit and chocolate of infinite variety.

"Well—yes, I suppose it is." Lady Connelton smothered another yawn. "One feels the gradual process of going abroad this way. Air travel is very comfortable, but rather abrupt."

"It is very convenient, nevertheless," her husband said a trifle irritably. "And much less tiring. If the doctors hadn't forbidden it, I should certainly have chosen to fly."

Elinor was very, very sorry about Sir Daniel not being

well enough to fly, but she simply could not help being glad on her own account that *some* reason had dictated their travelling this way. And more than ever did she feel this when—after an enchanting toot from a horn, instead of the more familiar whistle, the train started on its way, and they went along to the dining car for breakfast.

In all the world, she thought, there could never have been a more delicious meal than the scrambled eggs with ham, the crisp rolls with creamy butter, and the hot fragrant coffee served in big thick cups with which they regaled themselves as the train sped on its way past the fields and canals of Holland.

Every minute the light was strengthening now, and when she began to see distant windmills, Elinor almost cried aloud with delight.

The houses in the small towns through which they passed enchanted her, with their clean, brightly colored exteriors and their large and shining windows. People were already beginning to go about the day's business, and several times, as they ran over level crossings, Elinor saw fleets of cyclists waiting to pass.

Presently they began to enter the outskirts of a much larger place than any they had passed so far. And, as Elinor gazed eagerly at the distant liners which could be seen in dock, beyond the austere but attractive buildings of the city, Sir Daniel said briefly, "Rotterdam."

"There's a great deal of building going on here, isn't there?" she said, after a moment.

"Yes, there is," Sir Daniel agreed. "The Dutch are a very progressive people."

Presently the train drew into Rotterdam station and Elinor watched fascinated while throngs of travellers left the train and equally as many joined it. The bustling activity of large stations had always excited her, and this was no exception.

While the train was in the station, they left the dining car and made their way back to their own compartment, and Elinor settled down in her corner seat keenly anticipating the many wonderful sights that lay ahead. To her surprise, she dozed for a while, rousing herself from time to time to gaze at some specially beautiful line of poplars etched against the winter sky, or a gay windmill with turning sails. But, as they neared the frontier about nine o'clock, she became wide awake once more.

At this point the Dutch officials came on the train, to stamp passports and check currency. Then the train moved slowly across the narrow "no-man's-land" between the two frontier towns, and the German officials came on board. They too were very polite and correct, and presently the train moved off again on the next stage of the long journey.

Kenneth, who was sitting opposite her, leaned over once to ask, quite solicitously, if she were getting tired. But Elinor shook her head emphatically.

"No, it's lovely! I'm enjoying every bit of it."

"The loveliest part will soon be beginning," he told her. "After we leave Cologne. See—you can already glimpse the spires of the cathedral."

Elinor looked where he pointed, and in the distance, across the flat fields, she saw two beautiful, fretted spires pointing into the clear sky.

"I thought somehow that the cathedral was destroyed."

"No. A great deal of the rest of Cologne was. But though it was heavily blasted when so much of the nearby railway was destroyed, the actual fabric of the cathedral was preserved. You will have a better view presently."

"And then—after Cologne—what next?" she asked eagerly, unable to hear too much of the joys that lay ahead.

"On down the Rhine, through Bonn and Coblenz to Frankfurt, and for a great part of the way we follow the actual course of the Rhine. That's what I meant when I said the loveliest part of the journey was soon beginning."

In a short while, Elinor found this all too true. Once they had left Cologne behind and were out in the country once more, she began to notice a great falling away of the ground on the left, as though a deep valley wound its way through the scene. Once she thought she caught a glimpse of water. And then, almost without warning, they drew suddenly nearer, until they were running alongside the depression—and there, stretching before them for miles and miles, were the wide, silvery, slowly undulating waters of the Rhine.

Nothing could move Elinor from the window after that. Sometimes the ground was comparatively flat and they glided past enchanting riverside villages, with red-roofed houses and ancient church towers and little landing stages for the many river craft. Sometimes the banks became very steep on either side, curiously and regularly marked out in lines which, Kenneth explained, were the bare poles of the vineyards, later to be covered with foliage. And sometimes great cliffs towered above them, or across the river from them, and at intervals they passed incredibly romantic-looking castles or ancient ruins, which looked like something straight out of all the adventure stories she had read as a child.

No one disturbed her as she gazed, enraptured, at the tremendous and ever-changing panorama. The Connel-tons were both dozing, and Kenneth left her in peace to take her first long look at the greatest and most beautiful waterway of Western Europe.

Only once did he interrupt her absorption. He pointed out the lovely wooded rock known as the Lorelei and told her briefly of the legend of the Lorelei who used to sit there, combing her hair and luring the unsuspecting traveller to his doom.

Bonn and Coblenz had been left far behind, the shining waters of the Moselle had merged with those of the Rhine, the towers of Mainz lay behind them and Frankfurt not far ahead, and still Elinor was watching, when Sir Daniel roused himself and said it was time for lunch. And Elinor found that it was one o'clock and that she was ravenously hungry.

In the dining car once more—now beginning to be known to Elinor as a "Speisewagen"—she was struck afresh by the variety of languages being spoken around her. She even began to pick out which was which.

French was easy, because she had learned a good deal at school, and her small stock of German words enabled her to pick out similar sounds and identify the language. She thought she also detected some Italian—or it could have been Spanish. But as for the interesting-looking couple in the corner, she simply could not imagine what they were talking.

The two intrigued her and she wished she could have known more about them, but it seemed unlikely that she ever would. There would be dozens—perhaps hundreds—of these casual contacts before her adventure was finished.

However, during the late afternoon, Elinor went and stood in the corridor for a while, partly because the scenery was more beautiful on that side and partly because she thought the Conneltons and Kenneth might like a little time to themselves, and immediately she noticed that the couple who had attracted her so much were standing there too.

After a few minutes, the girl smiled and said something to Elinor in German.

"I'm sorry. I don't speak German," Elinor said, but she smiled, because there was something so extraordinarily attractive about this girl, with her slim, indefinably elegant figure, her long, laughing eyes, and her curiously wide cheekbones.

"Oh—I said that this is the part of the journey which always seems to drag," the girl replied in perfect English, with hardly a trace of any accent.

"Does it?" Elinor shook her head, still smiling. "Not for me. It is the first time I have ever done it."

"The first time!"

"How fortunate for you." The young man also spoke almost without accent and in a charmingly friendly way. "It must be wonderful to see the world for the first time."

"Oh, it is," Elinor assured them, with such fervor that they both laughed, as though they found her as intriguing as she found them.

"And where are you going first? Munich?"

"Only for an overnight stop. Then we go on to Ehrwald, which is a little place in the Austrian Tyrol."

"Yes, I know it. We also are going there," the man said.

"*Are* you?" The coincidence surprised and delighted Elinor. But she had the odd impression that the man's companion was equally surprised.

"It's a delightful place for winter sports," the man went on. "Not too fashionable and spoiled."

"It sounds lovely." And then, because her curiosity suddenly got the better of her, Elinor turned to the girl and said rather shyly, "Do you mind my asking what language you were talking in the dining car? I couldn't identify it at all. It—it sounded so strange. I couldn't help listening to a few words."

They both laughed at that.

"It was Hungarian," the girl told her.

"Oh, then—you're Hungarian?"

"No, not really. We're Austrian, but we had a Hungarian grandmother and spent quite a lot of our childhood in Hungary. When my brother and I want to talk without being overheard we usually speak in Hungarian. It's a fairly safe bet that no one round will understand, even in a continental dining car."

"Nowadays it is," her brother amended rather bitterly. "Most Hungarians are securely fastened away behind the Iron Curtain."

"Oh." Elinor looked startled. She had heard these expressions before, of course, and vaguely accepted their tragic meaning. But she had never expected to talk to people to whom they were personal facts—part of the pattern of their own lives.

She would have liked to go on talking to the handsome couple, who seemed to her like people in a book. But just then Lady Connelton drew back the door of their compartment and glanced out into the corridor for her.

"I must go now." Elinor smiled a regretful goodbye at her companions.

"Perhaps we shall meet in Ehrwald," the man said with a little bow. And before she could stop herself Elinor replied sincerely, "Oh, I hope so!"

It was just after six-thirty when the train at last entered the big, well-rebuilt station of Munich and their long day's journey was at an end. By now, even Elinor was willing to call a halt, for it had been too dark to see anything from the windows during the last hour, and she was eager for her first night in a foreign city.

In the crowd that poured out of the train she caught

sight for a moment of the brother and sister who had spoken to her, and was pleased that they both waved before going off in the wake of their porter.

Taxis seemed to be a great deal smaller and more cramped than in London, and as the Conneltons had a good deal of luggage, they went in one taxi, leaving Elinor and Kenneth to follow in another.

Again, Elinor felt a little self-conscious, left alone with him, but she gazed out on the town with genuine interest, and thought it looked extraordinarily gay and well lit, with fine shop-window displays and, in some cases, the shops themselves still open.

Once they passed a big open space where rebuilding was evidently in progress and, in the glare of great arc lamps, workmen were going about their business as though it were midday, and with a speed and energy that made Elinor gasp.

"Why—they're still working as though they mean to be there for hours," she exclaimed.

"They probably do," replied Kenneth Brownlow dryly.

"You mean that they go on building—and all that sort of thing—far into the night?"

"Of course. How else do you suppose they could have made such a comeback? They are almost the only race left on earth who've accepted the unpalatable fact that there is no substitute for hard work."

"Then—" Elinor suddenly saw a dry, economic fact presented to her in simple, practical terms—"they must produce more cheaply and efficiently than most other people?"

"Certainly. It is simply a question of what you want in life, of course." Kenneth said, still dryly. "Those who think the most important thing is to work shorter hours must not expect to do so well in a wicked world as those whose ambition it is to produce better, faster and more cheaply than anyone else. That's what is called realism. But it isn't very fashionable," he added, with a sudden, almost roguish smile.

They arrived at the hotel at this moment, and Elinor found that Sir Daniel—who was obviously tired after the journey—and Lady Connelton intended to dine there and go to bed early. Both of them had had enough for one day.

"But there is no reason why you two young people should do the same," Lady Connelton said kindly. "If you want to go out somewhere more interesting, just do so."

"But I'm really here to keep you company, Lady Connelton," Elinor said doubtfully.

"Tonight it isn't important." Lady Connelton actually patted her cheek indulgently. "I shall go to bed almost directly after dinner."

Elinor began to say that perhaps she had better do the same. But at this point Kenneth took a hand in the conversation.

"Suppose you let me take you out to supper," he said, glancing at her with a touch of amusement. "We could go to one of the local beer cellars."

"But I don't drink beer," Elinor explained.

"You won't have to," he assured her.

Lady Connelton seemed to take it for granted that she would now go. And so, with some trepidation, Elinor went off under the guidance of Kenneth Brownlow on her first exploration in a foreign city.

It was certainly interesting. The "beer cellar" turned out to be a picturesque place, with scrubbed wooden tables, shining copper utensils on great oak dressers, a fascinating tiled stove at each corner, and the most delicious food Elinor had ever tasted.

She was not, it seemed, expected to drink anything more alarming than "Apfelsaft," the delicious ice-cold apple juice found everywhere in Germany and Austria, though most people round her were drinking the famous, foaming Munich beer from great pottery tankards.

There was a good deal of laughter and much talking and, threading through it all, string music from three players in Bavarian costume who sat on a low platform at one end of the room, but remained in very intimate contact with the regular patrons.

From time to time there were songs in which most of the people joined. Some of them gay, but others with that simple, nostalgic melancholy found only in folk songs. And no one seemed to be in a hurry here. A meal was something over which you took your time—an end in itself, not something through which you hurried in order to go on somewhere else.

It was fairly late by the time they finally rose to go, and when they stepped out once more into the glittering, frosty air, Elinor realized suddenly that she was sleepy.

"You can sleep late tomorrow," Kenneth told her, noticing her weariness. "My uncle and I have business to attend to in the morning, and our train for the Tyrol doesn't leave until midday."

"Is it another long journey?" she inquired, trying desperately to smother a yawn.

"Oh no. About a couple of hours to Garmisch, and then Ehrwald is not far beyond that."

"I'm really almost glad," she admitted, as they reached the hotel. "I feel I simply must settle down and digest some of these glorious impressions before I try to take in any more. You know, Ken—" She stopped, astounded at herself, blushed and added hastily, "I'm sorry. I mean Mr. Brownlow, of course. I wasn't—"

"That's all right." He gave her that quick, amused smile. "Ken or Kenneth will do. I don't think I could be Mr. Brownlow for the next few months. Good night, Elinor."

He parted from her at the door of the elevator, leaving her with the distinct impression that, on this evening at least, she had not bored him.

The train that they took the next day was a much less luxurious affair than the express of the previous day. It was even a little primitive-looking, but with an engaging air of leisurely enjoyment about it, as though it were a rather amateur sort of train, given over to pleasure trips more than the serious business of life.

Most of it was composed of third-class carriages with wooden seats, and the passengers were in every variety of dress, from the neat, respectable garments of rural poverty to the smartest skiing kit.

The route wound through heavily wooded country—the very green grass powdered with snow, and the trees leafless against a clear, pale sky. Occasionally there were glimpses of breathtakingly beautiful lakes, but what made Elinor cry aloud with joy was the first sight of towering mountains sketched on the far horizon.

As they drew nearer, the track wound steeply upwards and the snow, lying lightly at first, became deeper, crisper, and finally covered everything. From Garmisch onwards they travelled through a fairyland of sparkling snow, a frozen, Christmas-card world, with fir trees bending beneath the weight of their soft, white burden, and little mountain villages, with their shining, onion-shaped church towers, clustering under the thick white carpet which would cover them from now until spring came to release them.

At the frontier the Austrian officials who came on board the train could hardly have been more friendly or casual. They made one or two jokes in their soft, beautiful German, and generally gave the impression that Customs duties were simply a game in which they had to indulge, even though it was not really much fun. And they finally departed with that most moving of all greetings and farewells—"*Grüss Gott*."

The train then puffed on a little farther in a leisurely manner and presently arrived at a pretty, wooden station, which looked more like a large toy than anything Elinor had ever before regarded as a station. This, it seemed, was their destination.

A number of people got out here and among them Elinor was charmed to see the two to whom she had talked on the train the previous day.

Not that she really had eyes or ears for mere people in those first few moments. She stood on the open platform, waiting while the luggage was slowly taken off the train, and gazed awe-stricken at the mountains that rose on every hand—their jagged summits reaching into the clear, bright blue of an exquisite winter sky. And as she did so there came to her, borne on the fresh, still air of the late afternoon, the enchanting sound of innumerable, softly tinkling cowbells.

"Well, Miss Connelton, how do you like your first glimpse of Ehrwald?" said a pleasant, faintly foreign voice beside her, and she turned to find the Hungarian—as she still called him to herself—smiling at her.

"It's all so wonderful, I hardly know how to take it in," she admitted. And then she suddenly realized what he had called her. "But I'm not Miss Connelton," she added with a smile.

"No?" He looked rather unexpectedly taken aback. "But isn't that Sir Daniel Connelton you are travelling with—and Lady Connelton?"

"Yes, certainly. But I'm not their daughter, you know. I am Sir Daniel's secretary, and my name is Elinor Shearn."

"Is that so?" He smiled and looked as friendly as ever. He even called his sister over and explained the mistake they had made. But Elinor had the curious impression that the information she had given him had shaken him more than any information about a virtual stranger had any need to do.

CHAPTER THREE

Elinor wrote a few days later to her family.

I wish I could find words to tell you how beautiful it all is here. I am sitting now on the glassed-in balcony of my room, where I bring my typewriter each morning. The sun is quite hot, and the snow is sliding from the branches of the fir trees with a soft plopping sound.

But it is still very much a white world. The snow on the mountains is so thick and so deeply frozen that I suppose it will be a month or more before the real thaw sets in. However, at least the little stream below my window is unfrozen and all day long I hear it chattering over the stones. In the morning and the evening the tinkle of the cowbells sounds above it— and that really is the sweetest sound I think I have ever heard, even in this enchanted place.

She paused and gazed away into the white and gold and

heavenly blue of the world beyond her window. She had been pretty busy during the first few days and only now had she had time to write in any detail, and it was important that she should find just the right words to bring the scene before them all, so that she could feel that the family, in some measure, shared these marvellous experiences of hers.

The hotel is a lovely chalet-type of building with lots of polished wood, color-washed walls both inside and out, and great tiled stoves that reach almost to the ceiling.

I think it is patronized mostly by knowledgeable travellers like the Conneltons. For, though there is a much grander hotel quite near, where they have a string orchestra in the dining-room and dancing at night, I gather that we feel rather "uppish" about that, and consider that we are more exclusive and typical of the district!

There are balconies and fantastically beautiful views to all the rooms, but I really think I have the loveliest view of all. From my window I can see right across to the Zugspitze, the highest mountain in our vicinity. There is a cable railway up to the top—Kenneth says the highest in the world—and from where I sit I can see the cars (there goes one now!) swaying up or down on the overhead cable.

Kenneth is going to take me up one day, but it won't be for a while because he is going off tomorrow on a brief tour of some of the holiday centers. I expect we shall miss him.

But Lady Connelton is an absolute darling to me, and Ilsa and Rudolf von Eiberg are charming. Did I tell you about them? They are the brother and sister I met on the train, coming out. They seem to live most of their time in Vienna, but they are partly Hungarian.

How I wish I could talk foreign languages the way they do! Which reminds me to ask—if it's not a tactless question, Deborah, dear!—how are the French irregulars coming along? The von Eibergs speak such wonderful English that I feel rather self-conscious about my few scraps of German, though I am beginning to pick up quite a reasonable supply of everyday words and phrases.

Except for the fact that I miss you all, I just could *not* be happier. If only I could rush home and tell you all about it instead of just writing, it would be perfect. I keep on wondering about Deborah and Henry at school, and Anne at the shop and Edward at the bank. Be sure to tell me *all* the details when you write. I am longing for news of all the little everyday things.

Wasn't it funny?—the von Eibergs thought I was the daughter of the Conneltons!—which will show you how kindly they treat me. I think they were rather taken aback to find I was only the secretary. I am not quite sure why, for it made no difference whatever in their friendliness. It seems that Rudolf is quite an exhibition skater, and he says he is going to teach me. I can't really suppose that an expert would enjoy stumbling round with a beginner, but it would be nice to learn. As it is—

Suddenly Elinor became aware that someone was knocking on the door of her room.

"Come in," she called, and Ilsa von Eiberg came into the room and across to the balcony.

"Hello." She stood smiling in the doorway. "How hard you work! Do you have to type all through this lovely morning?"

"Oh, no, I don't have to. In fact, I wasn't really working at all," Elinor explained. "Only writing a letter home." And then, as casually as possible, she took the sheet of paper out of the machine, in case Ilsa should see her own name on it.

Her visitor was quick to notice the gesture, casual though it had been, but she mistook the motive.

"Don't tell me you type your love letters!" she said with a laugh.

"My—oh, *no*! That wasn't a love letter. It was really a letter home—to my family, I mean. I haven't any love letters to write, in any case," Elinor added with candor.

"No?" The other girl seemed both amused and

incredulous. "How do you manage that, when you're young and pretty and far from home?"

"By being only two of those things," replied Elinor, with unexpected humor. "I'm not really pretty, you know. I've never been called that before."

"No-o, perhaps not, strictly speaking." Ilsa looked consideringly at Elinor's soft dark hair, her wide gray eyes and her unexpectedly red mouth. "You're something more. You're piquant—what the Americans call 'cute.' And then sometimes, quite without warning, you are very pretty. That's much more intriguing and dangerous than being pretty all the time."

"Is it?" Elinor was dumbfounded. Never in her life before had she heard herself described as intriguing—much less dangerous! And yet this girl said these things with an air of careless conviction there was no gainsaying.

It made Elinor feel strangely excited and yet more self-possessed than she had ever felt before. As though the mere fact that Ilsa von Eiberg found her interesting actually made her so.

"Why, of course," Ilsa affirmed amusedly. And it seemed as though she were prepared to elaborate this fascinating subject further when a clear whistle sounded from the garden, just below the balcony, and she exclaimed instead, "That's Rudi. May I, please—?" And, crossing the balcony, she pushed back the upper half of one of the windows and leaned out, to speak in German to her brother below.

After a moment she looked back at Elinor and said, "He wants to know if you will come skating with us."

"I—I should love to, but—" the self-effacing and shy Elinor suddenly returned, ousting the eager and self-possessed girl she had become for a moment or two—"I don't know the first thing about it. You go together," she urged. "I'm sure it's no fun for experts to have to bother about a beginner."

"But we want you to come. Perhaps we shall make of you an expert too," Ilsa declared good-humoredly.

"No, really!" Elinor was in full retreat now, all her shyness returned. "You had much better go on your own.

I'll come down later and watch, perhaps."

Ilsa turned away again to speak out of the window to her brother. But when she drew in her head once more, she said positively, "Rudi declares he won't go unless you come too."

"Oh, but—" Elinor laughed and bit her lip, indescribably flattered and touched that the charming Rudi should make this absurd assertion. "Then I'll come," she said, with sudden decision. "Can you wait just five minutes while I put on something more suitable?"

"Of course. I'll wait downstairs with Rudi. You only need a very wide skirt and some woollies. We'll see about skates when we get there."

Ilsa went out of the room and, full of excitement, Elinor changed quickly to a flaired black skirt and the really beautiful white and scarlet sweater and jacket, which were among the things Anne had insisted on her buying. There was a tasselled cap to go with these and even mittens. And, as Elinor caught a glimpse of herself in the glass, and saw how her gray eyes shone and that her cheeks were flushed, she could not help remembering what Ilsa had said about its being more intriguing to be pretty sometimes than all the time.

A sudden wave of gratitude to the von Eibergs flooded over her. Here was she, the shy, reserved Elinor Shearn, being taken out of herself willy-nilly, and being made to feel that she was someone important and attractive. Why, at home a charge of gunpowder would have been necessary to get her on to a skating rink! But here she was going willingly and happily, in a mood to enjoy herself.

That was what it was, of course. They created the mood of enjoyment, and then caught her while it was still strong upon her. It was sweet of them to bother so much, and their timing was perfect.

Not wishing to waste a moment of this glorious, exhilarating mood, Elinor ran out of her room and along the passage. As she turned the corner she cannoned into Kenneth.

"Oh, I'm sorry!"

"That's all right. I was just coming to look for you." He had some papers in his hand, and he glanced at these,

50

apparently completely oblivious of the fact that, for once, she was (intriguingly and dangerously) pretty. "This is an urgent job. We'll need—"

"Oh, can't it wait?" Elinor cried.

Never before, in the whole of her official career, had she reacted thus towards urgent work. But this was her Moment! The moment which she felt she should seize.

Kenneth hesitated, perhaps impressed by her manner, even though he probably took no special count of moments, with or without a capital "M."

"I—I was going skating," Elinor explained eagerly. "With the von Eibergs."

"With whom?"

"The von Eibergs."

"Oh." She could not have said why, but that one syllable somehow conveyed amused disparagement to a degree that infuriated her.

"They are good friends of mine," she reminded him, in a tone that shook slightly with both anger and disappointment.

"Quite," Kenneth said. But she had the extraordinary impression that in that moment he finally made up his mind against concession. "I'm sorry, but I'm afraid you will have to put them off this time."

It was perfectly justifiable, of course, that he should commandeer her for official work. This was, even, the sole purpose for which she was here. But the circumstances were such that Elinor could hardly hide her resentment.

"Well, then, I'll go down and tell them I can't come," she said, and she tried—not very successfully—to sound less cold and angry than she felt.

"If you would. I'll be in the sitting-room," Kenneth told her.

Not trusting herself to say more, Elinor brushed past him with something less than her usual gentle air and went downstairs to make her excuses.

"But surely the work can wait?" Rudi said when he heard the explanations. "Work is always there, while ideal skating conditions can change within the hour at this time of year."

"I'm afraid not." Elinor bravely concealed the fact that this was also rather the way she felt about the incident! "I did come here to work, you know."

"Nonsense. Like a sensible girl, you also came expecting to enjoy yourself," Rudi retorted with his perfectly charming smile. "But I know there are some things with which one cannot argue. Kenneth Brownlow is one of them, I have no doubt."

Elinor was not entirely pleased to have Kenneth referred to as a "thing," and at another time she might have protested. But, if he were really purposely keeping her away from the von Eibergs (as she suspected) then he deserved to be called anything.

She went upstairs again into the private sitting-room of the Conneltons' suite. Kenneth was alone there, sitting at the improvised desk, frowning over some papers.

"Where is Sir Daniel?"

She really had not intended to sound suspicious or abrupt, but Kenneth looked up with raised eyebrows.

"He's out, I suppose."

"I thought . . . I thought that since the work was so urgent it would be for him too," Elinor said, faintly confused.

"No."

"I see."

Again the tone was most unlike her usual pleasant, obliging one, and, pushing back his papers, Kenneth regarded her with a glance that disconcerted her.

"My dear girl," he said, "there's no need to sulk the very first time you have to work instead of going out to enjoy yourself."

This was most unfair, of course, particularly as the first few days had involved much work and no play at all.

"I am not sulking," Elinor replied composedly, and immediately felt a great and quite unfamiliar desire to do so.

"Very well." Kenneth looked very slightly ashamed of himself, as well he might, and then began to dictate at a rather more rapid pace than was usual with him.

Fortunately, however, Elinor was equal to the demand and she even felt something like a perverse pleasure in making her pen skim over the pages in response to Kenneth's spate of words. No one observing them would have supposed that they were two very angry people. But, under the conventional surface of this official scene, Elinor was disturbed by the unexpected currents of feeling flowing.

He was finished at last. And then he said in his most formal manner, "Three copies, please. One for my uncle, one for myself, and one for the London office. Shall I fetch your typewriter for you?"

Elinor usually did her official typing in the sitting-room because there were reference books and files there.

"No, thank you. I can fetch it myself."

"Don't be silly," Kenneth retorted unexpectedly. And, without more ado, he went and carried in the typewriter for her.

She thanked him without looking at him and set to work with such purpose that no conversation was possible. And presently Kenneth got up and, without saying any more, went off on some affairs of his own.

Elinor went on typing doggedly. She was still doing so when the Conneltons came in nearly an hour later.

"What, still working!" Her employer glanced at her kindly. "You must remember to take some time to enjoy yourself too, you know."

"But as this work was needed at once, Sir Daniel," Elinor explained—with dangerous demureness, had he but known it—"I thought I had better stay in and finish it."

"What work is that?" Sir Daniel came and looked over her shoulder. "Hm . . . yes . . . very useful for future consideration. But not vitally urgent. Another time, you had better ask me and make sure."

"I will, Sir Daniel," Elinor assured him. And, in that moment—contrary to all her usual gentle and conciliatory ways—she determined to have this thing out with Kenneth.

The opportunity came after lunch, at which she had not addressed any word to him that was not strictly necessary. As they strolled out of the dining-room in the wake of the Conneltons, she said softly to him, and with more composure than she felt, "I found out about the lie you told me this morning."

"Lie, my dear girl?" He looked both astonished and amused, but not in the least guilty or ashamed. "What lie was that?"

"You know perfectly well!" She bent upon him a glance of much more serious displeasure than she knew. "You told me that work was urgent, and it was nothing of the sort. Sir Daniel said not."

"Did you ask him about it?"

"Certainly not. He volunteered the information himself, when he came in and asked why I was still working."

"Oh."

"Is that all you have to say about it?"

"I'm afraid it is."

Elinor gasped.

"But don't you think it was extraordinarily mean of you to—to do me out of my morning's pleasure?"

"I didn't look at it that way, exactly."

"Do you mind," she said, in her coolest tone, "telling me in what way you did look at it?"

They had reached the small, deserted lounge by now and, while the Conneltons went on up to their own rooms, Kenneth and Elinor paused.

"Really, I'd much rather not, you know." He smiled down at her, quite unrepentant. "You won't like what I'm going to say. But, if you insist—the fact is that I don't have the same high opinion of the von Eibergs that you have."

"You don't need to," Elinor retorted. "They are my friends, and you don't have to like them."

"I don't want to make heavy weather of this," Kenneth said. "But my uncle and aunt are in a sense responsible for you and—"

"You are not," she put in quickly. "I am perfectly capable of looking after myself, in any case, and I resent being treated like a child. Besides, what have you against my two friends? What makes you think they are a couple of criminals?"

"Oh, not criminals, Elinor!" He laughed protestingly.

"Good heavens! I suppose there's no real harm in them, in the strict sense of the word. But—they're a type, my dear, that you can't possibly know and probably don't know how to handle. They're a sort of leftover from a world that no longer exists. It's their misfortune, I daresay, rather than their fault. But, quite frankly, I think they live on their wits. They probably thought you were the daughter of my uncle and aunt—"

He stopped, because Elinor had made a slight involuntary movement. However, she said quite firmly, "They knew almost immediately that I was not."

"But they thought so in the beginning? Before they arrived here?"

"Yes," she admitted, "but I don't see why that—"

"Well, never mind. We've talked about them much more than I ever intended. And the fact is that it doesn't really matter which of us is right, because they're leaving the day after tomorrow, aren't they?"

"Leaving!" She could not hide her disappointment.

"Yes. I heard them saying something about it at the desk just before lunch."

"O-oh." For a moment Elinor was too nonplussed and put out to say more. Then she rallied and said with some spirit, "Then you needn't concern yourself with my affairs quite so deeply, need you? In future please don't try to control my friendships. After all, you wouldn't like it if I suddenly started interfering between you and Rosemary, would you?"

"Rosemary?" He looked startled. "What do you mean by that, exactly? What do *you* know about Rosemary and me?"

"Hardly anything," Elinor told him lightly. "About the same as you know of the von Eibergs and me."

And, laughing in a provoking little way that would have astonished her family, she went off, while Kenneth stood looking after her with a rather complicated expression.

Emboldened by the success of her exit line, Elinor sought out Ilsa and asked her if it were true that they were leaving so soon.

"Unfortunately, yes." Ilsa smiled, but she looked

genuinely regretful. "We are off to Vienna the day after
tomorrow."

"I thought you were staying much longer," Elinor
could not help saying.

"So did I." Ilsa still looked smilingly regretful. "But
sometimes plans do change quite suddenly, don't they?"

Elinor hardly knew what to say to that. It was not her
experience that plans changed with quite so much speed
and abruptness. But of course that was the business of the
von Eibergs themselves.

"I'll miss you," she said with a sort of shy candor.

"Oh, you nice girl!" For a moment Ilsa's hand rested
on Elinor's arm with a gesture of such sincere good
feeling that Elinor found herself wishing Kenneth could
have seen it. "We shall miss you too. If only—" She
stopped, sighed and then gave a little laugh, as though at
herself. "Well, that's the way life is. Perhaps you will
come to Vienna later, and then we shall meet again?"

The prospect sounded entrancing, Elinor could not help
thinking, but she smiled and slightly shook her head.

"I don't think we are going there. I wish we were. It
sounds such a romantic city. I've always wanted to see
it."

"It has a charm all its own. My grandmother used to
say that no one who had not known Imperial Vienna in
the early days of the century could imagine *how* charming
and elegant it could be. But it still retains a little of its
elusive beauty."

"You make it sound . . . sad, somehow."

"Well, it is sad," Ilsa said. "At least, it has that touch
of melancholy that clings to all things that represent a lost
and lovely age."

Elinor said nothing. For suddenly she thought that
described the von Eibergs too. That was partly why they
appealed so much to her warm and affectionate heart.
Kenneth would have laughed at her for it, but the feeling
was strong upon her.

The next morning Elinor slept unexpectedly late. Her
employer had told her the previous evening that he would
not require her, and, with a mind free from responsibility,
she slept dreamlessly and long. To complete the

indulgence, she had her breakfast in her room—or, rather, on the sunny balcony looking over the snowclad scene to the Zugspitze.

When she finally sought out Lady Connelton, it was to be greeted with, "Ken asked me to say goodbye to you. He left about half an hour ago to catch the train to Garmisch."

"He has left? Already?" She was far more dismayed than she wanted to be. "I thought he was going by the later train."

"He changed his mind," Lady Connelton said equably.

Elinor told herself it did not really matter. If they had parted on strained terms, that was his fault, not hers. But it depressed her not to have made it up, as she phrased it to herself.

There seemed little the Conneltons required of her that day, and in the afternoon Rudi took her for the promised skating lesson. Ilsa was packing, so they tramped off together through the crisp, glittering snow, their breath clouding in the still, clear air, and their eyes bright with laughter and mutual interest.

The atmosphere was exhilarating to a degree and, by the time they reached the frozen meadow, which did excellent duty for an outdoor rink, Elinor had, astonishingly, become convinced that she *could* skate. She had never felt so gay and confident in her life before, and the feeling undoubtedly had something to do with the way her companion's handsome eyes surveyed her.

Her unusual sense of confidence even survived the lacing on of hired skating boots and the first stumbling to her feet in this unfamiliar footgear. Then Rudi took her crossed hands in his, the strength of his wrists making her feel unexpectedly secure, and, after a little initial sliding and slithering, to her amazement she found herself skimming along for whole stretches, feeling, she thought, as a bird must feel as it swooped over the icebound earth.

"It's glorious!" she cried, laughing aloud for sheer pleasure—and then almost immediately sat down hard on the ice.

They both laughed inordinately over that. Then he pulled her expertly to her feet, and for a moment she was almost in the circle of his arm, close against him, so that she could see the color under his fine olive skin and almost feel the pulse of the vitality which emanated from him.

It was a curiously exciting and disturbing moment, one which left her tingling with something other than the sparkling cold. But it was over almost before the impression was registered, and presently they were skating off together again, Elinor not even noticing that the fringe of spectators watched her and Rudi rather more than they watched anyone else.

All too soon the afternoon light began to fade, and the brief, lovely experience was over. As they walked homeward, Elinor tried to tell him how much she had enjoyed herself. But he brushed her thanks aside.

"You're a natural skater," he told her. "If only we were staying longer—" He broke off, just as his sister had, and sighed regretfully.

Elinor felt sorrier than ever about their going. And more than a little puzzled too. For she had never met anyone who appeared more footloose and fancy-free than the two von Eibergs. Why, then, should they have forced on them a departure which apparently neither of them wanted? It was all very odd.

There must be very much more in the background of their lives than appeared on the surface, she supposed. And now she was never likely to know more about them, for tomorrow they would be gone.

She tried to remind herself that she was lucky to have known them at all, that she was bound to meet and lose many delightful acquaintances on this trip. But none of this ready-made philosophy served her very well, and she felt unreasonably that there was nothing that she wanted quite so much as to know Rudi and Ilsa really well.

For once Lady Connelton seemed to want her company for most of the evening. And, while Elinor very willingly acceded to the modest demands that her kind employer made upon her, she could not help noticing that the von Eibergs obviously went off for an evening's dancing, down at the big hotel.

It would have been wonderful fun to have gone too. But this evening it was somehow impossible to make the suggestion. And tomorrow they would be gone.

Elinor dined quietly with Sir Daniel and his wife, sat knitting and chatting with Lady Connelton in the lounge, and went to bed early. Just before undressing, she went and stood by the open window of her balcony and listened to the faint sound of dance music borne on the still air from the hotel farther down the valley. She thought she could imagine the scene. He probably danced as well as he skated. "Ilsa too, of course," she added perfunctorily to herself. It was a pity.....

Well, it could not be helped. She undressed and went to bed, where she lay rereading the batch of letters that had come from home that day.

It must have been nearly an hour later, just as she was thinking of putting out her light, that a cautious tap sounded on her door.

"Hello!" Elinor leaned up on her elbow. "Who's that?"

"It's Ilsa. May I come in? Or are you more or less asleep?"

"Come in! I'm wide awake," cried Elinor, who was indeed so all at once. And Ilsa came into the room.

It was a rather pale, fatigued-looking Ilsa, however, and Elinor noticed at once that there was a long, wet smear all down her pretty bright red cape.

"Why, Ilsa! What's happened?"

"It was an accident—no, nothing terribly serious. But Rudi and I were knocked down by a car on our way back from the dance. It only grazed me, but Rudi's knee was hurt. Either a small bone broken or else a bad sprain. The doctor is having a look at him now. But, whichever it is, there's no journey for us tomorrow." Ilsa pushed back her hair from her forehead and laughed a little shakily. "We'll be here for some time longer."

CHAPTER FOUR

"Oh, Ilsa, I am sorry! About the accident, I mean. I can't help being delighted, of course, that you are going to stay longer, after all," Elinor exclaimed frankly. Then, noticing how tired and shaken the other girl looked, she added, "Sit down, dear, and let me get you something."

She was out of bed and reaching for her dressing-gown before Ilsa could make any protest. It was second nature to Elinor to look after people, and she took Ilsa's wet cloak from her, settled her in the most comfortable chair in the room and rang for hot coffee—Ilsa having rejected the suggestion of hot milk with a shudder.

"Won't coffee keep you awake, rather than steady you?" Elinor suggested.

"I don't care if it does. I shan't sleep for a while, anyway. Do you mind my staying here with you? I feel my own company isn't just what I want at the moment."

"Of course you must stay! Unless you prefer to go to bed in your own room, that is, and have me come and sit with you."

"No. I like it better here, thanks." Ilsa glanced round her almost curiously, and said with a sigh, "How restful your room is!"

"Yes, it's lovely, isn't it? And by daylight I think I have the most beautiful view in the place," Elinor said.

"It isn't that. Oh, it's a nice enough room, of course. Rather like my own, as a matter of fact. But you've impressed your own personality on it. I don't know quite what you've done, but . . . it's you. That's why it is restful."

Elinor was touched. This was the first time she had thought of Ilsa as being in the least in need of anything that *she* could supply. Until now the situation had been very much the reverse—the sophistication and experience of the other girl being something on which she herself instinctively leaned. Now Ilsa seemed, in some curious way, to have something in common with Anne when things went wrong at the shop. Or even with Deborah when school and her studies became too much for her.

The coffee was brought by a sympathetic maid who explained that the Herr Doktor had just left Herr von Eiberg, and it seemed that the injury was not a very serious one—only somewhat incapacitating.

Most of this was detailed at length in German, though she courteously threw in the few English words she had, for Elinor's benefit. As hardly any of these fitted the situation, however, Elinor was little the wiser, and Ilsa had to explain when the girl had gone.

"Then it really isn't a major disaster," Elinor said consolingly. "As I said before, I can't help being glad for my own sake that I shall have you here a little longer. I hope it doesn't upset your own plans too much. Was it vital that you should go to Vienna just now?"

"Vital—no. Nothing's ever really vital, as you put it." And again Ilsa pushed back her hair with that weary, slightly disillusioned air.

Elinor regarded her gravely.

"Why, Ilsa, you make that sound as though nothing really matters very much."

"Well, does it?" The other girl laughed shortly.

"Why, of course it does!" Elinor was a good deal shocked at such a view. "I think almost everything matters," she added earnestly.

Ilsa looked half-indulgent, half-impatient.

"Oh, you're so young!" she said.

"Not all that much younger than you," Elinor protested. And then, as some sort of inner knowledge touched her, "Am I?"

"About ten years in actual fact, I suppose." Ilsa smiled dryly, but not unkindly. "And about a hundred in experience."

"Oh, nonsense!" It was Elinor's turn to smile, indulgently. "That's just the way you see things at the moment. You're a bit shaken and depressed after the accident, you know. You really ought to be in bed."

"I don't want to go to bed," Ilsa retorted almost fretfully. She was as obstinate—very nearly as childish—about that as Deborah could be. "Go on talking to me. You soothe me."

Elinor laughed. Obligingly she asked, "What do you want to talk about?"

"Anything. Your philosophy of life; whatever it is that makes you so serene and—caring about what happens to people."

"I don't know that I have a philosophy of life," Elinor said slowly. Certainly she had never thought of herself as having anything that sounded so impressive! "When you say I am serene and gentle, I suppose you mean that I'm quiet." She smiled reflectively. "I come of a dear and noisy and busy family who are all passionately interested in their own affairs. I'm interested too. I like to hear about them, rather than to do things myself, quite often. I am used to listening, Ilsa. And so it comes naturally to me to be . . . I suppose 'passive' is the word."

"Oh, indeed, it isn't!" Ilsa dismissed that with a laugh. "If you were passive you would be dull. It's because you are *actively* interested and yet quiet that you fascinate people like me and Rudi."

Elinor was silent. She had not known that she fascinated him—them. But it was both moving and exciting to hear that she did.

"Go on," Ilsa urged.

"Well, I am genuinely interested in people," Elinor said at last. "I don't have to pretend to be. I just am. I was interested in you and Rudi the very first moment I saw you in the dining car. I thought you were like people in a book, and I longed to know what language you were talking and where you came from. I was thrilled when you spoke to me in the corridor. I don't know quite how I could have been anything else. Is it so surprising? Don't people usually like you and find you interesting?"

Ilsa smiled and shrugged slightly.

"Oh, we're reasonably attractive, I suppose, and people like to have us at parties because we pull our weight socially and that sort of thing. But they don't care about us or what happens to us as individuals. Why should they? You somehow give the impression of caring about people for themselves. Oh, I'm not expressing it well, of course, because there is really no way of describing these intangible things."

"I think you express it very well," Elinor told her. "I do care, as you put it. Of course I care about people. Whom should one care about if not 'people'?"

"Oneself, I suppose," the other girl retorted frankly. "That's what nearly everyone does, you know."

Elinor smiled.

"Well, I won't pretend I'm not interested in myself and what happens to me," she conceded. "That would be either stupid or insincere. But that doesn't rule out an interest in—even concern for—other people. Why should it?"

"It could do. What if your own interests conflicted very sharply with those of someone else? What would you do then?"

Elinor considered that. She had never before indulged in so much self-analysis, and this conversation half intrigued, half disturbed her.

"It all depends on the rights of the case, Ilsa," she said at last.

"There you are!" Ilsa laughed. "To most people the 'rights of the case' and their own interests are the same thing. That's what makes you different."

"But thousands of people argue the way I do," Elinor insisted.

"And millions argue the way I do," retorted Ilsa rather mockingly. "But never mind—you're sweet! And all the sweeter because you don't even know that you're unusual. I feel lots better now." She got up, stretched and yawned a little. "I'll look in and see how Rudi is and then go to bed. I think I shall sleep now. Good night, and thank you." And, quite unexpectedly, she kissed Elinor.

"Good night."

Elinor returned the kiss, once more curiously touched. She did not think Ilsa often kissed people. At least, not as though the kiss meant anything. And she could not help feeling that there was some sort of genuine emotion behind the impulse.

Ilsa went out of the room, and, left to herself, Elinor returned to bed, and lay there for quite a long time thinking about Ilsa and Rudi, infinitely glad that she was to see more of them, after all.

The next day, the chief topic of conversation in the place was Rudi's interesting accident. A broken arm or leg on the skiing slopes would have been a very ordinary affair. Such things happened any time. But to be knocked down by a car in Ehrwald was something of an event. For one thing, cars were not particularly numerous, and those that did appear usually negotiated the village street with care.

"I hear it was a girl who was driving," Lady Connelton said, over the breakfast table. "She isn't staying here, but at the big hotel." Thus was the shame attached to a rival establishment.

"Someone said she had only just arrived," Elinor contributed. "She was driving in."

"A somewhat unfortunate debut," observed Sir Daniel dryly. "Who is she?"

No one seemed to know that, though Liesel—who waited on table and liked to join in conversations—volunteered the information (unsupported by any evidence, so far as anyone could see) that she was probably American.

After breakfast, Rudi spent a delightful morning holding court. He lay in a long chair on his balcony and almost everyone in the hotel visited him to commiserate with him and hear details of the accident.

Elinor was, reluctantly, an exception, because there was some work sent by Kenneth from Munich, and, by some obscure action of conscience, she felt bound to attend to this first before going to see Rudi. Had Kenneth been there to say that work must come before visits she might even have argued the point. But, as he was not, she felt bound to be specially scrupulous.

She promised herself a visit after lunch, but then Rudi was resting, on the doctor's orders, and so it was late afternoon before Elinor finally went to make inquiries and express her sympathy.

He had evidently not long woken up, because he gave her a lazy, singularly sweet smile that made her heart beat unusually quickly, and said with rather less than his customary alertness and vitality, "Please come in, *Liebling*"—which even Elinor knew meant nothing more nor less than "darling." "I thought you were not coming to see me at all. Everyone else seems to have been torn with anxiety about my state of health, but you very properly dismissed my sprained knee as a minor matter. Is that it?"

"No, of course not." She stood smiling down at him, as though she could not help smiling when she looked at him. "I had some work to do and—"

"Work—work!" he mocked. "Does that always come first with you? Are your poor friends nowhere?"

"Don't exaggerate," Elinor told him equably, refusing to take his reproaches seriously. "Of course I found out from Ilsa at breakfast how you were. And, judging from the number of people who seemed to want to commiserate with you, I should think it was just as well that one person at least put off the visit until the afternoon."

"But did it have to be the one person I most wanted to see?" countered Rudi, his fine dark eyes sparkling with reproachful amusement.

"I suppose you would have kept that nice little speech for *whoever* came last," Elinor retorted. But she colored a trifle, in spite of herself, and hastily changed the subject by inquiring how he was feeling.

"Wonderful, since you have come!" he told her. "And I hear you were also inordinately kind to my dear sister when she most needed it last night."

"I hardly did anything," Elinor assured him, "except make a little fuss of her and see she had a hot drink and let her talk a bit. She had had a mild shock, you know, and didn't want to be alone. I know—I have two younger sisters who get like that when anything goes wrong."

"And younger brothers too?" he wanted to know, with a smile.

"Well, my younger brother is the most self-sufficient of us all. He doesn't often need anyone to whom to pour out his heart," Elinor explained, recalling Henry with a smile. "My elder brother does, though. He's rather inclined to fall in and out of love at the moment. I usually hear of the advent of each new divinity—and sometimes a little about her departure too."

Rudi laughed aloud at this, which made Elinor laugh

too. He seemed to be enjoying her talk of family.

"I almost wish you were my sister," he said. "Except that it's nicer to have you someone else's sister."

She refused to take up the implication of that. Instead, she said lightly, "Would *you* tell me about your falling in and out of love, if I were your sister, then?"

"I might. Except that I don't often do it."

"No?"

Perhaps she looked faintly sceptical, because he said, "Does that surprise you?"

"A little. You look the romantic kind who might," Elinor told him candidly. "If I may say so," she added demurely.

"Indeed you may say so." He laughed again, rather delightedly. "You are enchanting when you say these things. But let me convey a hint of cynical wisdom to you, *mein liebes Kind.* The people who look romantic are nearly always the most hard-headed, hard-hearted creatures on God's earth."

She looked at him consideringly, and, for a moment, her clear gray eyes showed that she was weighing him up in real earnest.

"Are you hard-headed and hard-hearted, Rudi?" she asked, with such a calm assumption that he would tell her the truth that, for the space of a few seconds, his laughing gaze wavered.

"Do I answer that in all seriousness?" he wanted to know.

"There is no point in answering it any other way," Elinor told him. "Since you yourself brought it up, that is. You were going to impart some cynical wisdom to me, you remember."

"You little wretch, you are laughing at me!"

"No. Or only a bit. But you are hedging now, and trying not to answer my question."

"Am I hard-headed and hard-hearted?" he repeated slowly, that slight smile of something like self-mockery just touching his handsome mouth. "I suppose I am a litte of both, Elinor. And not quite enough of either."

"And what do you mean by that, exactly?"

"Oh, dear child! If one can be entirely hard, one can do

very well for oneself, even in the world that has been left us. If one can be good and gentle and well-wishing like you, then at least the decisions are made for one. But if one is neither one thing nor the other—" He broke off suddenly, frowned, then laughed and said, "Here, how did we come to talk like this, anyway?"

"I think," Elinor said gently, "I asked you a probing question. And you were kind enough to reply quite seriously."

"Not too seriously," he countered quickly. "You must never take anything that we—Ilsa and I—say with complete seriousness, you know."

"But why not?"

"Oh—" he ran a hand through his thick, dark hair, making it stand up rather boyishly—"we rather feel that anyone who takes this crazy life quite seriously must either *be* mad or *go* mad. So mostly we live and think and feel on the surface. It saves one from crashing too badly when the disasters come."

"But do they have to come?"

The moment she had said that she would have liked to recall it. In some way, she knew it was the easy generalization of one who had never had to face stark disaster.

But Rudi smiled at her, and again it was that smile of unusual sweetness.

"Perhaps they don't have to come to everyone," he said, and he put out his hand and touched her cheek gently. "Never, I hope, to you. But Ilsa and I are almost the sole survivors of our family. We have seen our people, our home, our class and our country go. Better to live on the surface after that and pretend that nothing matters very much."

"You—" Elinor stared at him, and, without her even knowing it, tears filled her eyes and spilled over on to her cheeks. "You say that—that—"

"Don't," he exclaimed almost roughly. "You're crying. Why are you crying?"

She put up her hands and was surprised herself to find that her cheeks were wet.

"I don't know," she began. And then—"Yes, of course

I do. It was because of 'what you said. The completeness of it. About—about everything going.''

"Oh, my child—'' He put out his arm and drew her to him. "Does anyone still weep for the heartache of others? How very foolish and sweet and touching of you." And then he kissed her.

Unspeakably moved, Elinor kissed him quite naturally in return. She even hugged him for a moment in an impulse of unspoken sympathy. Neither of them noticed the slight knock on the door. And both of them started apart as they realized that someone had come into the room—a completely strange girl, who said, "Oh, excuse me—'' and prepared to depart once more.

Naturally it was Rudi who recovered first and, with sufficient presence of mind to try to make the episode seem of no special significance, he said quite calmly, "No, do come in. Were you looking for me?''

"Yes, I—as a matter of fact, I came to make my apologies in person. I'm afraid it was I who knocked you down with my car last night."

"O-oh." Rudi was completely himself again, and eyed the girl with a quizzical smile which had no trace of embarrassment in it, while Elinor, covered with confusion, would willingly have fled from the scene. Her more experienced companion, however, had no intention of letting her impart an air of guilt to a basically innocent occasion, and, with a slight gesture of his hand, he detained her when she would have slipped away. To the other girl he said, "Do sit down. I was told that my aggressor was an American girl. But now I see that she is not, I think, American."

"No, certainly not." The girl, who was very pretty and self-possessed, laughed too. "I had come straight out from London, and I'm afraid that, after two long days' driving, I was probably just that little bit less than careful."

"Not quite the moment to come charging into an unknown village at sixty miles an hour, Fraulein," Rudi said dryly.

"It was nothing like sixty!" the girl exclaimed indignantly.

"It felt like a hundred when you sent me flying," Rudi assured her.

"I am sorry! I came to apologize and so I won't argue about speeds. But I thought I had really just cleared you."

"You very nearly had. It was only a glancing blow from your mudguard. Otherwise," he added cheerfully, "you would probably be bringing a handsome wreath instead of your personal apologies."

The girl shuddered a little. But more for effect than from genuine dismay, Elinor thought.

"Please don't say such things."

"No? But surely the remark is the measure of my good fortune in escaping," Rudi said carelessly. "It was kind of you to come and apologize in person. Did you stay on in Ehrwald specially to do so?"

"Not exactly. I expected to meet a friend here. But, as a matter of fact, he had left. I shall probably stay for a day or two, all the same."

"Then I hope I shall see you again, Fraulein."

It was second nature to Rudi to make himself agreeable in this way, but Elinor experienced a slight stab of something almost like jealousy when she heard him being so nice to someone else. Someone who had knocked him down with her car too!

The girl, however, took the remark as a friendly dismissal—as indeed it was—and rose to go.

"The doctor tells me that you'll be laid up for a few days—" she began. But Rudi interrupted her with a smile.

"You are too kind! Do you mean that you have actually already discussed your victim with the doctor?"

"Of course. There's the question of my responsibility for extra expenses incurred, you know."

"Fraulein, I don't think we shall quarrel over those." Rudi held out his hand to her. "It is true that your—intervention prevented my going to Vienna today, as I had intended. But, in that admirable mood known to the British as 'making the best of it,' I have come to the conclusion that, after all, what I really want to do is to stay on here. I am indebted to you for making this clear to me." He was in no great hurry to return to Vienna.

The girl laughed at that and, as though she could not help it, her glance slid for a moment to Elinor, standing silent and as inconspicuous as she could make herself in the background.

"Well," she agreed good-humoredly, "things do sometimes work out that way. But it is generous of you to regard my carelessness in that light. Please express my regrets to your—other sister. The one I also knocked over."

"Thank you, I will," Rudi said gravely. And then the girl inclined her head to Elinor and went out.

"Why did you let her go away thinking I was your sister?" Elinor blurted out.

"It hardly seemed worth while undeceiving her in the circumstances," Rudi replied calmly. "She will be here only a day or two. We shall probably never meet again. If she likes to think that she came in to find me affectionately kissing my sister, well and good. If she even mentions the fact to anyone, no one will be the wiser. Altogether a very satisfactory solution of a slightly tiresome problem."

"I don't think she really believed I was your sister," Elinor could not help saying.

"Very likely not," Rudi agreed carelessly. "That also doesn't much matter, I think. We just found a pleasant formula of words which covered the slight embarrassment of us all."

Elinor could not help feeling that her own embarrassment had been increased, rather than reduced, by the final subterfuge, but she felt it would be ungracious to press her own views further, when Rudi evidently thought he had saved her rather neatly. At least the girl was a complete stranger.

"You don't even know her name, do you?" she asked rather anxiously.

"I did hear it last night, but I don't know that I recall—" He frowned and made an obvious effort to remember. "Rosalind something. Rosalind—Rosaline— No! Rosemary—that was it. Rosemary Copeland. Quite a charming name. It suits her somehow."

"Rosemary?" Elinor said slowly, passing the tip of her tongue over her lips and finding them unnecessarily dry. "Are you sure it was—Rosemary?"

"Quite sure." Rudi seemed rather pleased with himself for having remembered it. Then he glanced at Elinor. "Why? Do you know the name?"

"No," Elinor said quickly. "I really must be going now. Lady Connelton may be needing me."

Rudi bade her a lazy, almost affectionate farewell, evidently believing that no further embarrassment could possibly result from the scene. Elinor hoped he was right.

The name was not *so* uncommon, she assured herself. It was ten chances to one that this was not Kenneth's Rosemary.

At first she thought she would tell Lady Connelton about the girl coming to apologize for having run Rudi down. She could mention the name quite casually and see if there were any reaction. For, she remembered from the overheard conversation in the library, Lady Connelton had evidently had some acquaintance with Kenneth's Rosemary, whoever she might be.

But when she actually came to framing the sentences she was overcome by sudden shyness and knew that she could never carry off the scene with calm self-possession. So she decided not to say anything at all—just to leave things as they were, and hope that the girl would leave the village again without their meeting.

This was too much to hope in so small a place, however. The very next morning proved how vain a hope.

Sir Daniel had sent Elinor down to the countrified post office to inquire about a parcel expected from the London office, and as she stood at the counter, a friendly, familiar voice greeted her. Turning reluctantly, Elinor saw that the girl in the charming black and yellow skiing outfit was Rosemary Copeland.

She responded to the greeting and tried to look as amiable as possible, but Elinor was well aware that the glance bestowed upon her contained an element of mischievous interest and curiosity with which she could well have dispensed.

"How is . . . your brother today?"

"Mr. von Eiberg isn't my brother." Rudi might be able to keep up this sort of thing, but Elinor could not. "I think he is going on quite well," she added a little stiffly. Then she turned back to the counter and inquired about her parcel.

It had arrived, it seemed, but there were some formalities, which involved giving both the name of the sender and the recipient. Elinor determinedly focused her attention on the matter in hand, and hoped that the other girl would have drifted away by the time the transaction was completed.

This was not the case, however. As Elinor turned once more from the counter, Rosemary Copeland, who had obviously been waiting for her, fell into step beside her and accompanied her out of the post office.

"I couldn't help hearing the name you mentioned when you collected that parcel," she said, as they started up the village street together. "Do you know Sir Daniel Connelton well?"

A most disagreeable sensation invaded Elinor—a feeling of the inevitability of something very unwelcome to come. But it was useless to prevaricate.

"He is my employer," she said, as calmly as she could. "I am his secretary."

"*Are* you?" The other girl stopped in her tracks for a moment. Then, as she trudged on again through the snow, she laughed on a note which held something of mischievous amusement and something of genuine annoyance. "So you are the girl the particular Connel-tons chose in preference to me."

CHAPTER FIVE

It was quite the most uncomfortable moment Elinor had ever experienced. In the usual way, of course, she was the last sort of girl to be involved in a questionable situation and she had no idea how to cope with this one. She could only think how mortifying it was that this girl, of all people, should have been the one to see her do something which, innocent though her motive had been, would take some explaining even to someone who knew her well.

There was an awkward little pause, while Elinor tried to think of something graceful and casual to say. But, long before she could do so, the other girl went on, with the faintest note of amused malice sounding in her voice, "I like your Rudi von Eiberg. Is he one of the party?"

"Oh, no. We met him and his sister on the journey out. They happened to be coming to Ehrwald too."

"How very nice—for you," the other girl said, and this time her laugh clearly recalled the circumstances of their first meeting.

Try as she would to appear unaffected by this, Elinor felt her cheeks go crimson. And then, in a burst of candor that came naturally, if ill-advisedly, to her, she exclaimed:

"I know one doesn't usually go out of one's way to explain private affairs to strangers, but, since you must have got an entirely wrong impression yesterday, I'd like to say that I am not at all on—on kissing terms with Mr. von Eiberg. I was just—moved by something he told me—and it made me cry. And he—I suppose he thought that the best way of consoling me. It all sounds dreadfully silly put into words, but—"

"It doesn't at all," Rosemary Copeland retorted lightly. "It sounds immense fun. I think I shall try crying a few tears of remorse on his shoulder. I shouldn't a bit mind being consoled the same way." And she laughed.

"But I *assure* you—" began Elinor. And then she saw that it would have been much, much better to have left all this clumsy explanation unsaid.

She looked indescribably chagrined. At which the other girl, laughing and patting her arm—a familiarity which Elinor resented—exclaimed, "Don't worry. I'm not the kind to tell tales."

Immediately Elinor knew that she was. She would tell them amusingly, and only just the least bit maliciously—but completely damagingly. Further protestations, however, would be less than useless, and in any case, they had now arrived at the hotel. Elinor was glad.

"Are you coming in to see Sir Daniel and Lady Connelton?" Elinor asked stiffly. "You know them, don't you?"

"I have met her once or twice—not him. But no, thank you, I don't think I'll come in without the moral support of Ken. Anyway, I've decided to leave Ehrwald today. I'm going on to Vienna."

Elinor could hardly disguise her relief.

"Perhaps we shall meet there?" Rosemary went on.

"I don't think so," Elinor said quickly. "I haven't heard anything about our going to Vienna."

"One never knows," Rosemary Copeland said rather wickedly.

Then they parted with a few cool words, and Elinor almost ran into the hotel, hoping profoundly that she would never have to see that laughing, brightly inquisitive face again.

To her surprise, she found Ilsa and Lady Connelton chatting away in the lounge like old friends, though previously they had not seemed to have so very much in common. And, as Elinor approached, Lady Connelton looked up and exclaimed, "Here she is! Come here, my dear, and let us hear what you think of our little plan."

Elinor came and sat down, smiling and happy once more to be with people who neither disconcerted nor alarmed her.

"How would you like to visit Vienna?"

Lady Connelton dangled the prospect before Elinor as one might dangle a toy before a child. And, in the ordinary way, Elinor's reactions would probably have had something of a child's delight and astonishment in them. As it was, following so immediately and with such disturbing coincidence on Rosemary's talk of meetings in Vienna, the proposal had an alarming, as well as a fascinating quality to it.

"I should . . . love it, of course," she began soberly. Then she glanced from one to the other. Both, she thought, had a slightly conspiratorial air. "Is it Sir Daniel's idea?" she inquired.

Lady Connelton rubbed the bridge of her nose

reflectively, a habit of hers when she was considering her words.

"Not exactly," she admitted. "Not yet, that is. But I believe I might make him think it was, which is always such a big help, of course, when you want a man to do something. He doesn't know anything about it yet. But I must say that I find the idea most attractive."

Elinor thought of seeing Vienna with Ilsa—and Rudi. She too then found the idea so attractive that she almost managed to thrust into the background the vague, uncomfortable possibility of running across Rosemary Copeland somewhere in that city.

But the fears refused to be entirely banished, and so she inquired, with a casualness which had considerable anxiety, "Would Kenneth come too, do you suppose?"

"Oh, I expect so. I don't think he has an unlimited capacity for enjoying snowy scenery and rural peace any more than I have," Lady Connelton replied briskly. "It is very lovely here, of course. But—" her eyes sparkled—"I want to do some shopping, and Vienna is a woman's shopping paradise."

"You could either pick up the Arlberg Express," Ilsa suggested helpfully, "and go by train from Innsbruck. Or you could have a car and go at your leisure by way of Salzburg and—"

"That's it!" declared Lady Connelton, full of energetic good humor. "I think my husband has some business to attend to in Salzburg. We will all go together."

"You don't think he ought to have a longer rest here first?" Elinor felt bound to say, though her desire to make this trip was rising every moment.

"No, no," declared Sir Daniel's wife, a trifle cavalierly. "He is as right as rain by now. Just a little bored, which makes him think about symptoms he hasn't got. This change will do him a world of good too. We'll have a care and take our time—that's an excellent idea. But mind—" she added to Elinor—"nothing about this to my husband for the moment."

"Of course not!" exclaimed Elinor, who would never, in any case, have taken it upon herself to volunteer information to her employer unasked.

"I'll choose the best time and circumstances to let him know what a good idea he has had," Lady Connelton said, with a twinkle in her eye.

Then she took the parcel that Elinor had collected and went off with a satisfied air—possibly to find out if the circumstances were propitious for her husband's immediate enlightenment.

As she departed, Ilsa met Elinor's glance, and gave her the slightest roguish wink.

"Ilsa! What is that for?" Elinor wanted to know, as soon as they were alone.

"Comment on a neat piece of work," Ilsa retorted carelessly. "Now we shall have you in Vienna at the same time as ourselves. Rudi told me I was to see about it somehow."

"Rudi did?" Elinor was shocked. "Do you mean that this is a—a sort of put-up job?"

"Only in so far as all one's little plans to get one's own way might be called that." Ilsa smiled and shrugged. "You obviously couldn't come without your employers. Equally obviously your employers must be made to see how much they would enjoy such a visit."

"Ilsa, you are shameless." Elinor laughed protestingly, and a trifle uncomfortably.

"Not at all. They will enjoy themselves immensely. We will even go to great trouble to see that they do. I like your Lady Connelton."

"Oh, so do I!" Elinor agreed emphatically. "She is a darling to me. More like a very nice aunt than my employer."

"It would be rather fun," Ilsa said reflectively, "if we could all go together."

"By car?"

"By car."

"There would be six of us," Elinor pointed out doubtfully.

"There are six-seater cars to be had," Ilsa replied coolly. "I am sure Sir Daniel knows how to get hold of one."

Elinor was silent, again feeling rather uncomfortable. It would, of course, be lovely to have Ilsa and Rudi with them, and if the Conneltons had of their own accord offered the von Eibergs a lift to Vienna, that would be one thing. But she could not quite escape the impression that Ilsa was once more getting ready to pull strings and that she was merely making use of the Conneltons for her own and her brother's convenience.

"Well, we'll see what Sir Daniel has to say about the whole thing," Elinor said. And if there was a faint hint of reserve in her manner, Ilsa apparently did not notice it.

Sir Daniel said "yes." Not, Elinor was relieved and pleased to find, because he was taken in either by his wife's good-humored scheming or by Ilsa's more subtle arranging, but because he genuinely liked the idea.

"I can't say I ever need much persuasion to go to Vienna," he told Elinor, with a reminiscent smile, when he broached the subject over dictation a morning or two later. "First place abroad I ever visited."

"Was it?" Elinor smiled at him sympathetically.

"I was a schoolboy then, before the First World War," Sir Daniel went on reflectively, as though in retrospect he looked at another world. As indeed perhaps he did. "It's the most romantic city in Europe, I suppose. London's the finest, Rome's the most beautiful, but Vienna is—or was—the real city of romance. You'll probably fall in love there—" he glanced indulgently at Elinor— "everyone does. That's when the Danube seems blue, you know. That's what they say—it's blue only when you're in love. Rather a muddy gray most other times, to tell you the truth. Well, well, it was blue enough for me that first time." He chuckled a little to himself. "I've forgotten what her name was," he added elliptically. "She was a dancer at the Opera, and old enough to be my mother, I expect. But she said six words to me at the stage door—and, I can tell you, the Danube was blue."

Elinor laughed delightedly and looked at her employer with new eyes. She had long ago decided that she liked him very much, but she had not before suspected him of quite so much humor and understanding.

"I am sure I shall adore it all," she said. "And I'll try not to fall in love more lastingly than you did."

"Well, there are plenty of other things to do too," Sir

Daniel told her. "You can go shopping with my wife. She thinks she arranged this trip." And he laughed good-humoredly. "Fact is I meant to fit in some days in Vienna all along. I suppose we may as well take that good-looking Hungarian pair along with us. It will be easier for them travelling by car, with that injured knee of his."

"I think they would like it very much," Elinor agreed gravely.

"Of course they would," her employer said good-humoredly. "That was probably her whole idea in suggesting the plan to my wife originally."

"Oh—" Elinor colored a little on Ilsa's behalf, both amused and put out that Sir Daniel read her friend so well.

"No harm in it," Sir Daniel observed tolerantly. "She is amusing and good company. There are a great number of people in the world today scrounging very much more than car-lifts without wanting to be even agreeable in return. Graciousness and good manners are extra-ordinarily acceptable, even if one is being made use of a little."

"I suppose they are," Elinor said soberly, not having thought of this before. "And Ilsa has lots of very good qualities too, you know."

"Very likely, very likely," agreed her employer absently, as he glanced through some papers on his desk, the subject of the von Eibergs finished so far as he was concerned. "I'll have a word with Kenneth on the 'phone this evening. He should be back the day after tomorrow, and I'll suggest to him that we set off for Vienna the next day." There was evidently no doubt in Sir Daniel's mind that Kenneth would accompany them. "He can drive. I don't doubt that both the von Eibergs can too, but he won't want to overstrain that knee of his yet. We can do the journey in a leisurely way, stopping one night in Salzburg, as my wife says."

And so it was arranged.

The von Eibergs accepted the invitation to join the party with an air of pleasure and surprise that did them credit, and, as Ilsa had so confidently predicted, Sir

Daniel was able to arrange for the hire of a big car without apparent difficulty.

Everything has worked out splendidly (Elinor wrote to her family). As we shall be coming back here, we are leaving most of the heavy luggage, which makes the travelling arrangements much easier.

Rudi's knee is much improved. He still limps a bit, but is quite active again, and declares that he will be fully able to show me round Vienna in a few days' time. I am sure he—and Ilsa too, of course—are going to be the most wonderful guides. It seems they still have their stepmother living in Vienna. All their real relations are dead, as I told you. But this stepmother remains, and I think they mean to take me to see her.

I can't help feeling most curious. Rudi describes her as "fabulous"—whatever he means by that.

This afternoon I went down to the village with Ilsa to buy some souvenirs. They have some charming woodwork here, and hand-painted tiles, with designs of the local flowers on them, and of course the Tyrolean pottery. Ilsa bought a lovely cottage scene carved in wood—like a picture in three dimensions. I thought it was charming, but not quite what I would have expected Ilsa to choose for herself. And then she told me it was for Deborah—from Rudi!

Wasn't it sweet of him? I had told him about Deb trying so hard in her French test and doing unexpectedly well, and he said she ought to have a prize. At the time, I suppose I laughed and explained that prizes were only given at the end of term and that, in any case, Deborah had never had one. And it was his idea that she should have one now—from him.

I won't send it, Deborah, because it might get broken, but I thought you would like to know that it is coming. I wish Ilsa and Rudi would come to London one day. I should love you all to meet them. Well—who knows? Somehow I feel that our friendship can't possibly begin and end here.

Rudi's interest in the family and his charming and good-humored gesture toward Deborah had completely won

Elinor's heart, and since the Conneltons also appeared to take considerable pleasure in the company of the two von Eibergs, it seemed that the proposed trip to Vienna should please everyone. Except perhaps Kenneth.

Elinor awaited his return with feelings bordering on anxiety, for a variety of reasons. First, they had not parted the best of friends, and with Elinor this was such an unpleasantly novel situation that it troubled her. In addition, she was afraid the inclusion of the von Eibergs in the party would irk him. And, finally, she could not help feeling uncomfortable whenever she thought of Rosemary Copeland speaking of their possibly meeting in Vienna.

But when Kenneth did arrive, suddenly all her misgivings were swallowed up in a sort of shy pleasure in seeing him again. Somehow, she had not quite expected it to be like that, and the discovery was something in the nature of a delightful shock.

She had never been one to hide or dissemble the warmth of her feelings in her own home circle, and so, when it came to her turn to greet him, she said with patent sincerity, "Oh, Kenneth, I am glad to see you back!"

"Are you?" He laughed—a curiously pleased laugh—and, for the first time since she had known him, he flushed. "Well, I'm remarkably glad to see you, come to that. And to find that we're on speaking terms, after all."

Elinor blushed in her turn then, but fortunately he had turned away to hear Lady Connelton's plans for the projected journey to Vienna.

"You will not have to do all the driving," Sir Daniel told him. "I understand Miss von Eiberg is an expert driver too."

"Who?" Up went Kenneth's eyebrows.

"The Hungarian girl," Lady Connelton explained composedly. "Ilsa."

"But—I don't quite understand. Is she coming too?"

"Yes. And that amusing brother of hers also," added Lady Connelton. "But as he injured his knee recently in an accident, I don't think we must count on him for too much driving."

"I see." Kenneth's glance rested reflectively on Elinor for a moment, and again she felt her color rise, though she would have given anything to appear indifferent at the moment.

"Well, the plans seem to have been very well worked out," he conceded. "Whose idea was it, by the way?"

"Mine," replied the Conneltons simultaneously. Then they both laughed and Sir Daniel added, dryly but good-humoredly. "Perhaps, my dear, we both had a little prompting."

"Very likely," Lady Connelton agreed indulgently.

"Very likely," repeated Kenneth. And once more his glance rested on Elinor for a moment.

She wanted very much to assure him that she had nothing to do with this business. But, remembering the disastrous results of her over-explaining herself to Rosemary Copeland, Elinor remained silent and had to let Kenneth think what he would.

The next morning they made an early start, for they wanted to break the journey at Innsbruck, so that they could have at least a glimpse of the beautiful provincial capital of the Tyrol.

It was a clear fine day, with already a hint of spring in the air. That indefinable impression of life stirring and sap rising, even though, as yet, nothing was putting forth green shoots.

Everyone appeared to be in excellent humor, and if Kenneth felt some reservations about the inclusion of the von Eibergs in the party, he concealed the fact admirably, and even sparred rather amusingly with Ilsa.

At Innsbruck they stopped for lunch, and took some time to stroll along the celebrated Maria-Theresian Strasse, with its matchless view of the snow-capped mountains that surround Innsbruck.

Much though Elinor would have liked to linger, there was no time to take more than a glance at the Imperial Castle and the famous Goldenes Dachl—that fairy-tale structure with its fire-gilt copper tiles that make it look as though it is literally roofed with gold. For the days were still short and they wanted to complete the first stage of their journey by daylight.

So they drove on through the bright, clear afternoon, and came at length to Salzburg, that flower of all festival cities, where all the cultural streams of Eastern and Western Europe seem to have united. And, as Elinor gazed for the first time on that lovely baroque city of the plain, surrounded by picture-book mountains, Rudi said, half-smiling, half-serious, "No wonder Mozart was born here. Heaven could not have chosen better."

The light was beginning to fade, but the outlines of the castle on the hill were still discernible. And, as they drove along by the hurrying, chattering Salzach, Sir Daniel explained to Elinor how, in former years, when the *Glockenspiel*, or silvery peal of bells in the town, used to play a Mozart air at sunset, from far away in the castle on the hill, the organ would reply with the same air, so that the sound, borne faintly on the breeze, would seem like some celestial echo of harmony from another sphere.

"They don't do it any longer." Sir Daniel shook his head sadly. "Organ out of repair, I suppose, or something equally prosaic. But it was part of the magic of Salzburg—and one's youth."

"They'll mend the organ one of these days," Lady Connelton declared cheerfully. "There's no need to get melancholy and nostalgic, dear."

This annoyed Sir Daniel, who had been rather enjoying his little bit of melancholy nostalgia. But before he could reply sharply, Ilsa leaned toward him with her sweetest, most understanding smile and said, "Half the charm of Austria lies in its nostalgic memories, doesn't it?"

"Of course, of course," Sir Daniel agreed, and evidently thought Ilsa had justified her inclusion in the party.

Their hotel was situated in one of the superb seventeenth-century squares, and, as Lady Connelton remarked with satisfaction, it seemed that the comfort within equalled the picturesqueness without.

"I am all for beauty and fidelity to period until it comes to beds and plumbing," she confided to Elinor. "That's one point where I do find myself so much in sympathy with the American tourist. The hardy and uncomplaining British have been touring the Continent for generations, you know, and putting up with exactly what they found there. But not so the Americans! When they started going abroad, they expected to find comfort and cleanliness along with the culture. And what the tourist expects and will pay for, he can always find on the Continent. They found their comfort and cleanliness all right, and we have all benefited since. Particularly the very superior people who talk about the almighty dollar," added Lady Connelton with characteristic humor, "and pretend there is some virtue in being poor and inefficient."

Elinor, who loved Lady Connelton's trenchant comments, chuckled over this, and admitted that she too was by no means superior to the attractions of sheer comfort.

Over dinner, plans were made for the following day, and, as these included a comparatively early start, Elinor had already resigned herself to seeing no more of Salzburg than could be managed in an early morning walk. However, when she announced her intention of getting up early for this purpose, Kenneth immediately said, "If you like, I will drive you round. You will see much more that way."

"But—" she looked rather doubtfully at him—"if you are going to drive during most of the day, you won't want to take me on a tour first."

Rudi began to say at this point that it would be very simple for him to take Elinor by taxi. But Kenneth merely repeated that he would make himself responsible for Elinor's seeing something of Salzburg.

"What time do you want to start? Half-past seven? Quarter to eight?" he inquired, and Elinor had the distinct impression that he was not at all displeased to be cutting out Rudi in this particular respect.

"Half-past seven—if you really don't mind starting so early," she said.

"I really don't mind," Kenneth assured her. And so it was settled.

That night, just as she was going to bed, Ilsa looked in to bid her a final good night, and, smiling a little quizzically at Elinor, she said, "Your Kenneth is becoming a trifle masterful, isn't he?"

"Masterful?" Elinor flushed at the word. "Toward *me*, do you mean?"

"Of course. Who else?" Ilsa looked amused. "He was very determined that no one else should show you Salzburg."

"Oh, that—that's just his manner."

"He feels he has some sort of proprietary rights in you, since you are part of his family group?" suggested Ilsa.

"Dear me, no!" exclaimed Elinor, who could not feel that any of his experience with her could have given him a feeling of proprietary rights. "It's just that when he's made up his mind to something, he doesn't let anyone else come in between."

"Which is rather how I should define masterful," retorted Ilsa with a laugh. Then she went off, leaving Elinor to think that over in the few minutes before she fell asleep.

The next day Elinor rose in good time, to find the morning clear and sunny, with a sky of pale, heavenly blue overhead and a springlike sparkle to everything on the ground. When she was dressed, she ran quietly downstairs through the still silent hotel, wrapped warmly in her burgundy-colored travelling coat, with a smoky blue scarf over her head, which imparted the faintest blue tinge to her eyes.

Kenneth was already waiting in the hall, and, coming up to him, she said a little breathlessly, "I'm not late, am I?"

"You are punctuality itself," he assured her. And, taking her lightly by the arm, he escorted her out of the hotel to the waiting car.

Elinor was very much aware of his hand on her arm—of the slight pressure of strong fingers through the thickness of her coat. And suddenly, for the first time in her life, she knew that a touch could be as exciting as any word or glance.

Long afterwards Elinor was to remember that early morning drive round Salzburg with Kenneth. And, even years later, she had only to close her eyes in order to see once more in recollection the wooded slopes of the Kapuzinerberg, the rushing waters of the Salzach, the rich, ornate lines of the buildings around the Residenzplatz, and, above all—from every part of the town and often with breathtaking suddenness—the fairylike fortress of Hohen-Salzburg, towering above the town.

Perhaps the fact of her having an attractive man to act as guide had something to do with the pleasure of the experience. Perhaps it was partly the magic of the clear, early spring morning. Or perhaps it was just quite simply true that Salzburg was the loveliest place in the world.

That, at any rate, was how it seemed to Elinor then, and every building and monument and vista which Kenneth showed her that morning took on a special charm, which ever afterwards remained in her memory.

"Rudi says it was no wonder that Mozart was born here," she said rather reverently, as they paused for a few minutes before the tall, narrow house where that rare spirit over whom all the Muses of the eighteenth century hovered first saw the light of day.

"A little fanciful and studied of our Rudi," Kenneth replied, in the specially matter-of-fact tone which he reserved for comment on the von Eibergs. "But I see what he means."

Elinor bit her lip.

"I don't know why you have to be so critical always of Rudi," she said severely. "He has been extraordinarily kind to me."

"I am sure he has," Kenneth agreed politely. But his tone left no doubt of the fact that a recital of Rudi's excellences would bore him profoundly.

So Elinor said no more as they drove slowly onwards. And presently they crossed one of the many bridges, back to their own side of the river, and a few minutes later they stopped once more outside their hotel, and the magic hour was over.

"Thank you so very much for taking me," Elinor said, as she got out of the car. "It was a wonderful experience, and I shall never forget it. Not *any* of it."

He gave her a half-puzzled, half-amused look at that, and said curiously, "You funny child—I believe you mean just that."

"Of course."

"Do any memories last so long?" he asked—lightly, and yet as though he really wanted an answer.

"Not all of them, I suppose. But there are some things you remember always. You can take them out again and again, years afterwards, and look at them and find them as fresh as ever. I think," Elinor said slowly, "that perhaps they are the only things in life that nothing and no one can ever take away from you."

"I suppose they are," he agreed almost gently. Then he took her hand in his and smiled down at her in a way that suddenly caught at her heart. "Thank you, Elinor, for letting me give you one of those memories."

CHAPTER SIX

THE rest of the party was just coming down to breakfast as Elinor and Kenneth came in. And Lady Connelton, with a slight yawn, said she supposed that if only they had all had the same energy as Elinor and gone out early they would be looking as blooming and sparkling as she did now.

"*Do* I look like that?" Elinor smiled.

"Exactly like that," declared Rudi, coming up behind her. "When we get to Vienna, I am going to have my turn at devising early morning distractions. We'll go riding in the Prater. Or maybe we'll find one of the last of the open horse carriages and drive in the Ring and pretend the world hasn't changed from the days when the motor car came in and romance went out."

"That will be lovely," Elinor admitted with a smile. But she was rather glad Kenneth had not heard this last speech. She had an idea he might have characterized it as another of Rudi's "fanciful and studied" sayings.

In addition, she supposed that perhaps she ought to explain that she had never ridden a horse in her life, and could not quite see herself cantering elegantly in the Prater, whatever that might be.

But, on reflection, she decided that the whole effect of Rudi's nice little speech would be wasted 'if she started going into such mundane detail. So she contented herself with the general and enthusiastic comment which she had already made.

From Salzburg they drove that morning to Linz, through lake and mountain scenery that' held Elinor speechless with wonder and delight, and from time to time Rudi pointed out to her features which were obviously familiar to him but took on fresh beauty because someone was seeing them with fresh eyes.

It was hard to say where they first picked up one of the many tributaries hurrying along to swell the mighty waters of the Danube, but by the time they reached the lovely old medieval town of Linz, Elinor realized that they were already in the far-famed Danube Valley.

For a while, as they drove on that afternoon, the valley remained unexpectedly narrow. But then it began to widen out and presently, as they crossed and recrossed the shining, turbulent or muddy waters of the river—varying according to the type of country through which it flowed—Elinor began to understand how, of all the waterways of Europe, the Danube had somehow taken on a particular character of its own, so that it was regarded more as a personal force than a geographical feature.

"No wonder there are so many legends about it," she exclaimed to Rudi. "It is almost human!"

"It is superhuman," retorted Rudi with a smile. "While it lives I *think* Austria cannot die."

She glanced at him quickly.

"Is there any fear that it might? Why do you say that, Rudi?"

But, characteristically, he made no attempt to continue the melancholy subject further. Instead, he pointed out something of interest to Elinor, and was so amusing and gay about it that she thought she would never understand him, or his extraordinary facility for turning from sadness to gaiety within the space of minutes.

They were all tired by the time they came at last, late in the evening, to Vienna.

In spite of this, Elinor roused herself and tried to follow

the eager, rapid commentary which the von Eibergs kept up as they drove through the streets. But it was difficult to see much by lamplight, and what really interested her most at that moment was the fact that she would catch at any rate a glimpse of their house—or, rather, their stepmother's house—since the first stop was to be made there, before the Conneltons drove on to their hotel.

When they arrived, however, she could see little more than a stone gateway, leading into a flagged court. Over the gateway hung a lantern of ancient and beautiful design, and when Rudi pulled a long brass bell-pull at the side of the gate, a door on the far side of the courtyard opened, sending a further beam of light into the darkness.

By this light they saw an old man, wearing a green baize apron over a neat suit, come across the yard to take the luggage. At the sight of Rudi and Ilsa, his rather worn old face broke into a smile, and he welcomed them with a mixture of respectful affection and familiar severity which greatly intrigued Elinor, who was quite unused to the attitude of the old continental servant towards "the family" he served.

Goodbyes now had to be said, and, although the von Eibergs promised to call at the hotel the very next day, Elinor felt regretfully that a link was being broken. Ilsa kissed her goodbye, and then, rather unexpectedly, Rudi did too—under the somewhat quizzical regard of Kenneth.

Then the brother and sister followed the old man-servant into the shadows, and the car drove on.

"A very agreeable couple," commented Sir Daniel presently, breaking a few minutes' silence. "They both made admirable travelling companions."

"Very," agreed Kenneth non-committally.

"I wonder what their *background* is, exactly?" Lady Connelton said. "One couldn't tell much from the outside of that place. It could have led almost anywhere."

"Probably that was the courtyard of some old palace," Sir Daniel said.

"*Palace?*" Elinor was both impressed and startled.

"Yes, yes. Most of them have been turned into flats long ago," her employer explained.

"Is that their own home?" Kenneth inquired, more perhaps to make conversation than because he had any special interest in the von Eiberg background.

"No. It's their stepmother's home," Elinor said.

"So they have a stepmother?" For some reason or other, he laughed. "What sort of a stepmother?"

"They both describe her as fabulous," Elinor told him soberly. "She was an actress, I think. Her name was Leni Mardenburg."

"Leni Mardenburg!" exclaimed both Sir Daniel and Kenneth simultaneously. And then Kenneth added, rather unreasonably, "They would!"

"What do you mean by that?" Elinor was immediately up in arms on behalf of Rudi and Ilsa.

"Only that they have a genius for raking up dramatic detail about themselves," Kenneth said, somewhat unfairly. "Leni Mardenburg was indeed fabulous. She was one of the stage darlings of Imperial Vienna, years before the First World War."

"Must be about a hundred," remarked Sir Daniel reflectively.

"Oh, no. Somewhere in her eighties, surely," corrected Kenneth. "But no one ever knew her age, did they? I understand she looked round about thirty for something like twenty-five years. My father said he saw her play Portia when she couldn't have been a day under sixty. I suppose that was about the period she married the father of this pair."

"And collected all the family money," suggested Lady Connelton shrewdly.

"Could be," Kenneth said thoughtfully. "Though she must have salted down a good deal of her own, one way and another."

"There have been two wars and several depressions during her lifetime, don't forget," Sir Daniel said.

"That's true," Kenneth agreed.

And then they arrived at their hotel and, to Elinor's regret, this fascinating conversation came to an end. But she secretly determined that, if it were humanly possible, she would know more of the extraordinary personality who, a generation or more after her heyday, still had the power to make even Kenneth sit up and take notice.

The hotel where they had elected to stay had that air of faintly *passée* grandeur which clings to so many places in Vienna. But it was very comfortable—Lady Connelton had seen to that when the choice was made. And, although they had arrived very late in the evening, it seemed to be the concern of everyone to see that they should be made to feel welcome.

In her big quiet room, with what seemed to her to be slightly oversized furniture, Elinor took stock of her surroundings and thought, "It is like stepping into a novel. Almost an historical novel." And already she began to sense why it was that Sir Daniel found the place perennially fascinating.

It was the first time Elinor had ever stayed in a really big hotel—the "guest-house" at Ehrwald and the hotel in Salzburg being very much less intimidating places—and she was a good deal overawed by the unfamiliar surroundings.

Lady Connelton had said something about meeting downstairs for a meal, and Elinor supposed there would be no real difficulty in finding her way. But she found herself wishing that she had someone—Ilsa, preferably—who would accompany her this first time, and make her feel less alone as she started off down the immense, thickly carpeted corridor toward the elevator.

She pressed the bell timidly, and an elevator about the size of the drawing-room at home rose majestically to her floor. The operator drew back the wrought-iron gate and invited her in, with all the honors due to a visiting royalty—though perhaps a minor one.

Feeling very small, Elinor stepped in and, with a certain amount of creaking, the elevator sank once more to ground level. Here she was bowed out into a desert of rich, though rather worn red carpet and—now feeling almost exactly like Alice after she had nibbled the wrong side of the mushroom—Elinor left the comparative shelter of the elevator and started out across the red carpet, hoping that she would find her way to the dining-room without too much difficulty.

For a moment she could see no one in sight of whom

she could inquire, and wished now that she had ventured to ask the operator in English. Then, suddenly—with a degree of relief she had not previously associated with him—she saw that Kenneth was standing beside a table, reading a newspaper stretched on a curious wicker frame.

She made for him at once, with all the instinct of a homing pigeon. But, before she could reach him, someone else came running out of a side passage, with a delighted cry of, "Kenneth! I guessed you'd stay here if you did come on to Vienna. What luck that you came so soon!"

And the next moment Elinor had the surprising, and somehow most unwelcome, experience of seeing a pretty girl fling herself upon Kenneth and embrace him very heartily.

With feelings of unmixed dismay, she recognized the newcomer as Rosemary Copeland.

If Kenneth's transports of delight did not reach quite such fervent heights as Rosemary's, at least he kissed her back again with cordiality.

This left Elinor completely at a loss. She could not now intrude on the two—indeed she was terrified that her presence might provoke Rosemary to some mischievous disclosure—and the only thing she could do was gracefully change course for another part of the lounge, hoping that neither of them would notice her.

Even as she made the first movement, however, Rosemary caught sight of her and, with a half-friendly, wholly mocking smile, she called out, "Hello, there."

Someone rather more experienced than Elinor might perhaps have got by with a smile and a wave. But she made the fatal error of pausing, and, at the same moment, Kenneth turned and saw her.

"Why," he said, in considerable surprise, as Elinor came reluctantly forward, "do you two know each other?"

"We met," Elinor conceded, "in Ehrwald."

At the same moment the other girl said gaily, "Indeed we know each other. Quite well. I even know some of Miss Shearn's naughty secrets. Don't I?" And she appealed to Elinor for confirmation of this with a laugh that was frankly malicious.

The immediate attack was so unexpected that Elinor felt herself color violently with alarm and distress. But, while she groped ineffectually for some sort of casual reply, Kenneth came unknowingly to her rescue.

"Don't be silly," he said bluntly to Rosemary. "Miss Shearn is not at all the kind of girl to have naughty secrets, as you put it."

"That's all you know!" Thus challenged, Rosemary was at once upon her mettle, and when Elinor made a slight gesture of appeal and protest, she simply answered with the mischievous inquiry, "And how is your handsome beau? The one I pushed over with my car."

Elinor bit her lip.

"Mr. von Eiberg is quite well again now," she said stiffly. While, to her surprise, Kenneth exclaimed impatiently, "Don't use such silly and offensive expressions, Rosemary. Von Eiberg is a chance travelling acquaintance and nothing more at all."

Even at that moment, Elinor thought he was taking a good deal on himself to assert this so confidently. And Rosemary was provoked by the retort into still further argument, though all the time she was laughing.

"Oh, oh! Don't be so naïve, Kenneth," she warned him amusedly. "I believe you actually think Miss Shearn is as demure as she looks."

"That will do." Kenneth frowned. "You are embarrassing her."

"Not nearly so much as I did when I came in and caught her kissing the chance travelling acquaintance in his bedroom," retorted Rosemary lightly.

"Oh, *please*—" At the look of astonished distaste on Kenneth's face, Elinor could have wept with chagrin and embarrassment. "How can you say anything that makes me sound so—so horrid and cheap? You know quite well—"

But before she could justify herself, even in the stumbling phrases she was finding, Lady Connelton's cheerful tones interrupted her.

"Why, here you are! I've been looking for you everywhere. If everyone else isn't dying of hunger, I am. Come along and let's see if they can produce some genuine *wiener schnitzel* for us," urged Lady Connelton.

Elinor glanced round almost wildly. For a moment she thought she must break away from them all and run off back to her big, silent room, where no one could make dreadful-sounding accusations, like Rosemary Copeland, or look so freezingly incredulous as Kenneth now did.

But here were both the Conneltons, pausing only briefly for the necessary polite exchanges with Rosemary, and then moving on, obviously expecting Elinor to accompany them. She would have to go with them to the dining-room and make pleasant conversation as usual, even though she felt like weeping. And because they so obviously expected it, somehow she managed to make herself go with them.

Kenneth did not come immediately. He stayed behind to say something else to the laughing, bright-eyed girl who had already made so much mischief. Elinor would have given almost anything to have known what was said. But, when he rejoined them a few minutes later in the dining-room, she could not think, from his rather grim expression, that the subsequent conversation had done much to clear her.

It was a delicious meal, but once or twice Elinor thought it would choke her.

She tried to tell herself that Kenneth's good opinion was not of such overwhelming importance, but it was no good. She knew perfectly well that *anyone's* good opinion was of importance when it came to a question of a doubtful situation. She might feel as annoyed with him as she liked because of his glum expression and his presuming to judge her; she might tell herself over and over again that it was too bad that a perfectly innocent matter should have been reduced to these terms, to provide a malicious joke for someone she hardly knew; but the fact was that she had been made to seem cheap, both in Kenneth's estimation and her own. And the sensation was as disagreeable as it was novel.

"Are you tired, dear?" inquired Lady Connelton suddenly at this point, and Elinor realized that her manner must have become preoccupied indeed for her employer to seek some explanation for it.

She roused herself to say, "No—not really." And after that she managed to smile and contribute a few reasonably cheerful remarks to the conversation. Though she suddenly became completely dumb again when, turning to Kenneth, Lady Connelton said, "And what brings Rosemary here?"

"Who is Rosemary?" inquired Sir Daniel, before Kenneth could answer this.

"Rosemary Copeland, dear. Ned Copeland's girl," his wife explained in hasty parenthesis. "You've just met her."

"Oh, yes—yes," Sir Daniel agreed, obviously without much interest in Ned Copeland's girl. "He's a great bore," he added, as though Rosemary were somehow responsible for this.

"Well, she can't help that," his wife said generously. "But I'm rather interested to know why she turned up out here."

"It seems she came out to join friends for some skiing," Kenneth explained a little coolly. "Then, at the last minute, they were prevented from coming by some family complication. She stopped in Ehrwald for a day or two, rather expecting to see me there, and then came on to Vienna."

"Stopped in Ehrwald, did she? While we were there? It would have been polite of her to have let me know she was there," Lady Connelton remarked dryly. "After all, we do know each other."

"I think," Kenneth said slowly, "that she didn't want to thrust herself on you when I was not there. She tells me she met Elinor in the village and left it to her to mention her presence, so that you could see her or not, as you pleased."

"Elinor!" exclaimed Lady Connelton in great astonishment. "You never told me anything about it, dear."

They all turned and looked at Elinor then.

Taken completely off her guard by this fresh contretemps, Elinor went crimson and then rather pale.

"I . . . Miss Copeland made it perfectly plain that she preferred not to make any contact until Kenneth arrived," she explained hastily and a little breathlessly. "She—she certainly didn't suggest that she wanted me to mention anything about—about her being there."

"I suppose she thought you would do that anyway," Kenneth said rather impatiently. "It was the natural thing to do."

"Except that she . . . she implied that she wanted to . . . to make her introduction, in her own way, when you were there."

"I think you must have misunderstood her," Kenneth replied coldly, and Elinor felt perfectly miserable until Lady Connelton said cheerfully, "Anyhow, it was just as well, so long as the child didn't feel slighted, and she doesn't strike me as sensitive. If I had known of her presence I'd have had to do something about it, as her father is a member of Dan's club. In the circumstances, we were both spared a meeting which I should probably have found tiresome and she would undoubtedly have found boring."

And, on these philosophical words, she rose from the dinner table, thus breaking up the discussion.

So, it was over at last, and Elinor began to think gratefully of escaping upstairs under the protecting wing of Lady Connelton's presence. But, as they reached the dining-room door once more, Kenneth unexpectedly put his hand lightly round her arm and said—pleasantly, but in a manner not to be denied, "Just a moment. I want to speak to you."

It was her impulse to pull her arm away and say, "No!" But the Conneltons were already saying a brief good night to her and Kenneth. Then, as they left her, she found herself being guided into the big silent writing-room, whether she liked it or not.

At this late hour, and at an out-of-season period, there was no one else there, so that it was without any likelihood of interruption that Kenneth indicated a chair to Elinor and said, "Now, do you mind telling me what silly position you have been getting yourself into?"

His air of having the right to inquire carried such conviction that, for a moment, she almost conceded that right to him. Then some instinct, stronger than all her inexperience and natural diffidence, came to her rescue and warned her not to rush into nervous protests and excuses. Instead she replied, with a quietness and even a touch of dignity that astonished her, "How dare you speak to me like that? As though you had some right to question any behavior of mine, or berate me if you didn't find it to your liking?"

"I'm sorry." Kenneth was visibly astonished by this reaction. "But—" he stuck to his guns—"you won't deny, I suppose, that you and von Eiberg were seen in the sort of compromising situation one just does not get let in for, and—"

"I could," Elinor interrupted almost gently, "tell you to mind your own business, Kenneth, and leave me to mind mine. But that is not the way for . . . friends—" she chose the word deliberately and saw it had its effect on him—"to behave to each other. Any more than it is right for friends to speak the way you did to me, or suspect each other of almost anything, on the strength of a few mischievous words."

"They were not just a few mischievous words," he protested, but she had not before seen Kenneth's self-confidence so shaken.

"But it would still have been more friendly of you to have come to me and asked for my version of the facts, before condemning me unheard."

"That is just what I am doing," he reminded her. "Asking you for an explanation."

"But in what a tone, Kenneth! As though you knew I had been involved in something disreputable—and what had I got to say for myself now that you, the clever fellow, had cornered me?"

He actually flushed at that.

"I didn't mean to sound like that at all," he said stiffly. "I was a little . . . upset." He looked slightly surprised by the admission himself. "If I chose my words badly, I apologize."

She thought she would not split hairs by telling him that it had been his manner, even more than his words, which had been at fault. Instead, wondering dazedly how it was that she had somehow managed to become mistress of a situation which she had dreaded all through supper, she said coolly, "If you now want the real explanation of what Rosemary Copeland saw and reported so unkindly, the fact simply was that, when Rudi von Eiberg was injured, I—like everyone else in the hotel—went to his room to inquire about him—"

"But you were there alone."

"All right. I happened to be busy that day and was the last person to go to see him. We talked a little and—I don't even remember how the subject came up now—he said something about always taking things lightly, because then, when real disaster struck, one had not so much to lose."

Kenneth looked for a moment as though he were going to interrupt here. But he obviously then thought better of it and let her go on.

"I said—a little naively, I suppose," she admitted sadly, "that there was no need to suppose that disaster necessarily always came. But, the moment the words were out, I knew that I was a happy, normal creature, talking to someone who knew disaster in a sense I could never understand. In about a couple of sentences he described how he and Ilsa were the only survivors of their family—rootless figures from a world that no longer existed. The way he put it was so laconic and yet so—heart-breaking."

Kenneth bit his lip, but he said with a frown, "He really had no right to play on your sympathies like that."

"I don't think he played on my sympathies, Ken. He *had* my sympathy. Sympathy—like trust—is something one gives freely, and without criticism."

"Is that a rebuke?" he asked with a slight grimace.

"If you feel it is deserved—yes."

He swallowed that with some difficulty, she saw, but he did accept it, and after a moment he said, "Well, go on. What did you do then?"

"I cried."

"Oh, Lord!" He seemed both touched and annoyed by that.

"Not much—but it was a sort of shock. A sudden understanding, I suppose, of how terrible the world could be. And I think he was a good deal moved too, and that was when he kissed me. Whereupon Rosemary walked in, and drew what conclusions she liked."

"I . . . see."

He was, she thought, struggling with the unfamiliar sensation of being in the wrong. There was a short silence. And then, with a self-possession that the old Elinor would never have known, she said, "If you want to apologize, don't let me interrupt you."

He flushed at that, and his rather bold, bright eyes fell before her almost serene glance. She had never expected to see him so put out, and the knowledge that it was her own work was almost intoxicating.

"I am extremely sorry," he said slowly. "I realize that I was both smug and unjust, both of which are quite insufferable—"

"Oh, please!"

"But the only thing I can say in extenuation," he added with a slight, wry smile, "is that if I had not liked you I should not have bothered to interfere—mistakenly or otherwise."

"Oh, Ken!" The apology was so handsome that she forgot all her anger and distress and took both his hands in hers. "You couldn't put it more charmingly. Please don't say any more."

"I wasn't going to," he told her with a flash of humor. "Abasing myself is not my long suit."

And then they both laughed, and she felt his fingers clasp hers strongly.

"Am I forgiven?"

"But of course!"

"Good. Then I shall sleep tonight." And, even though she knew that was only a joke, she felt indefinably flattered that he should even laughingly suggest that he could lose a wink of sleep over her.

He came with her to the elevator after that, but as it appeared no longer to be running, she bade him good night and ran up the stairs with an indescribably lightened heart.

At the bend of the staircase, she turned and waved to him, and then went on once more, aware by some inner instinct only just awakened, that Kenneth stood looking after her, half-amused, half-puzzled, and wholly intrigued.

CHAPTER SEVEN

THE next morning Elinor awoke to a feeling of indescribable well-being. She lay there in bed for a moment or two, watching the pale sunlight filtering through the slatted shutters outside her window, and wondering why it was that she felt so satisfied with life.

Then suddenly she remembered her encounter the previous evening with Kenneth, and she knew that what made her feel so reassured—so elated, even—was the surprised realization that she had handled the whole thing extremely well. Less than a month ago such a thing would have been a sheer impossibility for her, and if this was what foreign travel did for one's morale, Elinor was all for foreign travel!

As she got up and dressed she hummed to herself. She felt that, in some way, the episode had given her some new light on Kenneth, and she remembered some of the things he had said with the keenest pleasure. (Not all of them, of course. But the less acceptable ones she dismissed from her mind.) What had pleased and surprised her most of all was his remark to the effect that he would not have presumed to interfere in her affairs if he had not liked her. The compliment might be oblique, but it was unmistakable.

Presently she went to the window and, pushing back the outer shutters, she looked out for the first time on what Sir Daniel had called the most romantic city in Europe.

Before her, in fascinating profusion and magically unstudied grouping, rose towers and domes and steeples. Almost immediately opposite her was the world-famous façade of the Opera House—still the heart and soul of

Vienna, though all except the façade had been destroyed during the war and then painfully and slowly rebuilt. And soaring over all, in isolated majesty and irreducible splendor, was the great Gothic steeple of the Stefanskirche—St. Stephen's Cathedral.

Suddenly Elinor felt she could not wait to explore it all. Shyness and reserve were all forgotten as she almost ran out of her room and along the wide corridor to the elevator. Even this spacious and gilded affair no longer held terrors for her. The man who was on duty that morning smiled at her and wished her "*grüss Gott*," and, following his instructions, she found her way to the breakfast-room.

None of the others was down yet, but it was an understood thing that they did not wait for each other in the morning, so she sat down alone to enjoy her coffee and rolls.

Hardly had she poured out her first cup of coffee, however, when Rosemary Copeland came into the room. She stood in the doorway for a moment, looking round. Then, seeing Elinor, she came over to join her.

"Good morning," she said, with unabashed amiability. "Ken said I was to come and apologize to you when next I saw you."

"Did he?" Elinor's tone was a little dry, in spite of herself. "And do you usually do what he tells you?"

"Mostly." Rosemary admitted. "It's habit."

"Habit?"

"Oh, yes. Ken is a bit like an elder brother to me." She pulled out the chair opposite Elinor. "May I come and sit with you?"

Elinor could easily have dispensed with the other girl's company, for she still felt sore about last night's incident. But it was difficult to see how she could refuse point-blank, and in any case, she was curious to hear more about Kenneth's being like an elder brother to her. So she indicated that Rosemary might join her and watched her slide into the seat opposite.

"How does Kenneth contrive to be like an elder brother to you?" Elinor inquired, before Rosemary could start any other, less absorbing, subject.

"Well, you see, during the war my parents sent me to the country to live with Ken's people. They were friends of theirs. Ken used to come home there in his school holidays, of course, and as he had no sisters, he used to treat me as sort of kid sister. The relationship continued to a certain extent as I grew up and so—" she grinned mischievously and rather charmingly—"I do tend to do what he tells me."

"And he told you to apologize to me?" Elinor smiled faintly.

"Yes. And really I do—in full style," Rosemary declared. "I didn't *quite* mean to make the scene between you and Rudi von Eiberg sound so startling."

"It was very unkind of you. Especially as I think you guessed it was entirely harmless," Elinor said, a faint tremor of indignation sounding in her voice even now.

"Yes, of course," Rosemary conceded carelessly. "Anyone could see you aren't the stuff of which flirts are made. Any girl would see it, I mean. Of course Ken is as stupid as most men about these things. I'm sorry if you were really upset. But—" she grinned suddenly—"it was a great temptation to make a drama of it, with you looking so solemn and Ken going bail for your good behavior in that most unusually rash way. I never heard him do it for anyone else."

"Am I supposed to laugh about it now and say it's all right?" inquired Elinor, trying to remain severe but somehow finding herself regarding Rosemary in much the same way as she would have regarded Deborah after some misdemeanor.

"I wish you would," the other girl admitted frankly. "After all, when you come to think of it, the whole incident wasn't so *very* important."

"You made it sound so!"

Rosemary laughed.

"I didn't mean it that way. I meant—well, did it matter *so* much what Ken thought, one way or the other?"

"Of course it did."

Rosemary stared at Elinor in sudden, wide-eyed interest.

"Are you rather sweet on Ken?" she inquired at once.

"Certainly not!" Elinor flushed with indignant amusement. "I just don't like being misjudged or thought cheap by any reasonably nice associate."

"Oh, I see. That's all right then."

Elinor glanced at the other girl with uncontrollable curiosity.

"Why is it all right?" she inquired, wondering—as she had several times before—whether Rosemary considered she had a proprietary interest in Kenneth.

"Just that—I was going to say it's so little good getting sweet on Ken. He never falls in love with anyone."

"Doesn't he?" Elinor said politely. And so strange and inexplicable a thing is human nature—that she immediately found Kenneth much more interesting than she ever had before.

"Oh, no. I've seen the most attractive and desirable creatures make passes at him," Rosemary declared. "He's very polite and sometimes quite charming and amusing in return, but he never loses his head."

"Perhaps that's just as well," Elinor suggested.

But Rosemary didn't seem to think so.

"His mother says—and I'm inclined to agree with her—that men of Ken's age should fall in and out of love a bit. I guess he's been a little spoiled, you know, with being a good deal run after."

"Perhaps," agreed Elinor, who would never have presumed to think of Kenneth as spoiled. And then the Conneltons and Kenneth came in, and this most interesting topic had to be abandoned.

"It's a wonderful day for shopping," declared Lady Connelton in a satisfied tone, as though there were some relation between the weather and the buying impulse. "I hope neither of you men wants Elinor today because I do."

Both disclaimed any intention of appropriating her time, though Sir Daniel did inquire curiously in what capacity his wife required her.

"Just to help me make up my mind about several things, dear," explained Lady Connelton vaguely, though everyone present knew that no one was better able to make up her own mind than that same Lady Connelton.

"I take it you are buying extensively?" grumbled her husband good-humoredly.

"Extensively," Lady Connelton agreed, without going into anything so debatable as detail.

She then turned to Rosemary and asked kindly if she would like to join Elinor and herself. But Rosemary, it seemed, had interests of her own—in fact, she was obviously a very self-sufficient young woman in most ways—and so, though she thanked Lady Connelton quite charmingly, she refused the offer.

Elinor was not sorry. For, although she no longer cherished any resentment against Rosemary—it was difficult to do so in the face of the disarming air of friendliness which Rosemary had now adopted—she was looking forward very much to a morning on her own with Lady Connelton.

They set off together from the hotel, Lady Connelton declaring that at least she knew her way to the Karntnerstrasse—the nearby heart of Vienna's shopping district. And, in a matter of minutes, Elinor found herself walking slowly along that strangely narrow but fascinating street, gazing in shop windows at the loveliest blouses and scarves and handbags she had ever seen.

"One could spend a fortune here!" she exclaimed.

To which Lady Connelton replied that, if she did not intend to spend exactly a fortune, she did mean to have a very pleasant and extravagant morning.

Elinor enjoyed every moment of it. She began to understand why Sir Daniel claimed—as he did—that the Viennese women were the smartest in Europe. Never in her life had she supposed that there could be so many enchanting dress accessories, and never, she thought, had she seen more attractive, elegant clothes.

Beside Lady Connelton's purchases, her own were modest. But she did buy a very lovely scarf for her mother, and the most fascinating little fob ornaments for Anne and herself.

To her mingled embarrassment and delight, Lady Connelton insisted on buying her an exquisitely embroidered organdie blouse.

"Nonsense, dear!" she said, in answer to Elinor's protest. "Why shouldn't I give myself the pleasure of making you a present? And, in any case, this was absolutely made for you. It reflects just that combination of the demure and the intriguing which somehow suggests you."

"Oh, Lady Connelton! You are an angel to give me anything so beautiful and to pretend at the same time that you are only pleasing yourself. But I don't think anyone else would agree with you about my being intriguing," Elinor felt bound to add. "I'm sure no one at the office ever found me that."

"Perhaps office life was not calculated to bring out the most attractive side of you," Lady Connelton suggested. "There has been quite a change in you in the last few weeks, you know."

"Has there?" Elinor looked doubtful. "I *feel* different, it's true. But I didn't know I showed it."

"Perfectly natural development, dear child," Lady Connelton assured her. "Nothing tends more surely to bring out a girl's natural charm than a little masculine appreciation. And you've had two decidedly attractive men taking more than a passing interest in you lately."

"Oh, Lady Connelton!"

"Of course you have. Don't be so depreciating about it," her employer advised her, with a sort of brisk amusement. "First there was that nice, amusing Rudi von Eiberg—who will, I am sure, turn up this afternoon with some agreeable suggestion or other—and now there is Ken, I think."

"Lady Connelton," Elinor protested, "Ken hasn't even a passing interest in me."

"Don't you think so?" Lady Connelton laughed good-humoredly. "Well, judging by my tiresome nephew's usual indifference to our sex, I should say that rather more than a passing interest just about describes his attitude to you."

"But Rosemary, who really seems to know him very well, says that he . . . he is never really interested in anyone."

"I know. So you got as far as discussing the subject with Rosemary?" Lady Connelton shot an amused glance at Elinor.

"Not really . . . no! She more or less volunteered the information," Elinor explained, blushing slightly.

"Very obliging of her, I'm sure." Lady Connelton rubbed the bridge of her nose with a reflective forefinger. "But it's more or less correct. In the ordinary way, he is too much run after, you know. I daresay he found you different and therefore intriguing. You see"—she laughed—"we are back at the same word."

Elinor smiled and shook her head.

"I still can't feel the word applies," she said.

"Well, we won't press the point," Lady Connelton conceded. "I don't want to make you self-conscious. But don't underestimate yourself, dear child. One can take that sort of thing a little too far. We both like your modesty and your quiet manners, but there is no need to let that self-advertising young woman who has just arrived push you aside."

Elinor did not really see how she was to prevent this if Rosemary were so minded. But she was infinitely pleased to learn that Sir Daniel, as well as Lady Connelton, approved of her so pleasantly.

Laden with purchases which Lady Connelton, who had an almost childlike gusto over these matters, could not bear to have sent, they returned to the hotel for a late lunch. And hardly had they detailed their adventures to Sir Daniel and Kenneth when the von Eibergs arrived.

Familiar faces are always welcome in a foreign country, so that they were welcomed, even by Kenneth, more or less as old friends, and, over cups of delicious Viennese coffee, future plans were discussed.

"No one goes in for masked balls any longer, I suppose," said Sir Daniel, shaking his head with enjoyable regret over the vanished joys that the present-day youth could not hope to sample. "Dear me, how romantic and exciting they were! Great fancy-dress balls at the various Embassies—and, of course, the Opera Ball. Nothing like that now."

"Don't be tiresome, dear," his wife adjured him

cheerfully. "There is probably some present-day equivalent." And she looked hopefully at the von Eibergs, as though expecting them to confound her pessimistic husband.

"I'm afraid there is nothing quite so grand and elegant nowadays as the sort of thing Sir Daniel has in mind," Rudi told Lady Connelton with a smile. "But I was going to suggest that, if you feel in a dressing-up mood—"

"*I?*" exclaimed Lady Connelton. "Not at all, dear boy! My days of being a Columbine or a gipsy girl are definitely over. I was thinking more of Elinor. Or Ken, of course," she added, thoughtfully regarding her nephew, as though assessing his age in terms of fancy-dress balls.

"Ilsa and I thought we might make up a party and go to Wimberger one evening," Rudi explained. "It's not elegant, in the sense Sir Daniel means. But it's gay and it's fun—and it's very Viennese. Would you like to come?" and he turned to Elinor, with a smile which said that her consent was the essential part of the arrangement.

"I should love it!" Elinor's eyes shone. And then, as though aware suddenly of a silence beside her, she turned to Kenneth and said, "You will come too, won't you?"

This time the effect of heavy silence came from Rudi's direction. So Elinor added quickly, "With Rosemary perhaps," and hoped that she had redressed the balance satisfactorily.

"That would make six, with Ilsa and her partner," Rudi said, beginning to plan in real earnest.

"It sounds an attractive idea," Kenneth said. "Though I'm not sure," he added with a dry little smile, "that I don't feel rather like my aunt—that my days for this sort of thing are over."

"Don't be absurd! You are just as young as the rest of us," exclaimed Elinor. And then was so surprised to find herself uttering anything so personal that she blushed scarlet.

"It's a question of temperament, rather than years," Ilsa put in lightly. "I don't think Kenneth need start calling his age in question. Provided he won't be all British and self-conscious about dressing up, he will enjoy a masquerade as well as any of us." They looked at him.

"Is this a challenge?" inquired Kenneth, meeting her glance.

"Or a suggestion," Ilsa retorted with a shrug.

"Challenge and suggestion both accepted," Kenneth answered with unexpected promptness. "And now I suppose we all start racking our brains about costumes. What—or whom—are we all impersonating?"

Various ingenious, preposterous and enjoyable suggestions were made, and then Sir Daniel said, "There are six of you, you say. Why don't you go as the complete cast of *Cosi fan Tutte*?

Both the von Eibergs cried out with delight, for as part-Viennese, they naturally knew their Mozart well.

"It's a wonderful idea!" Ilsa exclaimed. "Lovely eighteenth-century costumes for us all. Kenneth can be Alfonso, the cynical philosopher, who doesn't believe in anyone—"

"Thank you."

"No, he can't!" exclaimed Elinor indignantly. "That's not fair. He isn't a bit like that."

Everyone laughed over this, so that Elinor blushed again. But under cover of more chatter, Kenneth whispered to her, with not unkindly amusement, "It's only make-believe, remember."

"Elinor must be Fiordiligi, of course," Ilsa went on. "All good principles and fidelity."

"She sounds very dull," Elinor said, still a little sore about the insult to Kenneth.

"Oh, she's a *darling*!" Ilsa insisted. And she and her brother began to sing snatches of the opera across the table to each other, until they remembered that they had not cast the other parts.

"I shall be Fiordiligi's pair, of course," Rudi stated firmly. "I always forget which of the men it is, because everything is such a muddle by the time they have changed their identities. But I am whichever Fiordiligi gets in the end—" and he smiled at Elinor. "You can be Dorabella," he added to his sister. "Fickle, charming creature—that's you exactly."

Ilsa accepted this without objection, and merely said,

"That leaves Despina for your friend, Kenneth. What was her name?"

"Rosemary. Rosemary Copeland."

"Perfect!" Rudi laughed immoderately. "Has Rosemary turned up again? The girl who pushed us into the ditch, Ilsa. She will do wonderfully as Despina. She will be charming in a cap and apron as the maid who makes mischief."

"I didn't know you knew her so well." Kenneth looked at Rudi without favor.

"We met only once," Rudi admitted. "Twice, if you count the time when she knocked me down with her car. But such an introduction rather cuts through the social niceties, you know. Who will you include for your partner, Ilsa?" he asked, turning to his sister.

"Anton Mardenburg. I thought first of Ferdinand, but he hasn't the right legs for knee breeches and silk hose. As it is, I expect the men will have to hire costumes. Despina's won't be difficult. And as for Elinor and me—I imagine we can find something among Leni's costumes."

Everyone looked respectfully interested at this, and Sir Daniel said, "I hear that your stepmother is the famous Leni Mardenburg."

"Yes. Anton is a great-nephew of hers."

"I saw her several times on the stage. A wonderful artist," Sir Daniel stated sincerely.

"Thank you." Ilsa smiled at him. "I'll tell her what you said. She still loves to hear about the people who admired her. She is very old now, you know, though she doesn't like one to think so, and it isn't often that she sees anyone. But perhaps, if she had a good day while you are still here, you and Lady Connelton might like to come and see her."

Both the Conneltons received this suggestion warmly. And Lady Connelton said, "Well—so everything is more or less settled now about the fancy-dress ball?"

"Except that we haven't made sure yet that there is one, have we?" Kenneth said. "I take it this place von Eiberg speaks of doesn't have them nightly?"

"Oh, no. But I found out about that before we started the idea," Rudi explained. "There is a Carnival

Dance—it's not as grand as a ball, Lady Connelton—next Tuesday."

"And this is Friday. Not too much time to prepare," Lady Connelton observed.

"It's enough," Ilsa declared easily. "But if you will spare Elinor, Lady Connelton, this afternoon, I think it might be a good idea if she came back with us now, and she and I will look through my stepmother's costumes."

Lady Connelton readily gave permission, the party broke up, and Elinor—full of a sense of delighted anticipation—accompanied the von Eibergs back to their stepmother's home.

That it was her home and not essentially theirs was obvious from their conversation, and Elinor felt more than ever curious about the legendary figure of whom Ilsa had spoken.

"If you say that your stepmother doesn't often see people now, will she mind my coming?" Elinor inquired a little timidly.

"Oh, you won't see Leni," Ilsa assured her. "She keeps to her own room most of the time. We'll just go and look through the theatrical trunks that are stored in the attics, and if we find what we want, I'll ask her permission to borrow the things at a propitious moment."

"Is she so . . . difficult, then?"

"Difficult . . . no. But, like all retired stage favorites, she throws a temperament from time to time. It's just a question of knowing when to speak and when to keep silent."

Thus reassured, Elinor was conducted through the gateway she had seen the previous evening and across the courtyard to another smaller entry.

This admitted them to a stone passage and wide stone staircase, with doors on either side which were obviously the front doors to separate apartments. Each of them had a glazed hole through which one could observe whoever was outside before admitting them.

"No elevators in these old places, of course," Ilsa explained, as they mounted to the second floor, where Rudi took out a key and opened one of the big oak doors.

He stood aside for Elinor to enter, and, as she

afterwards wrote to the family, she stepped back fifty or sixty years.

> You can't imagine the crowded magnificence and elegance of the place. I have never before seen such furniture and pictures and china and knick-knacks. She must have collected things all her life, and kept them because she liked them or felt some sentimental attachment for them. Some of the things are exquisite, and some are just trash, but they are all crowded together, as though in some overstocked museum where no one has ever had time to arrange things properly.

By the time she wrote describing this Elinor had sorted out her impressions a little, but the first impact was almost a physical shock. The other two were obviously so long used to it that they hardly even noticed its effect on her.

A silent, elderly maid appeared from somewhere. But, after a few words with Ilsa, she disappeared into the shadows again.

"You'd better come to my room," Ilsa said. "If we're going to try on things, we shall need mirrors. And, as a matter of fact, darling," she added, turning to her brother, "though I hate to tell you so, we shall *not* need you."

Grumbling a little, Rudi accepted the practical good sense of that. And presently, at Ilsa's suggestion that he should "look up Anton and let him know what we've arranged for him," he took himself off again out of the apartment, leaving the two girls to do their exploring on their own.

They left their hats and coats in Ilsa's room—which was slightly less oppressive, but almost as crowded as all the other rooms—and Ilsa led the way up an inner staircase to a couple of huge, dusty rooms with skylights in their sloping ceilings. Here, piled on top of each other, were trunks and boxes of every size and shape.

Ilsa seemed at home here, however, and selected one or two of the trunks unerringly. Into these she dived with such assurance that Elinor had the uncomfortable impression she must have rather often gone through her stepmother's things—though with or without the old lady's permission, it was impossible to say.

After ten minutes or so of examining and rejecting, she drew out a panniered dress of blue taffeta, elaborately looped with rosebuds over a white, stiffened petticoat.

"Here is the thing for you, dear! Fiordiligi should wear blue. I'm not quite sure why—but she nearly always does." And she draped it authoritatively over Elinor's arm. "Take it down and try it on. If it fits and will do, I needn't look further for you. If not, we shall have to find something we can alter more easily."

"I—I'll wait for you, shall I?" Elinor suggested rather anxiously.

But Ilsa dismissed that idea.

"No, you may as well start the trying on. You know the way down, don't you?"

Elinor said reluctantly that she did.

"Well, then, you don't need to wait for me. Come back if this won't do, and I'll try again. But meanwhile I'll look for something for myself."

Thus adjured, Elinor went out of the attic and carefully down the winding stairs, taking great pains not to brush the beautiful blue dress against anything as she passed. It was quite the loveliest thing she had ever seen, she thought! If it really did fit her, she would look—well, really, she could not imagine how unusual and enchanting she, or any other girl, would look in it.

She reached the rather gloomy magnificence of the hall and hesitated for a moment, trying to remember which of the several doors led to Ilsa's room. As she did so, a peremptory, but indescribably full and sweet voice called out something she did not understand from a nearby room.

With her heart thumping almost audibly, Elinor stood stock still. She thought that could not possibly be the voice of an old lady—and yet who else but the mistress of the place would call in that authoritative manner?

As she waited, the words were repeated, and although Elinor did not know their meaning, there was no mistaking the tone.

"She heard my footsteps, and she's calling *me*!" thought Elinor, in sudden scared comprehension.

With frightened reluctance, and yet unable to resist the command in that tone, she went forward to the door. Here she hesitated again, but as she did so, the voice said unmistakably, "Herein!" And even Elinor knew that was an order to come in.

With the blue taffeta dress still draped over her arm, she pushed open the door and entered.

CHAPTER EIGHT

It was not until later that Elinor looked around and noticed anything about the room itself. In the first moment her attention was riveted by the sole occupant—a slim, straight, exquisitely elegant woman who sat in a high-backed chair by the window, her beautifully modelled hands resting with natural grace on the arms of the chair.

Her hair was white and piled rather high on her head, but her skin had the warmth and texture one associates with a young woman, and the beautiful bone structure of her face and the almost terrifyingly keen dark eyes gave an air of alertness and vitality impossible to attribute to a woman in her eighties.

"So," she said, speaking in English, but with an accent, "you are the little English girl of whom Rudi and Ilsa were speaking?"

"Yes, Madame," agreed Elinor timidly, instinctively according her this form of address.

"There is no need to be afraid. Come here and let me look at you. I am curious to see anyone who can make Rudi fall in love with her."

"Oh, Madame!" Elinor obediently came nearer. "Rudi is not at all in love with me. He thinks I am quaint and nice because he has not met anyone like me before. But that is all."

"Sometimes it is enough," said the old lady, and laughed softly. A laugh so infinitely attractive that Elinor guessed she had once been famous for it.

"You are very young. And very serious for one so young. Young people should be gay," went on the old lady arbitrarily.

Elinor smiled then.

"I am twenty-one," she said. "And I am not always serious. I was a little—scared to meet anyone so famous as you are."

"Ai, ai! My fame, as you call it, was fading before you were born. What do you know about it?" was the reply, but she was not displeased, Elinor saw.

"I was also feeling a little guilty because you find me holding something which belongs to you—" Elinor indicated the blue taffeta dress—"and I feel that I ought to have had your permission before I touched it."

"So? Ilsa gave you this, of course?"

"We . . . we were both looking for something to wear at a fancy-dress dance," Elinor explained, bravely taking half the blame. "Ilsa thought you would not mind, provided we asked your permission before we actually borrowed the things."

The old lady laughed sarcastically.

"Ilsa is not always so correct. The von Eibergs are all the same. They take first and explain afterwards. All the charm in the world, but no real stability. Don't marry Rudi, child. They don't make good husbands. I know—I married one."

Elinor felt profoundly uncomfortable at this casual disclosure.

"They are delightful and amusing. They are even warm-hearted in their way. But as husbands—" she shook her head and smiled reminiscently—"no!"

"I assure you, Madame, I have no intention of marrying Rudi," Elinor exclaimed. "Also I am perfectly certain he has no intention of marrying me. So—"

"No?" The old lady looked considering. "In practical fact, of course, he cannot think about it, because it will be necessary for him to marry money whenever he does marry. But, though I have seen many girls intrigued *by* Rudi, this is the first time I have known him speak as though he were intrigued in return."

Elinor thought passingly of Lady Connelton's use of the same word.

"Please don't tell me any more," she begged. "It embarrasses me, and will spoil my very nice friendship with him. Will you tell me instead if you mind my trying on this very beautiful dress, which I'm afraid I really have no right to be carrying."

"Not if you let me see you in it."

The old lady put out a hand and softly smoothed the folds of the dress Elinor was holding.

"I looked very well in it," she said without false modesty, and smiled. "A very stupid play, I think, if I remember rightly. All about Marie Antoinette as a girl. But I made all Vienna cry in the scene where I left my native Austria to go and marry in France." And she repeated a few phrases to herself in German, and the incredible voice took on the fluting, melancholy tones of a homesick girl.

"Oh, I wish I could have seen you!" Elinor exclaimed.

"Well—you see me now."

"But I mean on the stage—when you were a famous actress."

"Before I became old and ugly," suggested Leni Mardenburg, secure in the fact that she was still infinitely attractive.

"No, of course I didn't mean that! You are marvellous still. And when you said those few phrases you sounded like a girl. I just meant that I wish I had known you before you retired."

"Ai, ai—" the half-sighing exclamation seemed a favorite one with her—"that was a long time ago, my child. I retired soon after I married Julius von Eiberg."

"That was the father of Rudi and Ilsa?"

"Yes."

"Was he—like them?"

"He was good-looking in the way they are. He had even less sense of responsibility," the old lady explained without rancor. "By nature he was a gambler."

Elinor looked slightly startled and said quickly, "They are neither of them that."

"They cannot afford to be," was the dry retort.

"Were Rudi and Ilsa just children when their father married you?"

"They were in their teens. Rudi was already as handsome as the devil, and Ilsa a very pretty girl. They came to Vienna sometimes, but we preferred, their father and I, to have them remain in Hungary with their grandmother as much as possible."

"Why?" Elinor could not help asking.

She received an amused glance from those brilliant dark eyes.

"For one thing, I liked, as you English say, the center of the picture, and intelligent children in their teens are very much to be noticed. For another thing," she added practically, "I thought it was not good for them to see how their father wasted his money. This is something very easy to learn and not so easy to forget."

"You thought of their own good, then?"

"At this date, I could not tell you whether I thought of their good or mine," the old lady retorted with smiling candor. "I did not have them—that is all. Now, of course, they are welcome to stay here from time to time. But they are really no concern of mine." And, although she continued to smile, she seemed almost literally to wash her hands of them.

"I should have thought," Elinor ventured to say, "that it would be nice to have them as part of one's family."

"But that, I don't doubt, is because you are a kind, warm-hearted child," replied the old lady, her dark eyes snapping and sparkling with amusement. "In all probability, you think naturally in terms of family life."

"Yes," Elinor said soberly. "I belong to a very happy family myself."

"This is something different." An almost indulgent look came into the older woman's eyes for a moment. "For me there was never anything like that. All my life I stood alone. I worked—as only stage people work—for everything I have now around me. I owe nothing to any man, except perhaps to the stage director who gave me my first chance. For such as I am it is better to remain alone."

"But you did marry," Elinor pointed out.

"We all make one mistake," was the quick retort. Then the old lady laughed, without rancor. "He was charming, and I will not say that I would wish to have been without the years with him. But you will find, my child, as you grow older, that there are really only three kinds of people in every country and every society. They are the able, the weak and the lazy. If you are yourself among the able, you pity—you may even love—the weak or the lazy, but you will always in your heart despise them." She paused for a moment. Then she drew herself up slightly and said, with a simplicity that was somehow superb, "I was among the able."

"I think," Elinor said slowly, "that no one could improve on that as a final verdict."

"Well—I am aware that it is not complete." Again the dark eyes sparkled with amusement. "In my time, I have also been vain and selfish and capricious." She said this carelessly, almost as though she were listing virtues. "But I have never been lazy. That is why you see so much that is beautiful in this apartment now. And that," she admitted with a faintly malicious little chuckle, "is why it amuses me to keep them all guessing about what is to happen to all this when I am gone."

"O-oh," said Elinor, to whose warm and generous heart it seemed a rather doubtful form of pleasure.

"Sometimes they think I will live forever, and they are a little impatient—"

"Oh, no! I am sure they are not!"

"—but until I am gone none of them will know how all this—" her comprehensive yet graceful gesture seemed to embrace the whole of the crowded apartment—"has been left. And so they are all nice to me, and make me feel important still."

Elinor was somewhat shocked by this frank exposition of the situation, but she looked upon the one-time fêted, admired and courted Leni Mardenburg with compassion too. For it must be sad, she thought, to know in one's heart that one's principal power now rested simply on the

116

promise of favors after one's death or the threat of their withdrawal.

She was just wondering what suitable comment she could make upon it all when they both heard Ilsa's light, quick step coming down the stairs.

"There is Ilsa. Call her in," the old lady said commandingly.

So Elinor went to the door—somewhat startling Ilsa, obviously, by her appearance there—and said, "Your stepmother would like you to come in, Ilsa. She called me in when I came downstairs first, and she has been talking to me."

Ilsa recovered herself almost immediately—it took a great deal to disconcert her entirely—and merely murmured as she passed Elinor and came into the room, "Don't mind her if she tries to scare you. It's just her way of feeling power still."

Elinor thought that, on the whole, she had not found old Madame Mardenburg frightening. Only very interesting and a little startling in her unexpected confidences and her frank expressions of opinion.

Upon Ilsa the old lady bent a rather sarcastic glance. And, although she spoke in German, Elinor thought from the tone that she was being somewhat caustic about the easy appropriation of her property.

Ilsa, however, was smiling and apparently at ease as she made some explanation.

Elinor, watching the expressions with all the more attention because she could not follow the words that were being said, saw the old lady smile dryly in her turn. She inclined her head, as though accepting the explanation, but as Ilsa turned away, Elinor saw those bright, knowledgeable dark eyes follow her with a glance of speculative amusement that was completely without illusion.

To Elinor, however, she said quite gently, "Go now, child, and try on the dress. And then come back and let me see you in it."

"Thank you *so* much." For a moment Elinor stood beside the handsome, high-backed chair, and smiled into those beautiful, dark, yet disconcerting eyes which had seen so many, many things and people. "I hope so much that it fits me. I can't even imagine what fun it must be to wear anything so perfectly lovely."

"It is fun," the old lady agreed, giving the word a peculiar and engaging intonation. "Particularly when there is someone special there to share the fun. But—" she glanced after her stepdaughter who was just going out of the room, then, leaning towards Elinor, she added, with a charming air of conspiracy—"but not Rudi, remember, except for very light and passing fun."

Then, with a peremptory little nod, she dismissed Elinor, who, half-embarrassed and half-amused, flushed slightly and laughed, but made no real reply before going off in the wake of Ilsa.

Back in Ilsa's room once more, they began immediately to change into their masquerade dresses, and while they did so, Ilsa asked how it was Elinor had come to be involved in a visit to her stepmother.

Elinor explained.

"I suppose she felt curious about you," Ilsa said. "Sometimes she is like that. And then at other times she obstinately refuses to take the faintest interest in anything we are doing."

Elinor smiled and made some suitable reply. She saw no necessity to repeat the old lady's remark that "she was curious to see anyone who could make Rudi fall in love with her." That, after all, was simply the inquisitive and rather mischievous fancy of an old lady who had nothing better to think about. Instead, she said, "She was very kind to me, really, and spoke most interestingly about the time when she herself wore this dress."

Ilsa smiled.

"You see? She has the most prodigious memory for anything that concerns herself. She remembers all her roles and most of her costumes. But there is no one who can forget more completely if she wishes to do so."

By now they were both arrayed in their costumes, Ilsa in an infinitely becoming red-and-gray striped satin dress of the period, and Elinor in her blue taffeta.

"Dear girl! It might have been made for you!" Ilsa laughed with delight. "Sit down here and I'll redress your

118

hair for you. It will be more comfortable if we can manage with our own hair. Powdered wigs are so hot."

So Elinor sat down before the mirror, secretly enchanted and astonished to see how subtly and yet unmistakably the blue dress changed her. Not only was it in itself a lovely creation, but it gave her an air of elegance and poise which made her feel that the reflection in the glass had nothing to do with young Elinor Shearn, who went home each day from the office, and rather worried her mother because she never seemed to have anything very exciting to do with her evenings.

"Why, I could just be anyone in this!" she exclaimed to Ilsa. And, although this might not be very lucidly put, Ilsa evidently understood what she meant.

"That is the whole purpose of a masquerade dress," she declared, with a laugh. "You feel like another person, and so you are gay and fresh and a little outside yourself. Come now and show Leni."

She had finished with Elinor's soft, dark hair, which she had drawn back and lightly secured on the top of her head so that her very pretty ears were left showing, her face looked a little longer and less childlike, and the hair itself made a long, graceful line behind her ears and on to the nape of her neck.

"It is sufficiently a compromise, if not entirely in period," Ilsa explained. And then, together, they returned to the other room.

Madame Mardenburg surveyed them both with bright, critical glances that missed nothing. She made one or two suggestions for slight alterations, all of them very much to the point. But she was obviously tired now—in the sudden way old people do become tired—and, having expressed the final approval briefly, she dismissed them both almost peremptorily.

Back in Ilsa's room once more, they changed again into their own things, and Ilsa said, "You had better leave your costume here. It will be easier for you to come here and dress beforehand, so that I can do your hair for you. Besides—she is funny about these things. Because the dresses are really hers, she will want, as you say, to have a finger in the pie, right up to the end, and will expect to see us when we are all ready before we go on Tuesday.''

"That's quite understandable." Elinor smiled. Then she remembered her own nice employer, who also liked to have a finger in any entertaining pie that was going. "But I am sure Lady Connelton will be disappointed if she doesn't see me in the dress also!"

"We can arrange it," Ilsa assured her. "You come here and dress. Then Rudi and Anton can drive us over to the hotel, where we will pick up Kenneth and Rosemary. Then the Conneltons can see all of us in our glory."

This plan seemed to meet every requirement, and so it was arranged, and Elinor went back to report the various decisions to a very satisfied Lady Connelton.

"So you actually saw the fabulous Leni Mardenburg?" she said over dinner that night, when all five of them—for Rosemary seemed now to have joined the party more or less permanently—were discussing the day's events. "Tell us what she is like now?"

Elinor gave as accurate and attractive a word picture as she could, but she felt that this fell short of the original.

"One can't really describe her," Elinor declared. "It's not only that she looks unusual for a woman of her years. In personality she just isn't like anyone else I have ever met."

"Well, I suppose she is the personification of a vanished epoch," Kenneth said, with rare understanding.

"What is her attitude toward the von Eibergs?" Sir Daniel inquired curiously.

Elinor thought of the way the old lady had spoken of Rudi and looked after Ilsa.

"I think she is not unattached to them, in a rather sardonic way," Elinor said cautiously. "Though she often speaks critically of them."

"Which aspect of them?" inquired Kenneth, a little too quickly, Elinor thought.

"It's difficult to say." Elinor was not going to give them away in detail. "I don't think she had any illusions about their father, even though she was fond of him, and she is a little inclined to attribute his weaknesses to them too. I have the impression that, by the time Rudi and Ilsa came into her life, she had made all the really close contacts she ever intended to make. She tolerates them, but she doesn't love them, and they are more like familiar visitors in her house than members of her family."

"Very acute observation," remarked Sir Daniel, looking at his secretary with amused approval. "Did she like you?"

"Yes."

"Did she say so?" inquired Kenneth, amused in his turn.

"No." Elinor was surprised to find that her conviction was so complete, although nothing had been put into words.

"You just sensed it?"

"Yes. She would like you too, I am sure," Elinor added, with the same conviction.

Kenneth raised his rather strongly marked eyebrows.

"What makes you think that?"

"Oh, I don't know. She spoke rather disparagingly about people who are all charm but have no real stability. And I thought. . . ." Elinor's voice trailed away doubtfully, as she became aware that this sounded like a back-handed compliment.

Kenneth grinned, as he obviously made a mental effort to disentangle this statement.

"If I have this right, you mean that I, on the contrary, though devoid of charm, am a good, solid fellow?" he suggested teasingly.

"Oh, no!" Elinor was taken aback. "I don't think you're devoid of charm. I just—"

But both the Conneltons laughed heartily at this point, and Kenneth unexpectedly touched her hand and said not unkindly, "Don't enlarge on that. I rather like it as it is."

"He's supposed to have oodles of charm, when he turns it on," remarked Rosemary to no one in particular. But Kenneth frowned at her, and the subject was dropped.

During the next few days Elinor saw a good deal of Vienna and its beautiful environs. With the Conneltons she did the more obvious sight-seeing. The Cathedral, the Hofburg—where the Emperors used to live and where, even now, the magnificent crown jewels might still be seen—and some of the fine museums and art galleries.

These last, however, were pronounced by Lady Connelton to be a joy to the eye rather than the feet.

Rudi took Elinor driving in the Ring, as he had promised, and also showed her the out-of-the-way corners and streets and courtyards which only the real native of a city ever seems to know. And in his company she went to the beautiful Stadtpark, to pay her respects, as Rudi put it, to the statue of Johann Strauss, whose waltzes have for so long been so much an expression of Vienna that it is impossible to think of one without the other.

All these experiences Elinor enjoyed immensely. But once or twice she thought of that early morning tour round Salzburg with Kenneth, and she was not at all sure that that was not the loveliest sight-seeing experience yet.

On the Tuesday Lady Connelton showed as much interest in the preparations for the evening as if she had herself been going, and when she elicited the extraordinary fact that this was, in reality, Elinor's first dance, she found the whole thing so romantic that she could not help indulging in some sentimental recollections of her own.

"Not that you will want to hear about *my* first dance, dear," she said to Elinor—who protested to the contrary. "But I remember, as though it were yesterday, how I cried because my mother insisted on my wearing white, and I wanted a gorgeous red affair which was entirely unsuitable but very glamorous in my eyes."

"Oh, *how* Deborah would sympathize, if she were here!" declared Elinor, laughing with a sort of nostalgic affection as this recollection somehow brought her little sister almost before her. "She is passionately addicted to what she calls 'glamorous' clothes, and believes the height of happiness is to be dressed like an adventuress —whatever she thinks that is."

"She sounds such a nice, individual sort of child. I must meet her when we get home," Lady Connelton said.

"She would love that. And so should I," Elinor said. And then she wondered if life would ever be quite the same again. It was impossible to imagine herself going back into her shell and simply observing what other people did.

Here she was, carelessly and confidently arranging for Deborah to meet Lady Connelton, and not finding it either strange or frightening.

She *was* a little frightened, of course, when she actually came to the delicious crisis of the evening. But she kept on reminding herself that in the lovely blue taffeta dress she would hardly be herself, and that therefore she must regard herself as playing a part—and just enjoy the moment.

Dressing with Ilsa, in the bedroom of Leni Mardenburg's incredible apartment, she already began to feel that sensation of tingling excitement and unreality which belongs to all the loveliest pieces of "make-believe"—from the dressing-up of childhood to the most elaborate masquerade.

"The men's costumes are really wonderful, too," Ilsa informed her, with all the satisfaction of a good producer. "Rudi and Anton look born for theirs, of course. They have just that rather picturesque, nonchalant manner that makes fancy dress seem quite natural. Kenneth was the one I was worried about, to tell you the truth. He is so very uncompromising and twentieth-century. But he is splendid in Alfonso's rather austere get-up. Have you seen him?"

"No. He hasn't even talked about it much."

"Oh well, you'll see him in a very little while now. I went with the three of them when they chose their costumes. That's how I know. Now I think we are ready. Let's collect Rudi and Anton, and go and show ourselves to Leni."

In answer to Ilsa's peremptory call, Rudi, looking quite extraordinarily handsome and very much at home in satins and laces, made an appearance, followed by a pleasant and humorous-looking young man who seemed to be having some trouble with his sword.

He was introduced to Elinor as Anton Mardenburg and, after Ilsa had secured his sword for him, they all went into Madame Mardenburg's room for a last-minute inspection.

She smiled at Elinor and told her she was "*sehr schön*,"

and after a critical suggestion or two, declared that the others were excellent too.

"I wish you were coming!" Elinor exclaimed. "You are far more in character for this sort of thing than all of us put together."

The old lady laughed softly.

"My masquerade days are over, dear child. But yours are just beginning. Play your part well tonight." And, unexpectedly, she drew Elinor down and kissed her.

She did not kiss any of the others. And when they had all departed to install themselves in Anton's impressively big car, Ilsa said thoughtfully, "I never saw Leni do that before, did you?"

"Do what?" Anton inquired.

"Kiss someone in that almost impulsive way."

"She's never seen anyone like Elinor before," Rudi said lightly. "I can quite understand wanting to kiss her in an impulsive way—especially as she looks now."

Elinor laughed and colored. But a beautiful, light-hearted feeling of confidence began to take possession of her. She looked, she knew, more attractive than she ever had in her life before. She was young, she was happy—and the first breath of spring was wafting through the streets of Vienna.

Arriving at the hotel, they all went in, causing a good deal of admiring interest, and were taken up in the lift to the Conneltons' private sitting-room.

"Come in, come in! Dear me, how splendid you all look," exclaimed Lady Connelton in delight. "Kenneth and Rosemary should be here any minute now." And, even as she spoke, Rosemary entered in her turn, indescribably pert and pretty in a short-skirted rose-pink dress with a frilly apron and the sauciest of frilly caps perched on her hair.

A chorus of approval greeted her appearance, and they were all still congratulating each other when the door opened again and Kenneth appeared in his Alfonso costume.

This was the signal for a concerted shout of delight and amusement from those who knew the opera well, for nothing could have been more piquantly suited to the part

than the thin, dark, faintly sardonic good looks of
Kenneth.

He withstood the outburst of laughter and excla-
mations calmly, looking quite at home in his costume.
Then, as he glanced round, his eyes lighted on Elinor,
standing there smiling and curiously self-possessed.

The whole width of the room divided them, but
something in his glance told her that her appearance was
a surprise—in some inexplicable way, almost a shock—to
him.

It was some minutes before he came and spoke to her,
and when he did so, all he said was: "I like your dress.
What a wonderful blue it is."

She smiled without answering—only touching the folds
of Leni Mardenburg's dress with a sort of tender
appreciation. It was Sir Daniel who, speaking in an
amused tone behind her, remarked, "I think perhaps
that's the blue the Danube is when one is in love."

CHAPTER NINE

"Well, shall we go?"

Rudi, suddenly taking over the main direction of things
from Ilsa, spoke rather more abruptly than usual. But as
everyone was absorbed in telling everyone else what they
thought about the costumes, no one noticed this.

The signal for departure was, however, immediately
accepted. And, accompanied by many good wishes from
the Conneltons, they all piled back into Anton's car,
which proved equal to the occasion, and the addition of
two more.

When they arrived at the place of Rudi's choice—an
immense, brightly lit, gaily decorated place rather
removed from the center of the city—dancing had
evidently been in full swing for some time, and Elinor
thought she had never seen so bright and colorful a scene.

Hundreds of people, or so it seemed to her, attired in

the most amazing variety of strange or beautiful eccentric costumes, mingled together, laughing, talking, dancing, sometimes wreathed with paper streamers thrown by friends, sometimes throwing balloons to each other across the room and over the heads of the dancers.

It was her first experience of uninhibited carnival spirit, and she felt the last of her shyness and self-consciousness slipping from her. When Rudi put his arm round her and swept her on to the dance floor, she never thought about the fact that it was the first time she had ever danced in anything but a sedate dancing class, and she found herself following his expert guidance without difficulty and with the utmost enjoyment.

"You dance as naturally as you skate," he told her above the cheerful hubbub of voices and music.

"It must be largely because of your guidance. This is the first dance I've ever been to."

He didn't say that he found this extraordinary or pitiable or queer or anything like that. He just said, "How wonderful! You've all the fun in the world before you, and I can't tell you how much I appreciate being the first one to take you on the dance floor."

She laughed, and said, with a frankness she would never have employed in any other circumstances, "Rudi, you are *nice*! You never make one feel odd or self-conscious."

"Darling, why should I want to make you feel either?" he replied, lightly and yet with a note of warm feeling in his voice. "You are sweet and unusual, but you are not in the least odd. And, if you are shy, why should I not respect that instead of making you more so?"

"It's as I said. You argue that way because you're nice," Elinor told him, with a quick, flashing smile that was probably the most self-possessed glance she had ever bestowed on any man. "I feel just now as though I'll never be shy again."

"Not with me at any rate, I hope."

"I expect it's partly the effect of the dress," she went on, following her own thoughts, rather than picking up the somewhat personal line he had offered. "I feel a little as though I'm someone else. Almost as though something of the poise and success of Leni Mardenburg goes with the dress."

He smiled down at her.

"You like Leni, don't you?"

"Yes. I think she's perfectly fascinating."

"She liked you too. She told me so."

"Did she?" Elinor glanced curiously at him. She had not, somehow, thought of the two of them discussing her. "Do you talk to her a lot? I mean, are you on rather close terms with her?"

"More so than Ilsa is. My sex would always be easier of access to Leni than Ilsa's would," he admitted with a laugh. "And yet I can't tell you if Leni likes me."

"I am sure she does!"

"She doesn't approve of me."

"That's a different thing."

"Of course." He laughed again, but a trifle doubtfully. "I find that I often tell her things I wouldn't tell anyone else. I don't know why, because she is astringent, rather than sympathetic."

Elinor was silent. Suddenly she remembered old Madame Mardenburg bidding her come forward, with the words that she was curious to see anyone who could make Rudi fall in love with her. She had pushed that to the back of her mind as the mischievous conjecture of an inquisitive old lady. Now she wondered all at once if it were based on something Rudi had said.

"It's partly, of course," Rudi went on, pursuing his own argument, "that one feels she has known and seen so much. To speak to her of one's—joys and fears is to put them into their right perspective. Everything passes."

"Rudi, do you *have* to talk melancholy philosophy in the middle of a carnival scene?" inquired Elinor.

"*Liebling*, I am sorry!" He bent his head and lightly kissed her cheek with an air of contrition.

At any other time Elinor would have been slightly startled at this form of apology. Here, and in these particular circumstances, it seemed so right that she almost kissed him back again.

Not quite. That would have given too solemn a character to what must essentially remain a light occasion. But she tightened her fingers on his and they exchanged a smiling glance that was not so far short of a kiss.

"I wonder where the others are." She turned her head to see if she could find them in the whirling throng.

"I have no idea. And I really don't mind. Do you?" Rudi said.

"Not much—at the moment," Elinor laughed. Then she added more conscientiously, "I expect we shall find them by suppertime!"

"It is possible," Rudi agreed indifferently.

But it was not yet suppertime when, as they paused between dances in an alcove where it was possible to sit down in some degree of coolness and quiet, Kenneth and Rosemary made their way toward them.

"Hello," Rosemary greeted them both cheerfully. "We were wondering—at least Kenneth was—where you two had got to. I was telling him that it's impossible to keep a party together at an affair of this sort."

"We ought to make some plan about meeting for supper, though," Elinor declared. "Have you seen anything of the others?"

It seemed that a tentative arrangement had been made with them to meet in the supper-room in an hour's time, and Elinor and Rudi undertook to be there too. Then, before there was any question of their separating again, Kenneth said, "Don't I see anything of you until suppertime, Elinor? I was hoping you would have a dance with me."

"Which means that he's about to abandon you to the girl who tried to kill you," Rosemary informed Rudi.

"A risk any man would gladly take," Rudi informed her gallantly. "May I have the pleasure of leading my assailant on to the dance floor?"

With some laughter, they changed partners, and Elinor found herself circling the room with Kenneth, dancing with the same happy confidence that her first experience with Rudi had given her.

The realization brought a smile to her lips, and immediately Kenneth asked, "Are you finding this all very amusing?"

"I am enjoying myself immensely, if that's what you mean," Elinor assured him. "But I shouldn't think it's possible to do anything else at such a gay gathering."

Kenneth greeted this with silence.

"Oh, Kenneth—aren't you enjoying yourself?"

"At the moment, naturally," he assured her. But, though Rudi could say those things and make them sound gallant and charming, when Kenneth said them one always wondered if there were a sting in the tail.

"Why did you come, if you were determined not to enjoy yourself?" Elinor asked rather crossly.

"Because you were coming," was the unexpected retort. "And, anyway, the determination is not so irrevocable as all that."

"You came because—because *I* was coming?" She glanced up at him doubtfully from under her lashes—a glance which Leni Mardenburg would have applauded because she would not have been able to believe that it was not calculated. "Is that a joke?"

"No, of course not. Don't you think you are sufficient reason to bring anyone to a dance?"

"No," said Elinor with great simplicity.

And at this Kenneth laughed so heartily that Elinor thought perhaps the carnival spirit was having its effect upon him after all.

"At least, I shouldn't have thought I was sufficient reason to bring you to do anything you didn't want to do. I thought you came to please Rosemary."

"Did you?" He smiled faintly. "Who gave you that idea?"

"You did, I suppose. At least, I just drew the general conclusion. After all, you terribly wanted her to come on this trip instead of me and—"

"That's another idea I'd like to pin down. Where did you get that one?"

Elinor looked rather nonplussed.

"Well, the time I overheard you talking to Lady Connelton in the library, I thought—"

"You shouldn't eavesdrop," he told her, smiling. "Information obtained that way is always unreliable."

"I *wasn't* eavesdropping, at least, not on purpose. The

maid had shown me into the other half of the room, and I was overhearing your conversation before I realized what was happening. It was then you made the insufferable remark about—about nice, quiet little girls being boring."

"Well, so they are."

"Thank you!"

"Don't be silly. As I told you in the beginning, you're not a nice, quiet little girl at all. You're a bit of a spitfire, in a concealed way. And tonight you are a beauty."

"I . . . oh, thank you," she said again, but in quite a different tone this time. "It's the dress, I expect."

"I have an idea it's not only the dress," Kenneth retorted rather moodily. Then he added abruptly, "Elinor, may I ask you a rather personal question?"

"No, I don't think you had better," Elinor told him gently.

"Why not?"

"Because, if it's about Rudi, I might not know the answer," Elinor said.

And then the music came to an end, and Rudi claimed her once more, relinquishing Rosemary to Kenneth again.

But, although Kenneth passed out of Elinor's sight, he remained disturbingly in her mind. She wondered with passionate interest what it was he had wanted to ask her—and, still more, why he had wanted to ask it. And she experienced a flash of quite personal resentment when Rudi remarked carelessly, "Brownlow's a dull dog, isn't he?"

"No. I shouldn't describe him as that at all!"

"But he takes life so seriously."

"Someone must take it seriously," Elinor replied a little sharply. "Life doesn't consist of being a playboy and having a good time always."

"Are you reproving me?" he inquired, smiling.

"Why—why, no! Did you think the description fitted?" Suddenly she was horribly afraid that it did.

"I think I should ask that. Did *you* think the description fitted?"

"I don't know, Rudi. I don't really ever know quite

what to make of you. Sometimes I wonder a great deal. Then I tell myself that it isn't my business. But, since you ask me, I must say quite frankly that you are the only man I have ever known who doesn't seem to have a purpose—a plan of life—a . . . *job*. Don't you even want one?"

"Something that would tie me so many hours a day and so many days a week? I can think of nothing more horrible," he told her lightly.

"But it's a means to an end."

"What end?"

"Well . . . all the stable, permanent, everyday things that life's made up of, I suppose. You don't suppose many people do a regular job because they *like* being tied, do you? They do it because it provides the essentials for a full and useful life."

"People like Kenneth, you mean?" He was smiling.

"I was thinking of my father," Elinor said simply. "I daresay he had his romantic and hopeful and adventurous impulses once. But I suppose you might say he traded them for a wife and children. And, because my parents both played fair over that, they made a home that's the most important place on earth to five other people. You can't have it all ways."

"How true, my little philosopher."

There was a short pause. Then she said, "You mean that you think it was a poor bargain?"

"No, darling. I don't mean that at all. I hope your father thought it all worth while. I expect he did. Only I am the sort of tiresome, selfish creature who does want it both ways. Perhaps Fate will be kind to me one day and let me have that."

She started to say that she thought this a rather shocking point of view. But just then the music slowed once more, and she thought that perhaps a carnival dance was not the place for so serious a discussion. In any case, Rudi announced that it was suppertime, and so they went to find the others.

Everybody appeared to have been having a wonderful time, Rosemary declaring, with truth, that Anton Mardenburg was the best dancer in the room.

It struck Elinor that, in order to make this discovery, she must have left Kenneth and Ilsa to dance together, and she could not help wondering how they had got on. But then the sorting out of these personal complications became too difficult, and she was about to abandon them in favor of simply enjoying herself when Anton, by asking a perfectly conventional and likely question, brought them all back again.

"When," he inquired politely of Elinor, "do you and the Conneltons have to leave Vienna? I hope you are staying a long time."

"Not very long, I'm afraid. It was never meant to be more than a short visit. But I haven't heard anyone talk about leaving yet," Elinor said.

"I was talking it over with my uncle this afternoon," Kenneth put in at this point. "We are expecting to leave by the end of the week."

"So soon?" Elinor exclaimed, and a feeling of dismay invaded her, while all the others looked at Kenneth as though he had deliberately spoiled the fun.

"Unavoidable, I'm afraid." Kenneth, looking rather deliberately in character for Alfonso, shrugged and smiled slightly. "Business considerations come into it. My uncle and I ought to be in Rome in a week or ten days' time."

"Does one really go to Rome, of all heavenly places, for business?" Rudi inquired, a little disdainfully, although he smiled.

"Certainly one does. There's a lot of very useful business done in Rome, I assure you," Kenneth countered dryly. "Particularly if you're in the touring world."

"Rome—" Elinor said almost to herself. And for a moment the thought of Rome consoled her for the threatening loss of Vienna. Then she remembered that in Rome there would be no Rudi or Ilsa, and her spirits sank. "It will be lovely to go to Rome," she said, feeling that somehow blame seemed to have attached itself unfairly to Kenneth. "But I shall hate to leave Vienna."

"We shall hate to lose you." Ilsa glanced at her with genuine affection.

"We may turn up in Rome before you have time to

move on," Rudi said impulsively, and Elinor thought there was even a touch of rashness in the way he said that.

"You do get about, don't you?" Kenneth observed, speaking almost with a drawl. "For someone who is not in touring, I mean."

"I must see about getting into it," Rudi declared lightly. "It seems a wonderful way of combining business and pleasure. Are there any vacancies?"

"For those who are ready to work hard," Kenneth said. "It's not all running around enjoying oneself." And although the words suggested that he was merely giving useful information, the tone implied that Rudi was thus ruled out.

They went back and danced again after that. But a little of the brightness had gone out of Elinor's evening.

Only during the last waltz all of it came back again, because Rudi said softly and thoughtfully, "Shall I come to Rome, *Liebling*?"

"If you would like to, Rudi—of course."

"But would *you* like me to?" He seemed to have forgotten his sister for the moment. "That is more important."

"I'd love you to," she said, without coquetry. "You know I'm going to miss you dreadfully. But it's rather a long way to come just because I say I'd like to see you there."

"Men have changed their whole way of life for less," he told her, half-laughing, half-serious. "Wasn't that what we were talking of earlier in the evening? The idea of changing one's way of life because someone else's wishes mean so much?"

"I don't think we put it as categorically as that," Elinor said, trying to make herself sound matter-of-fact. And then they were silent, and perhaps he let the lilt of the waltz, the feel of his arm, and the knowledge that the lovely evening was nearly over, all speak for him instead.

A million stars were shining overhead as they drove home to the hotel, but the first cold breath of dawn was stirring as they said goodbye to each other on the pavement.

"Don't bother about the dress, darling. I'll collect it

sometime tomorrow—or, rather, later today," Ilsa said, as she kissed Elinor good night. "Anyway, I'm going to ask Leni if you can keep it. No one else will ever look half so lovely in it, and I don't know what good it's doing anyone, stored away in an attic."

"Oh, no, please don't suggest such a thing to her," Elinor exclaimed. "It would sound exactly as though I were cadging. I was so happy to borrow it, but that's all."

"You're sweet," Ilsa declared, as though she noted, but did not understand, Elinor's point of view. Then good nights were said and, suddenly unable to keep from yawning and overwhelmed by pleasant fatigue, they separated.

"You were talking Greek to Ilsa," Kenneth remarked as they made their way to the elevator.

"Greek?" repeated Elinor, too sleepy and muddled to work that out.

"Never mind." Kenneth smiled at her and, incredibly, ruffled her dark hair with a rather gentle hand. "Good night—or rather good morning. Sleep well."

And so she said good night and went to her room. But only when she had carefully undressed, hung the lovely blue dress on a hanger, and crept wearily into bed did she realize what he had meant. It was the last thing that she thought of as she drifted into sleep. That and the knowledge that the touch on her hair had been both amused and approving.

Inevitably she slept late. But, even so, she found Lady Connelton still at the breakfast table when she came down.

"I breakfasted late on purpose," that lady explained. "I guessed you wouldn't be early, and I do want to hear how everything went."

Very willingly Elinor re-lived her wonderful evening, describing in detail to her delighted employer all her experiences and reactions.

"M-yes, of course." Lady Connelton rubbed the bridge of her nose reflectively. "I suppose Rudi von Eiberg would be the ideal companion for such an occasion."

"It was a very nice party altogether," Elinor stated impartially, and something about that appeared to amuse her employer a good deal though nothing was said then.

"It's a pity we have to go at the end of the week. Did you know about that?" Lady Connelton asked.

"Kenneth told me. I'm sorry too. But even the best of things have to come to an end, I suppose, and we never expected it to be a long visit. Besides—" Elinor hesitated, wondering if she could make this suitably casual and then deciding that at least it was better to make the statement now—"Ilsa and Rudi think they might manage to come to Rome while we are there."

"Is that so?" Lady Connelton's expression became rather complicated. "Was that your suggestion or his?"

"His, of course, Lady Connelton! I shouldn't have made such a suggestion."

"Not even if you wanted him there very much?"

"Not even then," Elinor assured her firmly.

"Well, I don't know. He's a remarkably attractive young fellow, of course," Lady Connelton said, with apparent irrelevance. "No visible means of support, though, as my husband says. And one doesn't even know how the old lady has left her money, so one can't even bank on prospects."

"Oh, Lady Connelton, don't talk like that!" Elinor begged. "In any case, Madame Mardenburg is so delightful and . . . and vital, one doesn't want to think of any time when she would be . . . otherwise."

"Of course not," agreed Lady Connelton, who had quite obviously been thinking of just such a time. "But one must be practical. All old people die eventually. And all rich old people leave their money to someone. Unless of course it's cats' homes or something like that," she added. "But I don't think Leni Mardenburg is the sort to think in those terms."

"I am sure she's not," Elinor agreed with a slight smile. "But I don't know quite how we came to be talking this way."

"Don't you, dear? I do, exactly," Lady Connelton said cheerfully. "I was wondering quite frankly how fond you are of Rudi von Eiberg and whether, if he suddenly became well endowed with this world's goods, you would begin to take a practical, as well as romantic, interest in him."

"The situation doesn't arise, Lady Connelton," Elinor said quite firmly. Upon which her employer good-humoredly abandoned the discussion—and left Elinor wondering at her own social aplomb.

Later that day Ilsa came; partly to hold an enjoyable inquest on the evening before, and partly to tell Elinor that she was to keep the dress.

"I didn't say anything to Leni about it," she assured Elinor, before she could protest. "It was Leni's own suggestion. She said that when she saw you in it she remembered for a moment just how she herself had looked—and she doesn't want anyone else to have it, ever."

"How sweet of her!" Elinor's warm heart was touched. "May I come and thank her myself before we leave Vienna?"

"I'll try to arrange it," Ilsa promised. "But she's very tired again now and is keeping to her bed for a day or two. She sometimes has these spells, you know. It's nothing, really, only that she's so old. But I'm afraid it won't be possible for the Conneltons to visit her, after all. I'm so sorry, but the doctor says that she must not be tired when she is like this."

"Of course! I'm sure they will understand," Elinor said. Though secretly she was sorry too, for she knew how Lady Connelton would have enjoyed meeting the old lady, while Sir Daniel would have been able to indulge in the most nostalgic of his reminiscences.

The last few days slipped away all too soon, though each one was so packed with pleasant experiences that there was not even time for regrets.

Elinor was not alone again with Rudi, and for this she was not quite sure if she were sorry or relieved. He was beginning to have an effect upon her which was disturbing as well as delightful, and—as Lady Connelton's very practical words had indicated—there was no really solid basis to justify such feelings.

All the arrangements had been made for the Conneltons' party to leave on Friday morning, and there was a final dinner party with the von Eibergs as guests on the Thursday evening. The journey to Rome was not to be made direct, of course, as it was necessary to return to Ehrwald, hand over the car and collect the rest of their luggage.

"We shall probably be a day or two in Ehrwald," Sir Daniel explained to anyone who was interested to listen, "and then go by way of Munich and Verona to Rome."

"When we come—" began Rudi, and then stopped.

"Are you coming?" inquired Kenneth without much enthusiasm.

"Oh, we might." That was Ilsa, looking very faintly confused for once. "At least, we're pretending so to ourselves, and then we shan't feel so melancholy, saying goodbye."

Everyone—except perhaps Kenneth—seemed to think this did their sensibilities great credit.

"I do hope you manage it!" exclaimed Elinor. "And you must give Madame Mardenburg my most affectionate thanks and greetings."

For unfortunately it had not proved possible for Elinor to visit the old lady again, as the doctor still considered it unwise to allow visitors.

Both Ilsa and Rudi promised to convey this message. And then, suddenly, it was time for the goodbyes, and Elinor found her heart thumping in the most unaccountable way, and a big and almost uncontrollable lump in her throat.

She kept on telling herself that it was a good thing there was no possibility of emotional scenes with so many people present. But she was wishing, really, all the time that she could have just ten—five—two minutes alone with Rudi.

When he came to her, however, he simply took her hand, smiled down at her, and said in an undertone that made her heart thump harder than ever, "I'll come and say goodbye to you in the morning. Will you be down early to breakfast?"

"Very early. Before all the others," she promised quickly. And then he had passed on and was bowing over Lady Connelton's hand and kissing it respectfully.

It was not so difficult to say goodbye to Ilsa after that,

though they kissed each other with genuine emotion on both sides. And Ilsa promised once more to convey Elinor's friendly messages to her stepmother.

They were gone at last, and even Lady Connelton sighed and said, "I hate saying goodbye to anyone with whom I've enjoyed myself so much."

Elinor found a sympathetic echo to that in her heart. But, as Kenneth looked elaborately noncommittal, she decided not to put her feelings into words. In any case—she was to see Rudi once more for a few minutes on her own next morning. And, with that thought to cheer her, she could not be entirely downcast.

To ensure that she was down before everyone else on a day of departure was not quite easy. But Elinor was so determined to achieve this that she arrived in the breakfast-room next morning while it was still silent and empty.

However, a waiter appeared almost immediately to take her order. And then, for what seemed like hours, she sat there dawdling over her coffee and rolls, while her nervous impatience grew, and she asked herself how Rudi supposed he could have any time alone with her if he did not hurry.

The hands of the big clock in the dining-room crept on. One or two early risers drifted in. The waiter came to ask if she would like anything else. And still no Rudi appeared.

Instead, at last, Kenneth came in and, to Elinor's immense chagrin, joined her at the table.

"Hello, you did make an early start," he said, seeing her empty plate and cup.

"Yes, I . . . was awake early," Elinor told him, trying not to look self-conscious.

"It's often the way on the day of a journey," he agreed, without appearing to see anything unusual in her manner. Then he ordered his breakfast, and a few minutes later Elinor got up, saying that she had some last-minute packing to complete.

She went out of the breakfast-room and waited in the big entrance hall, glancing at the newspapers which she could not read and the one or two notices which hung near the reception desk. And all the time she felt a slow anger against Rudi mounting.

He had no right to put her in this mortifying position! He had said he would come early—that he would make sure of seeing her alone. And what girl with any proper pride wanted to have to hang about a hotel entrance, waiting on the chance of seeing someone who treated her so cavalierly?

It was desperately disappointing not to have those last few words with him. But there was such a thing as pride. And, on this reflection, Elinor started resolutely for the elevator.

As she did so, the big doors at the entrance revolved quickly and Rudi came in. A slightly pale, almost agitated-looking Rudi, who obviously saw her with relief and came straight across to her.

"Elinor, I'm so sorry—"

"I was just going," she told him a little coolly.

"Yes—I don't blame you. But it wasn't my fault that I'm late. Something very distressing has happened. Leni died in her sleep this morning."

CHAPTER TEN

"OH, RUDI!" Chagrin and annoyance were immediately forgotten in a rush of remorseful sympathy. "I am so terribly sorry." She put her hand on his arm in a quick gesture of friendliness.

"Yes. It's a shock, of course." Almost absently he covered her fingers with his. "One tells oneself that someone very old cannot, in the nature of things, be there much longer. But then, suddenly, when the end comes, the shock is just as great as if there had been no preparation."

"I know—I know. And you were so fond of her."

Rudi hesitated a moment. Then he said, "Yes."

"I mean—there was a real bond between you, wasn't there?" Elinor hastily amended, for she felt, a little embarrassedly, that she had presumed to overstate Rudi's feelings.

"Of course. Stronger than between her and Ilsa, at any rate. Though—I don't know—" Again he seemed curiously absent, as though he just could not fix his whole attention on what they were saying. "Perhaps she didn't really care much for either of us. Perhaps it was Anton."

"Perhaps—what was Anton?"

"Whom she really liked," he explained almost impatiently.

"It's no good trying to guess such things," Elinor said, seeking to comfort him. "And, in any case, it hardly matters now, does it?"

"My unworldly child, of course it matters." Rudi smiled, a quick, slightly strained smile, but again there was a note of impatience in his tone, "Leni had it in her power to be very—generous to the one she loved best."

"Why—why, yes. I suppose she had," Elinor agreed, a good deal taken aback.

She tried not to be shocked. She told herself that he was only being realistic and that, in families where there were no strong feelings as in her own, perhaps people did think along these lines. But no self-argument could quite reconcile her to the fact that, within a few hours of Leni Mardenburg's death, Rudi could already be conjecturing—even aloud—on the way in which she had left her money.

Elinor stood there, curiously at a loss for something appropriate to say. Not because she could not put her sympathy into words, but because she had the almost embarrassing impression that further expressions of sympathy were not really greatly needed.

Then, to her immense relief, Lady Connelton came downstairs. Surprised to see Rudi, to whom she believed she had already said goodbye the evening before, Lady Connelton came across to ask if anything had happened, and, on hearing the news, said with just the right degree of regret, "My dear boy, I am truly sorry! I know it is the way we would all wish to go, and of course she was a great age. But it is bound to be a sad occasion for you both. How is your sister taking it?"

Rudi said that Ilsa had recovered from the initial shock and was trying not to be too much upset. At this point Elinor found she had a curious and almost irrepressible urge to say she felt sure Ilsa was succeeding.

Then, in genuine remorse, she chided herself for thinking so censoriously of her two good friends, and assured herself that she had misjudged, or even misunderstood, Rudi a few minutes ago. After all, it would be unkind and absurd to examine anyone's words and manner too closely at a time like this.

Lady Connelton, with characteristic kindness, was already considering if there were any way in which they could be helpful.

"It would be rather awkward to postpone our journey at this point, I suppose," she said doubtfully. "But I'm sure if we could be of any real use to you, my husband would try to rearrange things. Perhaps—"

"By no means. Though it is very kind of you—and just like you." Rudi gave her his most brilliant smile, and spoke with that slight, charming formality which he often adopted toward Lady Connelton. "There is actually nothing which Ilsa and I cannot do. Of course we should be glad of any reason which prolonged your stay. But there is no real necessity at all. Instead, let us all—" he smiled at Elinor then—"look forward to meeting in Rome, in happier circumstances."

Lady Connelton said that no doubt that was the sensible way of looking at the situation. And then Sir Daniel and Kenneth arrived almost simultaneously from opposite directions and converged upon the group.

Fresh explanations and expressions of regret were forthcoming, Sir Daniel adding that he would willingly have stayed to pay his respects at the funeral of a great and affectionately remembered artist, only it had become too late for them to alter all their arrangements without some difficulty.

Once more Rudi protested that there was no need whatever for them to stay on, a view which evidently commended itself to Kenneth, whose expression became rather complicated at this point. Then goodbyes were again said all round, and Rudi—with a final hand-squeeze for Elinor—left the hotel, while the others dispersed to their rooms to make their final preparations for departure.

Elinor rather mechanically put on her hat and travelling coat, pushed the few last odds and ends into her overnight bag, and rang for a porter to collect her luggage. She was trying to concentrate on the minor things of the moment, but slowly growing on her was the chilling realization that she had now said goodbye to Rudi—though in circumstances she could never have foreseen.

He had spoken again of their meeting in Rome. She thought he certainly intended that they should meet there. But the break had been made, and who could say how future events would develop? She might even have said goodbye to Rudi for good, for all she knew. The idea hurt badly, and she thrust it away from her.

Then she wished that she had not had such a curious—perhaps such an unfair—impression of him at the end. Of course he had not *really* meant that the most important thing about Leni's passing was the division of what she had left. It was just—just—

"Are you ready, dear?"

Lady Connelton, dressed for the journey, appeared in the open doorway, carrying a very beautiful but rather oversized handbag which she had rapturously acquired in Vienna, the home of such articles.

Elinor assured her employer that she was ready, and the two went down together, to wait in the car while Sir Daniel and Kenneth saw to the luggage and supervised the final arrangements for departure.

Presently the two men joined them—Sir Daniel taking his seat in the back with his wife, while Kenneth, with a friendly little gesture, invited Elinor to join him in front. Then, taking their last regretful glance at Vienna, they drove rather slowly out of the city and headed westward once more.

"Well—" Sir Daniel leaned forward to address his young secretary with a kindly smile—"so you enjoyed your first visit to Vienna?"

"Immensely, thank you." She smiled bravely in return,

although the melancholy of departure was strong upon her. "It was one of the places I always wanted to see and—now I have," she ended rather lamely, feeling that this did not in the least express the joyous experiences of the last week or so.

"You will come back many other times, I daresay." That was Kenneth who, though apparently concentrating on the driving, still, it seemed, had attention to spare for conversation.

"I don't know," Elinor said slowly, wondering whether it was purely fancy which made her feel that the Vienna chapter was ended. "Some things never—repeat themselves."

"Oh, nonsense!" Her employer scouted this notion good-humoredly, because, to tell the truth, he rather liked to have the monopoly of pleasing regrets himself. "Vienna will always be there, I hope."

"Elinor was speaking figuratively, rather than literally, I think," Kenneth said, with rare understanding. But, before she could be either embarrassed or touched by this, Lady Connelton declared, with kindly common sense, "We are all feeling a bit melancholy because the visit ended on a sad note. Leni Mardenburg seemed a real personality to us all, and even if she had no close connection with us, and certainly lived to a gratifying age, we naturally feel with our two young friends in their loss."

"I understand she was not *so* close to them," Kenneth said.

"N-no, I suppose not," his aunt conceded. "But it is bound to mean a big change in their lives."

"It could mean a tremendous change, I suppose," Kenneth said dryly.

"Oh—financially, you mean?"

"Of course. If she left more or less everything to the von Eibergs, I imagine they would be very comfortably situated, without the necessity of raising a finger for the rest of their lives."

"Hm—yes. I'd forgotten that for a moment." Lady Connelton glanced at Elinor, but was tactful enough to glance away again immediately.

"It's not very good for anyone to be left like that," observed Sir Daniel, voicing an unpopular truth as though it were an original thought.

"I doubt if the von Eibergs would agree with you, Uncle," Kenneth retorted good-humoredly.

"Or anyone else similarly placed," added Lady Connelton in all fairness.

"Sir Daniel really meant that it isn't good for anyone, however well provided for, to feel that they don't need to pull their weight in *some* way," Elinor put in soberly. "He's right, of course."

"And, much though we all like the von Eibergs," said Lady Connelton, arbitrarily including her nephew in this, "we rather instinctively feel that they might react to prosperity that way."

Elinor bit her lip. She longed to defend them, but the words just would not come. Oddly enough, it was Kenneth who said, with a fairness amounting to generosity, "One can never say how anyone will react to prosperity. Or disaster either, come to that. It could be that our charming, rather problematical couple would become thoroughly valuable and worthwhile people once they were freed from the day-to-day problem of scraping a living."

"Finest discipline anyone can have," growled his uncle argumentatively.

Kenneth smiled.

"I'm not going to do violence to my own view by arguing against that," he assured Sir Daniel. "But you can't take exactly the same measuring rule to everyone."

Sir Daniel seemed to think one could. So Lady Connelton called their attention to the very beautiful country through which they were passing, and the discussion gently petered out.

"Thank you," whispered Elinor to Kenneth, on inexplicable impulse, then wondered how on earth she was to explain herself if he asked what she meant.

He did not ask, however. He took one hand from the wheel and patted hers as they lay in her lap. And after that they drove on in excellent harmony.

They made a very long day of it and contrived to do the

whole journey in one. This involved only the briefest of halts for meals and an arrival in Ehrwald considerably after dark. But, since Kenneth had preferred it that way and declared he could drive quite easily for that length of time, the others willingly accepted the arrangement.

For the last two hours both the Conneltons dozed in the back of the car, but Elinor remained bright-eyed and wakeful beside Kenneth.

Once, toward the end of the drive, when the road had become monotonous, he laughed slightly and said, "You'd better talk to me. This is rather sleep-inducing."

Elinor roused herself from her own somewhat complicated reflections and reminiscences.

"What was Rosemary intending to do after we left?" she inquired. "I managed to say only a brief goodbye to her, and didn't hear her final plans."

She meant to stay on with friends near Vienna for a while, and then make her way home by leisurely stages, I think. She has a good many friends in Paris. I suppose she might well go there."

"She wasn't thinking of . . . of coming to Rome?"

"No."

"Are you disappointed, Ken?"

"No."

Elinor was silent, for few things are less encouraging to conversation than monosyllabic replies.

"Nor," volunteered Kenneth, breaking the silence on his own account, "am I in love with her."

Elinor was slightly startled.

"Why did you think you had to tell me that?" she inquired.

"Because you seem to have got hold of some odd ideas about me and Rosemary. I thought it was time to straighten things out a bit."

"I had no ideas about you and Rosemary at all," declared Elinor, a little too quickly and with palpable untruth. "It was just that the time I—quite inadvertently—" she added with emphasis—"overheard you telling Lady Connelton that she would be much better on this trip than I should, I naturally thought you had some special interest in her."

"I simply thought she would be fun on a journey of this sort."

"And that I shouldn't?"

"My dear girl, I didn't know you. As my aunt described you, you didn't sound at all as though you would be fun. And, even when I first met you—"

He paused so long that she said, "Yes?" as casually as she could.

"I'd never met anyone at all like you before, Elinor," he said, frowning. "I didn't know what to make of you."

"But I'm the most ordinary and uncomplicated type," exclaimed Elinor with genuine astonishment. "I don't see what there could be about me to puzzle anyone."

He laughed a good deal at that.

"Perhaps that was the point," he said. "That you were uncomplicated, I mean. For ordinary you are not. But I don't want to embarrass you by analyzing you to your face."

"It doesn't embarrass me in the least," declared Elinor, surprised to find that this was so. "I rather like it. It makes me feel important," and she smiled rather mischievously. "I don't think anyone before ever found me interesting enough to analyze."

He gave her a glance of mingled amusement and, strangely enough, a sort of exasperation.

"Perhaps you never encouraged anyone to do so," he said.

"*Encouraged*?" She queried his choice of word as though it faintly shocked her. "Does one deliberately encourage someone else to be interested?"

"Of course. Though the degree of deliberation may vary, I suppose. And possibly," he muttered, half to himself, "the less the deliberation, the more the charm."

"What did you say?"

"It doesn't matter. Do you know that you've changed a good deal on this trip, Elinor?"

She hesitated, remembering that Lady Connelton had said something the same of her.

"Have I?" she said doubtfully. "Do you mean—for the worse, Ken?"

"No. Of course not."

"For the better?"

Again he gave her that half-amused, half-vexed glance.

"Perhaps changed wasn't quite the right word. You haven't actually altered in character. You've just developed enormously—if I may say that without sounding insufferable."

"Yes, you may," Elinor assured him, and a very slight dimple appeared in the cheek nearest him.

"When I first met you, you were like—like a nice tight little bud on a rosebush—"

"Thorns and all?" suggested Elinor.

"Look here, you horrid child, are you laughing at me?" he demanded suddenly.

"Just a bit."

"Well, I suppose I deserve it." He laughed reluctantly himself then. "I don't usually talk in this fanciful way. It must be the moonlight and the lateness of the hour and the general romantic quality of the Austrian landscape. But what I wanted to say was—"

"Dear me, we must surely be nearly home!" exclaimed Lady Connelton, waking up at this moment and leaning forward to try to see where they were. "What is the time, Ken?"

"Just after ten, Aunt Millicent," Kenneth replied with admirable self-control. "And we shall be home in less than half an hour."

"We shall none of us be sorry for that." Lady Connelton smothered a yawn. "It's been very dull for the last hour or so, but one can't expect anything else, once the light goes."

Elinor suppressed a rebellious denial to this. She liked—really loved—Lady Connelton. But at the moment she could have done very well without her.

Why did she have to wake up just then? Ken's simile of herself and the nice little rosebud had been most engaging. But she wanted him to develop the subject further—at least to the point when the rose came out!

This idea amused her suddenly to such a degree that she caught her breath on a private laugh. For Elinor was not without her own special sense of humor, which did not usually desert her even at disappointing moments.

"What's that for?" inquired Kenneth, leaning his head rather close to hers and speaking in a whisper.

"Several things," whispered Elinor back again. "But none of them malicious."

He laughed too at that.

"Of course not. There's not a grain of malice in you," he replied. Whereupon she immediately wondered perversely if he would have preferred her to have just a small admixture of amusing malice in her.

"Do you wish there were?" she asked, on impulse.

"No. I wouldn't have a thing about you changed," he told her curtly. But so curtly that she suddenly found she could not ask him anything further.

They arrived in Erhwald soon after that, and it was undoubtedly very pleasant to step out of the rather cramped quarters of the car and stand for a few minutes in the cool, starry silence outside the hotel.

But they were all tired, and soon hurried in—to a welcome meal and then, very thankfully, to their rooms. Elinor was glad to find that she once more had her "own" room, as she privately called it, where she could look out on to the moonlit slopes of the towering Zugspitze. But it was too late to linger even over that marvellous view, for the next day was to be a full and busy one. So she went almost immediately to bed—and dreamed that she was back in Vienna, dancing with Rudi.

It had been decided that they should go to Munich to pick up the train to Rome, because, although this would involve their retracing their journey as far as Innsbruck, it would enable them to board the night train at a more convenient hour.

"If we're lucky, we should all be fast asleep when we reach Innsbruck," Lady Connelton said. "It will be nearly two o'clock in the morning."

Elinor really thought it was a pity to have to sleep and miss any of the journey. But, by the time they had cleared up everything in Ehrwald, and travelled to Munich, she was beginning to feel that a night in the train would have to include *some* sleep at least.

To Elinor, who had never travelled all night in a train, the cosy intimacy of her sleeper was at least as attractive as her cabin on the ship had been. She experimented a little with the lights and the taps, she put her blind up and down, and finally she went to bed in the narrow but singularly comfortable bunk. Here she lay for some time, with the light out but the blind up, and watched the passing, moonlit panorama of the Tyrol for the last time.

She would, she thought, always remember Austria with affection, and that touch of enjoyable nostalgia which Sir Daniel had assured her she would find there. Now they were travelling rapidly southwards toward Italy—another country of romance and charm. But a more full-blooded charm, Elinor thought, from all that she had heard. If Austria might be viewed in pastel colors, Italy should have all the color and richness and warmth of an oil painting.

How lucky she was to see both. How incredibly lucky she was to have these wonderful experiences. No wonder they had changed her. Or, rather—no, developed was the word dear Ken had used, though he had been a little diffident about it.

There was a time, not so long ago, when Ken had showed no diffidence at all where she was concerned. If she had changed, so had he. Or else it was that he viewed her somewhat differently. She smiled a little at the thought, and her heavy eyelids drooped.

The train rushed on through the night, and long before they reached the lofty, remote loneliness of the Brenner Pass, or started the long, slow descent into the plains of northern Italy, Elinor was fast asleep.

She was up early, however, and when the train stopped at Verona, she came out into the corridor already dressed. Kenneth was just coming out of his compartment, and he smiled and said, "Good morning. Are you coming for a stroll on the platform? We stop here some time and there'll be a chance to stretch your legs."

Very willingly Elinor came with him, and, in the early morning sunlight, they strolled up and down while they exchanged reports on their excellent night, and he told her a little about Verona.

"We—you must come here again in the summer," he told her. "It's confoundedly hot, but there is a fascinating short season of opera, given in the open air in the Roman arena."

"Really Roman, you mean? From ancient times, that is?"

"Oh, certainly. Rather like the Colosseum in Rome, though, as a matter of fact, it is in a better state of preservation. I believe Verona is supposed to be the architect's idea of Paradise. There are the most wonderful churches and archways and things," explained Kenneth a little vaguely. "It's also the city of Romeo and Juliet, of course," he added irrelevantly.

"*Is* it?" said Elinor, to whom this somehow seemed to have a special sort of significance, though she could not have quite said why. Then the train showed signs of resuming its journey once more, so they ran along the platform and jumped in, laughing and rather breathless, just as the Conneltons came out of their compartment in search of breakfast.

All that morning and until well on in the afternoon they travelled onwards. Through Bologna, where Elinor glimpsed the buildings of the ancient University, and on to Florence, with its pink and white-washed houses, its miraculous domed Cathedral, and the soaring lines of Giotto's Campanile. As they stayed some time in the station, she even heard the faint, silver-sweet sound of the bells from the Campanile borne on the afternoon breeze. And then on again, to the glory and majesty of Rome.

The great station seemed disconcertingly modern. But, as they drove through the streets to their hotel, Elinor gazed in fascinated awe on buildings and vistas so famous and familiar through countless reproductions that it seemed incredible she was seeing them in actual fact at last.

"However long we stay, we shan't be able to see a tenth of this properly," she exclaimed at last.

"No, of course not." Sir Daniel smiled cheerfully at her, for Rome did not appear to make him nostalgically reminiscent. "See what you can and enjoy it. There are three Romes at least, you know. Ancient Rome, Renaissance Rome, and modern Rome. Well, well, Ken ought to be able to find time to show you something of each of them. In the intervals of work, of course," he added, suddenly recalling that they had not all come to Rome for the sole purpose of enjoying themselves.

Elinor smiled. Then she twisted round on the taxi seat to look rather shyly at Kenneth. He said nothing, however, and so she looked away again very quickly, in case he might think she were showing an undue amount of expectancy.

They had been going uphill for some time, turning and twisting along a road which had a curiously countrified look, even though it led straight out of one of the main thoroughfares. Now at last they arrived at their hotel, which stood high on what Elinor could not help hoping was one of the famous Seven Hills of Rome.

Her room, she found to her delight, was on the top floor, and from her balconied window she could look across the confused mass of the city to the shining dome of St. Peter's with the tremendous sweep of curved colonnades on either side. She stood there for some time, intoxicated by the warmth and color of a Roman spring. Then at last she turned to unpack, and presently, having bathed and changed to a cool, patterned frock, she went downstairs in search of the others.

It was a quiet, faintly somnolent hour of the day and not many people were about. So Elinor went through the almost deserted lounge and stepped out into a formal paved garden at the rear of the hotel. Rock plants grew in every crevice, and she saw a small, bright-eyed lizard dart along the warm, sun-drenched wall. In the center of the garden was a fountain, where the figure of a nymph held aloft a shell from which water fell ceaselessly, with a soft, tinkling sound that was like cool laughter.

Although the place was small, it was curiously secluded, and Elinor strolled about for a few minutes, enjoying the peace and stillness after the continual movement of the train. Then she stood to watch the water falling from the nymph's shell. And here, at the edge of the little pool Kenneth found her.

"Well, is your room comfortable?" he asked her, coming to stand beside her.

"Yes, lovely, thank you. And I have a wonderful view

again. Not like the view of the mountains, of course—but a glorious glimpse of Rome and St. Peter's in the distance."

"You must let me take you there."

"But of course—if you want to."

"Why should I not want to, for heaven's sake?" he demanded a trifle irritably.

Elinor counted ten and reminded herself that he was probably tired after the journey, and the long day's driving before that.

"You needn't snap at me," she said composedly. "I didn't mean anything special. But when Sir Daniel suggested that you should take me sight-seeing, you didn't pick up the suggestion, and I thought you didn't want to be stampeded into having to do so."

"I am not the sort of man who gets stampeded into doing anything he doesn't want," Kenneth pointed out rather heavily.

"Very well."

"You enjoyed the time we went sight-seeing in Salzburg, didn't you?"

"Immensely—of course."

"And it wasn't my fault that that confounded Rudi von Eiberg did all the sight-seeing with you in Vienna," he added, unwisely displaying a very slight sense of grievance.

Elinor turned her head and looked coolly at him. None of her family would have recognized that look, in its composure and its self-possession.

"You are in a bad temper, aren't you?" she said pleasantly.

"I suppose I am," he agreed crossly. And at that point he leaned forward and kissed her.

CHAPTER ELEVEN

ELINOR gasped slightly, wished that she could say something very cool and sophisticated and to the point, and finally produced nothing more striking than, "I never gave you permission to kiss me."

"Did Rudi von Eiberg always ask permission?" was the highly provocative retort.

"I don't know what you mean by always," returned Elinor with spirit. "Rudi hardly ever kissed me, and never without a good reason. And, anyway, that has nothing to do with it. It's not very nice to speak in that cross, nagging way to anyone, and then kiss them as though a . . . a rather impudent sort of salute naturally makes up for everything."

Kenneth looked startled at this description of his conduct, and then faintly sulky.

"I'm sorry," he said stiffly. "It wasn't meant to be impudent at all."

"Well, that was how it felt," Elinor declared severely. Then she suddenly remembered that the light touch of his lips on her cheek had felt rather nice, really, and because she was both impulsive and truthful, she added, "No, it didn't," and put up her hand experimentally against the cheek he had kissed.

He laughed at that, with immense relief, which made her laugh too, rather doubtfully. Then he took her hand—as nearly diffidently as was within his nature to do—and said, "I am really sorry if I annoyed you. I didn't mean to. I think the trouble was that I very much wanted to take you sight-seeing in Rome, but I was still jealous about the way Rudi monopolized you in Vienna, and I didn't want my uncle to start pushing what one might call my family claims if you were going to find someone else to take you around here too."

"But who else should I find?" Elinor asked with simplicity.

"Oh, I don't know. An attractive girl like you can always find someone."

Elinor looked at him in surprise and thought that, suddenly though quite inexplicably, he looked like her brother Edward when his latest girl-friend had puzzled and disillusioned him, or—even more inexplicably—like young Henry when his experiments had gone wrong.

"Don't worry," she said, and she patted the hand which held hers with a sort of encouraging tenderness. "We just got each other wrong. Let's start again. Would you like to take me sight-seeing when we both have some time? Because, if so, I'd love to come. I never enjoyed anything more than that morning in Salzburg together."

"Thank you, Elinor. Nothing would please me better," he replied gravely. And then his eyes twinkled irrepressibly, and he added, "Do we retrace our steps to the extent of letting me kiss you again—this time with all proper respect?"

She laughed and colored a little.

"If you very much want to."

"I very much want to," Kenneth stated. And, without more ceremony, he put his arm around her, drew her against him, and kissed her firmly on her smooth, flushed cheek.

It was true that he did not do it with the light, unoffending charm of a Rudi. But it was extraordinarily nice for all that.

Then the Conneltons came out into the garden—fortunately just a few moments after they had drawn apart—and conversation became general and followed the now familiar pattern of satisfied comments on the hotel and plans for the evening.

"Now we are in Rome and should obviously do as the Romans do," Lady Connelton said with a laugh, "what *do* we do?"

"Go to the Opera," suggested her husband.

"If it is not too long and inaccessible," agreed Lady Connelton.

"I will find out what is on," Kenneth said obligingly, and went in to make inquiries at the hotel desk.

He came back with the information that the performance that night was *Lucia di Lammermoor* with Maria Callas in the name part, and that it would have been quite, quite impossible to secure tickets for the performance if the hall porter had not just happened to have four excellent seats with which he was willing to part—for a consideration, naturally.

This being, as Kenneth and the Conneltons well knew, the recognized method of attending almost anything worthwhile in Italy, the bargain was struck.

"A full dress occasion, I take it?" Lady Connelton said reflectively. "Somehow the late losers of the war are always so much smarter than the late victors."

"Let us keep our end up, by all means," agreed her husband, "even in victory."

From which Elinor gathered that here, at last, was the occasion on which she should wear the ivory lace evening dress which Anne had, so providentially, insisted on her including in her wardrobe.

Fortunately the lace dress had stood up well to all the travelling and packing and unpacking, so that when they gathered for dinner Elinor was looking fresh and cool and enchanting. There is something in the sheer "dressing up" for a festive occasion which imparts a certain charm and glamor to almost every personality.

It was almost the first time Elinor had ever worn full evening dress. Certainly it was the first time she had worn it with confidence and a natural, graceful enjoyment. And, as she came in, Lady Connelton—very handsome in black and some good though unostentatious jewelry—said, "Dear me, child, you are indeed quite a beauty in your way."

"Of course she is a beauty." Sir Daniel looked at his young secretary indulgently. "I don't doubt that we shall have von Eiberg chasing after us soon, in tribute to the fact."

To her surprise, Elinor caught herself smiling apologetically at Kenneth. Then she thought how nice and distinguished he looked in his evening clothes and was glad that he smiled back at her, even if he did frown a little first at what Sir Daniel had said.

It was a perfectly delightful evening after that. The most luxurious evening, Elinor told herself afterwards, that she had ever spent. They dined leisurely and well, since the performance did not start until late, then they drove down to the theater, past beautiful colonnaded buildings, through superbly planned streets and squares—with an occasional glimpse of some breath-taking fountain or superb frontage or even just a doorway, caught, as it were, and preserved as the wave of modern Rome had overtaken the Rome of the past.

The theater itself was handsome, without being specially memorable. But the scene in the promenade and the auditorium was the most glittering and impressive Elinor had ever witnessed. Splendid dresses and jewels seemed the rule rather than the exception, and from their excellent seats in the stalls they could enjoy that rare spectacle that used to be called "a well-dressed house."

"It isn't always like this," Kenneth explained to her, seeing her almost awe-stricken surprise. "But tonight is definitely a gala night, and a gala night at the opera is not something to be lightly dismissed in Italy."

"Does the opera more or less follow the Walter Scott story?" Elinor inquired, glancing at her glossy and rather impressive program.

"Less, rather than more, if I remember rightly," Kenneth assured her cheerfully. "And I expect the Italian idea of Scottish legend will have its moments of amusement. But the action is simple and easy to follow—and, by all accounts, we should have some wonderful singing from the soprano."

They did. Elinor, who was no expert, sensed instinctively that here was quality of a very high order and, without bothering herself about finer points—over which she was, in any case, humbly ignorant—she enjoyed herself enormously, and heartily joined in that wave of almost riotous enthusiasm which occasionally sweeps over an audience, carrying both sophisticated and simple along with it.

"Enjoying yourself?" inquired Kenneth, with a smile, in the interval.

"Oh, enormously!"

"As well as in Vienna?" he wanted to know.

"Why—why, yes. Though in an entirely different way," she conceded. Then she thought suddenly about

Rudi and wondered whether his presence, if obtainable, would have added anything to her pleasure.

Perhaps, in an oblique way, that was what Kenneth had meant.

After the performance, late though it was, they walked part of the way home, just to enjoy the warm spring air and the subtle, intangible glamor of the Roman night. It was, Elinor thought, one of the loveliest experiences yet.

At one point, as they crossed a crowded road, Kenneth took her lightly by the arm, and, when they reached the other side, he did not immediately relinquish her. They strolled along together, two or three paces behind the Conneltons, and, many though the impressions were which were crowding upon Elinor in this magic city, she felt that the outstanding one was the sensation of those strong, friendly, supporting fingers on her arm.

The next day it was not possible to embark at once on a program of pleasure. A good deal of work had accumulated, and fresh aspects of it presented themselves now that they were in a new place. Lady Connelton declared that it was a shame to stay in when the weather was so superb. But there was no getting away from it; work had to come first for a while, and Elinor was exceedingly busy.

I don't really mind (she wrote to the family). No one ever worked in happier surroundings. Both Sir Daniel and Kenneth are so kind and appreciative, and I know they will see to it that I have time to enjoy myself later. After the wonderful time in Vienna, I can hardly complain. I doubt if any girl ever had a more wonderful trip than I have had.

Don't think that I am not still looking forward to every bit of it that is left, but sometimes I am quite violently homesick now. It seems that I have been away such a long time. (Well, I have, of course!) And I want so much to see you all and talk to you.

That goes for the home side of things, but when I think about the office, I wonder how on earth I am ever going to settle down again. Not that I expect to earn my living the rest of my life in these fantastic circumstances, but—I *feel* so different from the rather mousy girl who used to type schedules for Mr. Prynne and say "yes" and "no" to Sally Pascoe, and listen enviously while the others all talked about their much more interesting affairs.

Does that sound rather horrid and "above my boots"? I really don't mean it that way. I'm just wondering how I am going to fit myself into my little niche once more. Well—we shall see when the time comes. At present there is still Rome to enjoy, and there has been no talk as yet about our even thinking of coming home.

Once she had put all this down on paper, Elinor studied it rather soberly and wondered if this were what Kenneth had meant when he declared she had developed greatly from the "tight little bud" stage. The last thing she wanted was to seem in any way discontented when she, inevitably, had to return to earth. But—it was not that. It was—she sighed rather perplexedly. And Lady Connelton, coming in at that moment, wanted to know if anything was wrong.

"Oh, no!" Elinor looked up and smiled immediately. "I don't know what could be wrong in the lovely life I'm living now. It was just—I was thinking about going back to the office."

"But you are not going back to the office yet, dear child," Lady Connelton pointed out with her usual practical cheerfulness. "And things are never so bad as we expect them to be in any case."

"I didn't mean it quite like that," Elinor explained, because one could explain things very easily to Lady Connelton. "I don't really mind going back to the office when the time comes. At least—not in a discontented and resentful way. But I can't quite *see* myself as I used to be."

"Well, you aren't as you used to be," Lady Connelton said very sensibly. "You probably never will be again. We all change as we grow up. You grew up suddenly. That's all."

"I hope the others won't mind," Elinor said, with a

touch of characteristic humility. She was very serious.

"Probably they won't notice much," Lady Connelton told her with amusement. "As you are a nice, tactful child, you will almost certainly keep most of it to yourself. But whereas before I suppose you kept silent about your own affairs because they were almost non-existent, and listened respectfully to what the others had to say, now you will still listen because you are kind and know that what nearly everyone wants is to talk a little bit about themselves. But, instead of feeling blank and mildly envious, you will have your own experiences to think about, and sometimes you'll talk a bit about them too, and people will just think what a much more interesting girl you have become."

"Oh, Lady Connelton, do you really think so? You're such a comforting person!" Elinor exclaimed.

"There is no situation, my dear, which kindness and common sense cannot reduce to manageable terms," Lady Connelton declared in her rather positive way.

After a week during which it was possible to snatch only brief intervals in which to visit such obvious places of interest as St. Peter's or the Colosseum or one or two of the superb medieval or Renaissance churches, Elinor found herself at last with a completely free afternoon.

Unaware that anyone else was equally free, she was turning over in her mind what she would most like to do when Kenneth came in and said, "Everything finished? Then will you let me take you out to the Villa d'Este? It's too hot to do any sight-seeing in the city, but it's sure to be cool out there."

"I'd love it!" Elinor jumped up immediately. "Where is it, and how do we get there?"

"By car," said Kenneth, answering the second question first, and thereby showing that, as usual, he had somehow managed to get hold of a serviceable car. "And the Villa is out at Tivoli—about forty-five minutes' drive. There is a more or less ruined house and marvellous terraced gardens with fountains everywhere and cypresses that look as though they've been there since the beginning of time."

"I'll be ready in ten minutes," Elinor promised.

"No need to hurry. We have all afternoon," Kenneth reminded her. And, though she could not have said why, this last statement made her feel very happy.

Indeed, they embarked on the expedition in the most leisurely and restful way, and in the end they took very much more than the suggested forty-five minutes to drive out there. On the way, Kenneth suddenly started to tell her something of his earlier visits to Italy, and from that went on to an account of the Far East, where he had done his National Service.

Elinor was a born listener who, it must be confessed, had had excellent training from her devoted family, and in consequence she made as charming an audience as a man could wish to have. In addition, Kenneth, who was a keen observer and had a nice turn for description, really talked with interest, and Elinor had no difficulty in playing her role of listener with enthusiasm.

Presently, however, he broke off, laughed at her absorbed expression, and said, "I'm talking too much about myself. Why didn't you stop me?"

"Because I was enjoying it," Elinor told him with engaging simplicity. "Please go on."

So Kenneth went on. And if either of them remembered why it was Othello first fell in love with Desdemona, neither of them remarked on the fact.

It was cool and enchanting, as Kenneth had forecast, in the cypress-lined walks of the Villa d'Este gardens, and the ceaseless sound of a hundred splashing fountains so delighted Elinor that she exclaimed, "You do choose the most heavenly places to show me, Kenneth. Just as you did in Salzburg."

He smiled and, though he said nothing, his expression was so peculiarly gratified that she added impulsively, "Did you really mind that it was Rudi who showed me so much of Vienna?"

"I should have like to do so myself, naturally."

"But—it was very much his own home city. It seemed so appropriate that he should do so."

"Of course."

She trembled on the edge of feeling exasperated again, but firmly drew back.

160

"I should willingly have gone with you too if you had asked me, Ken."

"Would you?" He took her hand, swung it and smiled at her. "Well, I shan't grudge him his innings in Vienna. I am having mine now in Rome," he said lightly, and the subject was not pursued further.

During the next week or ten days, Kenneth interpreted what he called his innings in the most delightful manner. Work was not nearly so pressing and—sometimes with Sir Daniel and Lady Connelton, but often alone together—Elinor and Kenneth explored the thousand beauties of Rome.

They wandered among the sun-drenched ruins of the Forum, they climbed the steps to the Trinità dei Monti, they drove out along the Appian Way, where Caesar's legions marched, and visited the ancient Catacombs, and they spent hours admiring the beauties of the Villa Medici and then the matchless panorama of the city which was to be seen from the gardens.

Elinor could hardly believe it was possible to concentrate so much beauty and so many wonderful experiences in so short a space of time, and she almost literally felt her mind expanding and her spirit soaring.

She knew, though she tried not to dwell on the fact, that office matters at home in London would presently claim Kenneth's presence. But, although Elinor could see from various letters received that he might well decide to leave at any time, Kenneth said nothing and so she went on enjoying his company while she was lucky enough to have it.

In all this she did not forget that part of her duties consisted in being a companion to Lady Connelton, and the two of them spent many enjoyable hours wandering about the beautiful shops, or simply sauntering through the streets in the bright, clear sunshine.

It was after one of these morning excursions, when they had returned a little late for lunch, that, as they entered the hotel, Elinor suddenly saw two familiar figures standing at the reception desk. Even from the back, they were quite unmistakable, and Elinor was aware of a rush of pure friendly delight as she recognized them.

"Look who is here, Lady Connelton!" she exclaimed, enchanted. And, at the same moment, Ilsa and Rudi von Eiberg turned at the sound of her voice and rushed across to greet her and her employer.

Lady Connelton shook them both heartily by the hand, and they embraced Elinor with frank affection.

"Why didn't you let us know you were coming?" Lady Connelton wanted to know. "We would have been in to greet you."

"We thought a surprise would be nicer." Ilsa smiled from one to the other, and Elinor thought she had never seen her look more happy, bright-eyed and generally attractive. "Where is Sir Daniel? And Kenneth, too," she added as an afterthought.

"I don't doubt my husband is in the dining-room impatiently awaiting our return," Lady Connelton said. "Ken has gone to Naples for the day on business. He won't be back until some time tonight."

She then invited the von Eibergs to join them for lunch, an arrangement which put Sir Daniel in high good humor when he saw them come in, though previously he had been glancing continually at his watch and feeling in rather a bad temper.

There was no denying that, if Kenneth had to be absent, he could hardly have chosen a better day, for as it was, there was no second opinion whatever to disturb the general feeling of content and satisfaction around the lunch table.

Elinor, sitting opposite Rudi and catching a frank smile from him from time to time, could not help thinking how happy and sweet-tempered and charming he was looking. This was exactly how she remembered him and liked him best. And suddenly all the vague, unwelcome impressions which she had—most unfairly, no doubt—carried from that last meeting faded away, and she could only think how much she liked him and how glad she was that he and Ilsa had come to Rome to join them.

Presently, consumed with a curiosity which only good manners kept in check, Lady Connelton asked whether they had had very much difficulty over the settling up of their stepmother's affairs. At which Ilsa and her brother exchanged a quick smile, and Ilsa said, "I can't describe to you what a task it is to go through all the personal belongings in the apartment. The listing and valuing and sorting is quite distracting. It will be months before it is all finished. On the other hand, there are some wonderfully interesting things there, and, although I left it all willingly when Rudi suggested we should come here for a week or so, I really don't mind finishing it at my leisure when I go back."

"In any case, Leni has been very good to us," Rudi said, in such a warm, appreciative voice that Elinor wondered how she could ever have been critical of his attitude toward his stepmother. "We want to arrange everything just as she would like."

"Of course," Lady Connelton agreed, and obviously controlled her impatience with the greatest difficulty when her husband side-tracked the issue by embarking on a long account of an occasion when he had been unexpectedly made executor of the will of some remote acquaintance, who had left his affairs in great confusion.

"As though we wanted to hear about Dan's difficulties over poor stupid Bob Eldon's affairs!" she exclaimed impatiently to Elinor afterwards. "I couldn't possibly get the conversation back to where we started, after that. And I do so want to know if Leni Mardenburg left those two everything. And, if so, how much."

Elinor laughed.

"There was her great-nephew, Anton, too, you know."

"Oh, dear, I hope there was enough for the three of them," said Lady Connelton. "But I think our two had a . . . a rather satisfied look, don't you? One doesn't want to sound heartless, but, since she *is* dead, I should like to know if Leni Mardenburg left them—Rudi, anyway—sufficiently well off to make any necessary plans for the future."

At one time, Elinor would have been a good deal embarrassed by this very transparent, match-making way of putting things. But she had learned by now that, while Lady Connelton conjectured enjoyably on all sorts of matters, she never actually interfered in other people's affairs. So it was perfectly easy just to smile non-committally and go on thinking her own thoughts.

Both Ilsa and Rudi would have liked Elinor to join them for the afternoon. But, as she had been out all the morning with Lady Connelton, she felt bound to deal with some work which had been left over from the day before.

Even to herself, Elinor was not quite willing to admit that there was a certain charm, not to say relief, in keeping events in enjoyable suspense, as it were. It was enough to know that Ilsa—and, still more, Rudi—was there. She was not particularly anxious to have developments go further than that, for the moment at any rate.

It was all very well for Lady Connelton to conjecture about their new status and whether they had come to Rome for any purpose other than casual enjoyment. For her part, Elinor thought she would rather not know anything about any particular purpose, especially if this were something which might involve herself in any major decision.

So she typed away devotedly in the private sitting-room where she did most of her work, and profoundly hoped that, when Kenneth returned, it would fall to the lot of either his aunt or his uncle to tell him that the von Eibergs had arrived from Vienna.

Fortunately for Elinor, her work was sufficiently exacting to demand most of her attention, so that the afternoon slipped away without her noticing much how time was passing. She was, indeed, just drawing the last sheet of paper from her machine when the door opened and Kenneth came in.

Even so, she was astonished to see him back so early—and one glance at his rather unsmiling face told her that someone had already imparted to him the unwelcome news.

"Why, hello, Ken." She strove to make her welcoming smile completely unconcerned. "You're back early, aren't you?"

"Yes. I got through sooner than I expected at the Naples office, and caught an earlier train."

He came over rather slowly and stood beside her desk,

fingering one or two things on it with a somber aimlessness.

An unusual sense of impatience assailed Elinor, and she felt almost annoyed with him. Really, did he *have* to make such heavy weather of the von Eibergs' arrival and look as though he had just lost a near relative?

There was a short silence. Then she said, in a rather briskly cheerful tone, "Is there anything the matter?"

"I'm not feeling exactly elated, naturally. I've just been talking to my uncle—about what's happened," was the somewhat cryptic retort.

So Sir Daniel had told him.

"Well, really, it isn't exactly unexpected, is it?" she said, wishing, not for the first time in her life, that people with either confidences to make or grievances to air would come straight to the point, instead of talking round it in a rather reproachful way.

"I'm glad you feel so philosophical about it."

"Why shouldn't I?" inquired Elinor, all the least patient part of her rushing to the surface. "You can't expect me to be sorry about it."

He looked for a moment as though she had slapped his face.

"Funny—I thought you might be," he said. And, turning on his heel, he went out of the room.

A good deal distressed as well as annoyed, Elinor looked after him. It was too exasperating of him to take this unnecessarily tragic tone over nothing more unexpected and disastrous than the arrival of the von Eibergs. He had liked them well enough when they were all together in Vienna. At least he had tolerated them socially. Why behave now as though she were in some way a traitress if she did not share his own view of them?

Elinor was not given to displays of temper, or she would probably have slapped her papers down on the desk and banged the cover on her typewriter. Instead, she stacked her work neatly, covered her typewriter carefully, stretched her aching arms, and decided that the long hot afternoon's work had tired her enough for a rest in her own room until dinner.

By that time perhaps Kenneth would have realized how

unreasonably he was behaving, and they could resume a more sensible and friendly relationship.

She had not really meant to sleep. But as soon as she lay down on her bed, all the warm languor of the late afternoon seemed to settle on her eyelids, and she drifted immediately into the most profound and contented slumber.

From this she awoke more than two hours later, with the sweet, varied, syncopated sound of all the church clocks of Rome chiming eight o'clock.

Hardly able to believe that she had slept so long, but greatly refreshed, and feeling able to deal with even the recalcitrant Kenneth, she hastily changed and made ready to go downstairs.

"I'm so sorry," Elinor said. "I slept much longer than I meant to. I think it was the typing and the hot afternoon."

Lady Connelton smiled indulgently from the doorway.

"Then perhaps we were right not to wake you to say goodbye," she observed kindly. "Kenneth declared you had already said everything that was necessary."

"Kenneth said—?" In astonishment which slowly began to change to dismay Elinor regarded her employer. "But—why should Kenneth—say goodbye?"

"He had to go back to England this evening. Quite a sudden crisis at the office, I understand. But he said you knew about it." Lady Connelton looked a little puzzled. "He left about an hour ago to go to the airport."

CHAPTER TWELVE

"It's not possible!" Elinor actually felt herself go pale. "Lady Connelton, you don't really mean that Kenneth has gone? Back to London?"

"Why, yes. More than an hour ago, as I said. But he declared you knew about it."

"I didn't! I completely misunderstood him. Oh, I wish

I could remember exactly what I did say." Elinor pushed back her hair distractedly. "I thought he was being tiresome and—and gloomy about Rudi and Ilsa coming. I told him that he couldn't expect me to be sorry about it. Oh, what must he have thought? I must speak to him somehow—explain."

Lady Connelton glanced at her watch and shook her head slightly.

"I'm afraid you wouldn't get him now, dear, even if you telephoned to the airport."

"But he'll think I was glad to get rid of him because ... because—" Elinor broke off, and then, snatching at least at a straw of comfort, she asked, "Did he know that the von Eibergs had come? Perhaps at any rate he didn't know about that further aggravation of the position?"

"I don't know." Lady Connelton wrinkled her forehead. "We didn't have time to talk about anything much except his departure. And of course my husband talked to him a good deal about business affairs."

"But no one mentioned Rudi and Ilsa?" Elinor pressed.

"I don't think— Oh, yes, I remember now. Just as he was going we met them in the hotel entrance. He stopped only for a word or two with them as he was already late."

"But he realized that they had come much earlier in the day?"

"I suppose so."

"That was all that was needed!" Elinor declared despairingly.

Lady Connelton glanced at her with kindly curiosity.

"Is it so very important, my dear?"

"Oh, of course it is, Lady Connelton! He will be so hurt and angry. And quite rightly so. He will think I was telling him that I didn't mind about his going back to London because now I had Rudi to take me around. I wouldn't have given him that impression for the world."

Lady Connelton rubbed the bridge of her nose in that reflective, characteristic gesture.

"Then you had better write and tell him so."

"Write?"

"Of course. Wrong impressions can always be removed if one likes to take the trouble."

"It's not—a question—of trouble," Elinor said doubtfully.

"Of what then?"

Elinor considered that. She supposed, confusedly, that her pride had something to do with it. It was difficult to write post haste after Kenneth without giving him the impression that his opinion of her was worth a great deal. If that were not so. . . .

But it was, of course! She might lose patience with him over his attitude to Rudi and Ilsa, she might argue with him sharply about minor matters, but to be misunderstood by him over anything so basic as this shook her whole world in a way that almost frightened her.

Lady Connelton was silent. She knew exactly when not to hurry one.

"I don't want to seem over—over anxious," Elinor explained uncertainly. "I should hate him to think that I was attaching too much importance to . . . to—"

"The fact that he was hurt?" suggested Lady Connelton.

"Oh, no! I couldn't attach too much importance to that. I meant—the whole incident, I suppose. It might embarrass him if I—"

"Ken is very difficult to embarrass," stated Kenneth's aunt positively.

"Or to hurt?" suggested Elinor.

"No. That's different. If you want my opinion—which you probably don't, because someone else's opinion about one's most intimate feelings is always tiresome—I think he was probably feeling very sore and wretched when he went away. I didn't know at the time why he should do so, but I thought he was extraordinarily depressed and wordless."

"Oh, Lady Connelton!" Elinor's kind heart—no proof against this—was wrung by the thought of an unhappy, bruised Kenneth going off alone into the night. "I will write to him and try to explain. I don't mind if he does think me rather . . . rather—"

"He won't, dear," Lady Connelton said, not putting her to the embarrassment of finding the right word. "No explanation based on a kindly desire to undo a hurt has ever come amiss. Now we had better go down to dinner, because, really, one must eat, even if one's private affairs have got into something of a tangle."

"Would you—would you mind very much if I wrote the letter first and joined you later?" Elinor asked pleadingly.

"Not at all," said Lady Connelton, nobly refraining from pointing out that this would in no way hasten the departure of the letter since the last post had already gone. "I had better leave you his private address."

Whereupon she extracted from her handsome bag a pencil and a scrap of paper and, with a comfortingly matter-of-fact air, wrote down an address. This she put on the dressing-table and, with a friendly nod to Elinor went out of the room.

With fingers that trembled slightly because of a remorseful emotion, Elinor took out her writing case, and, without even waiting to think about restrained and dignified wording, she wrote:

Dear Ken,
    I can't tell you how unhappy I am to find that I gave you a completely wrong impression a few hours ago. I had no *idea* that you were going back to London when you came in and spoke to me. I thought you were just being rather cross and tiresome—oh, I'm sorry! but you are sometimes, you know—about Rudi and Ilsa turning up again.
    I must have seemed perfectly horrid to you, and I can't imagine what you must have thought when I said you couldn't expect me to be sorry about what had happened. I *am* sorry, Ken! I'm dreadfully sorry about your going away so quickly and suddenly, so that I didn't even have time to thank you for the lovely times we had here together. Rome isn't the same place at all without you.

She paused and considered that, wondering if she had gone a little too far. But it was true—Rome was *not* the same place without him. And, in her desire to abase herself and remove all misunderstanding, she saw no reason why Kenneth should not have full credit for all the pleasure he had given her.

I do hope I didn't hurt and anger you too much by my seeming ingratitude. It's so difficult to apologize by letter, but it is the best I can do. I just could not let you go on for days and days supposing I didn't care at all about your sudden departure. I shall miss you very much indeed—

Suddenly the paper and her own writing became all blurred, because the complete realization of *how* much she would miss him came home to her all at once as she wrote down those words, and she felt tears rush into her eyes.

He was gone. Kenneth was really gone. And, however nicely she might write to him and explain and perhaps quite successfully put things right between them, the lovely, carefree, intimate days were over. When she saw him again she would be one of the girls in the office and he would be the nephew of the Managing Director, and himself one of the heads of the firm.

That was how she had always known it would have to be, of course. She had never expected to prolong their happy times indefinitely. But it had all been snatched from her so suddenly that she had to wipe away a tear or two at the thought.

She finished her letter, and carefully addressed it as Lady Connelton had indicated. Then she went downstairs and joined her kind employers, and because she knew that it was part of her duty to be pleasant and cheerful, she did her best not to let either of them see that her heart was heavy and anxious.

Presently Rudi came in and joined them, with the news that Ilsa had gone out to see friends of theirs. He was in his most charming and amusing mood and, in spite of herself, Elinor felt her spirits rising, while it was obvious that both the Conneltons found him as entertaining and welcoming as ever.

In that quick, sensitive way which was characteristic of him he evidently realized that Elinor was in some way depressed. At any rate, he was specially kind and attentive to her, and, when the Conneltons said good night and prepared to go upstairs, which they did rather early, he took Elinor lightly by the arm and said, "Come and talk to me for a little while. We haven't had any time together."

She was not completely in the mood for this, to tell the truth. But the alternative—going upstairs to her own room and brooding over her misunderstanding with Kenneth—was not to be borne. So she let herself be persuaded, and came with him into the little flagged garden, where a few lights shone on the dark glossy leaves of the trees and shrubs, and here and there a seat or two could be found in a convenient patch of warm shadow.

He was so kind and considerate with her that she nearly started to tell him about the misunderstanding with Kenneth. But she remembered in time that this would be altogether too stern a test of his sympathetic interest. So she smiled at him in the rather dim light to show her appreciation of his attitude, and she let him do the talking.

Presently they sat down on one of the benches, from which they could see the nymph in the fountain, trickling water out of the shell in her hand. And after a short pause, in which there was nothing but the sound of the running water, Rudi said quietly, "Things have changed very much for me, Elinor, since last I saw you in Vienna."

"Have they, Rudi? For the better, you mean?"

He nodded.

"I'm so glad. It will make up for—so many things you have lost, won't it?"

"Yes." He was silent again for a moment. Then he said, "Leni left everything she had to be divided between Ilsa and me. There was a great deal more than any of us had expected."

"I'm very happy for you." Elinor spoke from her heart, and, putting out her hand, she touched Rudi's lightly and sympathetically. Then, suddenly remembering something, she asked, "But what about Anton?"

"What about him?" Rudi inquired idly.

"He was actually a blood relation. He rather expected to be remembered too, didn't he?"

"Oh, yes. But his luck was out," Rudi explained carelessly. "Although, I suppose, he was Leni's favorite in a way, he did something which annoyed her very much a few months ago. She changed her will."

"And left him nothing?" Elinor was a good deal shocked.

"Left him nothing," Rudi agreed.

"But—Rudi—it wasn't about anything vital, was it? I mean, if she had lived, she would probably have forgiven him and changed round again, wouldn't she? She seemed genuinely fond of him."

"Oh, yes, I expect so," Rudi agreed. "That's just the luck of the thing. Like staking on the wrong card."

"It's nothing of the sort!" Elinor sat up and spoke with energy. "I thought you—you liked Anton."

"Why of course we do."

"Then aren't you going to put things right?"

"In what way, Elinor?"

"By redividing the money, of course. Except for a temporary annoyance, which might come to any old lady, Leni loved him equally with you and Ilsa. Surely that has something to do with it?"

"I don't quite follow. She left the money to us, Elinor."

"I know she did! But if she'd had time to think a little longer, she wouldn't have cut out Anton. You as good as admitted the fact yourself. Do you mean to say you are satisfied for him to have *nothing*?"

"She left him nothing."

"But there is even more than you expected. You could well afford to be just—to be generous—over this."

"Darling, there is never enough to be as quixotic as that." Rudi laughed. "It's been a gamble all along. We won, Ilsa and I. That's all. I didn't know you were so much attached to Anton and his fortunes."

"I'm not! I mean, there is nothing personal about it. He's a nice fellow, I believe, but I hardly know him more than that. Only—that isn't the point, Rudi. You *know* it isn't."

"The point, my darling," said Rudi quietly, in a tone that suddenly silenced her, "is that I now find myself a comparatively wealthy man—with the power to do all the

172

things I have always wanted to do, without having to
study every minor, frustrating consideration."

"Yes, I know, that's wonderful," Elinor agreed
uncertainly. "You mustn't think I don't rejoice for you,
or that I . . . that I presume to tell you what you should do
with your inheritance. But—"

"Suppose I offered you the right to tell me what to do
with some of it, anyway?" Rudi said quietly.

"I don't understand."

"Don't you, *Liebling*? Would it be such a surprise to
you if I told you that I have it in mind to offer you myself
and my fortune, to do with what you will?"

His arm was round her now, and Elinor felt, as she had
once or twice before, the full force of his personal
fascination.

"Rudi, are you . . . asking me to . . . marry you?" she
said slowly. And, as she did so, a voice out of the recent
past—a soft, laughing, indescribably beguiling voice—
said, "All the charm in the world, but no real stability.
They don't make good husbands, child. I know—I
married one."

Against the background of that voice she heard Rudi
say, "Of course I am asking you to marry me! Didn't you
know that was what I was crazy to do all along? Only,
until Leni died and left me half her money, it was just a
lovely, impossible indulgence which I could not allow
myself."

Elinor was silent, groping in her mind and consciousness for the right reply.

His attraction was indescribably strong upon her. She
knew she had only to turn her head and his lips would be
on hers. Already she savored the moment with a delicious
thrill of anticipation. But, even while the feel of his
nearness excited and fascinated her, his words blew a
strange, chill breath upon her eager enthusiasm.

A lovely, impossible indulgence! That was how she had
seemed to him, if it meant working or making sacrifices
for her.

"You mean," she said gently, "that you love me very
much, so long as marrying me entails no discomfort for
you?"

"Elinor! I don't understand you. What possible discomfort could marrying you mean for me?"

"None—now. It would have been quite different if you had had to work for me."

He frowned.

"You're being rather hard on me, my darling. I never pretended to be other than I am. I'm not the stuff of which struggling, self-sacrificing husbands are made. And, frankly, I'd never ask any woman I loved to share such an existence. But the position doesn't arise now. I can offer you myself—and a reasonably comfortable life. I do that, with all my heart. Must you hold it against me that I'm not offering you a noble and struggling existence?"

"No, Rudi. I don't hold it against you. I like you very, very much as you are," Elinor said slowly. "I just don't love you—or else I shouldn't be so regretfully aware of the weaknesses in you."

He drew away from her sharply.

"You do love me! Only you've set some sort of ridiculously idealized standard of behavior that you think I should live up to. You mustn't expect people to be heroes, *Liebling*. Take them as they are and love them with their faults as well as their virtues."

"I do," Elinor said, almost gently. "But I couldn't really love and marry a man I didn't respect."

Most men would have been angry at that point, but Rudi took the implied criticsm quietly.

"You don't respect me, then? Because I can keep you in reasonable comfort without working for you?"

"No." She smiled a little. "I'm not so unreasonable as that. There are certain things which test us—and our friends, Rudi—and however much we like them and excuse them and try not to judge them, we assess our friends by the way they react to those tests."

"And, to you, the test was that I wouldn't ask you to share my life until I knew we could do it in comfort together?"

"I was thinking of Anton, too," she said almost absently.

"Anton? What has he to do with this?"

"Only that it was more to you to have *all* the money, knowing that Anton had been done out of his share by a fluke, than to have part of the money and the reassuring knowledge that Leni's real wishes had been carried out."

"The will was explicit enough," Rudi exclaimed impatiently.

She did turn her head then and look at him, but her expression did not encourage him to kiss her.

"We are not talking the same language, Rudi," she said, in that curiously gentle tone. "You have been a good and charming friend to me, and I know that I owe a great deal to you for the—development of the last few weeks. I'll always be grateful to have known you, and you've given me the most wonderfully happy hours—you and Ilsa. But I am not the wife for you, my dear, and you are not the husband for me. We think and feel too differently ever to *be one*. That's all there is to it."

He stared at her in wordless astonishment, longing evidently to find words in which to refute her arguments. But, even as she spoke and he remained silent, the balance between them seemed subtly and curiously to shift. She was no longer the young, unknown girl, feeling her inexperienced way under the careless, kindly guidance of the man of the world. She spoke from some inner wisdom beyond his grasp—and it was he who seemed suddenly young and unsure.

"I'm sorry." He got up, accepting defeat as gracefully as he had accepted all the other unwelcome things in his life. "There's nothing else to say, is there?"

"Nothing. Except that I shall always like you and remember you." And, putting her hands on his arms, she reached up and kissed him almost tenderly.

"Darling—" his arms went round her—"are you quite sure of your decision?"

"Quite sure."

"It's the other fellow, isn't it?—Kenneth."

She thought of Kenneth, speeding through the night, carrying with him the anger and hurt which she had inflicted upon him, and she winced as though she herself were hurt.

"Perhaps. It isn't for me to say."

Rudi smiled down at her. "He'll never love you with quite the romantic understanding that I should, you know. It isn't in him to do so," he said with a touch of outrageous self-appraisal.

"If he should love me with the integrity that is in him, I shouldn't ask more," Elinor retorted. Then she regretted the frankness of her confession, and putting her hand against Rudi's lips, she said, "Please don't say any more, I have said too much already."

Even then, Rudi would have held her and pleaded his cause again, but she gently freed herself from his grasp.

"Good night, Rudi."

"Good night." He caught her hand for a moment. "There is always tomorrow, and I shall not cease to hope."

She did not answer that. It was not for her to start a fresh argument by the assertion that for them there was no tomorrow. Instead, she smiled at him with all the genuine friendliness she felt, and then left him and went to her room.

As soon as she was there and safely alone, she went over to the open window and stood looking out over the shadows and lights of the city. A subdued hum drifted up to her, that indefinable mixture of sounds which belongs to every city and which holds a different note for each.

"I feel *old*," Elinor said aloud. "At least, I no longer feel young and inexperienced. It isn't only that I've had my first proposal and refused it. It's that, however stumbling my words and explanations might be, I arrived at my own scale of values and measured it against that of someone else. I wish," she thought, with a sigh, "that I'd been half as sensible and well-balanced in my dealings with Kenneth."

And then she fell to thinking what Rudi had said about her being in love with Kenneth, and for the first time she allowed herself to reflect how much Kenneth had come to mean to her in the last—days—weeks?—which was it?

Hard to say exactly when it was that each thought and action had taken on a special significance if associated with him. He had just been there and so she had taken him a little for granted, she supposed now. But how completely at one they had been during these happy days in Rome. How inevitably they liked the same things, thrilled to the same discoveries.

No wonder he had looked as though she had struck him when he thought she was telling him that it was nothing to her if he went or stayed.

"If only I could take that back," she thought restlessly. "Take it back much, much more quickly and completely than by letter."

Even though she had written at once, it must be so long until he knew that a mistake had been made, and that she was not the callous, uncaring girl she must have appeared to be.

Not that she wanted him to know *how* much she cared. Just . . . that she cared. Just to put that right, and then to go on from there. Perhaps with a much more formal and remote relationship, such as there was bound to be in the office, but at least with kindness and understanding between them.

She stepped out on to her little wrought-iron balcony and leaned her arms on the rail. It was quiet in the street below, and quieter still in the grounds of the big villa opposite, so that the sound of a taxi turning the corner and drawing up before the hotel sounded unnaturally loud.

Idly Elinor leaned over further and watched while a man stepped out of the taxi and stood there for a moment paying the driver. Then he turned, as someone came from the hotel to collect the luggage, and in a moment was gone from her range of vision.

But even the glimpse had been enough. Or surely, surely she was right in thinking it was enough! By every rule of cause and effect, Kenneth should be in the airplane, halfway between Rome and London by now. And yet—she *could* not have been mistaken—surely it was he who had stepped from the taxi and come into the hotel below.

Turning back into the room, Elinor ran to the door and wrenched it open. She left her handbag on the bed, her key in the lock, thereby violating every rule Lady Connelton had carefully instilled into her about caution when travelling, and ran along the corridor to the elevator.

There was no answer to her urgent ringing of the bell, and, unable to wait, she started down the several flights of stairs.

She could not have been wrong, she told herself as she ran. However unreasonable her belief might be, it refused to be shaken. Kenneth had come back, for some inexplicable reason, and she must see him and explain.

The last flight of stairs stretched before her, and beyond them an uninterrupted view of the almost empty entrance hall. Almost empty—but one person at least was there. The only one who mattered. As she literally jumped the last three stairs, Kenneth came toward her.

"Oh, Ken—Ken—" She ran to him with outstretched hands, all thought of reserve or discretion gone in the immensity of her relief. "You came back—you came back! It wasn't true that I didn't mind your going. It was a mistake. I though you meant something else. I hated your going. I—"

"For heaven's sake, my darling!" He stopped dead as he saw her coming. Then he opened his arms and she ran straight into them, aware suddenly that she was crying and that he was kissing her over and over again.

CHAPTER THIRTEEN

"I DON'T understand a thing you're talking about." Kenneth said, kissing the top of her head, as she gave a luxurious sob or two against his shoulder. "But it isn't necessary, I daresay, if you feel like this."

"Where did you *come* from?" Elinor gasped, hugging him tightly. "I thought you were miles away."

"I should be. But there was engine trouble and we had to turn back. I've been cursing all the way from the airfield. But now I'm glad. Here—" suddenly he became aware that a delighted and romantically inclined clerk at the reception desk was watching and enjoying all this immensely—"suppose we go somewhere where we can talk."

Inevitably he led her toward the little paved garden. But so absorbed was Elinor in the joy of the moment that she forgot all about the fact that it was here that Rudi had proposed to her no more than an hour ago. And although they sat down on the very same bench together, she never even noticed the fact until long afterward—when the thought gave her more amusement than embarrassment.

"Now," Kenneth said, taking out his handkerchief and drying her tears with more efficiency than romantic tenderness, "will you tell me what this is all about?"

So she told him—still catching her breath on an occasional after-sob—how she had thought he was referring to the arrival of the von Eibergs, when all the time he was gloomy over the sudden necessity for his own departure for England.

"And when I found that I must have made you think I didn't mind if you went or stayed, I didn't know what to do! I wrote at once, but I knew it would be ages before you got the letter. I couldn't bear to think I'd hurt you so much and couldn't—"

"Did you know how much?" He smiled and ruffled her hair very gently. "Did you know that I thought the girl I loved best in the world had just given me the brush-off?"

"Oh, Ken . . . is that true? That . . . that you think of me like that, I mean?"

"Of course, it's true, my silly little sweet. Didn't you know it?"

"One never knows until it's actually said, Ken." She smiled rather tremulously at him. "One wonders, of course . . . and hopes—"

"Did you hope, darling?"

"I wanted you to love me," Elinor said simply.

"Oh, how sweet you are! You never pretend," Kenneth exclaimed and scooped her up in his arms. "What about that confounded Rudi von Eiberg now?"

"Nothing about him," Elinor said, smiling more certainly this time.

"You mean that he still philanders charmingly but

never comes directly to the point?" Kenneth replied.

"No. I mean that, having become financially secure after the death of Leni Mardenburg, he followed me up with—what I believe are called honorable intentions."

"You—" Kenneth actually paled a little. "You mean that he asked you to marry him?"

"I suppose it's mean to tell another man so, but—" she put up her hand and touched his cheek lovingly—"you deserve a little reassurance, my poor darling. He did, which was very honorable and nice of him, but I refused, because I loved you and only liked him."

He held her close at that, as though he perhaps believed—though quite incorrectly—that he had almost lost her.

"And there are no regrets whatever for his charm and his graceful way of paying court?" Kenneth asked, kissing her anxiously.

"None whatsoever. I enjoyed being petted and flattered," Elinor admitted with a smile. "But I'd rather be kissed by you, and have you dry my tears, even if you did make a very brisk and workmanlike job of it."

They both laughed then, and for quite a long while there seemed nothing more urgent to do than to exchange reminiscences of when they had first begun to love each other. Then a clock struck twelve somewhere and Kenneth said, "Good heavens! Is that the time? I suppose we ought to break this up. We're engaged, aren't we?"

"I had thought so," Elinor admitted demurely.

"When will you marry me?"

She hesitated.

"I suppose it depends when we go home. I don't want to make your uncle and aunt feel I'm impatient, after the wonderful time they have given me. And then—"

"They won't," Kenneth assured her. "As a matter of fact, it was largely because of you that they decided to stay on here, instead of coming back to London almost straight after me. I think my uncle would rather like to be home now. He is feeling perfectly well again and is hankering after his own solution of some office problems. But they both thought it was a shame to rush you off once more, particularly as they thought perhaps they had done just that in Vienna. My aunt nearly drove me mad—in the nicest way possible—by hinting at a romance between you and Rudi. They didn't either of them want, as they thought, to blight that a second time."

"What an *extraordinary* idea!" exclaimed Elinor, for all the world as though she had never entertained romantic thoughts toward Rudi. "If they would really like to go home quite soon, I should love it—in spite of all the wonderful experiences."

And suddenly, at the thought of walking into the shabby house that was home, and seeing all the dear faces again and telling the family all her adventures, Elinor felt that, though she had enjoyed every moment of her wonderful trip, she would trade it all for the welcome back that must be waiting her.

"I'll see what can be arranged," Kenneth promised. Then he went with her to the elevator, and kissed her good night under the approving eye of the attendant. After which she was wafted upwards, with the vague and delicious feeling that she was indeed being taken heavenward.

Not until the next morning did she find how literally Kenneth had meant that he would see what could be arranged. Though she came down early to breakfast, both the Conneltons were earlier still. And, to her mingled delight and embarrassment, not only Lady Connelton but Sir Daniel too kissed her very heartily and told her how happy they were to hear the news.

"And, of course, it alters all the future arrangements, dear," Lady Connelton said. "We really have no one to consult but ourselves, and, for various reasons, we are all beginning to feel the tug home, I think. Kenneth has been phoning the airport to see if he can get a seat on today's flight, but it seems doubtful. And so the simplest thing is for us all to take the midday train. We shall be home tomorrow evening."

"I can't believe it!" Elinor was divided between delight and astonishment. "Do you mean that we can really arrange it—just like that?"

"Not much good running a tourist agency if you can't arrange a little matter like that," Sir Daniel declared in high good humor.

And then Kenneth came in, to say that there was no question of his getting a place on the early plane and that, therefore, they would all be travelling together.

"A much better arrangement, in the circumstances," stated Lady Connelton, and neither of her menfolk had the temerity to point out that Kenneth's presence in the London office was pressingly needed. Romance had definitely taken precedence over business, in Lady Connelton's view at any rate.

In spite of the rush, and in spite of the necessity of saying goodbye to a city which had won her heart, Elinor could not feel anything but wildly happy over the sudden development. She allowed herself the indulgence of a long and expensive telegram home, so that the family would at least be prepared for her sudden arrival and the fact that she had become engaged.

"Will your people mind?" Kenneth asked, with an anxiety that was unlike him.

"Mind? Why should they mind? They'll be delighted," Elinor said.

"But they don't know a thing about me. They've never seen me, and may distrust the idea of anything that has happened so suddenly. For that is how it's bound to seem to them."

"Not entirely." Elinor smiled to herself. "I wrote quite a lot about you from time to time, Ken. And, anyway, they will like you on sight. Anyone would."

"You didn't," he reminded her with enjoyment. "You flew at me and berated me like anything."

"There were special circumstances," Elinor stated firmly, at which Kenneth laughed delightedly, and then kissed her, just to show there was no longer any ground of difference between them.

It was a long journey home. But for Elinor every hour was made bright by the fact that Kenneth loved her. Even now she could hardly believe that she was really engaged to him. Only, as they sped through France—regrettably fast, for she would have liked to see more of it—he told her that he would bring her back here on her honeymoon. And somehow that made it all real.

The Conneltons were exceedingly kind, and left them as much as possible on their own, and showed no surprise if the two of them chose to stand for long hours in the corridor talking to each other.

Even on the boat, they retired tactfully to seats in a sheltered part of the deck, leaving Kenneth and Elinor to saunter up and down, watching for the first faint outline of the English coast.

"There it is!" exclaimed Kenneth at last. And although it was still nothing but a smudge on the horizon, Elinor said, "How lovely it looks! I thought when I left it that I must be the luckiest girl in the world. Now that I'm coming back, I know I am."

He laughed, but he put his arm round her at that.

"There'll be many wonderful journeys in the future, I hope, darling, and many happy homecomings. And all of them together."

They were both silent then, in contented contemplation of the radiant future ahead, and Elinor's heart was so full of the happiness of this home-coming that she thought she would retain a little of the glow of it all her life.

Neither of them noticed that the Conneltons observed them and then exchanged a smile of amused satisfaction.

"Extraordinary how it has all worked out," Sir Daniel remarked. "I left the choice of secretary entirely to Prynne—the most unromantic of creatures. And he must needs pick out the one girl who, in her quiet way, swept Ken off his feet from the first. Chance is a strange thing."

"Very," agreed Lady Connelton. "But here and there it needs just a little assistance." And she rubbed the bridge of her nose, with the satisfied air of one who had not disdained to assist chance occasionally.

I AND MY HEART

I
AND
MY HEART

Joyce Dingwell

To tell the truth, Jane was fed up with submerging her own desires to accommodate her glamorous half sister, April. This time, Jane was to go to Ceylon, where April had mysteriously stopped off on her way back to London. April's latest conquest — the wealthy Portuguese, Rodriguez — needed the assurance that she had a respectable family background. Oh well, Jane thought philosophically, the trip should be interesting.

On the flight out she met Senhor Joao Camoes and tried to divert his kind but forceful attentions. She never suspected that he was Rodriguez's even wealthier uncle and that she and April would end up as rivals for his love!

CHAPTER ONE

IT had been different in the assembly hall when Mr. Lennox had handed Jane the award.

Handsomely engraved, with many curlicues, swirls and touches of gold, it had announced that this year's star pupil in the Ackland School for Advertising was J. Winter.

Mr. Lennox had read out the citation, rerolled the scroll, then handed it, with the envelope, to Jane.

There had been applause.

On top of the world, her mind scurrying in a million directions—and none, Jane had answered to Mr. Lennox's kindly, "What next, my dear?" a fervent, "Overseas, of course!"

"It's only two hundred dollars," Mr. Lennox had reminded her of the contents of the envelope, to which Jane had said, "It's my beginning, now I can do the rest."

Over coffee afterwards, her fellow students milling around her to offer their congratulations, Jane had still known wings. When she had done the Ackland test paper—this year it had been an advertisement for selling engagement rings—she had felt her effort was good. But never, she had thought, *that* good. Award-good. Two hundred dollars good.

As she had sat in the examination room biting her pen she had remembered a newspaper her half-sister had sent from Colombo—the *Sinhalese Observer* was printed in English—and how interested she had been in the matrimonial advertisement, horoscopes to be interchanged, dowries to be stated.

She had begun her advertisement: "I am Aquarius and I offer Fifty Rupees . . . " and from that had proceeded to western troths of diamonds and platinum at much more than fifty rupees.

Mr. Lennox, in the citation, had praised her for adopting such a novel approach, and Jane had thought a little wryly that for the first time in her life April, if unconsciously, had done her a good turn.

However, it had not been the time to be ungenerous, it had been smiling time, top of the world time.

But of course the coffee and praise had finished. Mr. Lennox had gone back to his office. The class had gone home. And among them, Jane. On the top of the bus, naturally on top when she was in these elevated spirits, Jane had started out in triumph. Only the elevation hadn't lasted. Not even for two stops.

Jane had come back to earth.

Most certainly, she realized, she could not go overseas, nor anywhere much. As Mr. Lennox had said the sum of two hundred dollars, one hundred pounds, was insufficient. And she had nothing more. The rest had gone to April.

"Janey," her mother had said . . . how often had Mother drawn a breath and started the bad news, for Jane, like that?

"Yes, Mother?"

"It's April, darling. We must give April her chance. That voice—that lovely voice—"

Once it had been April's health, actually superb, and once it had been a love affair that had never really been on. Had April's voice been as ephemeral, Jane might have rebelled at last, but the fact was that her half-sister April *did* have a voice, how good, Jane, a lover but never an authority on music, did not know, but appealing enough, and perhaps promising enough as well.

"Jane, we must give April her chance."

Jane had known what her mother had meant. There had been a nest egg left for Jane by her mother's second husband and Jane's father, only a small sum, but handy. It would have been very handy, with her two hundred dollars, now.

But it was gone. Gone with April. Gone to England where April was to have her chance. If April had taken her chance less luxuriously, tourist class instead of first, a less fabulous wardrobe, there might still have been something to supplement the award. But there was nothing at all. If her mother's money had not been paid weekly there would have been none of that.

"I can't help it, Jane," Mrs. Winter had defended

plaintively, "not with my paradise bird. Don't think I love my two daughters any differently, darling, but you are my little brown wren."

She had been wrong there in one instance. It had been the loving differently, for Jane was well aware that she was indeed a brown wren—compared to April, anyway, April of the flame-red hair and the turquoise eyes. Jane was acorn, three acorn freckles on the small, rather undecided nose. No coral wash on perfectly moulded cheeks, just fair skin. No full red mouth. Just a wren.

But the not loving any differently, that *had* been wrong. Never had Mother loved Jane as she loved April.

For one reason, April had been Vernon's child, and Vernon, the girls' mother had admitted had been her dear, dear love.

"Just like in books," she had related often, "it was a whirlwind romance, and it lasted only as long. April was just born when Vernie, darling Vernie, died."

"Lots of people were astounded when I married Paul Winter so soon. But I was very young, very lonely, and I thought that Paul—"

Her voice had always trailed away at this juncture, but you gather that she had relied on Paul to keep and cherish her, not just to give her another daughter, then die, too.

For the second husband had done just that, died leaving only a small income to his wife and a nest egg, now gone to April, for Jane.

"He was a good man," Jane's mother had assured her, "but you must understand, little brown wren, that there's only one real love."

Mrs. Winter was given to such romanticisms, something that cool-headed April was not, which made Jane think that April took after her father, Vernon Winthrop, though in looks April's and Jane's mother certainly hoped her elder daughter took after her. Who could question such a fervent hope? Not when one was claiming a paradise bird.

There was only a year between them, between April and Jane. And a wide, wide world.

When they had been young Mrs. Winter had used April's seniority as an excuse for favors—"April first, little wren, she's older than you"—but after they had been nineteen and eighteen, she had dropped the pretence.

"Jane, we must give April her chance."

All this came to Jane now as she sat on the top deck of the bus and realized, as her spirits plummeted, that she shouldn't have climbed the stairs, that the lower level was more in keeping.

Yet perhaps, she thought, she could keep the hundred pounds secret. After all, it wasn't being selfish, she could buy Mother something except that Mother wanted nothing except something for April. But I'll still keep it quiet, determined Jane. Mother takes no interest in any of my friends, she need never know from them.

She opened the paper she had bought, wondering wistfully, for she always had longed to see England, how it would be to sit in the top deck of a bus in London and open a paper, which, if she could only augment what she had in her envelope by careful budgeting, by extra work, she might be able to do even yet. The thought brought back some of the elevation.

Then she saw it. Only on a slack news night would the papers have bothered to feature it.

Miss Jane Winter . . . "I am Aquarius" . . . offers Fifty Rupees and wins Two Hundred Dollars.

"Oh, no!" said Jane.

She slipped the paper down behind the seat and stared out at the slowly darkling streets. As she got off the bus she thought hopefully that she still might escape . . . escape, how silly she was being, wasn't she twenty-one now, an adult with a mind of her own? Her mother's intimate friends were like her mother, card devotees, practically non-readers, they probably would never see the item, pass it on.

It's deceitful, she thought, but I can't . . . I won't . . . keep on helping April. She turned in at the block of flats.

Usually Mother was playing bridge upstairs, or, if there was no fourth available, sitting under the lamp trying her hand at solitaire. But tonight Mrs. Winter opened the door. There was sherry on the table and two excited pink spots on her mother's cheeks. If Jane had looked closer she would have seen there was an aerogram in her mother's hand. But Jane's eyes were roving around for a newspaper.

"Darling little wren," said Mrs. Winter at once, "I just happened to turn on the radio, and there you were! Jane—my Jane! The Ackland Award! Two hundred dollars! One hundred pounds!"

"And a scroll," Jane said dully; she felt dull. But she held out the citation.

"Of course, pet." Mrs. Winter did not even glance at it. "Oh, I'm so proud!"

She was pouring the sherry now . . . fussing, praising, telling Jane she always knew she would make good, dear Paul had been similarly talented, words had come easily, too, to him, and only that he had died so soon. . . .

It went on and on, the story Jane knew so well through repetition. It left her father Paul to concentrate on her mother. How it would have been hard enough to bring up *one* fatherless child, but when it came to two. . . .

"And the first such a child as April. I mean, my wren, just one look at her and you know she must have her chance."

Fleetingly Jane thought of Jeff . . . Jane was to have married Jeff, only suddenly April had been interested, so had been given her chance. She had lost her interest, of course, and returned Jeff to Jane, only Jane had lost interest, too.

"April is something that doesn't happen very often, darling," her mother was babbling, "I know you understand, wren."

"Mother," interrupted Jane, suddenly aware that something was going to be disclosed, "what is this?"

As Mrs. Winter, at a loss for once, could find no immediate words, Jane reminded her, "She has enough money to start her off in London."

"But, darling, she's not in London."

"She will be next week."

"But she won't, Jane. You see, the naughty girl got off at Colombo. Oh, dear, it's very dreadful of her, but"—the pink spots quite red now—"a wonderful chance."

"For what? Is there a musical opening in Ceylon?"

"Not musical, darling, but matrimonial. April—well,

April has an offer," her mother answered dreamily.

Quite stupidly Jane asked again, "For what?"

"I told you, dear—marriage. April doesn't say so in bare words, but—well, read it for yourself."

The letter that Jane had not seen in her mother's hand was put in her own hand. Certainly there were no *bare* words.

This man her half-sister had met had tremendous possibilities . . . he was a Portuguese trader and exporter, as charming and as rich as you could dream. He had fallen in love with her, and April was quite sure she was in love with him. Yes, remembered Jane, as April had been sure at first with Jeff. Only there was an obstacle. The Portuguese were very formal. Not darling Rodriguez, of course, but it appeared he had a strict uncle. . . .

Rodriguez had suggested that if April could bring over one of her family it might make a good impression . . . especially with a representative like Jane, April had written on her own account, quiet, respectable. Jane added, "dull."

"When I read the letter I burst into tears," admitted Mrs. Winter. "How, I thought, can Jane go? I have a little put aside, but very little, Jane has a little, but very little, and both put together is still not enough, and then just by chance I put on the news, and darling, darling wren—"

"I'm not going." Jane broke this in rather heatedly for her; she was usually a calm person. "I'm using the money for further study. I'm—I'm—"

"The news spoke about how you based your winning paper on April's *Sinhalese Observer*. Quite clever of you, Jane, though the real credit must go to April."

On it went. On. On.

It wasn't as though Jane was being asked to *give* the money to April, why, she was to have the pleasure of it herself. Then there was nothing to stop Jane, after she had made her appearance, done her duty, of going on to London. Mrs. Winter spoke hurriedly of this in case Jane interrupted, "On what?"

"Then, who knows," finished Mrs. Winter triumphantly, "you mightn't go on at all. April might find you somebody suitable, in a position like she would have once she married this man that would be easy."

Yes, some under-clerk would suit Jane . . . and April . . . quite well.

"I'm not going," Jane said again.

"Darling, your own sister—"

"No."

"Our paradise bird—"

"No, Mother."

"But, Jane, we must give April her chance."

Give April her chance . . . give April her chance. . . .

Tossing in bed that night, Jane heard nothing else, even the traffic boomed it, the bedside clock ticked it. Give April her chance.

Well, she supposed wearily at last, at least, as Mother pointed out, *I* will be using the money, and it's the first time I'll ever have done that.

Then if I still hold out, don't agree to go, will I use the money at all? She saw it eking away, in cablegrams of regret, in compensating presents, in endless correspondence with something as well as words tucked within the envelopes, and all done with sighs, ahs, dabs to eyes and reproachful looks.

Oh, what was the use?

Colombo, Jane tasted next. It sounded interesting enough. But just interesting, though, simply places faraway, never—never London. Still, it could be a beginning, one could always go on from there, if one raised the extra money, if one didn't fall to the attraction of that under-clerk that April might produce. In the darkness Jane gave a wry smile. But she knew . . . defeatedly . . . there was no other way out, no alternative. It was either Ceylon for her, or nothing. She had been a brown wren for too long not to recognize that.

In which case she would not prolong the misery, neither Mother's, nor hers. She came out to breakfast and forestalled her mother's pathetic, "Wren darling—" with a resigned, "All right, I'll go."

"Jane, you mean it?"

"I've just said so."

"You're so sweet, so reliable. Just like Paul, your dear

father, except that I could never, well—" A sigh. "And I'm sure you will be just what April needs, someone quiet, respectable—"

"Dull."

"Well, we all can't be paradise birds, and you will have the satisfaction of knowing you've given April her chance."

Yes, her chance. Jane put down the cup she had taken up and went to the window. It was a rather poor flat with a very indifferent view, but with money spent regularly on April there had been little choice.

For a moment Jane wondered about her mother. *She* lived in this poor flat, too. She looked tenderly at her . . . and wistfully. With the money she would have to put out on getting to Ceylon the two of them. . . .

But Mrs. Winter's eyes were shining now, she did not care about views, only April's view. View—to what?

"A wonderful chance," she was purring.

The moment of tenderness left Jane. There was something terribly mercenary in planning to settle an affair in such a deliberate way as this.

"You'll be very circumspect, Jane . . . but as though you could be anything else . . . it's just, darling, that sometimes even the most reticent of girls change when they leave their home for a foreign country, and in a case like this—"

"Of giving April her chance, you mean? That kind of case?"

"Yes, darling." Mrs. Winter's eyes were a little puzzled as they rested on Jane.

"Don't worry, Mother." But Jane said it abstractedly.

Give April her chance. The message was ringing in her again. Give April her chance. But who, she wondered bleakly, would give Jane hers?

For a rather frail woman, or so her mother always had implied, suddenly Mrs. Winter changed to a dynamo. Pushing aside her cards that were never removed from the table, she sat down and leafed over the telephone directory.

"It will have to be air, of course, ships take too long."

"They're cheaper." As she answered Jane remembered April's luxury suite on the *Fairhaven* which had been dearer.

Mrs. Winter was frowning slightly. Cheapness, when it was not for April, rather attracted her. However, there was the time factor to be considered: time, according to April's letter, *mattered*. "Make her come, Mummy," April had written. She had sounded in haste. Even if Jane managed a ship berth immediately she still could not hope to be at Ceylon and in Colombo under two weeks, whereas by air. . . .

Already Mrs. Winter had selected an air agency and was dialling the phone.

"I wonder," she said to Jane as she waited for a response, "How long it takes to Colombo. Ah!" Into the receiver now. "I didn't realize you were there. Only that much time, you say? Thank you so much. Now, will you give me departure details. Just twice a week . . .! Friday and Saturday? But that's days and days away." It was Tuesday morning.

"Mother, it would take me that long to—" But even as she began to say it Jane realized that she could have left that morning. She had had all the necessary vaccinations. When April had made her overseas preparations, the injections had upset her so much that in the end, on her mother's suggestion, Jane had accompanied her and been injected, too. With a slight smile Jane now recalled that her own small pox reaction had put April's to shame, but nonetheless she had not regretted the precaution at that time, for—who knew?—she might need it sooner than she thought. And, as it was happening, she was needing it.

Or—the look at her mother's shocked face—was she? For her mother was delving now into fares.

"Three hundred and sixty dollars," she echoed, "a hundred and eighty pounds. You're sure that's the economy rate?"

Jane was squirming with embarrassment even though there was no one to witness her discomfort. When April had left Sydney even the best hadn't been good enough. The phone went down, and suddenly contrite, her mother assured her, "I'm just thinking of you, darling, with your award plus all you can add to it, plus all I can spare, that terrible fare would still leave you very little to spend."

Or to give to April?

Mrs. Winter, despite Jane's insistence that the rate would be the same wherever she applied, was now going through all the agencies in the pink pages. All at once unable to listen to the protests, Jane went out of the flat and down the stairs.

She remembered at the bottom step that she had not told Mr. Everett about the award . . . nor what was to happen to her because of the award. That is, wryly, if Mother and the airline could come to terms. Even if they did not come to terms, and she remained here, Max Everett would still be interested in her success, then if they did, and a passage was booked, he must know at the earliest possible moment because he would have to look for a replacement for the position she had filled.

Mr. Everett "arranged" things, parties, tours, projects, entertainments, lectures—the list was seemingly endless. Jane had spent three nights a week, from six to eleven, helping him with his accounts, all day Saturday. In this way she had been able to attend the Ackland Institute, and, because of the unusual thus better-paid hours, her weekly pay envelopes had been as fat as if she had a daily nine-to-five job.

She found Mr. Everett busy on a pile of tickets. He was more often on tickets than anything else, so Jane, not so intrigued as she might have been had she not written up for him similar forms for faraway places, got straight into her news. Though before she could say much Max Everett got in first.

"Congratulations, Janey. I saw it in the paper. I suppose you're here now to tell me you won't be working for me any more."

"I would be working for you if I wasn't going away. Two hundred dollars isn't a fortune."

"Then," interrupted Mr. Everett, "why are you leaving work? Leaving me? No, don't tell me." His smile was edged. "April. Stranded somewhere. In need of our Jane."

"Yes," Jane said.

"Well, it's been nice knowing you, Janey, and heaven knows where I'll get a girl to toil the hours you did, but if you're going, you're going."

Jane put in, "*If* I'm going," and told him how much the award had been a second time and then the lowest fare to Colombo.

"Colombo? Ceylon?" He looked up with interest from his tickets. "I'm working in that direction right now— a charter flight to Madras." He looked down again and read: "Sydney . . . Darwin . . . Singapore . . . Madras. The usual Air-India route, though this time in a private craft instead of the company Boeing."

"How many in the charter?" Jane's interest was instinctive; she had liked working on flights with Mr. Everett.

"It's a trade conference," he told her, "and the full load was to be fifty souls, but two drew out. I sold one of the seats at once to an outside . . . out of the trade, that is . . . and I reckoned at the rate I was getting from him that a complement of forty-nine travellers would be fair enough." He started to smirk, then stopped suddenly to look, instead, at Jane. "Or do I reckon that?" Now the satisfied smirk had grown into a speculative grin.

Jane grinned cheerfully back, not at all impressed. She knew these charters of Mr. Everett's, they were always run on strictly luxury lines, for which a passenger paid strictly luxury prices. No economy rates here—despite that contemplative expression on Max's face certainly no seat for her.

"You're wrong, Janey." The agent had evidently read her thoughts. "If I was satisfied with forty-nine for my party, it only stands to reason I'll be more satisfied still with forty-nine and a half. In other words you can have the seat for half fare."

"Which is—?" asked Jane, still unenthusiastic, expecting from Max Everett as much plus a little more than the economy rate of a public craft.

Max said, "A hundred and fifty. Will that do?"

"A hundred and fifty?"

"Yes."

"Pounds of course."

"Dollars."

"S-seventy-five pounds!" gasped Jane.

"You're right, Jane."

"But in the charters you arrange," half-laughed, half-cried Jane, "that's only a third fare."

"In this instance it's actually a quarter, it's a real slap-up trip. But I reckon"—with a pat on Jane's shoulder—"you're worth it." He became busy again. "How about health requirements? You'll only need smallpox from Australia, eight days after primary, up and to three years after secondary."

"I've had that, and cholera and typhoid as well, with April."

"Good girl! How long do you intend stopping? If it's under a month you won't need a visa." At Jane's uncertain look, he added, "You can always apply over there if you overstay your time, so that's no concern."

Jane was glancing through his charter list to give herself time to collect her senses. She was feeling that everything was going much too fast for her. "All of these tickets are for Madras," she said, glad to find a hitch to halt the bewildering speed. "If I went would I have to go to Madras first and then find my own way back to Colombo?"

"For a special girl I think we can arrange a special call."

"When the special girl is only paying a special quarter fare?" asked Jane, still unsure.

"Why not? The other outsider is making up for you . . . monetarily, I mean; I felt he could afford it." Max Everett shrugged. "After all, I got him included in a hurry so he must expect to pay for speed. Not that Senhor Camoes would ever argue over money . . . he's too much the bland gentleman for that."

"Senor? He's Spanish?" asked Jane.

"It's Sen-hor, Jane, and he's Portuguese."

"That's a coincidence. I'm to fly to Colombo because April—" But Max Everett was not listening, he was busy including Jane on his list.

"You're not wasting any time," Jane said nervously.

"And you can't either. The charter leaves at noon."

"What?" Jane was aghast.

"Noon. Still want that seat?"

"Of course . . . though twelve o'clock is only a few hours away."

"Three. While I'm making out your certificates, your entry endorsements, currency declarations, the rest, you better run home and pack your bags. No need to tell you about that." He smiled, for it had been Jane's special job at the Agency to advise on what and what not to take.

As Jane still stood, he snapped his fingers under her nose. "Everett for speed. Remember our slogan? Get going, girl, because I have a lot to do for our quarter fare."

"Max . . . Max, you're sure you're not losing over me?"

"All I'm losing is losing you. Don't be an idiot, Jane, it's the least I could do for the best secretary I've ever had. The charter leaves at one p.m., really, but you'll be required at Mascot an hour before that. Now scram, Janey, else I'll offer your fourth to Senhor Camoes, and probably he'd snap it up."

"Is he that large to need it?" she laughed.

"Yes, he is large, as a matter of fact, but I was speaking more in the manner of exclusiveness, if this Portuguese gentleman could have chartered the entire craft I know he would have done so."

"You mean he doesn't like people?"

"My dear Jane, I issue tickets, arrange flights, not delve into people's characters. Now, home with you, and back here at eleven. No, to make sure I'll come round to the flat, I'll drive you to Mascot myself."

"You are a dear!" she smiled.

Max grinned again. "Don't let my dearness go to your head," he reminded in a mock-business manner as Jane hurried out of the office. "You still have to part with that quarter fare."

A quarter fare! Less than a child's fare! A luxury flight at that. It was, as the girls at Ackland would have said, "a steal."

As she scurried back to the flat Jane wondered briefly

if she would keep some of the money facts of the trip to herself . . . she could tell her Mother that Max had offered her a reduced fare . . . she could say it was half, not a quarter, the usual rate . . . she could say. . . .

But no, it was no use. The custom of sharing was so inherent in her that the moment she walked in she announced, "It's all right, I can go." Then, to dispel the dejected . . . and defeated, by the closed-up pink pages . . . look on her mother's face: "Seventy-five pounds."

"Seventy—Oh, darling. Oh, darling, darling wren!"

Darling *April*, deciphered Jane.

Together they packed, though Jane would have been quicker and more accurate, without her mother. Kindness, however prevented her from refusing the unsuitable cape that her mother pushed on her, embarrassment stopped her from pointing out that her travelling clothes were totally unsuitable for a luxury charter, that she should race into town and splurge some of the savings she had won on a sophisticated suit. She looked ruefully on her office-y navy linen with the almost schoolgirl white collar.

As though she read her thoughts her mother said anxiously, "No one looks when you're travelling, darling, and once you get to Colombo, then April can advise you. I've no doubt that there's lots of her things that she would be glad—I mean, you're both the same size."

She really meant that April would be willing to pass over her present wardrobe and use Jane's money on a second issue, but she did not say it, of course, and Jane did not voice it. Of course.

A cup of tea . . . a last look round the flat that after all, was home, then Max Everett tooting impatiently at the front door, Jane reiterating to her mother that she needn't come to bid her farewell, her mother reiterating that she must see her brown wren away though really meaning that she must repeat right up to the last moment how Jane must be very circumspect, very *everything* that April desired, the two of them descended to the courtyard, got into the car, and were whisked off to Mascot.

Max talked for all of them all the way in, fortunately so, for Jane felt suddenly apprehensive and unsure of herself, and her mother was undoubtedly not with them but miles across the sea.

After Max had checked Jane's luggage for her, however, gone through all the details, put Jane and her mother in comfortable chairs to await their summons through the loudspeaker, he stopped talking and instead pressed Jane's hand. More than that he pressed, with a fatherly affection, his lips to Jane's cheek. Then he left before Jane could bid him goodbye. Dear Max Everett, she thought a little dewy-eyed. He had been a good boss.

"Gone!" said her mother astringently. "I thought at least he would be taking me home."

"He has a business," Jane reminded her. "Also we have a half hour's wait."

"All the same—" complained Mrs. Winter. She decided not to pursue the grievance but to spend the half hour briefing Jane.

"Darling, you will remember how much this means to April? She never said so in actual words, but I do think this Rodriguez of hers must be quite—well, quite—"

Jane said for her, "Rolling."

"Jane!" A punitive pause. "Not of course that money counts. I mean take Vernon, darling. Take—well, take Paul."

"Did you know my father had no money when you married him?" asked Jane abruptly, and was shocked at the look in her mother's face. Or could she be shocked? she asked herself. A marriage so soon, so desperately soon, after real love.

"Jane!" her mother said again.

It was hard going after that. Mrs. Winter tried rather deflatedly to repeat April's cause, and at last Jane put the two of them out of their misery by pretending to hear her flight called.

Her mother knew she hadn't, but rose at once.

"This is it, then, darling. Give my paradise bird all of my—I mean give April my love. And—and Jane—"

"Yes, Mother, I'll do all I possibly can." At least, thought Jane, I can afford Mother that.

"Thank you, darling. Goodbye little wren." A flutter

of a handkerchief at the terminal door and Mrs. Winter was gone.

Jane sat, aware of a great relief. It's terrible, she thought, but it's like a load off one's shoulders being rid of Mother. Fleetingly she wondered how she would feel if she were April and being farewelled by a parent who loved her with all her being, not just—not just—

But the thought was unbearable, and she turned away from it. Turned, literally, into the darkest eyes she had ever seen.

They were set in a smooth olive face, a face crowned with thick, shining, very black hair. That the owner, a man, was extremely tall was evident in the length of the legs stretched from Jane's neighboring chair almost twice as far as her own legs, had she stretched, could have reached. For the rest, he was impeccably, if rather soberly and utterly formally, dressed. And he had a small, clipped moustache.

Undoubtedly this was all Jane might have gleaned of him as her glance flicked his had he not said at once, in a voice she could not quite put a finger to, so correct, so perfect it was: "That was exceedingly neat. May I congratulate you? If the occasion arises I too must hear a summons in the air."

She looked at him furiously at first, but quickly hiding the anger in an innocent raise of her eyebrows. She *had* hurried her mother off, though her mother had been in a hurry to go but it was none of this man's business and the best way to tell him so was to appear uncomprehending.

She was unsuccessful. Even though she did not know him she had the feeling that it would be very difficult to evade an issue with him.

"Come," he said a little impatiently, "I am not reproaching you, I am praising your skill."

"What do you mean?" she queried distantly.

"Undoubtedly the position was becoming tedious. How much more honest your handling of the situation than the usual polite humbug that more often than not takes over the controls. It was clever of you." He made an acknowledgment.

But Jane was annoyed. She was not pleased with

herself over her dismissal of her mother, even though her mother had rushed the opportunity to go. She was less pleased that this man had edged himself into the act.

"I fail to see," she said coldly, "what any of it has to do with you."

"You are right, of course, but I was placed in this seat by my representatives, and the Australian voice, I find, is very clear."

Australian voice. Then he was not Australian himself. Though, of course, that had been obvious from the first. That perfect English, no short cuts, no drawl or slur.

Jane said tersely of her own Australian voice: "Clear—or loud?"

"I did not say loud," he reproved.

There was a silence between them. Jane wondered if she could get up and find another seat, but then her two bags were at her feet, and if she did he would probably, being the gentleman he undoubtedly was, rise to help her, and she would feel more embarrassed again.

At that moment fortunately a noisy band of travellers arrived, by the affluent appearance of them probably Max Everett's trade bunch, and even if she had wanted to put the man in his place Jane doubted if she could have done so. The chatter drowned all but the official announcements; this time the Australian voice *was* loud.

Then:

"Flight 507, special charter to India," was being intoned over the public address, "please go to Gate Number Four," and Jane rose as she had wanted to, first reaching for her bags.

But, as she had expected, the man beside her rose, too, took the bags for her.

"It's all right," he answered as she protested, "my own already have been attended to. I have empty hands."

"But—but you can only take them as far as the barrier, and you'll lose this seat." It was a busy departure hour, the terminal was packed.

"I do not need the seat," he shrugged. "I am leaving, too."

"Then"—with a show of cordiality that she found rather hard but after all she would not see him any more—"you must be leaving around the same time as I am."

"That could be."

They had reached the gate by now. An officer was examining Jane's ticket . . . for a hysterical moment Jane wondered if it stated quarter-fare . . . then the checkclerk was saying politely, "thank you, madam. And" . . . to the man bearing Jane's two bags . . . "thank you, sir." They both passed through.

There was something wrong here. This was a chartered flight. They were all conference attendants, specialists in trade, only one outsider, except herself. Only one outsider, except—except—

But no, it couldn't be. And yet—and yet *Senhor* Camoes, Max had said.

She looked quickly and covertly at the man now striding beside her, noted the unfamiliar look. Portuguese? Quite feasibly. But, thank goodness, going to Madras in India, not Colombo in Ceylon. She was the only traveller for Colombo, so at least she had not put her foot into it, into April's ambitions, right from the start.

For, although he had commended her, spoken of her honesty and lack of humbug, Jane had had a feeling that the praise really had been damning, that for all his praise, as he had expressed it, that actually he had strongly disapproved.

However, Madras was India, and Colombo was Ceylon, and never the twain and all that. With luck this Rodriguez of April's, or at least Rodriguez's family, need never know that their new daughter's sister had not started off as far as they nationally were concerned in a suitable . . . Portuguese . . . manner.

The thing to do now was to avoid the man, sit as far from him as possible. Conversation, however hard one tried to be circumspect . . . that favorite word of Mother's! . . . often got into the wrong channels.

"May I sit—" began Jane to the bowing, sari-clad hostess who greeted her at the door.

"But yes, it has been arranged," came the smiling answer before Jane could finish her request. "The others, they are all of one mind." The hostess gave a graceful gesture. "They are all trade. After all, it is charter Flight. But you two certainly can be spared details in which, naturally, you are not interested." She was leading Jane down the passage.

Before Jane could protest, explain, before she could say a word, she was comfortably seated—Senhor Camoes seated by her side.

CHAPTER TWO

ALL the pre-departure things were being performed . . . the placing of the rest of the passengers, the adjustments of headrests, the fixing of seats and belts, the fastening of doors. None of it took really long, and yet the silence between Jane and the man now beside her seemed to grow so abysmal that Jane wondered if the conversation could ever climb out of the depths.

But it did—by Senhor Camoes saying abruptly, "Admitting that my presence is a surprise, and not a pleasant one, it is still surely insufficient reason for dumb dismay, senhorita." He paused. "I assume I am right in that?"

"In the dumb dismay?" she managed to ask.

"The dumb dismay has been established. No, I refer to senhorita. You are senhorita?"

Stiffly Jane said, "I have no knowledge of Portuguese, but if you ask am I miss, then I am."

His lifted brows indicated that he would like her to complete the self-presentation, but Jane left it at that.

He gave a slight shrug, said, "I am Senhor Camoes," then, leaning forward deliberately to consult her neat card, "I am Joao Camoes, *Miss J. Winter.*"

"Jane," complied Jane unwillingly, "Miss Jane Winter."

"So," he said.

The engines were whirring. The plane was slowly taxiing down the long runway. Ordinarily Jane, singularly

206

unused to travel for the average youthful Australian, would have been quivering with excitement, but not this time, not with the probing black eyes of Senhor Camoes on her.

"So sophisticated," he remarked of Jane's studied calm. "The young women of my country would have been in vapors of fears and pleasure."

At that moment the craft left the ground, and in spite of her determination not to show any emotion in front of this man Jane thrilled at her first experience of wings.

"So," he said once more, a little amused smile flicking the corners of his long sensitive mouth. He said nothing else, just that low, discerning, "So."

Jane was annoyed with herself that she felt obliged to offer explanations.

"I've never known anything like this," she half-stammered. "I've never flown before."

"I can believe you have never flown previously, you are very young, senhorita, but not to know such things—" His quick gesture took in the obvious luxury of the expensive arrangements of the interior of the plane. He smiled a kindly reproof.

Jane understood at once. The very fact that she was on such a luxury flight made a travesty of her words. She began searching for a dampening response, one that would put him, and his deductions, in their right place, but he added before she could a formal, yet approving, "It is well you are not experienced in travel, I think, for although I find the young spirit of your young country very commendable, I still believe in our own Portuguese safeguarding of those of the tender years."

"Safeguarding or cloistering, senhor? And am I not a little beyond 'tender years'?"

"If you were, senhorita, then undoubtedly it would be cloistering, but my eyes tell me that the bloom is still very much there." He made a gallant inclination of his dark head.

A little embarrassed, for Australians did not pass such suave compliments and she was unused to them, Jane blurted, "But you're very wrong, of course—if not in the age, then in the appearance. My name, senhor, may I remind you of my name?"

"Senhorita?"

"Jane." She summoned up a wry smile for him.

"What is that, senhorita?" He looked puzzled.

"Plain Jane. Don't you have that in Portugal?"

"Plain Jane! You mean uncomely Jane? But you joke, of course. Or"—a searching glance—"you are being coy?"

"I'm never coy." That was true. With a sister like April it was no use trying tactics.

"Then I do not understand." He shook his head.

"I am *plain*, senhor," Jane said quite crossly. It was all right to admit indifference in looks in bright repartee, but not such fun to have to announce it in unadorned words. "Thank you for the 'bloom and tenderness'," she accepted drily, "but it still doesn't alter an unassailable fact."

"You must please yourself over that so-called fact," he said a little carelessly, "but I still award you bloom and youth."

"Tenderness was also a word."

"But not yours?" His brows raised quizzically. "Yet tell me, senhorita, is there not a tenderness in you right now? Have you not left behind you, as all young women do, part of your heart?"

"I have left none of my heart, I and my heart are travelling together."

"So," he said.

The travellers were unbuckling their seat belts, forming their little groups. Each of them seemed to know someone else and the greetings were hearty.

"We are an island," Senhor Camoes said softly.

The plane now had found its rhythm and its engines beat out the theme; the sari-clad hostesses moved like exotic butterflies in the rich Oriental decor.

The senhor was watching Jane, smiling slightly. "Yes," he said, still in the soft voice, "in such a setting you are not Miss J. Winters but Maharanee."

"And you a Maharajah." She had caught the spirit.

"That calls for a royal toast." He smiled at a soft-eyed attendant. "A red wine for Miss Winter. I think perhaps"—he gave a name and vintage.

"And you, sir?"

"Since we are an island, we must take the same."

"Sir?" The hostess's dark eyes were bewildered.

"We will both have the red wine." There was an errant note of laughter in his voice, and though errantry was the last thing she would have believed in this smooth sophisticated man Jane found herself, too, concealing a smile.

"Our fellow travellers are relaxing," pointed out the senhor presently, for the cigaret smoke now was weaving the groups together in a closer more hospitable circle. "You, too, will have a cigaret, senhorita?"

"Thank you, no." Something in his face as she refused made Jane ask, "You seem disappointed, but surely you don't approve of smoking in the young and tender?"

"You are not one to forget," he remarked mildly of her own remark. "Yes, I am disappointed. Although I approve of the young and tender, as you put it—"

"No, *you* put it."

"Not smoking," he continued, ignoring her interruption, "I must admit I am wishing to smoke myself."

"Then do so by all means, Senhor Camoes."

"You may not be so approving when you see my cheroot."

"My employer smoked cigars, and that's what cheroots are, aren't they, and I loved the aroma."

He had taken a case from his pocket, removed a long cigarillo from it and was clipping the end. "Employer?" he half-frowned. Before she stumbled an explanation he said, "But of course, you are Australian, and in Australia the girls do not sit at home and work fine lace."

"Do they in Portugal?"

"In many places of Portugal."

"Is—is that good?" Jane dared, and was relieved when he actually turned and smiled at her.

"I don't know," he admitted. "Perhaps I thought so once, but now I am not so sure."

"This was your first trip to Australia?" she gathered . . . but gathered wrongly.

"No. But"—a pull on the cheroot whose aroma Jane found quite as pleasurable as Max's cigars had been—"this is the first time I have actually observed."

"And why is that, senhor?"

"I have become interested. Very interested," he returned.

"That sounds," bantered Jane frivolously, "like something to do with a woman."

"It is," he affirmed soberly.

The red wine arrived, but before it was poured the senhor tasted it critically.

"Yes, it will do." He handed Jane the glass, took up a glass himself. "Will our toast be," he asked, "to the young and tender? Or will it be to a whole-hearted traveller? Your words quite definitely this time, senhorita. You said: 'I and my heart.'"

"A whole-hearted traveller will do," agreed Jane with a small shrug. She wasn't going to drink to the young and tender, she considered herself years beyond that.

Yet not so many years. . . . The throb of the engines, the contagious serenity of the composed and gracious hostesses, the lazy buzz of conversation, the blue drift of smoke and the aromatic air of the cheroot closed her eyes for her. She opened them with difficulty when the senhor made some remark, but her reply was hazy, unconnected. The lids closed again. The red wine loosened her fingers, set her gently adrift. The last thing she heard was the senhor intoning something in his soft formal voice.

The first thing she heard again was a teasing yet still formal: "So you are not young, my child. On one small glass of wine you have slept four thousand kilometers."

"Four thou—"

"We have arrived at Darwin, where we have twenty minutes' stopover. Shall we walk around, look at the terminal displays?"

He asked her, but at the same time helped her to her feet. A glance around her showed Jane that the plane already had emptied, so evidently it was expected that she would alight.

She followed the senhor to the door and down the steps to the airfield. It was still bright light, but of course it would be. They had left Sydney early afternoon and by air the Northern Territory capital was only four hours away. All the same Jane felt a surprise. All those kilometers that the senhor had told her . . . though she found she could only think in miles . . . and still the same daylight. She was glad, though, she had not expressed her surprise. It would make her seem, to him, more the child still.

But perhaps he sensed it in her, for, looking down on the still sleep-dazed eyes, he promised with a hint of amusement, "Night will not catch up with us until we are approaching Singapore. But do not be disheartened, senhorita. By Madras I can promise you a big gold moon and many silver stars."

You needn't bother, Jane said to herself, for I won't be seeing them, not in Madras.

It was too hot to leave the airport, and anyway, twenty minutes was too short a time for any sightseeing, so Jane simply looked at the souvenirs that departing travellers could take with them if they wished . . . and if they had sufficient means. She had not.

She stroked the soft ears of a furry koala, but her eyes were on a flashing opal bracelet that Senhor Camoes was examining closely. Was he interested in it because of that interest he had spoken about? "Something," she had interpreted boldly, "to do with a woman?"

Evidently not—or so he presently implied. He explained, Jane still fondling the bear: "I trade in gems."

"Is that a good piece?" she asked.

"Excellent, though perhaps not as valuable as a black piece would be. The black opal is more popular, so, of course, its monetary value soars."

"I prefer this." Jane touched the deceptive pearly stones, deceptive because suddenly fire broke out from the gently gleaming depths, flashes of purple and gold.

"Yes," he said, regarding her and the bracelet, "the white opal would be for you, never the black."

"Milk for a mouse." Jane smiled faintly.

"Senhorita?"

"You would need more than Plain Jane to show off the black variety, senhor."

"You are being coy again."

"I said before, I'm never coy."

"Yes, you said it," he agreed blandly, and, annoyed, Jane put down the koala and went to examine some carved nulla-nullas.

Almost at once he joined her. "Are you so angry with me," he asked, "that you take this revenge?" At her look of surprise he reminded her, "The nulla-nulla was once a killing stick . . . see, a Portuguese knows that Australian lore better than a native daughter . . . and although I deserve reproof I think that the extreme action would be rather unfair. Especially,"—putting the bear she had fondled into her arms—"when I am a Portuguese bearing gifts."

Mollified, Jane accepted the bear; she told herself that at least she could do that. "But you shouldn't," she added banally.

He shrugged . . . a frequent gesture of his, she had noted . . . and the summons came to return to their plane.

They left Darwin . . . and Australia . . . and began winging their way through larkspur-blue skies over larkspur-blue water, a water that turned into a pale turquoise as they went farther and farther north. Once the plane flew lower to let the passengers see the dreamy, spicy islands that rose from the glassy seas, the trade ships that passed in almost endless procession: junks, sampans, some of the sampans with complete little houses built on them.

The sun set several hours before Singapore, set in a blazing triumph of crimson and gold.

"Soon," said the senhor, "you will have your moon and stars."

Jane could not remember expressing a wish for moon and stars, only a secret satisfaction that the moon and stars she would see would be Sinhalese, not Indian. Not that she did not wish to include India in her experiences, but not in the company of this formal man. Even kindly as he undoubtedly was, as in all honesty she must admit he had been to her, he was still almost formidably formal, undoubtedly a force to be reckoned with. She had no wish to do any reckoning. She was going to have her hands full as it was. Full of April.

The triumph of crimson and gold gave way to eggshell

212

pallor, then, in the way of the tropics, night came almost like the drop of a curtain.

"Instant evening," the senhor smiled.

An exciting Indian meal was served, a curry very unlike the curries Jane had had at home, and so spiced and hot that but for the poppadoms that the senhor suggested she eat quite liberally with it perhaps a little too exotic for Jane's taste. But the delicious slices of tropical fruit helped, the cooling papaw and mango, and Jane at last put down the fork and sighed.

"That was lovely."

"You like the new flavors, senhorita?"

"Very much."

"Then that is good. You will enjoy India, too."

Only I'm not going to India. I am getting off at the next exclusive, exclusive for everyone but me, stop. She should have told him this, it would not have hurt her, but for some reason she could not have explained Jane kept silent.

"You will be stopping in Madras only?" he asked.

"No." That was true enough.

"Then that is good, too. To see India you must see more than the English metropolis."

"English metropolis?"

"I exaggerate, of course, but Madras is more English than the other cities of India. Understandable, when you realize that it was founded by the English. Bombay was founded by my own people. Though they both are India, there is still, even after almost three centuries, a national difference."

"Obviously you prefer your own Bombay," deduced Jane.

"But I do not live there, senhorita," he said rather in surprise.

Disconcerted, and in some way vaguely uneasy, Jane asked Senhor Camoes to tell her about Madras.

"To tell would be to spoil," he smiled. "I would not deprive you of the beauty that awaits you in Pantheon Road. It is a beautiful place, and only for the fact that it is not my place—"

His voice obviously halted for Jane's polite inquiry as to where was his place, where that is outside of Portugal, but she could not bring herself to do it.

"Then at least," she suggested brightly, "we can talk of Singapore."

"Singapura, the Lion City, yes, indeed. It is a pity, senhorita, that again you will not have enough time to see it, though I promise you that the airport will be brighter than Darwin's, and that there will be more than a bracelet and a bear to buy."

"But you didn't buy the bracelet," Jane reminded him.

The Indian hostesses were coming around to help with seat belts, so there was no time for Senhor Camoes to reply. The plane put down.

Once outside the airport confines Jane could see what the senhor had meant when he had promised more brightness than at Darwin. It was a lush, tropical night, the sky fairly blazing with stars, and, the way it was in the tropics, shadows were more than dark here, they were indigo, they were deepest violet; light did not just gleam, it sprung out.

"It is a pity you could not have seen the Botanical Gardens, but at least you can look at the Malaysian dancers, hear some of the pedlars calling their wares," the senhor said.

Jane watched a dance, marvelling at the delicate finger-work, refused lychee and sugar-cane juice from a drink pedlar and was glad that the summons to reboard the plane came before she succumbed to a shimmering jade green cheongsam that was being pressed on her at a quite ridiculous price. But ridiculous, or not, it was still money, and she did not know how long she might need her money. Or April might need it. She turned at the summons and went back.

"You have a cool small head," commended the senhor.

No, thought Jane, I have a slender purse. She hugged the bear to her, finding more pleasure in his soft fur than she believed she would have found in the satin moulding of the cheongsam.

The plane taxied off again. Coffee was served, little

sweet cakes. The senhor insisted on more red wine, but this time Jane did not fall asleep after it. She gathered her things together instead.

"We have still some time to Madras," the man beside her said lazily, his own eyes closed.

Jane did not reply. She did not know whether, as she had, he slipped off into sleep, but if he did he was certainly awake when the plane put down, strictly briefly this time, at Colombo.

The air hostesses were round Jane, making sure she had everything, and the senhor, opening his eyes, but not looking sleep-dazed as Jane had, so probably he had only been resting, said, "But this is not Madras."

"Colombo, sir."

"We do not go to Colombo."

"A special stop, sir. Not long enough, I regret, if you wished to shop."

"I have no wish to shop. Good heavens, why would I when— But I did not know the trade conference was calling, too, at Ceylon."

"Not the conference, sir."

"Then—"

"The young lady."

"There is only one young lady."

Jane thought the rather unhappy hostesses had had enough. "Yes," she intervened calmly, "I am the one."

"You—But you are going to Madras."

"I leave the plane at Colombo, Senhor Camoes."

"You never said so."

"I don't remember you asking."

He went to reply, reply quite hotly, must have had second thoughts and closed his lips.

"You are being met, of course." A full minute had gone by and all Jane's bags were accounted for.

"It is not," said Jane, feeling her nerves so taut that if she didn't speak out she would cry out, not caring if the hostesses heard or not, "any business of yours."

"But of course it's my business. It is—" he looked at his watch—"after nine o'clock. You saw for yourself how dark it was in Singapore, and that was barely nightfall. Now it will be pitch black. The tropics always are."

"Presumably," said Jane cuttingly, "the city will be lit."

"It pleases you to be flippant, senhorita, but it does not please me. I repeat . . . and I would like to do more than repeat, I would like to question you closely, find out why you deceived me—"

"I did not deceive you, senhor, I simply kept my own business to myself."

"All right, then." His voice was testy. "But I repeat, and I demand an answer, and I also feel so strongly about it that if you do not satisfy me with that answer I will leave the plane here also: *Are you being met?*"

"I," said Jane meticulously, "am being met."

"Are you sure of that?"

"Quite sure." Though even as she said it Jane knew she was *unsure*. Her mother as likely as not would have forgotten to cable. April, being April, would be late, or wouldn't turn up at all, or—

"Senhorita, I am coming to the terminal with you." The senhor must have read her uncertainty.

"If you do the trade conference will complain that they were not told, either, of any stop at Colombo."

He did not reply to that. He strode down the aisle to the steps that had been wheeled up, had a few brisk and to Jane indecipherable words to one of the pilots who had emerged from the controls, then preceded Jane to the tarmac, across the tarmac to the terminal.

"Your friend?" he asked shortly. "You did not say which sex."

Not a friend, a relation, female, a sister, a half-sister. Jane could not have explained, but a quick searching glance had told her that April had done it again, done what she always did. She had not turned up. Perhaps she would come late. Or perhaps she would have forgotten altogether and Jane would have to make her own way. But one thing was certain . . . and with flaming-red hair like April's beautiful hair it was easy to be certain . . . April was not there.

"Senhorita?" The senhor's cool but barely leashed voice reminded Jane that she had to do something, and do it quickly. Otherwise she would either be returned to the plane and taken on to Madras, or, and the prospect for some reason was worse still, the senhor would leave the plane with her.

"My friend," said Jane flatly, "has arrived. I thank you for your company. You've been most kind. I also"—clutching the koala tighter and finding a small reserve of courage in his touch—"thank you for the bear."

"But your friend, senhorita?"

"You won't have time to meet—" Jane glanced at the only European she could see—"him."

The Portuguese was looking too. He appeared surprised. "You mean—"

"Yes," Jane said.

"In that case I shall not be meeting him." If she had thought this man formal before, all Jane could have described was that then he had been indulging in high jinks. Bowing stiffly, he took Jane's hand and kissed it, but such a thin scornful kiss that it was more a derision than a salute, then, turning on his heel he strode away.

But only for a few steps. He paused, turned again, came back.

"You do not entirely satisfy me, senhorita."

"Do I have to?"

"Yes. I would like to see you greet this friend."

"By all means." Jane's heart was sinking. Nonetheless, clutching the bear as though for courage, she walked across to the tall loose figure leaning indolently by the doorway, then, because the senhor was close on her heels and could hear if she spoke aloud, she rose to her toes and pressed her lips on a cheek she had never seen before, but not to salute him but to whisper, "Please, *please!*"

She was uncomfortably aware of blue eyes too close to her for her peace of mind, tired eyes, slightly bloodshot, and just now impudently amused. But the man came up to scratch.

"Honey, I didn't see you. Forgive!" He kissed Jane back, and made no idle semblance of it. He kissed her again—on the lips.

"Senhorita Winter. Senhor Marsden." It was the Portuguese speaking. He bowed. It was a derisive bow.

Even Jane, unused to being bowed to at all, could not fail to see that.

Then the Senhor Camoes turned and went.

Vaguely Jane heard the whirr of the plane's engines . . . she had come to recognize its sound now . . . and she knew that the special Madras charter had started on its final leg. But what she could not realize was that she was here and not there, no longer in the comfortable, and comforting, lavish surroundings, that, in a few hours, had become a kind of home—a very delightful home.

Not that the terminal lacked the usual amenities, but, being a smaller port than Singapore, and being experienced at a later hour, there was an air of emptiness that rather worried Jane. She felt, as she had not felt previously, on foreign land.

Also there had been the company of Senhor Camoes, formal, it was true, yet just now Jane would have welcomed formality in place of the unashamedly bold blue eyes looking her up and down.

"Senhorita Winter, wasn't it?" The rather slack mouth twisted into a wry smile.

It was then that Jane remembered that the Portuguese had addressed this man, still leaning against the wall in the same indolent fashion as when she first had seen him, by name, too. Joao Camoes had acknowledged in a stiff, expressionless voice, "Senhor Marsden," and rather expressionlessly herself Jane now echoed the name he had intoned.

"Terry Marsden," the man introduced himself.

He was looking at her in question, and seeing he had come to her rescue she supposed that at least she should return the courtesy.

"Jane Winter."

"Countess? Duchess? Surely an Honorable at least?"

"Miss," she told him.

"I didn't mean the matrimonial state." He smiled—he had a rather fascinating smile even if it was faintly crooked. "I meant the rank."

"I'm Australian."

"No, rank . . . oh, I see what you mean, you don't go in

for titles Down Under, but you still could be Her
Ladyship at least."

"I'm not. You look surprised."

He didn't really look it, obviously he was only
pretending it, but she went along with him. "Why are you
surprised?" she asked.

"His Nibs," Terry Marsden explained briefly. "Senhor
Camoes himself."

"Well, what about him?"

"He isn't—isn't just Senhor. He's no less than a Count
who prefers anonymity, but of course, that sort of thing
gets around. My surprise was that he took upon himself a
plain Miss."

"He simply conducted me to the terminal," said Jane
rather crossly. She felt sure this Terry Marsden was
teasing her, and she was not amused. A Count!

"Simple!" The man took her up on that. "To avoid
him you come to me, a perfect stranger, for help.
Simplicity, my foot." He was lighting a cigaret with
nicotine-stained fingers that twitched slightly as he
fumbled with the match.

"I can explain that," she said haughtily, hoping the
brushing-off attitude would discourage him.

But he said, "I'm waiting."

"Really—" she began, but he intervened.

"Yes, really, Miss Winter, you pick me up, you use me,
then you expect me to accept being put down again at
your convenience and not bleat back one word of Why?
When? How come? Well"—exhaling—"where will it be?
In the coffee lounge here or in town in some hotel?" At a
look at Jane's face, "It has to be somewhere, girl, you're
not going scot-free."

It appeared by the April-empty terminal that she was
not going anywhere, but Jane said, "Here, then. I'm
being met."

He did not question that, but he did raise his brows.
"Bit late, isn't he?"

"It's my sister." There was a sudden quiver to Jane's
mouth, she felt all at once very lonely, quite bereft, and
with an unexpected gentleness that was hard to believe in
this brittle, tough man, Terry Marsden said, "Sorry kid,

she'll probably turn up. Meanwhile, we'll take a cup."

He led her to a deserted lounge where he had to wake up an attendant and prod him into producing an indifferent brew.

"There's no craft expected in until early morning," shrugged Terry Marsden of the coffee, and he took out another cigaret.

Considering the less than busyness, Jane wondered what he was doing here. He must have anticipated the question she did not ask, for he drawled, "I'm a journalist. I meet the planes."

He was frowning as he said it, his fingers twitching again, and to tide over a rather awkward moment Jane asked, "Do you represent the *Observer* by any chance?"

"I see you know something of us. By your bewildered look I should have thought you were new to the Pearl's bright shores."

"Pearl's?" she queried.

"But Ceylon is the Pearl, surely you knew that? At least, it used to be, but now the tendency is to drop the last letter and call it the Pear."

"You don't like it?"

"I have no feeling one way or other, it's just a place I happen to be in. But don't talk about me, you'll hear it all whether you're interested or not, talk about you. Why are you here?"

"I told you—I'm visiting my sister."

"The one who hasn't turned up to meet you?"

"Yes."

He frowned slightly. "Can't say I've run into her."

"I didn't think you would. She hasn't been in Colombo all that long."

"Nonetheless I would have known; it's my job. But then she may be married?"

He meant, of course, that April's name might not be Winter. It was not, but Jane didn't bother to tell him so.

"She's not married," she offered, "and what do you mean that you should know because it's your job?"

"Just that. I meet the planes, write up the important people."

"But April isn't—"

"You're going to say that your sister isn't a V.I.P., that she's the same as you. My reply to that is that anyone who is personally conducted into a terminal by the Count Joao Camoes, who has apparently travelled in the same craft, which undoubtedly would be a luxury aircraft, can't be anything else but a V.I.P. All right, young Jane, your turn."

Jane sighed, but complied. It seemed she had to. Not only was the man persistent but the terminal was still April-empty.

"I'll tell you," she said, and did, leaving out, of course, April's real reason for wanting her in Colombo in a hurry, that reason of impressing her family-to-be, or so April planned.

"Well, that's a bare-bones story if I've heard one," he accepted when she had done, and drained his cup. "I think, Jane Winter, there's a few things you haven't told. However, I'll let you off, I'll even believe your incredible quarter-fare story if you'll tell me why you need to put the Count off *that* much."

"H-how much?" Jane blurted.

"As claiming me." He lit up again. "You couldn't have done a more damning thing had you struck him across the cheek."

"I don't understand."

"You will if you stop here long. Every city has its rake, its crook, its hard-time Harry. In this Pearl, or Pear, take your pick, I'm the one."

"You mean," interpreted Jane, "you haven't the best of reputations?"

"Smart girl." He nodded.

"But that couldn't affect Senhor Camoes," said Jane, even as she protested remembering again . . . and hollowly . . . the Portuguese addressing Terry as Senhor Marsden. "He's a resident of Madras."

"Colombo." Terry exhaled.

The Portuguese had said he did not live in Madras but he had known all about it . . . he had been going there . . . and she had disbelieved him.

"But I'm sure," she argued, "that he . . . I mean the plane was bound for—"

"There would be a branch at Madras. Bombay, Calcutta, many more, no doubt. But the Camoes have always centered their activities in Ceylon."

"I—I suppose there are many Portuguese here." Let there be enough, anyway, to make it improbable, quite, quite remote, that Senhor Camoes knows April's Rodriguez.

"I'll let you know the number." Terry's voice was dry. "Oh, yes, Sinhalese statistics is a branch of my newspaper duties, along with haunting the airport in the chance of an interesting character. Also classified ads."

"It sounds interesting."

"It's hell. I was a top-grade journalist on the— But you don't want to hear that."

Sympathetically she encouraged, "I might."

"You'd be sorry, and the sorrow wouldn't be for me but for yourself for listening. I told you about—"

"The rake, crook, hard-time Harry?"

"Yep. I brought it on myself. You know"—whimsically—"I wouldn't tell everyone that, in fact I've never told anyone before, but you look, right now anyway, a lost sort of kid, as lost as Marsden himself."

He ashed his cigaret and got up, took Jane up with him.

"But we'll find the lost girl, will we? What address?"

"It's here in my bag." Jane fumbled in the bag's recesses and brought out April's letter. His dry "Humph" rather disturbed her. "Is it—is it—"

"A bad address? Heavens, no. Just a very average one. Bread and butter standard. Definitely no jam. Which proves, I suppose"—he flashed her a sudden and rather sweet smile—"that your quarter-fare story could be true. No sister to a genuine luxury passenger such as you appeared to be would stop at the Ranick. It's respectable and patronized by government servants, medium grade, no higher. Certainly no glamor."

"Then it wouldn't suit April," declared Jane.

"Only her purse, eh? Well, we'll find April." He paid the attendant who was almost asleep again, then conducted Jane out of the terminal.

Many of the Sinhalese slept just where sleep had claimed them, in gutters, across footpaths, under dry, dusty trees. But many were still wide awake, even trading among themselves, and when they saw Jane they rushed at her, exhibiting their wares, mostly bean necklaces, wooden flutes, woven bags and the inevitable small black elephants.

They clamored, they cajoled, they insisted, and Jane shuddered to think how she would have got on without the man at her side, now ridding her of her tormentors with a practised word here, a gesture there. She understood why Senhor Camoes had been so concerned at her arriving unaccompanied at a late hour on a private flight. With a routine arrival there would have been a small crowd to share the attentions of the pedlars, the airport would have had several guards on duty, porters and guides. Too late Jane regretted tossing back at the Portuguese when he had objected to her leaving the plane that unforgivable: "It's not any business of yours."

"Scram! Vamoose! Get cracking!" Terry Marsden was snapping his fingers as he said it. When he succeeded in forcing a path for Jane he snapped his fingers for a cab.

The driver, like the coffee bar man, was still half asleep, but a wave of a ten-rupee note under his nose took the dust from his eyes. He nodded without enthusiasm when Terry Marsden directed the Ranick, which made Jane think that Terry had been right, that it was not a glamor hotel, or, as the cabman would be thinking, very promising for a large tip.

They drove through dark streets occasionally interspersed with bright markets, where, the same as at the airport, trade was being pursued over prone figures sleeping where sleep caught them.

"Why not?" said Terry. "That's what sleep is for, strictly for sleeping. Ever slept under the stars?"

"Often, but it wasn't like this."

"You mean you had a bag, an air mattress, all the cons. But I'll bet you didn't have stars that size."

"No," agreed Jane, "nor such a moon. Is it always perfect weather like this?"

"There are monsoon periods, but the climate is always tropical. No woollens needed here, except in the Hills where it's much cooler, but I hardly think that someone who stops at the Ranick will be making a habit of that."

"A habit?"

"Of going to the Hills for a cooler."

"Is it exclusive?" asked Jane.

"Not as much as it was once, perhaps, but then none of Ceylon is." He shrugged. "Besides the Hills, the streams and coast now have a following, too."

"But what do you mean, that none of Ceylon is the same as it was?"

"Just that. All the world over it's happening as it's happening here. The British . . . or the French . . . or what-have-you leave the country, and for a while a rot sets in. But from that rises a braver, more independent state. At least"—cynically—"that's the idea. It's supposed to be just a matter of time."

"You are British, Mr. Marsden?"

"Terry, Jane. Yes. There are a few of us still here."

"As unhappy as you?"

"My unhappiness is Marsden, not Ceylon. No, I don't think they're unhappy. The place is looking a little tatty just now, but, like a small boy, it'll spruce up all right one day, and believe me, here there's some of the most glorious scenery in the world. Do you recall the beautiful background in that *River Kwai* film? In *Elephant Walk*? Then wait until you see the setting at Mount Lavinia—creamy surf, coconut trees, just everyone's dream of a tropical paradise come true. No, there's no reason to be like Marsden. Ah, here we are at the Ranick now."

Jane peered out and saw an indifferent building, all the more indifferent because of the flamboyant setting, a circle of wind-ruffled palms with stars caught in their branches. One had spiked the full gold moon.

But the hotel was not flamboyant, it was distinctly dull. The man beside her must have read Jane's thoughts, for he assured her, "It's quite all right really, as I said, it's just strictly non-glamor and making no bones about that fact. If your sister's in the same quarter-fare category as you affirm you are what else did you expect?"

"April has a Ritz taste," admitted Jane. "It's hard to see her here."

"*Is* she here?" he asked.

"It says so in her letter."

"Well, that's the right letterhead," he conceded, glancing at the piece of paper that Jane held aloft. "I'll go and ask at the desk."

He was gone before Jane could tell him to ask for Winthrop, not Winter. She bit her lip.

When he returned his face was a study.

"Look, Jane, she's never even signed in, no Winter at all."

"I know," said Jane, ashamed now that she had not confided more in this helpful man, rake, crook, hard-time Harry though he might be. "Her name is Winthrop. We're half-sisters."

A light had come into his eyes, to Jane it looked like recognition, but all he said was a reproachful, "You might have told me."

"I might," she agreed humbly, and got out of the car and walked up the steps to the vestibule herself.

But when the clerk, questioned, gave his answer, she was glad that Terry Marsden had come up behind her. When the Sinhalese behind the desk said in perfect English: "Miss Winthrop has left, she has gone to the Shangri-la, gone this afternoon," Jane was glad to have Terry to turn to, to lean on once more.

April, she thought, doing the same old thing, even in Ceylon. April, never reliable, never where you expected her. Where was this Shangri-la? What sort of place? Why had she left the Ranick Hotel?

When—if—they traced her at the new hostelry, if hostelry it was, what then?

CHAPTER THREE

TERRY had led Jane back to the taxi . . . and that was another thing, taxis cost money. Jane had no idea as to how much they cost in Ceylon, and the little money that

Jane had in her purse might be needed for a long time.

Putting nicotine-stained fingers lightly on hers, Terry said, "Not to worry, the bill's on me."

"That is a worry."

"All right, Miss Independence, on my expense account then, if I word you as an important person we'll get this taxi free."

She gave a rather wobbly smile, then, still disturbed by that recognition, or she had thought it recognition, in his face when she had corrected, "Winthrop," she asked, "You've met April, haven't you, Terry?"

"I've seen her," he agreed. As her eyes clouded in worry, he assured her, "That's why I get a weekly pay packet, goose, to see people—it's my job, and teeming though Colombo is with Sinhalese, Moors and Malays, the proportion of Europeans is not so large that I could fail to notice one flame-haired, turquoise-eyed girl."

"Undoubtedly," said Jane of his description, "that is April."

When they had returned to the taxi, Terry had instructed the driver to the Shangri-la, and much more cheerful now, probably with a very large tip in view instead of the mediocre one associated with the Ranick, the Sinhalese began threading his way through the city, each turn of the wheels taking them through a more favored area of Colombo.

"As you must perceive," drawled Terry Marsden laconically, "your sister's second choice of an hotel is in a very different end of town." His glance at Jane, had she noticed it, was narrowed, speculative.

But Jane did not notice. She was nagged with possibilities and probabilities to do with her half-sister.

"Why did April move?" she fretted to herself, but in her concern still loud enough for Marsden to hear. "If this is a better hotel, as it seems it might be by the better neighborhood, where did she get the money?"

"It is," interrupted the journalist quite flatly, "not just a better hotel but a luxury hotel. No, take that back. It's a *super* luxury abode."

"But—but—"

"Exactly," he agreed significantly.

His eyes were narrowed again on Jane, the cynical twist back on his lips. He seemed sourly amused at his own thoughts, but—after a long, long look at the girl beside him—he did not express those thoughts.

"Where did you see April?" Jane asked him.

"I cover the ships, too. Your sister, if I remember rightly, came in the *Fairhaven*."

"Yes. She was to go right through to Southampton. I can't think why she disembarked here."

"Can't you?" Another look, then an abrupt softening in the hard face. "Young love and all that," Terry lightly suggested.

"You mean, of course, this Rodriguez?"

"Oh, so you do know about it." Once more the tight estimation.

"Just—just that she's fallen in love. No details of where they met, when they met. Nothing at all, really, not even his name, or connections, not anything."

"Ah." It was only a half breath really from Terry Marsden. He looked faintly amused.

"They would meet," he informed Jane, "when Miss Winthrop came ashore with the rest of the tourists to see Colombo."

"But surely the ship wouldn't stop long enough for—for—"

"For two people to fall in love?"

"For April to make such a big decision as to leave her ship less than halfway through the trip."

"It depends," said Terry Marsden drily, "on the prospects."

"What do you mean?" Jane's acorn eyes that matched her hair exactly were wide and troubled.

"Prospects, Jane. Hasn't love many prospects?" He made it a laughing evasion.

She smiled with him, and he asked a little cagily, "But where do you come in? I mean why have you flown over? Not even come leisurely by ship? No, don't tell me, it's to impress the family, isn't it? You've come on a sisterly crusade, and why not? You've got just that sweet, impressing look that would win a mission, you're not at all like April."

"That could be. We're only half-sisters. April is our paradise bird. I'm the brown wren."

"In England we think highly of our brown wrens."

"Well," said Jane with an earnestness there was no mistaking, "I trust the Portuguese will think highly of me."

"And through you your sister?"

"Yes." A little challengingly, "Is there anything wrong in that?"

"No," said Terry Marsden. But he added to himself, "Except that you've made a very unfortunate start."

The taxi was coming to a halt, and already the driver was arguing over the fare.

"Take no notice," advised Terry. "It's always like this. Finally we come to a mutual agreement."

But Jane was barely listening. She was looking . . . a little aghast . . . at the Shangri-la. If the Ranick had set her back with its air of respectable seediness the Shangri-la set her much further back with its grandeur. Why—why, the place was literally a palace.

Imposingly large, blazing white, lavishly flanked by tropical palms and Temple trees, which were necklaced, now it was night, by strings of colored lights, fountains playing in paved courts, an orchestra stringing a dulcet tune, dark waiters in long robes with green cummerbunds and with sandals on their feet, a truly remarkable red carpet on which to enter, the Shangri-la had the effect on Jane of making her want to shrink back into the car.

"Oh, come!" grinned Terry crookedly. "Your sister would walk down like the duchess I believed you were."

"How would you know?" asked Jane. "You haven't met her."

"I told you I'd seen her, and I must now add to that statement, for I must have met her, mustn't I, to have introduced her to Rod."

"Rod?"

"Rodriguez."

"You—you introduced her to this man?"

"Yes."

"But how? I mean you two hadn't previously met—"

"That's easy." His voice was laconic. "She asked me to."

"She—" But Jane did not go on. Flushing with embarrassment, she saw in her mind what she had seen with her eyes many, many times—April using people. April riding roughshod over people to get what she wanted. April, seeing this Rodriguez no doubt getting out of a lavish car, for it would take more than good looks to attract April, turning to the journalist who had met the tender from the *Fairhaven* to write up any important people and demanding, for April always demanded, to be presented.

"I'm sorry," Jane said impulsively.

"For what? She was pleased. He, undoubtedly, was pleased."

"And you?"

"I was amused."

"Amused?" she echoed.

"At the thought of her stricken look, after the presentation, when Rod would tell her, as undoubtedly he must tell her, being a true Portuguese and always solicitous toward the fairer sex, that her presenter was a rake, a crook—"

Jane murmured, "A hard-time Harry. But you're not, are you? You're—you're kind."

He looked at her with a soberness she had not seen in him before. "Thank you, Jane," he said. "And now shoulders back, head up. You may not be a duchess officially, but you are—to me." He pressed her arm and together they went down the fabulous red carpet.

Halfway to the reception desk an imposing figure in tropical hotel uniform hurried across to them.

"Madame? Sir?" A deep bow.

"Miss Winthrop," said Terry, and Jane held her breath. If April had gone on from here. . . .

But of course April hadn't. She might have known that April could not tear herself from such luxury.

"Certainly, madame, sir. The Rainbow Suite on the third floor."

Oh, no! groaned Jane inwardly. Oh, no, not a suite!

Terry's fingers were under her arm again, quite firm this time, affording her strength. To the hotel official's

"Shall I call Miss Winthrop?" he answered casually, "Don't bother, we'll go up."

But at that moment Jane saw that it would be of no avail to go up, because April was not in her suite, she was sitting, alone, in a corner seat of one of the lavish lounges—the Kismet Lounge, Jane read in gold lettering, and, ostensibly, she was listening intently to the orchestra. But Jane, knowing April, knew that she was only listening to her own thoughts, that any attention left over from that was on her physical self, what effect she was having on the other loungers, whether any of them would be worth the fanning of those quite fabulous lashes over those perfect coral-washed cheeks, the pretty pushing-back movement she practised on her flame-red hair.

Still, that was April, and for all her infuriating though enchanting gestures she was still Jane's half-sister, the family's paradise bird. I suppose, thought Jane, despairingly, I love her, I must do to let her worry me like she does.

Terry had seen her, too . . . how could he fail to miss her loveliness, all the more spectacular now in a shimmering lamé suit of red-gold to match her hair? That suit! Jane had never seen it before. April must have been buying up, she thought apprehensively. That ensemble would have cost the world. April did not have the world, nor anything like it.

"Come along," said Terry.

They walked along another red carpet to the Kismet. Jane said, "April," and her half-sister looked up.

She made a charming little moue of shame when she saw Jane, began an apologetic "Darling, I completely forgot—" then her glance fell on Terry.

"You," she said.

He wasted no time on argument or reprisal, he just said briefly, "I'll have your bags sent up, Kid," to Jane, flicked April a long derisive look, bowed to them both and went.

"That man!" fumed April. To Jane she said, "Sit down, for goodness' sake. You look terribly travelled."

"I am," reminded Jane.

"Well, I said I was sorry. Jane, sit down, people are looking."

Tired, knowing she was showing the signs of her journey, Jane said, "Isn't that what you want?" but still obeyed.

April flicked a signal to a waiter in that experienced way of hers, then turned to her sister.

"Really, Jane, how could you embarrass me by arriving with *him*!"

"You mean—" said Jane deliberately, "that he's a rake, a crook, a—"

"Here, in Colombo, he is not thought well of," said April haughtily, "and being in the position that I am I think it's very unkind of you to make a show of me like this."

"In what position are you?" asked Jane carefully.

"You know very well. That's why you're here. I'm practically married into the richest family in all India and Ceylon."

"Don't you think," asked Jane, "if it's still not quite clinched" . . . April shuddered delicately . . . "that you're rather foolish sitting here unescorted in a hotel lounge? Keeping in mind, I mean, that the Portuguese are careful about such things."

April's turquoise eyes indicated triumphantly that she would not have been unescorted very long, but to Jane she tossed, "Roddy wouldn't care. He adores café society like I do. He's a pet, Jane, I really do love him to distraction, it's not just the prospects." For a moment her turquoise eyes looked purely into Jane's acorn. . . .

Jane, rather touched, leaned across and squeezed her hand. "I'm glad of that. But if Rodriguez is so open-minded why are you angry that Terry Marsden came to my rescue tonight? Especially"—taking her hand away—"when he came to *your* rescue when you wanted to meet this Rodriguez of yours."

April pouted her full red lips. "Terry Marsden is just one of those people who isn't done. You know what I mean. Roddy doesn't particularly object to him, but he did tell me after we had been introduced and Marsden had left us that he was not widely accepted, and most certainly not accepted by his own family, nor, and most important of all, by his uncle."

"Have you met this important uncle, April?"

"He's out of Colombo just now. Roddy seems a little uncertain of him, but I'm not. You know how I've always been with old uncles and things." She gave a gay little laugh. She sobered at once, though. "But all the same I don't want to start on the wrong foot, and you coming in with that person is the wrong foot."

"Then I'm sorry," said Jane, "but I still think it was preferable to waiting in the airport all night."

"Darling, you could have found your own way."

"To the Ranick?" Jane's eyes reproved April.

"That place was dreary. Roddy agreed with me when I said I simply must move. I was a little let down when he didn't . . . when he. . . ."

Jane thought she knew what April was *not* saying.

"Where are you getting the money for a suite in this hotel?" she asked at once.

"Why, darling, not from Roddy, of course. Not from anybody. I mean in a position such as I'm in now I must be very circumspect." Circumspect—Mother's little word.

Jane looked at her half-sister shrewdly. She could see that she was disappointed that Rodriguez had not presettled the bill. But Jane instead was relieved. Even though April would lightly dismiss it as a loan, it was still something that must not be done, especially, as April had pointed out, in her position.

But if Rodriguez was not paying it, nor anybody else, who was?

"April, have you been singing on the ship? Earning money?"

"In that luxury suite? I would have looked a fool. No, I just signed in here and they took me gladly. After all, just to be accompanied by Roddy is enough. And then you must admit I don't appear as poor as I am." Again a gay laugh.

"Not in those clothes, anyway. April, are they—"

"Darling, nobody pays cash these days. Please don't fuss. Look upon them as an investment, the biggest investment I've ever made. Roddy's family, which really stops, apart from distant relatives, at the uncle, and thank heaven, for I'd loathe a lot of encumbrances like brothers, sisters and aunts, is quite tremendously rich. They're agents, only Roddy says that's really a misnomer because they own and don't just represent, and Jane, the things they deal in! Not just tea and coffee, rubber, coconut, mahogany and satinwood, but"—her turquoise eyes glowed—"jewels. Roddy told me about the sapphires. Then rubies, Jane—the sought-after pigeon's blood."

"April," interrupted Jane anxiously, "you did say you really liked Rodriguez?"

"Oh, yes." April did not hesitate. "I love him, Jane. I'll not deny that I was attracted by what he has. After all . . . but he's very sweet, and we took to each other at once."

It was not the ideal basis, but, for April, it was as substantial as one could hope. And the good thing was that in the beginning April had been attracted by the young man himself, plus car perhaps, and chauffeur, but not by the sapphires and rubies. They had come later.

"When we go upstairs we must delve into the money problem," Jane frowned. "I don't like taking credit like this."

"It's an investment, as I said, but I do think a money conference is a good thing. We'll go at once. How much have you brought?"

"Not much—" began Jane, then she asked, worriedly, "Where am I to sleep?"

"Here, silly. I booked for you as well, hence the suite." April got up in her graceful way and preceded Jane out of the lounge to the elevator. At the third floor they traversed more red carpet to a satinwood door. April opened it, and this time let Jane go ahead.

It was what Jane would have expected of April, large, lavish and reeking of extravagance. She stifled a sigh.

April threw herself down on the bed and laughed, "How much is not much, darling? Break the bad news."

"It is bad." Jane told her.

But April was not so concerned as Jane had thought. "I hoped for more, but I didn't really think there would be. Poor Mummy, if you can't win in two attempts what hope have you? I mean, Jane, for your father to be poor as well as mine! For us both he left only a pittance!" Jane forebore to remind April that only she, Jane, had been left anything, even though it hadn't turned out like that. "One thing"—April resumed narrowly—"that won't happen to me." At the look in her half-sister's face she reassured her, "But I do like him, I like Roddy tremendously, and you will, too. You will want to do what I want you to, Jane, help me impress this uncle so that he gives his blessing. It must be Portuguese tradition that the relatives wholeheartedly approve. So far as I'm concerned, I'd snap my fingers, but Roddy says it's important we do the right thing. And I suppose it is, too, for after we're married we intend leaving Ceylon . . . it's fun for a while, but frightfully limited."

"With all those shrines to visit, those plantations, those—"

"I mean society, silly. It's the same old set. Roddy says that Monelva, fairly near their old family home, is really smart, then, of course, everyone knows that Lisbon is international. We'd like to go amicably, so there won't be any finger-snapping, just April looking demure and presenting a sister in whose mouth most assuredly butter would not melt. Darling Jane, thank you for being what you are."

"Dull?"

April took off her gold suit and while Jane hung it up said magnanimously, "I forgive you for turning up with that Marsden man, anyway. I don't think many noticed."

"No, they would be looking at you."

"Yes," accepted April quite calmly. "But don't do it again. I mean it's bad enough to start on the wrong foot, but it would be catastrophic to continue the mistake."

After she had snapped out her bed light Jane remembered, on leaving Sydney, thinking rather in the same strain. She had not wanted to start off in an unsuitable . . . Portuguese unsuitable . . . manner. The fear had come, she recalled, when she had discovered that the man who had been walking beside her to the plane was Portuguese. At the moment it had seemed just too much of a coincidence, only, fortunately, he had been going to Madras, not Colombo.

Then at once, and rather hollowly, she was recalling Terry Marsden remarking that the Camoes had branches also in India, at Bombay, Calcutta, other places, but that the center was in Ceylon. She remembered asking him if there were many Portuguese in the island . . . remembered Terry forgetting to tell her.

A cold finger touched Jane.

"April!" she called.

No answer.

"*April.*"

"Oh, really, Jane!" April came reluctantly out of her first light sleep.

"Your Roddy—what's his name?"

"Rodriguez, of course."

"But his next name—his surname?"

April giggled a little. "I can't pronounce it properly yet—isn't that mad? I'm going to marry him and I can't pronounce his name."

"What is it?"

"Carreras. I'll be the Senhora Carreras and I'll live in this beautiful home in this *avenida* that Roddy has told me about. Jane, are you asleep?"

Jane was not, but she felt she would be asleep quite soon. It had been a long day, a tiring day, and tomorrow was tomorrow and not to be dealt with until then. Especially when April's Roddy was Rodriguez Carreras, not Camoes as she had feared.

Jane felt her limbs slacken.

She wakened in the same cheerful spirit, wakened to iced lime juice, slivered papaw, a jug of coffee, cream, a rack of crisp toast. There was a small dish of marmalade and a curl of butter, all served on a silver tray. It was rather nice to be treated as though you were rich, Jane thought.

April came in from her bath, even more beautiful without her careful makeup. She sat on Jane's bed and buttered a piece of her toast and ate it. "If you're hungry I'll ring for more."

"Where's your own?" Jane was rather hungry.

"I'm breakfasting on the terrace, with Roddy. I'll

bring you along next time, darling, but this morning —well, I haven't seen Roddy for two days, he's been in Madras."

Madras.

However, Jane was determined not to cloud her new cheerful spirit. She smiled at April, said something foolish about young love, and when April directed her to come just at the end of the meal to meet Roddy . . . "looking sweet and serene and every inch the lady, Jane" . . . she agreed.

April went through Jane's clothes, snorting her disgust.

"Mummy shouldn't have let you come like this!" she exclaimed.

It was, thought Jane, actually the first time April had mentioned their mother.

"I'll find you something of mine. No need to panic, it will be one of the articles I brought from Sydney, so at least it will be paid for." April heaved a sigh and said, "I'm so glad I don't limp through life."

"If limping means paying one's way—"

"Oh, Jane, spare me. This is going to be quite a day, I'll need all my resources. Roddy will have seen his uncle, no doubt have something to report. Don't needle me before I start."

"If loving Rodriguez is going to affect you like this," demurred Jane, "I think you should do some serious considering, April."

"I've considered," assured April, "and don't worry, once I'm Senhorita Carreras someone else will do the worrying. And I"—she smiled wickedly—"the needling. This doddering, dependent old uncle, for instance—"

"How do you know he is dependent?"

"If not exactly on Rod's money, I mean if he has a little money of his own, then assuredly he is dependent on Rod's youth. Firms are always like that. The young carry the old." April pulled a bright-orange sheath over her head, a tangerine that should have clashed with her hair, but, because it was April, became part of her.

As Jane watched her, her own bright spirits diminished. April was too young and too lovely to be so coolly calculating. She felt too young herself, if not lovely, to be a party to such connivance.

"April, I don't like it," she said.

April, about to toss something astringent at her, changed her mind . . . and changed Jane's with her next words.

"Just wait till you see Roddy, Jane, see him—with me." Her turquoise eyes appealed, and when April appealed. . . .

"All right," Jane agreed.

After her half-sister had gone in a mist of fresh morning fragrance . . . April was very clever with her perfumes . . . Jane got up and went to the window. In the starlight and moonlight of last night she had only received a hazy impression of the part of Ceylon, of the dropped pearl to which she had come, so now she looked out with curiosity. With a little dismay. Yet withal an extent of thrall.

The dismay was because of the seediness . . . the same as she had sensed last night . . . making a pear of the pearl, and not a very appetizing pear at that. For beyond the lavish grounds of the Shangri-la a different story unfolded, the story of a too sharply divided economy, told, once beyond the hotel's handsome gates, in teeming crowds and clamoring, scantily clad children. But the thrall was in the bare bones of the picture, if you could overlook the seediness, in graceful palm and Temple tree, in the distant glimpse of a Buddha in meditation, of a sky so blue that it seemed part of a postcard and not existing in fact at all.

A rickshaw went by, a very small coffee-colored boy in tiny pants but carrying a huge umbrella, an oxen wagon, a girl with a red oleander in her black hair.

The same articles of trade with which she had been pestered last night at the airport were being clamored. Jane wondered that any business was transacted, for surely everyone in Ceylon already had a bean necklace, a wooden flute, a small black elephant. Drinks were being peddled . . . probably lychee juice, sugar-cane juice. Little portions of dried seasoned fish were becoming even drier in the blazing sun as they waited to be consumed by some hungry customer.

Laughing a little, Jane withdrew from the window, then saw, rather to her dismay, for April liked her plans to go off like clockwork, that she had delayed longer than she should. She hurried into the pale green, button-up linen that her half-sister had allotted her, buckled sandals on her bare feet, ran a comb through the soft, straight, acorn hair and hurried out to the lift.

She found her way to the breakfast terrace and was relieved to see that she was in time. Indeed, by April's gay signal, she had timed it well. The pair, Rodriguez and her sister, had finished the meal and were sipping coffee.

But as Jane came nearer to the table beneath the striped umbrella April did not look so gay. Her eyes now were on the apple-green linen she had given away, and they were sulky.

Rodriguez, as Jane approached, had got smartly to his feet to bow gallantly. He insisted that Jane take his seat while he called for another chair. When one did not come he murmured a word of apology and hurried off to question the delay.

"That green," said April, "doesn't suit you, you're too brown, Jane."

"Yes, a brown wren. We can't all be paradise birds."

That mollified April slightly. A look in her handbag mirror mollified her a great deal more.

"What do you think of him?" she asked.

"We haven't met yet."

"Yes, but what do you think?"

"He looks very nice." He had looked very nice —young, straight, faintly olive-skinned, smiling-eyed, boyishly fresh and clean. Nice.

"There was nothing much to report," reported April, "except that the uncle is returning to Colombo today. We'll meet him, Jane. You'll do your gentle refined act."

"And you?"

"What I would like to do would be to put him in his place. I must admit that Roddy's deference rather maddens me. Anyone would think. . . . However, Roddy persists in being repectful, so I suppose it's an old Portuguese custom. But I can tell you, Jane, that once I'm Senhora Carreras—Here's Roddy now."

Behind Rodriguez Carreras came a steward with a chair. The young Portuguese sat down, ordered more coffee, for three this time, replied to Jane's protest laughing, "But no, sister of April, at least if you will not eat with us you will drink with us," then turned to April for introductions.

"Jane." His hand was in Jane's, warm, sincere, a good friendly grip. Yes, he is nice, thought Jane again.

They talked busily together about many things, but when the conversation centered on Ceylon topics, the country's national and religious festivals, their cottage industries, April became bored. She sat it out until Jane asked Rodriguez about the ruined cities, a subject that always had intrigued her.

"My uncle knows much more than I do. You must get him to tell you of Anuradhapura, the ancient capital."

"Of course he would know more, Roddy," pouted April. "He's older."

"But not two and a half thousand years older," said Rodriguez with delight. "You are a dear, mad girl!"

April gave a pretty moue, asked to be excused to comb her hair and ran off. Rodriguez watched her go with unconcealed adoration. He *is* in love, Jane thought. But when he turned again to Jane the delighted amusement had given way to a small frown of concern.

"Your sister seems to think that my uncle is Methuselah," he proffered troublously.

"When one is twenty-two, anything over that does seem rather old."

"But you are younger than April."

"Not much."

"Yet you do not think like that?"

Jane got over the hurdle by smiling, "Is it that important?"

"Not at all, but—but something else is. It's April's attitude to my uncle. Jane—I may call you Jane?—I have a feeling that April doesn't realize, appreciate, understand that—"

Jane understood without Rodriguez explaining any further. Obviously he was worried by April's carefree, one could say careless, attitude to people. To be concise, to Rodriguez's uncle.

"I think you're making a mountain out of a molehill," she smiled encouragingly. "I wouldn't worry, such an attitude *is* April. She doesn't really mean it, of course. She's thistledown, Rodriguez . . . do you have those in your native Monelva?"

His face had brightened again. "So April told you!"

"Yes. And of the beautiful home in the *avenida*."

"But the home," said Rodriguez, "is just that, it is not like my uncle's. I mean—" He stopped. April was returning to the table, and the morning sun was catching the pure flame-gold of her hair.

"Yes. A paradise bird."

"She is so lovely," he said almost painfully.

They lingered over their coffee, for Rodriguez said there was no hurry to go out to the airport to meet the plane. He commended April on having such a sister as Jane. "My uncle will be favorably impressed," he smiled. "It is a splendid idea to have a member of the family present, and such a member." He bowed. "My uncle," he explained, "is very Portuguese in his views. I am, too, I suppose, but being junior—"

"Not junior, darling, just young." It was April —pouting, not liking Rodriguez to be a junior in his firm.

"When he comes into the terminal," continued Rodriguez, "and sees Jane—"

"But I'm not going out to the airport." The airport was the last place that Jane did want to go to. Her memories of last night were too recent—and painful. She heard again that frigid: "Senhorita Winter. Senhor Marsden." She saw the tall, straight back of Joao Camoes returning to the Madras-bound plane.

"But of course you're coming!" It was April and Rodriguez together.

The Portuguese said, "It is most important, Jane, that April has a companion. It is also important, and you must forgive me, that the companion is not like her sister. I mean—well—"

"Roddy means that the companion is essentially a lady." April's turquoise eyes laughed at the young man and their glances merged.

Feeling distinctly a third, and very uncomfortable, and *still* anxious not to go, Jane offered to meet the gentleman in question at the hotel.

"It won't do," refused Rodriguez.

"You promised," declared April.

With a sigh Jane complied.

As the plane was not scheduled until noon, the three of them wandered out to the paved courtyard where they sat for a while near the playing fountain, then on Jane's request they went to the nearby fish-pond to observe the beautiful tropical specimens that Ceylon had to offer, then later on Rodriguez's suggestion to the datura tree, just now in full bloom.

While Jane was delighting in the convolvulus-like blossoms . . . snowy-white at morning, related Rodriguez, but turning pink and purple as they faded at the end of the day . . . April decided it was time she changed her dress for her meeting with Roddy's uncle.

"But you look so beautiful," he pleaded.

"And unsuitable?" she teased. "No, darling, I intend wearing a silk suit."—Silk suit! Jane flinched. There had been no silk suit in April's original wardrobe.

"Also, when I get back, Jane must change." April's eyes on her sister were suddenly narrowed.

"But surely Jane is very suitable," protested Rodriguez. "That spring green is definitely Jane."

That was the trouble. It was. April said flatly, "I'll lay something out. Oh, yes"—to the young Portuguese—"I often do that. Jane has no sense for such things."

"If I come now you can tell me," offered Jane a little tightly.

"Two women in one room dressing together?" April, who had shared her room with Jane all her life in their modest flat in Sydney, threw up her hands.

"It's a suite, not a room," said Jane.

"All the same, darling, after the space we've been used to—" She shuddered. "No, I'll leave your frock in readiness."

When she had gone Rodriguez took Jane to see the lotus pool, for Jane had never seen lotus before in her life, only read about them.

"Actually they're much better in Burma. Also there they play a bigger role in temple worship than here, but they are lovely, aren't they?"

Jane bent over and touched the almost unbelievably satin petals, some pink, some white.

"We'll sit here if you like," said Rodriguez, "unless you would sooner the cooled lounge."

"I love the sun."

"You don't find it oppressive?"

"Why, no. I'm Australian, remember."

"April finds it too much. She would like us to live in Portugal after we marry."

"Would you?"

Rodriguez said a little uneasily, or Jane somehow sensed it was uneasily, "We must see, of course. It all depends."

He did not say on what it depended, so Jane changed the subject and at the same time broached the subject of the airport again. She definitely did not want to go.

Rodriguez insisted what he had insisted before. "Also," he finished, "you gave your word. Why are you so reluctant, Jane?"

"It was unpleasant last night arriving and not being met," mumbled Jane unwillingly.

"But," reminded the young Portuguese gently, "that was your fault. You never told April when you were coming, so how was she to know?"

It was such a silly little lie it was not worth correcting, all the same it irritated Jane sufficiently to prompt her to announce: "But for Mr. Marsden I'd have been in a spot."

As Rodriguez frowned, she asked, "Why are you so antagonistic to Terry Marsden? April was quite livid when he brought me here."

"April appreciates the position," said Rodriguez with a formality that sat rather absurdly on him. "Actually" —relaxing a little—"I like the fellow, but to many people in Colombo he is quite beyond the pale. In April's and my position we both feel we must be careful."

Jane said forthrightly, "Why? You love each other. You intend to marry. What else is there? What else to concern anyone but yourself and April?"

"Quite a good deal," Rodriguez admitted.

Jane was nonplussed. She could understand her sister's attitude, to dislike anyone who did not come up to her personal standards, and undoubtedly Terry Marsden would never come up to her standards, was simply April.

But she could not understand Rodriguez. He was young. He was easy-going. In his own words he "liked the fellow." Yet he practised a caution that was foreign to him, though a caution that came instinctively to April. There was something here that Jane could not understand.

She became aware that Rodriguez was looking at her, wetting his lips preparatory to saying something.

But it was not to be said. At that moment April came down the broad staircase . . . a more effectual entry than from the elevator . . . and the silk suit was glowing pink, not the color for a hot climate, not the color for flame hair, but on April simply superb in spite of everything.

While Rodriguez was struggling for words, Jane went upstairs. A gray cotton with a demure white collar was laid out. Jane regarded it, then said aloud, "But you're wrong, April. I'm a brown wren, not a gray mouse."

She was past caring, however, and got into it without bothering to check her reflection, which was a pity, for that reflection would have lent her confidence, would have explained the pout that again settled on April's full red lips.

"We will go now," decided Rodriguez, and they got into his car, a good car but not lavish, observed Jane. She observed that April was observing this, too.

It was not a gay journey to the airport. April was still pouting, still observing the less-than-luxury car, Rodriguez was preoccupied and not very cheerful, Jane was frankly hating going into the terminal again.

But three reluctant people made no difference to the turning wheels. The wheels still bore you there, bore you through narrow streets, sometimes thronged so thickly that you literally had to inch your way through the crowds, bore you past afforestations that Rodriguez said were jaggery palm that yielded a sort of rough brown sugar from its sap, bore you through orchards of limes, shaddocks, grenadillas and plantains.

It would have all delighted Jane had she not felt so oddly heavy . . . prescient . . . as though something was going to happen.

What could? Everything that might occur, that is everything unpleasant, or at least unfortunate, already had occurred. Until her sister married her Rodriguez, or departed for Portugal to marry him, Jane felt she had had her share of misfortune, or misdirection, sufficient unto the day, and the week, and the month.

Rodriguez parked the car and they entered the building. It looked different by daylight, brighter, less foreign. Nonetheless Jane averted her eyes from the coffee lounge, from the wall against which Terry Marsden indolently had leaned.

"Flight 17 from Madras," intoned a voice, and Rodriguez said, "This will be it. It's a domestic line—Air-Colombo."

Now the unease was really disturbing Jane, her hands were damp, but her throat was dry and tight.

"Jane, are you all right? You look ghastly. You shouldn't have sat like that in the sun." It was April and she seemed a long way away.

"I'm all right. Of course I'm all right," Jane said—but only with her lips. She was far from all right. How could she feel right with that man coming from the tarmac through the terminal door?

He was tall, broad, olive-skinned, infinitely suave, he had a small moustache. Jane did not need April's quick little intake of breath to tell her that Rodriguez's uncle was much taller, much broader, much more blandly attractive than his nephew who had left their side to hurry across.

For he must be the uncle. Who else? Rodriguez had gone straight to him, taken his hand. He was leading him back.

Had she not been so concerned with herself, with the last time she had seen this man, Jane might have found a little wry amusement in April's gasped, "But I thought he'd be old!"

Old and doddering, had been April's words. Someone whom she intended to put in his place the moment she married the young nephew.

But it was April who was being put in her place—coolly, formally, ever so politely. *But in her place.* With the barest click of his heels Senhor Camoes took April's hand and brushed his lips over the white skin. He took his time over the gesture, but one had the impression that it was because he would always be unhurried, not because he wished to eke out the salute.

But, realized Jane with shamed certainty, as at last he stepped back then turned to her, it was neither a romantic nor unhurried nature that had made him take his time over April, it was a reluctance to greet the sister.

The click of the heels was the same. The salutary brush of the lips on a sunburned, square-nailed hand this time, the same. But the eyes. . . .

The eyes challenged hers.

CHAPTER FOUR

THEY were in Rodriguez's car and drawing away from the airport. Jane had only a confused idea of the sequences that had taken place after Senhor Camoes had released her hand, stepped back to bow briefly, coolly, again, then turned to his nephew.

The actions had been like the flick in a deal of cards, like the quickly turning facets of a kaleidoscope. She had been aware of a porter taking the senhor's bags, of Rodriguez saying, "The car is waiting," of a faintly uncertain April, uncertain for the first time in her life?, moving forward, and she, Jane herself, moving mechanically as well.

As they had crossed the terminal another card had flicked. It had been Terry Marsden—not leaning indolently this time but sitting lazily, legs pushed out, his notebook in his hand. He had waved the book airily to the party and April, by Jane's side, had visibly stiffened. Rodriguez had saluted back, Senhor Camoes had inclined his head formally, and Jane given a rather wobbly smile, at least she believed that that was what had happened. The turning facets of the kaleidoscope had been too quick for her to be certain.

At the car there had been a small delay as the bags were stowed and the party seated.

For Rodriguez, who was driving, there was no arrangement, but April had stood hesitant . . . not knowing whether to climb in with her Roddy, or sit at the back.

For the briefest of moments Joao Camoes had kept them waiting. Would he get in the rear with April where he could further the acquaintance? April's eyes had lit up. Or in the back with Jane, leaving April to sit with her fiancé-to-be, thus establishing his approval of the match? Again . . . though with slightly *less* enthusiasm, Jane saw . . . April glinted.

But the senhor did neither. Politely he helped the ladies in, April first, Jane next, then he seated himself beside Rodriguez. The car edged off.

A quick glance at her half-sister had disturbed Jane. There was a look on April's beautiful face that she had seen before. It had been the time she had brought Jeff home to the flat, and April . . . April. . . .

April was looking at the two men in front of her, and it had not needed Jane's experience to know that April was comparing, that she was weighing up, that she was reaching a sum total that was causing two little creases across her usually smooth white brow.

Jane regarded the men herself. Joao Camoes was far taller, far broader than Rodriguez Carreras, he was much more mature. There was also an air of worldly assurance about him that had not settled yet on Rodriguez's slighter, younger shoulders, an experience, a wisdom, an unmistakable and unarguable affluence. A subtle superiority, and not only in the impeccable cut and material of his formal lounge suit as compared to Roddy's more casual attire, but in the man himself.

Jane saw now there were three creases on April's brow.

She tried to turn her attention to the scenery—after all this was new, fresh country—but her eyes kept coming back to the two men sitting in front of her . . . and to April.

Presently Senhor Camoes began speaking in Portuguese to Rodriguez Carreras, asking, of the back seat, formal permission first.

"Perhaps you will appreciate the fact that we have many business things to say," he explained. "I have been overnight and early morning in Madras ironing out a problem, and naturally I can discuss the result with my nephew more flexibly in my own tongue."

"Of course," smiled April, to whom the apology had been addressed. Jane, since he had not even looked at her, said nothing. She heard the smooth interchange of words she could not understand; a rather musical and flowing language this Portuguese, she decided.

April had stopped weighing up the situation and was weighing herself up instead, looking in her handbag mirror, adjusting here and there, ridding her brow of the three creases. When Senhor Camoes turned to speak in English again she was beautiful, serene and smooth-browed.

"We will take you to your hotel and the four of us have luncheon there," said Joao Camoes. "You are in which hostelry, senhorita?"

"Shangri-la." Rodriguez said it for April.

"So." There was no frown on the senhor's brow, but there was an enigmatical look in his dark eyes that did not escape Jane—or April.

April wetted her lips with the tip of her tongue prior to saying something. Then, after a moment's thought, she said nothing. It was that unrevealing "So," that enigmatical look, that silenced her. She did not know whether to explain the Shangri-la, whether to praise or regret it. Or, Jane knew, too, whether to put it all down as a whim of her sister's, which, for April, would be her expected form.

She must have decided to bide her time, see how things went, for, when Rodriguez's car was put in the Shangri-la

porter's hands to be driven away and garaged, she
followed the men docilely into the big hotel, Jane a little
to her rear.

Last night Jane had been a little aghast at the obvious
luxury of the hotel, now she found herself more aghast at
the too lavish displays, the too apparent affluence, the
slight trend to the showy and the ostentatious. Her sister
was no fool, she sensed it as well. And she realized what
had been meant in the senhor's "so."

Softly, yet loud enough to be heard by the man in front,
she said to Jane, "Darling, why did you? We were quite
comfortable enough before. This place is—well!"

Rodriguez took no notice, he was looking for a steward
to arrange a table, but Joao Camoes could not help but
overhear.

Jane wondered what his reaction would be to the ornate
dining room, but a few words in Portuguese must have
ordered Rodriguez as to his requirements, for when the
party was bowed in it was to a small, more subdued,
private annexe, much less marble to it, a more sober
decor, only one fairly simple arrangement of
flowers—Temple flowers. In Australia they were called
frangipanni. They gave up their faint, sweet temple air.
Jane went across to smell the gentle breath, and over the
creamy flowers with their golden hearts she looked up to
meet the eyes of Joao Camoes. April and Rodriguez were
standing by the window together. They were saying
something in soft voices, they were absorbed in each
other. For a moment the senhor and Jane were quite
alone.

"You were not," observed the Portuguese in his formal
voice but a much lower voice now, "so anxious to meet
the Senhor Marsden this time, Senhorita Winter. Not a
disagreement, I trust? Not what the English, so no doubt
the Australian, calls a tiff?"

Jane had time to reply only a bare "No" before April
and Rodriguez turned. But even if she had had the opportunity what else had she to answer to what he asked?

The table was set and the meal was brought in. Jane
had the impression that it was simpler than customary
but more meticulously and fastidiously served. The

248

waiters moved silently and carefully, and but for their
frequent anxious glances at the Senhor Camoes they
might have been automatons.

That he was not the ogre that undoubtedly their
superiors had warned them was borne out by a rupee note
that he handed across between the final red wine and the
coffee. Jane, not yet used to Sinhalese rupees, could still
tell by the pleased faces that it was a substantial reward
for their services.

"Thank you," they bowed.

The table was cleared, only the coffee appointments
left. April poured gracefully, aware that a woman can
look her most charming attending to such rites.

At first the conversation was desultory, and then it
became more pertinent. Senhor Camoes inquired from
April how she had come to Colombo, evincing interest
when she said by ship. Which ship? The weather, the ports
of call followed. Had Senhorita Winthrop liked
Singapore . . . and for the briefest of moments Joao
Camoes was looking not at April but Jane.

Soon . . . any moment . . . he would say, "But your
sister did not sail, she flew. In the same plane as I flew,"
and April's turquoise eyes would widen, then narrow.
Narrow on Jane.

Jane felt she could not wait for that. She wished desperately that she had told April last night, but
how could she? She had not known then that Senhor
Camoes. . . .

"If I may be excused I'll go upstairs." Jane rose, rose
definitely before she could be stopped by any protests, by
more coffee, by being sucked into a new conversation.
The two Portuguese gentlemen got to their feet and
bowed. April did not protest. Handling two men by
herself rather pleased her.

But when she came up to the suite half an hour later,
Jane back at the window trying to be diverted as she had
been diverted this morning, April was not pleased. So
Joao Camoes had wasted no time telling her!

But April's first words refuted this. Had she been told
April certainly would not have started first on another
strain.

"I don't know what to think," she began rather in a wail. "I really don't. What's your impression, Jane?"

"Impression?"

"Of Joao Camoes, of course, who else? He's certainly not what I thought, not what Roddy gave me to expect."

"Did Rodriguez really give any impression, April, or did you build one up yourself?"

"Well, I ask you, *an uncle!*"

"An uncle can be even younger than a nephew," reminded Jane.

"Joao is older," April said reflectively, her eyes glinting again. "I like a mature man," she said definitely, and Jane shrank—for Rodriguez. April had said exactly the same words just before the Jeff episode had come to an end.

"Definitely he liked me," said April.

"Then that augurs well for you and Rodriguez."

"I wasn't thinking of that." Now April's voice was a little short of a wail again. "Jane, you have to help me."

"How?"

"Find out about Joao . . . what exactly he is in this firm of Roddy's. It could be he's as important as Roddy, I mean—well, I mean Roddy's "sir" each time he addresses him."

"That could be Portuguese respect," suggested Jane.

"It could be, and yet—Oh, I don't know." April went restlessly round the room, picking things up, putting them down again. "I wish—" she said helplessly.

Jane had a fair idea of what she wished, but she could not be worried about it, she had her own wish on her mind, the wish that she had confided in April before Joao Camoes eventually did.

One thing . . . *now* . . . she could not let the pretence go on any further.

"April," she said clearly, "Mr. Camoes and I had met previously. We came on the same plane."

"Well, obviously you didn't impress him," shrugged her sister. "He didn't even recognize you." She was still self-absorbed.

"But he did," gulped Jane. "He spoke about Terry Marsden . . . asked why I was not so anxious to meet him this time."

Now April's attention was on Jane. She looked at her furiously, and Jane's heart sank. April had a quick, sharp temper.

"What do you mean? Tell me at once. You mean to say that you flaunted this man in front of him? What did you say to Joao on the trip up? That is"—sarcastically—"if you did speak."

"We sat together."

"You . . . Oh, so that's it, is it? You're trying to warn me hands off."

"Hands off? April, what on earth—"

"You could see, as I could see, too, that Joao—that Rodriguez—that Joao—Oh, you're the sly one, Jane. So you flaunt that man, that Terry Marsden, to start me off in a bad light!"

"If what you suppose was true," pointed out Jane reasonably, "wouldn't it be I who was in the bad light?"

April absorbed that and brightened slightly. Because she had to live the next few weeks with her half-sister, and because she knew from experience that unless one lived fairly amicably life could be unbearable, Jane took advantage of the brightening and said, "I'm sorry for anything that has happened, April. Believe me, none of it was intentional, I wouldn't have embarrassed you for the world. If I can help you now I'll be glad to do so. I like Rodriguez very much and I'm sure—"

But now April was darkening again, losing the smile in her turquoise eyes.

"Just forget Roddy for a while," she said, "and find out about Joao. I mean I can hardly go and ask—ask—"

"Ask what?"

"If he's married, engaged. The most important of all—"

"Yes?"

"What he is? Whether he could be what I think he could be, and I can tell you, Jane, that if he is—"

April went across to the window from which Jane had withdrawn and for quite a while did not speak. But when she did her words shocked Jane, though, she thought drearily, she should have expected them.

She said, fastening down her bottom lip with her white, even teeth:

"I never did like young men, and Rodriguez Carreras is very young, quite immature—almost a boy. But Joao Camoes—"

Words were on Jane's lips, words like, "April, you're not going to drop Rodriguez like you dropped Jeffery, are you? Drop him because all at once somewhere else the fields are greener?" But she never uttered them. For one reason she was a little afraid to, for all her instinctive feeling for the young and obviously in-love Portuguese, afraid of April's anger. The other reason she held her tongue was because April gave her no chance to do otherwise. She monopolized the conversation, examining Jane closely as to her trip and what had taken place between her and the Senhor Camoes.

"Nothing did." Jane remembered the tour of the shops at Darwin, their mutual, hers and the senhor's, admiration of the opal bracelet. His gift of a koala bear. She told April about the bear in case she found it, and inquired, and April said rather sharply, "An odd gift. Are you sure there was nothing else? What did you talk about on the journey?"

"Very little. You see, I slept."

At that April tossed back her red-gold hair and laughed delightedly.

"You are a strange girl, Jane—you sit beside this Joao Camoes and what do you do? Sleep. Now I'm beginning to believe your job with Max Everett was just that after all, a job."

"What else?"

"Darling, from six to eleven every night! Now you're angry. Please don't be, because I really love my little sister very much, and you know it, Jane."

Jane did not know it, but she knew that she herself had a lot of affection, deserved or otherwise, for April. She knew April knew it, and would trade on it. And she, Jane, being vulnerable and unable to do anything about it, would let her have her way. But not the way she wanted now. She would *not*, she thought, pump Joao Camoes.

She said so definitely, and April shrugged.

"Perhaps you're right, it might give him ideas that you yourself are interested. I'll get it out of Roddy. I wonder what those two men are talking about down there. I was practically sent up here like a small child. That Joao is certainly used to authority." April gave a little moue that was not entirely displeasure. "We'll soon find out!"

They found out within the hour. A message came up that the senhor would like to see the Senhorita Winthrop in the coffee lounge.

"Why can't he come up here?" pouted April; she had put on a very charming negligee.

"He mightn't approve of that, nor approve of Rodriguez coming, either."

"Oh, Roddy!" April was flicking back her frocks . . . a large collection of frocks, much larger than the number she had brought from Sydney. She chose a cool lime with a narrow white belt. White sandals, and she was ready.

"You do look lovely, April. But that dress—"

"Singapore, darling. They measure you and deliver the frock to the ship."

"Was it expensive?"

"Their clothes are ridiculously cheap. That's why I bought so many."

"So many? But, April—"

"Jane, don't fuss. It was essential."

"I can't see why. At that time you hadn't met Rodriguez."

"Please don't keep on about Roddy." April was irritated. "I've been bidden to go down to see Joao Camoes, Jane. Doesn't that indicate anything?"

"No," said Jane.

"Well, *you* haven't been asked, have you, for all your advantage of knowing him first."

Jane, nettled, said, "I think he's asked to see you because you are senior. I think he has something to say."

Now it was April who was nettled. She was always sensitive to being a year older.

"We'll see," she smiled blandly, giving her hair a last flick.

Jane went with her to the door. "April, I don't want you to tell any more lies about me—not to Senhor Camoes."

"Why not to him more than anyone else?" April's eyes were narrowed. "Anyway," she defended, "I told no lies."

"Not directly, but you indicated that I'd been responsible for the change of hotels."

"Darling, you're too sensitive. It was just something to say, I hate hollow silences. Besides, all's fair. Remember, Jane?"

"You mean"—Jane looked incredulously at her—"'all's fair in love and war?'"

April nodded wickedly, her eyes laughing. She looked quite irresistible, Jane thought.

"But you love Rodriguez, April—"

"Of course, darling, and to win him I had to butter up Uncle." April's evasion was butter-smooth, for she had not, and Jane had known it, been thinking in that strain.

"Cheer up, Janey." April kissed her lightly. "I have a feeling I'm getting somewhere at last. And"—with smiling promise—"where I go my little sister comes, too.

"Now to find out a few things. Why Joao is Camoes but Rodriguez Carreras."

"We're Winthrop and Winter, remember," said Jane.

"But not aunt and niece. Also, Joao's position, marital and otherwise."

"Otherwise?"

"In the firm, silly. Wish me luck, Jane."

"Luck?" Jane looked at her a little stupidly. Why would April need luck? But before she could question her, she was gone.

Jane spent the time until she came back tidying her clothes. There were literally rows of them. How much money could April have left of the joint sum that she and her mother had raised for her?

She unpacked a few things of her own, taking out the koala bear and putting the furry souvenir in the wardrobe. She cleaned April's shoes in the hope that if they were bright and attractive it might encourage April to hold on to them longer.

April came in at last in fair to moderate spirits.

"He's a close one," she shrugged, "but I've discovered he's not married. I explained our half-sistership, so he was obliged to explain the Camoes and Carreras. Roddy is the son of his older sister. Much older, I'd say, for Joao isn't all that much senior to Roddy. He's really a quite fascinating young-old."

As Jane did not comment, she went on with her report.

"I don't know what he is in the firm, he was very cagey, but I'd guess he's some sort of adviser to Roddy. In which case—"

So Rodriguez was on again, Jane thought.

"Yes," said April reflectively, "I think that could be it. I think Roddy's 'sir' is, as you suggested, Jane, just Portuguese formality. I feel nearly sure about his being an adviser, because already he's advised, no, one could say *ordered*, us to go to another hotel." April tossed airily, "So you can begin to pack, Jane."

"But—but we've—I mean you've changed once already."

"On your insistence, Jane." April went into peals of laughter, reminding Jane of her implication earlier today, but, at a look in Jane's face, became instantly repentant.

"I'm sorry, Janey, but you know how important all this is to me. I could see how Joao despised the Shangri-la, so what else could I do?"

"But Rodriguez didn't despise it."

"No," agreed April quite calmly.

Jane looked levelly at her half-sister.

"April, who is it you want?" she asked directly.

April was hunting round for words. If they had been honest words they would have been, "The highest bidder." But April did not deal in honesty.

"How can you ask such a question, Jane?" she reproached plaintively. "You know how essential it is that I stand high in the family regard."

"Meaning you lied only for Rodriguez?"

"Jane, don't fuss—unless it's over clothes. The taxi will be around in an hour."

"Where are we going?"

"Some very select and elegant and no doubt as dry as dust hotel in the other end. But I rather think"—April astened her teeth over her bottom lip—"it won't be for ong."

"How do you mean?"

"There was a mention"—now April's turquoise eyes were glowing—"of going up to the Hills. That's where all he people who matter go, Jane, to take the air." She did a graceful little dance. "Oh, I do love mattering, don't you?"

But Jane stood stolid. "Where would we stop?"

"Joao's bungalow—or so I gathered. Oh, for goodness' sake get a move on, darling, the taxi will get here before we're ready."

Jane gathered up some clothes and began to fold them. Typical of April, she went to the window, not offering to help. Still, thought Jane, just to have her in a good mood is all I ask.

Then April was speaking quite furiously, her good mood gone.

"That man is in the courtyard and he actually had the nerve to look up and wave. Oh, I could choke him! If Joao happened to see him he would be quite livid."

"What man?" Jane was tucking in shoes now.

April's reply made her glance up quickly, not because April said "Terry Marsden" because Jane rather had expected Terry's name, but the manner in which April said it.

A manner angry beyond all proportion for the simple act of waving, furiously angry—yet something else as well. Somewhere in it a protesting, a futile, almost Jane could have said, a *desperate* note.

Desperate! Why desperate? Jane had never known a man yet whom April could not file in his allotted drawer.

The Senhor Camoes might prove the exception, but then Joao Camoes was exceptional himself. But Terry Marsden, well, he was definitely run-of-the-mill. A rogue undoubtedly. She, Jane, personally found him a likable rogue . . . but certainly never a threat to an intelligent, and April was extremely intelligent, girl.

Jane had pondered over it all as she had finished the packing, had received the call to proceed down to the lobby, had crossed the city to their new headquarters.

The Sterne Hotel proved just what April had said, very select and very elegant. But April never mentioned the dry as dust, because Joao Camoes himself conducted the girls there, saw them established.

"It's charming," April said dutifully of the very chaste for the tropics, building. "Such refinement, so much quieter than the Shangri-la."

Undoubtedly it was much quieter. There were no courtyards noisy with gay diners seated under gaudy sun umbrellas, no marbled bars bearing the names of Rainbow, Kismet, Nemesis . . . where young ladies could sit and toy with long exciting drinks. Instead darkened cooled rooms were set aside for tea-taking, and a quick glance told Jane that even over tea a young lady did not sit alone. There were no bands and no glittering uniforms, only a soft-footed, calm and faultless service. And no fabulous red carpet.

However, when April came up to their suite after thanking the senhor she was not as irritable as Jane had expected. At least, not at first.

She said, "By no means could you call it madly exhilarating, but I'd say there's not one guest here who is far from a millionaire."

"April, how are we—"

"Jane, don't bother me with details. I told you it was only a brief stay."

"But even a day here—" protested Jane.

"Darling, even your dim brain must have absorbed by now that I've been 'accepted.' In which case doesn't it only stand to reason that I must be especially protected, particularly when my protector is Portuguese? I really mean, Jane, everyone knows the fastidiousness of the Portuguese, how they guard their fair sex."

Jane said directly, "*Which* Portuguese?"

What her half-sister would have answered to that, either a sharp rebuke, a bantering rejoinder, or the stark truth with which April occasionally surprised you, Jane would never know, for there was a knock on the door. At a nod from April, Jane answered it.

Terry Marsden stood there.

Because their suite had its own tasteful sitting-room, Jane asked the journalist in, receiving black looks from April as she did.

"You didn't take long to cross half of Colombo." April opened the encounter in the rude manner she could when she chose to.

The newspaperman was quite unperturbed. "As long as you did," he drawled. "I tailed you."

"Well, what do you want?" April asked next.

"The routine things, Miss Winthrop." Terry smiled blandly. "How, when, where and why. Don't"—as April looked quite thunderous—"take this as personal. I cover the Sterne along with the Shangri-la, Kandy, Galle and Grand Oriental. If I failed to write you up as a Sterne guest I'd be out on my ear."

April said pointedly, "Again."

Terry smiled implacably, "Again."

"Don't you ever want to settle anywhere?"

"Don't you?"

"I'll be settling quite soon."

The journalist took up his notebook. "Can I quote you on that?" He paused, rather diabolically, Jane thought . . . "And can I say—with whom?"

Jane had asked almost the same question, but it was different for a sister. She was in sympathy with April when April fairly threw him out of the room, if a slender girl could throw a large man like Terry.

Following after the reporter, Jane said reproachfully, "You deserved that, you know."

"I know." He grinned. "I apologize to you, Janey, but not to her. I know how she ticks. I should do, I tick rather the same way myself. We're both one of a sort. She was not so much insulted as furious at being found out, found out in the waiting game, waiting to know which one will make The Bid."

"Which one?"

"Of the Portuguese gents."

"You're quite wrong," defended Jane. "Already Rodriguez—"

"I refer to the bid that matters," said Terry smoothly. "Believe me, honey, one bid matters much more than the other, and I think that's what our lovely April is after."

"Do you know the answer?" asked Jane pleadingly.

"What, want to do a spot of fishing yourself? No, take that back, kid. You're not the sort. You're only asking for your sister. Yes, of course I know. Everyone here knows."

"Will you tell me?"

"Whether Rodriguez has the money or Joao? No, I won't. Let April do the dirty work."

"The trouble is—" began Jane, then stopped. She had been about to say, "The trouble is she expects the information from me." But she was too loyal.

She need not have bothered. Terry laughed at her, lit a cigaret, called, "See you in the information library, Janey," waved an indolent arm and left.

When Jane returned to the suite, April was sitting at the phone, and she looked pleased again.

"We're all running out to Mount Lavinia, Jane."

"All?"

"Joao, Roddy, both of us."

"I really think I should stop here and write to Mother," demurred Jane. "She'll be anxious for news."

"No news yet, so why waste time and postage? You are asked, too, and I'm glad of that. A threesome is an awkward number. I'll probably need you to take Roddy off my hands."

"Rodriguez?" echoed Jane.

"Yes. I'll have to get what I want out of Joao myself, seeing you won't."

"Can't you ask Rodriguez straight out?"

"I've tried, and he hems. No, I'll go direct to the source."

In preparation April ran to her as yet unpacked case and began selecting a dress.

Jane, remembering Terry Marsden's description of Mount Lavinia . . . "creamy surf, coconut trees, everyone's dream of a tropical paradise come true" . . . thought her sister's choice of a nasturtium silk shift very apt. For herself, she did not bother, save to remove the jacket of the brown and white striped cotton suit she had worn for the trip across town.

April carefully painted on an exactly matching nasturtium mouth, loosened her lovely flaming hair to a shoulder-length silken sweep, then went to stand by the window to watch for the men.

"This is certainly a very dull hotel," she pouted presently.

"Millionaires notwithstanding?" teased Jane.

"I expect that's an exaggeration, and that they're only very rich. No doubt Mount Lavinia will prove an exaggeration, too."

"I don't think so. Terry—" Jane remembered how April loathed Terry Marsden, so did not finish. But as Terry's words concerning the beach resort flashed back again there came another flashback—*that April would have liked.*

Were it true . . . But Jane could not believe it was true. It was just *Senhor*, not *Count* Joao Camoes.

She became aware that April had turned her attention from the window to her sister. The turquoise eyes were speculative.

"What are you thinking about, Jane?"

Jane wondered a trifle hysterically what April's reaction would be if she announced: "Portuguese Counts."

April, fortunately not waiting for an answer, went on a little querulously, "I don't feel I know you like I used to. I'm beginning to think it wasn't such a good idea bringing you here."

Before Jane could remind her that she had brought herself on an award, also brought a further sum to help her sister, April snapped, "What have you done to that dress?"

"This dress?" Jane was startled.

"What other? Have you altered it or something?"

"I've removed the jacket."

April stared a long, rude moment, then turned to the window to look out again. What had happened to Jane, she was thinking. Plain Jane. Acorn-brown Jane. April's long nails pinched into her palms. For one thing, she resented Jane wasn't having the make-up trouble that she was, her powder did not streak in the humidity for the simple reason that she wasn't wearing any. The child had always had a good skin—her sole asset, really. April brightened a little and decided to be magnanimous. Jane could be very helpful, she reminded herself.

"You look quite nice," she praised, "but you want brightening. Wear my crystals."

Jane did not want the crystals. They were triple-stringed and glittering and they did not suit the simple brown and white stripe.

"Wear them," April insisted, fastening the clasp.

At that moment there was a soft knock on the door, a soft voice informing the ladies that the gentlemen were waiting, so Jane left it at that.

When they descended to the Sterne courtyard . . . no gay umbrellas and playing fountains, just stone benches under clipped shade trees . . . it was to a long sports model instead of the car that Rodriguez had driven. And Joao Camoes was at the wheel. He wore an open-necked shirt of dull cream silk, but at the throat he had tucked a pale cinnamon cravat that almost blended in with the very deep olive of his skin. His hair, sleek and shining, was brushed immaculately back. His teeth gleamed white below the small clipped moustache. He looked, thought Jane, aware by April's erect stance by her side that her sister was thinking the same, relaxed, assured . . . vitally alive.

In comparison Rodriguez Carreras appeared a little untidy . . . hair blown, tie carelessly knotted. Or was it the air of Rodriguez that gave this impression? He seemed a little ill at ease, somehow. Unsure.

To April's undoubted delight she was beckoned in to sit beside Joao. Actually relieved, for she felt she could not have found anything to say to the Senhor Camoes, Jane got in beside the much more approachable . . . well, she found him so . . . Rodriguez. They set off.

The skyline enchanted Jane; it was almost fairylike, even though, as Rodriguez archly pointed out, some of the silhouette was supplied by twentieth-century radio towers that were intermingled with the old mosques.

Nearer to earth it was less enchanting. There was

squalor here, overcrowding, and yet, Jane noticed, infinitely impressed, the children were beautiful, the women walked in grace and the men in pride. And they smiled.

"I love it," she said impetuously, and Rodriguez looked incredulous.

But the Senhor Camoes turned briefly in the driver's seat, so briefly his eyes barely left the road, and looked at Jane. Jane knew she must have been mistaken when she thought afterwards in retrospect that those dark eyes had glowed at her.

They passed rickshaws and ox-carts, and once a double-decker red London bus that Rodriguez explained would have been bought second-hand. It was only a matter of some eight miles to Mount Lavinia, but every yard to the splendid headland Jane found quite fascinating . . . then when the beautiful hotel loomed up, she was more charmed still. The eggshell blue and white she had seen on several Sinhalese edifices, but it was a loftier instance this time, pillared, terraced, many huge fans ensuring cooled air.

They went through the long corridor with the inevitable . . . Jane already had discovered . . . touts, or scouts, to clamor at you to patronize a certain shop. Joao dismissed them kindly enough but quite definitely, and veered his party to a cool terrace and a cooler lime squash.

Sipping it, April complained that the Colombo shopping was not like Singapore's.

"I saw only wooden flutes, suppercloths and baskets in the corridor 'shops,' " she shrugged, "and the jewelry —why, it was only bean beads."

Looking up from watching the ice growing smaller in her long frosted glass, Jane found Joao's eyes on her. Not really on her but on the glittering string that April had fastened round her neck. She flushed. She had known it was wrong, and undoubtedly this man, this immaculate, fastidious, knowledgable man, knew it, too. She lowered her gaze again.

The drinks finished, they walked by the beach. It was, thought Jane, dismissing her discomfiture, just as Terry had said, a dream of a tropical paradise come true. Some of the coconut palms grew right to the edge of the water, the graceful crowns wreathing rhythmically at each gentle breath of the salt wind. Under a tropical sun the sea took on a deeper brilliance, and the green vegetation of the headland interspersed with the trails of bright-yellow sand made it inexplicably vividly beautiful.

Winsomely April had thrown off her sandals and run down to the creamy rim of the sea. Taking the sandals up, Rodriguez laughingly ran after her. Jane and Joao walked on, and presently they were in a small thicket of palms, nothing in sight except bending, swaying leaves, occasionally framing in deep sweet green an inch of brilliant-blue sea. The only sound was the sough of the palm fronds and the sea wash, no human voice at all until Joao Camoes said: "So you like Colombo, little Jane?"

"Yes." Jane was a trifle confused, a trifle uncertain of herself at his low, rather teasing use of her name, but never uncertain of this pearl of an island. "Oh, yes," she said ardently again.

"I am glad of that. It is well that we are of the same mind."

We? He was referring, of course, to April. As he was Portuguese, and almost fiercely family, or so Jane, through the intense respect of Rodriguez for his uncle, had gathered, the fact that she was April's sister, even though only a half-sister, was sufficient for him to include her.

"And this Mount Lavinia," he asked. "It, too, pleases you?"

"It enchants me."

"Then you must have a memento of it." He reached in his pocket to withdraw, unwrapped, a string of bean beads. A simple string, yet . . . and Jane saw it at once . . . the only adornment for the simple cotton dress she wore. Her hands went instinctively to her throat, foolishly trying to hide the wrong glitter of the triple swing that didn't belong there. She felt her cheeks burning.

"I think," he said softly, "that these will be right, little one. May I?" Without waiting for her permission he put his long, sensitive, olive-skinned hands round her neck and unfastened the clasp of the string she already wore. His fingers were cool—yet warm. The touch was cool. But the feeling, even after he had taken the hands, and the crystal necklet, away, tingled her skin.

He held out April's trinket to Jane and she took it. She stood quite still as he doubled the bean beads round her neck. No need for fingers to fasten this time. But they brushed her skin as they slid the string from their grasp, and again the touch was cool—yet warm.

"Ah, that's better." He was standing back regarding her.

It was better. "Cottage beads on a cottage dress for a cottage girl." Jane murmured it aloud.

"That is what you want, senhorita?" His voice held a rather odd, small concern, Jane thought. "You want a cottage?"

"Yes." She laughed, trying to hide the curious tension she felt building up in her. "But I'll settle for a castle in Spain."

"I can offer you neither," he said quite solemnly, "only a *palacio* in Portugal."

"That sounds like a palace," she laughed again, not taking him seriously. "When did you buy these beads, senhor? I did not see any transaction."

"A Sinhalese sale can be very quick so long as one does not bargain. I"—his eyes were rather narrowed on her now—"never bargain. I know what I want and if it is there I pay the price."

"Your price?"

"If I want it," he persisted, "I pay the price."

Now was the time, thought Jane, while the subject was more or less to do with money, to find out what April wanted to know. But even if she had found the words Jane still could not have uttered them. She stood fingering her new necklace, aware of his deep look, so vividly aware that at last she said a little agitatedly, "I can't, of course, take these."

His brows soared in question.

"These beads," she explained.

The brows remained raised.

"It's very kind of you, but—" Her hands went up to uncoil the string, but at once his own hand shot up to prevent her.

"What is this? You took another gift."

He meant the souvenir bear. But that was different. Jane went to say so, but the words were not said. April and Rodriguez came through the palm thicket looking for them, April's lovely face a study even before her sharp glance fell on the bean beads.

Something has angered her, Jane thought. She found out what it was the moment the door was closed on their suite at the Hotel Sterne. But before that she tackled Jane about the beads. She was furiously angry, even though Joao Camoes had arranged for a theater party that night, a Sinhalese dance recital that sounded very exciting, and an invitation that April had accepted with charming enthusiasm.

But she was not charming now. She turned on Jane and took hold of the beads.

"Where did you get these?" she demanded.

"At Mount Lavinia."

"I didn't see you buy them. Why did you waste your money? You already wore a very beautiful necklace. *My* necklace. Where is it? Did you lose it, Jane?"

"Here it is." Jane handed it across. She said, hoping to appease April, "The thing's only made of beans."

But April was not to be appeased. The simple trinket on the simple dress did something for Jane, something that April could not put a finger on, and that fact infuriated her. Suddenly the cottage look, as Jane had said of herself, made everything else, and that included what April wore, exaggerated and showy. In a burst of anger, April pulled her hand down sharply and the next moment the beads were all over the floor.

With a little cry Jane went down on her knees to retrieve them, but as she crouched there she knew it was hopeless. She could never gather them all up, little more than seed-size as they were. Even if she did, she could not restring them.

April at least had the grace to be sorry.

She said so, but added, "Flimsy things, not worth worrying about. How much did you pay?"

"I didn't," Jane said a little thickly. She was upset over the beads. "The senhor bought them."

"Joao?"

"Yes."

"Bought them for you?" All at once—and fortunately—April decided to make a joke of it.

"First a teddy bear," she scorned, "then a string of bean beads. Kindergarten stuff!" She patted Jane's head, and the bean incident was closed. Though in the closing Jane all at once remembered Joao Camoes saying when she had tried to reject the bean beads: "What is this? You took another gift."

But only of a bear, as April has just said. Kindergarten stuff. And yet, recalled Jane, he had looked very adult when he had reminded her of a previous bestowal. However, she did not have time to ponder over that look. Not then—for April was on another tack.

"I don't know what to think." It was the old theme again. "I worked Roddy, but as usual got no results. I don't know whether he has or has not. You know what I mean, Jane. Probably he has, but I'd like to know for sure. And I'd like to know how much it is in comparison to what Joao has."

"April!"

"Oh, don't look so shocked. I bet you'd be interested yourself in finding out how many dollars . . . no, pesetas or something, isn't it . . . each of the Portuguese runs to. I know that Joao at least has this Hills bungalow, and that to have a Hills bungalow here, well—" She spread her hands. She went to the window . . . a favorite spot when she had a problem.

"It's tricky," she admitted. "Joao could have only the bungalow and an income and Roddy could have the entire export firm. But on the other hand. . . ."

She stood staring out on the courtyard. When she next spoke her voice had changed from concern to irritation, the same irritation as the last time she had stood at a window.

"He's there! That odious Marsden person. Writing up his little bits and pieces. There's a failure for you if you like. One thing"—a derisive laugh—"there would be no choosing him."

Jane, who had crossed to stand by April's side, looked

down, too, on the journalist. From the courtyard below he looked back at them, then, almost as though he had heard April's scornful words, he shut his notebook, turned without acknowledging either of them and left.

CHAPTER FIVE

For some time afterwards Jane felt an odd little regret for the somehow bereft look of Terry Marsden leaving the Sterne Hotel. The sense of loneliness disturbed her, the air of failure and despair. His defences had been down, there had been no cocksure, don't-give-a-damn quirk, no bantering, no giving back as good as he was given.

"What a man!" April had taunted, and there had been no sympathy in her, only a leashed, barely leashed, anger. There was something, puzzled Jane, about the journalist that got under April's skin.

She wished she could dismiss Terry as apparently April dismissed him, with an uncaring shrug, but she couldn't. She kept seeing him again, hollow, empty . . . until a care of her own, not Terry's, took the spotlight.

It happened as she reached up to bring out her shoes to wear to the theater. The bear that she had placed there tumbled down. Bending to retrieve him, her fingers closed on the soft grey fur . . . and on something else. Something she had not noticed before fastened round the soft bear neck. A bracelet. A bracelet of white opals. The bracelet that Senhor Camoes had examined at the Darwin airport, Jane felt sure of that, that he had invited Jane to examine as well. The bracelet of whose flashing depths of purple and gold in a milky sea he had said: "The white opal would be for you."

But how . . . *how* had it got here?

He had handed it to her to examine. Had she forgotten to give it back? But if this had happened how could it be fastened securely now round the neck of the bear? It could never have found its own place there. Jane looked again, double-checked. No, it was impossible. Not only was the clasp fastened but it was safety-chained as well.

At the same time that she suddenly, and tremblingly, recalled the senhor's comment at Mount Lavinia on her objection to the bean beads, that surprised: "What is this? You took another gift," April's enthralled voice, enthralled because of the opal bracelet, cut into Jane's painful recollection.

"That's quite exquisite! It's absolutely beautiful! How much did it cost? Where did you buy it?" A pause. Then, in a dangerous voice: "Jane, did *he*—"

"No. No, of course not." Jane knew she protested with her heart as well as her lips. He couldn't have . . . he mustn't have. . . . And yet the bracelet was in her hands.

In April's hands really. Thank goodness Jane had removed the circlet from the bear's neck before her sister could see the meticulous care with which it had been fastened. Otherwise Jane's subsequent, "I don't know how it got here. I'm very worried about it . . . I saw a string like this in Darwin, but—" would have rung very hollow.

But now all April's response was a gay, "Well, pet, don't worry. Darwin is Australia, and if the worst comes to the worst you can always explain."

"Explain what?"

"How you came by it, and that is entirely by accident. Also you can explain in English, Jane, not struggle in Sinhalese. All I can say is: *Ma palathe nama mokakda. . .* What is the name of this place? Joao taught me today, but it wouldn't be much use squaring off an opal bracelet, would it?" April laughed. She was pleased about the beautiful piece of jewelry. As Jane did not join her pleasure, she offered magnanimously, "You're still worried! Look, I'll wear it tonight for you and break the ice." Without waiting for Jane's permission she put it on, and, knowing April, Jane knew that that was the end, for her, of the opal bracelet. Still, she thought dreamily, though unconscious of dreaming, I have the bean beads, if not in my hands, then in my thoughts.

"They're not really my choice," April was admitting.

"I go for the black opal, but this is such a beautiful piece, Jane."

Remembering the sharp eyes of the senhor, anticipating the quick lift of his eyebrows as he saw the bracelet on April's slim wrist, dreading what he might comment but dreading more what April would say later, Jane appealed to her sister, if she must wear it, not to flaunt it.

"I feel guilty," she explained.

"Poor darling, I never do. I promise I won't even lift my wrist. Anyone would think you'd been given it by a secret lover."

"I wasn't given it at all," said Jane, not knowing whether she spoke the truth or not, but feeling that surely she must be speaking it, for Joao Camoes might give her a cheap bean necklet, but never more than that, and yet—frowning—that lock and chain. The bear, she thought a little hysterically, could never have done that.

April was whisking out an emerald chiffon, pouting at a crease.

"Darling, could you—" she coaxed.

"Yes," said Jane, needing occupation, diversion, "I'll press it for you." She took up the green filmy folds and went along to the laundry unit.

April, her dress attended to, her wrist adorned, was in an angelic mood. She cast Jane no reflective glances as Jane dressed, and the pearls she offered her for the unadorned white sheath that Jane pulled over her head were right.

Amicably the girls descended to the lobby. Even the quiet brownness of it, the lack of orchestra, pomp and show, did not discourage April. She was radiant when the men appeared, and Joao Camoes remarked on the radiance, bending gallantly to kiss her hand. It was, Jane observed thankfully, not the hand with the bracelet. Even though she knew she must broach the subject of the opal piece, she wanted to do it in a more tactful manner than April holding up her slender arm with the milky circlet of flashing stones.

A car was waiting and they sped through the darkling street to where the dance recital was to be held. In the lushness of the tropical night the seamier side of the overcrowded ways lost its squalor and became, with its lights, a Sinhalese version of the Arabian Nights.

At the theater they were shown to comfortable stage-side seats, and almost at once the dance fiesta began.

First there were Indian dancers, resplendent in richly gemmed breastplates and Turkish trousers, and it was impossible not to be carried away by the slap of the drums that beat out the rhythm for their jewelled feet.

A Kandyan troupe performed next. This, whispered Joao Camoes to the girls, was one of the most ancient art forms in existence today.

"The dancing is still pure," he explained, "despite over a century of foreign contact."

Jane watched in fascination at the graceful sinuous movements. It was totally different dancing from the Indian fiesta, it was more aesthetic.

A Devil, or Bali, dance brought the feast to the long interval. This was a dance of masks, ranging from kings to demons, and it depicted the barbaric and grotesque.

The dancers took their bows, the ornate curtains drew together, and the audience drifted out for cool drinks on an open terrace.

"It was delightful,"enthused April, "though I must say I found the last one a little uncivilized."

"It is supposed to represent a faith in the supernatural. That is one of the characteristics of the Sinhalese villager—a very inherent trait." The senhor took out his cheroots, offering one to Rodriguez, who refused and instead lit up a cigaret. Joao took his time over his cigar, then said, "Speaking of villagers brings the subject to where a villager lives." He smiled slightly. "A village, naturally."

"Yes, Joao?" April's eyes were wide and shining, her red lips slightly apart.

"I wish you to experience a village."

"Any special village?" It was April again, still waiting on his words.

"Yes, senhorita. Our own." *Our* own. So April was still not to find her answer. "Not actually our own, of course, but the grounds of Ambanta are so extensive that they comprise practically all the land, and, in maintenance, employ all the villagers."

"Tea?" asked Jane in interest.

"Yes, senhorita. Also a little coffee, though after the coffee failure in the end of the last century tea is preferred by the planters. Also, seeing our estate is extensive, and in a small island like Ceylon one crop must come on top of another, there is as well some rubber and coconut. All this is not counting our strip of jungle where we have been emulating Burma and planting teak. Though"—with a smile—"if you come, that part of Ambanta will be strictly taboo without Rodriguez or myself and several guides."

"But why, Joao?" Once more April.

"This is still a wild island in parts," related Joao. "Aside from losing yourself in those forests of blackwood you could come face to face with a sloth bear, even a leopard. In the creeks, and there are many, a crocodile. In the grasslands which fringe the jungle even a rogue elephant."

"A rogue?"

"A wild one. Ordinarily elephants cannot be shot without licences, and that is right, but with a rogue no permission is necessary."

"It all sounds very fearsome," said April.

"But wonderful." Jane was not aware that she was sitting forward in her chair, her eyes like stars. She was soon brought to heel. Annoyed at the animated picture she made, at the men's rapt attention at Jane's almost little-girl thrall, deliberately April held up her hand with the opal bracelet on it, ostensibly to adjust her shining flame hair, but no doubt to break up the unpleasing . . . to her . . . tableau.

"That is a pretty piece," Rodriguez said admiring the bracelet.

April smiled. Joao said nothing.

They went back to the dance feast, to more beating feet, swaying bodies, and vibrant, thrilling booms of drums. They had coffee in a city restaurant, after which Rodriguez by devious, yet very obvious, methods managed to spirit April into a car of his own arranging instead of his uncle's. The look on April's face as he triumphantly bore her off was rather a study. Jane did not relish her sister's return to the hotel that night.

"The conquering hero looks very happy," remarked Joao Camoes drily, "but I would not say that about the conquered, would you?"

Jane answered uneasily, "She was just taken by surprise."

Thinking this could be an opening, Jane went on, "As I was taken by surprise tonight, senhor. I was lifting down my souvenir bear when I found around its neck the opal bracelet that we were examining in Darwin. I have no idea how it got there, and I'm very upset. Do you think I could cable the firm?"

"For what reason, Miss Winter?"

"To ask them if—if—"

"If an opal bracelet has been stolen?"

"Mislaid," substituted Jane.

He had been smoking his cheroot, but abruptly he put it down.

"You are not serious, surely?"

"Certainly I am."

"You really want me to believe the bracelet took you by surprise?"

"It did, senhor."

"You had not noticed it before?"

"No."

"And even when you found it securely fastened and chained you still thought it could have got there by mistake?"

"I thought that unlikely, but—how else?" Jane was distressed.

"This is quite unbelievable," he frowned. "You did not argue with me today at Mount Lavinia when I said that you must accept the bean necklet because you had accepted a gift before."

"I—I thought you referred to the souvenir bear. Had I known, senhor, that an opal bracelet was included I certainly wouldn't have accepted that."

"That I can believe," he commented drily, "for you have not accepted it now, you have passed it on to your sister. If you are so proper, senhorita, for yourself, why is it that you are not so careful for Miss Winthrop? Oh, I know she is not a full relation, but there is still a very close tie. As a Portuguese, I cannot understand this trait in you. To us family is everything; first the closer family, and then, like the aureoles of a circle, the kith, as you call it, and the kin."

Nettled, Jane said, "I won't argue about that, instead I will question the opal bracelet. Why did you buy it, senhor? Fasten it on the bear?"

"I could have wished to bring it here without paying Customs." He yawned deliberately.

"But that wouldn't be true." It would not, Jane knew. This man would be the last man in the world to use tactics to beat Customs, he would be far too arrogant, too formal, too proper. Besides, had he not said of himself that he never bargained? Anyway, Jane doubted if on a personal string of opals any penalty would be required to be paid.

"You are discerning, senhorita. No, I did not do it for that. The piece appealed to me, so I bought it. But gems like those must be worn, not stored, otherwise they lose their vitality, so I bought them. For you. For your own sake, since you are still very naïve, child, one could almost say gauche, I spared you the embarrassment of presenting them to you personally. I used"—he took up the cheroot again—"our mutal friend the bear."

"But—but, senhor, they were expensive."

"I told you at the time a black string would be dearer."

"Yet still quite a sum."

The cheroot went down once more.

"There is something I must say to you, Jane, something I sense is very important to you"—a pause—"and your sister. It is this: Money is of no concern to me. By that I do not mean I do not value and appreciate it, but rather that I have enough never to have to think about it. In other words"—he took up the cheroot, inhaled, exhaled almost lazily—"I am well-situated." A deliberate pause. "I am rich."

His black eyes sought and held hers, they probed, they extracted.

She knew she could not let this pass. "What—what do you mean, senhor? To what are you referring?"

"You ask me that? You on whose lips such a question trembled today at Mount Lavinia. The question of my means."

She was silent and ashamed. For the words *had* been there. The words—for April.

He watched her closely, reading her guilt, and his lips thinned.

"Now," he said at length, "you can rest assured that I am worth the bother."

"Senhor!" she gasped.

"You can also inform your sister."

"Really, Senhor Camoes—"

"Yes, Miss Winter?"

But Jane could not find the words. She sat infinitely troubled until, quite unexpectedly, very gently, he leaned across and touched her hand.

"There, little one, I am harsh with you. My real reason is that Rodriguez, of whom I am inordinately fond, has become restless of late, dissatisfied. Not only these things but as well very demanding."

"Demanding?"

Joao Camoes smoked a moment.

"You must understand," he said presently, "that in a business like ours one must succeed slowly for a success to be established permanently. Rodriguez has recently wished everything at once on his plate." Through the weave of smoke the black eyes searched Jane's. "Would you know why?"

"Of course not, senhor." Jane knew she protested too quickly.

A few moments went by in absolute quiet. Then the senhor shrugged: "Well, at least you are Portuguese in that."

"In what?"

"You protect your family."

Jane got up abruptly, preparatory to leaving. Upon her rising he rose formally as well.

"You wish to go back already. But surely the young lovers will be later than this."

"I wish to go, senhor. As for the young lovers, aren't you presuming?"

"If you say so." He bowed. "I had formed my opinion by my nephew's attitude. Rodriguez, to say the least, is extremely keen. Perhaps your sister will be equally keen when you assure her that as young men go Rodriguez is favorably placed."

But that, knew Jane, would never satisfy April. Its range was too wide. It could mean just comfortable . . . or it could mean reasonably affluent. But could it mean, as Joao had said of himself, *rich*?"

Probably Rodriguez as he grew maturer would become rich. But April . . . April had to have everything at once. Suddenly something seemed to turn in Jane's heart. Did April have to have it from this man now standing beside her, helping her with her wrap?

But Joao Camoes was scornful of April, derisive.

Almost eagerly, and she was ashamed of it, Jane said, "You don't like my sister."

"On the contrary"—his voice was undeniably warm—"I admire her tremendously. She has quite fabulous beauty, and she is, I think, an honest person."

Honest? April?

"She has come to terms with herself, which in a woman is refreshing and rare. You, for instance, look in a mirror but never in your heart.".

"Is that required?" Jane's voice was stiff. She did not understand this man . . . but she did understand that for all his arrogant criticism of April he was still deeply interested in her. She remembered how he had added to his information as to his own monetary standing: "You can also inform your sister."

Did that mean he wanted Jane to tell April that he—that he—

Joao Camoes broke into her thoughts with a cool, "Tomorrow I will arrange for us to go to the Hills bungalow."

"You are too kind, senhor." She was equally cool.

"By no means kind. It is essential. Even if the family was not personally interested"—the family, noted Jane, not just Rodriguez—"even if you were merely two young ladies in Colombo, I still could not allow you to remain here. And now"—before she could argue—"I feel you might be later than Miss Winthrop, and that, for a younger sister, is not the thing."

It certainly was not the thing. One look at April's face as Jane entered their Sterne suite told Jane that.

"Where have you been? Why were you so long? Why did you let Rodriguez monopolize me like that?"

"But, April, isn't that what you want?" Jane unfastened April's pearls and handed them back to her sister. "Also we went nowhere."

"Neither did we." April was pouting. She was also troubled. "I wouldn't have minded so much if Roddy had gone on to some night club, but—" She paced the room restlessly. "Jane," she said at last, "I just don't think he has the money."

"Then, darling"—Jane felt she'd better reassure her—"he has."

"You found out?"

"Yes."

"He has the money?"

"Yes, April, he has."

But before Jane's eyes a strange thing was happening. Instead of being reassured, relieved, April seemed more troubled. She went to the window, came back. Jane had a shrewd idea of what she was thinking. She was wondering *how* much? How much compared to—to Joao Camoes?

But when April spoke it was of neither of the Portuguese gentlemen.

"He was in the lobby when we came in—that Marsden. Book, pencil and nothing else." The laugh was a little harsh, slightly hysterical.

Then April repeated derisively:

"Nothing else."

By ten the next morning they had left the Hotel Sterne—and Colombo—for Joao Camoes' Hill bungalow in the village of Ambanta.

To Jane's surprise it had been April who had held back at the last moment, April to whom this very significant move to a private abode Jane would have thought would have comprised a considerable triumph. But April, even while Jane had packed, had demurred.

"Don't you think several cases will be sufficient? We could leave the remainder at the Sterne."

"I think Senhor Camoes wishes us to take all of them." Jane repeated to her sister what Joao had said to her.

He had stated definitely: "Even if you were merely two young ladies in Colombo I still could not allow you to remain here."

"How dull," said April.

"What do you mean—dull?"

"I don't mean Joao or Roddy, of course." April's answer had been quick. "But I do mean the Portuguese protection. Such a boring word, protection."

"But, darling"—Jane had been worried, for after all, if she married a Portuguese April must learn to agree as well as decree—"protection is one of their characteristics, and if you're really serious—"

"Of course I'm really serious. What on earth gave you the idea I was not serious." Irritable—to Jane's idea—beyond all proportion, April had fairly flung herself across the room to stare moodily out of the window.

"It's all right for you," she said presently, "you'll be really interested in all those barbaric things that Joao told us about. You'll remark on the tea crop, the rest of the odious industries, and mean it. I'll be near to tears."

"But being April won't show it," said Jane with determined cheerfulness. "Look at it this way if you can't raise any other enthusiasm: your make-up will remain perfect. You're always complaining of the stickiness here."

But April was not to be jollied. She simply stood at the window while Jane finished the last case. But when, having been bidden by the hotel porter, the girls descended to the lobby, and the car into which they were ushered proved a larger and more expensive version than any that they had driven in yet, April began to become her old self.

Her quick, acquisitive turquoise eyes took in the quiet

resplendency of the limousine, the immaculate uniform of the smiling Sinhalese who opened the door. She saw years of such service, such resplendency, her only immediate problem which of the two charming Portuguese would ensure the greater grandeur. Forgetting the boredom she had foreseen in Joao's Hills bungalow, April for the present chose the maturer man and stepped in beside him in the seat immediately behind the driver. Jane got in with Rodriguez in the rear compartment.

There were glass divisions, but they were not pulled up. Jane could hear April's gay chatter as the car travelled through the Colombo streets. She was temporarily silenced, however, as another car, a shabby sports model in London bus red, eased past them from the opposite direction.

"Terry Marsden," said Rodriguez by Jane's side. "He must be after a story."

April was pulling out her cigarets, fumbling with the lighting of one. With a little low laugh the Senhor Camoes took over and presently April looked her bland beautiful self again.

Jane turned her attention to the scenery. They were still in the low country, and around the coastal flats through which they were travelling she knew to expect coconut palms and later fields of paddy. She asked Roddy about it all, but found him disappointingly vague. Either that or his attention was on April.

Yet somehow he did not seem so absorbed with her sister as he had seemed before. He looked, or so Jane considered, almost introspective.

At her third attempt to inquire about the paddy fields, Joao Camoes, at a gesture, stopped the car.

"This is scandalous," he said in mock-rebuke to his nephew, "here we have a thirsty student and no spring of information at which to quench her thirst."

Rodriguez mumbled something about never having found very much to interest him in the Sinhalese cultivation, a statement that brought a frown to his uncle and a concealed quirk of amusement from April.

"We will change positions," said Joao Camoes. "You will sit where I am sitting, Rodriguez."

He had got out as he spoke, and now stood impatiently waiting for Rodriguez to change seats. Once more the limousine set off.

Now Jane did not have to ask, she was told, and told so graphically that she found herself leaning forward in her seat to follow every gesticulation of the senhor, every wave to some new aspect.

"The flowers of the rice," indicated Joao, "are borne in a tuft, each on a separate stalk. The threshed paddy is sifted and winnowed clean and then separated into husked rice by hulling."

"Are these crops," asked Jane about the submerged fields, "watered by rainfall or irrigation?"

"We are fortunate here in the more mountainous south with our monsoon rains from May to September, the lowland north is less rainy, so cannot depend, as we can, on natural methods."

Now the car was beginning to climb, and with every grade there was an almost startling change of scenery. Presently they came to a gigantic mass of rocks, and the driver stopped, evidently anticipating their interest. However, only Jane and Joao got out to admire the vista, Jane catching her breath at train lines set on mere shelves hewn from the scarped precipice.

"Why, yes," said the senhor, surprised, "there is a train, did you not know? We are quite proud of our comfortable and extremely scenic service." Abruptly he left Jane staring out at ravines, crags and serrated edges to speak with the driver. Then he spoke with April and Rodriguez. Finally he came back to Jane.

"We are in luck, a train will be coming along fairly soon. It can take us some of the way to Ambanta. The car will await at an arranged station to pick us up again. You would like that?"

"Oh, senhor, yes, yes!" Jane's eyes were shining.

"I would like it myself," he smiled, pleased at her eagerness, "I am fond of trains."

"All boys are."

"Boys, senhorita?" He was laughing openly now.

"Men are only big boys."

"I bow to the knowledgable female." He actually, and laughingly, did bow.

"But how," he asked at once, "do you explain my nephew Rodriguez who prefers to travel in the car?"

"I would explain that by saying that my sister prefers to remain as well," proffered Jane.

"Love, senhorita?"

Jane knew that in April's instance . . . just now, anyway . . . the reason was comfort, April hated to move around more than she had to. However she did not correct the senhor.

"Perhaps," she agreed. Then, to change the subject, "But how can we take the train? There's no station."

"It is well concealed behind that thicket of splendid satinwood and mahogany, and its name, my man tells me, is Paraka."

"Then," said Jane gaily, "by all means let us take the train from Paraka."

She went back to the car to get her handbag and was rather surprised to receive from April instead of the glowering look she rather expected a listless one instead.

"Darling, you make me feel quite exhausted," April mildly complained. "You're actually going to walk to a funny little station and catch an odd little train. Well, it's your choice." She leaned back against a nest of cushions that her Roddy thoughtfully had arranged.

Jane and the senhor set off down a narrow track and the big car resumed its journey again. Scarcely had it turned a bend in the road than the senhor asked rather abruptly, "Your sister, Miss Jane, she was wholehearted, too?"

The "Miss Jane" surprised Jane, but the question that came after her name surprised her more.

"Wholehearted, senhor?" she queried.

"You told me on the journey from Sydney that you had left nothing behind you, that you and your heart travelled together."

"I and my heart," concurred Jane.

"And Miss April? Pardon me if I sound probing, but she is—well—" He searched for a moment, then said with triumph: "Preoccupied. Correct?"

"Yes. And I agree with you that she is just that. But I think it may be the heat."

"When it is not hot? Not up here. Had you not noticed?"

Glad to be done with the rather edgy subject of April's moods, Jane acclaimed, "Why, yes, it's hot no longer, it's quite pleasant." She stopped abruptly, excited. "Senhor, is that a monkey?"

"It is, child. It is a small variety called the macaque. The larger ones are called wanderoos, and they have black eyebrows, white beards and short hair."

"But a monkey!" Jane beamed.

Joao shrugged tolerantly. "Monkeys are everywhere in Ceylon except the settled areas."

"What else could I meet?" Jane begged.

"It would be very unlikely that you would encounter an elephant, for they are, unfortunately, dying out in our dwindling jungles. I have, however, one at Ambanta that you will see."

"Perhaps a leopard, senhor?"

"So near to the rest-house . . . yes, there will be a rest-house at the station . . . very improbable. But deer, perhaps, many wonderful birds, and, with extremely good fortune, a loris."

"Loris?"

"A lemur about the size of a squirrel."

"And why the extreme good fortune?"

"Because it is said that if you catch a tear from the eye of a loris you can make a love potion."

"Is that," asked Jane, "another of the things in which you trade?"

"Love potions? No. But thank you, senhorita, for the idea. Look, we are through the track and at the rest-house. There is the small station, and if your eyes can see a long distance down to the grasslands you will glimpse a moving spot that is our train."

Jane looked beyond the simple building and the small shelter to an aspect that fairly grabbed at her heart. Imposing cliffs, ribbed with rock, laced with tumbling waters, clad in unnumbered trees and knee-deep in flowers that almost accosted her in their brilliant regalia.

"Joining the train at Paraka," informed Joao Camoes, "you will be spared Sensation Peak where the train crawls round a sheer ledge just wide enough to permit the track and where you can feel the wind blow. Even as it is, senhorita, you will travel several curves where the guard and the driver can exchange civilities in passing. Have you a brave as well as a whole heart?"

"I will look only at the beauty," she assured him. She said it seriously, for she knew she had never known such beauty as this.

He nodded as gravely back again, then put his long, fine brown hands together as in a prayer and bowed very slightly. "*Ayubowen*," he said.

"That is?"

"A greeting. A Sinhalese greeting to you for loving this lovely land."

On an impulse Jane turned again to the vista, joined her own hands together and bowed. "*Ayubowen*," she repeated.

When she turned back to the senhor it was to dark eyes so deep, so warm that for a moment she knew a strange yet curiously sweet trembling. In that moment their gazes met and held . . . held until a small Sinhalese boy trotted up, proud in a white jacket over white shirt and sarong, to announce something to the senhor.

Joao nodded, then said a little diffidently to Jane, if this proud Portuguese knew diffidence, "The rest-house has made tea. We have time before the train climbs the mountain."

Suddenly shy herself, not understanding why, Jane followed the man and the boy to the verandaed building. There were several other small boys watching them from the shade of a golden bamboo, but obviously they were not as important as the small messenger, for their sarongs were just tubes of cotton, and they wore no shirts.

"Yes," smiled the senhor, "they envy our escort."

"Class distinction in Ceylon?"

"Quite a lot, as a matter of fact. The 'trousered' class is more esteemed than the saronged, and, of course, the takers of life, like hunters and fishermen, are what you might term on the outside."

"Well," smiled Jane, "on the outside, is the more pleasant in this rest-house." She had glanced into the rather dim, through lack of sufficient windows, interior. "Can we sit on the patio?"

"By all means." Joao Camoes clapped his hands. He gave the order in Sinhalese, then turned to Jane.

"They will bring black tea which we will take with lime. Does that please you? I know that usually it is China tea that the English palate associates with the sliver of lemon, but you will like the tang, I am sure, of these local limes once they marry with the Souchong blend I have ordered."

His choice of the word "marry" reminded Jane of the advertising school award and how she had borrowed from the *Sinhalese Observer*. She laughingly told the senhor about it.

"Yes, it is true that in Sinhalese marriage the planets must be favorable, it is as important really as physical and mental compatibility. Dowries, of course, are excluded." He took out his cheroots. "The Sinhalese husband," he remarked, snipping off the top of the cigarillo, "assumes the authority over his wife that was exerted by her father. The wife"—he lit the cheroot —"defers in all ways to her lord."

"Lord, senhor?"

"He is that—to her. She walks a few steps behind him, never sits in his presence or that of his friends." A weave of blue smoke. Then: "You wrote this exercise, senhorita, on a suggestion from an *Observer* that your sister had sent you?"

"Yes."

"Why had your sister come alone to Ceylon?"

"Alone? She was on a ship."

"You choose to misunderstand me." The depth and warmth had gone from the black eyes. "I am well aware that there would be many on the ship, that she would be indeed surrounded, but that does not make for chaperonage, senhorita."

Which is very important in Portugal, interpreted Jane, and very important to you.

Aloud she said rather bluntly, "She came by herself as I came by myself."

"But you came for a reason: to be with your sister. A worthy reason, I think. But for what reason did your sister come?"

Here could be a trap, recognized Jane. If she answered back, as she felt dangerously like answering back: "What does it matter?" it could matter—for April. These things mattered to him, to the senhor, and he could make them matter for her sister.

It seemed a time for truth to Jane, so she answered the truth. She told him of April's ambitions for the theater.

"A singer?" he said, surprised. He smoked a while. "Yet she disembarked at Colombo."

"She met Rodriguez."

"He is not a singer."

"I didn't say he was."

"You misunderstand me again. How would my nephew meet your sister?"

Exasperated, Jane burst out, "How do young people meet, senhor—have you forgotten?"

It was an unfortunate rejoinder, for she saw the red mounting slowly from his throat, and knew he was very angry.

"I do not know, senhorita, how young people meet in your country, I only know how they meet in mine."

"Dully." She said it deliberately, for she was desperately angry with herself and her clumsiness, and it made her tongue acid.

He must have thought it acid, too, for after the tea and lime had been left before them he looked long at the lime, then said, "Cream would have been a blander choice."

Jane did not reply. She knew that the Souchong and delicate sliver of fruit was very refreshing, but in her present state of emotions it almost choked her.

She was glad when he told her not to toy with her cup but drink the contents as the train was climbing the last rise.

She did so, then followed him to the small station just as the little puffing engine and its several carriages came to an exhausted halt.

He helped her into the one first-class compartment,

then after a brief spell and some water the train set off.

It was quite as delightful . . . and hazardous . . . as Jane had anticipated. The British, the Portuguese said, had done this masterpiece of engineering, had thought out its ledges, its boring through mountains, its crossing of ravines, its climbing to dizzy heights. As for the beauty, the Pearl itself had supplied that.

On the rim of the tea district, at a tiny station very much like Paraka, Jane and Joao left the train and climbed a short track to the road. There, as Joao had planned, his car awaited. April sat in the car, but Rodriguez was standing some yards away talking to a man. Some yards away again was a shabby sports model whose London bus red hue brought instant recognition. It was Terry Marsden's. The man was Terry.

Jane half-stopped.

"What is it, senhorita?" It was Joao Camoes, cool, poised, waiting.

"That—that man—" she stammered.

"Yes. Mr. Marsden."

"Why—why is he always—"

"Yes?"

"Nothing." Again Jane had need to bite her lip.

"I think you are trying to ask why do you always seem to encounter him. But that is understandable, surely? A journalist must be here, there, everywhere."

"Even up in the Hills? The tea district?"

"We are not actually in the tea district yet, but yes, there, too. Possibly he is doing an article on the tea estates of Ceylon. There are not so many now, the days of the big resplendent holdings are gone, but there are many smaller acreages that are very lovely, and I think he might be doing a series for an English publication, who knows, even coming to Ambanta for copy, for our home, as you will see, senhorita, is very lovely."

"You—you speak almost as though you approve of him, senhor."

A look of surprise. "But I do."

"Yet on the night of my arrival—"

"That was entirely different." The voice now was stiff. "Any disapproval then was for you."

"It sounded for him as well."

"Then if it did it was because he was with you. As man to man I like the man. I know he is not regarded well in all walks, but I like him."

"As man to man?" hazarded Jane.

"Exactly."

"But when a woman is involved it's changed?"

"Yes. Is there anything unreasonable in that?"

She did not reply. She was too busy trying to decipher April's expression now that she had come near enough to read it. As before she found it not as easy as April's usually was to read. All, indeed, she could say was that April was no longer listless.

Terry waved a casual arm to Jane, then went back to his rather vulgar model. Rodriguez held the door open, then he and Joao got in together, and they resumed their journey.

Rodriguez said, "Terry Marsden is doing a tea series for an English syndicate. I said by all means to come to Ambanta. That was right, sir?" April's brows met as they always did at her Roddy's deference.

"Perfectly right," nodded Joao. He smiled perfunctorily at Jane. "You see, I was correct."

"How far have we to go now? I'm tired." April added a plaintive tremor to her voice to hide the fretfulness.

But any fretfulness should have been wiped away the moment the car rounded the plantain-planted drive of the Hills home of Joao Camoes. As at the rest-house looking down on the splendid vista of the rock-ribbed, water-laced mountains, Jane's heart was grabbed up in the exquisite pain of the very beautiful once more.

The grass, greener than green, framing the splendid house . . . no mere bungalow this . . . the formal shrubs, the permitted intrusion of native flora, the Portuguese addition of stone benches, urns of spilling flowers, a fountain, a lily-pond, the profusion of terraces, summer houses and seat-encircled trees, reached at her. Surely the scene must reach April, too, even a little. At least take that unrest away.

But in the suite to which their bags were carried April might just as well have remained in the Sterne, before

that in the Shangri-la. She went at once to the window to
stare out . . . but not, and Jane knew it, at the loveliness.

"That man—" she said, as Jane had said, but much
more troublously. Strangely, inexplicably troublously.

"Well, what about him?" Jane asked practically.
"What does it matter that he's writing a series up here in
the Hills? I mean, April, what can it matter to you?"

She expected a sharp retort, or a shrug of indifference,
or a cutting criticism . . . anything but what April *did*
reply.

For:

"You don't understand!" April cried more than said.
"You don't see that I—that we—"

She wheeled sharply and went out of the room. The
next moment Jane heard her laughing in the hall with
Rodriguez. But the laugh had a high unnatural note in it,
it rang too gay.

Too gay, thought Jane, at a loss, for turquoise eyes that
had slid away from hers to hide their tears.

April . . . April of all people *crying*!

CHAPTER SIX

By dinner that night April was entirely recovered. She
had been taken on a tour of the house and grounds, and
what had met her eyes had evidently settled a question.
No longer did she laugh over-gaily, or slide her troubled
glance away. Her turquoise eyes were wide and bright,
and she asked innumerable questions over the special
Sinhalese meal that Joao had had his staff prepare.

As the staple Ceylon diet was rice, it was offered now in
the form of *buriani,* made, the senhor said, from rice,
mutton, ghee—which was buffalo milk butter—onions,
cardamon and lemon-grass. A very hot *sambol,* made of
chillies and lime juice, accompanied it, and a *pilau,* which
was saffron rice with raisins and *cadju,* or cashew, nuts.

Jane, for her part, for the dishes were extremely

satisfying, was glad that the sweets comprised only a dish of fruit that was new to the visitors—sour-sop, jaks, rambuttans, plantains from the trees that bordered the drive and pomegranates. As she peeled a plantain, coarser than Australian bananas, Jane let her glance rove round the large room, furnished entirely in cool rattan, but, because in these hills the air was more moderate, with the warm addition of fabric curtains instead of the coastal bamboo.

In the choice of drapes she saw the touch of the Portuguese, that trend to the heavy rather than to the airy, to rich, flowing brocades in glowing colors of clarets, russets, dark plums and dull golds.

Seeing her interest, Joao Camoes smiled, "We had to have a touch of home. You see, this house was English-built, and though we love it, it was still not our own brainchild."

"English-built? Yes, I can see that now." Jáne remembered wondering slightly upon arrival here at the faintly Tudor air. "So the English came before the Portuguese."

"On the contrary, senhorita, we were the first, in 1501. The date is carved on a rock which is now preserved in Colombo. But our particular family came after an English tea-grower, so, of course, the house was already built." He smiled sincerely. "I do not think we could have improved on it had it been the other way about."

"It's a very beautiful place." April was looking around her with charming enthusiasm. Only Jane, thought Jane, would glimpse the measured, the acquisitive look.

As though all at once she was unable to bide her time any longer, April asked with a sweet childish candor and naïveté of the senhor: "Is it *your* house?"

"Mine."

"Not Roddy's as well?"

"No, mine."

With a deliberation that was so determined that every action seemed marked, seemed emphasized, the senhor took out his cheroots, adding, "*And* the firm, too, Miss Winthrop. *And* the tea estate."

There was a little silence in the room. Jane felt herself

stiffening—for April. Really, the senhor could have chosen a better time to tell her sister where she stood!

Then quite charmingly, very gallantly, Joao Camoes said, "But Rodriguez is quite excellently placed. His jewels, I should say, are far worthier than mine."

The little pulse that had begun to beat fiercely in April's fair brow at the news that Senhor Camoes had given her at once lost its fevered tempo.

"Roddy told me about his jewels," she said eagerly. "They—they are really his?"

"Very much so. Rodriguez always has taken far more interest in that side of the business. He has an excellent collection of zircons, amethysts, topazes, moonstones."

"Rubies and sapphires." April barely breathed it. Her lips were parted in anticipation, her eyes dreamed.

Rodriguez, looking at her in positive enchantment, said softly, "They are yours for the asking, I assure you of that."

April smiled softly back at him, all radiance, all sweet young love.

"For myself," the senhor remarked, though only Jane now listened, the other two were gazing at each other, "my preference goes to a string of bean beads."

He in his turn was looking at Jane, and, embarrassed, Jane came back with, "Not an opal bracelet?"

"What is that?" he asked blandly. "I have never seen one save on the wrist of your sister, Miss Winter."

Still the other two remained unconscious of the interchange, so Jane, to break the tension, inquired busily, "Where are these jewels found?"

"Ceylon's minerals are scattered in many districts, but we are fortunate enough to be able to mine in our own land. Ratnapura, into which the Ambanta property extends, is one of the most promising sources of this Isle of Gems, as it was once known. Sinbad"—he smiled at Jane—" reputedly found many of his jewels here."

"Is that true?"

"As true, I expect, as that Lanka—"

"Lanka?" she queried.

"Sri Lanka, meaning the resplendent land, and meaning Ceylon, was the original Garden of Eden, and as true as the belief that Solomon took his gold, silver, ivory, apes and peacocks from these very shores.

"For myself, as I said, it matters little. I prefer—"

"A bean necklace," said Jane.

"With a firm cream throat to hang it on."

"But I'm sallow," Jane blurted. Suddenly sallow no more but a flaming pink, she added, "I mean—if you were speaking of me—I really mean—"

"I was," he said clearly. "And you are not."

What she could have answered to that, Jane did not know. She was grateful that the interchange of looks between April and Rodriguez came to an end, that with the arrival of liqueurs the talk became general.

The girls went to bed early. Joao Camoes had planned a tea growing and packing inspection for the following day. He also wished to speak on business matters with Rodriguez.

"But do not feel you must go to your rooms on that account," Joao bowed.

"We must," laughed April. "Well, I must, anyway. Beauty sleep, senhor."

"That I can believe," he said admiringly, and, indeed, April had never looked more beautiful. The talk of gems had animated her. Rodriguez's devotion had given her a radiance.

In the suite afterwards she was still in the same sweet mood.

"All those jewels, Jane," she thrilled, "and all of them dear Roddy's! You know how I've always felt over jewels. Roddy, too, is excellently placed, Joao said so himself. Undoubtedly the senhor has the greater wealth, but it would be tied up in this estate, and, darling, I'd be bored to tears. Besides, Roddy is fun, and"—a winsome glint—"very easy to handle. Oh, yes, I think everything is fine."

She even kissed Jane in her gay mood.

Yet, crossing to the window for a brief moment before she got into bed, the mood dropped from her like a discarded cloak, and she stood suddenly childish somehow. Vulnerable. Unsure.

There were no moods, even brief ones, the next day as Joao and Rodriguez showed the girls over the estate.

Even though April could hardly sustain the interest she pretended, could barely wait for the inspection to be over so that she could see the jewels that Roddy had locked in the Ambanta strong-room and which he had promised to show to her, she was still sweet, gracious, and, outwardly anyway, enthralled.

It was not until Terry Marsden made an appearance that her veneer cracked . . . but that was hours away.

They set out after breakfast in two jeeps, April in her present mood going instinctively to Rodriguez's rover, leaving Jane perforce to climb into Joao's. It was a macadamized road for lorry transport, but very soon Joao, in the foremost jeep, turned into a cart-track, one of literally scores of such tracks, all steep of gradient, occasionally crossing bridges over ravines, over culverts, over "Irish drains" which were paved crossings where the amount of water to be taken off did not justify the expense of more than just that.

The jeep went past storage for tools, storage for fertilizer, carpentry shops for the building of more and more dwelling houses, although there were many distributions already of small neat accommodation huts. They went past the nursery where the young tea plants waited, past Tamil boys working on boundary fences to keep out stray cattle and buffaloes. Everything, Jane noted, was done with almost mathematical accuracy, and this, Joao told her, was the pattern of the tea estates.

"Some 'contour,' " he said, "some 'slope,' but always we work by compass and line."

Close planting, Jane found when they reached the first work section, was practised, enough breathing space for the tea bushes to grow to their full stature, but not too much, for they were also expected to provide an umbrella for the soil.

"In my matured fields," said Joao, "I do not like to see any ground. Not"—a little sadly—"that even green umbrellas in rhythmical rows can bring back one small iota of the natural beauty that once was."

They proceeded along to the plucking, and here even

April did not have to pretend enchantment. It was like looking at gay butterflies fluttering above green grass to see the pluckers working their way along the rows. They carried large bamboo baskets slung to their backs by means of a cord wound round their foreheads, and as most of the pluckers were young, pretty women whose taste ran to vivid colors, the rows of green tea bushes were interspersed with brilliant reds, purples and golds.

The bushes themselves, trained to a height of three feet by pruning, yielded a crop every two weeks. This "flush," or crop, demonstrated Joao, comprised of a tender closed leaf bud and the next two leaves, young and succulent. They alone were plucked. It was fascinating to watch the women's fingers darting over the surface of each bush, gathering the crop in small heaps, then throwing them over the shoulder into the waiting basket. The leaf was not to be crushed, not to be bruised, and Jane marvelled that with all the speed this was never done to the tender plants.

The leaf next was weighed on the field and then transported to the factory. There it went through five processes that took the party the entire morning to examine . . . the withering, rolling, fermenting, firing and finally grading.

Jane, standing at last beside a fragrant heap of black, crisp tea, waiting for sorting, sifting then packing, said thirstily that that was all she could now ask: a cup of green umbrellas reduced to an amber beverage.

"And you shall have it," Joao assured her.

He was in a happy mood, as elated over his tea as April had been over Rodriguez's gems last night.

April smiled brightly but a little pityingly at his enthusiasm. Jane knew her sister was thinking that it had all been very interesting—if you liked that sort of stuff.

Sipping the tea that Joao had ordered to be served in the overseer's office, April's full mouth kept up its happy quirk. She was thinking of pigeon's blood rubies, no doubt, thought Jane tolerantly, grateful that at least April could smile, could forget her moods.

Then the curve was going quickly downward. The mood was returning. Returning with Terry Marsden

strolling casually into the office, greeting everyone yet no
one, giving April a long cool stare, seating himself
without being invited, helping himself to tea, taking out
his notebook.

"I'd like your opinion," he was saying in a clear
arresting voice to Senhor Camoes, "as to deep-forking.
Heresy? A waste of good top-soil? What method do you
use"—he paused—"your Excellency?"

He had chosen his moment. The question, intelligent,
to the point, had silenced the tea-drinkers so that Terry's
voice cut knife-sharp into the quiet.

The effect was almost electric, even to Jane, who had
been told of the senhor's rank before. She had neither
believed, nor disbelieved, it. She had not been really very
interested. But April. . . .

April's cheeks were drained, her eyes were so big they
seemed to use nearly all her face. She looked from Terry
to Joao, then back to Terry again.

Into the silence came Terry's voice once more. "That's
true." The Englishman grinned.

There was another silence, a silence fairly screaming
out to be broken, broken by a denial . . . or an agreement.
An agreement it was.

Completely bored, quite indifferent, Joao Camoes
tossed, "Quite true. I am the Conde de Camoes. Your
question again, Marsden? Oh, yes, deep-forking, was it
not? In my opinion, and on my estate—"

Jane did not hear the rest. Her attention was on April,
April rising slowly, almost, it seemed, with difficulty,
from her chair, crossing to stand at the door to look out.
She did not turn back until, the deep-forking question
settled, Joao Camoes issued an invitation to Terry
Marsden to move into Ambanta and finish his series
there.

"We have ample room. You can have the quiet that
writing demands."

"But your other guests—" Terry demurred falsely, for
his eyes were gleaming wickedly—glinting at April.

What else could April do than murmur a politeness?
Jane smiled at Terry, to which he responded with a sly
wink.

On the way back to the big house Jane found herself in the showy red sports car. Marsden quite impudently had placed her there, but, apart from a momentary stiffening of the straight back, a brief disapproving line to the long mouth, the senhor paid little attention. Even if he had wished to keep the previous arrangement, he had no opportunity to do so. Making some excuse, April got in beside Joao, leaving Rodriguez to travel back alone.

Starting the noisy engine of the car, Terry smiled sourly.

"She's wasting no time," he said.

"What do you mean, Terry?"

They were on the cart-track now, Terry keeping within seeing distance of the jeeps for the connecting tracks wound intricately and it would have been easy to get lost.

"Oh, come off it, Jane, you know what I mean. You saw milady's face just now."

"When you—when you—"

"Spilled the news of the peerage? Yes. You could see change of mind flicker across that lovely face just as unmistakably as if it was written down in words of one syllable. Two syllables really." He laughed harshly. When Jane did not inquire, he said, "Count-ess. With emphasis on the *ess*."

"Oh, Terry!" she exclaimed reproachfully.

"But it's true, isn't it?"

"Not true." Jane spoke determinedly. "She's going to look at Rodriguez's jewel collection this afternoon."

"Betcha!" Terry inserted almost brutally.

"I beg your pardon?"

"I bet you the title wins over the rubies."

Jane did not reply. The title would win—when it was April. How could it not win? She wanted to feel indignant against her sister, but all at once, she could not have said why, she felt inexpressibly sad. For herself.

"Terry," she asked presently, "why did you do it?"

"Had to, Janey." His words were a little thick.

"Had to?" Jane could not understand.

In a staccato voice now Terry tossed, "When . . . if . . . I mean if pigs fly . . . you understand . . . well, I'd want to have everything levelled out."

"I don't know what you're talking about, Terry."

Marsden said with an attempt of lightness, "That makes two of us."

As they came down the drive of plantains he asked Jane what she would be doing that afternoon.

"I told you." Jane was cross. "April will be inspecting the jewels."

"Not unless Joao inspects them, too. Anyway, I never asked about milady, I asked about you."

"And why? It won't matter to you. You'll be writing in some quiet corner."

"Not me. It was good of Camoes to invite me, and I rushed the invitation, but I'm a newspaperman and I need no quiet corner, my love."

"Don't call me that."

"Why not, Jane? Is it because you are someone else's love?" His eyes probed hers.

She did not answer. She just stared steadily . . . and candidly, or so she thought . . . back at him. She was surprised, and a little dismayed, when presently he said softly, "Poor kiddo, poor little Jane."

"What, Terry?"

He did not explain, and in some odd way she was relieved for that. She got out of the sports car, did not wait to hear his proposal for the afternoon but hurried along to her room.

The moment she entered the room, which adjoined April's by a communicating door, her heart sank. April was standing in the middle of the room, no dreaming by the window now, and she was furious.

"That Marsden has edged himself right in this time. Of all the insufferable louts!"

She paced the room, then said, not quite so angrily, "And yet in a way he's done me a service. I didn't know . . . I never dreamed. . . ."

"You mean," said Jane flatly, "the Senhor Camoes being a Count."

A word of two syllables, she thought, Count-ess. Count-*ess*.

"Of course," April said.

"It makes a difference?"

"Darling, don't be completely naïve. Money will buy Roddy's rubies and sapphires, but money will never buy Joao's title. The Countess. *The Condesa*." Quite unashamedly April thrilled.

"But he doesn't use it. Joao doesn't go by his title."

"Not now, but when he's married it could be a different tale."

"It would be redundant at Ambanta, and he loves and intends to stop at Ambanta."

"That also could be a different tale. Oh, if only I'd known all this before I wouldn't have wasted the time that I have."

"You mean—"

"Yes, my little greenhorn, I mean just that. Don't look so righteous. Wouldn't you?"

"No."

"If you had known Joao was a count?"

"I did know. At least"—at a sudden narrowing of April's turquoise eyes—"I'd heard Terry mention it."

"Oh, so that's it! That's why you haven't left any stone unturned to worm your own way into Joao's attention. That's why you stopped back with him at the restaurant after the dance fiesta, travelled in the train with him, rushed to be in his jeep this morning, asked questions aimed to alert him as to your intelligence, for it would have to be intelligence, wouldn't it, Jane? You certainly have nothing else!"

"April!"

"You little brown nothing, how dare you pit yourself against me. Oh, yes, you did. Deliberately you withheld his title from me, for you saw yourself in the role of countess. You! Plain Jane! That's a laugh." But April did not laugh.

"You nearly fell over yourself telling me how Roddy was well-placed, you wanted a match with Roddy and me so that you—that you—"

"*April!*"

This time Jane's voice did reach her sister, and the lovely girl stopped her pacing to come and stand by Jane.

"I'm sorry." Typical of April, she could subside at once. "None of it's true. You probably are the greenhorn

that I said, the fact that Joao is a count would mean
nothing to you. I should have remembered how you
always were a rather sweet imbecile, Janey. Take it all as
unsaid. I don't know what's come over me. I always was
an acid drop, but never as acid as this."

"Does all this mean that you're not—will not—"

"No, it doesn't, if you're referring to my plans—with
Count Camoes." April lit a cigaret then exhaled slowly.

"They go right ahead. I start this afternoon, Jane.
When Joao spoke on the way back about his wretched
elephant I immediately clamored to see it . . . implied that
cold things like rubies were nothing to a big clumsy beast.
Only I said something like the noble jungle king." She
laughed.

"No doubt," she resumed harshly, "Roddy will be
desolated. I only hope he doesn't take it out on the jewels
and fling them away. Not that it matters to me, I'll never
wear them. Though I've been thinking. . . ." She stood
there absorbed in her thoughts.

Then she turned to Jane and said without a trace of
embarrassment, "I've been thinking about tiaras, Jane,
and whether a Portuguese Countess. . . .

CHAPTER SEVEN

As it turned out four, not two, went to see the Ambanta
elephant that afternoon, April, Joao, Jane and Terry.
Rodriguez either had other business to attend or was
sulking because of the treatment he was receiving. When
Jane spoke to him at lunch she saw some sulkiness but
much more conjecture. The rather boyish glance every
time it turned on April held an almost estimating glint.

April had put on, for the inspection, perfectly tailored
jodhpurs that Jane had not seen before. Beside them her
own slacks looked shabby, and, no doubt through wear,
rather baggy. But April was pleased with her sister's
appearance, seeing it as a sharp contrast to her own,

and she forgave Jane for her being included in the party.

She did not forgive Terry, though. After giving him a sharp loathing look when he joined them on the veranda she never intentionally glanced his way again.

Joao took the lead through the bushes and the others followed in file, April behind Joao, Terry at the rear. The elephant, Joao related as they clambered down the gully reserved for Vasco . . . the Ambanta elephant had been given a Portuguese name . . . was not a ferocious king of beasts. "I must beg your pardon," he paused turning to the girls, "but the elephant has always been that to me, and not the lion. No, on the contrary he is entirely vegetarian. He eats wood pulp from tree branches."

April said naïvely she was pleased about that.

"Yes, you would make a tender dinner," smiled Joao. Terry's wicked eye caught Jane's and ticked up a point for Jane's sister.

"Wild elephants are still around," related Joao, "but when I say wild I do not mean savage, for elephants are seldom that. There are rogues . . . we have one on the rim of the grassland worrying us now . . . but it is an exception, never a rule."

"How did Vasco come to Ambanta?" called Terry.

Joao smiled. "He simply came. In all the animal world there is always a certain one, an 'Elsa,' shall we say, who needs more than a fellow beast, who needs man. Vasco just came, as I said, came, I really believe, for love."

"We never fenced him . . . we left the way open for him to return to his haunts, but the years went on and he stopped. So"—Joao shrugged—"this became his gully and we did enclose it. Fortunately there are many trees, thus a lot of wood pulp, for our Vasco has a large capacity."

They were almost at the bottom of the gully now and Jane called out that she could hear water.

"Then we are lucky. I hoped we would be. Vasco will be bathing. Elephants bathe very regularly, they are quite Roman in their allegiance to the bath, but Vasco is almost an addict. It is an extremely pleasant sight to see an elephant enjoying his bath. I'm sure you will enjoy it as I do."

"Have you really made a bath for him?" asked April facetiously. Fecklessness suited her, made her a winsome little girl.

"We have blocked up a stream," smiled Joao, "big enough for Vasco's outsize. Hush!"

But there was no need for any hushing. The wallowing, snorting, trumpeting and rolling could not have been missed even if one wanted to miss it. Turning a bend of the rough track, they came in full view of the elephant cleansing, relaxing and having fun all in the one go. It was delightful to watch, and Jane laughed aloud in her pleasure. April did, too, but from farther back. She did not want splashes on the silk shirt she had tucked into the new jodhpurs.

"Our elephants are smaller than Indian and African, and the tuskers are not very prevalent. Vasco is a tusker, though in India and Africa such minor tusks would be scorned. I have seen some tuskers also among the wild ones."

Vasco began rolling, playful as a puppy, but when he got up, forefeet first, then his hind feet, any likeness to a puppy was dispersed, he was a veritable mountain of beast, a great gray dome, even though, being Sinhalese, he was a smaller breed.

He came up to the party, allowing Joao to fondle him. Then he looked at the girls.

"He would like to pick you up," invited Joao. "I assure you that once you get used to it there is nothing like an elephant ride. It is a quite superb sensation being borne as high as the topmost leaves of the tree."

April had shrunk back, and so not to embarrass her, also with a thought to what she might say later, Jane refused, too.

Disappointed, Joao said, "I am so heavy for this small one." None the less he submitted, and the small one took him up with ease and put him on his back.

At that moment there was a bellow that froze the girls and Terry to the ground where they stood. It came from the bottom of the gully, and there was no mistaking the sound. It was the same noise that Vasco had made, but this time it was angry, raging.

As if propelled by automation Joao slid from Vasco's back, calling at the same time for Marsden to retreat with April and Jane.

"I told the Tamils to see to the boundary at the gully bottom," Joao was calling as he backed the unwilling Vasco. "They must have forgotten—either that or the beast down there in his raving has broken the fence."

A moment later there was no beast down there, it was literally upon Vasco, upon the four of them, for the party found it much harder to climb up than clamber down, and April at the rear, or rather the front now in the retreat, in her frantic fear was making little progress, slipping back as fast as she strained up, delaying the rest.

With an oath Joao pushed past to her and pulled her up into his arms.

"Move. *Move!*"

Taking his cue, Terry did the same with Jane. An enraged bellowing stopped them. Whether still in danger, or not, they simply had to turn and see.

The wild, or rogue elephant . . . a tusked one . . . was raging down on Vasco, his small eyes like fire. They stood in horror as his great shape crashed out at the Ambanta elephant, his tusks gleaming in the slates of sun forcing their way through the thick leaves of the trees like white flames. He was seeking to sink the tusks into Vasco, but Vasco had other ideas. With unbelievable maneuverability for a huge gray dome he stepped back, then as the rogue having misjudged slipped past him he did some tusk work of his own.

Now the bellowing fairly shook the jungle, but, tasting his own medicine, the invader must have decided he had had enough, for he turned and fled. Vasco chased him, then as they all still stood wordless, looking at each other, came lumbering back again. He sidled to Joao to repeat his tricks, but instead Joao cut down some green wood and gave it to him.

"I think," he said, "we've had enough, old fellow, today."

"What will you do about that other dreadful beast?" asked April when they reached the top once more. "Send someone out to shoot it?"

"That would be rather difficult, it could be far into the grasslands by this time. No, there has been too much elephant slaughter already. No doubt the so-called rogue has suffered some wound, and in his blind pain has been momentarily mad. As I said before, mostly they are easy beasts."

"Easy for Joao to say that, I'm sure," April grumbled as the girls changed for dinner. "How could you stand down there looking as though you enjoyed yourself, Jane?"

"I did . . . until the incident occurred."

"I didn't at any time. I hated it. I hate the great outdoors."

"Then April—"

"Don't say it, Jane. I have my own foolproof solution. I think you know what I mean."

"Back to Portugal?"

"England, France." April took a long deep breath. "The world. With Joao's money and with Joao's title there's no limit, no limit at all."

Then, quite inconsequentially, with no pertinent reference at all . . . April added: "Let Marsden write an article on that."

At dinner that night April again was to suffer a shock. Last night it had been the shock of the announcement, by Joao Camoes, that it was the Camoes money and not the Carreras, the Camoes tea estate and the Camoes exporting trade.

The jewel talk had softened the blow, and the shock had become a turning point. But now, with the turn made again, the turn currently to the count and not his nephew, a nephew evidently well out of the running on his own accord as well as April's, to judge by Rodriguez's more enlightened than disillusioned look, a barrier and a possible hitch cropped up when Joao Camoes, the coffee having arrived, leaned intentionally over and said to April, "So you are a singer."

There was no opportunity to dart Jane a quick and inquiring glance, so April marked time by saying sweetly, "More or less."

"More or less? But you were on your way to further your career."

Whether to agree, or protest, to be ambitious or to shrink from possible success. For really the first time in her life, Jane thought, she watched her sister and saw indecision. She wanted desperately to help her. It was no use, she knew wretchedly, one can't arrange one's heart, and I'm really fond of April.

"She sings beautifully," she put in proudly.

"And yet," frowned the senhor as he had frowned before, "she stops her journey at our island where there is no opening for a singer at all."

There were a few moments of silence round the table. Rodriguez's attention was on his cup. Jane was waiting for April's move. Joao was reaching for his eternal cheroots. Terry Marsden was leaning back, his lips twisted in a wry grin. Why, he's enjoying himself, Jane thought.

April's face was a study. She was no fool, she had perceived by this time what value a Portuguese puts on social behavior, especially social behavior in a young unmarried girl. As an Australian she might call it stuffy, but as an Australian with an eye for another nationality, for—yes, she admitted it to herself, and to Jane—a title, she would forgive the stuffiness. Now that she had made her final decision she could not offer the romantic excuse of Rodriguez, of her eyes encountering his, and after that ... after that. ...

No, most certainly that would not do.

What then? *What?* She had lost her money, so had to get off the ship? She had been in indifferent health and had decided not to go on?

No, money could be replaced, at least as far as the senhor knew, for she had never told him of their straitened circumstances, it could be replenished, and as for her health, it obviously was, and had been, good. Besides, everyone knew that these days the medical attention on ships was as excellent as on shore. What then? What?

All at once it came to April. She knew. Hanging her head a little, biting her lip, she managed a small crystal

302

tear, just, Jane remembered, as she had been able to manage tears when she was young and wanted something that she could not have. But, Jane remembered hollowly now, finally got.

"What is it, child?" The senhor had got up from the table to cross to April. "Child," he said gently, "you are distressed."

"I—I never wanted to come. I—" There was a pause, a long tremulous pause. "I never wanted to sing."

"You . . . but I don't understand. What is this?"

In a voice so soft that it could barely be heard April whispered lies that Jane could not believe she was listening to with her own ears. How all her life dear Mummy—yes, she was that for all that she was an ambitious mother—and darling Jane, who always asserted that the next best thing to success was to be a sister to success, had pushed April.

"Because"—now April lifted the turquoise eyes with the crystal glint of tears in them—"because you see, Joao, I really had such a little voice. Such a very unimportant, such a small voice. That, anyway, was obvious to me. A voice only destined to—to—"

"Sing lullabies?" It was Terry Marsden, his lips twisted in the old derisive grin.

"Marsden!" It was the senhor.

"Sorry, Joao. Sorry, milady."

"*Marsden!*"

"I beg your pardon, Miss Winthrop, do please proceed."

"I suppose I could have held out, should have held out, but—but I loved them, Joao, and they had sacrificed a lot for me. Lessons, you understand, and then finally the money for this journey. But—but I found I couldn't last out, that I couldn't go through with it, so—so when the ship reached Colombo, I—I just got off."

"And your sister, Miss Jane Winter, instead of coming as I understood, to join you, to chaperone you, came instead to urge you to go on?"

April's "Yes" was so low and so troubled it barely could be heard at all.

Presently Joao turned to Jane, just as she had known

he would. But though she had known, she had still not prepared an answer to the question she knew he would ask.

"Is this true, Miss Jane?"

Jane sat very still. What was the use now of speaking the truth? she thought miserably. It would do her no good and it would do April harm.

"I suppose," she evaded, "it is more or less like that."

"Like what?"

"Like you just said."

"And like your sister said?"

"More or less."

"If that is meant for a clever evasion I do not find it so."

"It was just meant as a reply. Really, senhor, aren't you making a great deal out of nothing? A mountain from a molehill? It is, after all, of no importance at all."

"No importance?" He stood quite furiously above Jane, and for some reason in his gray suit Jane thought of the height and bulk of the gray dome down in the jungle gully. Joao's king of beasts.

"No importance!" said this king ... no, Jane thought a trifle hysterically, this *count*. "I consider it of vast importance. In fact I am very concerned over this what you call small affair. To force a person ... or should I say oblige a person ... to do what they do not want to do is little short of criminal. How much have I seen of it in my own country? An estate handed to a first son whose interests were in medicine, in engineering, in anything but the cork and lime groves. And then the second son, with his heart fairly crying out for the soil, sent to some business house instead.

"My own sister did it with Rodriguez. Nothing would please her but that he come out here, where obviously he is not at home."

Rodriguez glanced up, but only just that. He looked down on his cup again.

"He was born for an *avenida*," went on Joao, "an avenue, for urban activities. Is that not so, my boy?"

"It is true," admitted Rodriguez. "All I ask is my car to run up to the mountains, to run down to the coast, to run into the city. The usual pleasant things a civilized place bestows. This Ceylon. . . ." He got restlessly up and went to the window.

"You see," said Joao, "he is not happy and never has been. That is why. . . ." He looked down on April's lovely flaming hair but, discreetly, did not finish his words.

"You will understand then, Miss Winter, why I have 'exaggerated.' I was very angry with my sister for her lack of intuition."

"Then," said Jane coldly, "why did you not fight it, refuse to accept Rodriguez?"

"She was my senior." He was as cold as Jane.

"But you," she came back, "were male."

Terry Marsden chose to intervene then, and his intervention brought April's head up again, her eyes dark with hate for the journalist.

"All very interesting," Terry yawned, "but the proof of the pudding, as they say, is in the eating."

"What do you mean, Marsden?"

"Shouldn't we judge by letting the lady sing?"

"I don't wish to sing," April said with a little shiver.

Terry said deliberately, "No, I bet you don't."

"I do not follow," said the senhor. "If Miss Winthrop is too upset to sing then of course she must not sing."

"And we must all believe her story since we cannot hear her, her story that she has not, as she insists, any voice. And,"—flicking a glance at Jane—"disbelieve her sister."

That was a poser for the senhor. He studied his cheroot for a moment, then said very gently to April, "You could perhaps sing a small song to satisfy our cynical visitor?"

Terry, undismayed by the tag, simply sat on and grinned.

"Of course I'll sing," agreed April docilely. "You must understand, Joao, that actually I love to sing. It's just that I'm not, and never will be, what has been put upon me. And that is a real singer. A singer in the true meaning of the word."

Terry put in, "Can *we* judge that?"

"By all means, but"—triumphantly—"I only sing to an accompaniment."

"I can accompany you," said Terry. "These ink-stained fingers can rattle a scale as well as write poems."

"A scale!" April shuddered. She added—softly for Terry—"A poem! You?"

He shrugged, untouched, and April went on aloud more triumphantly again, "There's no piano."

"Ah, but there is." It was Joao now. "In the other wing. Quite a good one, I have been told by visitors who are musically inclined. If you have finished your coffee, ladies, shall we proceed there now? That is"—with solicitude to April—"if all this is not too presumptive, too much of a burden, an imposition, dear child."

The dear child smiled up at him, a rather wobbly, pathetic, tremulous smile, and said, "I'll try. But you know what to expect."

"I'm sure it will be charming."

"If uneventful?"

"I do not ask for an event."

"Thank you, senhor."

They walked to the other wing, where the senhor called for drinks, and while they talked desultorily April looked through some music that Rodriguez had found. The young man was more friendly now, his resentment was gone, he was looking upon April as another ill-cast performer in life, a fellow sufferer, in fact.

April found a song that Jane had never heard her sing before, in fact had never heard at all.

"This." She handed it to Terry. "Is it too difficult for you?"

"I can promise you a note here and there."

"That will be enough." She gave him a brittle smile.

But Terry played more than a note here and there. He played fluently, quite excellently, with feeling. Jane, recalling how April had at least been genuinely carried away with music, though whether the carrying away had been artistic or not she never had had the art herself to judge, wondered how April would be able to resist putting everything into the song she had chosen.

For putting nothing was what April planned, Jane felt sure of that. She would have to prove to the Senhor Camoes that small, unimportant, trivial voice. And, cleverly, cunningly, with little brow-creasing pauses here and there, difficulties, wrong notes, wrong timing, convincing passages of music now and then to vindicate to a small extent her mother's and her sister's selfish attitude, sufficiently, anyway, not to make a fabrication of it all, she stumbled, smiled, started again, finally got through the song.

That it was an ordeal was evident by the carnation pink patches on her fair skin. Again the turquoise eyes glinted with tears. She looked lost, troubled, infinitely sweet. An appealing child.

Rodriguez fussed around her, said comfortingly that she had done very well, that really it was a very nice voice. The senhor said softly, gently, "Now I understand."

But Terry Marsden, back from the piano stool now, downing the brandy that had been brought for him while he accompanied April in one vicious gulp, said . . . but only Jane could hear: "You lying, you damn lying girl!"

Once she had made her decision April proceeded on her chosen path without pause or deviation. There was something quite unnatural and ruthless in the single-minded way she went about achieving her goal.

Even for April it was a little too much April, Jane thought, dismayed. Her half-sister had always been a selfish girl, but there had been chinks in her armor. Now there were no chinks. She was completely encased in a hard, impenetrable shell. Hard—for everyone save Joao Camoes.

There had been a few words between the girls on the night of the piano incident, but they had been brief and to the point—and mainly April's.

"I'm sorry about the showdown this evening, Jane, but in a way you have only yourself to blame. You should never have spoken to Joao about my voice. I had no alternative other than to do what I did."

"Make ambitious pushers of Mother and me?"

"You're over-sensitive. I wasn't that hard, I simply implied that you both saw in me what was not really there."

"Isn't it there, April?"

"A voice? Oh, one of a sort."

"But not the sort you used for Senhor Camoes."

"The Conde de Camoes, Jane, and there is your answer. *Count* Camoes."

April had wheeled round and gone to her own room, indicating that the matter was closed.

As regarded the senhor, of course, it was only just opened. The following morning April began what Terry Marsden impudently tagged . . . to Jane . . . the Peerage Pursuit. At times more impudently still: the Royalty Race. Without the shade of a doubt the pursuit, or the race, went very well; the senhor was kindness and solicitude itself to April. Sometimes it seemed that April had only to ask and it was given . . . but if she asked for the removal of Terry Marsden, which Jane considered likely, that was one thing that was not given. The newspaperman stayed on.

That it infuriated April was evident very often to Jane, when, in the safety of their suite, April had need no longer to contain herself.

"That man . . . that wretched man, why does he stay on?"

"It's his work, April, he's doing this series for an English syndicate."

"So he says! Look, Jane, you're interested in writing yourself, can't you get in with him and see whether he's really doing these articles or imposing on our hospitality."—*Our*, noted Jane.

"I'm quite sure he's here to write," defended Jane.

"And I'm quite sure he's not."

"Then what?"

"He's here to—to—" But April could not, or would not, finish.

"I loathe him," was all she said.

Out of fellow interest Jane did speak with Terry, and found, as she had said to her sister, that he indeed was writing a series of articles.

"So milady had her doubts, did she?" grinned Terry maliciously. "What does she think I live on, young Jane?"

"Just now she thinks you're living on her hospitality."

"Her?" Terry was nothing if not quick.

"Actually April said 'our,' " Jane admitted.

"Of course. And now she's anxious to be rid of me. Right?"

"Well—"

"Don't hedge, little one, I'm tough."

"Then—yes."

"Good for her and bad for me. But the Count wants me here, so good for me and bad for her. And keeping in mind that as in Ceylon as well, the Portuguese male has the first and last word, I think we can say with assurance that the newspaperman stays on."

"Has he?" asked Jane with interest. "Does the Portuguese male—"

She stopped, embarrassed. Terry, always restless, always moving somewhere else, had left her, and unnoticed, Joao Camoes had appeared.

"Senhorita?" he asked, brows raising. "You were saying?"

"I was saying it to Mr. Marsden, senhor."

"But surely, being a Portuguese subject, a Portuguese can answer more fully. You began 'Does the Portuguese male—' "

It was simply no use trying to evade this man. How many times had Jane tried it before?

She said, with the hint of a sigh, "Does the Portuguese male, like his Sinhalese counterpart, have complete authority?"

"You mean over his female partner?"

"Yes." Now Jane's cheeks were flaming. Why did she always have to flush like this?

She awaited his lofty reply, his arrogant assurance that most certainly the Portuguese male held the reins. So much so did she anticipate the answer that when Joao Camoes spoke, said what he did, it came as a shock. For quietly, almost tentatively, the big man said: "We like to think, Miss Jane, that we meet halfway."

A surprising but very comfortable position . . . for both sides . . . had become established between April and Rodriguez.

Since the night of April's poor little performance a

kind of *esprit de corps* had risen between them, the fellow feeling of misdirected lives, on one hand the subjected singer, on the other the obligatory alien. They exchanged little sighs of unwilling concession, little moues of unhappy resignation, and both obviously preferred their new relationship.

"He's quite a nice lad," April said to Jane . . . and Jane smiled secretly. It seemed impossible that only several weeks ago her sister had declared she loved the young man. But that, of course, had been before she had known that Joao was Count Camoes.

The very thought of the senhor being a count intoxicated April, but not so much that she did not pursue her course soberly and with meticulous care. She became more out-of-doors, accompanied Joao on estate inspections, spent a day with him in one of the tea tallying rooms, drove with him in the jeep to see to the boundary fences, when she knew he would be coming out on the patio for an evening smoke bribing a Tamil boy to drive her past the bungalow in a cart, the while she sat gaily at the boy's side laughing irresistibly like a bright young schoolgirl.

That he was amused by it all was evident by his gay rejoinders, his frequent smiles as though he was inwardly as well as outwardly entertained.

April even nerved herself to be picked up down the elephant gully by Vasco, and, knowing April, surely there was no deeper sacrifice, Jane thought, on any woman's part. But when Joao proposed . . . no, not proposed, *arranged*, for the Portuguese senhor, in spite of that assertion that the Portuguese male and female met half-way, still, in Jane's opinion, more often decreed than agreed . . . that the house-party make a pilgrimage to Adam's Peak, for the first time April quailed.

She had been told all about Sri Pada . . . the Sacred Footprint . . . and how the eight-mile ascent which was literally an eight-mile staircase was enough to tire a healthy athlete let alone . . . let alone. . . .

In the privacy of their rooms April shuddered.

"I can't. I can't! Why isn't the wretched Peak up in the north of Ceylon and not so horribly handy to here?"

"It can't be so bad, many of the Buddhists carry their children or support their ailing relatives up the trail. It's the attitude to it that counts, April. It's not to be approached as just another peak to be conquered, but a pilgrimage."

"Well, let the pilgrims do it. I'm not one."

"Then tell Joao. I'm sure he'll understand."

"Oh, Jane, don't be naïve!"

April toyed with a dozen excuses. Health? No. Just now she was sure that the Count . . . she always called him the Count . . . was quite delighted with her sturdiness. How many times had he said that she deceived her fragile look. A strained ankle? No, he was so meticulous he undoubtedly would summon a physican and have the foot examined.

Perhaps she could suddenly find the prospect of the emotional side of the Sacred Footprint a little too disturbing for her delicate senses. No, that would not do. Joao had commended her practicality.

There seemed no way out but to suffer, and to April eight miles was a lot of suffering. Then, with typical April-luck, April escaped. It happened on the very morning of the expedition, April even dressed for the adventure, so that no one, not even Jane, could doubt April's integrity.

Rodriguez was taken ill. The doctor who attended the neighboring tea estates was summoned and diagnosed a mild food poisoning, then traced the source. He said that most certainly Rodriguez must stay at home, that any other members of the household who had eaten of the particular suspect spice should take a similar precaution, for even though they had no ill effects as yet, it could be very uncomfortable for them once on the steep track.

It was literally manna from heaven for April. With a stricken expression she clapped her hand over her mouth and called, "I ate that dish!"

Hardly were the words out of her mouth than Terry Marsden called, "I ate it, too."

"Three out of a party of five," demurred Joao, "makes it no party at all. I think we must call off the expedition till later."

April, restraining herself with difficulty from flicking Terry a furious look, changed the look to quick appeal . . . to Jane.

Jane knew that even though April did not want her sister to be with Joao, she still wanted Jane to clamor to go, and so cancel the Adam's Peak expedition as far as April was concerned. And why not? thought Jane. The anticipation of the Peak had enthralled her right from the first. She had read all about the ringing of the bell at the entrance of the temple, once for every time a pilgrim had climbed Sri Pada, and she yearned to begin to ring.

The longing must have shown in her, for she became aware that the senhor was looking at her with understanding.

"You are disappointed, child?"

"Yes. But it doesn't matter."

"It does. And you will not be disappointed. We will leave these too greedy children and go to Sri Pada ourselves."

Now April, for all her meaning looks, was not so pleased, but there was nothing she could do about it. Either the party was cancelled for today and they all went later on or Jane and Joao went and April escaped the ordeal she dreaded. She decided the latter the better of the two evils, and followed Jane and Joao out to the car that Joao would drive himself over the ranges, Rodriguez remaining listlessly on the patio, Terry sauntering rather jauntily behind the girls and Joao, to call to the adventurers to be very careful, darlings, and please, dear Jane, to take great notice so that she could be told everything, every beautiful detail of Sri Pada which, unhappily, she was to miss.

At that Terry gave an impudent grin.

The car skimmed down through the drive of plantains then turned northwest into terrain that Jane had not yet experienced. For a while they still traversed the tea estates, and then the mountains enfolded them with deep misty valleys and pyramid-shaped peaks, later a plateau, or a *murg*, whose shoulders were clad in dark-green juniper and rhododendron, and then rolling country with mountains rising in the distance again. There were delicate buttercups on the Horton Plains that surprised Jane in a tropical country, but Joao reminded her that here the mornings could be bitterly cold, that she was no longer in the sleepy lagoon region of Ceylon.

They reached Hatton, then took the road to Laksapana, the foot of the Peak. Here they rested a while, Joao taking out a hamper and thermos of tea that he had had packed.

"You must eat hugely, little one," he smiled, "for there is enough for five. Also"—as Jane protested—"before you there is a climb of eight steep miles." He poured the tea and handed it to her.

"It is important that you know of Sri Pada before you pay homage. Tell me how much is in that funny little head."

Jane wondered whether he would have spoken so amusedly to a beautiful flame-gold head, but she was lit with interest in Sri Pada and had no objection to conceding to his request.

"It is venerated by Buddhists, Hindus, Muslims and Christians," she answered. "On the summit is a great boulder in which there is a footprint-shaped depression."

"You are a good student," nodded Joao. "You would know also that the Buddhists believe it is the mark of Buddha, the Hindus the mark of Siva, the Muslims the footprint of Adam."

As they ate and drank a family began the quest. They travelled slowly, for there was a cripple among them. Though Jane and Joao lost sight of them in a turn of the track they heard their voices raised in "*Saddhu!* . . . *Saddhu!* . . . " which Joao said was Hallelujah.

"You can see now," said Joao, "it is not just a climb but an exaltation. It is a brotherhood. It could be done by a hardy hiker in commendable time, but that would not be the purpose."

"I didn't come for a record," offered Jane soberly. "I came for that human understanding, for it must be, mustn't it, for Buddhist, Hindu, Muslim and Christian all to climb the same height."

"Such a wise brown head," he said back, "such an understanding brown wren."

In surprise Jane asked, "How did you know I was called—" then stopped and flushed.

"Mr. Marsden told me," replied the senhor.

"Terry? But—"

"We were speaking of home. I expect you could call our conversation Home Thoughts from Abroad. Because you were a brown wren you entered our mutual thoughts. Entered quite nostalgically." The senhor smiled.

"Nostalgia?" she questioned.

"In Portugal, as in Mr. Marsden's England, we have such small brown birds. Here in Ceylon the bird life is different, here are bold, strident birds, clever, cunning birds, gorgeous blue kingfishers, big fan-tailed pheasants, splendid, colorful creatures one and all, but no small sweet wren.

"Well, little brown bird, are you ready to fly?"

"I suppose," smiled Jane, "flying would be much easier, but not, I think, the same deep satisfaction."

"You have understanding," he said gravely, and helped her out of the car.

Climbing from the Hatton side, Joao told Jane, there were no dangers and only some three and a half thousand feet to conquer. From the other side, from the valleys of Ratnapura, the ascent was from sea level and much more severe.

That it was not to be easy, though, Jane found in the first few yards. The climb was uncompromisingly steep; it simply went up and up.

"A normally strong walker could reach the summit in three hours," said Joao. "I thought we would allow four, then half of that for the descent."

Almost at each step Jane found the air growing cooler in spite of her warm efforts, in spite of a blazing sun. She saw that the nature of the terrain was changing to wilder grandeur, tremendous boulders flung around, deep gorges suddenly at one's feet, lush jungle growth and huge trailing creepers.

They stopped for a breather, silent for a while in the strange beauty of it all.

"Even April would have appreciated this." Jane said without thinking, then clapped her hand over her mouth.

"It is all right, little one," smiled Joao, "I understand. Your sister indeed would have appreciated it, for it is said that none can stand on the summit without worship in his soul, and Miss Winthrop is intrinsically a fine as well as an exceedingly beautiful woman."

"Yes, senhor," Jane said a little unwillingly, hating herself for her lack of alacrity, wondering at her sudden heaviness.

Joao Camoes leaned across and pulled a stem of grass which he peeled then bit into with his strong white teeth.

"I love her." He said it reflectively . . . to himself . . . but Jane heard.

Suddenly the beauty around her was not there any more, only a blank hollowness bordering on utter despair. The peace was unpeaceful. Nothing was right. What is the matter with me? her heart cried out.

You know, her heart cried back.

Yes, she knew. Unbidden, uninvited . . . even unwanted, her heart had reached out to this big, rather aloof, rather arrogant man. Why, I love him, she knew. I love the man my sister intends to marry. I love the man who intends to marry my sister, he must intend that, for he has just said, and I have heard it: "I love her."

"Senhorita, you are suddenly quiet." The senhor's voice broke into a pain that Jane had never experienced before. She looked up at him. He seemed no different, no more emotional than he had been when he was driving the car. And yet he had just said of April: "I love her."

Obviously he had believed he spoke only to himself, for there was not the least glimpse of embarrassment, of an emotion admitted, in his smooth olive face.

The only thing to do, knew Jane, was to be as smooth back to him. He must not know she had heard his thoughts.

"It's this place," she offered, and he accepted that.

"Yes, it is silencing. If you are rested, shall we go on?"

Jane went heavily for a while, but soon, like all those who climbed these heights, she found her own thoughts slipping away from her, something finer . . . that exaltation Joao had spoken about? . . . taking its place.

The path now was stepped with granite, but the steps

were steep, they went ruthlessly up. The trees were thinning away, but the impact of the sun was lessened by the refreshing air.

They passed a nun battling bravely up, a devout Sinhalese calling out pious ejaculations at the steepness . . . or Joao assured Jane that they were pious.

But when they reached the little family that had begun the climb as they sat in the car, the father helping a crippled parent, the mother holding the hand of a child, Jane caught at Joao's arm.

"No," she begged.

"What, senhorita?"

Jane flushed. "It's not the place to shoulder others aside. It's—it's—"

"I am glad you have said that." He was looking at her with deep eyes. "You mean," he went on, "it is reverence, unselfishness, consideration, fortitude."

"Yes, senhor."

"And you mean also that we proceed behind this little unit, that we help them, not go ahead."

"Yes, senhor."

"Then we shall do that. Only—" He paused.

"Yes?"

"It will make us late. Very late."

"Does it matter?"

He smiled back at her. "That is the answer I wanted."

Now the steps were really demanding. Jane knew by the strained faces of the pilgrims, none of them robust, that they found the last lap of the climb almost torture. On an impulse she took the weary child into her arms. At the same moment Joao took the elderly cripple in his.

The look on the faces of the man and wife was reward enough without the shower of words.

At that moment there was the clang of a bell above them, and its resonance gave them all new strength.

"A pilgrim has reached the top," Joao smiled.

"*Saddhu!*" called the little party.

An hour later, which was extremely slow going, but they could travel no faster with the handicapped and the child, they climbed to the Peak, clanged the bell, passed by the holy footprint, stood at last on the summit.

It was as superb a vista as Jane had anticipated, probably, suggested Joao, because everything fell away so quickly and sharply, leaving nothing else to absorb the eye. Beneath them an immense, undulating carpet of earth spread itself out, parts here and there enveloped in eddies of fog.

It was not the hour, the senhor said regretfully, for the fabled Shadow of the Peak, a freak of nature at sunrise when the cone of darkness shortened rapidly, but Jane had no time for regret, she simply stood sufficed, rewarded.

"Well, child," the senhor was consulting his watch, "even though you said you did not mind being late we must start down again."

"Descending will be easy," returned Jane.

But she was wrong—tremblingly wrong. Her knees shook, in fact quite frequently they threatened to give way altogether. The bottom seemed to reach up for her.

"Steady," said the senhor, and she was grateful for his hand.

Down at last, they went thankfully to the car to sit a long exhausted while before Joao Camoes once more took out the hamper. It was not until he was packing the food away that he said quite casually, "We will not of course return to Ambanta tonight."

"Why?" she asked in surprise.

"You will find the rest-houses exceedingly comfortable, if simple."

"What do you mean?"

The note in her voice must have reached him, for he turned puzzled eyes on her.

"But you distinctly said," he reminded her, "when I warned you we would be late if we delayed that it did not matter."

"I know but I didn't think, I mean—"

"What did you mean, senhorita?" The voice was stiff now, uncompromising.

"I thought you—you just meant we would be late getting home."

"So we would. A night later. We would arrive the following morning."

"Oh, no!" It was more a little cry than a spoken word.

The senhor's brows were one black line. "What is this, Miss Winter?" he asked. "You tell me yes, we will not hurry, but now you sing a different tune."

"I don't sing any tune at all," said Jane a little frantically, "except that I want to get back."

"Your objection, please?"

"Isn't it obvious?"

"No, it is not. For a Portuguese young woman, to any similar young woman cluttered up with convention and rules a thousand years ago, yes, but you are not one of those. Your country is new, unfettered, fresh."

"We still," said Jane with restraint, "concede to certain standards."

"Like?"

"Like not—well—"

"Sheltering in a rest-house with an attendant hand maid, attendant room maid, attendant bath maid, attendant clothes maid . . . oh, I could go on and on. But I will not. I will just assure you, senhorita, that we do not camp overnight, as Australians camp, I believe, in any old tent."

"Then you're misinformed." Jane's voice was cold. But her hands were hot—hot and trembling. She must not stop. She knew that. It was not just the knowledge of April's wrath, though that was cause enough, it was—it was something else. *She must not be near this man more than she could help.*

He was looking at her with kinder eyes now. When he spoke she saw that he was under the misapprehension that, childlike, she had been laboring under a wrong impression, but now was convinced, and happy to be advised by him.

"It would be too much for you to return tonight, little one. To tell you the truth I myself would not relish the journey back over the range."

"All the same, that is what we will do."

Her voice was absolutely calm, and she marvelled at it. How could it be calm with this trembling inside of her?

He was looking at her incredulously, with utter disbelief. Then the look was altering, a shuttered, withdrawn expression taking its place. Of course he would feel like that, she thought wretchedly. Of all the circumspect, prudent people in the world, this man would be the most circumspect, the most prudent. Propriety to him would be a second skin.

Yet I have questioned that in him. I—I have shamed him. Her cheeks burned.

He said nothing, however. He said absolutely nothing all those long hours, those long miles home to Ambanta, the dark ranges slipping past them, all the hazards of the mountainous journey magnified in the blackness of night.

Now Jane knew she had been a fool. It had been dangerous to return like this, and he had known it, but because of a stubborn, wretched girl—

"I'm sorry." She said it once as he swore softly at some hidden hindrance in the dark that dangerously rocked the car. Still he did not reply.

They did not stop for rest or refreshment, they went grimly, relentlessly on.

Cramped, unbearably tired, thirsty, hungry, Jane longed to cry out to him, but she resisted. If he could resist, she could. After all, it was entirely her fault, she had brought about all this. She must have dozed at the end, for opening her eyes after she had shut them for a minute, or so she had thought, at a particularly hazardous stretch, she saw that they were out of the mountains and once more in the tea country. Half an hour later the familiar plantains of the Ambanta drive were enclosing them. They were home.

It was into the small hours of the morning. Jane, looking sleepily at her watch but not registering the exact time, saw that.

The household, she thought, would all be in bed long ago. But, climbing to the patio, opening the door and going down the long hall, they passed the lighted room, there was wine on the low table, chairs drawn up. April was laughing as Jane had never heard her laugh before . . . gay, caught up with mirth, outside of herself.

Rodriguez was not there. He must have still been ill and gone to bed.

Terry sat there. The room was filled with smoke, and

filled with their happy relaxation. Jane could feel the relaxation almost as if it was spelled out to her. But, she thought stupidly, applied jointly to Terry and April, it just didn't make sense.

Still, April was like that. If she was bored, she would fill in time just to relieve the boredom. That was what Jeff had been, simply a relief from boredom. That was what Terry was being now.

With Joao she entered the room. At once the atmosphere changed. April's mood clouded over like the eddies of mist below Adam's Peak. Considering the displeasure Jane had anticipated if she did not return, the displeasure now that she had returned was quite unnerving. Why was April so unmistakably shaken, so annoyed?

It was more obvious again after the girls, bidding good night, went to their rooms.

"Why did you have to come back just then, you little fool?" snapped April, incensed.

"I didn't think you'd like it if I didn't come back."

"I wouldn't have had a moment of speculation. Not with you. Oh, this is awful! What will Joao think? What could it lead to?"

"You should have thought of that before." Jane's voice was cold. Really, April was going too far.

"Yes, I should." April stood quite still in the middle of the room. "I must have been mad! I dislike him. I dislike everything about him."

"About Senhor Camoes?"

"Jane, you idiot, *him*! Marsden. And yet . . . and yet . . . . Oh, I must have been fed up. That was it, sheer ennui. All the same . . . all the same *that man must go*. Otherwise," April continued, an almost hysterical note in her voice now, "otherwise I—I—"

Wheeling sharply, she went through the communicating door to her own room.

CHAPTER EIGHT

From that moment on there was no deviation on April's part in her drive to be rid of Terry Marsden.

Shrewdly, insidiously, she used every trick up her sleeve, and April had many such tricks, to belittle him in Joao Camoes' eyes. She found him out wrong, rude, tactless, overbearing, indeed, the very antithesis of a welcome guest. When Joao shrugged these failings off as just that, failings, she cloistered herself with Joao in his study so long that Terry in his turn shrugged and told Jane he'd better begin packing.

"But why?" she asked.

"The writing's on the wall, young Jane. Camoes, being the polite fellow he is, won't actually kick me out, he'll suggest I find a greater degree of peace and quiet for my writing elsewhere."

And that was exactly what happened.

Over sundowners on the terrace that evening Joao said to Terry, "The Lalanda house over the other side of the hill is vacant, Marsden, while the Reynolds are in Hong Kong for a spot of shopping. I know they would like someone there as a protection, and I thought what an excellent opportunity it would be for you to have some real peace and quiet for your work."

Terry's I-told-you-so glance at Jane came at the same time as his glib, "Why, thank you, Joao, Miss Winthrop's chatter certainly was undermining my output."

If he expected to bait April into a sharp rejoinder he was unsuccessful, she just played with the long cool drink she held with her delicate hands and gave him a stare as frosty as her frosted glass.

But Jane was indignant for Terry. He was being victimized, and she told April so.

"Keep out of this, Jane. If ever I knew what I was doing I know now."

"I'll go to Senhor Camoes and tell him what I think, April."

"Go by all means. But I think you'll get a shock."

"You mean. . . ." Did she mean that the senhor had spoken *to* her in the same way as he had spoken *of* her to Jane on their way to Sri Pada? Did she mean he had not said "I love her" but "I love you"?

It all made sense. If he had, naturally he would want to be rid of Terry Marsden, if not on his own account then certainly on April's, for when one loved one could not do enough for the loved.

"Go," flung April triumphantly, "go and ask Joao for your answer!"

And suddenly driven to it by an urgency of her own, Jane did.

He was walking around the garden, an extremely beautiful garden, for as well as cool air to encourage the more delicate flowers, there were numerous butterflies. Ceylon had more than its share of these glorious things . . . the magnificent black and yellow Darsius, the cobalt-blue Parinda, many other diaphanous wings.

"It is said," said the senhor as Jane approached, "that once a year flimsy legions of these wend their way to Sri Pada to die. It could be true, for I have seen the hordes on their fluttering way myself, and a butterfly always flies to his greatest height before death." He must have been in a whimsical mood, for he went on, "And yet so easy not to die, senhorita.

> "He who has seen a white crow,
>   The nest of a paddy bird,
>   A straight coconut tree,
>   Or a dead monkey,
>   Will live for ever."

"By the dead monkey is meant a monkey who has died. It must happen, but where?"

"That," he concluded with a smile, "is a very old Sinhalese village saying."

She could have listened . . . and listened. She was always fascinated when he talked like this. But there was something she had to say herself.

"Senhor—" she began.

"No, little one, I won't find you the nest of a paddy bird."

"*Senhor!*"

He saw the intent in her face and stopped his bantering. "What, Miss Winter?"

"Mr.—Mr. Marsden," she stammered.

"What of the gentleman?"

"You're sending him away."

Coldly he said, "I have never been so discourteous to a guest."

"Not in actual words, but in intent."

"In that either. Really, Miss Winter, you are being very discourteous yourself."

"Then I'm not sorry. I was very upset this evening to see how Terry was being cast out."

"You call being provided a more suitable workshop being cast out?"

"That was only the veneer," she flung. "Actually you were ridding yourself of him. Or"—as an after-thought—"ridding April."

"You are very interested in Mr. Marsden, senhorita," he said keenly. "Do you think that is wise?"

"I'm not interested in him—I mean not in the way you imply."

"Did I imply? It was unintentional."

She ignored that. She concluded, "Anyway, even if I am interested it's no business of yours."

Swiftly he came back, "On the contrary, it is of very real interest. For two definite reasons."

"Your own and April's," she said with more bitterness than she had known was in her. She was surprised at the extent of the bitterness . . . but more surprised still at the small smile that all at once twisted his long, sensitive mouth. He seemed somehow pleased. But of course he would be pleased, pleased at being coupled with her half-sister. Had he not said: "I love her."

All the same she had expected a fairer attitude than this from the senhor, for whatever he was he was always strictly fair. But April's assurance had had firm ground. Whatever Joao Camoes had said to her when they had been cloistered together in his study had been sufficient for April to toss triumphantly, "Go by all means . . . you will receive a shock."

It hadn't been a shock, though, for she had known before. But it had been . . . and turning blindly away Jane felt it sharply . . . a hurt.

"Senhorita . . . Miss Winter!" His voice followed her as she hurried through the clusters of flowers. "Jane!"

That nearly halted her, but only nearly. Why not Jane, she told herself. You can't keep on calling your sister-in-law senhorita or Miss Winter.

Your *sister-in-law*. . . .

"Well?" April's eyes were snapping. "Wasn't I right? Doesn't he want the fellow to go?"

"You were right. He wants him to go. But it isn't fair."

"All's fair," laughed April, "in love and war." Her laugh was a little hollow, though, even for a rather hollow girl like April.

Terry gathered his things, got out his absurd red roadster, waved an impudent goodbye and went thundering much too fast down the road, then along a cart track to the Reynolds' empty house.

"Good riddance," said April.

It was all too much for Jane. Suddenly she knew she had had her fill. April no longer needed her, she had established herself, she had found her place. In short it was all over bar the shouting, and Jane shrank from being around when the time came for the shouting. She decided she would move out, either on to England . . . fortunately she still held a little money, for April had not needed, not under her pampered circumstances, to call upon her sister as Jane had anticipated . . . or back to Australia.

But first she must let her mother know, tell her that she had done everything she had come to do, and now she was bowing out.

Without telling April she wrote the letter, then she asked one of the Tamil boys how one went about posting it. He talked a lot and made a lot of gestures that left Jane none the wiser, and into the conversation came Joao Camoes.

She heard the Tamil explain, "Missy ask *'Thapal Kanthoruwa Koleda?'*" then heard Joao say, "So she wants the post office. I'll attend to this."

After the boy had gone he said, "There is none here. We have to take mail to the nearest depot, which is rather a distance away."

"I can't wait very long," Jane explained.

The brows had risen in the old manner.

"So urgent? And yet you told me this was a whole-hearted journey, that you had left nobody behind."

"My mother." Jane's own voice was infinitely cool.

"Ah, that is very different. We must of course take your letter to the depot."

"And take it urgently," added Jane. "I'm in a hurry."

"A hurry, Miss Winter?"

"To leave here. Also although I'm Australian, senhor, I still would like my mother to know my plans." Her voice reminded him sharply of the few comparisons he had drawn between the young of the two nations.

"I expect," he accepted mildly, "I deserve that jibe. We will not take your letter to the depot after all, we will take it to a private airfield I know, who in turn will take it quickly to the Colombo airfield for instant despatch to your home."

"Thank you, senhor." Jane turned away.

"You will come with me to this private airfield?" he invited.

"Thank you, no."

"It is an interesting drive."

"I said no," she said stiffly.

He gave a stiff acknowledgment and pocketed her letter. She went and sat on the patio with a magazine waiting for the sound of his car as he went down the drive of plantains with the letter.

When an hour went past and there was no departing car, she got up to demand a reason why her letter had not gone. But her reason came from April, not the senhor.

Typical of April, April who never shrank from doing the most unheard-of things, her sister was sitting on the bed with Jane's *opened* letter in her hand.

"April!" gasped Jane.

"Oh, yes, I know it's dreadful of me, but when Joao told me you had an urgent letter to send and perhaps I, too, had written something which could go at the same time, I got your letter from him . . . it doesn't matter how, I just got it . . . and here I am, doing the impossible, reading someone else's words. Sorry, pet, but it had to be. You see, this letter's not going."

"What?"

"Because you're not going. Jane, you just can't leave me."

"But why, *why*? You've got what you want."

"Not actually. Not yet."

"Near enough, then."

"It isn't. It won't be until . . . until . . . look, you mustn't go, it—it wouldn't be correct."

"You're talking about being correct!" Jane could not believe it, not in April. "Anyway," she reminded her, "Rodriguez is here to make a third."

"A third isn't worrying me, a fourth is. And that's what it would be with you gone."

"April, what are you talking about?"

"Terry."

"But he's left."

"Only as far as the other side of the hill. Look, if you can't see what I'm getting at, then I can't make you see, but please, even if it's blindly and without comprehension, stay on and help me, Jane."

"Help you?"

"Help me not to—not to—Oh, just help me. Please, Jane. Please, wren."

Jane stood in an agony of indecision. Everything in her called, no, *shouted*, for her to go, but that look in April's face, a look she had never known before, not at any time, under any circumstance, halted her.

"Oh, April," she said weakly.

"Don't leave me yet, Jane. Promise. Promise!"

"I feel I must get away."

"Promise!"

A minute of unhappiness, of unease . . . of prescience. Then: "I promise," Jane said wearily.

She went outside to the patio again and sank down on the nearest chair. She felt suddenly terribly tired.

When the rest of the household gathered that evening

for sundowners . . . the chair in which Terry had always impudently squatted back to front empty for the second night and apparently nobody noticing him gone but Jane . . . Joao Camoes said, "Tomorrow evening at this time, instead of taking long drinks I intend, with good fortune, that we shall all take a long look."

"What do you mean, Joao?" asked April in the enthralled voice that, through repetition, was becoming second nature with her whenever it was the senhor to whom she spoke.

"We are going to lie by a water-hole. I have been observing for some time a likely source, a quite large indent of water in an outcrop of gneiss down the valley. The·weather has been very dry of late, so the animals have to look farther for their supply than their customary source. This appears to me the supply they have found, for I have examined the spot closely and observed several tracks."

Jane sat almost breathless with the anticipation of it all, to lie low and watch the wild animals come to water stirred her deeply even before it happened. But, remembering how she felt about Senhor Camoes, she determined stubbornly, in spite of a longing to anticipate, not to go. So instead of voicing her pleasure with the others . . . how well April did that pleasure when Jane well knew that all she really felt was distaste . . . she remained stiff and silent.

The drinks came and were drunk. The shadows of night began to fall, and April, and after her Rodriguez, got up to go indoors to dress for dinner.

Jane rose, too.

"Senhorita!" Joao Camoes' voice stopped her.

"Senhor?"

"You did not join in the chorus of enthusiasm just now."

"For a reason—I'm not enthusiastic. And"—at a look in his face—"I'm not going."

"Oh, yes, indeed you are. I let you have your way the other day when you refused to come with me to the airfield, but this is one occasion on which I insist."

"And one in which I desist."

"Senhorita, you are still coming, believe me. It is something that no one should miss, given the opportunity, and most particularly you."

"Why should I be singled out?"

"Because there is something deep and clear in you, something that wants to know and feel and experience and learn. You desire to see these animals watering. Admit it, now."

She could not deny it, so she did not attempt it. Instead she said without any attempt of adornment : "I do not wish to see them with you."

"Thank you for your candor at least. I like it better than your evasions. However, seeing there is no one else to conduct you down there, I shall."

"I shan't go," she insisted.

"You will cut off your nose to spite your face? See, I have the English clichés."

"If you mean will I deprive myself, then yes."

"But you won't," he replied quite calmly. "you will come. You will come, senhorita, if I carry you every step of the way. There will be no need to gag you, for once you are there the magic of it all will take your breath away. See, your eyes already are shining. You *long* to come. Why are you stubborn like this?"

"Because I won't be ordered. Just because you're Portuguese—"

"Aren't you forgetting something?" he came in quickly. "Aren't you forgetting that although I related to you the Sinhalese male superiority, I did not say the same of my own race. Indeed I said, senhorita, that in my country we prefer the man, the woman, to meet halfway. Will you meet me halfway in this?" His smile all at once was quite disarming. He could climb down when he wanted to, she thought grudgingly, this big, arrogant man.

Disarmed in spite of herself, Jane dared, "And if I don't?"

"Then," he said, "I will come all the way to you." As she went to the door he added softly, "A promise, Miss Winter, not a threat."

She could not help becoming excited every time she

thought of what lay ahead. It would be an experience, she knew, not given to many. But it was not that special fact that gave her the thrall, it was the pre-knowledge that she would be so near to nature that every vestige of veneer would be stripped from her. She would feel elemental, primeval, at the very beginning of things. Because of this, she listened keenly to Joao's directions the next day, issued at the breakfast table to April, Rodriguez and Jane.

"Once you have taken up your position down there, which must be a safe time ahead of the expected watering, there must be absolute silence. No talk of any sort. Also, bites or stings or scratches from bushes must be borne without even the slightest movement or protest. No brush, no slap, no cough, no sneeze."

April was fidgeting. Several times she darted an appealing look at Rodriguez. He and his food poisoning had got her out of the ordeal of the climb to Adam's Peak; could Roddy again find an escape?

But Rodriguez's eyes were sparkling, he was as keen as Joao. "We will take our guns?" he asked.

"Only in case protection is needed. To shoot an animal which comes down to drink is murder. By the way, ladies, no insect repellent—animals are sensitive to strange scents. And no perfumes or powders."

"Really, Joao!" pouted April.

"To my way of thinking you do not need them at any time." Joao made a gallant gesture, to which April responded with a soft smile.

She was not so amiable, though, after he went out to the estate, taking Rodriguez with him, though even had the younger man remained Jane doubted if April could have prevailed upon him to think out an escape. He was looking forward to the afternoon as much as April was dreading it.

"Not even insect repellent! I'll be covered with blotches. And I look awful without any make-up at all."

"I think you'd better wear your jodhpurs," advised Jane to keep her from dwelling on the unhappy ultimatum. "It could become chilly."

"Just to see some old bear or something!"

A bear! Jane felt her blood tingle.

Late in the afternoon, but well before the first faint shades of evening, the four started down the narrow track to the valley of Joao's choice. At the very bottom and along no track at all now they forced their way through coiling vines and rotted trunks, keeping an eye out for snakes, to a platform, or mesa, that the senhor had had built in the branches of a tree. There they climbed, one after the other, stretched out on their stomachs, then that was that.

At least that was what April's sulky eyes telegraphed to Jane. These mosquitoes, said the turquoise eyes. The hardness of the boards on your limbs. That branch that's scratching my head.

But Jane could not return the look; she was in a seventh heaven.

Almost at once a family of monkeys had come, too, to watch . . . later she was to be told that monkeys enjoyed watching water-holes as much as human beings. It was delightful to observe their antics . . . alert when they believed an animal was approaching, bored to the extent of tantalizing each other when nothing eventuated.

Then . . . a faint stir in Rodriguez beside Jane . . . something *was* happening. Jane held her breath in thrall.

A sambhur, or variety of deer. A huge, noble fellow with fine antlers and a splendid stance. Hardly had he gone than a Ceylon bear came along, smallish, rather scruffy and very nervy. He drank quickly, then disappeared. The buffalo some half hour later not only drank he immersed himself, wallowing until Jane feared no other animal would care to drink from the muddied depths.

But the hole soon cleared after he had lumbered off, and even if it had not, by the time they received their next visitor it would have had time, had rain fallen, to refill. For they were to lay prone and waiting for almost two more hours.

At the end of the hours even Jane's previously unprotesting limbs were protesting. April, at the end of her tether at last, not caring any more, sat up.

At the same moment the Ceylon leopard, with no

perceptible movement or approach, reached the waterhole, stood a poised moment in lithe beauty, then, though not dangerous to man under ordinary circumstances, alarmed by April's movement, leaped up instinctively before it leapt instinctively away and into the jungle again.

But it was the upward leap that did the damage. The enormous spring missed April, missed Joao, missed Rodriguez, but caught Jane's arm. It was only a glancing blow, but the pain was all-encasing. Jane felt the red-hot sear of it, gave what she believed was a cry but was only a small sigh, then knew no more.

When she opened her eyes it was hours later and she was in bed back at the bungalow. April sat at the side of the bed, her eyes worried. The doctor who had attended Rodriguez for his food poisoning waited beside April. Rodriguez sat on the left. And at the foot, so pale she did not recognize him at first, stood Joao.

CHAPTER NINE

Jane's consciousness did not last long.

Barely had the weaving faces around her taken shape, begun to belong instead of to nebulous people to people she knew, than the mists rolled in again, enfolded her in unawareness and unreality. She seemed weighed down with lead, though at times she felt herself soaring lighter than air. On these occasions she realized rather drunkenly that the sedative, or whatever it was the doctor had given her, must be wearing off, for she was dimly conscious of pain, and she saw people again.

She saw Joao. Always she saw Joao.

Sometimes it would be April who was with him, sometimes Rodriguez, and once, she recognized him even in her muzziness, it was Terry. But every time her heavy lids opened, the Senhor as well was there.

At length there came a time when the lids were less heavy and they stayed open.

The doctor examined her again, re-dressed the arm.

"I'm not having any more drugs," protested Jane.

A very charming Sinhalese, trained, he told her, in Australia under the Colombo Plan, he smiled back and promised to insert no more needles.

"Unless," he added, "the arm needs it. As for shock, you haven't any."

"The arm is sore, but not that bad."

"Nonetheless it will need close attention. In a tropical country like Ceylon, infection can come very rapidly. I could wish, for all that I was desperately homesick when I wintered there for my warmer birthplace, that it was July in Melbourne."

Joao Camoes had entered silently, and his eyes glinted keenly.

"No wishing that now," he put in, "for it is summer during this month in Australia. But"—a pause—"it is winter in Albufiera."

"Albufiera?" Jane and the doctor asked together.

"*My* birthplace." He smiled and bowed. He made the usual polite interchanges that visitors do with patients, insisted that Jane ask for anything she required, then told the doctor he would see him on his way out.

Terry came along, his smile, thought Jane gratefully, as good as a tonic. She would never know, laughing weakly at a ridiculous joke, why April did not like him.

"Well, Janey," he grinned, "the leopard incident might have put you to bed, but it at least got me back into the house."

"Are you back?" she asked.

"No. But I was on the night they brought you up from the jungle. There's no grapevine in Ambanta, but the news spread just the same. The word that Missy had been savaged brought me breaking all speed limits to be here to write up the scene at the deathbed."

"And I disappointed you!"

"You did, as a matter of fact. I thought it was April. I had a very smug feeling in me when I thought of looking down on that girl instead of her looking down on me. But"—a shrug—"it was you instead."

"Still busy on the tea articles, Terry?"

"Yes, but not so busy that I can't do a piece on 'The day I looked into a leopard's eyes.' Though"—regretfully—"being a woman of letters yourself probably you've reserved all the rights."

"No," admitted Jane, "I haven't. I've never written very seriously. In fact"—ruefully—"you could call me rather lackadaisical. I'm not ambitious, Terry."

He did not answer for a while, which was unlike the voluble journalist, then when he did he said, rather oddly, or so Jane thought, "That's good, Kid. In my book that, in a woman, is my pipe dream."

He did not stop long after that. He planted a light affectionate kiss on Jane's brow, then left.

Rodriguez came in. He was a little excited, but evidently he had been told not to divulge the cause of his excitement, for he kept strictly to the same visitor-patient pattern that Joao had.

At length, tired of trivialities, Jane asked, "What happened to the leopard?"

"Dear Jane, don't upset yourself."

"I'm not upset . . . but I would be if I thought it had been shot. It couldn't help doing what it did, it was alarmed."

"It was not shot, it ran into the jungle. As far as being shot—well, it's extremely unlikely it will water there again even if we placed a posse. Which, of course, Joao would not countenance. He's very keen on wild life, though I must say"—a sigh—"it, or Ceylon, is not to my liking. However—" His eyes brightened and he wet his lips as though to make a statement. But, on second thoughts, he did not. He, too, kissed Jane lightly and went out.

The doctor came again. The nurse.

When, thought Jane a little crossly, is April coming? But it was not until early evening that her sister finally visited her. Jane was sitting up now, feeling, apart from a stiffness and a rawness in her arm, quite fit.

April perched on the side of the bed and said at once in a breathless little voice, "Jane, we're going to Portugal."

"What? April, are you ill yourself? You look very flushed."

"It's excitement. It's happening at last!"

"What is?"

"Joao has arranged a private charter for the four of us to leave, the doctor permitting, and his last examination said that you were definitely sufficiently fit, for the Algarve.

"The Algarve is a Portuguese province, darling, down in the bottom corner." That was typical of April, no points of the compass for that lovely flaming head. "The capital is Faro—fruit, fishing, wine, salt." Her voice was unnaturally high and it held a note slightly bordering on hysteria. "But it's Albufiera we're going to."

"That's the senhor's birthplace," recalled Jane.

"Yes. Actually his *palacio* . . . yes, Jane, it's what it sounds, a palace . . . is back in the hills from there, but he has this beach place where he wants you to recuperate."

"Me? But I have no need to recuperate. I feel wonderfully fit."

"A leopard leaps out at you and you feel fit! Don't be ridiculous, Jane."

"I'm not being ridiculous, I'm being truthful. I have no need to go to Portugal."

"Then for pity's sake, for my sake, don't say so."

"What do you mean, April?"

"I mean I must go."

"Then go."

"But I can't, can't you see that? I can't go unless you go. It all depends on you, Jane."

"Why does it depend on me?"

"Because Joao is only going because of you. He has this thing that you need further medical attention, and what better medical attention to a Portuguese than the attention in Portugal. It's quite reasonable when you come to think of it. We would feel the same."

"Very well, then, I'll go back to Australia for my treatment."

"Jane, you can't!"

"I can. I will. That is, if I have to undergo treatment elsewhere. Anyway I would feel it was a slight to the good Sinhalese doctor, and I wouldn't be a party to it."

"But that's all settled. The Sinhalese doctor suggested a change of climate himself."

"But not particularly Portugal."

"If not, then certainly not Australia, for it's summer there. A cooler, more moderate air, he said, to assist healing."

"I am healed."

"Then, Jane"—April got up from the bed and went to stand at the window in the way she used to—"do it for me. I have to go. Can't you see?"

"Yes, I can see," said Jane slowly, "I can see the whole distasteful design of it all. But what I can't see, April, and I won't, is my part in the wretched thing. I won't help you to clinch your deal. I'm sorry if the words are raw, but that's how I feel."

"They are raw," admitted April, "but it still makes no difference to me. You see I just have to get away from here before—before it's too late. That it happens to be Portugal offering an escape is just coincidental. I—I mean, Jane, even though that distasteful design you just spoke about is pretty true, it's not my real reason. Jane—Jane, can't you see *why* I have to get away?"

"I know." Jane's voice was stolid.

"No, not that, not that. . . . Oh, oh, what's the use?"

Something of the driving panic in her half-sister reached Jane. She looked at her curiously.

"You sound almost as though you're running away from something, but that couldn't be true."

"No," said April, "it couldn't be true." Her laugh was high and unnatural again. She sat on for a while, but she made no other attempt to persuade her sister.

But when the nurse came . . . a smiling-eyed Low-Country girl with shining black hair caught up in a knot beneath her white veil . . . she left Jane to have her arm re-dressed, only pausing at the door to look back in silent entreaty, an appeal that reached across the room to beg and implore.

It only remained for the senhor to add his piece and he did so when the nurse had finished.

"More comfortable now?" He had pulled up a chair by the bedside.

"I'm a fraud. I should be up," smiled Jane.

"I am glad you feel that well, senhorita, otherwise I would have had second thoughts on allowing you to fly tomorrow."

"Then have second thoughts, senhor, for I am not flying." Jane paused. "Not, anyway, to where you have planned."

"And where have I planned?"

"Portugal."

"I see already you have been told."

"Not told," persisted Jane stubbornly, "acquainted. Acquainted of your plans."

"You are in the mood to correct. Then I will be, also. I have made no plans . . . plans are tentative things . . . I have made definite arrangements. The private small plane will take us down to Ratmalana airport and from there we will take a private charter to Lisbon. From there another small craft to a field very near my home."

"Is a *palacio* a home?" Jane inserted sharply.

"An Englishman's home is an Englishman's castle," he returned evenly. "I see no reason why that should not be reversed for a Portuguese. Could not"—he swept her a look that only for the idea being too ridiculous Jane could have categorized as appealing, appealing? the senhor? . . . "the castle of a Portuguese be his home?"

"It could be, but I won't be finding out."

"I agree. I have decided that rather will we go to my cliff house at Albufiera. There the weather will be both bracing and temperate."

"Senhor Camoes," broke in Jane, "I am not going at all."

"But Miss Winter," he said, still even, "you are. What happened in the jungle, the leopard incident, lies entirely on my shoulders. Not only the territory was mine but the arrangements for the expedition mine also. Can't you see that I am responsible for you, that I do not *dare* omit the precaution of removing you from Ambanta?"

"Oh!" Jane could not help a certain deflation. "Then it's really a matter of—of liability."

He did not answer for a moment. Then he said, "And something else."

But he meant some*one* else. Jane knew that. The fact that her injury could be attended at the same time was just something that had happened rather conveniently, since the senhor, being the senhor, would never have taken April home without someone else of her own sex.

And he wanted . . . and intended . . . to take April home. Had he not said: "I love her? *I love her.*"

"Senhorita?" His voice broke in, asking for her decision, even though his decision . . . for her . . . had been made.

Jane made one more attempt.

"I don't like to discard the Sinhalese doctor, he has been very good to me."

"You will not be discarding him, child. Do you think I would take the risk of changing medicos mid-course? He, of course, will come as well."

Jane just lay wordless. What else was there to say, to protest?

The small plane took the party down to Ratmalana airport the next morning. As Jane changed crafts she could see working elephants, urged on by mahouts, padding the road down firmly, and she thought how lucky Vasco was in his private valley.

At once the big craft set out, and then it was like the turning pages of an atlas, the countries beneath them taking the same shape as the remembered shapes in the atlas. Almost, thought Jane, you looked down to pick out the appropriate colors, pink for India, yellow for Persia, just as you had as a child.

Karachi . . . Cairo . . . briefly at Algiers . . . hours of drifting sleepily, waking refreshed, then Lisbon rising up, but no chance to see it, for the next small plane was waiting for the final leg. For that private strip belonging to the Conde de Camoes at Albufiera.

That last, anyway, was what April's glittering eyes were telegraphing to Jane. Once during the journey she had whispered, "Pinch me, Janey, is all this true? Not only a private plane but a private doctor as well. That man must be positively rolling! And to think I had my ideas on little nephew Roddy!"

"April—" began Jane.

"Darling, I'm beyond being reproached. I am, thank heaven, beyond all that has happened before this moment. I'm safe."

"Safe?"

But April had only kept glittering.

It was a brief hop to the province of Algarve. The plane made a smooth landing, the party got out and boarded two waiting cars. How well the senhor did things, thought Jane grudgingly, but the smile on her half-sister's face was not grudging, while no doubt, Jane knew, April was not thinking of Joao as the senhor but as the Conde.

They ran swiftly through a forest of eucalyptus that reminded Jane of home.

"Acclimatized, of course," said the senhor, "but these cork are our own."

They passed big imposing gates that Rodriguez said led to the *palacio* . . . an *avenida,* or avenue, of magnolia wound round concealingly as far as the eye could see, and though she did not glance at her, Jane could imagine April's shining eyes. But the *palacio* remained withdrawn from sight, though the cliff house, when it was reached, certainly indicated that the Camoes' main stronghold should be something quite breathtaking, for even the seaside home was in its way a minor castle.

Even April was silent as she followed Joao down the long corridor, lofty, as most less modern Portuguese buildings are, and given to much fretted oak and baroque.

There was sufficient accommodation for thrice their party, and, as at the bungalow at Ambanta, April and Jane had rooms with communicating doors. The furnishings were purely Portuguese, rich of color and fabric, nothing airy. But the view through the window dispelled any sense of heaviness, floating blue, the blue of both sea and sky, drifted in until, instead of the rather ponderous reds and burgundys, it became a blue refuge instead. At least a blue refuge it seemed to Jane. She felt at once infinitely at peace here.

But not, surprisingly, April. April stood, brow creased, uncertain, on edge.

"It's all too much," she said more to herself. "I can't feel myself think."

Suddenly touched by her confusion, if not understanding why she was confused, Jane asked gently, "Do you want to think?"

"No, I don't. Thank you, Janey, for reminding me, keep on doing that, wren. And now shall we unpack?"

Dinner was eaten in a long, high-ceilinged room facing the sea. There was a great fire burning, for it was a cold night. When, during conversation, Joao anticipated doing some swimming in the week they would be here . . . where, then? wondered Jane briefly . . . April gave a little shiver of protest and inquired about icebergs.

"You will be surprised," Joao smiled, "at the temperature on the beach compared to that on the cliff. Down there the winter sun shines hotly. You can lie in your bathers and look eighty feet up to people in thick coats."

The meal over, the young doctor took a look at Jane's arm, then having proclaimed his satisfaction at her progress, he suggested that she have an early night.

"For after all" . . . a flash of white teeth in a smiling brown face . . . "it has been a journey of many miles."

To Jane's surprise, for Rodriguez had excused himself and gone out and her sister could have had her Count to herself, April said she would go to bed as well. She even saw Jane into bed, plumped her pillows, then did something she seldom bothered about, she kissed her goodnight.

"Thank you, Janey," she whispered before she clicked out the light. "You've helped all you could, it's not your fault that—"

"What is it, April?" Jane sat up, the sudden movement hurting the arm. "April, is anything wrong?"

"In these surroundings of riches? Don't be foolish, darling."

"You sounded unhappy."

"I'm as happy as I deserve."

"Is that an answer?"

"It's all the answer I can think of. I'm terribly tired, Jane, don't fuss. I'm going to sleep in until ten o'clock in the morning. Roddy told me that it's bitterly cold on the beach until that hour because the sun doesn't get over the cliff. Goodnight, kid."

But she didn't sleep. Jane, not sleeping either, knew it because she heard her tossing restlessly, once she heard her walking round her room.

Walking to a window again to look out?

But in the morning, none of the household venturing out into the very cold air until after Rodriguez's correct ten o'clock, April was a different person. She was quite enchanted.

Hurrying down to the beach, and shivering with every step, suddenly, like walking out of a refrigerator, it was summer in winter. April, lying back in a brief bikini, stretched luxuriously and with all the grace of a cat.

"But this is wonderful!" she thrilled.

While she and Jane sunbaked, Joao, Rodriguez and the young doctor swam the length of the exceedingly pretty beach. Then they came back to the girls, and the five of them basked, talked desultorily, often slept. It was an idyllic existence, utterly blissful, utterly lazy, and it set the pattern for the week.

Blazing fires at night. Hot sun by day. Always the sough of the sea, and the sight of the steep and picturesque fishing cottages, all in dazzling white but each with a differently designed chimney. Each day followed in the same pattern, though after the third day they were only four, Rodriguez having deserted them for pastimes of his own.

"I must tell you," smiled the senhor, "that there was a childhood friend very precious to Rodriguez. Will it disturb you"—to April—"if I whisper that it was a girl?"

"You can sing it aloud," April assured him. "I wish him luck."

"And I," put in Jane, "wish him no return to Ceylon, for he seems happier here."

"Yes," nodded Joao, "and I will have some words about that with my sister. I do not believe she will be difficult. Her only brother being unmarried, I think she was under the misapprehension that I needed Rodriguez out there. But now it is different. I intend not to need to borrow anyone else's family." His eyes were closed, so neither April nor Jane could read the dark depths, but their own glances met. . . .

The doctor took a run up to Lisbon to inspect the medical university. Rodriguez was away so much they barely saw him, even at meals.

"I think," shrugged Joao, "the romance must go well."

It was that day, the girls having ensconced themselves on the beach with rugs, cushions, magazines and the huge hamper that Joao always had brought down, the senhor taking his usual beach-length swim, that Jane, leaning back on the sand and daydreaming, opened her eyes as she always did to enjoy the luxury of seeing people eighty feet up in overcoats, saw—saw—

No, it couldn't be!

She closed her eyes again. But when she opened them once more, with clearer focus, more deliberation, she still saw the figure, and it still looked like—

But now it was gone.

She sat up and unscrewed the thermos. A cup of coffee, she thought. I must be seeing things.

April, a little greenishly pale, though that must be the reflection of the flawless pale-blue water on the flawless pale-yellow beach, said quickly, "No, you'll strain your arm. Let me, Jane." And did—spilling the entire contents on the sand.

"Oh dear, how stupid! Now I must climb up for more."

"Not for me, April."

"But certainly for Joao. He looks for a cup when he comes out."

That was true, but all the same Jane did not think that Joao would make an issue of it if by accident it was not there. Still, if April wanted to do the service, let her climb the eighty feet.

"Please yourself," she smiled.

"Oh, I am, Jane. Jane, I *am*!" It was an odd rejoinder but one that Jane did not think about. Not then. She watched April climbing up. She watched her out of sight.

Joao came out of the water and rubbed himself dry with an immense towel. Jane explained about the coffee, and he nodded, and they both lay in the sun, and Jane, anyway, slept.

When she awoke the sun was much lower. April was not there, but the thermos was.

"Has she come and gone again?" asked Jane, still a little stupid with sleep.

"No. Just gone."

"But the flask is here."

"It never went. I noticed that when I came out of the water. She never took it up."

"But—but I don't understand. That's what she went for."

"No, she never went up for that."

"Joao . . . " Jane always addressed him as senhor, but this time a puzzled urgency unloosened her tongue.

If he noticed her use of his name he did not show it. "Come, little one," he said, "come up the cliff to the house. I cannot tell you, for I do not know myself—not yet. I can only think—"

"Think what?"

"What I have observed and sensed and felt."

"What? *What*?"

"It is not my prerogative to tell you. It is hers."

"April's?"

"Your sister's, senhorita. Come, and we will see if she has done that thing."

"*Done* it? Why, you sound as though she won't be there, as though if she has anything to tell it will not be by mouth but by—by—"

"By note. By letter. Yes, and I think it will. Now, can you manage that cushion? I will carry the rest."

It was useless to try to hurry up to the cliff top. Apart from the rugs, the magazines and the hamper, Jane's arm had to be protected. Today it seemed to the suddenly desperate Jane that the senhor fussed inordinately at each rocky bend, protected her too much.

"We're twice the usual time," she cried out at last in dismay.

"There is plenty of time," he assured her. "A lifetime, I believe." At least Jane thought it sounded like that.

But at last they were there. Walking the last few steps into the cliff house. Jane was going through the rooms calling April's name. And April was not responding.

A servant spoke in Portuguese to Joao, and Joao nodded soberly.

"Upstairs," he said to Jane, "there is a note."

"A note?"

"For you, senhorita. Senhorita Winthrop left it."

"Left it?"

"When she left here herself." With delicacy he asked, "Do you want to read it alone, or shall I come with you?"

Jane stood perfectly still, feeling somehow suspended, weightless, not there or anywhere, outside of herself. But she had to come down to reality. She had to go upstairs and see that April really had gone. Why? Where? And she had to read that note.

"Come with me," she said jerkily, suddenly very young and wondering and needing help, and, protecting her injured arm, he went with her up the steps.

CHAPTER TEN

"Dear Wren, I have left for England with Terry Marsden. I'm marrying him tonight. You thought you saw him when you were down on the beach. I knew I saw him, and I knew that I had been waiting only for that.

"I love him, Jane. I did right from the moment I first met him, but I fought it with all my power. I'd had enough of not enough, I wanted to be important and rich.

"I admit none of this is what I planned, or ever would have planned, but it's no use, little sister, it's stronger than I am, and even if Terry and I are poor as church mice we'll be together, and though it will be hard for you to believe it of me, that's all I care about.

"Don't worry about Mummy throwing a fit, she'll see in Terry and me Father and herself all over again. Remember that love she used to prate and I used to sneer about? But it's true, small Jane, it's true.

"Yet what am I doing telling you and Joao?"

—Inserted under this was a man's writing, evidently Terry's. It read: "What, indeed?"

Then they both had signed: "April, Terry."

Jane, still dazed, suspended, weightless, put the letter down. She permitted Joao to lead her to the windowseat, gently press her down.

"It's not true, is it?" she asked vaguely.

"Quite true. I knew it on the sands, I knew it as you slept."

"Then—"

"Then why didn't I awaken you? What could you have done?"

"Stopped them."

"Stopped a dream? For it is that, child. I have observed this pair, reckless, feckless, selfish, unthinking. They were still made for each other, and they will succeed. It is all for the better that April has fought against it, it makes the losing more a triumph, a triumph of love. I believe that Marsden will come good, and very good. He was empty before, purposeless, now he has April to solidify a future that was barely the glimmer of a hope."

"But April. . . ."

"She has him in her turn. That she needs him, and needs him desperately, has been proven in these last weeks. Why, otherwise, did I agree to come here, child? I could see her desperation, her last bid to live her own life, not a life with him."

"It was not only her own life she was thinking about," put in Jane tremulously. "It was yours as well."

He smiled carefully. "Oh, that! First Rodriguez, then me. Do you think for a moment that I—"

But Jane was still worried.

"April can't live like a church mouse, she's not the sort," she protested.

"*Was* not the sort. She has changed now. She is half a person, and Terry is the other half. Anyway, what is this talk of church mice? He is a fine journalist, and your sister has a quite remarkable voice."

Jane looked at him in astonishment. "A voice? But you said . . . you said. . . ."

"Of course. As the English—and no doubt the

Australians—put it, I played along. April, if the extra money is needed, will be able to earn it. Though I have a feeling that the new April, with Marsden beside her, will be content with less.

"Well, little one, what is the next frown on your brow?"

"Mother," sighed Jane.

"Your sister explained that. I don't think you are really worried."

"No, I'm not. What April does is always right with Mother. And money has never really concerned Mummy very much." The unremarkable flat, Jane remembered, the ever-present pack of cards, the living on the past—and her Vernon. Those first happy days. She felt suddenly sorry for her own father. Those who kiss and those who are kissed.

She was not aware that she said that aloud.

"What is it, Jane?" he asked. She told him, and he nodded. "It is sad, yes, and yet to either it is the next best thing."

"To loving equally?"

"Yes."

She thought that over, sad herself. It had to be the next best thing for her. For she loved this man.

But also, she remembered, it had to be next best thing for him. He loved April. He had said so.

"I'm sorry, Joao," she sighed.

"Sorry?"

"For you. I—I remember going up to Sri Pada."

"So do I. How could I forget?"

"You said it then."

"Said what?"

" 'I love her.' You—you said it about April."

"Said it of . . . why, yes, I did. And I meant it. Indeed, I meant it."

"Poor Joao!"

"Wait, little one, wait. I never finished that day. It should have been 'I love her because she brought me you.' "

"Brought—" she began.

"You—*you*, Jane. Plain Jane. The little brown wren. I

don't know about that, all I know is that every time ever since when I have been with you I have cried *Ayubowen* in my heart and put my hands together in prayer."

"But, Joao—" she faltered.

"Can't you see, child, you are the one I want to kiss, and seeing you have nothing to give in return all I can hope is that giving and not receiving can be my next best."

"But I have it to give, oh, I have, Joao! I just didn't understand . . . I never dreamed . . . I couldn't dare hope . . . ."

"But surely I told you, told you a hundred times? A Portuguese, I said, is not a Sinhalese, he comes halfway, and he will come, if needed, and if love is waiting there, all the way to a heart that is whole. You had said your heart was whole."

"It was." Jane looked up at him shyly, then, seeing his lean, sensitive face, the face she loved, she said with rising strength, "But not now. I and my heart are not whole any more." Slowly, with conviction, with knowledge, "Not ever any more."

"For which I say *Ayubowen,* for which I join my finger tips again." And Joao did.

Standing in the blue-washed room, they stood all at once instead on Sri Pada . . . by the Sacred Footprint . . . having clanged the bell of the temple.

Having reached the top.

WINDY NIGHT, RAINY MORROW

Windy Night, Rainy Morrow

Ivy Ferrari

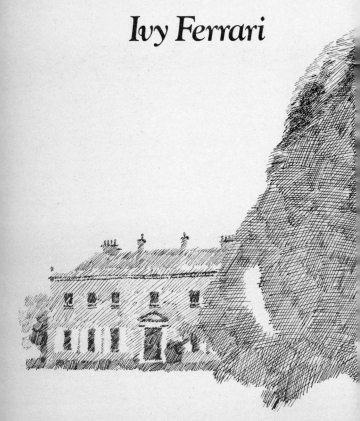

"I'm not retracting my invitation," Alan Copeland said grimly. "Unfortunately the cable misfired and you're here so I consider I still owe you hospitality. But," he paused, "I forbid you to visit my sister on any pretext whatever. She has had enough heartbreak."

Tina Rutherford listened in furious dismay. When her brother Bruno was tragically killed she had decided to leave Rome and come to Northumberland, where he had been working. There she would meet his fiancée, Helen Copeland, and clear up his affairs.

Now it seemed, she would have to clear his name — and this she was determined to do in spite of all the restrictions imposed by the arrogant Adam Copeland!

CHAPTER ONE

"Go if you must, darling," Mark Rutherford said gently to his daughter. "But I can't help wondering if it's wise to visit England so soon."

Tina moved restlessly about the large salon of their Rome apartment. The city sweltered in spring heat, but they were aware of the sun only as a distant dazzle behind drawn blinds.

"You mean—wise to go where it all happened, to meet the Copelands?"

"Better to wait, perhaps. It's all still so shocking, so painful. You could always stay with your Aunt Lucia. Of course in my case—"

Her father glanced at the expensive luggage piled near his desk, at the passport folder on the table, the labels with a New York destination. His eyes held a resigned acceptance.

Behind his chair an English grandfather clock ticked off the seconds with a quiet insistence that impinged on the roar of traffic outside. Tina flung herself into an armchair, shook back her ebony fall of hair and wished passionately that time might be set backwards, that it could be still a fortnight ago, with her father anticipating his lecture tour and her own life a happy careless existence of secretarial college, outings and parties with friends.

Unwillingly her gaze slanted to her brother's photograph. She saw a clever, sweet-tempered face, with clear strong lines of brow and jaw. Bruno—impossible that he could be dead, wiped out in seconds in an English car accident. He had been only twenty-three, five years older than herself.

Like herself he resembled their long-dead Italian mother. Her photograph was on the desk too, in her bridal headdress. She could have been Tina all over again. But Regina Rutherford's blood had been wholly Latin. Tina's was mingled, for Mark Rutherford was a quiet self-possessed Englishman, with the controlled emotions of his race.

"Of course you must go to the States, just as you planned," she reassured him. "This lecture tour has always meant so much to you. And now there's nothing you can do—for Bruno."

She heard her father's sharp sigh. Never yet had he broken down, even when the cable came from England; at least not in her presence, but she had watched the paling of his tan, the desolation in those so-English blue eyes under the graying thatch of hair.

Although Tina had Regina's magnolia skin, wide sensuous lips and poised graceful body, her eyes, soot-fringed, were of a soft flower blue, subtly echoing her father's.

"Like English forget-me-nots," he always said. And often he had spoken to her of Coventina's Well, on the Roman Wall in Northumberland, with its smother of wild forget-me-nots in late spring; Coventina the little Roman water-goddess, so real to those Roman soldiers stationed on the Wall all those centuries ago that they had thrown their precious coins as offerings into that ancient spring.

And so Mark Rutherford had called his daughter Coventina, in memory both of her Roman ancestry and those far gray moors he loved.

Those same forget-me-not eyes, soft and troubled now by grief, were actually deceptive, suggesting a mildness and docility very far from the truth. For Tina was wilful, spirited and halfway to being spoiled, her father's darling and so lately her brother's delight. Life had been utterly pleasant and taken for granted, Bruno's friends had vied for her favors. There had been money, a lavish spending allowance, as much education as she wished. Until now, life had denied her little.

If she had been wholly of her mother's blood her sudden tragedy would have brought swift passionate tears, a total abandonment to grief and then a sure healing. Tina had cried, but not for long. Her father's stoical courage, like a vein of ore, streaked through her southern emotionalism. She was his daughter too.

Mark Rutherford roused himself to speak again. "I still think it might be the wrong decision, you going over there. But you won't be alone. I know Chris will look after you, bless him!"

"I feel I ought to go, though in a way I'm dreading it. But Bruno *was* engaged to Helen Copeland—that makes us—well, almost sisters. I feel I owe it to her. And then there's Bruno's unfinished work on the dig—"

"It was all so sudden, wasn't it? Bruno falling in love, becoming engaged—" Mark Rutherford broke off, his thoughtful face a little bewildered. A distinguished archaeological scholar, a world-wide authority on the Roman occupation of Britain, he had an endearing habit of being constantly surprised by real life.

"That's what I mean," Tina said slowly. "She's almost one of the family now. And her brother too, of course. Remember what Bruno said in his letters, how he admired Adam Copeland? . . . Yes, I think I must go, Dad. You needn't worry about me. After all, I almost know the place."

Tina tried to speak brightly, but her young heart sank a little. She had been to Northumberland once, nine years ago, while on holiday with Bruno and her father. Details were lost now, but she remembered a gray spring, the moors lying heavy and sullen under a leaden sky. She could just recall glimpses of the great lonely bastions of Hadrian's Wall, built by the Romans who had sacked and occupied those sad northern moors sixteen centuries ago.

Her knowledge of the Wall, however, had nothing to do with that long-ago visit. While she and Bruno were still small children their father had built for them a large relief model of the original Wall, big enough to fill their playroom and exact down to each turret and milecastle, each bridge and gateway, temple and bathhouse. Though the real Wall was ruined now, long stretches of it non-existent, Tina never doubted her ability to find her way anywhere along its length, from Milking Gap to the Cat Stairs, from the heights of Sewingshields Crags to the shining sands of the Solway. Already she had pinpointed

354

Hadrian's Edge, the home of the Copelands, lying west of Chollerford.

"Chris will be glad of your help at the dig," her father mused. "And you know so much about it already, from Bruno's letters."

"Chris has already suggested it—that I should work on the dig, I mean. After all, I've got to do something while I'm there—I can't just sit around getting in the Copelands' hair all day." Tina thought with relief of Chris Irwin, a friend and fellow lecturer of Bruno's, who had been assisting him on the archaeological dig on Hadrian's Wall. Chris was so efficient, so uncomplicated. She would be glad to have him around as a comforting background. Besides, he knew the Copelands already, which would be an undeniable help to her.

She saw the familiar mask of grief settle again on her father's face and said quickly: "It's time for tea. You know you always look for it at four and it's nearly ten past—you stuffy old Englishman, you!" But she slipped to the arm of his chair to drop a kiss on the top of his head.

They had just begun tea, served by their voluble Italian maid, when Chris Irwin arrived.

"Trust an Englishman to smell tea!" Maria lifted her solid shoulders expressively. "I bring another cup."

Chris gave her his usual quiet grin, greeted Tina and her father and sat down to light a cigaret. He was a tall, easy-boned Londoner with a relaxed personality, his coloring fair to medium, his eyes a forthright gray. He and Bruno had both taken a year off from their work as lecturers in a Rome Institute of Archaeology to carry out field work on the dig at Hadrian's Edge. Chris had travelled back to Rome for Bruno's funeral but was now due to return to the dig.

Bruno had been in charge of operations, though Chris had spent longer in England, having opted to go out first and make the preliminary arrangements. He had been restless and rootless since the break-up of his marriage to a beautiful Italian photographic model. Some years older than Bruno, he had always treated Tina with the amused indulgence that an elder brother would have shown her.

Tina, knowledgeable without being too committed, listened in silence to the conversation of the men. They were talking of Bruno's plans, of the work already done, the discoveries made. Both men were subdued, almost listless, though the dig showed exciting promise. Tina felt impatient. Interested as she was in archaeology, for owing to her father she had almost cut her teeth on it, she yet thought of the dig emotionally rather than otherwise. It was the scene of Bruno's final labors, his last enthusiasms. And now his work was finished. Others would have the recognition, the praise. And the cold Northumbrian wind would blow uncaring over Hadrian's Edge. . . .

At last Chris spoke directly to her. "So you've decided to come with me, Tina?"

She braced herself for criticism. "The Copelands have been kind enough to invite me."

"I'm not so sure it's the right decision, for all that. Though of course I'll be glad to have your help. That is if you promise to behave yourself," he said crisply.

"On Hadrian's Wall? Have I any choice?"

He smiled. "No night clubs or bright lights, I grant you. That wasn't quite what I meant. You know that trouble has a habit of following attractive girls around."

"And good-looking young men?" she parried.

A shadow crossed his face. "I can't say I've had any trouble like that yet. Even if I *were* interested, girls are pretty thin on the ground round Hadrian's Edge—except for the students on the dig, of course. And usually one can't see *them* for mud."

Tina poured out more tea. "You'll hate the weather too," he warned her.

"It's still spring," her father protested. "Summers up there can be warm, you know. But I grant you spring is usually bitter."

Tina shivered, imagining hail on the wind, huddled sheep, a sad and shrivelled turf. She had never minded exciting weather, rainbow and tempest, the battling of the elements. Italian storms were exhilarating she felt.

Her father excused himself to make a phone call. Chris turned to her again, stubbing out his cigaret.

"I meant that, you know—about behaving yourself. Otherwise the deal's off."

"I can look after myself," she said loftily. But even as she spoke she remembered escapades in the past from which Chris had rescued her. Since his separation he had always been around if she needed him and, like Bruno, she had expected him to pamper her whims. He had been indulgent, affectionate but not at all blind to her many faults. "Anyway," she finished, "I shall be at the house and you at the hotel, so you can dodge me whenever you like. Fair enough?"

He shook his head at her. "Why did no one spank you when you were small—good and hard? No, don't tell me. You looked at them out of those fragile blue eyes—and they just hadn't the heart. A pity for your sake, Tina."

"Why?"

"Because one day you're going to meet a man who has a trick for every one of yours, who will hurt you like hell—"again the shadow crossed his face—"and make you wish you'd never been born. You'll see!" he said all this with a hint of relish.

"Sounds fun!" Tina said lightly. Then her eyes swung to Bruno's photograph and her voice softened again to grief. "You *do* understand why I have to go, Chris? I can't just resign myself to—what happened. Not like you and Dad. I've got to go there—it's just as if he's telling me. As if he's still there in spirit, and somehow troubled. And there's Helen. I've never met her—and I want to. We ought to be friends. You liked her, didn't you—and her brother?"

"Yes, I liked her. I'm not so sure about her brother."

"You mean Adam Copeland?"

He nodded. "He rules the roost up there, a kind of country squire and uncrowned king rolled into one. You might say he bestrides the Wall like a Colossus. The Copeland family has been known and respected in the area for generations. They've been magistrates—he's a local J.P.—local squires, served on the County Council. The local church has more than one Copeland on its memorial tablets. Mention his name up there and you have everyone touching their caps. But Bruno probably told you all this in his letters."

"You must be joking. His letters were all about Helen. But he did say Adam Copeland liked to rule *her* life."

"You could say that too." Chris hesitated. "You're sure you're doing the right thing, accepting this invitation of theirs? You don't think it would be better to wait, until everyone concerned has had time to get over it all—"

"No, I don't. I've told you—" Tina began collecting the cups to place on the tray. "I've got this strong feeling I must go—"

"You always were one for following your instincts." He shrugged. "And I suppose you can always practise your wiles on Adam Copeland."

"I might." Her smile was half sad, half teasing.

"I doubt if you'd get anywhere. He's a hard-headed Northumbrian, not a susceptible Roman. And a land agent, of all things, his feet in the soil, his mind on estate problems. Don't deceive yourself about him, my dear Tina. You'll find yourself up against something as impregnable as the Wall itself." And with this warning he got up to leave.

A few days later, when Mark Rutherford had already flown to the States, Chris drove Tina to Milan, where they stayed a couple of days en route, as Chris had arranged to lecture there before returning to England. From Milan they flew to London Airport, with a further short lap to Newcastle. Here Chris picked up his car which he had garaged in the city and drove her out to Corbridge-on-Tyne.

Corbridge in the rain—a gray steepled town perched along the northern escarpment of the river. The Romans had called it Corstopitum and made it their supply base for the building of the Wall.

Rain, bitter spring rain—the gutters ran, the drenching trees swayed about the ancient church, the river ran steely over its pale pebbles under the wooded heights across the valley.

Tina sat huddled in her blue anorak, shivering and drinking tea in the lounge of Chris's hotel. She was tired and depressed after the journey. The outer door was opened five times in as many minutes, swinging draughtily in the wake of other drenched tea-seekers.

Chris had gone to telephone Mrs. Butterfield, Adam Copeland's housekeeper, who combined her household duties with enthusiastic archaeological activities. In Chris's absence she had been in charge of operations at the dig.

Tina pulled a face at the thought of her. She had met female archaeological enthusiasts many times at the flat in Rome, and usually escaped by the back stairs. Interested in the subject as she was, there came a limit to one's enthusiasm in the presence of these excitedly-babbling ladies.

At the moment, though, the thought of Carrie Butterfield merely hung on her mind like an irritating burr she was too listless to brush off.

Something bigger was troubling Tina, one of her dark sinking misgivings. Already she had grave doubts about her journey. Back in the Rome sunshine it had seemed an overwhelming necessity. Now, in this chill northern rain, her reasons for coming seemed suddenly impulsive, without reason. It could be just because she was chilled and depressed, already missing the light and warmth of Italy. It was difficult to understand how these Northerners felt any emotions at all in weather like this. And sympathetically if inconsequentially, she thought of those miserable legionaries fresh from Rome to do duty on the Wall centuries ago, and with no recreations except gambling in the bath-houses. How they must have hated this cold northern clime! Yet she remembered too that many of them had married Briton girls from the wild countryside bordering the Wall and when their time-serving duties were over had settled down to farm and raise families. It was odd, she mused, how traces of that same Roman blood must have shaped the Northumbrians today, perhaps accounting for that warmth which her father insisted was one of their best-known virtues.

Warmth! She shivered again as the hotel door crashed open for the umpteenth time. . . .

Tina found herself arrested by the sight of the tall man who stood there. With an easy authority his gaze moved over the occupants of the lounge, as if looking for someone. He was well but negligently dressed in drill trousers, a white sweater and a waterproof jacket, and the clothes had the look of being moulded to his hard muscular body.

A man who spent most of his time outdoors, Tina guessed. His tan had a weathered vitality that suggested storm and wind rather than exposure to sun.

His gaze had reached her now, measured, almost insolent. Cold gray eyes surveyed her from under a dark sweep of hair. Tina saw the hard implacable curve of jaw and temple, the heavy eyebrows. He was too racy-looking to be handsome. Tough but interesting was her final summing-up, and almost automatically, being Tina, she widened her forget-me-not eyes.

His gaze settled, his expression changed. Those heavy eyebrows lifted fractionally and a smile touched his mouth, a smile which made Tina hot instead of chilled. It was amused, condescending and somehow utterly disconcerting.

"Do you happen to own a blue Fiat?" he demanded, and repeated the registration number.

"My friend does. I have the car keys here." Tina, a capable driver, had been at the wheel on the road from Newcastle.

"Then perhaps you'll kindly park it in a more sensible situation. I want to get my car out."

He had already moved to the door, somehow conveying without moving an eyelash that he had no intention of being kept waiting.

She moved toward him with deliberate languor.

"And put a jerk into it, my lass!" he shot at her. "I happen to be in a hurry."

Tina winced. She waited imperiously for him to open

the door, saw a further flicker of amusement in his face.

Outside he waited, hands in pockets, while she manoeuvred the car. She had parked it badly, she realized, and the knowledge annoyed her. She supposed the mud-splattered Land-Rover nearby was his vehicle. That meant he was probably a farmer. Yet she was shaken, not having visualized a moorland farmer in quite that mould.

"Thanks," he said, almost as if conferring a favor. He added carelessly: "Staying at the hotel?"

She stood beside him, pulling up the hood of her anorak against the rain. "No, I'm going on to Hadrian's Edge. My friend's staying here. He's going to drive me up."

"For the dig, are you? Then don't trouble him. I'm going up there. You can have a lift if you like."

The stranger had half turned away, as if expecting her to refuse. And this too had been her first instinct. Then she hesitated. This man had stung and intrigued her. Also she had failed to impress him. This was a novelty so foreign to her she felt piqued enough to challenge it, tired and depressed as she was.

"I'll have to go in and leave word first—if you can wait."

He was already opening the door of the Land-Rover. "Make it snappy, then."

Having explained the situation to Chris, who was relieved to be spared further driving, she returned and got her suitcase from the car. The stranger heaved it into the back of his vehicle.

"No gilded chariot, as you see." The seat bounced as he settled his weight beside her. "Shove those ledgers in the back, and mind that can of chemical. Come far?"

"Oh yes—quite a way." Tina did not consider he deserved more details.

He backed into the road, drove with careless ease through narrow streets and a cobbled market square, took a dangerous bend as if in his sleep and then the Land-Rover was climbing out and away to the higher land. The sagging clouds lifted, the rain became a mere drizzle. A bleak soft light lit the rolling countryside. As they climbed the contours of the valley became more marked.

"Been up here before?"

"Once—years ago."

"We're on the Military Road now—it was built by General Wade during the Stuart rebellion. It runs along the top of the original Wall at this point." He spoke tersely and clearly, without any special enthusiasm.

Tina's glance went knowledgeably to the contours of the rolling fields, noting the declivities that marked the old lines of Roman Vallum and ditch skirting the Wall. "Yes, I did know that," she said quietly.

He gave her a sideways glance. "Done it all at school, I suppose?"

Without warning he swung the car into a lay-by where the road had mounted the brink of a high plateau. The view opened out so suddenly Tina gasped. Now the rain had lifted she could see for perhaps twenty miles on either hand, with wooded hills to the southwest and far away to the north a faint blue range she guessed to be the Cheviots. Ahead was wilder moorland country, mounting to the crags which she knew belonged to the limestone strata known as the Whin Sill. And now again, as the light sharpened, she could see the Wall itself, a faint gray line mounting peak after peak of the crags. Tears stung her eyes. It was an emotional moment. So many centuries ago her mother's countrymen had toiled and fought and died on these cold northern moors, leaving a monument for all time. . . .

"You can see the causeways of the Vallum quite clearly here." Her companion spoke with condescension, as he might to a schoolgirl. "I suppose you know what the Vallum is?"

"A wide ditch between two mounds," she said. "Designed as an obstacle to any barbarians approaching the Wall."

He was startled, then grinned. "You *have* mugged it up, haven't you?" Then abruptly, after scanning her face: "Your eyes are the exact blue of forget-me-nots. Ever been told that?" His direct question surprised her.

"Frequently." She met his stare as calmly as she could.

Now his eyes held a lurking suspicion. "But you're not English. That hair and—" His gaze took in her ripe young figure.

"My father is English."

"But a Continental mother, I'd guess. Well, they've all kinds up there at the dig. The Youth Hostel's like a League of Nations. They've Irish, Poles, an African or two—"

"You sound resentful."

He offered her a battered packet of cigarets. She wondered where his hurry was now. He seemed quite content to sit at the wheel and relax. "You don't smoke?" He lit one himself. "Resentful, you say? Perhaps we Northumbrians have arrogantly assumed rights of ownership of the Wall. After all, some of our ancestors helped to build it as slave labor."

"And some of the not-so-distant ones helped to destroy it," Tina protested. "Even as late as Victorian times, the local farmers were pulling it down to build their barns."

He surveyed her again with that easy amusement, that slight lift of black eyebrow, which so infuriated her. "Quite a little know-all, aren't you? I can't imagine why you bother. One flicker of those long eyelashes would impress any man so much more."

Her eyes widened. He laughed openly. "Oh, not me, my dear. Or shall we say I'm impressed but not devastated. And I'm also afraid I have no more time to chat." He started the car and drove on.

"I suppose you know the length of a Roman mile too?" he asked suddenly.

"The Wall is eighty Roman, seventy-three and a half English miles," she said almost mechanically.

"You're quite a girl, aren't you? Should be able to hold your own up at the dig. Not to mention setting the Youth Hostel by the ears!"

"But I'm not going to the Youth Hostel." As Tina spoke rain lashed the windscreen again with vehement force, blotting out the landscape. His hand went out to switch on the windscreen-wipers to see the road ahead.

"Not the Youth Hostel? Then where? I hope you've booked in somewhere. Accommodation at Hadrian's Edge is almost nonexistent."

"Oh, you misunderstand me. When I said Hadrian's Edge, I didn't mean just the place. I meant the house of that name."

She sensed his sudden check. His gaze swung to her face, then front again. "You mean—*my* house?" She heard his swift indrawn breath. "Then you must be Tina Rutherford."

"I am." The truth hit her. She said faintly, "Then —you're Adam—Adam Copeland?"

He nodded, his gaze still on the road. A chill seemed to steal over the car. And if anything, his face had hardened.

She was appalled. This then was Adam Copeland, Bruno's friend, Helen's brother, the man who might have been her brother-in-law by marriage, almost one of the family. And she had been pert, coquettish. This was awful! She was genuinely grieved. Scoring off a stranger was one thing. But *Adam Copeland*.

In a flash, all Chris's warnings fell into place. A kind of country squire and uncrowned king rolled into one. . . . Yes, she had already learned his arrogance, his almost regal orders and demands No doubt the chill she now sensed came from disapproval on his part.

She realized an effort was required of her. "I'm sorry. I didn't realize. . . . It's a bit late to exchange polite greetings now, isn't it?"

"More than a bit late, I'd say." The words were an edged drawl, suggesting neither warmth nor welcome. Tina's heart quickened. Something was wrong. She could feel it in her bones.

"I take it you didn't get my cable, then?" he demanded.

"Cable?" she faltered. "No, I haven't had any cable. We stayed two days in Milan on the way over here. Chris had a couple of lectures to give—"

"Chris Irwin? Where is he now, then—oh, of course, your friend at the hotel. . . . But I know *his* car. That one you were driving—"

"It was new just before he came out to Rome. I don't suppose you'd seen it." She returned to the cable. "What was the message, then?"

"It told you to cancel the trip."

Told, not asked. And cancel, not postpone. "But why?" she asked.

"I'll explain later. Now we've got this far we may as well go on up to the house."

His tone was quite final. She subsided into dismayed silence. His driving was now a matter of grim concentration, with occasional savage outbursts of speed which she was certain betrayed his anger.

After more switchbacking of hills, he whipped the car suddenly up a side-track. It dipped into dark plantations, emerged on a bare plateau and dipped again. The woods grew thicker as the road took another twisting climb, emerging at last to heights where blue views could be glimpsed through the thinning trees. At the end of a steep drive they reached a high-standing house of dark stone, gabled and turreted, its upper storey naked to the gales. This, Tina recognized from Bruno's snapshots, was Hadrian's Edge, turning an impregnable face to wind and storm and facing the moors toward the Cheviots.

For a moment the man beside her sat immovable. Then he said: "Before we get out, you'd better hear what I have to say." He eyed her in such cold challenge her heart sank. The amused tolerance of only minutes ago might never have existed.

She faced him proudly, but with huge misgivings.

"Since we wrote inviting you here"—his tone was abrupt—"something has happened. Something highly unpleasant and unexpected. I warn you to prepare yourself for a shock."

"I—don't understand." What could have happened, now the worst had drained her of tears? Bruno was dead, part of her happy life was gone for ever. What else could there be?

He paused to light another cigaret, perhaps also to consider his next words. And in the brief reprieve Tina remembered one of Shakespeare's sonnets she had studied at school and which had always clung in her memory. Fragments of the words came to haunt her:

> "—*Ah do not, when my hearth hath 'scaped*
> *this sorrow,*
> *Come in the rearward of a conquered woe.*
> *Give not a windy night a rainy morrow*—"

Adam Copeland was speaking again. "What has happened may make a difference to your stay here, may even make it impossible. That was why I tried to reach you by cable." He turned to face her.

"But what could happen? Bruno—"

"Pay attention and listen," he commanded. "Since the inquest someone has come forward with news that has been most upsetting to us all, particularly to my sister. We have discovered your brother was not alone in the car the night he was killed."

She eyed him dumbly, her heart in agitation.

"Not alone," he repeated. His gray eyes seemed to darken. "He had a girl with him, and she was seen by at least two different people."

Tina was bewildered. "Who was she?"

"We don't know that. It was a filthy night, fog and rain. No one got a good look at her. But it does explain something else—a letter found in Bruno's room, written on the notepaper of an Edinburgh Hotel—and confirming the booking of a double room."

"Oh!" Tina felt the color rush to her face. "You mean—he—"

"We know no more. The girl was obviously unhurt, and made herself scarce after telephoning for an ambulance. It looks as if it were some rather sordid escapade."

"I don't believe it!" she gasped. "He loved Helen—he was engaged to her."

"We understood so," he rasped. "But I had forbidden Helen to marry until she came of age, for good reasons of my own which he was inclined to question. Your brother—"

His gaze suddenly stilled, his voice dropped a tone or two, became less harsh. "your brother is dead and I hate to say this. But it's quite clear now that he was deceiving Helen, that he wasn't prepared to wait—in fact that his feelings were very shallow indeed."

"That isn't true!" she flashed. "He *loved* her—I know he did. It was plain enough in his letters."

He went on evenly and coldly, his profile now turned away. "I can well imagine those letters. Italians can no doubt make an overwhelming passion out of a very small attachment. This love, as you call it, could not have been very deep if he was prepared to be unfaithful at the first temptation. . . . But we won't argue about that. You haven't heard the end of it yet."

Tina's brain whirled in sick misery. So there was still more! She waited.

"Helen, as you know, was very distressed by your brother's death. That was why we couldn't attend the funeral. But this discovery has caused a complete breakdown. She's now in a nursing home and her recovery could take months, if not longer."

"I'm sorry!" With Helen she could sympathize. Helen too was mourning Bruno. "But she can't really *believe* this. Bruno wouldn't hurt a fly. He's gentle and kind and—"

"Unfaithful?" he supplied relentlessly. He stubbed out the half-smoked cigaret. "I'm telling you this now because in the circumstances you may feel you would rather not stay with us. But understand that I'm not retracting my invitation. Unfortunately the cable misfired and you're here, so I consider I still owe you hospitality. There is another reason." He paused. "As you can imagine, local gossip has been busy over the situation. I have done my best to suggest that your brother was merely giving a lift to a hitchhiker. Your presence here would add weight to this supposition and would save my sister humiliation. It might also occur to you that it would be kinder to your brother's memory. On the other hand, if you would prefer to stay at the hotel with—your friend—"

Tina said hotly: "In a double room? Is that what you mean?"

A faint amusement warmed his eyes. "Quite a little spitfire, aren't you? All right, which is it to be? Go—or stay?"

He ran a cloth over the misted windscreen, got out to clear the outside of the glass; and possibly also to give her time. Tina sat wretched, shocked, watching his tall body moving about in her field of vision, glimpsing that stony profile, the heavy brows drawn over eyes narrowed in concentration. She was angry, resentful, a little afraid of him. Yet, only minutes ago, she remembered the warm boldness of his smile, his bright mocking eyes. He had been different then, arrogant, conceited, but human.

And now he was at the open door, looking in.

"Well?"

She got out at her side, walked round to join him, the wind searing her like a knife, so that she looked wan and shivering.

She had had no time to think after all, and as usual relied on instinct. "I'll accept your invitation to stay. But I'd like to tell you why."

His frown was impatient. "All right, my lass, but don't make a speech of it. I've work waiting to do."

"I'll stay," she repeated proudly. "Because one day—and soon—I hope to change your opinion of Bruno. Whatever you say—or guess at—I know him better than you do. He couldn't possibly treat a girl he loved like that. There must be some other explanation and I mean to find it."

He shrugged. "Please yourself, of course. But if you take my advice you'll confine your investigations to the dig." His tone was like a slap in the face. "Who knows, you might otherwise find something you don't like."

Her face flamed, she could find no words.

"Bruno was no plaster saint, my dear. In these last few weeks I've been hearing gossip about him. You're sure to hear it too. So don't say you haven't been warned."

The clouds above them had darkened. Suddenly lightning flashed, the sky cracked in thunder and far across the moors she saw the misty splendor of a wild rainbow. And she too was caught up in a storm, helpless in the tempest of her emotions. She told herself she hated this man, who had already patently rejected her along with her brother. But in that flash of lightning came a revelation, that there was another, darker reason for her staying—because no man yet had shaken her with such power and force, because not once in her young pampered life had she been spoken to like this, set at nought like this. No fluttering of forget-me-not eyes could dispel this man's dislike. And the knowledge was an equal pain to his disclosure about Bruno.

"Perhaps your sister wasn't a plaster saint either!" she said with spirit, between two thunderclaps. "Hasn't it occurred to you Bruno might have had good reason for—pulling out?"

His eyes held hers, with a still anger. "I promise you here and now, my dear, that if you try to blacken my sister's name, or do anything to distress her, I shall personally see that you regret it. Is that clear?"

Tina's chin went up. She eyed him in silence, flinching only as lightning forked in a blinding flash above them. "And one more thing," he continued. "I forbid you to visit my sister on any pretext whatever. She has had heartbreak enough."

The rain descended, with a force and fury that made more words impossible. He took her suitcase from the car, grabbed her by the elbow and more or less ran her through the open front door of the house. A collie stood waving a plumy tail, looking for notice. He threw the dog a gruff word, then called in paradeground tones:

"Carrie, are you there?"

A slim active woman appeared. Tina noticed with relief that she had a kind if preoccupied face and couldn't have been much above forty.

"Oh, there you are. Carrie, it seems Miss Rutherford did not get my cable and has arrived after all. I'll leave her to you." Then, rather in the manner of having disposed of a crate of chickens, he talked across Tina's head. "Did Robertson of High Haugh ring about those drainage rights?" he wanted to know before he left.

"Yes. But he said he'd see you at Scots Gap mart anyway."

"Right. I won't be in to supper, Carrie. If Barton calls tell him the new rails are down at the sawmills."

Without another glance at Tina he had gone, walking into the deluge with an utter disregard of its effects. The car's engine revved into a powerful roar, the shabby vehicle circled the drive and disappeared into the trees and into the storm, to the accompaniment of a full barrage of further thunder and lightning.

But now, Tina saw, the rainbow had gone.

She turned blindly toward Carrie Butterfield, and something in her face sent a quick spark of sympathy into the older woman's eyes. 'Hallo," she said quietly. "In a bit of a mood, is he? Not to worry. You come into the warm and have a cup of tea."

"Her voice was brisk and educated, but warm and friendly. She guided a bewildered and upset Tina down a back passage and into a small sitting-room.

"Now, sit down. Or better give me that damp anorak first." She walked into the passage again, calling: "Isa, are you there?" Joining Tina again she said quietly: "He's told you, I see. Men can never choose the right moment for bad news. You look tired to death after your journey."

Tina's lips trembled. After the scene she had just experienced, kindness threatened to break her. Only that vein of ore, her father's courage and determination, came to her rescue. "Thank you," she said. "Yes, I am tired."

A plump, heavily-boned woman appeared in the doorway, stared stolidly at Tina from under sandy eyebrows and said: "What is it, Mrs. Butterfield? And who's yon?"

"Some tea, please, Isa. This is Tina Rutherford, Bruno's sister."

"Oh, aye. So she's come after all? She's like him—like as two peas." Isa backed out, still staring.

"You mustn't mind Isa," Carrie Butterfield said. "She's a rough diamond, but you'll get used to her ways."

Tina began to notice things about her, to relax just a little. It was a pleasant room, with a floor-length window set deeply in the wall between folded white shutters, and overlooking steeply-descending woods. A log fire flamed in the hearth, but apart from a few conventional watercolors, Tina found the decor of the room was rather strange.

Over the mantel was a huge propeller of polished wood, with an Air Force crest in the centre. Pictures of wartime aircraft, of young people in uniform crowded the bureau and bookcase tops. And standing about on occasional tables and shelves were many glittering model aircraft, some brass, others white metal. Perhaps, Tina reflected, Mr. Butterfield had been in the Air Force.

Isa arrived with a large tea-tray, still staring. "By, she's like him! *And* bonny!" She set the tray down and sighed gustily. Tina heard her muttering as she left.

"What did she say?"

Carrie, busy with the cups, smiled. "She was quoting a text. Isa's always quoting texts. Her father was a travelling preacher and she must have had texts from her cradle. You'll seldom ever see her smile. She's a born pessimist but very good at heart."

"What was the text?" Tina gratefully accepted a cup of tea.

Carrie hesitated. "It was: "Set not thy foot in thy neighbor's house, lest he weary of thee and so hate thee." Proverbs, I think."

"Oh," said Tina, and shivered. The feeling of doom returned.

"Oh, no one minds Isa! It's just that she has an uncanny habit of sizing up a situation and finding a text to suit. Do you take sugar?"

She offered a cigaret, lit one herself and sat down. Hazel eyes twinkled frankly at Tina, matching a mass of untidy waves rising from a very definite widow's peak. The face was too bony and determined for beauty, but was fascinating and full of character.

"Drink your tea and relax," she advised. "There —feeling better now?"

Tina set down the cup, again on the verge of tears. She was still wildly upset. Her shock at finding herself in Adam Copeland's company, his behavior toward her, the revelations he had made, were still too new and wounding. Added to this had come the strain of new surroundings, the need to control herself before strangers. Now her face crumpled a little.

"I didn't know who he was!" she burst out. "He offered me a lift—I didn't know—"

"And then he told you?"

Tina nodded, blinking back her tears.

"I can imagine it. He'd steamroller you with that tongue of his until you'd wonder what hit you. Not that I blame him, in some ways. He thinks the world of his sister, you know. He feels her humiliation and heartbreak just as if it were his own. They've always been very close. But there, we won't talk of it now."

She turned the conversation toward Rome. Tina brightened. They discussed her father's lecture tour.

"Best thing for him," Carrie Butterfield nodded. "Best to get away from it all. Close the hangar doors."

"What was that?" Tina looked up, puzzled.

"Oh, just an old Air Force expression. You'll hear plenty of them from me. I suppose you've noticed this room's almost an R.A.F. museum?"

"Well, yes. Was Mr. Butterfield—"

"No." Her companion's voice was sharp. "No. *He* wasn't in the Air Force. We were divorced some years ago. Don't bother to make sympathetic noises, my dear. It's all past history now. But we might as well get the record straight. I've been looking after Hadrian's Edge ever since, combined with some lecturing and field work, of course."

"Oh, I see. Then—"

"Then why the Museum? Because I served in the W.A.A.F. during the war—the latter end, anyway. But that story can wait. You'll want to go to your room now and have a rest before supper."

The house was large and lofty, a wide corridor running

its full length upstairs. Tina's room was in the east gable, overlooking the same descending woods at the back of the house. From the window she could see beyond them to the hollows and heights of the gray-green moors and far beyond the misty blue line of the Cheviots.

The room was comfortable, not in any sense modern but solid and charming, the window seat upholstered in blue patterned chintz to match the bedspread and armchair. There was an electric radiator and a washbasin.

"You might like to sit here sometimes," Carrie Butterfield said, "but come down to my den any time you like. Adam doesn't use the living-room much. He is usually still working in his office most evenings. That's the room to the left of the hall."

"What exactly does he do? Bruno said in his letters he was a land agent." Tina unhasped her suitcase.

"He is just that—agent for the Willingdon estate, and that means he has fifteen tenant farms on his books. And answerable for all of them to Sir Walter Willingdon. And I can tell you this—the estate runs like clockwork. He's actually up to the eyes at the moment. Helen usually does his typing and office work. Thank heaven I'm no use bashing the keys or he would have roped me in!" she smiled. "Well, see you at supper."

The meal, cold meat and a tempting salad, was laid out in the small dining-room next to Carrie's den.

Rested and a little less disturbed, Tina roused herself to make conversation, and found herself telling Carrie about the scale model of the Roman Wall. "It was so real to us. A toy and yet not a toy. It was quite a thrill to glimpse the real Wall today—or some of what's left of it. But possibly I'm due for some disillusion."

"I doubt it." Carrie spoke abruptly. "You'll get Wall Fever, just as I did, and generations of other searchers."

"How did you begin?" Tina was curious.

Carrie poured more coffee. "Scratch a woman for a motive and ten to one you'll find an emotional one. I don't tell everyone this, but—well—" She eyed Tina calmly. "You've just had a bad loss. You'll understand. It might even help you, just to know how someone else had to face up to it. . . . It so happens I first came to the Wall with someone I loved."

Mr. Butterfield? Tina wondered.

Carrie lit a cigaret. "It's a long story, but I'll try to shorten it. When I was just eighteen it was still wartime. I joined the W.A.A.F., as it was called then, in 1944, and went parachute packing on a station in Wiltshire. It was an M.U.—Maintenance Unit to you—with none of the drama of Bomber or Fighter Commands. Just a bunch of men and girls isolated on the Wiltshire downs, with nothing to do in our spare time but fall in love. As I did."

She pushed aside her coffee cup. "His name was Laurence Ames, but he was always called Lofty. He was tall and had smashing looks. But that wasn't all. We had lots in common, walking and poetry—quiet things. Then I found he was an amateur archaeologist. He used to yarn on for ever about the Roman Wall. Oh, he had Wall Fever all right. . . . Well, we both managed to get seven days' leave together and he took me to walk the Wall, from Wallsend to Bowness on Solway. It was no piece of cake in wartime, I can tell you. Some stretches we had to by-pass—War Department property, rifle ranges, barbed wire sometimes. But we did it—together, and my Wall Fever was born. Possibly because that was almost the last time I saw Lofty." Her voice had slowed and dropped.

"What happened?" Tina was intrigued, her own troubles receding a little.

"He was posted suddenly to the Far East. Later he was missing, believed a prisoner. You've probably read about the conditions in those Jap prison camps?"

"Yes, I have."

Carrie tapped the ash from her cigaret. "I haven't heard from that day to this what happened to him."

"Oh, I'm sorry. Didn't the War Office or whatever it was—"

"They had to presume him dead, eventually. But it's just—not really knowing. And the last thing he said to me was: 'If we don't meet again until the war's over—or if we ever lose touch—you'll find me one day up on the Wall, on a fine summer's day, with the wind whistling over Sewingshields and Crag Lough blue in the sun.' "

Tina was silent, awed. Carrie went on softly:

"He was joking, in a way. But maybe that's the answer. If he'd survived I would have found him again, somewhere on this middle stretch of the Wall, his favorite part—from Chollerford to Birdoswald."

She paused a moment. "That's how I come to be here, you know. After the war I began studying the Roman occupation. I went out on all kinds of field work, learning all I could about the things that motivated him. And every weekend I came up to the Wall—walking and looking and—hoping."

"Then you married?"

"Yes." Carrie gave her a wry smile. "After a year or two of that I told myself I couldn't live on dreams."

"I married and was divorced two years later—sheer incompatibility. And there were no children. I'd long ago given up hope of seeing Lofty, but I had a hunger to see the Wall again—I'd been living in Birmingham, of all places. So I came back, took this job and kept up my archaeological interests. I'm contented and happy. No heights or depths, but I'm living the life I enjoy, the life that holds meaning for me."

"But you've given up looking for Lofty?"

"In a way. Except that he could still be here, in spirit. After all, heaven has its own shape for all of us. For Lofty it would be the Wall and the summer moors with the gorse in bloom and the wind over Cuddy's Crag. But don't imagine I'm just mooning around, thinking thoughts like that. I've told you, the Wall is my life now, my past and my present. I'm happy in my own queer way. Daft Carrie, they call me round here, because I'd much rather muck about in the mud, finding the past, than live a sensible life attending Women's Institute teas. . . . And that's enough about me. You look tired again and need your sleep after that journey."

Tina found her bed so comfortable that despite the still whirling conflict in her mind she burrowed beneath the covers to instant sleep. So much to fret about, so much to do, but tomorrow was another day. . . . She fell asleep.

She was awakened by the sweet ragged sound of children's voices, singing on the wind. At first the words were indistinguishable, then resolved into:

> *"She's a big lass, she's a bonnie lass*
> *And she likes her beer—*
> *And they call her Cushie Butterfield*
> *And I wish she was here. . . ."*

Tina remembered it as a much-loved old Tyneside song her father used to sing to her when she was tiny. She heard the words die away in a chorus of giggling and, wide awake now, she jumped out of bed and flung back the curtain.

At first she could see no one in the gravel courtyard below, with its high wall of hewn stone. Then beyond, in the woods, she saw a flash of color up a tree, followed by a scrambling movement and further giggling. Two small figures slid to the ground, clad alike in dark jeans and scarlet jerseys. They ran off down a ride between the trees, the girl's fair hair streaming in the wind, a mongrel dog yapping ecstatically at their heels.

Carrie entered with a cup of tea, grinning ruefully. "Not to worry, it's only the Finch twins—cheeky little brats. They're thoroughly wild, but you've got to hand it to them—they know how to live."

Tina took the teacup and nestled on the bed. "I remember now—Bruno mentioned them in his letters. Quite a family of them. He seemed to go there quite a lot."

Carrie nodded. "Oh yes, Bruno was very friendly with the Finches." Her tone was a little uneasy, Tina thought. She asked curiously:

"Don't you mind—about the serenading, I mean?"

"I'd be daft if I did. They mean no harm. Did Bruno tell you? They're by way of being poor relations of Adam's. And quite a thorn in the flesh, too."

"Doesn't he like them?"

"Let's just say he endures them. And occasionally

descends on them like the wrath of God. The trouble is Adam's so straightforward and efficient himself he can't stand shiftlessness in any shape or form."

"How many of them are there?"

"Five. Matt's the eldest, and the only dependable one. But he's a dreamer and inclined to be obsessed with his pigeons, anyway."

"Pigeons?"

"Racing pigeons. You're in the north of England now, you know. Pigeons are one of the men's favorite hobbies. There you are, look—"

Tina followed Carrie's pointing arm, saw a flash of gray and white wings over the far woods. "He's just released some," Carrie explained. "Probably young birds on a trial flight. . . . Where was I? Oh yes, and then there's Jamey. He's around twenty-two, and more than a bit wild. Then Francey—she's eighteen, a lovely-looking girl. Got the most gorgeous red-gold hair you ever saw. The local lads are always chasing her. But she's deep—I wouldn't trust Miss Francey farther than I could see her. The twins are just ten—their mother died when they were born. And a few years back the father ran off with another woman and left the family to fend for themselves. Matt does his best to keep the home going, but Adam doesn't altogether approve."

"Why not?" Tina asked a little sharply.

Carrie shrugged. "He isn't convinced it's the best thing, that the twins are getting a stable upbringing. He lets the family live at the Quarry farmhouse, as the Quarry Farm land runs with Tipstones now and no one needs the place. He found them a housekeeper—more than once—but no one would stay. Then he got Matt a good job as farm foreman, but he gave it up after a fortnight—said he hadn't enough time for his pigeons. Oh, they're not an easy family to help."

"And—Jamey?"

"I think Adam wrote Jamey off long ago. He's had several convictions for poaching—on the Willingdon preserves, too. Talk about biting the hand that feeds you! As for Francey—" Carrie hesitated. "Maybe if it hadn't been for Francey he'd have washed his hands of the family long ago."

"You mean—he likes her?"

"He's a man, isn't he?" Carrie said drily. "Very much of a man. And she's a very attractive girl. I once had an idea it would come to something, but he seems to blow hot, blow cold."

"Oh," said Tina.

Carrie had turned toward the door, but paused again. "Now Bruno—this'll interest you—Bruno was very much at home with all the Finches. The twins adored him. Funny about Bruno, though. Being Italian, or half-Italian, was no barrier there. He seemed to get right on their wavelength. It was the oddest thing."

"I don't know about that," Tina said slowly. "Perhaps the Finches are rather like the Italians—I mean just living for the day, being happy-go-lucky. Bruno was like that himself."

She felt a little cheered, convinced that she too would know and like the Finches. And from them she might learn all she needed of Bruno's last weeks at Hadrian's Edge.

Carrie was at the door now. "Just a thought," she said abruptly. "If you get too thick with the Finches, Adam won't like it."

Tina stiffened. Her chin went up. "Why not?"

"Because he's had trouble between the two houses too often, I'd say. There was a time when Helen couldn't keep away from Jamey Finch. Then the business of Bruno being down at Quarry Farm too much—which upset Helen. And—well, let's face it, my dear. You're a beauty—and trouble has a habit of following beauty around."

"Is Helen pretty?"

"Helen? No. Pretty is the wrong word. She's rather fragile, and very—bewitching. A little on the weak-willed side. Adam's always been inclined to overshelter her. All the same, I wouldn't underestimate her by any means. She's not a girl easy to forget."

Carrie added: "I know what's on your mind, Tina.

You're not satisfied that Bruno was entirely to blame. In a way I agree with you. That's why I've tried to fill in the background for you. But just don't deceive yourself that it's going to be easy, because it isn't. See you at breakfast."

Tina dressed in thoughtful mood, glad that she needn't fuss over what to wear. Jeans, a blue sweater and a matching ribbon to tie back her hair were about right for the dig.

Her mind was full of the Finches. A thorn in the flesh, were they? All the more likely that they would ally themselves on her side, and help her in her investigations.

Adam Copeland wouldn't like it, of course. He had warned her off the whole situation in no uncertain terms. And for a moment near-panic rippled through her. She was remembering Chris's words:

"One day you'll meet a man who has a trick for every one of yours; who will hurt you like hell and make you wish you'd never been born."

Again she was seeing the battered estate car riding off into the storm. The chaotic emotions of that moment returned to overwhelm her. Then she shook herself. She must be crazy. Adam Copeland was the last man on earth she'd ever be attracted to.

She braced herself to meet him at breakfast.

He was sitting at the dining-table reading the newspaper, and cocked an unimpressed eye at her. He did, though, have the manners to stand up, Tina noted.

"Good morning. Did you sleep well?" Without waiting for an answer he indicated a seat opposite and returned to the study of his newspaper.

"I slept very well," Tina announced. And added a slightly caustic: "Thank you."

Carrie came in at that moment, followed by Isa with a laden tray.

Isa stared, as before, in the intervals of setting down covered dishes and the coffee-pot. "You'll find the eggs a bit hard, I dare say, for I'd no' my usual letter from my sister in the post, and it upset me. . . . Did you sleep well, hinney?" This to Tina, who assured her that she had.

Isa backed out, her lips moving silently. Tina looked inquiringly at Carrie. "Another text?" she asked.

Surprisingly, it was Adam who answered, with a half-smile.

"Not yet, I'd say. Isa can't always call one to mind exactly when needed. Don't be surprised if you hear it half an hour later. It's a trifle—shall we say—disconcerting."

"So are the eggs," moaned Carrie. "I don't know why it is Isa always has to get upset when she's cooking."

He said lightly: "Hadrian's Edge wouldn't be the same without Isa, and you know it, Carrie. I think the price of a few spoiled dishes is not too high."

Tina looked at him in surprise. He sounded almost human again this morning, she thought.

Breakfast proceeded. Carrie excused herself to sit reading her letters. Suddenly Adam Copeland turned to Tina.

"Going to the dig this morning?"

"Yes, of course. I shall be working on it every day."

"Then a few words of warning won't come amiss. You'll be subject to the same rules as the others, since the dig is on Willingdon land, and near the game preserves. No trespassing beyond the wire fences, no damage to trees or walls, no undue noise or horseplay. And scrupulous avoidance of litter."

Tina's face flamed. "I'm not a child! And those rules are automatic as far as any serious archaeological work is concerned."

He returned her gaze with a vast and merciless patience. "Nevertheless I've told you, so there'll be no excuse for you to pretend otherwise. It will also help the smooth running of the house if you can bring yourself to be on time for meals. Otherwise you may please yourself what you do."

"Thank you," said Tina, with irony.

"Don't mention it!" For a second their glances locked. She was conscious more than ever this morning of the rocklike arrogance of his face, with its hard bony planes. Those intimidating gray eyes, she noticed, held green flecks, like the colors of a cloudshadowed sea. She found it difficult to withdraw her gaze.

"Making eyes again?" he asked pleasantly. "A complete waste of time, my dear. I should save it for the youths at the dig, or your friend Chris Irwin."

Carrie looked up, surprised, perhaps sensing the tension. "More coffee, Adam?"

He threw down his table-napkin. "No, thanks. I've more work than I know how to cope with this morning."

He gave them both a nod and left the room.

"He's the rudest man I've ever met!" Tina exploded.

Carrie shook her head. "He's never been rude to me. You must have somehow got under his skin. And if you don't mind a warning, he likes the women of the house to keep his rules. We've always found it a small price to pay for domestic harmony."

"I'm not his sister." Tina was mutinous. "Or his housekeeper."

"No, but you are his guest. And I'm afraid that means you toe the line like the rest of us," Carrie said firmly.

Isa stumped in with her empty tray, her solid face gloomy as before. Facing Tina, she struck something of an attitude and intoned: "Love not sleep, lest thou come to poverty!"

"Yes, Isa, we get the message," Carrie said. "Looks like you're slipping, though. It's taken you five minutes to think that one up."

"Aye, my memory isn't what it was. And that reminds me, Mrs. Butterfield, I broke another piece o' the Crown Derby yesterday—a tea-plate it was. The man on the radio had just said the Premium Bond winner was local, and I got fair excited. . . . I didn't win, for all that. I've only the one bond and I won *that* in the Chapel raffle. "Lay not up for yourselves treasures on earth." And breathing heavily, Isa began to load her tray.

When she had gone Carrie laughed. "You'll get used to her. We're an odd lot, I suppose"—her voice softened—"but I hope our hearts are in the right place."

"I know they are," Tina said, but mentally excluding Adam Copeland. "Shall I help Isa wash up?"

"No, she would never allow it. She likes to muddle along in her own way. I've a few things to see to, though, so I'll join you at the dig later—right?"

Tina walked into the hall, unhooking her anorak from its peg. Gyp lay in the shaft of pale sunlight before the open door. As Tina stooped to fondle her a voice said: "Off to the dig, then?"

She straightened herself, saw an open door on her left giving on to a not-too-formally furnished office. Adam Copeland stood behind an untidy desk, an open letter in his hand. His expression was derisive, she thought.

"I suppose you find the dig rather a nuisance?" she challenged him.

His eyes flickered. "The dig? I have no complaints to make. It seems to be admirably run. Perhaps I find this eternal questing into the past a little—shall we say—overdone at times."

"Then you can't have much imagination," Tina ventured.

His gaze became stony. "That's possibly better than having too much, don't you think?"

"You suggest that I—"

"Like all women, you tend to take everything personally. If new discoveries of Roman occupation provide you with thrills, far be it from me to criticize you. You will probably develop a quite acute case of Wall Fever. And, like a lot of other searchers, you will tend to forget one important thing."

He reached to the desk to light a cigaret. Tina lingered, stung but curious.

"And what's that?"

He raised his eyes coolly. "That the Romans did defeat this land once, but failed to make good their victories. They came, they saw, they conquered. But eventually they had to withdraw. That's why the Wall is a monument to failure as well as success."

"I don't quite see—"

"What all this has to do with you? I'm telling you, perhaps, because this new Roman occupation—your presence in this house—is unlikely to be more successful.

Dig as much as you like, my dear. We at Hadrian's Edge
have nothing to hide. And you won't find what you're
looking for. Not only that, you will only distress yourself
into the bargain."

"And if that's a risk I'm prepared to take?"

His face changed, softened almost to regret. "Then I'm
sorry for your sake."

Tina's anger flashed. "You couldn't possibly be wrong,
could you—about my brother, I mean? You can't even
envisage any fault on your sister's side?"

"None whatever. That's why I deplore this idea of
yours, to dig for a truth which can only give you pain and
humiliation." His voice harshened again. "I say again,
you are welcome to our hospitality, such as it is. I can't
prevent you from giving yourself even more grief than
you're probably suffering now. You are obviously an
obstinate and spoiled young woman. I'm trying to make
allowances for you—"

"Don't bother!" Tina blazed. "I shall try to keep out of
your hair as much as possible, Mr. Copeland. As for
digging into the past—neither you nor anyone else can
stop me doing that, either on the dig or concerning my
brother's life here. As for Wall Fever—"

She stopped for breath. Again she saw that infuriating lift of his black brows. "Yes, you were saying?"

"I've learned one thing already," she said, greatly
daring. "I've learned why they called the Wall a barrier
between the Romans and the barbarians!"

She fled from the house before he had time to reply.

Tina followed a path round lawns, past a dilapidated
tenniscourt and through a gate on to rising pasture. Free
of the trees, she could now see the vast tawny stretches of
the northern moors, patched here and there by acres of
dark forest. Looking below and to the west she saw the
site of the dig, Chris and his workers gathered in a knot as
he gave directions for the day's work.

This particular dig was on the site of an old civil
settlement below the Wall. Like all other sites it consisted
of buried layers of overlapping cultures, to be studied in
the light of modern knowledge. But Tina was seeing it

motionally. This was the scene of Bruno's last labors, his
opes, his inspirations, his successes. Now Chris was in
harge, and while she could not grudge him the position
e deserved, a bleak sadness overcame her. Some
noments passed before she could rouse herself to descend
he slope.

She walked down slowly, her practised eyes taking in
very detail. The site was being excavated on a grid
ystem, consisting of hollowed squares of a uniform size,
onnected by the crossings of the grass baulks between.
Vith this method students and other workers could be
given individual squares to investigate, the vertical sides
of the hollows providing evidence of the different levels of
civilization.

Drawing nearer, she saw the usual clutter of measuring
ods, photographic equipment, trays to hold pottery
inds, brushes and bowls for washing the shards.
Excavation work, she knew, included everything from the
irst sheer navvying to delicate towel work and the
ntricate keeping of records.

Chris looked up and saw her, covered the ground
between them with swift strides. "Welcome to the site,
Tina. Settled in all right?"

"Far from all right. I've got to talk to you, Chris. It's
mportant."

He studied her troubled face. "We can't talk here. But
here's rain coming. I'm afraid we won't do much this
norning. When we stop for elevenses I'll run you out
omewhere in the car—show you something of the
listrict."

Tina restrained her impatience. She supposed he was
right. They were facing south now, across the great open
aucer of the Tyne valley. A curtain of smudged cloud
moved sluggishly across a far ridge to the southwest.
"That's Cross Fell," he told her, and pointed out a few
nore landmarks. Depressed and chilled as she was by the
olustering wind, Tina saw only a vast bleakness, a waste
of hills and moors. An intolerable homesickness came.

Chris seemed to sense something wrong. "Come on
lown to the dig and see what we're doing," he suggested.

"Carrie will soon be here—she'll put you in the picture."

Tina shook off her gloom. Perhaps this was the answer to interest herself in immediate affairs, to try to forget Hadrian's Edge and the shadow over Bruno's name.

Later Carrie materialized workmanlike in trousers and anorak. She glanced keenly at Tina, perhaps divined her troubled spirit and led her briskly over to a trestle table where some previous finds were arrayed.

"We had quite a harvest in one of the far squares, right there on the perimeter. It must obviously have been in the area of the settlement's rubbish-dump. See these flanged rims of cooking pots. Pre-Samian ware, I would say. And look at this . . . a Flavian platter—late first century according to Chris. But we'll get the experts at the Museum on that. And what about this?"

Carrie produced with triumph a heavy jet ring, grey with the dust of centuries and carved to represent a twisted rope. "How would you like that for an engagement ring?"

Tina, turning it over in her hand, was thrilled as always by this pathetic reminder of the vanity of primitive woman. Someone had prized it, worn it always, was even perhaps buried with it still on her finger, for long after bones crumbled such objects remained unassailed by time.

Her eyes met Carrie's. "Makes you think, doesn't it?" the older woman said. "Makes you wonder why we fret and fume over anything. Time, in the end, looks after it all."

Tina sighed and handed back the ring. She felt a little steadied, taken out of her brooding sorrow. And for the next half hour was crouching with Carrie in one of the squares, patiently digging and sifting with her trowel, losing herself in the layers of the past.

At elevenses time the rain sent the workers to the shelter of the open shed which served as office and store. Chris drove Tina down the stony track which connected the dig with the Military Road, and turned westwards. Soon he swung the car up another narrow road to the right, curling past a farm under the brow of the rise. He stopped in a small parking area at the top of the ridge.

"This is one of the few points where it's possible to reach a stretch of the Wall by car." he told her. "if the rain clears we can walk as far as Crag Lough from that stile in the corner there. . . . Now, Tina, what's the trouble?"

She met his clear gaze. "Adam Copeland," she said. "You might have warned me what he was like."

"Is that all? Anyway, I did tell you he ruled the world hereabouts. Been dictating to you, I suppose."

"Worse than that. It was a toss-up whether I stayed as a guest at all." Suddenly Tina was spilling out her story, in tearful resentment. "He actually believes it—he believes Bruno would treat a girl like that—the girl he loved—"

Her voice choked. For a moment Chris was silent.

"Chris, did you hear what I said?" She caught at his arm. "We can't let him get away with it—at least I can't."

"I agree it's upsetting. Embarrassing too, as you're his guest. Wouldn't you rather pull out, come down to the hotel for a while?"

She shook her head. "I told you what he said, that it would look better if I stayed. But that's not my only reason. If I'm in the house I've a much better chance of finding out what really happened."

Chris said quietly: "And if you discover something you don't like—"

Her eyes flamed. "*Chris*, you don't actually—"

"Think the story's true . . . ? It's just possible there's enough of truth in this hitchhiker theory to excuse Copeland thinking so. And let's face it, Tina—he thinks the world of his sister. You can hardly blame him for feeling sore."

"I do blame him, for judging Bruno without proper evidence, for accusing a dead man who can't—who can't—"

She was suddenly overcome and hid her face in her hands. She felt Chris's arm cradle her shoulder. "I know, Tina. I know just how you feel." His voice was wretched.

"It's been hell for all of us who loved him," he said.

She mopped her eyes. "You'll help me, won't you, Chris? You want the truth brought out as much as I do."

He patted her shoulder and withdrew his arm, reaching for his cigarets. "Of course I do. But if you intend to stay on as Copeland's guest you'll have to watch your step. You know how impulsive you are. And you can hardly go round calling him a liar. . . . No, it's no use rushing it, Tina. I'd like time to think about it, maybe to make some inquiries of my own. And I promise you I'll let you know if there's anything new. But you won't do anything impetuous, will you?"

She gave a reluctant promise. For some minutes they discussed the situation afresh, then Chris broke in firmly: "And that's enough of it for today. Look, the rain's stopped. And you're about to set foot on Hadrian's Wall for the first time. . . . Come on, try to forget everything else. . . ."

Tina roused herself with an effort and got out of the car. The wind whipped her hair into a flag. Chris took her arm. "We make for that stile over there."

Tina climbed the stile and then gasped. She had stepped from its wooden platform directly on to the Wall itself, at this point fully six feet high and carrying a broad footpath on its face. Before her the dark gray ribbon swooped and climbed the rising crags of the Great Whin Sill, soaring up impossible heights, dropping steeply in incredible feats of engineering to swamp and hollow. She saw the exactitude of the masonry, the almost insolent regard for dangerous contours. She saw the pride and the strength of the barrier built so many centuries ago by her own countrymen, still implacable, undestroyed under the wild moorland skies. She was seeing the Wall as those Roman legionaries had seen it. Nothing had changed, no sign of civilization, the only movements the white spotting of lambs with their gray mothers, the movement of the leaves in the plantation behind them.

"Oh, Chris," Tina said. There were tears in her eyes. "Isn't it—Oh, isn't it—" Words failed her.

"Better than any plaster model, isn't it?" Chris said.

"Look, that water ahead at the crag foot—it's Crag Lough—we'll follow the Wall to it."

Tina moved on reluctantly, as if breaking a spell.

Chris pointed out a hundred things she might not have noticed, the exactitude of the masonry, the deliberate weaving of the stones, the corner pieces and angles, the outlined foundations of a milecastle, set back from the line of the Wall itself. His voice went on, reasoned, interested, enthusiastic, and yet she was only half listening, knowing that she too was catching "Wall Fever", that she wished she were alone to dream and wonder and that Chris would forget to lecture.

But now they breasted the last steep rise before Crag Lough, arriving panting at the summit. The Wall soared on toward the Hotbank heights, but they dropped down to a footpath along the top of the perilous crag.

Tina shrank away from the edge. It was a perpendicular drop of black rock, with the waters of the little loch so far below, now silver as the light lifted, now wrinkled and peat-dark as the wind sent the clouds scurrying. Ragged crows volplaned from the edge, swooping and circling and diving into that great airy nothingness. Apart from their cries there was no sound but the rustle of dead rushes in the clefts of the crags.

Chris said softly: "This was one of Bruno's favorite spots on the Wall. He had one or two tries to get a watercolor of the moors from here, but he always said the colors changed too much even while he was working—"

Tina understood, gazing beyond the lough to the pale patchwork of emerald and sapphire folds of the far-stretching fells. Chris pointed out the first black tongues of Wark Forest running into the clefts of the hills, and pale blue ribbons of small farm roads winding interminably over the moor.

"Did he bring Helen here?" she asked.

"I doubt it. She gave me the impression of being rather a hot-house plant. I should imagine she'd prefer a warm car."

"You must have really known her quite well," said Tina.

Chris shrugged. "Not really. And I didn't have much contact with her, even in the early days—Let's face it, anyway, our dig interests bored her stiff. She was always trying to get Bruno away from it."

Tina stood huddled in her anorak, watching the suicidal diving of the crows, and flinching in spite of herself at their sudden swoops into space. "Yet Adam Copeland is quite well informed about the Wall and archaeology generally, isn't he?"

"Oh; he knows it all. He also affects to laugh at what he calls our fanaticism. He once said his sense of the past, as with most of the locals living on the Wall, was sufficiently developed without having to dig with little trowels to titillate it."

"How pompous!" said Tina hotly. She glanced at Chris, his lean clever face whipped into color by the wind. "you don't like him much, do you?"

He shrugged. "My opinion doesn't count for much, at least around here. The local people seem to worship him. He can do no wrong."

Tina remembered what Chris had said in their Rome apartment. " 'He bestrides the Wall like a Colossus'."

And Chris had been right, she told herself reluctantly. His influence, his responsibilities, his bearing, caused him to tower like a giant over his kingdom of Hadrian's Edge. . . .

Her gaze sought the climbing Wall again. This was his country, his wild domain, for all the Romans had left on it their eternal monument. "They came, they saw, they conquered" . . . and eventually, as he had so triumphantly pointed out, they withdrew.

Her hands clenched tightly. She knew he expected her to withdraw just as ignominiously. And though she had given Chris her promise not to do anything impulsive she made a vow, standing there in the same wind which had chilled her countrymen centuries ago, that she would make him retract every word of condemnation against her brother.

Yet her heart quailed a little at the prospect before her. . . .

CHAPTER TWO

WHEN lunchtime came back at the dig, Chris joined his young workers for sandwiches and coffee. Carrie and Tina walked back to the house. Just before the path entered the grounds by the tennis court Carrie pointed across the moor.

"See that path? Quarry Farm's in the dip beyond. You can just see the chimneys. So if you want to visit the Finches, that's the way to go. Even now there's no proper road to the place. The path is a blind end so they don't get many visitors. And the last time the Health Visitor called Jamey let all the geese loose and she had to run for her life."

Tina laughed. "It doesn't look very far. Half a mile, would you say?"

"Nearer three-quarters. So you've decided to go?"

"Yes. I want to talk to them about Bruno."

Carrie glanced sharply at her. "I know one who won't make you very welcome, and that's Francey. You'll be a bit of a shaker to her, as she's always queened it as the local beauty. She'll take rather a dim view of competition. Matt and Jamey—well, they're just another cup of tea. And no one counts the twins. Go if you must then, but don't count on it being a piece of cake. I don't know how it is, but everyone who tangles with the Finches comes to regret it."

"I shan't."

Carrie shrugged. "Come on, lunch. I'm hungry."

Over salad and coffee they discussed the finds at the dig, though Tina's attention wandered, settling inevitably with a sick anxiety on thoughts of Bruno.

Suddenly Carrie said drily, "Why don't you tell me to close the hangar doors?"

"Oh . . ." Tina said softly. "Carrie, how long did it take you to get used to losing Lofty?"

"I wish I could tell you what you want to hear—that you won't always feel as you do now about your brother.

It's true that I said all the old trite things about time healing. But time is a very elastic thing. When we lose someone a day can seem an eternity. Then looking back, the years seem to telescope. . . ." She broke off. "Maybe as far as Lofty is concerned I ought to close the hangar doors too. Call an end of thinking about him."

"But—some day—someone might come along with news of him."

"I suppose miracles sometimes happen." Carrie changed the subject abruptly. "You were pretty upset at the dig this morning, weren't you? I can understand why. And if it's going to help you to talk to the Finches about Bruno then by all means go. But wait until evening when Matt's home from work. You'll get some sense out of *him*."

That afternoon on the dig Chris took Tina aside. "Look, Tina, I've had a bit of a talk with one or two locals in the pub. It's true that the countryside's buzzing with talk—about this girl seen with Bruno. Now brace yourself, Tina. I'm afraid it's more than just a tale. There *was* a girl. And the general idea seems to be that if he was only giving her an innocent lift she would have come forward at the inquest. Whereas she has just disappeared. It certainly looks odd."

"Chris, you can't honestly believe all this?"

"About Bruno's supposed motives? I hope I knew him better than that." He hesitated, his eyes uneasy. "But, Tina, Bruno could have had secrets from me, even from Helen."

"I still don't believe he would do anything to hurt her," Tina exploded. "He loved her—you know that. He was crazy about her."

"He was." Chris shrugged. "But Copeland was determined to make him wait for marriage, as Helen was under age. Isn't it just possible he got involved with someone else—in a casual way? And there's that hotel booking. It's not easy to explain away."

Tina shook her head. "It doesn't make sense, knowing Bruno. Except . . . Chris, do you think it might have been Francey Finch? Bruno knew her well, didn't he? Would she be the kind of girl to try and entice him into some—well, adventure of that kind?"

"Francey?" Chris frowned. "It's just possible, I suppose. Bruno did go quite often to Quarry Farm, and gossip says she's getting rather tired of carrying a torch for Adam Copeland."

Tina spoke with a spasm of irritation. "Another worshipper—does everyone make a God of that man?"

Chris sighed. "I wish I could make you see—this is why there's so much talk against Bruno. Local opinion is that he served Copeland and his sister very badly indeed. I really doubt if trying to dig up the truth is going to do much good. You might prove Bruno innocent, but who is going to believe you or even care? I think you'd be better to leave well alone."

Tina glanced at the students kneeling, digging, sifting the earth. "You don't ask your workers to leave the past alone. If they didn't dig they'd never find the truth. I'll find it too."

Chris shook his head. "The truth isn't always pleasant. Just as when we dig here we find a layer of peaceful living, then evidence of fire and bloodshed and sword. And once dug up the evidence can't be destroyed again. Better forget it, Tina. And after all, what will it matter, when we're both back in Rome, what a parcel of Northumbrians thought of Bruno?"

"It does matter," Tina said passionately. "Because Dad's a Northumbrian—Bruno had Northumbrian blood. Isn't that a good enough reason?"

Chris reached for his anorak. "There comes the rain. We shall have to call a halt to any more work today."

The rain came like fine needles on the force of the wind, drenching and chilling. By four o'clock all work on the site had stopped and equipment was stored under cover in a makeshift shed. Later that evening the wind strengthened from the west, blowing away the low curtain of cloud and revealing odd glimpses of chilled blue sky. After the evening meal Tina decided to visit the Finches. She had changed into a blue wool dress, swinging high above her dimpled knees, and slung a soft white cardigan sweater carelessly about her slim shoulders. "You'll freeze on the moor dressed like that," Carrie told her. "This isn't Rome, you know."

Tina, who hated coats, pulled a face. "You'll learn," Carrie sighed.

Tina followed the track through the woods at the back of the grounds, where Carrie had promised her she would find the path forking to Quarry Farm. Except for the sombre green of fir and spruce, the woods were bare and wintry still, even in April. And as Tina emerged on the open moor she shivered at the bite of the wind and wished she had taken Carrie's advice. She ran down the stony track to keep warm, and suddenly the farm lay revealed below, a low white house, roughly limewashed. A line of linen flapped in a rough garden, she could hear the gaggle of geese from outbuildings, and then, like grace notes above a line of music, there came a silver flutter of wings over the stables.

Racing pigeons, Carrie had said. It seemed a strange occupation to Tina, but then so much about her father's beloved homeland was strange to her.

As she approached the farm she saw that the front door was almost obscured by neglected creepers. She found a back one open on to a stone-floored scullery, smelling of paraffin. She knocked. A voice called to her to come in. Rather diffidently she opened the door opposite, finding herself in a high beamed room with an old-fashioned black grate. The furniture was old and scarred, the paintwork peeling, but there was an air of instant and rather pathetic homeliness about it.

There were also two young men, both staring at her the way all young men stared at Tina on first sight. She forced a smile. "I'm Tina Rutherford. I hope you don't mind—"

The taller of the two stood on the hearthrug, regarding her soberly. He had a thin, rather intense face, with a steadiness and depth to his eyes, she found reassuring. "You must be Matt." She held out her hand. He took it, his fair thatch of hair falling forward over his face. "Nice to meet you, Tina. This is my brother Jamey. We heard you were expected at Hadrian's Edge," he said to her.

Jamey perched on the table edge, his dark bold eyes frankly assessing her charms. He was black-haired, swarthy, well aware of his masculine vitality. And he did not so much grip her hand as hold it. "Well now, if I'd have known I'd have worn a clean shirt." His glance was warm, a little more than friendly.

Tina had assessed *him* at a glance. She had been approached by and carelessly brushed off dozens of such young strutting males at Rome parties.

Jamey reached over, tipped a ginger cat off a chair and turned it toward her. "Might as well sit down, now you're here."

"Thanks," she said coolly.

Matt spoke, a little uneasily. "Tina, we're all very sorry about Bruno. He was our friend, at least we were proud to think so." She recognised in his voice the rougher Northumbrian burr of the moors, subtly different from the more singsong accents of the Tyne valley. Jamey's voice was lighter, more impatient. "Aye, it was bad luck. A burst tire in the fog."

"He came here quite often, didn't he?"

Jamey nodded, his eyes admiring her brief skirt. "Francey brought him first. I think she had a bit of a fancy for him."

"Don't talk daft! Matt argued. "It was just friendship and you know it. Miss Copeland was *his* girl—much more his stamp, educated and all that."

Matt sat down in the sagging armchair by the fire. "Staying long?" he asked.

"I don't know." Tina hesitated. "That depends on Mr. Copeland." She rushed on. "Please don't be shy of talking to me about Bruno. I'd like you to tell me all about his life here."

Jamey drew on his cigaret, grunted. "That wouldn't be much. Bruno was a bit of a dark horse. You don't think he told us everything, do you, pet?"

Pet . . . a well-known Tyneside endearment and one her father often used. Like the more usual "Hinney" of the rest of the county it could cover a multitude of

relationships. She was not and never would be a pet of
Jamey's, but the word reached her without offence.

Matt began sorting a box of colored rings. His hands,
though work-worn, had a shapely strength Tina found
herself admiring. She guessed the rings were for the
pigeons.

"No, he didn't tell us everything," Matt said. "Nor did
we want him to. He was friendly—a canny lad, but a bit
above our level." And his glance, curiously defensive, said
plainly enough— "And so are you."

"You're bonny, I'll say that for you." Jamey was
plainly anxious to be more personal. "Bruno said you
were. You knock spots off Helen Copeland—or even our
Francey."

"Francey? She'd be all right if she didn't plaster her
face with all that make-up muck." Matt spoke shortly.

"Is Francey out?" Tina asked.

"You'd be lucky to catch her in, nights," Jamey
grinned. "Me either, for that matter."

Matt pushed the box of rings aside. "Would you like a
cup of tea, Tina?" He hesitated. "Or coffee, if you'd
rather. It's only the instant stuff."

Tina gratefully accepted the coffee. Matt pushed a
heavy kettle farther on the stove. His glance went to an
old wall-clock. "Time Rosie and Bobby were in. I
suppose they're up in the crags." He glanced at Jamey.

"Not after Hadrian chased Thompson's lambs. Old
Thompson said he'd shoot the dog if they went up there
again." Jamey spoke with a half grin.

"He'd be within his rights," Matt said grimly. "They
know better than to go near the lambs. I'll have a word
with them when they come in."

"I saw them this morning," Tina said hastily. "They
were serenading Mrs. Butterfield."

" 'Cushie Butterfield,' was it?" Jamey's laughter was
uninhibited.

"I'll tan them both if I ever catch them at it," Matt
promised. "I hope Mr. Copeland didn't hear."

"What's the odds?" Jamey asked. "Carrie doesn't
care."

Matt said: "Aye, Carrie's a canny lass. She doesn't take offence."

Jamey winked lazily at Tina, who had to repress a smile. Jamey was rather like a naughty but endearing dog playing for attention. Suddenly, though, he got up and efficiently produced three mugs of coffee of a strength to take the roof off her mouth.

Tina set hers aside to cool and appealed to Matt again: "Didn't Bruno ever—well, talk to you about himself?"

Matt, lounging against the mantelshelf, gazed soberly down at her. "No, he didn't. And look, Tina, it would be better for you if you didn't come here too much."

"Why?"

He shrugged. "There's nothing for you here, except maybe trouble. We haven't got much of a reputation."

"I don't care about reputations," Tina spoke spiritedly.

"Then you should."

"Don't frighten her off, man!" Jamey protested. "As far as I'm concerned she's as welcome as the flowers in May."

Light footsteps sounded in the scullery. A small slender blonde flounced in, heavily made up, and reeking of cheap perfume. She stared at Tina, catching her breath. "Who's this? Oh, don't tell me, I can guess. Bruno's sister, aren't you?" She dumped her handbag on the table, flung off her coat and slumped into the armchair opposite Matt.

She was lovely, Tina conceded, with a rough wild-rose beauty. Her hair was naturally curly and despite obvious attempts at straightening, it clustered in tiny rings about her ears and temples. Her eyes were dark by contrast, long-lashed and wide-set above a pert tilted nose. There was perhaps too much of the healthy peasant in Francey for glamor, but there was also Jamey's pulsing vitality.

"Welcome to the Palace," she drawled. "If I'd known you were coming I'd have baked a cake—eh, Jamey?" Their unbridled laughter brought swift color to Tina's face.

"Hold your tongue, our Francey," Matt ordered.

"And it's more of a pigsty than a palace, thanks to you."

Francey eyed Tina closely. "Come to work on the dig, have you? You must be daft! Catch *me* grovelling for old Roman rubbish."

But her gaze, settling on Tina's simple well-cut dress, held something of a hungry wistfulness. "Must be great to have money," she said. "And be educated and all that. And invited to stay at Hadrian's Edge." The last words held surprising venom.

So that's it, Tina thought. She hates the fact that I'm living up there.

She finished her coffee, got up and said: "I must go. But I'd like to come again." She avoided Francey's sulky stare. "You were Bruno's friends, so I'd like you to be mine too."

"I don't see why!" Francey got up and collected the mugs, slammed out a rather stained tablecloth.

"Francey, watch your tongue!" Matt's voice was a rasp.

Francey ignored him and turned to bring plates from the dresser. Tina sighed and prepared to go. Her visit had been less than a success. Jamey had nothing to offer but flirtation, Francey was openly antagonistic. Only Matt held any promise.

"Like to see the pigeons?" he asked suddenly.

She brightened. "I'd like to."

"You've asked for it," Francey said. "Love me, love my pigeons. You'll learn!"

Tina followed Matt into the yard. The light over the moor was waning, turning tawny shadows to russet, blackening the plantations tucked in the folds of the hills. A few pigeons circled in a desultory way above the loft.

"It's feeding time," Matt explained. He filled some shallow pans with maize, calling in a curious cooing chuckle. There was a rubbery sound of wings, then the pigeons were clustered and bobbing about the feeding pans.

"I've got eight pairs," he told her. "Four of them still at the trial stage. That's a Barless Blue. Those two are Barred Mealies, and over there are Blue and Red

Chequers. And that pair there are called Silver Duns."

"What pretty names!"

"Oh, they're just the names of the various strains. They've their personal names too. That's Storm Princess. She's Pearl of the Wind. He's Red Knight and this is Silver Cloud."

"You're quite a poet." She watched him pick up a bird here and there, stroking the wings with a gentleness she found touching. "You love pigeons, don't you?"

He smiled. "You can't beat pigeon-racing. It's not the prizes, nor the silver cups. It's waiting, in the dark and cold, in the loft—watching for your birds, knowing the canny wee things are battling through storm and wind to you. It's like having a share of the sky with them. Your heart's with them all the way, hundreds of miles, from the Highlands of the Lakes or up from the Sussex Downs—" He broke off, smiled again shyly. "We're all daft that way, all us fanciers. You might say we've only got one leg on the ground."

Tina watched a couple of Chequered Blues daintily pecking. "Did Bruno like them?"

"Aye, he did! He named yon mealie—called her "Moonlight." She'd just done her first two hundred miles."

Tina said hurriedly: "Matt, please tell me something. Do you think Bruno would treat Helen Copeland the way everyone suggests?"

He shook his head, seemed distressed. "I don't. But I didn't know him all that well, Tina. You might say we both kept something of ourselves back."

"I see." She felt suddenly blank and hopeless. "I suppose I'd better go."

"Like me to see you across the moor?"

She shook her head. "It's not dark. And you've the pigeons to see to. But I'd like to come again." After all, she thought, what could she have hoped to accomplish on a first meeting?

"I hope you do, though I doubt if it's wise." His honest blue eyes met hers wistfully.

She smiled a goodbye and ran down the long slope of

the moor, deeply shadowed now in every dimple and fold of the land. What a queer primitive household it was, she thought, and could well imagine the august Adam Copeland disapproving. Yet she felt drawn to return.

Over the next rise a mongrel dog raced barking toward her, then rolled on his back, all four paws in the air.

"Hallo, Hadrian." As she stooped to pat him, the twins burst into view. They pulled up short at sight of her. She noticed they were not identical. Bobby was the taller of the two.

"I've just been to your house," she told them.

"We know who you are." Rosie scraped her tangled hair out of her eyes. "You're staying with Cushie Butterfield. Did we wake you up singing?"

"You didn't call that noise singing!"

They giggled. Hadrian ran round them in circles, giving short barks of ecstasy.

"Did you go to school today?" Tina asked.

"No. We were up in our tree house in the woods."

"You mean Mr. Copeland's woods?"

"Aye—why not?" Bobby seemed surprised.

"Doesn't he object?"

"He doesn't know yet. Or else he turns a blind eye," Rosie explained carelessly.

"What do you do in your tree house?"

"We play real houses." Rosie's eyes shone. "We've got cups and pots up there."

Bobby was scornful. "She's aye wanting to play houses. But that's not all we do. We spy on people. It's great."

"But you can't surely keep missing school like that?"

"Now and again we do, then the Inspector comes to the house. Matt gets mad then and tells us off. Then Mr. Copeland comes and shouts at Matt."

"Charming!" said Tina.

They giggled again. "He threatens to put us out of the house. But he won't. He's gey sorry for us really."

"Aye. He got us a council house once, so we could have a proper bathroom," Bobby said importantly.

"What happened?"

"The Council put us out. People complained because we fought all the other bairns and Hadrian fought all the dogs. That was when we went to live at Quarry Farm."

"Wasn't Matt angry?"

"Not him!" Rosie stared. "It meant he could start his pigeons in the old loft."

"What did Mr. Copeland say?"

"He was fair mad. He said trying to help us was like casting pearls before swine."

Tina's mouth twitched.

"Now he's to put us in a bathroom, when the grant comes through. But Matt's mad because it makes us more in Mr. Copeland's debt."

"I see." Tina felt that the twins' revelations could now well be cut short. She had quite enough to think about for one night. "I'll be coming back to see you," she went on. "I might even bring you some sweets if you promise not to miss school."

"We'd rather miss school," Bobby explained kindly.

"Couldn't we have the sweets anyway?" Rosie appealed.

Tina studied her a little more intently. Though like Bobby, her fair skin was tanned by the moorland wind, there was a peakiness beneath it. Her cheekbones seemed too prominent and shadows lurked below her pretty blue eyes. Perhaps she was just growing too fast, Tina thought, but wondered a little uneasily if Francey took proper care of her. Knowing Francey she felt doubtful.

Next minute, as if to prove her fears ungrounded, Rosie turned a very showy cartwheel on the grass and bounded away down the hill, Bobby and Hadrian at her heels. Tina smiled, relieved that her fears were surely unjustified.

Her thoughts reverted to Adam Copeland. She felt mystified. The more she learned of him the more of an enigma he was. At first meeting she was impressed, attracted, almost overwhelmed. On learning his identity, his opinion of Bruno and thus obliquely of herself, she had been prepared to resent, almost to hate him. Now he had been presented as a friend of the poor and helpless, now she had learned he was determined to protect, to advise, and if necessary to threaten the Finches for their own good, she was bewildered again. Such actions showed a generous, forgiving nature, at absolute variance with his behavior over Bruno.

She tried to harden her heart. The Finches were not her concern—Bruno's memory was. She must not allow herself to be sidetracked into unwilling admiration.

The following evening Tina borrowed Carrie's car and set out to find Coventina's well.

"Or what remains of it," Carrie had warned her. "There's nothing to see but a few stones round a swamp now. You'll be disappointed."

"I'd still like to go."

"I know," Carrie nodded. "It's not what you see, it's what you picture in your own mind." Carrie had already shown her, earlier that day, the stone monument from the well in Chester's Museum, with its carved figure of the little goddess, holding in her hand a water-lily leaf. Like many Roman monuments found along the Wall, it had had to be removed to safe keeping because of possible defacement and vandalism through the years.

Tina drove eastwards until she saw the roadside sign pointing to Carrowbrough fort. Leaving the car at the lay-by, she took the path across a hilly pasture. Beyond the gap of the Tyne valley the hills of South Northumberland tumbled to the skyline, a waste of lavender and gray distances under the threatening sky. She paused a while at the fort excavations and the site of the Temple of Mithras, then paced her way to the site of the well, only to find the spring rains had turned the lower ground to bog.

Ripping off her shoes, she risked the ruin of her pantyhose and floundered across to a ring of ruined stones. And there it was, desolation indeed, a lonely spring in a smother of weeds and mud, once a noble fountain held sacred by Roman soldiers to her long-dead namesake.

Her emotions were mixed. It was all so strange, so unlike what she had imagined. Did any local people care, she wondered, or ever turn aside from their shepherding and farming to muse on that sad little water-nymph and her shrine? Almost furtively she dug a sixpence from her pocket and threw it in the pool, where it sank instantly from sight.

"Very touching!" a voice said just behind her.

She turned abruptly, almost losing her footing in the mud. Adam Copeland stood just behind her, his hands dug into the pockets of an old donkey-jacket. His leisurely gaze went over her.

"Paying homage, are you?" he asked. "I saw you cross the field and guessed where you'd be. At the moment, though, you look most unlike a water-goddess, except perhaps for your feet." His voice rose to a masterful rasp. "Was it really worth getting your feet soaked? This is northern spring, you know, not summertime in Italy. You'll probably get a stinking cold."

"I don't care." She faced him defiantly. "I've always wanted to see Coventina's well."

"And now you've seen it, I suggest you get back to your car as quickly as you can."

"I was just going anyway." Under his withering gaze she climbed the wall and sloshed through the swamp to higher ground, pulled her shoes on to her soaking feet. The damp penetrated uncomfortably. To her annoyance she sneezed.

"See what I mean?" he said.

As they climbed the path he glanced at her: "You had no difficulty finding the well? You learned it all from your plaster model. I suppose. Carrie told me about that."

Tina was silent, resentful. She had to hurry to keep up with his long strides, but he either failed to notice or he ignored the fact.

"A plaster model," he repeated. "It's almost incredible. Why, you've got to live a lifetime on the Wall to really know it. But you wouldn't understand that."

"I'm a Roman!" she flashed.

"Half a Roman, I believe," he corrected. "And when the Roman cohorts stationed on the Wall took Northumbrian girls as their slave-wives, *their* daughters may have looked much as you do. Maybe they even had eyes like Coventina's forget-me-nots too." His glance was inscrutable, but his voice had sunk to a grudging softness.

"There weren't any forget-me-nots," she complained.

"In early April? Hardly. I promise you there will be—in June."

"I don't believe it." They had reached the road again. Tina's gaze took in the bleak ridge of the crags, gloomy under trailing cloud. "I can't believe flowers ever grow here."

"See that gold at the roadside? Coltsfoot. And there are daffodils in the cottage gardens. Spring comes late on the Wall. When it does, I promise you'll be enchanted."

Tina shivered. They had reached Carrie's car and she saw the Land-Rover parked behind it. "How is your sister today?" she asked.

"About the same." His brow darkened. "There will be little improvement for quite a while yet."

"And you still refuse to allow me to visit her?"

His face grew dangerously taut. "I still refuse."

"And you expect me to accept that?"

"I not only expect it, I demand it. I expect you to keep my rules in my house."

"And a host? Has he no rules?" Tina was completely roused now.

"Not this one, my dear. I'm a law unto myself. But just in case you're still embarrassed by accepting my hospitality, I have a suggestion to make."

"Yes?" He was lighting a cigaret with smooth deliberate movements.

"I believe you are an expert typist?"

"I am."

"And I am without one since Helen's illness. Would it put you out at all to desert the dig for two hours every morning, while you give me a hand? Starting Monday?"

"I suppose I'm expected to say yes?"

He gave her an ironic smile. "I not only expect it, I've anticipated it. There's a three-day backlog of work piled up. . . . And don't bat your eyelashes at me, my dear. You're quite free to refuse."

"You know very well I can't." Her heart was racing. She wondered what it would be like to work with this man, in the close privacy of his office. Impossible to imagine, yet surely overwhelming.

"I'll give it a try," she said coolly.

"Thanks." His tone held little gratitude. "And now I suggest you get back home and change those stockings—or tights or whatever they are." He waited while she unlocked the car. "How do you get on with Carrie, by the way?"

"I like her very much." Greatly daring, Tina stressed the "her". "I think she's a very genuine person."

"Agreed. Though inclined to be a dreamer. Are *you* a dreamer, Tina Rutherford?"

She got into the car, faced him boldy. "No, I'm not. I like the truth."

"Be it bad or good?"

"Be it bad or good," she repeated.

He stood eyeing her, his mouth set, his eyes measuring.

"Yes, I think you do. Haven't you discovered yet how the truth can hurt?"

She shook her head.

"You will, Coventina. You will. Seekers after truth tread a hard road."

She got into the car and pulled the door to. "I'm going now, Mr. Copeland. Thanks for the lift."

He lifted his hand in a relaxed salute, but did not turn away. And because his presence flustered her she muffed her gears. His laughter was soft but audible. She drove back to Hadrian's Edge, her face burning.

A day or two passed. Rather to her surprise Tina found she had slipped easily into the life of Hadrian's Edge. It was a house of order and peace, though continually haunted by the sound of the wind, which made the heavy curtains and log fires seem an added comfort. She could sense the presence of former generations of Copelands, who had contributed their heavy antique furniture, and who must have often gazed as she did from the deeply-alcoved windows toward the hills, their far troubles and longings now lost on that eternal wind.

404

In Carrie's den she always found a friendly welcome. Carrie had the art of friendship without involvement. There among the Air Force souvenirs Tina could make a confidence without regretting it, or sit in silence without giving offence.

She found an equal if different welcome in the kitchen, which Isa had made very much her own domain. Two rocking chairs nodded at the hearth, a text or two decorated the high white walls, and under the window stood a small harmonium, flanking with incongruous effect a modern sink unit. Isa explained that she played the organ in chapel and must keep in practice.

"Though I can't pull out all the stops I'd like," she sighed to Tina. "For Mr. Copeland, now, he aye comes in and reminds me I'm not playing at the Odeon in Newcastle. "In quietness and confidence shall be your strength, Isa," he says. For he's a great man for coming up with a text himself. But then he reads the lesson in church once a month, and I think he saves them up to fair bamboozle me."

She often invited Tina to sit by the stove with the ginger cat Samson on her lap, while she served up strong tea in the kitchen cups. Though she was a natural gossip, her country courtesy made her respect Tina's affairs, but she was only too ready to talk of her own.

"I've never married," she explained. "For the lad I fancied, he fancied another lass. And the lad who fancied me, I couldn't take to him, though his mother offered me a whole kist o' the best linen, all drawn-threadwork it was."

"Don't you mind, Isa—about not being married, I mean?" Tina asked.

"No, hinney, I'm well content. For if I'd got wed, I could have had worse troubles—a man who drank, or got in a bad fettle if my pastry wasn't just right." She paused. "I'll say this for Mr. Copeland," she went on impressively, "he's a reasonable man about pastry!"

Tina hid a smile. Isa admired her dress. "By, I can see that cost something. . . . But then I'm fair lucky about clothes mysel'. For I was cook once to Mrs. Green-wood—they were big shipping people on the Tyne. She got all her clothes from Paris. Aye, and she passed so many of them on to me, for we were the same size, that I haven't had to buy a new dress for years. Mrs. Butterfield now, she says they're old-fashioned, for Mrs. Greenwood was older nor me. But, says I, they're the best quality and wortha mint o' money. I'm like to throw them away when the Hexham shops are asking ten guineas for a bit of a wool dress—so-called wool, for no Otterburn sheep ever went near it!"

Isa paused dramatically. "Some of them are on the dressy side. I'll warrant—I'm talking o' Mrs. Green-wood's dresses. There's a mito' bead and fancy bits on some o' them for a woman like mysel' who's strict chapel. . . . Aye, but ma conscience is clear, for when I'm off to play the organ Sundays I wear my plain black coat ower top o' them, so I don't get above mysel'."

Carrie grinned when Tina relayed the conversation. "Those dresses have to be seen to be believed. Pure twenties and thirties, most of them. She wears them sometimes in the afternoons—always reminds me of a character from Doctor Finlay's Casebook. But who cares, as long as she's happy!"

Then there were the evening meals in the dining-room, when Adam Copeland appeared. Just as Carrie's company was reassuring and Isa's amusing, Adam's was an uneasy challenge. Tina could not deny that his presence rounded off the day, gave point to the household's domestic activities. His ease as host, his racy tales of the countryside, his bland disregard of her reserved silence, both fascinated her and increased her resentment.

Sometimes he sat in the living-room afterwards. Carrie had a disconcerting habit of disappearing suddenly on ploys of her own, and then Tina found his presence, even if he were quietly reading, so overpowering that she too would escape to Carrie's den, a quiet sanctuary except for the wheezing of the harmonium from the kitchen.

Yet even then she was still aware of the man across the hall, so self-possessed, so arrogantly king of his castle.

She told herself firmly that though the rest of the household revolved round him she must resist being drawn into that dangerous whirlpool. She must remember he was her enemy. . . .

On Monday morning Tina presented herself at the estate office, deliberately choosing the hour of nine-fifteen.

Adam Copeland was talking on the telephone, significantly glanced at his wrist-watch and a moment later hung up.

"You're late! Please try to be here at nine tomorrow. I begin at eight-thirty." His tone was glacial.

"I thought this was a friendly arrangement," Tina said with spirit.

"It'll be a darned unfriendly one if you keep me waiting about, my lass. . . . Now, a quick guide to the office. These are the letter files, accounts the other side. Estate wages and maintenance in that metal cabinet. That's a map of the estate on the wall, with the names of all the farms. The sooner you memorize them the easier your work will be. This side door here behind the curtain gives on to the drive. Anyone coming on business rings the bell there. Right? Now, better get down to some of these letters. I read fast, but I expect you to be absolutely accurate."

"I begin to see why you had to get your sister to do the job," Tina said. "I suppose no other girl would stay."

"And you?"

"As I said, I have little choice. It's one way of repaying your rather reluctant hospitality."

His eyes darkened. "There would have been nothing reluctant about it had matters been different." His voice sank a little. "Even now, perhaps—"

Tina's gaze met his coldly. He broke off, resuming his former dictatorial tone. "Right. Letter one—to the Land Tax Commissioners. You'll get the address from the files."

By the end of the next two hours, when the letters were typed and ready for his signature, Tina had learned a great deal more about Adam Copeland and his work.

The letters had dealt with a cross-section of estate life, forestry, game reserves, farm tenancies, drainage laws, farm and estate workers' wages. She learned that Fairstones needed new field gates, that High Dunchester was plagued with rats, that a cottage eviction order was being sought at Romandyke.

Later the cottager himself, much distressed, had rung the side bell and Tina, busy at her typewriter, had heard most of the interview. She admitted that Adam Copeland had been scrupulously fair even while insisting on the farmer's rights. Eventually he had promised to try for an extension. There had been tears in the man's eyes as he wrung Adam Copeland's hand on leaving. "I knew you'd help me, Mr. Copeland. I knew I could rely on you."

She also heard him roar scathingly down the phone to a building contractor falling behind on his contract, and gave a silky assurance to the local Children's Officer that the twins at Quarry Farm were in no danger of being neglected.

At this Tina looked up, startled. His gaze met hers, bright with challenge. "Curious, are you? I heard you'd been to Quarry Farm and failed to get far with your inquiries." He smiled. "And now you're wondering why I side with them against authority? It's no secret. They're a darned nuisance at Quarry Farm, but they'd be a much bigger problem anywhere else."

"Francey's pretty, isn't she?" Tina said. "I suppose she bats her eyes at you, as you so charmingly put it."

He laughed with such good nature she was startled again. "Oh, she does! Make no mistake about that. And why not? Like you, she uses the only weapons she has."

"And—it works?" Tina found her voice unsteady.

"She thinks it does." He grinned to himself, then with one of those lightning changes of mood she found so disconcerting he said tersely, "You didn't get on very well, I hear—except with Matt. I would have said Jamey was more your line of country. And he's always eager to notch up another newcomer."

Tina's face flamed. "Jamey's a little too obvious thanks. And anyway, I'm not looking for—anything like that."

"Of course not," he said smoothly, pushing aside the papers before him and relaxing in his chair. "You'll content yourself with Roman remains and stirring up trouble—right?"

"If necessary, yes." She got up. "Your letters are ready." She laid the sheaf on his desk. "Is it all right if I go now?"

"When I've looked through them, yes." He riffled through the sheaf. "Excellent work, I see. Some Roman executive is going to get himself a perfect secretary. I may even write you a reference."

Tina lingered in the doorway, stung by his mocking tone, but magnetized into holding his gaze. "What would it say?" she faltered.

"Oh, the truth, of course. Miss Rutherford is an ornament to any office, but used to having her own way and completely spoiled. She ought to improve rapidly under strict discipline and a daily beating."

"You sound like the overseer of a slave-market!"

Her heart was bumping uncomfortably, but she stood her ground.

"Do I? It's certainly true that you've been over-pampered, that you have no compunction in using your looks to your own advantage. Take care, my dear. There may come a day when the formula no longer works."

"Thanks for the warning!" she flashed, and left the room. He was insufferable, she told herself. Yet the stinging truth in his last words stayed with her. "There may come a day—" It seemed to her that the day had already come, that he alone was amused and unstirred by her beauty. It was a curiously depressing thought.

That evening Carrie and Tina joined Adam Copeland for the evening meal, which Isa, with much heavy breathing, served in the small dining-room at the rear of the hall. Adam had been sitting on the local magistrates' bench that afternoon and wore a dark formal suit, which made him more impressive than ever.

"Good evening," He smiled at Carrie, nodded at Tina, eyeing in a brief but comprehensive glance at her white sleeveless dress with the forget-me-not silk scarf at the neck. She thought she saw a hastily-suppressed approval in his eyes. Carrie wore a suit in pale green, but as always with her clothes, seemed quite unaware of what she was wearing, not even quite inside them. She was usually much too preoccupied to give her wardrobe any particular thought.

"Well, how many poor victims did you send to prison today?" Carrie asked briskly, as Isa served the soup.

"None. A few probation orders, fines, the usual thing. This is a pretty law-abiding district. . . . Oh, by the way, Carrie, Sandy Armstrong's got another lodger."

Carrie groaned. "Let's hope he likes listening to the pipes, then." She turned to Tina. "Sandy's manager of High Moor Quarry—that's a couple of miles over the moor. He has a cottage right up in the woods above the dig, on the line of the Wall. In fact, one of the milecastles backs right on to his place, and I've a suspicion most of the stones in the cottage walls are from the Wall. I don't know if you've heard, but accommodation's hard to get round here, and Sandy often has people knocking on his door, asking for meals or a bed. So now and again he takes pity. Who is it this time, Adam?"

"Oh, a student walking the Wall from the Tyne to the Solway. Seems bent on making it, but he's laid up with pretty bad blisters for a day or two. The trouble is, half these people with Wall Fever haven't a clue as to the conditions they're going to find, especially up on the Whin Sil. You could wear out any pair of ordinary boots from Chesters to the Knag Burn Gap alone. . . . Anyway, Sandy picks and chooses. He doesn't take just anyone. Their aura has to be right, as you might say." Adam flashed a glance of sharp mischief at Carrie. "Sandy's by way of being a special friend of Carrie's," he said blandly.

"*Friend!*" Carrie exploded. "The day he and I see eye to eye is a long way off! I wanted to dig up a square yard or two inside his garden. I just had a hunch it was the site of the baking-oven in the south wall of the milecastle. But would he let me do it? Not on your life! He has no respect for the Wall at all, though he's not above making money out of it with his lodgers. Don't talk to me about Sandy Armstrong!"

Tina looked with surprise at Carrie's heightened color.

"Methinks the lady protests too much," Adam said softly. He turned with disconcerting suddenness to Tina. "I'm visiting my sister tonight. Is there any message you would like to send?"

She felt his tone was unnecessarily goading, a reminder that while he decreed there should be no contact between the two girls, any message she might care to send would have all the force of a spent rocket.

"Please say how sorry I am she's ill, and that I hope to see her soon."

"Certainly. But one hopes she will have patience, as a meeting just now is, of course, out of the question." He turned to Carrie again. "Any luck at the dig today?"

"One good-sized shard of pottery, three third-century coins and a Roman hair-pin," Carrie said briskly. "We're going to bring the notes up to date tonight in my den. No objection to Chris Irwin coming, have you?"

"Any friend of Tina's is, of course, welcome. You did say he was just a friend, didn't you?" He eyed her coolly.

"There is a friend that sticketh closer than a brother!" quoted Isa, as she panted in under the weight of a large apple pie. Adam grinned.

"We must have Mr. Irwin in for a meal one evening," he went on. "Very remiss of us not to have asked him earlier."

Carrie nodded. "I'll ask him, then. But I'll have to warn him to keep off archaeology, for your sake."

Isa cleared the plates. Carrie was dubiously poking at the pie.

"You'll find that pastry a bit on the hard side, Mrs. Butterfield," Isa announced. "I was down in the dumps when I made it, all along o' my knitting no' winning first prize at the Handwork Show. I always say you need a light heart for light pastry."

"But you won't find that text in Proverbs!" Adam remarked. "Just a small portion for me, Carrie, please, now I've been warned."

Isa stood over at the sideboard, placing out the coffee cups, a look of bovine complacency on her face. Carrie shot her an exasperated look. "If that's another text coming up, Isa, I'm not in the mood."

"Text—what text?" Isa looked affronted. "I was just waiting to say the coffee's ready and I'm off to the Chapel Social." She bustled out importantly.

Adam took only a half cup of coffee before excusing himself to make some telephone calls. Tina felt herself relax and watched Carrie light a cigaret. Suddenly she noticed a photograph on a bookcase in a rather shadowed corner of the room. "That photo—who is it, Carrie? I haven't seen it before."

Carrie got up and brought it over. "It's Helen—you may as well have a good look. It's a perfect likeness."

Tina saw a fair face, fragile, almost moody. The eyes held depths impossible to fathom, but there was a hint of petulance about the mouth, a weaker reflection of the arrogance of her brother.

"She takes after the mother's side," Carrie explained. "Adam is more like his father."

"She looks rather frail," Tina said.

"She isn't exactly bursting with health, even in normal times. She had polio as a child, and that's one of the reasons Adam is over-protective."

"One of the reasons?"

"There were—others, or at least one more. He made a pretty big blunder when he was still just a boy."

"Something to do with Helen, you mean?" she pressed.

"I shouldn't be telling you this. But it might help you to understand Adam more. He was just fifteen at the time it happened—or so he told me. He shut Helen up in an old quarry hut for a joke, then forgot about her. Sounds odd, I know, but he was asked to go and play football, and, lad-like, it put everything else out of his mind. It was after ten at night when he got back—he'd cycled over to Hexham for supper with friends. Naturally the household was in alarm and he had to confess what he'd done. Helen was in hysterics when she was found. It was pitch-dark in the hut. Since then she's always been terrified of the dark.

And even now she burns a light all night in her room."

Tina was intrigued. "Do you think he still has guilt feeling toward her, then?"

"I'm pretty certain of it. That's why he flew off the handle so much about this breakdown of hers. But I've a feeling Miss Helen is deeper than Adam imagines."

"Why?"

"I think she plays on the situation. She can put on a fine show of hysteria if she wants anything badly enough."

"And he actually gives in?"

"Not always." Carrie shook her head. "But there are times when she is genuinely upset and depressed. Sometimes he has to give her the benefit of the doubt."

"I suppose so." Tina hesitated. "I can't help wondering what Bruno found to love in Helen."

"You ought to know by now that a deep physical attraction doesn't have to depend on liking a person or even being blind to their faults." Carrie's eyes looked faraway and Tina got the impression that she wasn't thinking of Bruno and Helen at all but something much more personal. Lofty, perhaps?

"And you think it was like that?"

"I know it was. Your brother fell hard, but he was too intelligent to nurse too many illusions."

"But what about—before he came? Didn't she have anyone else? I wondered about Matt Finch—"

Carrie shook her head decisively. "Never in the world! You're flying right out of formation there. He was too slow and quiet for her and he'd have far too much sense, anyway, to offend Adam. I suppose she flirted around, here and there, but no one she was specially keen on."

She sighed. "I know—I know—you're looking for reasons to justify Bruno walking out on her, if he did. But I can't find you a male scapegoat, look as hard as I like."

Tina sighed. "So you think Bruno just tired of her?"

"I don't know. But men, even the best of them do these things. They may see a new face and be tempted to cut and run. Instant romance instead of ploughing through all the conditions laid down by Adam—the year's

engagement, the elaborate wedding expected of a
Copeland who is as near as anything we've got to a local
squire—the promise perhaps that Helen wouldn't be
required to live in Italy. It could have all got on top of
him. But you know the gossip—about this mysterious
girl?"

"I know," Tina said miserably. "But I'll never be
convinced the first fault was Bruno's."

Carrie said drily: "If you reveal Helen to be the serpent
in Eden you're not going to be very popular with Adam."

Tina set her lips. "He detests me, anyway. What have I
got to lose?"

"Detests you? That's not quite the impression I
got. . . ." She pushed back her chair. "It's Isa's night out,
so me for kitchen fatigues. Like to help?"

While carrying a loaded tray down the hall Tina
encountered Adam Copeland leaving his office. His
eyebrows lifted. "Useful as well as ornamental? Don't
carry your sense of a guest's obligations too far, will
you?"

Without warning he relieved her of the tray. "Much
too heavy for a Roman water-nymph."

Tina flushed. He jerked his head to indicate that she
preceded him into the kitchen. "Thank you," She said
stiffly as he set down the tray. "I suppose it's all right if I
carry the salt and pepper through?"

His dark brows lifted. "That's better. You're beginning
to relax and find your sense of humor. I hope it also
means you're beginning to feel at home?"

His tone was bantering, but something still and curious
about his eyes disconcerted her. Looming in the doorway
as he did, her exit was trapped. An answer seemed
expected.

The truth, she thought in a panic, was that he was right.
To tell him so was the last thing she was likely to do.

"Aren't you expecting rather too much, Mr.
Copeland?"

His eyes flickered coldly. He made way for her. She
was distressingly conscious of his chilled withdrawal, for
a moment wildly wishing she could retract her words. She

even hesitated beside him, searching for the necessary courage. But he was already striding up the hall. She heard the decisive and final click of his office door.

Carrie, arriving with another tray, glanced at her sharply. "Anything wrong?"

"Not a thing," said Tina lightly, blinking back the tell-tale tears.

The following morning Adam Copeland was terse and abrupt over his letter dictation. As soon as he had finished he reached for his jacket. "So much for that lot. I'll leave you to type them. There may be a phone call. If anyone wants me, be sure to say that I'm over at Rudchester—Bill Grant's place."

"Rudchester," Tina repeated. Then: "Vindobala," she said, automatically using the Roman name.

"Vindobala then, if you wish." His stare was sardonic. "There's something not a little disconcerting about all this pert knowledge of places you haven't even seen. If you visited them with me you'd learn things your scale model could never teach you."

"That's not very likely, is it?" Tina said flatly.

He gave her an unreadable look, then left. Immediately the room seemed emptied of vitality. Tina looked with distaste at her shorthand notebook, then lurked behind the curtain to watch the departure of the Land-Rover. She turned to her notebook again, saw a faint gleam of sunshine at the window and decided to leave the letters for the moment. As long as they caught the afternoon post she told herself there was no urgency. Besides, being Tina, she was drawn to idle in the sunshine. There was little enough of it on these bleak heights, she excused herself.

His warning about the telephone message was already forgotten. It had been casually given and just as casually slipped her mind.

As she left the office a twinge or two of guilt did bother her, but after all, she told herself, she was no paid typist. Yet her heart raced a little as she let herself cautiously out of the side door.

She followed the path from the back of the grounds

which led to the fork for Quarry Farm. It skirted the lip of an abandoned quarry, smothered now in leafless thickets and the pale ghosts of withered weeds. Beyond the quarry an unknown track led westward into the woods, toward the dig. She hesitated, then turned to retrace her steps. Better not risk that way, in case she ran into Carrie, and the moor track to the farm would be too exposed for idle loitering. Remembering a sunny sheltered bank almost opposite the quarry, she thought it might be pleasant to sit there for half an hour.

Something hit her quite sharply on the shoulder. She spun, startled, and saw a fir-cone at her feet. Another struck her arm, this time more gently. She heard a giggle from somewhere above, and laughed in relief.

"It's the twins, isn't it?" she called. "Where are you?"

"Come and find us." The voices seemed to come from a giant ivy-clad oak near the path. She remembered the tree house and saw two faces peering down at her.

"So that's where you are? May I come up?"

The twins deliberated in whispers. "Aye, you can—if you can climb the ladder. We're letting it down."

The rope ladder was makeshift but strong, with roughly-cut hazel stakes for treads. Tina scrambled up the ten feet or so to the fork of the boughs and found to her surprise that the tree house was quite a solid affair, a floor of saplings lashed together, and with others splaying at angles for the walls.

"This is good." Tina scrambled in, helped by Bobby, and an old piece of curtain was slung over the door-space. "You didn't build it yourselves, surely?" She lowered herself to a seat on an old cushion.

"Jamey helped us. We *made* him," said Rosie. Her thin little face was stained with green mould. Bobby wore an Indian headdress of pigeon's feathers.

"*Made* him?" Tina accepted a square of toffee from Bobby.

"Aye, we did. You see, we knew about—" Bobby began, but Rosie nudged him sharply. "It was something we knew about him he didn't want folks to know. So we said we'd keep quiet if he built us a tree house."

"But that's blackmail!" Tina's protest was mild. She felt that Jamey probably deserved all he got, anyway.

"Aye, that's what Jamey said," Rosie giggled.

"Aren't you going to school today?"

"We might this afternoon." Rosie banged her slab of toffee against a bough. "It was history this morning and we hate history. Francey said she might write us a note if we kept out from under her feet."

"Don't tell me you've got a hold over Francey, too?"

The twins exchanged a glance but remained silent. Tina peered through a gap to the path below. "Do you pelt everyone who passes with fir-cones?"

Bobby was scornful. "No. We mostly spy on them. We've seen poachers. And once we saw a badger come out of his sett—by the quarry there."

"We see lads and girls out courting," Rosie said triumphantly. "Then we whistle at them and they jump a mile."

"Thanks for the warning. Then I won't come courting here." A thought struck Tina. She hesitated, then said, her tone casual. "Did you ever see Bruno here—my brother?"

"Aye, we did." Again the twins exchanged a secret glance. There was a silence. Then: "We're right sorry he died," Bobby said soberly. "He was nice to us, wasn't he, Rosie?"

Rosie nodded. Tina thought she saw the glint of tears in her eyes. She had been wrong to mention Bruno, she thought, wrong to question them on impulse. And whatever they had seen from their hiding-place—if indeed they had seen anything of Bruno at all—it was unfair to upset them. She also had a strong suspicion that their silence could be one of loyalty rather than ignorance. She changed the subject abruptly.

"Does Mr. Copeland ever go past?"

Bobby laughed. "He walks past and looks straight ahead. But he's no' daft, is Mr. Copeland. We're sure he knows. . . . Look, Tina, if you ever want to come up on your own, the rope ladder stays coiled here. You pull it down by that bit o' string."

She felt this was a subtle dismissal and got to her feet. "Don't you mind me coming up here, then—on my own, I mean?"

Rosie said importantly: "You can come, but mind not to bring anyone else."

"I promise."

She left them in their hideout and walked back to her sunny bank. Here she lounged on a dry mat of pine needles, enjoying the pallid warmth of the sun and sheltered by the thickets on the quarry edge. She thought about the twins. She supposed it was all wrong, their absence from school, the blackmailing of Jamey and perhaps Francey, the determinedly blind eye of Adam Copeland. No one could call it an ideal upbringing for children. Yet they were surprisingly unspoiled and lovable, due perhaps to Matt's influence.

Tina dreamed a little, thinking with a pang of happy days in Rome before tragedy struck at their close-knit family. She wondered how her father was faring in the States and whether new scenes and interests were helping him control his grief. Eventually she fell into a half-doze, until a fitful wind, chill-edged, wafted into her sheltered retreat. She stirred, glanced at her watch. There might be just time to do some of Adam Copeland's typing before lunch.

Her arrival at the house, however, constituted a rude awakening. When she let herself in at the office door, a tornado of anger smote her.

"Where the devil have you been?" Adam Copeland rasped. He was ranging restlessly, looking bigger and more intimidating than ever, between the desk and the door. After a hard stare he stood slamming papers about, in a haze of cigaret smoke.

"Out!" said Tina, after the first shocked impact. "Don't worry, your letters will still catch the post."

"Letters! Did I mention letters? I thought I made it plain that I was expecting a phone call and that you were to give a certain message?"

Tina was dismayed. Of course, she remembered now—Vindobala. . . .

"I did forget," she admitted. "I'm sorry. No harm's been done, has it?" It seemed an unnecessary fuss about nothing.

"It so happens"—his tone was one he might have used to a three-year-old—"a call did come. Isa had to answer it and could give the caller no idea where I was. It's not her job to know my movements or my business. Those I entrusted to *you*." His voice took a razor edge. "Even if you were tempted to go out, you should have left the message on the phone pad. And it may interest you to know that the man who phoned needed to find me urgently on a financial matter. It may well be that your carelessness has cost him a sum of several hundred pounds."

Her face flamed. "I've said I'm sorry—and I mean it."

She saw in his eyes impatience, contempt and a disgusted acceptance that nothing better could be expected of her. "After all," she protested, "you didn't say how important it was."

"I didn't see the need. Even the most incompetent secretary makes a note of any directions she's given."

It was true. But knowing she was in the wrong only increased her resentment.

Her eyes sparked. "I'm not your paid secretary. You can't really hold me to blame. And anyway," she said it defiantly, "why couldn't the man look after his own affairs?"

He sat very still, regarding her. The dark curve of his moustache above his lip had a cynical twist, almost cruel, she thought. "I'll tell you why. Because it is my job to advise these people, because this particular man trusted my judgment and was prepared to act by it. Because it is my duty to protect the tenant farmers' interests. But more than all this, because he happens to be a friend. Does any of that mean anything to you?"

"I'm sorry," she said coldly. "If you'd explained—"

"I'm not in the habit of giving explanations. When I leave explicit orders I trust people to carry them out, without giving reasons."

"Orders?" Tina questioned. "Order?" But she quailed a little as she met his eyes.

"Directions, then, if you can't stand plain speaking. Was it so much to ask, after all? Especially when you'd already agreed to the arrangement."

"I agreed—yes." She felt warm and flustered now. "But I didn't mean—"

"I know exactly what you meant, my dear," he said with harsh deliberation. "What you meant was that you would oblige when and if it suited you. But the sun shone this morning, so your Roman lotus-eating temperament took over. Right? 'Work can always wait another day—today we sit in the sun'."

She colored. How well he understood her nature, her motives. Yet why should she be ashamed of her Roman characteristics?

He went on relentlessly: "Unfortunately, there is always our duty to others. Laziness is inexcusable, if it means others have to suffer. But perhaps you haven't thought very deeply on the subject."

"Shall I do the letters now?" was all she said, with a shaking hint of tears in her voice.

"If you please!" Abruptly he left the room.

She sat down blindly at the desk. She knew it was now necessary to redeem her fault by hard work. For she would not be helping Bruno's cause by allowing her normal rather spoilt young nature to assert itself. Now Bruno was dead Adam Copeland would judge the family by *her* actions.

And this, she well saw, meant altering her ways, being more thoughtful, considerate and punctual—all the virtues which her indulgent father and loving brother had never really required of her.

It was perhaps at that moment of truth Tina really began to grow up. . . .

CHAPTER THREE

ALONE in the office, Tina labored over Adam Copeland's letters. She was still distraught enough to make many mistakes, and much careful retyping was necessary. At last Carrie looked in.

"Lunch, Tina. You still at it . . . ? We had quite a good morning at the dig. Looks like we've found the corner of a memorial stone in the central section. There's an inscription showing up, but not enough to decipher yet—"

Tina was unusually unresponsive. Carrie rattled on for a few minutes, then said abruptly: "I've been thinking about that supper-party. What about Saturday? Adam could ask one of his women friends."

"Has he so many?"

Carrie grinned. "I saw a real touch of Latin cynicism in you there. . . . Well, as to friends, he has a number of hopers and wishers. I could name half a dozen now who would give their right hands to come."

Tina said coldly: "He shouldn't have much trouble, then," and thought Carrie gave her a curious look.

On that Saturday evening Tina dressed with care, wearing a pale primrose dress, perfectly plain except for a row of gilt buttons down one side. With it she wore a matching gilt bracelet. Her hair lay like black satin about her shoulders and she had been lavish with forget-me-not eye-shadow.

When she joined Carrie in the living-room she found her enjoying a sherry and a glance through the local paper. The older woman looked up approvingly. "I must say you look all continental glamor. I'm afraid I haven't tried very hard." She glanced down at a rather full air-force blue suit, almost as if she had forgotten what she was wearing.

She threw the paper down. "I see that fool Everard-Kipps is at it again!"

"Who is Everard-Kipps?"

"Oh, he's a local amateur historian and would-be journalist. Writes pieces for the *North Tyne Chronical* and considers himself an expert on the Wall. But he's dead wrong about the Vallum at Housesteads, and I shall write in to the paper and say so. We're always battling in print. I quite enjoy shooting him down."

Tina laughed. "There's Chris's car now. I'd better let him in."

Carrie stared at Chris, who looked unusually distinguished in a dark formal suit. "Heavens!" Carrie gasped. "We're all scarcely recognizable away from the dig. I suppose it does us good to be civilized for once."

She had just begun to pour sherry for Tina and Chris when Adam Copeland entered with his lady guest. Tina experienced a tingling shock. Even Carrie's eyebrows lifted.

For the lady was Francey Finch.

"Hallo." Adam spoke easily. He too was formally dressed in light gray. "We've all met, I think. Sherry, Francey?"

"Yes, please. Sweet for me." She stood rather defiantly in the centre of the room, her tough little chin well up. Tina was surprised to see her in a simple cream shift dress, her make-up quite underplayed; it was evident, though, that she had spent time on her hair. It was a gleaming sunset halo about her face.

Tina also noticed that Chris was eyeing Francey with some appreciation. They had met before, of course, but perhaps this was the first time he had seen her in civilized surroundings.

"Found anything wonderful on your dig yet?" she asked him.

"Oh, bits and pieces. But you're not interested, surely?" Chris gave her an indulgent smile.

"You're right—it seems an awful waste of time to me." But her eyes ogled him over her glass. Tina saw Adam intercept the look and wondered what Francey was up to. Was this an attempt to sting Adam to jealousy? If so, he looked remarkably unimpressed.

Isa looked round the door, heavily flushed. "It's on the

422

table, so don't blame me if good food goes to waste." Her
soured eye settled on the sherry glasses. "For strong wine
is a mocker!" she announced as she left the room.

"Isa's getting worse," Carrie sighed. "But then she did
badly at the whist-drive last night, so I expect we shall
suffer for it. Come on, let's learn the worst."

They trooped into the dining-room, where Isa handed
the soup-plates with a face of doom. She was wearing a
rather peculiar dress of mustard-colored velvet, with a
marabou-fringed neckline. The color was distressingly at
odds with her sandy hair and heightened color. Tina
smiled to herself as she saw Chris give the outfit a rather
stunned glance.

A large steak pie followed the soup. Carrie looked
resigned. "I'm afraid the pastry's pretty U.S.
Sorry—unserviceable in Air Force language. Anyway,
the steak and mushrooms seem all right." She began
serving it. At the head of the table opposite her sat Adam,
with Tina and Francey to right and left of him and Chris
next to Francey.

"Sorry we're still odd numbers," Adam remarked. "I
asked Sandy Armstrong along, but he's playing at
Hangingstones Barn Dance tonight."

"And a good thing too," Carrie retorted. "Or he'd
have been piping in the steak and kid instead of a haggis."
Was she disgruntled, because he had been invited, Tina
wondered, or because he had not accepted?"

Isa, bearing in a sauceboat of gravy, caught the last
words. "We have piped on to you and ye have not
danced!" she quoted as she made for the door.

Chris showed his astonishment. Adam's grin was
complacent. Only a man so maddeningly sure of himself,
Tina thought, could accept with such poise the
eccentricities of his domestic staff.

"That Sandy Armstrong!" Carrie exploded. "He led
me a fine dance when we first started the dig. He wasn't
above stealing down after dark and burying all kinds of
daft things in the rubble. Foreign coins, for instance. And
were our faces red when we'd cleaned them up! And once
it was a broken earthenware bowl. We thought we'd got

some Samian ware until we found the "Made in Stoke-On-Trent" stamp on the base."

Tina laughed. "All very well," Carrie grumbled. "If you ask me it's just childish—playing practical jokes at *his* age!"

As the meal proceeded all was not well with the conversation. Carrie, with no one to impress or entertain, had lapsed into some train of thought probably connected with the third century. Chris discussed a current film with Francey, who treated him to flirtatious looks between responses. Adam watched them both with a carefully blank expression. Was he actually jealous? Tina wondered, and the thought chilled her. Then he was asking her, lightly and ironically, "I hear you've been to Winshiels and Crag Lough. Were you impressed?"

"Yes, I was. Those crags are fantastic. And the Wall—" she faltered, lost for words.

"Magnificent, isn't it? Considering every stone was hauled by hand labor, it must still be the greatest engineering feat of all time. A bit different from the plaster model, I imagine."

"I admit it," she said stiffly.

"I used to do some climbing on the crags above the lough—the usual rope and tackle stuff. When I was a lad, of course."

"You mean you went down that—that awful drop?" She shivered.

"Nothing to it, when you know how." He went on to speak of Chesters fort. "You know, I suppose, that there's a local ghost story about it."

"No. What is it?"

"Oh, a troop of legendary Roman horsemen are supposed to emerge from some underground stables and roam the night countryside."

"Has anyone seen them?" Tina asked sceptically.

"You needn't sound so superior. What has been seen or believed to have been seen on moonlight nights along the Wall might surprise you. And, still talking of Chesters, you know, of course, who was governor of the fort in the second century?"

"Ulpious Marcellus," Tina said without hesitation.

"Go to the top of the class!" His tone was lightly mocking, but his glance, Tina saw, was for Francey, now in animated conversation with Chris.

"What about Ulpious Marcellus?" Tina asked coldly, determined in some pettishness to transfer that glance to herself, and when she had engineered it, to give him the full forget-me-not treatment.

He met her efforts with amused eyes. "As I was about to say, Ulpious Marcellus was quite a martinet. Before going to bed he used to write out a series of orders to be sent at intervals to his guards on the Wall, so they would think him still awake and watchful."

"Nice person," said Tina. She remembered her father telling her the same story. "Perhaps you'd like to do the same thing in your office, to make sure I stay on the job?"

"Certainly an idea." His gaze moved wickedly over her face, the curve of his mouth was more sardonic than ever. At this point Carrie intervened.

"I thought we weren't to talk about archaeology or Wall history," she complained.

"Sorry, Carrie." Tina heard genuine courtesy in his tone. "I'm afraid I forgot. We'll certainly close the hangar doors, as you would say!" He turned with some determination to interrupt the other couple.

"How is the family, Francey? The twins been in trouble again?"

"Nothing worth mentioning." Francey's voice was cool It was obvious she was deliberately playing off Chris against Adam.

"And Matt?" Adam persisted. "How are the pigeons?"

"Oh, flying as usual." This time her tone was pert and the look Adam sent down the table was clearly a warning. Francey dropped her gaze and fiddled with the bread on her side plate.

After a short silence Chris said pleasantly to Adam: "Nice place you've got here. I should imagine it's bleak in winter, though?"

Adam agreed. "The summer visitors to the Wall should see it in January and get quite another picture.

The winters up here were of course responsible for so many early deaths among the legionaries and slave labor."

"I thought the Romans had central heating," Francey said meekly, seeming determined now to placate Adam. But it was Chris who turned to explain: "That's true—it was the holocaust system—what we would now call underfloor heating. But that was mostly for the commandant's and officers' quarters. The men on the Wall guarding the forts and milecastles would have to do with open braziers." He caught Carrie's ironical glance. "Oops, sorry! We're away again. That's the worst of Wall Fever!"

Carrie laughed. "It was to give you a change I suggested we all avoid the subject. Seems I needn't have bothered. We'll have our coffee round the living-room fire. Anyone care for a game of cards?"

Tina declined. The others began a not too serious game of rummy. She crossed to the radiogram, put on a Brahms waltz very softly. Adam Copeland caught her eye and smiled. The smile was mild, appreciative and plainly said: "I like Brahms." Nothing else, yet it had the power to scatter her thoughts. She sorted through the discs to hide her face.

Tina helped Carrie serve the coffee. Soon the rummy game got lazier and petered out. Adam dispensed drinks, there was some desultory talk and then the evening broke up. Late nights were not a habit at Hadrian's Edge, Tina had already discovered.

Chris offered Francey a lift in her car. Adam, who was handing Francey into her coat said firmly, "Kind of you, but I think you'll find Francey prefers the quarry path."

Francey's golden eyes flashed. Her tough little chin tilted. "No, I feel lazy tonight. I'll take the lift, thanks."

Adam's face betrayed no emotion. The other two left with a chorus of 'Goodnights'. Carrie was already pushing the trolley along to the kitchen. Tina and Adam were left alone in the hall. He lit a leisurely cigaret, looked her over and said. "Better watch it. Your boyfriend seems smitten."

"He's not my—"

He held up a warning hand. "Please, no more protests. I believe I've already got the message. It might be kindness, though, to warn him he is handling dynamite."

"Oh, really?" Tina lingered, intrigued.

The collie thrust a loving face into Adam's hand. He caressed her gently. "Or perhaps you'd rather he found out for himself." His head was bent, so his expression was hidden.

"Found out what?" She was exasperated, yet a little excited. Was she on the verge of some discovery?

He lifted his head and looked her full in the eyes. His voice lifted to a savage rasp. "That Francey Finch is a charming little animal with sharp claws and no conscience?" He strode across the hall to his office and closed the door after him.

Tina stared at the heavy oak door, her heart floundering. Did he love Francey despite everything? And in what way had he been disillusioned? Because Francey . . . and Bruno? Her heart raced painfully now.

Yet if Francey had proven so treacherous, why invite her to the house? Because he couldn't resist her company, even now?

There was one way to find out. And being Tina, it was no sooner imagined than done. She tapped on the shut door and entered. Adam was reaching for a book from the wall shelves. He swung about to face her, his expression discouraging.

"Yes—what is it?"

"I want to ask you something." She tried to speak boldly, but her voice quivered.

"About—Francey Finch?

"How did you guess?"

"Elementary. We've just been talking about her. And now you want to know if she and Bruno were up to anything?"

"If you must put it so coarsely—yes."

"The answer is that your brother was a good-looking man, practised with women and easily able to sweep silly little girls off their feet."

"You mean—Francey?"

"Don't underestimate Francey, my dear. Or for that matter any of the Finches. Too many people, including myself, have made that mistake."

"Then what—"

"What did I mean? Why don't you ask Francey?"

"Because I thought you would know."

He threw the heavy book on the desk with a jarring violence. "If I knew exactly the extent of the chaos and unhappiness caused by your brother I would certainly tell you. Perhaps, like yourself, I'm still making discoveries."

The icy formality of his tone stunned her. She left the room, ran upstairs and collapsed in tempestuous Italian tears.

She had failed to make any sense out of his words. At one moment he had seemed to link Francey with Bruno, at the next he was disclaiming knowledge. But it was not the failure to find her question answered which upset her, but his entire change of personality and attitude at mention of her brother. His animosity had not only been plain, but wounding beyond measure.

By Monday morning it was as if that incident had never been. Adam dictated his letters in a normal manner and politely remarked on the change in the weather. Beyond the heavily curtained window huge clouds raced before a northerly wind, and Tina remembered that before breakfast she had seen a flutter of white wings on the moor, then the circling and mounting of Matt's pigeons, wheeling in a course due north for Scotland. They would have a rough passage, she thought, though Matt had told her pigeons rode on air currents to conserve their energies.

After dictating the letters Adam announced he had to go out, leaving directions as to his destination with a rather heavy insistence. Tina said: "It's all right. I'll be here," and slammed her typewriter carriage across with force. He ignored the action and left the office.

When he had gone Tina lapsed into thought. Seeing the pigeons had made her want to see Matt again. He had been so sympathetic, so quietly kind, had little but good to say of Bruno. She felt passionately that she needed reassurance often. There was also a less commendable reason. An open friendship with Matt might shake Adam Copeland's monumental self-complacency.

She typed his letters with care, determined to give no room for criticism, gave explicit directions as to his whereabouts to two telephone callers, and left the office in a neat and efficient state.

That afternoon she spent as usual at the dig. The wind held an icy quality as it skimmed over the southerly ridge to rake the site. The students, huddled in anoraks and scarves, knelt and dug, squatted and examined with their usual persistence. Eventually Tina made her way over to Chris, who was entering the records at a camp table, his papers held down by rough pieces of boulder.

"Well, how did you get on with Francey?" She turned over a few shards from a Roman lamp, traced with her finger the raised design on the glazed earthenware.

Chris did not look up, though whether deliberately or not she wasn't sure. "We found a stone laver in section sixteen—some kind of altar vessel. Cracked but otherwise intact. Alice is cleaning it now. . . . Francey Finch? She's quite the local beauty, of course."

"The Finches have rather an odd reputation round here." Tina was deliberately trying to draw him out.

"Watch those shards. I've got them in a certain order." He spoke with restrained patience. "And don't fish, Tina, please. I'm not interested in local gossip. And I found Francey quite good company. Satisfied?"

"I'll have to be, won't I?" She patted his arm. "Sorry. I'll get down to some work and leave you in peace."

The weather blew even colder, with now and then the sting of rain. Tina was glad of the undemanding company of the students, interested in the stone laver and in a bone Roman comb one of the boys had unearthed in his section. It had fine teeth, though much damaged, on both sides, with a rough form of rivet through the central portion. Carrie, now on the scene, examined it with intense interest. "It's smaller than others found—could have belonged to a child, one of the commandant's children, possibly. . . ." Standing with the comb in her hand she went off into a dream of her own. Tina guessed she was reconstructing some scene in perhaps the second century, with her almost uncanny gift for the past.

That evening Adam was missing from supper and Carrie announced that he was visiting Helen. His absence made Tina restless, though she could scarcely have said why. Perhaps Carrie noticed it, for she suggested a walk.

They wrapped up warmly and climbed the rise of the Military Road to Limestone Corner. Here the highway rode high on the base of the Wall, reaching the brink of a plateau giving vast views of the surrounding country. It was a clear still evening, though piercingly cold. Cross Fell loomed a chill blue to the southwest, the Cheviots were gray wraiths to the north, while the undulating land between was a circular frieze of palest green and sapphire landscape, serrated by the harsh darkness of forest.

"The best view on the Wall," said Carrie briskly. "But we didn't come to look at the view. I wanted to show you what's left of Milecastle Thirty, among other things."

They scrambled about in the fields on either side of the road, Carrie pointing out the line of the Vallum, which here was cut through solid rock, and tracing the Wall ditch on the opposite side, where the rock still bore evidence of the work of the Roman engineers.

They were both absorbed, fascinated, lost in thoughts of that distant past, but at last became aware that dusk was falling. As they walked back downhill Carrie said abruptly: "Gets you, doesn't it? To think that the men building the Wall looked at that same view, felt the same cold of an English spring, even marched where we're walking now. Lofty had a theory, you know—that the more you walked the Wall, the more you let the scenes of it seep into your mind, the more odd things began to happen, as if your eyes and ears were tuned to the past."

"Have you ever seen anything, Carrie?" Twilight was now shadowing the still fields, where ewes and their lambs called plaintively to each other.

"Not the ghostly company from Chesters, I'm afraid.

But queer things have happened to me. Sometimes I'm up on the Wall at dawn or twilight. They're the best times. It's just as if then the veil is very thin between the past and the future. Sometimes I've even fancied I heard Latin voices singing on the wind—"

Tina clutched Carrie's arm, her skin pricking. "Listen—what's that?"

Carrie had to wait until a car swished past. Then a sweet reedy sound came, seductive and wild. They glanced at each other, startled.

"Look!" Tina pointed. A tall figure stood in dark silhouette near the roadside wall. The seductive lament sounded again.

Carrie clicked her teeth. "It's only Sandy Armstrong, on his pipes. His cottage is just through the trees there. I suppose he saw us and this is his idea of a joke."

They walked toward him. A full-throated laugh sounded. "Do you no' like my serenading, Mrs. Butterfield?" He came to join them.

Tina looked at him with interest. So this was Sandy, whom Carrie affected to despise, Sandy the practical joker and happy bachelor. He was big, given to brawn and muscle, and had a soldierly stance. His hair was undoubtedly ginger and his craggy face alive with good humor. He smiled at Tina. "You'll be Miss Rutherford—I heard you'd come, hinney."

Tina shared a hearty handshake, looked with interest at the Northumbrian pipes tucked under his other arm; a black and white plaid bag, with scarlet fringes and brass-mounted keys. "How do you get your mouth down to play them?" she asked, mystified.

"My mouth, pet?" he laughed. "Why, you don't play the Northumbrian pipes with your mouth. You're thinking of the Scottish ones. With these you just finger the drones. . . . Aye, they're grand little pipes, these. What about a tune while I set you both down the road?"

"Anything but Cushie Butterfield, please," Carrie said sharply.

"What about this, then?" As they walked on he played a delicate air. "That's 'Sweet Hesleyside'," he told them.

"It's a song well known on the North Tyne. Ah, and Hesleyside's a bonny spot—I'll have to take you there one day, Carrie."

This was so patently an invitation that Tina smiled. But Carrie's reaction was a sniff. "I've more to do with my time than traipsing half way to Kielder, thank you very much."

Sandy seemed in no way abashed, but announced that he would play 'Blow the Wind Southerly'.

He sang the words softly under his breath:

> *"Blow the wind southerly,*
> *Southerly, southerly—*
> *Blow, bonnie breeze, my lover to me . . . ."*

Carrie dropped back. "Don't wait. I've a stone in my shoe. I'll catch you up."

Tina guessed she was upset. It was a sad song and one she knew well herself, having heard her father humming it often when she was small and his widowhood still raw and near. It clawed at her own heart, too, hinting in some way of joys and sorrows still untasted.

And Carrie? Was she thinking of Lofty, back there in the twilight, knowing only a miracle could bring him now?

Sandy glanced behind him, hesitated, then walked on. He had finished playing and said softly: "She's a canny lass, is Carrie. I think the world of her. It's plain she's had trouble in her life, though. Does she ever talk of her husband?"

"No, never," Tina told him.

"I've often wondered—" He broke off. "That was a sad case about your brother, pet. You've been through a bad time and that's a fact." He patted her shoulder. "You'll just have to stick out your chin and go marching on, like we did in the Army. And there'll come a day when it won't seem so bad. For nowt so bad if we face up to it—I've proved that time and again."

Carrie came up with them. "Tired of the pipes?" she asked. "At least the Romans were no pipe players. Far too civilized for that," she finished triumphantly.

"Get away!" He laughed loudly. "They hadn't the brains for the pipes. Take them all their time to finger a harp!"

"You'd better watch it. Tina's half Roman," Carrie warned him.

He turned to wink at Tina. "She's only mad because I won't let her dig up my garden to find a Roman bakehouse. She's never forgiven me for that. And what use would it be when it was found? A few stones held together with clay. Though I could keep my manure in it, come to think of it," he grinned.

"You're a fool, Sandy Armstrong!" Carrie said crisply. "No wonder you had to join the Army. The Air Force would never have had you!"

"What, the Brylcreem Boys? You should have heard what we thought of *them*!"

They reached the side-road to Hadrian's Edge. "Shall I walk you both up to the house?" he asked. "We could have another bit sing and a go at the pipes up the road there."

"No, thank you," said Carrie with great emphasis. "I don't want Isa frightened out of her wits, or Mr. Copeland thinking we've all been down to the pub."

"Then I'll say goodnight!" He gave them a gay salute and strode back up the hill, the thin sound of the pipes giving out a tune which was certainly "Cushie Butterfield".

As they went into the house, Tina couldn't help feeling the encounter had stimulated her, and she noticed that as Carrie passed through the hall she glanced rather self-consciously in the mirror and smoothed back a strand of hair.

On Saturday afternoon, as was the custom, work on the dig stopped for the weekend. The students dispersed to shopping in Hexham or more sophisticated delights in Newcastle. Carrie too was going to Hexham and even Isa was in holiday mood, bound for an outing with the Women's Institute.

Carrie mentioned that Sandy was playing at another

dance, up Bellingham way, and that he had actually had the audacity to ask her along.

"He must be out of his mind," she added. "Can you see *me* at a barn dance? I ask you."

"You've got to close the hangar doors sometimes," Tina said slyly.

"I've my own ways of closing the hangar doors," Carrie retorted. "I don't need any Sandy Armstrongs to show me."

Tina herself felt rather at a loose end. Adam Copeland was visiting Helen that afternoon and was later dining with friends at Otterburn. She felt that the day stretched endlessly ahead.

When he was in the house she was always tense, stretched to the limit of her powers and with a sense of battle and challenge in the air. Hadrian's Edge without these emotions seemed woefully flat.

In the end she decided to go to Quarry Farm. Even if Francey's welcome might hold a chill, the boys, she knew, would be glad to see her.

It was a brisk windy day, with more than a hint of spring in the air. Huge cloud masses raced across a bright sky. As Tina ran down the moor track she met two small trudging figures, Bobby and Rosie. They looked almost tidy for once, though still in jeans and jerseys.

"Hallo," Tina greeted them. "I was just coming to visit you all."

"You can't visit *us*," Rosie said. "We're off to Hexham on the bus, to spend our pocket-money."

"How much do you get?"

They exchanged glances. "*Officially*—" Bobby brought out the word with pride, "it's fivepence each, but—"

"But we get other money on the side," Rosie explained. "Jamey has to give us twopence each to keep us quiet, and Francey—"

Bobby dug his twin in the ribs. He went on proudly, "But we've got lots more this week. Mr. Copeland gave us fifty pence."

"To keep you quiet?" Tina asked ironically.

They stared. "No," Rosie explained. "Because he'd heard we'd been a whole week at school without being late or absent, and there'd been no complaints about us or Hadrian from the farmers."

"That was generous of him." But Tina despised him for this type of bribery. Bobby's next words, however, changed her opinion. "But Mr. Copeland said if we expected to get money every time we behaved ourselves we'd be sadly disappointed."

"What are you going to buy with it?"

"Some cups and saucers for the tree house. And cakes and things to eat for a picnic," Rosie gloated.

Bobby shrugged. "She's aye wanting to play house. I'm after a fishing line."

Tina dug in her bag. "Have an ice-cream on me." She handed out two sixpences. Rosie kicked the turf, her eyes downcast. "Matt says we haven't got to take money off folks. And anyway"—blue eyes raised hopefully—"the ices we like are ninepence!"

Tina laughed. "Well, I haven't got ninepence, so you'll have to pay the rest yourselves. And don't worry about Matt—I'll tell him it's all right. Is he in?"

"He's in the pigeon loft." The twins ran off, giggling at their own audacity.

Tina skirted the house. Hadrian, sprawled by the back door, thumped his tail at sight of her. She stooped to pat him. Pigeons were wheeling round the loft with a soft rubbery sound of wings. Matt's voice hailed her.

"Like to come up, Tina?"

Stone steps were set sideways to the wall, leading up to the open door of the pigeon loft. Tina mounted and joined Matt inside the doorway.

"Hallo!" he smiled. "Quite a surprise to see you. I thought I was on my own for the afternoon. I've some birds out racing and I've got to wait here at the trap. They should be in soon now. Here, take a seat on that box, if you'd like to watch. I've three due, but as soon as they're in we can go over and have a cup of tea."

Tina gazed about her with curiosity. The rough rafters and walls were whitewashed. She saw nesting boxes and water bowls and an erection of compartments up to the ceiling.

"That's the trap," Matt explained. "You've seen the bob wires hanging over the trap opening. The birds fly through but can't get out again. They land in this main compartment. I throw some seed down for them, and catch them as they're pecking. Then they've got to be timed by the clock and the thimbles."

"Thimbles?"

He smiled. "Not the ladies' kind. The pigeon's ring is slipped off as soon as he comes in and fitted in the timing thimble to record his arrival time. The longer you take to catch your bird the longer is chalked up for the race. That's why I've a warning bell on the bob-stays. If I do have to go over to the house I know in a second then that one of the birds has arrived."

"Do you win prizes?" Tina asked.

Matt pointed to some pigeons already on perches in the trap. "Red Biddy, she won a hundred and five miles. Dark Joy, though, she's a three-hundred-miler—"

"Dark Joy?" Tina was startled. "Did you think of that name, Matt?"

He looked a little confused, his quiet eyes avoiding hers. "Aye, I did. Why do you ask?"

"It's rather—poetical. But joy shouldn't be dark, surely?"

Matt shrugged. "It's the same as calling a thing bitter-sweet. You get to thinking a lot, alone in a loft, you know. It's the quiet and the waiting. And, come to that, I've found most happy things have a shadow on them somewhere—"

He broke off as the bell jangled. There was a bright flutter of wings at the bob-stays and a mealie and white pigeon swooped to the loft floor. Matt threw in a handful of maize and as the other birds fluttered down to join the returned racer, Matt opened a wire-netted door in the trap, reached in and secured the bird. The next instant he had the ring off and in the timing clock. He released the bird into the trap again.

"What's that?" Tina saw him unroll a tiny cylinder of

paper. He read its message, screwed it up and pocketed it. "Oh, they often send a message when they release the birds. It's quicker than the threepenny post and more reliable." He grinned. "I once had an argument with Mrs. Butterfield as to whether the Romans used pigeon post on the Wall."

"To communicate with Rome, you mean?" Tina was intrigued. "But surely a pigeon couldn't fly so far?"

"In this day and age they do. The first one to do that distance was in 1907, from San Sebastian. Eight hundred miles in fourteen days. I had one who did four hundred, but it's dead now."

"What did Carrie think?"

"She wouldn't have it. In any case, as she pointed out, they could flash messages by heliograph to Rome in six hours."

Two more birds arrived in quick succession, Sky Angel and Hope On.

"Hope On?" Tina repeated. "Why that name?"

"Because I keep hoping on they'll turn up safe. She's a bit of chancy hen, that one." His shapely hand caressed the glossy slate feathers. She sensed a certain embarrassment.

"You love your birds, don't you? Even more than people sometimes?" Tina asked curiously.

"That's a leading question." Gently he replaced Hope On in the trap. "Come on, we'll go and make some tea. Then we might have a walk. Have you been right up the Quarry woods yet?"

"No, not really."

"It's a bonny walk." They entered the back door. "I'm afraid the place is in a bit of a mess. Francey's off out somewhere."

Tina was undismayed by the dying fire, the uncleared table and the boots lying about. But she did wonder if Francey's date was with Chris, and if Francey knew he was still married.

Matt went with quiet deliberation about his preparations for tea, reviving the fire with a handful of kindling, setting the already bubbling black kettle on the flames and clearing the table. Tina reached for clean cups from the dresser. "Where's Jamey?" She asked.

"Oh, he's off to Haydon Bridge. There's a new lass in the guest house there. He quite fancies her." Matt took the cups from her, his warm fingers touching hers. "You shouldn't be doing this. I don't suppose you've ever done housework in your life, have you?"

Tina shook her head. "No, I've never had to."

"Then you'll never have to marry a poor man." His eyes were shy but insistent. "You should never have anything to do but just look bonny."

She pulled a face. "How boring!"

Yet she was touched, almost embarrassed. She knew it had cost Matt an effort to betray his admiration. He was obviously attracted but awed. Over the cups of tea and some rather stale shop cake she did her best to put him at his ease, describing her home in Rome, her life before Bruno died. He soon warmed into quiet talk.

"I'm glad you came, Tina. Saturdays I don't do much."

"Don't you ever go out with girls?"

He shook his head. "I'm not like Jamey. He's got to be proving himself all the time, scared he's slipping. If there's a new girl around he can't rest until she's eating out of his hand, like one of my birds. . . . Aye, and he'd chase *you* if he thought he had a chance. But you saw through him, first go off."

"I suppose I did," she hesitated. "Matt, don't you—haven't you got a girl, then?"

He shook his head. "I wouldn't marry yet, or even think of it. Not until the twins are turned sixteen and able to stand on their own feet. We've not much of a home, but it's all they've got."

Tina was moved. She believed him quite capable of such self-sacrifice, whatever the price to himself. Supposing, for instance, he had already fallen in love and had to deny his feelings? She couldn't help remembering her wonder over Helen and Matt. But all she said was:

"It's hard on you—and on any girl who falls in love with you."

"That's why"—his honest blue eyes met hers—"I make a point of telling girls how they stand. Then—well, they get frightened off. It stands to reason all girls want marriage, not friendship."

"I would," Tina said.

"You would what?" His gaze across the table was wistful but wary.

"I'd like to be your friend. I mean it. You were Bruno's friend, weren't you?"

"I was."

"And you might be able to help me," Tina rushed on. "About Bruno—and all this gossip. You might be able to help me clear it up."

"Is that why?" his face darkened.

"I'm not just using you—no!" she flared impatiently. "You're far too touchy, Matt."

"Aye, I'm touchy. Or so I've been told. When you've had to put up with a lot of humiliation, one way and another—when you've got to be beholden to folks you'd rather not owe a penny or a kind word to—you do get touchy."

"You mean—Adam Copeland?" She was startled.

His cup crashed into the saucer. He ignored her question. "What do you want to know about Bruno, Tina?"

"Did he have any other girls—besides Helen, I mean?"

"I've never seen him with any. But I'll tell you this—there were plenty after him. He was different, after all. Aye, and that soft Italian voice—he could have had his choice of girls."

"But—you don't think he did?" she faltered.

"I didn't say that." He took a crumpled pack of cigarets from his pocket and lit one. "I told you before, Tina—he wasn't the kind to give anything away."

"But you said you were friends. Friends usually confide in each other."

"I wouldn't say that. He respected my affairs and I respected his."

Tina said slowly: "If you ever do find out there was another girl—you'd tell me, wouldn't you?"

"I might." His voice had shortened.

Tina collected the cups. "And there's another thing I wanted to ask. Did you know Helen Copeland well?"

"Leave those cups, Tina. Francey can do them when she gets home—it's little enough she does. Helen? She was always a cut above me, boarding school and all that. And Adam Copeland's always been one to vet her friends."

"But he approved of Bruno at first," Tina reasoned. "For a man so sure of his own judgment—as he is—doesn't that just prove there couldn't have been much wrong on Bruno's side? Helen's much more likely to have been at fault."

Matt shook his head. "Are you trying to say she had some other man?" His eyes searched hers suspiciously.

"Didn't Jamey once—"

Matt stubbed out his cigaret. "I'll tell you what happened about Jamey. He enticed her out once—oh, it would be two years ago now. She was always a bit on the wild side, ready for any adventure. But Adam, he found out. He came right here and knocked Jamey down. And he promised him worse if he ever mixed with Helen again."

Tina stared her heart in her throat. "What did *you* do?"

"I left Jamey to take his medicine. Besides, after all Adam Copeland had done for us, I could hardly complain. Anyway, our Jamey's got a bad reputation where girls are concerned, though most of it's just talk."

"And Jamey hasn't been with Helen since?"

"Not on your life. He'd run a mile rather than try. Jamey's a fool in most things, but he has a healthy respect for Adam Copeland."

"But you haven't—is that it?"

"We'd be in a poor way without his help."

"And that's why you don't like him," she said slowly.

Matt got up with an impatient movement. "Come on, Tina. It's a fine night. Let's take a walk."

Tina now had the firm conviction Matt resented her questions. She knew an instant's despair, then told herself perhaps she had been too insistent, that patience was the answer.

They walked across the moor track to the Quarry woods, Tina's gaze drawn often toward Hadrian's Edge. The turrets and gables of the house were limned darkly against a sky of apricot and turquoise, rising like a witch tower from the dark lace of the tree tops. It was a fit eyrie for its master, she thought. Soon, though, they had turned away, past the tree house, to take the path leading into the gloom of larch and pine, of thickets still tawny with last autumn's leaves. The twilit peace of the woods soothed her.

"There'll be a whole sheet of bluebells here later on," Matt told her. "And primroses high up there, where the bank climbs. That's the best time, about May and June." He showed her the entrance to a badger's sett, identified various birds by their calls and plumage, spoke of an old fox he often met in the woods. Tina, ignorant of country ways, found his quiet informed talk fascinating. There was much more to Matt than she had realized, after all. In the sophisticated world of her former life he would have seemed clumsy, boorish, even ignorant. In his own element he showed a new confidence and assurance.

They came to a gate set in an arch of trees and overlooking the shadowed reaches of the moors. "Tell me about Bruno," Tina pleaded. "Anything you can think of—his favorite places, where he used to talk. . . . Did he ever come here?"

Matt looked at her soberly. "It must be rotten for you, Tina, never being able to talk about Bruno up there at the house. I'm sorry if I was a bit short with you before. I can't tell you much about his movements, apart from him coming to Quarry Farm. He was mostly out in the car with Helen. And about that time I was working over at Tipstones and didn't get home till late. But we'd some good nights at our place. I think he liked to get away from Hadrian's Edge at times."

Tina was startled. "Do you?"

"Why not? Oh, Adam Copeland had accepted him, but he'd still have to toe the line in a way. At our place he could relax. We'd get some beer in, play cards—just the four of us—and have some laughs. He was a right good mimic, wasn't he? That way he had of imitating an opera star!"

Memories burned and ached. "I know," she said. "I'm so glad he was happy with you all. I suppose Francey—"

"Aye, Francey liked him. Though it's always been Adam Copeland she's really soft on." He laid his big hand over hers on the mossed gate-top. "It could be like that with us, Tina—the way it was with Francey and Bruno. Just good friends."

Tina remembered uneasily that the time-worn phrase had lately grown sinister overtones, especially in newspaper gossip columns. But Matt spoke innocently enough. He held her hand in his warm grasp now, and she left it there, a sense of security stealing over her. Perhaps he was right. She was lost and bewildered, still grieving sorely for Bruno; *he* was islanded in a perpetual duty to his family. There was, perhaps, something even more than friendship they could exchange; an understanding and sympathy they couldn't find from their own sex.

Matt walked with her as far as the cross tracks. "Want me to come right up to the house?" She sensed his reluctance.

She shook her head. Twilight was now dimming the woods, and a champagne-colored moon had risen above the gables of Hadrian's Edge. "I'll be there in five minutes. No wolves in these woods, are there?" she teased.

"There probably were, when the Romans guarded the ridge there." He smiled, pressed her hand again. "Thanks for coming to see me, Tina. It's been—great. Be seeing you!"

She called goodbye softly and ran down the path under the roof of trees, the wind soughing eerily in the bare branches. Then she screamed as a figure sprang at her out of the thicket. Her heart seemed to stop. She heard Jamey's laugh. He put out a hand to steady her. "No wolves, I heard you say. Well, here's a human one." But he released her again, grinning in amusement at her flustered state. She began to scold him furiously.

"You beast, Jamey! I nearly had a heart attack. Anyway, what are you doing here?"

"Taking a short cut home." He shrugged. "Not much talent about tonight."

"Meaning no one would look at you, I suppose?"

He grinned. "So it's Matt now, is it?"

"No, it isn't," she snapped.

"No? So now you're going in to keep Adam Copeland company."

"Wrong again. He's out visiting Helen."

"Does he never take you with him?"

Tina said reluctantly, "I don't even know where she is."

Jamey lit a cigaret. "I know where she is, Tina."

"Then—where?" Her voice was hopeful.

"She's at her aunt's—Miss Coxon, an old battleaxe who used to be a hospital sister. Now she runs this convalescent home at Thornriggs, over Bellingham way. Turret House, it's called."

"How do you know all this?" Tina was elated but suspicious.

He laughed. "They'd have a right job to keep it a secret from me."

"Well, I'm always over there. Oh, not at the house. But there's a farm at the back of it run by a friend of ours, Charlie Philips. He's a bachelor and a bit sweet on Francey, as it happens. Pity she can't see sense and marry him, for he's doing well . . . I go there making deliveries for Dixon's."

"Oh, I see." Tina remembered that Jamey worked for a local cattle dealer.

"Charlie's like Matt," Jamey went on. "Another pigeon fancier. They sometimes swop birds. I often drop messages or a basket of pigeons for Matt. You see he won't go near Charlie's place now Helen's there. If you ask me he's scared Adam Copeland might get the wrong idea."

"And what about you? Aren't *you* scared of Adam Copeland?" Tina was remembering Matt's words.

Jamey went suddenly silent, watching the glowing end of his cigaret. "Be all the same if I was, wouldn't it? I've got to do my haulage work for the firm—delivering there." His voice lightened again. "Well, now I've done you a favor, telling you all this, what about coming dancing with me next Saturday?"

It was Tina's turn to laugh. "Has everything you do got a price?"

"Just about. Will you, then?"

"What do *you* think?"

"That my chances are pretty poor?" he chuckled.

"I'll let you know if I change my mind. But thanks for the information, anyway."

"You're welcome, pet! Be seeing you!" He went off whistling into the shadows.

Tina returned to Hadrian's Edge not a little satisfied. Now she knew where to find Helen, she meant to visit her without delay. It ought not to be too difficult to keep that visit secret from Adam Copeland.

As for Jamey, she couldn't help wondering about his calls at Turret House farm. As he said, it was all to do with his work. Yet what a convenient cover if he still meant to see Helen Copeland.

Jamey. . . . Yes, it was still a possibility. Matt could have been quite deceived about his brother. And Jamey, for all his reputation, was no fool. Tina guessed that where his own affairs were concerned he could be as deep and secretive as Matt.

Altogether, she felt that she had learned a lot. The visit to Helen might well reveal more. . . .

On Monday afternoon Tina was at the dig as usual. As always she became lost in the past, kneeling in mud and dirt, with the scent of bruised grass about her, handling with reverent fingers every significant scrap of evidence her "grid" might yield. Even the different layers of earth, of stones and gravel told their own fascinating tales of building and pillage, of restoration and further destruction.

Until almost tea-time she was so absorbed she hadn't noticed the change in the weather. The wind had roughened again and sagging black clouds raced to obscure the pale April sun. She had already planned to miss the evening meal at Hadrian's Edge and to find her way to Thornriggs before dark.

She glanced across at Carrie, busy in one of the other grids. The older woman was crouching on her heels, her sweater sleeves rolled up, a smudge of clay on one cheek, lost to the world as she peered at some fragment in her hand. All about her the students were easing stiff backs and producing their flasks and sandwiches. But to Carrie time meant nothing. She often missed tea altogether and Tina hoped that this would be one of the days.

She dusted the earth from her own hands, brushed back her hair with the crook of her arm, and approached Chris at his table.

"Hallo, going off?" he asked casually.

"Yes. I've entered my lot. There's a section of rubble you might look at. It could have been part of the camp rubbish dump, though the level isn't consistent. I got one or two more shards of that baking vessel, nearly all the rim. . . . Chris, any chance of borrowing your car tonight?"

"Sorry, Tina, I'm using it myself," he said firmly.

"Chris, *please*!" she pleaded.

"You ought to know better than to try your tricks on me, my girl. And as I've said, I'm going out in the car myself."

Tina teased: "Taking a girl, I suppose? Is it Francey?"

"Don't be nosey, my child. Can't you borrow Carrie's car?"

Tina hesitated. "I didn't really want her to know where I'm going."

Chris gave her a curious glance. "What are you up to, Tina? You know I promised your father to keep an eye on you."

"I'm not up to anything. I might just go sick-visiting, that's all." She tried to speak casually.

"You mean—Helen Copeland?" Chris eyed her rather more soberly. "Have you got her brother's permission."

"Well, he didn't say it was inconvenient." She began

edging away. "But I have got to go in for tea now—"

"But, Tina, wait a minute!" Chris's voice was raised in an authority she would normally have submitted to, but at that moment a student rushed up to Chris with news of a find and Tina was able to escape. The lack of a car would be a nuisance, but there were buses going Bellingham way, she knew.

She was glad to get out of the ice-edged wind and into the warm kitchen at Hadrian's Edge. Here she found Isa complacently viewing a tray of rather over-baked scones.

"Hallo—what happened?" Tina perched on the table and sampled one. "A bit burnt, aren't they?"

"Aye, they caught on," Isa said heavily. "And well they might, with me so upset."

"What are you upset about?"

Isa set the kettle on the hotplate and turned an indignant face. "Why, it's because I wasn't asked to be on the tea committee of the Ladies' Guild." She sighed gustily. "I knew I'd never turn out good scones the day!"

Tina said curiously: "Why don't you leave your baking until you've got over being upset, Isa?"

Isa stared. "Leave it? I'm no' leaving it. It helps to take my mind off things."

Tina found this logic more than a little confusing. She tried and abandoned a second scone.

Isa, now wearing her text-reciting face, intoned: "She looketh well to the ways of her household and eateth not the bread of idleness."

After a suitable pause Tina asked, "Is Mr. Copeland in tonight?" Better be certain *he* wasn't visiting Helen too.

"Oh, he'll be in for the supper. Aye, and there's a man from the County Planning calling to see him after."

"I shan't be in to supper, Isa. Perhaps you'll tell Mrs. Butterfield I'll be out for the evening."

Isa brightened. "Have ye got a lad already?"

Tina laughed, drank the tea Isa poured, but parried any further questions. After tea she consulted the bus time-table in the estate office. There was, though perhaps she didn't deserve this, a bus going to Bellingham in half an hour, with a return one two hours later. Studying the local map on the wall she saw that Thornriggs was up a side road on the way to Bellingham, roughly a mile and a half. Not so far, after all.

She longed to dress warmly, in trousers and a duffle coat, for instance. But the visit, she felt, called for an elegant dress and her white fluffy coat from one of the Rome boutiques. She hesitated beween delicate strip sandals and heavier casual shoes. The sandals won, which in turn needed the complement of cobwebby hose.

She was offered a lift along the Military Road as far as Chollerford by a dumbstruck young man in a green van. At the bus stop by the hotel a few women and one or two workmen waited. They looked her over but glanced away again in country courtesy.

Tina was glad to be on the bus at last, for she felt distinctly chilled in her stunning outfit. The conductor had some trouble understanding where she wanted to go. "Thornriggs, pet? Why, we don't go *there*. We'd as soon think of gannin' to the moon!"

"Why, aye! But yon's a mucky walk—and two miles or more. By, you diven't want to gan there the night! There's a storm brewing an' all! Why not change your mind and come into Bellingham wi' the rest of us? I could just do with a bonnie lassie to keep me company!" He winked broadly at the other passengers. But a stalwart country woman plucked at his sleeve. Tina heard the word "Copeland". Instantly the man's manner changed to reddened embarrassment.

"Just a bit of fun, miss. Thornriggs road-end it is. No offence meant."

Tina smiled, took the ticket and thanked him. She was surprised, a little awed. It certainly seemed, as Chris had said, that Adam Copeland's name counted in these parts. Less encouraging was the news that Thronriggs was a two-mile walk. Already rain flecked the bus windows. Whenever the door opened to admit another passenger a blustering draught sent everyone shivering. Wistfully Tina thought of the despised trousers and duffle coat. Would she ever get used to the dramatic changes of an English spring?

At Thornriggs road-end she was set down, pursued by a concerned goodnight from the cheery bus conductor.

She ducked her head against the driving spikes of rain and looked about her in dismay. The Bellingham road rounded a ridge which dipped into steep woods on the east. On the west, and the way she must go, a rough road, unsignposted and faced with a cattle grid, led over a desolate stretch of moor until it dipped out of sight. She picked her way over the cattle grid, then looked in dismay from her fragile sandals to the broken chippings of the road. There was nothing for it but to go on, hoping perhaps for shelter farther ahead. She tied her pale hyacinth scarf over her hair, turned up the collar of the useless white coat, and began to stumble uphill.

For perhaps half a mile she struggled gamely, her father's obstinate streak very much in evidence. Buffeted by the chill wind, half blinded by the rain, she emerged at last on the top of the rise. The moors opened out before her in a dramatic backcloth, fold after fold of dun and tawny and pale green hills, the far ones lost in drifting white cloud. Here and there climbed patches of forest, she glimpsed a far farm or two, crouched in its windbreak of trees, but nothing yet that looked like a village or small hamlet.

It was difficult now to even think coherently, so merciless was the battering of wind and rain. To be alone in such conditions, with the chance that her return journey must be made in twilight, was to Tina, child of the sunlit Roman squares, a frightening prospect.

She thought of Bruno and set her lips. She had to see Helen, and if this was the only way. . . .

The rain, without warning, became a deluge, falling with such brute force from the heavily sagging sky that Tina panicked. About a quarter of a mile ahead a dark plantation nudged the track. She stumbled uphill towards it. Half way a sandal strap snapped, rotted with rain. She bent to whip off the shoe, to limp, wincing now, over the stones, wet through to the skin, until she reached the shelter of the trees.

They were thickly planted larch and fir, so close

together that there was no hint of undergrowth, just a dark mat of pine needles still blessedly dry. In the shelter of the trees it was no less cold, but a haven from the tearing wind and the pitiless rain. Tina slumped to the ground and fought for her breath.

What a country! she thought. What merciless, terrible weather! And they called this spring! Deep down she was afraid. If only Chris was with her, if only she had managed to borrow a car. . . .

No wonder so many Roman legionaries had died so young! No wonder so many children's memorial stones were found on the digs. To work, to march, to live on the Wall in weather like this must at first have been a shocking ordeal for her countrymen.

Her damp coat was making itself felt. She took it off, shook it and wrapped it loosely about her. She also considered stripping off the soaking hose, but decided she'd be even colder without them. Her sandals were past salvation, the paper-thin soles like sodden cardboard after their soaking. The very last time she had worn them had been in blazing sunshine on the Spanish Steps.

She sighed and shivered. Somehow she must crouch here and be patient until the rain ceased. But Tina had never been particularly patient and never seen such rain. Gradually its force increased until it was a silver blinding curtain before the trees, the stones and chippings of the path washed in rivulets downhill. Above her the branches lashed, and now rain was seeping through the feathery leaves. And beyond the veil of rain a tangle of swollen clouds raced across a wild sky, gray upon dirty sable upon black, layers and layers of more rain to come and the promise of an early dusk.

Now she knew she had no hope of reaching Thornriggs, and very little more of regaining the Bellingham road and the chance of a lift. It would be madness to plunge back into this endless deluge, even if anyone were out driving in a storm like this, which she doubted. She had long ago given up hope of seeing a vehicle on this track.

She supposed this was what they called Wall Weather. How right Adam Copeland had been, and how little she had known of conditions on the real Wall, while she had traced milecastle and turret, ditch and vallum on a plaster model in a sunny Rome apartment.

Tears pricked her eyes. She huddled herself lower in her coat folded her shivering arms for warmth. Rome, the apartment, the loved streets and squares of the Eternal City, the Appian Hills . . . a rush of homesickness came. Why had she come here, and of what use had she been? Chris scarcely needed her help at the dig, she had discovered nothing to clear Bruno, had met almost hostility at mention of his name.

Then her aching heart stilled. Did she really want to go home, to leave Adam Copeland's roof at this point of their stormy relationship? How could she possibly leave him still despising, still resenting her brother's memory? That unresolved barrier between them would haunt her for ever if she could not destroy it.

"Don't dig into the past," he had ordered. "Seekers after truth don't always find pleasant things." And what of *his* past? What other women had there been besides Francey Finch? What had Carrie called them—the hopers and seekers? Had he ever in his whole life, she wondered, shown tenderness to a woman? Tenderness from such strength would be a wonder indeed. . . .

She jerked herself out of the daydream to find the rain had lightened. She walked shivering to the wood's brink. Should she make a run for it back to the main road and hope to pick up a lift? It would be dark soon. Through the slowing needles of rain she could trace now that high ridge where the Wall ran. It was easy in this dim light to imagine those ghostly legions on the march. . . .

Carrying both sandals, she limped and lurched her way down the puddled track, wincing occasionally as a stone rolled painfully under her feet.

Fifty, a hundred yards—she was almost in sight of the rise which hid her from the main road when the skies opened again and whole water fell. She spun in panic under its weight and force. Blinded and almost deafened, she essayed a turn toward the plantation again. Her soaking scarf plastered her face, her feet were in ribbons and there was blood on her toes. The rain had penetrated to her very skin.

The high whine of a car horn rent the air. She jumped blindly to the side of the track, seeing a dirty Land-Rover loom and stop. Her heart leaped wildly. In the driving-seat was Adam Copeland.

She stood helpless, saturated, her hair plastered cruelly to brow and cheekbones, her coat a soaking ruin. She knew, with misery in her heart, that her plight must be laughable.

But there was no laughter in his voice as she heard him rasp, "Are you out of your mind, wandering about in a storm like this?"

Without waiting for an answer he glanced at her bleeding feet, whipped her up into his arms and marched over to the Land-Rover, to dump her without ceremony in the passenger seat. His heavy body crashed down beside her, the door was slammed and for the next few moments there was nothing but the savage revving of the engine, the clashing of gears, as he turned the Land-Rover with what seemed like his own force on the narrow track. Only when the vehicle had bounced and torn its way down to the hard road did he speak again. "And where the devil did you think you were going?" he demanded. His slanted glance at her face was without mercy or sympathy.

Tina hesitated, mortally afraid. She had never met anger as violent, had never known such a lack of poise or courage in herself. Her forget-me-not eyes were drowned in misery and panic.

"I was—just walking," she lied.

"Just walking!" He approached and overtook a lorry before going on. "Just walking, you say? And a good eight miles from home. Oh yes, my dear, I believe you." She heard the weight of his sarcasm.

"I took a bus first. I—I'd never seen the country on the north side of the Wall."

His gray eyes scanned her face. She saw utter disbelief and more than a touch of derision.

"Don't try stories like that with me, my lass! Even you

would never go country walking in a town coat and beach sandals. *You* were dressed for visiting, and there was only one place at Thornriggs which could have interested you—"

He paused for breath, then rapped out with such force she winced: "It was Turret House, wasn't it? Despite my orders you were determined to visit my sister."

"I don't know what you mean," she faltered. Even now she could not find in herself the courage to admit the truth.

For a while he was ominously silent. At last he turned the car on to the Military Road at Chollerford. Not until they were in the lane leading to Hadrian's Edge did he speak again. Suddenly he braked on the verge. The windscreen wipers, until now inexorably swishing before them, were still. In a second the windscreen was awash, the outer world curtained off. In the eerie waiting silence, his face seemed almost brutal.

"Look, don't waste my time. I'm not gullible and I'm not a fool. Also your friend Chris told me what was on your mind. . . . *Well?*"

Tina tried to throw back her hair in the old gesture of defiance, but plastered to her head as it was, the action drew a sardonic smile. "Too bad, isn't it?" he goaded her. "You look like the wrath of God, my dear. And I may tell you here and now that none of those tricks are going to work. What I want to know is why were you so determined to go to Turret House—against my orders?"

"To see your sister, of course!" she flashed, now very near to tears. "To talk to her about Bruno. Why do you bother to ask, when you already know?"

"Why do I ask?" he rasped. "Because I doubted the evidence of my own eyes and ears. When I lay down the law, as I frequently do, I seldom find it so flagrantly disregarded."

Tina's eyes sparked dangerously. "I've told you before, you may be my host, but I don't take orders—at least not where anything to do with Bruno is concerned."

He lit a cigaret with a maddening deliberation. "And if you had made contact with Helen, if in doing so you had learned some unpalatable truth—well, what then?"

"I'd think your sister was mistaken," she said steadily.

He blew smoke toward the drowned windscreen. "Be careful, Tina Rutherford. Your late brother has already hurt my sister beyond bearing. I will not take such insolence from you."

"There isn't much you can do about it, is there?" She was recklessly defiant now.

"Isn't there?" His eyes glinted dangerously. She caught her breath at the sudden bracing of that sweeping jawline. "It happens to be getting dark and this road is very isolated. Doesn't it occur to you that I could humiliate you without mercy and that you could do damn-all about it, my bedraggled little Roman goddess?"

Panic swamped her. "You—wouldn't dare. I'm not Francey Finch, you know. You may treat her like dirt, for all I know. No man has ever made love to me against my will."

She heard him laugh softly in the gloom, and knew with a sinking heart that she had said a foolish thing.

"Never," he repeated. "*Never?* My poor deprived little Coventina! With all the grandeur and glamor which is Rome you have to come all the way to Northumberland to find a man who sees your vain struttings and posings as merely pitiful, who sees underneath all that eyelash-batting and Latin head-tossing, a silly spoiled schoolgirl. Someone who needs to be told what to do in no uncertain terms—who needs to be kissed without regard to her feelings."

"No—Adam. . . ." Why had she used his Christian name? Then all thoughts melted as he jerked her toward him with a movement at once brutal and deliberate. Her bones became water as he crushed her against his hard body. That merciless mouth was over hers and struggle as she might she received the full smothering force of his kiss.

Long after she thought all breath had gone, even as she felt faintness stealing over her, he held her imprisoned. Then, with just as sudden and violent a release, she was gasping and sobbing in hysterical reaction in her corner.

"Right," he said calmly. "That's the way we do it on the Wall. Maybe you're right and we *are* barbarians. It may teach you not to play me up again, my dear!"

Tina scrubbed at her eyes, gulped once or twice, then managed to control herself. "I hate you," she said clearly.

He switched on the ignition again, leaned forward to let in the clutch. "That is a sheer waste of a very useful emotion." The windscreen wiper came into play as he drove on, revealing the gray road winding into a blue stormy dusk. "Especially as it leaves me completely unmoved."

"I hope Francey Finch gets you," Tina muttered. "She's just about what you deserve."

He laughed. But when he spoke again his voice was level and sober.

"You know very little about me, do you? Like your imitation model of the Wall, I'm a kind of cardboard man—a hateful figure who has condemned your brother without mercy, who refuses to allow you to work out your extraordinary whims. And now something worse—a man who has kissed you without asking. You know something, Tina? When I was a little lad I had a toy theatre. The goodies were all colored blue and the villains red. You've been pretty busy sorting out heroes and villains. . . . Have a care, my dear. You'll discover as you grow older that we have the makings of either in each of us. We've all got mixed motives, guilty consciences. We can all be kind and generous one day, or as mean as a bat out of hell the next. I wish you joy of your digging for truth. And I offer you the same old well-worn advice—stick to Roman remains. They're safer."

The car screeched on the wet gravel at Hadrian's Edge. Tina, feeling the full effect now of sitting in her soaking clothes, sneezed three times in quick succession. The handkerchief she fished from her bag was so minute she found a large clean white one thrust into her hand. He was giving her a searching scrutiny, but this time his eyes seemed guarded, empty of both amusement and anger.

"Better run straight up to your room. I've had Isa leave a flask of warm milk there for you and the electric fire's been burning this last hour. I'd advise a hot bath first, though."

She got out. "Thank you," she faltered, a little stunned. Angry as he must have been when he came out to search for her, he had meticulously seen to her comfort first. The action was touching, generous and unexpected.

He made no response to her thanks. The Land-Rover shot away round the side of the house to the garage, his profile as composed as if nothing had happened.

Shivering and drenched as she was, Tina stood motionless, watching him go. The memory of that kiss seemed blasted into her mind and body alike. It had been an outrageous liberty, a violent punishment for her disobedience. . . .

Yet it had been more than this. She had sensed, too, an exasperated desire, a goaded passion. She knew now that Adam Copeland found her physically attractive, that he furiously resented the fact and that there had not been one atom of tenderness in that embrace.

Her shocked face crumpled as she turned toward the house.

CHAPTER FOUR

The next week passed quietly. Tina was subdued during her working periods with Adam Copeland. He in turn was abrupt but watchful. There was, she sometimes imagined, a certain curl of satisfaction to his mobile mouth, a glint of victory in his eyes. Obviously he imagined he had quelled for good any tendency to rebellion.

He was, of course, mistaken. Tina might look subdued, she might even feel subdued, but she was still set in a calm determination to go her own way. And if his guard had been lifted, so much the better. He would be less likely to expect further action.

Tina had felt sore with Chris, regarding his tale-telling to Adam, and one day on the dig had challenged him about it.

His response was impatient. "What did you expect me to do, young Tina? Cover up for you? And with the weather as it was that day, I expected you'd be glad to be rescued."

"But you didn't approve of me seeing Helen in the first place, did you?"

"No, I didn't. I think you should consider Copeland's feelings and keep away from her. There, you asked for it. And I did promise your father I'd keep an eye on you. So let's hear no more about it, shall we?" he spoke with cool authority.

"I thought you were on my side, Chris."

"No one's taking sides. Do have some sense, Tina. I've told you before there's very little we can do as far as this business of Bruno goes. You won't help matters by setting everyone by the ears, either. Now, if we've settled that, I've something else to tell you."

"About—Bruno?" She was instantly hopeful.

"Yes, but quite apart from what we've been discussing. I don't know if he ever told you in his letters, but he always had a hunch about that south section of the grid."

"A hunch?"

"That's what I said. I can't tell you any more at the moment, because I'm still going over his notes and making preliminary investigations. But I'll tell you this, if he was right—his name's going to mean something big in archaeological circles."

"Chris, what is it? Why can't you tell me?"

He smiled. "I wouldn't have told you this much, except for one reason. You may dig about as much as you like trying to clear his name. To my mind this is much more important, to press on along the lines of his last discoveries. If his notes prove to be right, this could be the crown of his life's work. . . . So, Tina, never accuse me of not caring, or of forgetting, will you?" He spoke softly.

Tina tried to speak and failed. Her eyes were misty. At last she said: "I'm sorry, Chris. I've misjudged you . . .

456

and I think you're right. This is a bigger thing you're doing. Only you do understand I've got to work for him in my way too.''

"I understand.'' He turned back to his littered table under the tarpaulin shelter. "But, Tina, don't do anything really crazy, will you? Try to remember I'm responsible for you.''

"I'll try.''

She felt vastly cheered by this interview, forgiving him gladly for his "tale-telling'', as she had thought it. Quite apart from his assurance that he had Bruno's interests at heart, she realized now that he was after all answerable to Adam Copeland for dig discipline, and as such could scarcely refuse Adam information concerning herself. As for the hint that Bruno might have been on the verge of a startling discovery, she was warmed and inspired by the news. True, it might come to nothing, but she doubted whether Chris would have spoken if his hopes hadn't been high. Her only saddening thought was that Bruno had not lived to reap any possible success. . . .

Meanwhile, Tina had not forgotten her vow to mend her ways, to be more punctual, assiduous and considerate in her work for Adam Copeland. Strangely enough, once she concentrated more, she became interested in the work for its own sake, quickly grasping the names of the farms and their tenants, becoming knowledgeable in matters of Ministry of Agriculture returns and anxious to be helpful with telephone callers.

She sensed Adam's surprise, but at first he made no comment, noting her efforts with what could only be called a poker face. She noticed, though, that he began to trust her judgment more, to explain less, and for the moment it was enough to redeem her former carelessness.

Her old resentment at the curtailment of her dig work had quite gone, despite the fact that out of doors spring was making brilliant thrusts into the dull days. The daffodils in the cottage gardens had given way to wallflowers, the hedges and woods were veiled in green and a subtle new bloom had come to the moor. Around Hadrian's Edge bird-song tangled in the budding boughs from dawn to dark.

One morning when the office work was over, Tina discovered that Carrie had not gone to the dig, but was bustling about upstairs, helping the daily domestic worker to turn out the bedrooms.

"Spring-cleaning?" Tina grimaced. She knew it was an English malady peculiar to the lightening days.

"Afraid so," Carrie said. "There's no future in it, but it's got to be done. If you're just stooging around you might help me move some blankets from Helen's room."

"That's the door at the end, isn't it? I've never seen it yet."

"It's much the same as yours, only in the opposite gable." Carrie threw open the door. "As Helen's likely to be away for another month or so I think I'll strip the bed altogether and send the blankets to the cleaners."

Tina followed her into a delicate airy room decorated in white and lilac. "Isn't it pretty? I love the rosewood furniture."

Carrie was already turning back the lilac silk coverlet. "Oh yes, Helen has expensive tastes, and Adam always indulged them."

Tina stood by the window, fiddling with a curtain-tie. "I suppose that's what really attracted Bruno—he was always attracted to very feminine girls."

Carrie was now half out of the door with the blankets. Tina, deciding she ought to be useful, began turning back the coverlet over the striped mattress. She lifted the pillows, meaning to fold the cover under and back over them in a tidy roll. As she did so something white fluttered to the carpet.

She found it to be a folded piece of paper. After a second's hesitation, curiosity won and she opened it, seeing a very feminine flowery writing.

"Darling," she read, "I know it's no use and I *do* understand how you feel. I hope one day you'll forgive and—"

The note finished there, as if the writer, whom Tina was certain must be Helen, had been interrupted. Or perhaps she had had second thoughts about sending the note at all and just thrust it under her pillow until she could destroy it. Possibly her breakdown had intervened.

Tina's breath came fast. To whom was the note written? Bruno? Or some other man? She felt guilty now at having read it—but there was exultancy too.

She slipped the note under the pillow and pulled the coverlet into place. On the dressing-table she had noticed an engagements book, and flicked it open. Yes, one glance was enough to see that this was indeed Helen's handwriting.

At that moment Carrie came back.

"Made up the bed—oh, thanks." She grinned. "I've just been down to the kitchen. Isa had a letter from her cousin this morning, inviting her there for her holidays. Isa's all cock-a-hoop, so I think we're in for a rather nice Eve's pudding for lunch." She looked critically round the room. "It looks neat enough now. You should see it when Helen's in possession. She throws her things all over the place."

"Who picks them up?"

"Oh, she's not above wheedling Isa to do it. Isa's so good-natured she can't see there's no future in it."

Tina followed Carrie down the wide, crimson-carpeted corridor. "Do you really like Helen, Carrie?"

"I've no illusions about her. Let's just leave it there, shall we?" They turned to descend the stairs.

"But do you think she was good enough for Bruno?" Tina insisted, unaware that there was anyone in the hall below. Too late Carrie nudged her. Below stood Adam, dressed for the fields in tweeds and rubber boots, Gyp waiting at his feet. He gave Tina one annihilating look.

"You might also ask," he said harshly, "was Bruno good enough for her. I warn you again, Tina, I detest this prying into my family affairs."

Tina's blood tingled. Carrie disappeared tactfully into the living-room.

"Yours *and* mine, Mr. Copeland," she said quietly. "You always seem to forget that. . . . Were the letters to your liking?"

"Excellent, as always. For such an intelligent young

woman some of your antics are surprisingly out of context. I can't fault your work—*now*. All that's lacking is the need to begin facing up to the truth about your brother. Emotionally, you're very far from being stable."

Tina's face flamed. Too shocked to answer, she brushed past him and went blindly out of doors. The wall between them loomed higher and darker than before. Despite all her efforts to avoid criticism, then, his opinion of her remained the same. Despite that mockery of a kiss, they were more at variance than ever.

Her first reaction was one of sour anger; then let him do his own work! If he insisted in his attitude toward Bruno why should she lift even a finger to help him?"

Yet she soon saw the folly of this. To show herself as childish and spiteful could only justify his accusation of emotional immaturity. No, she must go on as before, but must step up her efforts to discover the truth about Bruno, to prove Adam Copeland monumentally wrong. . . .

That afternoon Tina worked industriously at the dig, but her attention wandered sorely. Perhaps because of her depressing morning she decided to visit Quarry Farm that evening. During the week she had bought some games for the twins in Hexham. They might be glad of some distraction for the weekend.

After supper she took the path by the tree house. Just where the moor track forked she came upon Francey, loitering as if waiting for someone.

"Hallo," said Tina cautiously. One never knew quite how Francey would react. One thing though was evident—the other girl was dressed to kill in a vivid pink trouser suit, the effect spoiled by the scowl on her face.

"Where do you think *you're* going?" Francey eyed Tina's expensive white wool dress, the lush Italian coat slung over her shoulders.

"I'm just taking some games down to the twins. I suppose they like games?"

"Oh, they do. And *you* like to hand out charity to that scruffy crowd at Quarry Farm! I bet you took good care Adam knew what you were doing."

"Why should I?" Tina stared.

"You know very well why—to impress him. You needn't pretend to me you're not after him for yourself!"

Tina felt as though a hand had gripped her heart.

Francey spoke breathlessly. "I heard about you going off in that storm, so he had to find you and bring you back. You were careful to leave word of where you were going, though!"

Tina's anger mounted. "You've got a wonderful imagination, Francey. I suppose you wouldn't be waiting for him yourself?"

She found herself waiting in peculiar anxiety for Francey's answer.

"Yes, I've got a date with him, if you want to know!" Francey's green eyes flashed.

"What—at the roadside?" Tina guessed she was lying. It was just possible, though, that the other girl hoped to waylay Adam. "I hope he doesn't keep you waiting too long," she said.

"Well, you needn't hang about anyway." Francey's rudeness smacked of the village school playground. Tina wouldn't have been surprised if she had pulled a face or thrust out her tongue. For this snapping little animal was the real Francey, not the carefully controlled creature who had dined at Hadrian's Edge.

"I'm just going." She turned away down the moor path, wondering a little now if there might not be another explanation for Francey's loitering. Her boast of a date with Adam might have been cover for a meeting with Chris. Tina wasn't too sure Chris hadn't been attracted, and Francey must know he was married, which would call for a meeting in secret if she wanted to keep the affair quiet.

Not that Chris was likely to be serious, though. It was so obvious to Tina, who knew him so well, that he was still suffering from his broken marriage. The company of Francey might just be an antidote to loneliness. . . .

Or was all this wishful thinking, because she herself couldn't be reconciled to the picture of Adam and Francey alone in the spring beauty of the woods?

This new thought held so many frightening implications she dismissed it immediately, and ran the rest of the way to the farm.

Tina found the twins eating their supper, or rather, as she saw from the state of the table, having a cornflake battle. Matt, who had been reading a pigeon-fancier's journal, jumped up at her entrance. The twins, at a sharp scolding from him, lapsed into giggles.

"Hallo, Tina." He smiled but looked in dismay at the disordered table. "Sorry about all this. They've got a bit out of hand tonight while I was seeing to the pigeons." He jerked Bobby to his feet. "Come on now, you've had enough. Go and shut your rabbits up."

"I've had enough too." Like lightning Rosie left the table. Matt ordered her back. "You haven't touched your sandwiches."

She curled her nose. "Don't want them. I'm not hungry." She sidled up to Tina. "isn't that a bonny dress? What's in yon parcel?"

Tina smiled at her. She was such an engaging child, yet there was still that heart-catching look of delicacy about her. She had none of Bobby's robust color.

"It's something for you," she said. "But only if you eat your supper for Matt."

Rosie ran to the table and crammed a sandwich into her mouth. Matt snapped at her: "Rosie, where are your manners?"

She finished the sandwich at a more decorous speed. "I'm not hungry, Matt," she whined. "Cheese makes me feel sick."

"Drink your milk, then." He turned to Tina, shrugging. "Francey's out—she can manage Rosie better than I can."

Tina privately considered it wasn't good policy to admit such a thing in Rosie's hearing, but said nothing and opened her parcel. Rosie's cries of joy over the games brought Bobby in at a run. The twins, docile again, settled down at the table to play.

"Come up to the fire," Matt invited her. "It's warmer out than in today. This old place is always a bit damp."

Tina took the offered chair. "How are the pigeons?"

"Oh, fine. I'm racing Peerless Blue and Star Rocket tomorrow." He spoke of the race, the competition he would encounter, the rules followed. Meanwhile the twins' voices became raised in argument over the throw of the dice.

"That's enough," said Matt. "Bobby, you give in now."

"I've always got to give in—just because she's a lassie," Bobby scowled.

Matt said quietly, under cover of the barrage of childish voices: "I suppose I do favor her. She always seems to me to have come worst off out of all our troubles. Girls need a mother. And Francey hasn't got the mothering touch—though she's fond enough of her." His glance went soberly over his little sister's face. "I worry about Rosie."

Tina's gaze followed his. Rosie was triumphantly leap-frogging her ludo piece over Bobby's. "She's got plenty of life in her, though."

"Aye, but I'd be happier if she ate more. She just plays about with her food."

"Why don't you see a doctor?"

He shrugged. "If she seemed ill, I would. But you've just said yourself, she's got plenty of energy. It's just that she gets moods when she won't eat—says she feels sick. But she's tried that once too often to miss school—I never know when to believe her."

The children's play grew quieter, and the subject was dropped. "I saw Francey just now," Tina said, "She said she was waiting for Adam Copeland."

He flushed. "I'd hoped she'd learned more pride than to keep making a fool of herself over Adam Copeland. She hopes if she makes folks talk he'll have to marry her. But that's the last thing he's likely to do."

"Is she really in love with him?"

"She's daft about him, in her own way." Matt's voice was lowered again, so that the children couldn't hear. "But she doesn't say no to going out with anyone else she fancies—she is hoping to make him jealous, I expect."

"Is that what she did—with Bruno?"

He shook his head. "I've told you—they were just friends."

Tina was still not reassured. "I tried to see Helen." She told him of her abortive effort in the storm.

"Why should you want to go there?" His eyes looked suddenly wary, she thought. "She's not very likely to talk to you."

"I wanted to find out if she had been playing fair by Bruno. I would have asked her, straight to her face," Tina said doggedly. "Don't you think I have every right?"

Matt got up, turned his back to stare into the fire. "I'd leave well alone, Tina." He pretended the fire needed stoking and was busy for a full minute. Tina's suspicions were aroused again. She was still not convinced there had been nothing between Matt and Helen.

"Did you know Helen was a very nervous girl—inclined to be hysterical?" she asked.

"Aye, so Adam would have folks believe," he said drily. "There was no sign of that about her when she was with your brother. She was a different lass then. It was earlier, before he came on the scene—"

He broke off, with the consciousness of a man who has said too much, and turned to look at the twins. Bobby rolled the dice. "I've got a six. Wake up, Rosie—I've got a six!"

Rosie's head was on one hand. She watched in a listless way, then yawned. "I'm tired, Bobby. Finish the game."

"Better be off to bed, Rosie," Matt said. "Or you'll be getting behind in your lessons again, and get wrong from Miss Purvis."

Rosie got up, hesitated, then came across to Tina. "Thanks for the games."

Tina slipped an arm about her. "Want me to come up later and tuck you up?" The child's eyes brightened.

"Don't forget to wash, Rosie," Matt ordered.

Tina went upstairs after a few minutes, noticing how the upper floor, with its rough whitewashed wall and ragged stair-matting was even less devoid of comfort than downstairs. She found the child in a tiny single room, containing no more than a bed and a rough washstand. Rosie was curled up in a shabby nightdress on the unmade bed. It was only too evident she hadn't washed.

"What's the matter, Rosie?" she asked.

"I'm tired."

"Didn't you make your bed this morning?"

She sat up and stared. "We never do. Francey does it, if she can be bothered."

"Come on, let me help you. You go and sponge your face. I'll make your bed for you."

Rosie dabbed listlessly at the enamel basin. Tina was efficient when she cared to be and plumped the pillows into an enticing nest. The bed linen, though rough, was clean.

"By, that's nice." Rosie settled on the pillows, her hair still tousled. Tina found a hairbrush, persuaded her to sit up while she brushed the fine fair strands. "You've pretty hair, Rosie. Have you a ribbon so I can tie it back?"

"There was one, but I lost it." Rosie snuggled down again and pulled a girl's comic from under the mattress.

"Are you allowed to read in bed, Rosie?"

Again Rosie stared. "There's nowt to stop us."

The comic looked lurid and over-stimulating. Tina guessed Rosie was an imaginative child. Was she over-taxing her young brain? Could this be the reason for her listlessness?

Tina peered over her shoulder. "Do you get this comic every week?"

"Aye, and it's right good!" Rosie gloated. "I like the middle story best—see here." She spread out the picture-script. "It's all about a lassie called Denise Dawnley . . . Daring Denise, they call her. She's the same age as me, an' in this one she's joined a circus, an' the trick-rider lass, *she's* broken her leg. So Denise dresses up to look like her an' wears a mask an' then rides with the circus ponies. Only the lad on the trapeze, he knows, an' when Denise nearly falls off an' she's hanging by the stirrup, this lad—Lorenzo, he's called—comes swooping down on his trapeze an' just whisks her up. An' all the audience think it's an act they planned, like. So after that they do it every night."

"Goodness!" said Tina, amused by the fanatical glow in Rosie's eyes.

"Aye—an' last week she was in the jungle, among man-eating tigers. An' next week she's up in an aeroplane. . . . Look, it tells you here: Don't miss Daring Denise's next exploit. What dangers and adventures will she meet in the air? Order your copy now. On'y we don't. Bobby and me, we get our comics from the sweetie-shop in Hexham."

Tina laughed, "You'll have to let me know how Denise gets on, won't you? What about lying down to sleep now?" She bent to kiss her. "Goodnight, Rosie." As she reached the door Rosie called softly: "Will you go in and see Bobby? He'd like that."

The adjoining bedroom door was open and Bobby was sitting up in bed drawing.

"Hallo, what's that you're doing?" Tina asked.

Bobby displayed his sketch shyly. "It's one o' the pigeons. Forest Fawn—it's a mealie, see, and I'm going to crayon it after."

"That's very good, Bobby. But isn't it time to go to sleep now?"

"Why?" Bobby was clearly mystified. "I sit drawing while it's light. Then sometimes I light the candle—we've got no electric upstairs." He hesitated. "Thanks for the games, Miss Rutherford."

She pulled a face. "Can't you call me Tina?"

"Matt said we weren't to be cheeky. Bruno—" He checked himself and flushed.

"Yes, Bobby, what about Bruno?" Tina asked in a low voice.

Bobby looked embarrassed. "Matt said we weren't to talk to you about him."

Tina felt distressed. "Well, suppose you tell me this one thing you were going to say?"

"Oh, it was just that Bruno showed me how to get the shading right in my drawing. He used to come up and see us some nights and do shadow tricks on the wall wi' a candle."

Tina smiled in poignant memory. "Did he do the butterfly and the kangaroo—and aeroplanes?"

"Aye—how did you know?"

"Because he did them for me, when I was a little girl." The room blurred before her eyes. "I'm glad you were friends, Bobby." She gave him a soft goodnight and left the room.

Matt had been making coffee and poured out a mug for her. "It's good of you to bother with the twins, Tina. Bruno, he used to play with them by the hour. He'd the knack, somehow. Many's the time I've sat down here listening to them all laughing their head off up there. Aye, and they behaved for him. They'd do anything he asked them."

His voice faded as he saw the tears still in her eyes. He laid a gentle hand on her arm. "Tina, you're upset. I shouldn't have mentioned Bruno—"

"It wasn't that. Bobby was telling me about the games Bruno played with him—"

"I warned them not to mention him—"

"Why?" she demanded. "Why should they be warned off? They loved him—they still love his memory, as I do. . . ."

She broke down into unrestrained weeping. Matt's arms closed about her. "Oh, come on, Tina, come on, hinney. You'll make yourself ill."

She clung to him, groping for comfort. He had spoken softly and kindly, had shown true concern, and for the moment it was enough. She found deep solace in the knowledge that in this humble home Bruno had given and received affection.

Matt's jacket was rough against her face. He held her close, patting her shoulder. "Come on, Tina pet, this won't do."

He produced a clean handkerchief and mopped her eyes. Her tears subsiding a little, she rested against him. His rough endearing words went on, until suddenly she felt him stiffen. He set her gently from him and she turned to see Adam Copeland and Francey watching them from the kitchen doorway. Tina's heart jerked. She was aware of her red eyes and dishevelled hair. Francey's face was mocking.

And Adam Copeland's? He leaned against the door-post, almost lazily surveying the scene. His eyebrows lifted as he said: "Well, well, sorry we barged in! But we weren't to guess a strong emotional scene was going on!"

Despite the casual words, the glance he sent Tina was withering.

Matt released her. "It was nothing," he said. "Tina was upset, that's all. We'd been talking of Bruno."

The name dropped like a stone in an already troubled pool. Adam's face showed a determined blankness. Matt went on:

"Was there something you wanted, Mr. Copeland?"

The other man eased his long frame from the door-post and eyed Matt steadily.

"Yes, there was, apart from driving your sister home. She tells me she's been stood up by Chris Irwin. At least she insists she was waiting for him. . . . The other thing—that dog of the twins'." His voice was severe now. "I've had more complaints from the farms. This is your last warning. If you can't keep the animal under control you must find a more suitable home for him. I don't like to deprive the children of their pet, but the farmers have the right about this, as you well know."

Matt's face burned, but he spoke quietly. "I do my best, but Hadrian does give us the slip at times. I've never held with dogs being chained up, but I admit the twins get careless about watching him."

"Then I suggest you teach them better!" Adam Copeland rapped. "They're your responsibility, my lad. Yours and your sister's here. And she knows my opinion on that score only too well."

"There was a time, Mr. Copeland, when you yourself had a lot to do with Francey's neglect of the bairns. Times when you and she—"

"Have a care, Matt! Have a care what you say. Francey herself will tell you the times I've lectured her about the twins."

"You don't own us, Mr. Copeland."

"No." Adam's voice was quiet, but held a hint of cold steel in its depths. "I don't own you. Sometimes I think it might be easier if I did."

His glance, masked of all expression, rested for a moment on Francey's bent head. Tina's heart seemed to fall. Was it true then, as she had suspected all along, that Adam's conscience regarding Francey was still troubling him? And what about Francey's assertion that she was meeting Chris? To whom had she lied—to Tina herself, or to Adam?

Adam Copeland made as if to turn away, but swung back. "Oh, and please note, Matt, that your sister has been delivered safe and sound to your door. I've heard rumors that you consider I'm getting her talked about." His glance at Francey was now almost contemptuous. "May I point out to you that she's quite capable of doing that without my help."

"Adam!" Francey cried out in protest. But all he did was to push her, none too gently, into the room. "No more arguments, my lass. From what I can see your first need is an apron and some elbow grease." His gaze roved the messy tablecloth. "And if I do find you've been neglecting those children or their home I promise you I shall unleash all the powers of the Welfare Department at your door!"

"You'd better not try!" Matt was thoroughly roused.

Adam ignored him and filched Tina's coat from a chair. "This yours, Tina? It's getting dark. I'll drive you home."

"No thanks!" Her chin tilted.

He threw the coat with some force. "Get it on and don't keep me waiting. I'm sorry about spoiling the passionate love scene, but perhaps you can resume it at a later date." Then, as she still did not move, he took her firmly by the arm and propelled her forward. "Move, my lass! I haven't got all night."

Tina thought it expedient to obey. "Goodnight, Matt," she called. "I'll be back."

Adam's gaze went from one to the other. "Congrat-ulations, lad—she must have liked it!" And he strode out of the house without bothering to see that she followed. But follow she did.

Tina got into the Land-Rover. He drove it, bumping and clattering, to the meeting of the ways. Here he braked and sat watching her. "Getting quite involved with young Matt, aren't you?"

"He's a friend," she said coldly.

"That all?" There was a mocking curve to his mouth.

"Maybe a little more." No harm in letting him think so, she told herself in her hurt pride.

His laugh was somewhat subdued. "He won't do for you, Tina. Too quiet, too rough and ready—too narrow."

"*Narrow*? Because he stays at home and minds the children while Francey—and you—"

His eyes were sword-bright. "While Francey and I—do go on!"

"You must have encouraged her!" she insisted.

"On the contrary, she encouraged me." He smiled. "The trouble with Francey is she has no sense of timing."

"So you encourage her when you're in the mood, and drop her when you're not?"

"Something like that." He sounded almost complacent.

"Aren't you ashamed of yourself?"

"Not a bit of it, my dear. There are always Franceys around. Like the poor, they're always with us."

"You're callous!" she burst out.

"I'm truthful." But his eyes sparked with amusement. Was he merely teasing?

"In your case," said Tina heavily, "it amounts to the same thing."

This time he laughed without restraint, then examined her face closely. "Why this concern over Francey Finch? It couldn't be—jealousy?"

"Jealousy?" she faltered. "Why should it be?" But her face burned.

"I leave that to you to decide." He lit a cigaret, gazed reflectively into the gloom of the trees. The sleepy twittering of nesting birds was all about them. "So you really went to Quarry Farm to talk about Bruno?"

"At least he's spoken of there with kindness and affection." A tide of tears threatened.

"And this upset you?"

"Of course. After always hearing him condemned by you, it was very moving to know that there he was appreciated."

His face was cold and stern now, all mockery gone. "You said just now I was both callous and truthful. To tell you the truth about your brother perhaps I had to be callous. Yet there was a time"—he drew on his cigaret—"there was a time, my dear, when I could have spoken of him with just as much affection and praise as you may have heard from Matt. That time is past, unfortunately."

"You're so sure, aren't you?" Her tears fell now, unmanageable. "You couldn't be wrong. Adam Copeland could never make a mistake—the farmer's friend, the people's adviser, the county magistrate—*he* could never be wrong!"

"Oh, I can be wrong. But I never accuse without complete evidence. The evidence was there—"

"I won't accept that—I won't!" She turned away, her tears a flood now. Again a large clean handkerchief was thrust into her hand.

"Dry your eyes, Tina. We won't argue about it." His tone was final. "You're upset, and I've learned by now that your excess emotionalism is a fine show of Roman candles. I'm not in the habit of shouting down a weeping girl either, callous though I might be. Now take a grip of yourself. If I escort you into the house like this Isa will be certain I've seduced you and will no doubt produce an appropriate text!"

This incident at Quarry Farm gave Tina much to think about. Far from the tangle unravelling, it seemed twined into further confusion. Bruno's involvement with the Finches was deeper than she had imagined, but she was still far from drawing any conclusions about her brother and Francey; then too there was the enigma of Adam's feelings for Francey and even now a hint of complication concerning Francey and Chris.

All she could do was to wait, to be tuned in and watchful.

As the Easter vacation passed the students on the dig were replaced by other amateur archaeologist of mixed ages and occupations, some using a week or two of their summer holidays to pursue their hobby, others perhaps between jobs of waiting for university places.

Chris managed his shifting personnel with admirable aplomb, but his was no enviable position. Since Bruno's death his burden of responsibility was heavier and perhaps because of this he sought her company less. She had hoped he would take her on more Wall excursions, but each time she decided to ask him she was conscience-smitten at sight of his tired and preoccupied face. Better to wait, perhaps, until he had settled into his new position of authority.

Meanwhile Tina was still absorbed in her office work at Hadrian's Edge. She noticed that Adam Copeland was much more inclined to discuss estate problems with her, to include her in his routine affairs. He would say; "We must see to this—" instead of "I must see to this." It was "We must send them a letter. . . . We must look up those files. . . .

At these times Tina felt a glow of satisfaction, almost of reluctant delight. He had also further unbent to detailing stories of the district and some of its eccentrics.

"Bell, now, he's a queer one. He's the farmer at Heather Houses—"

"I know. And isn't it his brother who has Low Dene?"

He cocked an impressed eyebrow. "You're learning! . . . Well, this Bell I'm talking about—Alec—he's only a small man now, you might say. But in his heyday he farmed in a big way toward the coast. He had a housekeeper and maids in those days, but the housekeeper was a bit forgetful. One day he found no pepper on the table and roared at her to ask why. She said she'd forgotten to order any. By Gow! he shouted, I'll see you never forget again. And he ordered a ton of the stuff.

They say there's still some of it rotting in an old barn on that farm to this day."

After such a genial interlude he would say stiffly: "Sorry, this can't possibly interest you."

"But it does!" she wanted to cry, except that his reaction would surely be sceptical. He always seemed to forget her Northumbrian blood, or that she knew much of the county's folklore through her father's tales.

It was at these times, when the barrier between them seemed misty and transparent, that her conscience smote her. For she was still planning her secret visit to Helen. Reports on the sick girl's progress were good, and Adam visited his sister rather less than before.

Tina waited patiently for the right opportunity. It came perhaps sooner than she deserved.

Adam was to be away for the day consulting Sir Walter's solicitor in Newcastle. Tina, however, was not expected to extend her working hours. A young man from Hexham who was learning the estate business was to take over for the afternoon.

"Which suits me down to the ground," Carrie said with relief. "For I *have* done it in the past, and I must say it's a strain to be in the third century one minute and yelling down the phone about drains and County Councils the next."

Tina laughed. "I think I'll take an afternoon off from the dig myself," she said. "Any chance of borrowing your car?"

"Wall exploring? I'm afraid I've rather fallen down there—meant to take you myself. But it's good to be alone there, take it from me. . . . Where is it to be—Housesteads?"

"I'm—not sure yet."

Carrie gave her a shrewd look but said no more. Tina wondered if she had guessed her real destination.

This day's journey to Thornriggs was in marked contrast to the last. It was a dazzling afternoon, the clouds high and peaceful, the sunlight holding a new warmth. Along the Bellingham road the woods showed tassels of new green, the gorse on the moor was goldpangled and the new heather growths an olive carpet owing between the stony outcrops.

The car seemed to leap up the Thornriggs road, passing n a flash the plantation where she had sheltered, making hort work of the rough surface. The road dipped and urved again, mounted a low ridge which gave her her irst view of Thornriggs, a few stone houses round a riangular green, a church and a village school.

She parked outside the one shop, bought a bar of chocolate and inquired for Turret House. The directions vere simple. She drove between a pair of white gates near he green, up a long drive and found the house at the end. It was a secluded but smaller edition of Hadrian's Edge.

She rang the bell under the stone portico. There was a lelay in answering, giving Tina time to tremble a little und wonder at her own audacity. Eventually the door opened and an elderly woman stood regarding her.

She looked into severe gray eyes, saw the blue dress that suggested a nursing sister. "Yes?" the woman asked curtly.

Tina gave her name; then Helen's. Instantly the woman's gaze was affronted. "Did you say *Rutherford*. . . ? I'm afraid you can't see Miss Copeland. I have strict instructions that she has to have no upsetting visitors."

"I won't upset her." Tina spoke politely but with rising anger.

"I don't think you quite understand," the woman went on repressively. "I am Miss Coxon and am in complete charge of my patient. Mr. Copeland left strict instructions that you, of all people, must not be allowed access to his sister . . . and now, as I'm very busy, I'll bid you good afternoon."

Tina withdrew a step, but insisted: "Do you mind telling me when Mr. Copeland left that last instruction?"

"I see no point. . . . Oh, very well then, it was ten days ago or thereabouts."

The door was now closed firmly in her face. Tina drove back up the avenue, her feelings in tumult. At the village green she pulled up, knowing she needed to compose herself before driving on.

So Adam Copeland had guessed she would try again. The date of his instruction, coming after the previous attempt, proved it without doubt. And all the time she had thought his suspicions lulled!

Despair washed over her. Despite all her scheming he had been too much for her, had read her thoughts as easily as his own barometer.

She unwrapped her chocolate, eating it for solace rather than hunger. It was peaceful on the village green, the only sounds a restless cawing of rooks, and the faint singing of children in the school. Tina sat on, deflated and listless. There was no reason why she shouldn't go on to explore the Wall. But today the urge had gone.

It was as if Adam Copeland, after his genial relaxation of the last week or two, had slammed a steel door in her face.

She was roused by the sound of a vehicle. Glancing in her driving mirror she saw a lorry emerging from the white gates of Turret House. Next moment she recognized the driver—Jamey!

He did not glance her way as the lorry shot off with a hideous grinding of gears toward the Bellingham road. She remembered the farm at the back of Turret House, belonging to Matt's pigeon-fancying friend. Even as she eyed the dark turrets above the trees she saw a flutter of pale wings. Two pigeons mounted into the dazzling brightness and streaked eastwards.

As for Jamey, he had obviously been making some kind of farm delivery—innocent enough, possibly. Yet Helen could scarcely be a prisoner in the house, and if she knew the time of Jamey's deliveries what simpler than to stroll round the farm at that time?

Helen—and Jamey? Was it really possible that that old flare of interest was not dead? After all, Helen had a reputation for irrational behavior. And wasn't Jamey utterly ruthless where his own interests were concerned?

Or was she allowing her imagination to run riot in her anxiety to make Helen a scapegoat?

She finished her chocolate, temporarily dismissed Jamey from her mind and shook herself out of her despondency. She wasn't beaten yet. She could still write to Helen. No one could intercept a letter and to disguise the sender she could type the address. Much less satisfactory than a meeting, and Helen would be under no obligation to answer, but at least she, Tina, could state her passionate disbelief in Bruno's guilt.

She drove home slowly, still in no mood to finish her afternoon exploring, though to the south the dark ribbon of the Wall, plunging and climbing the contours of the crags, drew her eyes often. But no, she would go home and compose the letter. Only then could she find peace of mind.

At Hadrian's Edge, as there was no collection box nearby, it was the postman's custom to collect any letters from the house when he made his deliveries. Tina dared not risk leaving hers for the morning collection, as at most there was only a slim selection. The afternoon post, though, contained all Adam's business mail. It was easy to slip her typed envelope under the pile on the hall table. Adam was back from Newcastle, she learned, but had gone out again.

She walked into supper that evening to find him drinking a whisky at the sideboard. His stare was disconcerting, there seemed the old sarcastic twist to his mouth. She made a remark or two and moved toward her seat. Then she stopped as though stung. At her place setting lay the letter.

"A letter for you," he said. "And very silly of you, my dear. I happened to come in for a moment just before the postman, to check if young Groves had answered a certain letter. I found—that!"

She was silent under the shock. His tone roughened. "Do you take me for a fool? Even if it had reached Turret House my sister wouldn't have seen it. Miss Coxon has instructions to save all unfamiliar letters for my inspection. And it was equally stupid of you to waste time and petrol going to Thornriggs this afternoon. Why not accept defeat and save your dignity?"

Tina crushed the letter into her pocket, humiliated beyond bearing. Adam lounged against the sideboard watching the effect of his words. His heavy head of hair seemed blacker than ever above a pale gray town suit. His eyes dominated her.

"Well, lost your tongue?"

"No!" she exploded at last. "Dignity? Do you think I care about my dignity when it comes to Bruno's good name? If I did, do you think I should ever have come to this house, where daily I'm reminded that you—that you—"

"That I face truth—reality?" He straightened, drained his glass and set it down. "And come, my dear, don't tell me it's been one long penance. There have been occasions when I even thought you found glimpses of happiness here."

"Everyone has been most kind, I agree. That is—"

"Everyone except myself?" he asked quietly. "Yet apart from our main bone of contention it has always been my sincere wish that you should benefit from your stay in my house."

"Benefit?" she echoed. "When you prevent me at every turn from discovering the only things that can give me peace of mind!"

"Have it your own way." His voice held ice again. "Would you care for a drink?"

"No, thank you."

At this point Isa plunged in with the soup, Carrie followed and the conversation was closed.

Later Tina looked in at Carrie's den, but found her writing a letter. "Come in if you like, Tina, but I can't be very sociable. That fool Everard-Kipps has actually had the nerve to criticize that article I'd published on centurial stones. He calls my findings poppycock, if you please! I'll poppycock him!"

Carrie turned to the pile of tomes at her side, already oblivious to Tina's presence.

"I'll pop in and see Isa, then." Her words fell on deaf ears.

Isa was seated at the harmonium, wearing one of her "afternoon" dresses, of mole-colored crêpe-de-chine, with beaded sleeves. She turned with her usual gloomy nod of welcome. "Come away in, hinney. Sit by the fire. I was just thinking of taking a run through The Lost Chord, for it makes a right good voluntary at the chapel. They like summat solum, wi' a judgment-day sound to t."

Tina smiled and nursed Samson. "You go ahead, Isa—don't mind me."

She was to regret the words, for it was a thunderous rendering, with all stops out. For, as Isa explained afterwards: "Mr. Copeland's out, and once Mrs. Butterfield's got her nose in yon muckle Roman books, she'd never even hear the trump o' doom if it sounded."

Somewhat to Tina's relief, Isa left the organ and set the kettle on the hotplate. "We'll have a cup of tea, while we're at it. What did you think of yon apple-meringue at supper?"

"It was lovely, Isa. You must have been in a good mood when you made it."

Isa sat down, nodding complacently. "Aye, I was. And I'll tell you for why. Mr. Copeland, he's given me a rise. Said I was worth my weight in gold. . . ." She paused, her gloom returning. "I'm no' so sure now, though, that it's a good thing."

"Why, Isa?"

"It could mean changes. He could be buttering me up, like, so I wouldn't be likely to up and leave if he got wed or anything."

Tina said faintly: "He's not thinking of marriage, surely?"

Isa hunched her shoulders. "I'd a bad fright once—I thought he was set on yon Francey Finch. Aye, and if that had come about I'd have been up and away, organ an' all! For you know what it says in Proverbs: 'A virtuous woman is a crown to her husband.' Some crown *she'd* be. . . . But there, he's seen sense where she's concerned. If he's got summat else in mind, then he's keeping it dark."

Isa looked reflectively at Tina. "A lass like yoursel' now, I wouldn't say no to. For you'd understand my ways, and no' be expecting perfection. For it stands to reason if a woman's feeling down, then her pastry's got

478

to suffer. And as to the organ, why, I reckon you could turn as deaf an ear as Mrs. Butterfield, if you'd a mind."

Tina was embarrassed. "I shouldn't worry, Isa. It's no likely to happen."

"Aye, well, that's as may be. I'm just saying"—Isa paused impressively—"if you'd a mind that way it would suit me fine." She spoke, Tina thought, as though a possible last obstacle had been removed.

Her next words sent a shock through Tina. "Aye, and I've told Mr. Copeland the same. You could do worse, I said, for all she's a foreigner, or as near as makes no difference. And I made plain I'd be ready to stop on."

"What did he say?"

"Why, he made a joke of it, for he's a rare man for talking in riddles. Said he'd like to choose his own wife, when the time came, and he wasna' likely to settle for a Roman water-goddess. . . . But there, I couldn't make head nor tail of him, for he fair likes to bamboozle me."

Tina, unaccountably depressed, drank her tea and went up to bed. Why should she be upset? she asked herself furiously. He could have a hundred wives, for all she cared. . . .

The following evening she decided to visit Quarry Farm again, with the slight hope of discovering more about Jamey's visit to Turret House. On the way through the woods she heard a childish call from the tree house.

"Tina! Come up and see me!"

Rosie's head peered out from a bower of budding branches. "I'm here all by myself. Bobby's gone fishing."

Tina hesitated, glanced down ruefully at her crisp cream linen dress. Rosie's eyes pleaded. She smiled and scrambled up the rope ladder.

"My, you are playing houses, aren't you? Is this the new tea-set?"

"Yes. Will you be a lady who's come to tea?" Rosie's wistfulness was touching. "Bobby won't play houses. He says it's a lassie's game."

Tina entered with spirit into the play. There were two bright pink cups and saucers from Woolworth's, an old tea-pot with a cracked spout containing Coke. "It looks

ke tea," Rosie explained. Strips of bark served for
lates, holding a collection of chestnut husks, sappy leaf
uds and colored stones.

"They're the cream fancies," Rosie explained. "Like in
he café in Hexham. You've got to pretend."

Tina swallowed a little of the Coke-tea, which tasted
eculiar. She guessed the old tea-pot needed cleaning.
Ier delicate passes at the cakes and refined munching
nade Rosie's eyes shine. "You do it just like ladies in the
afé."

After simulating the polite conversation of the said
adies Tina at last ventured to ask: "Been to school today,
Rosie?"

Rosie nodded. "Miss Purvis told us the school doctor
nd nurse are coming Monday." She scowled. "I hate it
vhen they come."

"Why, Rosie?" Tina watched her closely, thinking it
night be a good thing for the child to have a proper
examination.

"'Cos Francey has to take me, an' they make her tell
ll what I've been doing—not eating, an' things like
hat."

"But surely it's better if Francey's there. All the other
girls will have someone.

To her surprise Rosie began to cry, kicking out at her
plates of "cakes" in a gesture of temper. "They might
ind something wrong with me."

Tina made no reply but collected the "cream fancies,"
giving Rosie time to compose herself. At last she lapsed
nto miserable snuffles.

"Here, borrow my handkerchief. It's clean."

Rosie brightened. "Is yon real lace?"

"I suppose it is . . . Rosie, is anything wrong? You're
not hiding anything from Matt and Francey, are you? No
pains or tummy-aches?"

"No, I'm not." Her voice was sullen. "But the nurse
and doctor, they might pick on me. They picked on Alice
Tate last time."

Tina glanced at her watch, feeling it would be better if
Rosie didn't dwell on such thoughts, "I shouldn't worry

about Alice Tate. I'm going down to your house now. Ar
you coming?"

"No. I've the washing up to do, down at the burn. The
I've got to hide my cups."

"Hide them?"

Rosie looked sly. "This isn't my only hidey-hole. I'v
got another secret place nobody could ever find. I kee
my things there."

Tina smiled. All children loved secrets. And alread
Rosie seemed to have recovered her spirits. She felt sh
could safely leave her, and even decided against tellin
Matt of the incident. Why worry him when the medica
examination was so near? If there was any cause fo
anxiety he would know soon enough.

She found him alone in the house, reading the sport
page of the local paper. He greeted her eagerly.

"Hallo, Tina. . . . I've done well this week. Peerles
Blue won again and Moonlight got a second. The rac
was from Sussex—like to see the report?"

Tina read the name M. Finch and the birds' timings i
a very minute paragraph. Matt was a little pathetic a
times, she thought, in his obsession with his birds. But sh
tried to show the proper enthusiasm. She accepted hi
offer of coffee, perching on the end of the old sofa whil
he made it. The kitchen was a little tidier, she noticed
Had Adam Copeland's advice about elbow grease mad
the difference?

Matt handed her the mug of coffee, his eyes suddenl
solemn under his fair quiff of hair.

"I heard about you going to Turret House, Tina."

She felt a little thrown.

"You—heard? Was it Jamey who saw me?"

"Jamey? No. Why, should it be?"

Tina explained about seeing his brother.

"Oh, he's often up at the farm for Charlie Marshall
And there's only the one way in at the drive. The farn
path goes off before you get to the house."

She frowned. "Then who did tell you—Adam?"

He shrugged. "You can't do much around here withou
someone noticing, Tina. And most people know you b
sight now."

She had to accept this to mean that some passing motorist had seen and recognized her. Matt's next words sent her thoughts at a tangent.

"I've told you, Tina, it's not wise to go there."

"So everyone tells me. Everyone seems so scared I meet Helen Copeland. No one gives me credit for any common sense. What I have to say to her is just as likely to be a comfort as the opposite."

"You don't know that," he said sharply. "Tina, you don't know Helen the way we all do. It's best to keep away."

"Best?" she repeated. "Or just more convenient for everyone?"

Matt frowned. "Don't make mysteries out of nothing, Tina."

"You never visit Charlie Marshall, then?" she demanded.

His shake of the head was angrily abrupt. "No, and I'm not likely to just now. If he wants to see me he comes here. Jamey's a fool to go to the farm so much. It could make talk, especially after that old affair."

"Perhaps the talk's justified. How do you know *he* just sees Charlie Marshall?"

Matt turned his face from her. There was a brief silence before he said: "I don't. But I do know Adam Copeland keeps a close eye on what goes on up there."

"Adam Copeland isn't infallible." Yet Tina spoke with the despairing knowledge that he was, or as near as made no difference.

"Let's not argue, Tina." Matt pleaded. "Have you seen the bairns anywhere?"

"Rosie's on her way. She's been playing in the tree house."

Matt seemed to relax, glad of the change of subject. He spoke of the impending visit of the school doctor. "It's a good thing she's having a going-over. And it'll upset her less than taking her along to our own doctor. When all the other bairns are lining up she won't think a thing of it."

Tina was uneasily silent. Should she warn Matt that Rosie was already showing alarm?

"Why should going to the doctor frighten her?" she asked.

"Oh, there was a bit of a scare when she was five. She'd a bad chest inflammation and the doctor spoke of taking her into hospital. She was a wild wee thing then and had hardly ever seen a strange face. They did take her in, just for a few hours, for treatment, but she was so upset—the poor bairn was nearly demented with fear. That's why she's still scared of doctors and hospitals."

"So that's really why—" Tina broke off, understanding having dawned.

"Why I've let things slide a bit?" He nodded, a little ashamed. "Only it was a toss-up. It seemed wrong to put her through all those fears again unless she was really ill."

"Most people would have felt the same, Matt. Anyway, you can relax now. She'll have a proper examination."

"Aye, that's right. And ten to one we'll find we've been bothering about nothing."

Rosie arrived then, flushed with running and looking so normal that Matt and Tina exchanged rueful smiles. On her heels came Bobby and as the children went to shut up their rabbits Matt walked with Tina to the yard gate.

It was still scarcely dusk, the thickets of gorse sending long blue fingers of shadow over the pale moor.

"I wish I could walk up with you, Tina, but I've the bairns to chase off to bed."

Suddenly he found her hand, seized and held it. "It's been great, Tina, you coming here. Though what you see in us all I can't think."

"I see Bruno's friends," she said quietly. "Please don't put me on a pedestal, Matt. I'm not good enough, and it would spoil our friendship."

He released her hand. "I'll try, then. But to have a girl like you walk into Quarry Farm—it doesn't happen every day, you know." His smile was wistful.

"Just as well," she teased. "You'd have no time for the pigeons!" With a parting wave she ran up the slope of the moor toward the darkening woods about Hadrian's Edge.

Two days later Adam detained Tina as she was leaving the office. "Have you been to Housesteads or Cuddy's Crag yet?" he asked.

"No, not yet. I was waiting for a spare afternoon. We've been pretty busy on the dig these last few days."

"Don't tell me you've found a whole new Roman bathhouse or granary?"

"No." She hesitated, said cautiously: "Only in the southeast corner we've come across some rather strange signs. It could be something important—some big break-through, or nothing much after all. But it's—exciting."

"You won't miss much in one afternoon, surely?" There was a touch of mischief in his glance. "Three shovelfuls of soil and half a Roman hairpin?"

Tina flushed. "The three shovelfuls of soil might contain the most significant clue so far. . . . And you seem to forget, the mere fact that I'm following up my brother's work means a lot to me."

"Sorry, I did forget. But I was going to suggest you come up to Housesteads with me this afternoon. I've a call to make on a farm close by."

Tina was startled. "You mean you want to show me round?"

"Why not? Just because I don't believe in getting coated to the eyebrows in clay doesn't mean I'm not interested in Wall history."

"Thank you." She was conscious of inner turmoil. "I'd like to come. I'll just have to take a chance they don't unearth something marvellous at the dig."

He smiled. "Your chances are pretty good, I'd say. It so happens I've teased you rather unmercifully about your cardboard Wall model. I also insisted I could teach you so much more. The time seems to have come to implement my words." He glanced at her feet. "Oh, and strong shoes or boots, please—it'll be rough going if we follow the wall westwards from the fort. Right. I'll have the car outside at two o'clock sharp."

At lunch with Carrie, she mentioned the outing.

"Oh, Adam's taking you, is he? Good. He's much

better informed about the local stretches than Chris."

"Better than *Chris*! But he's an expert," Tina protested.

"Granted, he's an expert on Wall history. But he hasn't got the feel of it the way local people have. And remember Adam's seen it in all weathers and conditions."

"I suppose so."

"Let's just hope the weather holds." Carrie begun to pour the coffee.

"Seen Sandy lately?" Tina asked.

"Yes, I met him up the top lane last night—by accident, of course—playing those wretched pipes of his. He actually had the nerve to ask me to a fancy dress dance at Elswhistle!" Carrie looked heated.

"Why not? It would be fun."

"It never seems to enter his thick head that I'm not interested in dancing. And fancy dress, of all things!"

"But you could watch. It means getting out—meeting people. Closing the hangar doors."

"Ah well, I've my own ways of doing that. I don't suppose he meant a word of it, anyway. You know Sandy and his practical jokes."

"But supposing it wasn't a joke?"

"Like to bet?"

Tina did not press the point. At two o'clock she was waiting in the front doorway, in blue trousers and anorak, zip-sided boots and a forget-me-not hair-ribbon.

The Land-Rover drew up. Adam Copeland surveyed her. "You look about sixteen with your hair tied back. . . . Those boots are a bit fancy, aren't they? Don't blame me if they get cut to shreds."

"I can always buy some more."

His smile was sardonic. "I forgot—poor little rich girl! Come on then. Put a move on while the sun's shining!"

She got in beside him. He hummed calmly to himself as the car switchbacked westwards along the Military Road. She decided to speak when spoken to. The consciousness of a whole afternoon in his company was a burden on her nerves and breathing.

She knew that Housesteads fort, or to give it its Roman

name, Borcovicium, was the most spectacular of all the preserved Wall forts. When Adam pulled in at the small carpark on the roadside she could see the exposed ruins about half a mile away on the crest of the Whin Sill. Adam led the way to a footpath climbing the sheep-bitten turf. Fat lambs bundled from their path. Half way they met two returning visitors, but as they mounted away from the road the peculiar silence of the heights enveloped them.

It was a gray afternoon, the skies a moving mass of ragged cloud, and a feeling of rain on the wind. "We'll leave the museum in case it turns wet," he announced, and having paid the entrance money they climbed on into the fort itself.

It was a site of five acres, the north wall of the fort edging the Whin Sill escarpment, and was laid out on the usual plan, four double gateways with one-time towers and guardhouses, the usual headquarters building, commandant's house, barracks and granaries, all well exposed to a height of six feet or so above the ground. Tina, thrilled at seeing it in reality for the first time, forgot Adam Copeland's intimidating presence, and ran about identifying the various buildings. He followed her with an indulgent smile. "I must say that plaster model of yours was quite something. But come over here with me—what about *this*?"

He pointed to the ground in the east gateway. There, in the stone base-work, were the deeply worn marks of Roman chariot wheels. Tina was stilled and awed. "All these centuries—it's hard to believe, isn't it?" She turned shining eyes to his face. "I knew about this—but actually *seeing* it—"

Words failed her. She had even to blink away a tear, which she was certain he saw. He said softly: "Your countrymen have made certain we who live on the Wall shall never forget them. I've something else to show you."

Walking eastwards, he began pointing out the complicated system of water supplies and latrines. The intricate stone channels had formed a precise and careful sewage system. "And remember all the water had to be somehow brought up from the Knag Burn at the foot of the hill there—not an easy plumbing feat. That is one thing I do admire about the Romans. They were centuries ahead of their time in domestic and health matters. Once their civilization had fallen it wasn't until the nineteenth century we even approached proper plumbing again."

They paused at the eastern wall of the fort. "And there you see the most famous view of the Wall," he told her. "King's Crag and the heights of Sewingshields. And down there you can see the Knag Burn, still flowing through the gap built for it in the Wall. You realize how steeply the Wall falls here before it climbs the crag again. This fact and the water gap made it one of the weakest points to defend—hence Housesteads itself."

Tina made murmurs of consent. Though she knew most of this information anyway, she sensed the pleasure he found in showing his local stretches of the Wall. Her eyes were misty again as she watched that gray ribbon rearing at fantastic angles up Sewingshields Crags.

He laid a hand on her arm. "Listen—a cuckoo. First I've heard this year. And can you pick up those other sounds, the peewits and the sheep, a lark or two over the moor—and of course the crows?" He pointed as a dark swerving mass rose from the rookery over King's Crag. "They're all the noises you'll ever hear on the Wall. And none of it has changed in sixteen centuries. Except that man's work has fallen into ruin." He looked significantly at the fort. "Make no mistake, though, we locals are proud of Housesteads. The way we go on about it, especially in the pubs hereabouts, you'd swear we'd built it ourselves."

Tina laughed. Gradually, as they wandered in the ruins, the rain came. They visited the museum, where Tina pored over the finds discovered during the excavation. They were amused by a stone relief of three hooded deities, looking exactly like old wives gossiping at a cottage door. Then Adam paused at a statue of Nemesis.

"Do you believe in fate, Tina?"

"I don't quite know."

"You prefer to think us all responsible for our actions?"

"Yes, I suppose I do."

"Nothing worked out in advance?"

"I think we make our own fates," Tina said.

"Your countrymen thought otherwise." He pointed to the English translation of a stone inscription. " 'To the Gods who dwell in this place.' No people were more superstitious than the Romans."

She said pertly: "You must allow us to have learned some wisdom over the centuries."

He laughed. "Come on, the rain's stopped. I want us to try to get as far as Hotbank Crags."

At the northwest corner of the fort they found the Wall again and mounted to the path along its crest. Here it plunged into a wood, perched on the crag's edge, tawny with dead rushes and bracken, the ragged Scots pines rearing above their heads. As they moved on in single file, Adam leading, the Wall nudged the very edge of the precipitous drop.

Tina's steps faltered. Adam was gaining on her. She had never been good at heights. Her knees buckled as she saw ahead the curvings of the Wall on the very lip of the ravine. This was worse than the Wall at Crag Lough, and a blustering wind made her even more uncertain. At last she stumbled and cried out.

Adam's voice was blown back to her. "This is Cuddy's Crag. We'll go on to Housesteads Milecastle, in the dip beyond the woods, then up to Hotbank. You'll get your first view of the Solway there, the end of the Wall. . . ."

She called faintly: "Adam, please stop!" doubting if he could hear. A black dizziness came. She staggered, tried to cry out and wondered as oblivion came whether she was pitching into that dreadful airy nothingness below.

She came to consciousness again to find herself half lying on the Wall, supported by Adam's arm. His dark face, intent and serious, was within inches of her own. He was trying to unscrew a small flask while still holding her, and now crammed it to her lips.

"Drink," he ordered.

She drank, coughed, felt a surge of life in her veins.

"I'm sorry—I was faint—no good at heights—"

"Save your breath—easy now! You won't be the first who baulked at the sight of that drop. I should have checked you were all right, or suggested you walk below the Wall on the other side. Trouble is heights don't bother me and I tend to forget they worry other people."

She was conscious of his physical nearness. A trembling assailed her. She remembered again his punishing kiss on the occasion of her first trip to Thornriggs. "I think I can stand up now."

Those green-flecked eyes examined her face, concerned, almost gentle. He helped her to her feet. "If you could just help me down into the wood, I'll be all right to walk on."

His arm still encircled her in a firm grip. "Certainly not. No more walking on today except down to the car and then home for some shock treatment—hot sweet tea." He jumped down to the floor of the wood, lifted her from the Wall. "I'm sorry, Tina, I was thoughtless. Perhaps because your countrymen must have had nerves of steel to build the Wall in such conditions, I forgot not all Romans might be equally endowed."

"I'm sorry too, for spoiling your afternoon. And I was enjoying it so much." Her words were faltering, for he was still holding her, imprisoned between the Wall and his body. She heard his sharp indrawn breath, a sudden tightening of his grip. He seemed to sigh as he released her.

"There are always other afternoons." He tucked her arm in his. "Now, take your time. We'll walk back slowly."

They emerged from the wood. The clouds had lifted, a shaft of sunlight crept stealthily over the northern moor, turning dun shades to gold in its path. Above Broomlee Lough, under the shadow of King's Crag, the clouds still trailed gray scarves of rain.

"Think you can make it all right to the car?" Adam turned to survey her critically.

"Of course. I'm fine now."

And in a sense it was true. Now that she had recovered

from her faintness, apart from a marked weakness at the knees her overwhelming sensation was the memory of his arms about her, confused moments when she had been aware of concern and tenderness. Yet she asked herself if it was any more than the gentleness he would show to a sick animal if the need arose.

They reached the car and he helped her in, but he seemed in no hurry to start. He gazed ahead up the Military Road, and at last said: "Sorry again about your fainting spell." He turned abruptly to face her. "But apart from that, did you enjoy the outing!"

"Yes, I did."

He bounced a restless fist on the driving wheel. "It *is* much pleasanter when we drop the barriers. Wouldn't you agree? Tina, why not be sensible? Why don't you drop all this animosity concerning your brother?" He spoke directly and firmly. "I have managed to quieten the gossip. Most people now believe the mysterious girl to be a hitchhiker who took fright. And your stay as a guest at my house has looked after the rest. Tina, don't you understand what I'm trying to say?"

A frigid misery came. "I'm—not sure," she said, wanting him to commit himself further yet afraid of the outcome. His expression was guarded now.

"What I'm trying to say is this. Need you insist on this business of clearing Bruno's name? I've already told you, the gossip is over and forgotten. Why go on punishing yourself, digging for a non-existent truth? It's going to do about as much good as throwing yourself against that Wall up there. No one condemns your brother now. So why not let him rest in peace and start living again?"

"You say no one condemns him. Does that include yourself?" she asked shakily.

He hesitated, his eyes sombre. "All right, I'll be honest with you. I still hold him responsible for my sister's unhappiness. We both know there was that letter from the hotel. You can't expect me to exonerate him altogether, however much I've tried—and believe me, Tina, I've leaned over backwards to still the gossip. I've also striven to smooth things over on the surface between us."

"You ask me to forget?" She was sick and roused now. "You expect me to accept it like that, all comfortably smoothed over, as you put it, while all along I know you still condemn him?"

He said quietly but with a touch of harshness: "Is my opinion so important, then?"

She was silent, trapped.

He too was roused now, the old arrogant glint in his eyes. "Come on, Tina, I asked you a question. Why should you care? Why turn your days upside down fretting over what *I* think?"

"I don't know." She spoke wildly. "But I've got to change your opinion—I've got to! For his sake if not for mine. . . . And now, please may I go home?"

"I'm sorry. I shouldn't have started all this. It was just that, for an hour, the barriers seemed to be down. The wall you built between us seemed to be crumbling just like those ancient stones up there."

"If there's a wall you built it too," she said bitterly. "And come to that, you laid the foundations in the first place. Never forget that!"

She had to turn away from his chilling stare. He seemed about to reply, then changed his mind and started the car. A silent journey began.

CHAPTER FIVE

As soon as he had garaged the car Adam disappeared into his office. Tina drank a cup of tea with Isa, then lay on her bed for an hour. She slept, but woke heavy-eyed.

Supper was a restrained affair, even Isa sensing the tension in the atmosphere and refraining from quoting texts. Instead she went gloomily to and fro with occasional sharp glances at Adam and Tina. Her dress was one Tina had not seen before, a plum-colored marocain with beige frilled modesty vest. As she left the room with the used plates Adam murmured: "Even Solomon in all his glory was not arrayed like one of these!"

It was a determined attempt to lighten the atmosphere. Carrie laughed. Tina did not respond. Adam threw down his napkin with one of his frightening displays of controlled anger. "I shan't take coffee, Carrie." His voice was like a slammed door.

When he had left the room Carrie said: "And just what have you done to upset him?"

Tina was silent. Carrie saw tears in her eyes and began to talk briskly of the day's work on the dig.

For a few days Tina was utterly dejected, nursing her hurt. Her work on the dig was mechanical, half-hearted. She was glad when the weekend came, with its opportunities of being alone. She declined an offer to go shopping in Hexham with Carrie and set out for a walk instead.

There was a needle-sharp wind which made her choose a westward path through the woods. She guessed it would eventually bring her out at the dig but walked idly, uncaring of her destination.

It was pleasant in this sheltered way, the occasional sunshine gilding the greenery of the larches. Everywhere underfoot was new growth and overhead the trills and chatter of nesting birds. She saw and heard these things, but was still locked in her own misery.

For so many weeks there had been, if not exactly a suspended truce, at least an unspoken understanding between Adam and herself that they could at least come to some kind of amiable compromise. Their working hours together would have been impossibly difficult otherwise.

Now in a few words at Housesteads, he had shattered that illusion.

She was angered that he expected her to lay down her arms while he refused to alter his opinion of Bruno by one jot. Perhaps, though, she persuaded herself, this new resumption of hostilities might be no bad thing. Wasn't it true, she asked herself guiltily, that she had lately permitted the situation to drift; had allowed that physical fascination of his to distract her from her search for the truth?

She found herself at a fork in the path and took the one plunging left and deeper into the woods. The white scut of a rabbit disappeared into a tangle of brambles. The path dipped into a dell where a small burn chattered over its pebbly bed. She took it at a jump, climbed the rising path beyond and found herself unexpectedly in a clearing where stood a trim one-storey stone cottage, its blue smoke a straight column against the trees.

She hesitated, wondering if this was private ground, yet admiring the cottage with its snowy paint, creeper-bowered doorway and a well-tilled garden inside its rough stone wall. A sound of sawing from the rear ceased and a voice called her name. To her relief it was Sandy who came forward, his hand extended in welcome.

"By, I didn't expect such a bonny visitor! Where are you off to, pet? There's nowt doing on the dig, is there?"

"I was just walking. Is this your cottage?"

"Aye, this is Quarry Cottage. I was just sawing up a bit of kindling wood, nothing that can't wait. So what do you say to a cup of tea? I'm old enough to be your father, or it wouldn't be proper to ask."

Tina accepted, glad to be jerked out of depression. The inside of the cottage delighted her, giving every evidence of the care of a methodical man, yet obviously masculine, with a gun or two about and a side table covered with evidence of some carpentry work.

"I'm making Carrie a cabinet for her aeroplanes. Only don't tell her, will you?" Sandy carefully poured water into a brown teapot. "But if I get many more visitors it'll be the autumn before I've finished it."

"Have you anyone coming this weekend?" Tina asked, as he handed her a heavy white cup.

"Not this week, no. I've a Scottish schoolteacher for two days next weekend. Then in about a fortnight I've an Aussie bloke coming, though where he got my address beats me. But yon guesthouse up the village is listed in the Wall guide, so they probably put him on to me, being full up themselves."

They drank their tea companionably and Sandy, after courteously asking permission, lit his pipe. "And where's Carrie off to?"

"Hexham, shopping. She said she really had to get something new to wear for the spring. She forgot last year."

"Aye, that's just her, now! That's just her! For half the time she isn't inside her skin at all, let alone her clothes. . . . Looks like she's changing, then. You wouldn't know if she—if she has anyone in the offing?" His voice was so dismayed Tina smiled.

"I'm sure she hasn't." She felt soothed by the peace of the cottage, the sleepy tick of a wall clock, the scent of Sandy's tobacco.

"You're very fond of Carrie, aren't you?" she ventured.

"Well, now it's not hard to spot, is it? Aye, I think the world of her, though she's an odd little body when you get to know her. It's just as if summat got snarled up in her life, all those years ago. She told me a bit about this Air Force bloke—at the time I think she did it to put *me* off—and it seems to me she's tried to spread that one bit of happiness too far and too thin. They talk of Wall Fever—why, hers is no ordinary Wall Fever. It's all tied up with yon chap she loved. And as long as she's so set in the past, why, Sandy's chances are about even with winning the Pools!"

"Unless Lofty came back, perhaps?"

"Came back, pet?" he exploded. "Why, that would be the end of it."

"No, I mean if he came back and things didn't work out—" Tina broke off. "But Carrie's right. Miracles don't happen."

"You could be right. But it's a miracle I'm needing, if ever she's to look twice at me. I know she thinks I'm some kind of a clown or a fool, always joking on and ribbing her about the Air Force." He set down his cup, looked suddenly despairing. "It's just that I'm no good at any other kind of approach. That's the way I always chatted up the lasses and I'm too old a dog to learn new tricks. . . . Why, if she but knew it, she's more than welcome to dig for yon old brick oven. But I pretended I was against it so that—well, one day she might do something for me in return."

"Like going to the fancy dress dance?" Tina asked.

His vivid blue eyes brightened. "She's not coming, is she?"

"I don't know—but she did mention it. I wish I could help, Sandy, but she's a very determined person."

Talk became general again. Soon Tina got up to go. She noticed a book on the dresser, gave it a closer look. It concerned the Roman occupation of Britain and was open at a page of military costume.

"Why, Sandy, I thought you weren't interested in Roman things?"

"Oh, that! It's a library book I got in Hexham." She detected embarrassment in his face and thought she understood. Had Sandy, tired of waiting for a miracle, decided in desperation to become a second Lofty, to study and try to understand what made Carrie tick? She was touched by the thought, pathetic though it was.

"Thanks for the tea, Sandy. I think I ought to go now."

"You're welcome, pet." He hesitated. "And—if there should be another mention of the dance, you'll put a word in for me?"

"I promise."

He walked with her to the gate, then returned to his sawing. Poor Sandy, she thought, as she walked home. She would gladly find him a miracle if any were going. Come to that, she could use one herself. . . .

No miracles, however, were forthcoming. Relations between herself and Adam continued cool, though she had recovered her spirits a little, determined to show him he had no power to make her permanently forlorn.

On Monday morning she remembered that it was Rosie's day to see the school doctor. She mentioned it to Adam during her mornings' work. Disconcertingly, he already knew about it.

"Don't forget I'm on the school board of governors.

And the health visitor is going to make certain both twins get a good going over." He paused. "That is, if they manage to catch them first."

Tina stared. "You mean—"

"I was referring to the twins' habit of staying away from school when anything unpleasant is in the offing. Let us just hope Francey will lead them there by the ears. Come to that, we can soon find out how things are." He whipped up the telephone receiver and dialled a local number.

"Miss Purvis? Adam Copeland here. I just wondered if the Finch twins had turned up for their medical. . . . What? Oh, I see. Bobby did, but not Rosie . . . I half expected it. No, I don't suppose there's a dog's chance of her turning up until after school hours. Thanks, anyway."

He replaced the receiver. "Francey set out with both of them, but Rosie gave her the slip. She'll be hiding up like a little vixen gone to earth."

"But surely Francey must have some idea where to find her?"

He shrugged. "The twins have their own secrets, though I certainly know about the tree house. But that isn't their only bolt-hole, you may depend on it. Just think of the woods, acres of them, full of old thickets. Then there are at least three disused quarries, overgrown for twenty years. Think of all the crannies in the moor. . . . No one in their right senses would even start looking."

"Poor Rosie," Tina said softly.

Adam cocked a sharp glance at her. "Would you like to elaborate on that remark?"

"Well, it's not Rosie's fault, is it—that she's scared, I mean." Tina began recounting the story of the hospital visit, but Adam waved an impatient hand.

"I know all about that. I still think they've given in to her far too much. Girls like Rosie need a firm hand. If I'd known she'd really give Francey the slip I'd have driven them to school myself. . . . Oh, they're a feckless lot!"

He turned again to the letters. "No sense in your fretting over the child. She's not your responsibility."

"Nor yours," said Tina.

His gaze was intimidating. "Only in that they're tenants and distant relations of mine. One tries to do one's duty."

"I suppose so. And I was just trying to be friendly. I think Rosie's sweet."

"Most people do, until she turns and rends them, like a wildcat. But I admit she's an endearing little savage." He permitted himself a slight smile. "But we shan't waste another minute over her. . . . Where were we? Oh yes. To John Forbes, Agricultural Contractors—Dear Sirs. . . ."

Tina felt deflated, more than a little annoyed. Yet she suspected Adam was more concerned than he admitted. She reflected too that Adam was surely the last person to criticize over-indulgence where Rosie was concerned. What about his own sister and her neurotic ways? Or this could be the very reason he saw the danger, possibly having paid bitterly for past mistakes of his own. She would never really know. He was as much of an enigma as ever.

She planned to run down to Quarry Farm after the dig work was over, just to see if Rosie was safely home. But when Carrie joined her for lunch all thoughts of Rosie were temporarily banished.

Carrie had an exulted look. "Well, we think we've solved the mystery in the southwest grids! Chris is almost certain now we've stumbled on another Mithraeum temple. The signs and the measurements are beginning to add up, though there's evidence of earlier work having been rebuilt." Carrie paused, her eyes shining. "The earlier stones would seem to be third century. . . . You know, Tina, Chris has just told me Bruno always had a hunch about that southwest corner. Of course the excavations hadn't reached that point when he—" She paused again. "If we're right, and of course we can't divulge anything yet, it'll be as spectacular a discovery as the one at Rudchester in the mid-fifties." She sat staring into space, her lunch forgotten.

"A Mithraeum temple!" Tina was no less excited. "Chris did say Bruno had a hunch about that corner. He was always terribly interested in the cult of Mithras. He read a paper on it at Padua University . . . I remember him saying it was the popular religion of the common soldiers and N.C.O.s of the Roman occupation."

She sat there musing on this strange religion, the central figure of which was the mythical Mithras, who after a miraculous birth slew a giant bull, from which came all the fruits of the material world. He thus typified the taming of wild nature to the needs of the common man. She remembered too that there was initiation by ordeal, followed by its members passing through successive grades of knowledge, in many ways similar to the freemasonry cults of the present day.

Carrie spoke again, still in that tranced voice. "Chris seems to think there's evidence of deliberate destruction in a later century, which would fit in with the idea published in the Rudchester report, that the worship of Mithras ended abruptly all along the Wall, due perhaps to a new wave of worship or a general order from the authorities."

Tina nodded. "Bruno thought that too, after studying all the evidence." She said softly: "Oh, Carrie, I hope you're right. Not only for our sakes, though it's wonderful to be in on something like this at the beginning. But I was thinking of Bruno. It'll justify all his work, all his ideas . . . and somehow I feel he'll know. . . ."

Carrie descended from her exulted sphere to give Tina a gentle glance. "I'm sure he will, somehow, somewhere. . . . But we've lots of work ahead yet. Mustn't let our imaginations run away with us. Oh, and by the way, keep this to yourself. Chris hasn't told any of the dig workers yet—we don't want advance news to leak out and then find we're wrong. But he said I could tell you, under promises of strict secrecy."

Later at the dig Tina managed, during all the heightened activity, to congratulate Chris. He gave her a calm smile. "We've some way to go yet, but Carrie and I are as sure as can be, even now. You may be sure I'll see Bruno's name is mentioned with honor when we publish the report."

"I know you will." They seemed suddenly back on their old friendly footing and spent the next ten minutes in intense discussion, while he displayed fragments and photographs, detailed the evidence so far and again cautioned her to immediate secrecy. There followed a busy afternoon of excavating, with what Tina's knowledge told her held several further exciting clues. It was only as the students and amateur archaeologists began to drift away that she straightened her back and realized how tired she was. And then she remembered Rosie. It was coming up to five o'clock. If she skipped tea for the present she could be down at Quarry Farm in fifteen minutes.

A light spring shower veiled the moor as she ran down the track, primrose scarf over her hair. As she approached the back door a babble of raised voices reached her. Her knock was unheard. She walked in to find Adam already there before her, a commanding figure on the hearthrug. Matt sat hunched in an armchair, his face sullen, and both Francey and the errant Rosie showed signs of tears.

A silence followed her entrance, the voices cut off in mid-air. Matt made the first effort to greet her. "Hallo, Tina. A pity you came just now. We're all at sixes and sevens."

"Think she cares?" Francey stormed.

"It so happens that she does." Adam's voice was now menacingly calm. "It's obvious she has come to see if Rosie's safe. You ought to make a show of appreciation, at least."

"I call it plain nosiness," Francey sulked.

"I think *you'd* better be quiet." Adam spoke on a low key but with such authority Francey slumped on to the sofa, snatched up a magazine and opted out of the conversation.

Rosie sidled up to Tina and reached for her hand. Matt scowled. "Tina doesn't want to talk to naughty girls."

Rosie now cried in earnest, and again it was a look from Adam that quietened her.

"Where were you, Rosie?" Tina asked.

Rosie's eyes hardened. "I'm not telling. I was in my secret place."

Matt stood up to face Adam. Tall as he was, the older man topped him by at least two inches. "You'll do no good here, Mr. Copeland. I've told you, Francey already slapped her and I've given her a good talking-to. We can manage our own affairs."

"Can you? I very much doubt it on the evidence."

Rosie, after a cautious glance at Adam's grim expression, stole into the parlor and closed the door. Adam instantly lowered his tone.

"You've admitted you were worried over Rosie and that doctors frighten her. Right, I've made special arrangements to fit her case. The health visitor will call here in the morning to look at the child. It's not her job to follow up fugitives from the shcool medicals, but in the special circumstances she has agreed. All I ask now is that you keep Rosie strictly indoors until the health visitor has been. It shouldn't be too difficult for you, Francey?"

His words rose to a pistol-shot suddenness which made Francey jump.

"Oh, all right. But she won't have to get wind of it, or she'll be off."

"In that case, I shall hold you entirely responsible," Adam said smoothly. "And now, as Rosie is safe and sound, we needn't disturb you further." He looked at Matt. "Unless of course Tina has any personal business with you?" His tone was gently sarcastic.

Tina's face flamed. "No. I'll go back with you. And I came to see Rosie, not Matt."

Matt's eyes, as they met hers, were resentful. She guessed he disliked her going off in Adam's company. Francey ignored her 'Goodbye' and Adam and Tina left the house in silence.

As the Land-Rover bumped and clattered up the track Adam said: "You know, there's quite a change in you since you came to know the Finches. At first you were entirely self-absorbed, both in grief and resentment, and with little consideration for others."

"Perhaps I was. Do you wonder at it?"

"I can't say I was too keen on you getting entangled with that lot, but excepting Francey, you seem to have impressed them all. You've even got Rosie eating out of your hand." He paused, his voice softened. "And you can't fool children, after all."

Tina was silent. His flattery, such as it was, hurt almost as much as his former criticism, she couldn't think why.

"Oh, by the way," he went on, "your friend Chris Irwin seems to have taken to squiring Francey around. I've seen her in his car a time or two."

"Does it annoy you?" asked Tina, greatly daring, as the Land-Rover grated to a stop in the front drive.

He laughed easily. "Why should I mind? My interest in Francey these days is confined to the welfare of her family."

"But you were in love with her once?"

He looked with a fixed gaze through the windscreen. "I prefer to call it an animal attraction. And flames like those die as suddenly as they flare. Being in love, now—" He swung to face her, eyeing her boldly. "You must agree that is a different emotion altogether. There must be a liking of the spirit too—"

He broke off. "Haven't you found it so?" His voice was now deliberately light. "Or perhaps you haven't been in love yet?"

Tina's gaze locked with his. She felt powerless, her breath gone. The long moment was unbearably tense. Then—"I don't know," she said lamely.

A shadow crossed his face. "You'll know, when the time comes." But his tone was abrupt to the point of coldness, and after she got out, his manoeuvering of the Land-Rover held a hint of savagery. Shaken, she found refuge in the house.

Though Tina wondered at intervals the next day how Rosie had fared with the health visitor, she was much too busy and absorbed on the dig to have time to make any inquiries, even if she had felt it wise to visit Quarry Farm again so soon.

Further intensive excavations had revealed without

doubt the outlines of a former Mithraeum temple, possibly rebuilt once and then destroyed in a later century. Chris was now sure enough of his discovery to allow news leakage to the press, and in the next few days it was expected that several eminent archaeologists would descend on the site to give advice and form opinions.

At supper that night both Tina and Carrie were tired. A day of alternating suspense and discovery, of feverish work and abnormal excitement, left them both drained and quiet. Adam had heard of the new discovery and shown a satisfactory if scarcely fanatical interest. But he also had news of his own to impart.

"I've just phoned the health visitor. It seems she gave Rosie a good going-over and discovered her tonsils and glands were in a pretty bad state. That little hussy must have concealed a good deal of pain at times. Anyway the upshot is hospital and the removal of her tonsils. The health visitor made no bones about it and it seems Rosie took it rather well."

"You mean she seemed to?" Tina asked. "Surely she's clever enough to conceal her feelings as well as her pain?"

He gave her an exasperated glance but remained silent.

"Poor little thing," said Carrie. "She must have suffered quite a lot. I suppose this was why she was eating badly?"

"Obviously. Also it seems the girl who sat beside her at school, Alice Tate, had the operation last year and made great drama out of it, thereby scaring Rosie more than ever. . . . A pity Matt or Francey hadn't the gumption to guess the trouble, but there it is. I admit myself there were times when the child seemed perfectly normal."

After the meal, Adam disappeared to his office and Carrie and Tina lingered over coffee. Tina thought the moment might be propitious to further Sandy's cause and mentioned the fancy dress dance again.

"When is it, Friday?" Carrie asked carelessly. "I said I might go, but would let him know the night before. He doesn't seem to understand just how involved I am with this terrific discovery at the dig. I wouldn't mind betting he's never heard of Mithras or his bull." Her tone was clearly derisive. "And when he does, he's sure to make some awful pun about it."

"It's just his way, Carrie. He says he can't seem to chat women up any other way—just has to tease them and make clumsy jokes."

"Well, he needn't practise on me," Carrie said decidedly.

"You might go to the dance, then?"

"I doubt it. But no harm in making him sweat a bit. Deserve him right for poking fun at the dig."

"Poor Sandy!"

"Poor Sandy, my foot!" Tina thought it best to desist.

On Thursday Carrie eventually sent Sandy a note begging to be excused from the dance.

Yet on the Friday evening, as she and Tina sat by the fire in her den, she seemed restless and kept alluding to it.

"After a day on the dig like we've had, it's just as well I didn't arrange to go," she said. "I'd have been a wet blanket."

Silence for a few minutes, then: "I don't say I'll never go to one of his dances, though. But I've too much on my mind at the moment."

They were both tired enough for bed by eleven o'clock, but the fire proved so soothing they lingered. It was nearly midnight when Carrie announced she would have a last cigaret and then go to bed.

She scrabbled in her bag. "Oh, blast! I haven't, have I? Yes, I have, though. Left my lighter on the dig. I know just where it is too—on a stone ledge in my section."

"It'll still be there in the morning, won't it?" Tina was surprised to see Carrie get up, obviously perturbed.

"I daresay. But I think I'll take a torch and find it now. I know you'll think I'm crazy, but I've had it a long time. It was a present."

Tina guessed at Lofty and understood. There would be no sleep for Carrie that night until the lighter was safe.

"Want me to come with you?" she asked.

"No, thanks. It's misty out. You'd better stay by the fire, or go to bed. Besides, you know me. I rather like the Wall after dark. I don't suppose I'll be above twenty minutes."

"I'll wait up for you," Tina said. She stretched out in her armchair, only now as she relaxed realizing how tired she was. She switched off the standard lamp. The clock ticked gently, the firelight danced off the shining models of Carrie's aeroplanes. Her eyes closed and she sank into a delicious state of half sleep.

She was awakened abruptly by the door crashing open. Carrie stood there, pale to the lips, yet with a triumphant shining in her eyes. Alarmed, Tina shook off her drowsiness.

"Carrie, what is it?"

Carrie shut the door and leaned against it, still in her old raincoat. She seemed to be struggling for breath. "I ran all the way home to tell you . . . I still don't believe it. But I saw it, Tina—saw it with my own eyes—"

Tina went over to her. "Carrie, please come and sit down. You've had a shock, haven't you?" She was more concerned than curious at that moment, intent on getting Carrie to a fireside chair and helping her off with her coat.

"A *shock*? I'll say I have!" Carrie leaned back and closed her eyes until her breathing came more evenly. When she sat up and looked at Tina again that shining triumph was still evident.

"I told you, didn't I," she said at last, "that things were seen along the Wall on moonlit nights that no one would believe. I'd always, hoped, dreamed, that some time that veil would lift and I would see something . . . but this!"

"But what, Carrie?" Tina knelt beside her, still concerned but now stirred to curiosity.

"I'll tell you, all in good time. Just give me a minute. Hand me those cigarets first. . . . Oh yes, I got my lighter all right. This happened afterwards—"

"Carrie, what *was* it?"

"I'm coming to it. I told you it was misty, didn't I? Well, so it is—ground mist in patches, actually, but the moonlight comes through quite clearly here and there. It was pretty eerie on the dig, I can tell you, with all those dark woods at the back. Only the sound of the wind in the trees and owls calling. I found my lighter first go off. Then I put my torch out—I don't quite know why." Carrie gazed at her in what was almost despair. "The trouble is you'll never believe it, never in a million years. But I swear I saw it. You know me—I'm not one of your hysterical sort."

She took another drag at her cigaret. "I was just standing there, on the west side of the dig, looking at the Wall. You know how it humps up over the rise there, then disappears into the hollow and then you see it climbing up to the sky again over Ewe Hill?"

"Yes, yes."

"It was there I saw him." Carrie's voice dropped in awe. "A white figure on top of the Wall, marching down the slope from Ewe Hill."

"A—figure?" A shiver ran like a mouse down Tina's spine.

"Yes, but that's not all. I was petrified from the first because he seemed to be wearing a helmet. The moonlight picked out the flash of the metal. Then he disappeared into the dip. It took him a few minutes to walk that bit. I just couldn't move. I don't think I even breathed. Then—Oh, my God—" she covered her face. "I wanted to run, Tina, but I was rooted there. He—he breasted the rise of the Wall and came down the bit where it joins the northwest corner of the dig. He—he was a Roman soldier, Tina—a sentry. I even recognized the uniform. The First Cohort of Tungrians—you know they were stationed at Housesteads."

Tina gazed at her, speechless.

"The First Cohort of Tungrians!" she repeated dazedly.

"That's right. The helmet, the folding of the toga, the breastplates and the crossed sandals . . . Tina, how do you think I felt? I couldn't see his face properly. He was just like a wraith under the moon, but I could hear his feet—this was the most eerie thing—just the sound of his feet marching. And then—he left the Wall where it crumbles away and just walked on along its line, into the woods. . . . Don't you *see*, Tina, what I saw was the ghost of a Roman sentry—" Carrie's voice sunk in awe—"patrolling the Wall between Housesteads and Chesters, just as he must have done sixteen centuries ago."

"A ghost, Carrie?" Tina was still trying to cope with utter disbelief.

"What else? Oh, this'll beat everything Everard-Kipps says he's seen. He'll never better this."

Tina shook her head. "I don't get it—Carrie, are you *sure*?"

"Meaning you think I dreamed it all." Carrie shook her head. "You've got to take my word for it—I saw him plain as if—as if he'd been on television." She turned to the telephone. "I've a good mind to ring Everard-Kipps now. He's never in bed until the small hours. . . ."

While Carrie, still breathless and starry-eyed, began to dial, Tina was conscious of a strange disquiet. There was something teasing her mind, some connection with a part of Carrie's story. But it wouldn't come. . . .

Neither could she rid herself of a strong sensation of trouble in the air. Even Carrie's understandable hurry to contact the pompous Everard-Kipps seemed unwise.

"Is that George Everard-Kipps? . . . Yes, I'll hang on."

Tina seized her arm. "Carrie, should you? I mean—just now, when you're so worked up about it. In the morning you—"

Carrie gave her a withering glance. "You think I'll call myself all kinds of a stooge in the morning, thinking I dreamed it all. Oh no, Tina—now, please, I'm trying to speak. . . . George, is that you? Carrie here. Now, just hold your horses. I've got something that'll really give you copy for the *North Tyne Chronicle*—"

Tina gave up and left the room, still oddly disturbed. Most ghosts, she believed, had a rational explanation. And there was still that strong feeling that something about Carrie's story rang a distant bell of recognition.

But no, she couldn't think what it was. . . .

She decided to leave Carrie to Everard-Kipps and go to bed. Half way up the stairs Adam hailed her from the office door. "What was all the excitement about?"

The door of Carrie's den was a little open, and the heightened pitch of her voice, though not the words, must have reached him.

"Carrie—well, she made another discovery. She'll probably tell you herself." No point in spoiling Carrie's story, she considered.

"Oh, you mean on the dig?" He shrugged resignedly. "I just wondered. . . . Goodnight, Tina."

"Goodnight."

Tina slept badly, haunted by Carrie's ghost, by a host of possible explanations, and still with that teasing knowledge that somewhere there was a tiny clue.

She woke early, reminded herself it was Saturday. And last night was Friday. . . .

And then, in a flash, she knew! There could be no lying in bed now. The house was still quiet as she ran downstairs, the dew heavy on the lawns as she ran toward the woods. She was glad to see Sandy's chimney smoke against the trees. Her tap at the door brought him out, pipe in hand.

"Hallo, pet! What's up?"

Tina was breathless from running. "Can I come in a minute? It's—important. Something about Carrie."

"Not hurt—ill?" She saw fear settle in his vivid blue eyes.

"No, she's fine."

"Better come in, pet, and have a cup of tea. I'm just busy with my breakfast." He moved the newly-opened copy of the *North Tyne Chronicle* and set out another mug.

"There, and help yourself to sugar. Sit down, hinney. You're all of a shake. . . . Why, you're laughing. What is it—some kind of a joke?"

Tina controlled herself. "Sandy—last night, did you go to the fancy dress dance—on your own?"

"Why, aye! I was playing there. I'd promised to give a turn on the pipes while the band had their supper."

"And you went dressed up? As a Roman soldier?"

"That's right." His eyes glowed, then faded. "It was to be a surprise for Carrie. Yon book you saw—"

"I know, Sandy, I know." Tina groaned. "That's how I guessed—I remembered it was open at a page of Roman uniforms—"

"Aye, and it looked a treat, pet. Here, look—"

He snatched up the paper. Tina's mouth was twitching almost uncontrollably, to Sandy's amazement.

"Just a minute," she begged, pushing the paper aside. "Did you walk along the Wall—over Ewe Hill?"

He stared. "Aye, I did. And I'll tell you why, though it beats me how you know. My old car conked out at Dyke Farm crossroads, and I couldn't get her started, so I just left her there and took the quick cut home. It was wet underfoot, and I just had yon cardboard Roman sandals I'd made—left my own shoes in the car. So I got up on the Wall for drier walking."

Tina made a strangled sound and hid her streaming eyes. "Oh, Sandy, you don't know what you've done!"

"What do you mean, pet?" He was alarmed now.

"Only that Carrie went to the dig last night, to find a lighter she'd lost. And she *saw* you!"

Sandy sat transfixed, his mug poised in the air.

"Don't you *see*—" Tina pleaded almost hysterically. "She saw you, but she had no idea it was you. How could she? She thought you were the ghost of a Roman sentry. I just guessed what had happened this morning, but I'm too late, anyway. Last night she rang up that man on the *North Tyne Chronicle*—"

Sandy set down his mug with a crash. His mouth dropped open. "Oh no, hinney!"

"That's why I'm here," Tina hurried on, still fighting a threatening convulsion of laughter. "If you keep quiet about it—about your fancy dress, I mean, there's just a chance she won't hear about it—"

"But it's too late, pet!" he exploded. "Look here!"

He folded the paper and handed it over. Under the caption 'Fancy Dress at Elswhistle' was a picture of some of the revellers, Sandy well to the fore in his Roman outfit. The smaller print read: "One of the most striking costumes was that of Mr. Sandy Armstrong, dressed as a Roman legionary. . . ."

"Oh no!" Tina slumped back in her chair.

Sandy took the paper from her, sat folding it with intense concentration, then raised his eyes to hers. A wild merriment sparked between them. Sandy threw back his head and roared. Tina ached and choked along with him.

"It's so f-funny and yet so awful," she gasped at last. "Poor Carrie, if it gets out that you were her ghost she'll be the butt of the district."

"Aye, she will." He sobered again. "And if I know it, I've put paid to my chances now. This'll finish her with me." He began to look positively gloomy.

"But it wasn't your fault." Tina too had controlled herself by now and was all ruefulness.

"It wasn't my fault—and yet it was. For I planned a surprise for her, and it was a surprise she got, right enough. Only the wrong kind." He paused a moment. "Do you get the *Chronicle* up at the house?"

"I'm afraid so. And Carrie always reads it at breakfast."

"Couldn't you make away with it? Lose it or summat?"

"No use. Isa has her own copy and *she* rakes it from cover to cover. It's sure to get out one way or the other. Better let her know and get over it."

"Aye, maybe that's best." He gave Tina a resigned grin. "It'll maybe teach her to come to the dances when she's asked. . . . I'll tell you another funny thing. It was because I was that disappointed she hadn't come I left the dance early. A trick of fate, you might say."

Tina got up to go. "Poor old Sandy! And you meant so well."

"Aye, but that's poor comfort. Here now, you'd best be away. It doesn't do to be seen visiting a bachelor before breakfast. I wouldn't like you to get yourself talked about. Oh, and Tina, if you get the chance, tell her I'm right sorry, and that I'll be seeing her to explain."

Tina nodded and left the cottage. Her feet dragged on the return journey and she walked into the dining-room in some dread. Her worst expectations were fulfilled. Carrie, with a face of doom, was staring at the photograph in the *North Tyne Chronicle*, while Adam supported himself against the sideboard, wiping his eyes, his broad shoulders heaving.

"Carrie, you'll be the death of me! First Cohort of Tungrians, eh? A Roman sentry doing guard duty! And all he probably had was an old sheet and some cooking foil!"

"I tell you it was misty!" Carrie slammed the paper down, turned to Tina. "And what are *you* smirking about? Now, wait a minute. Wait a *minute*! Last night . . . did you know?"

"Not then. It was this morning I remembered about Sandy having a book on Roman uniforms—and about it being the fancy dress dance last night—"

Adam's shoulders heaved again.

"He'd planned it to please you, Carrie," Tina pleaded.

"Please me!" Carrie echoed, her face crimson. "Why, the great stupid, blithering stooge! I'll never speak to him again as long as I live—and that'll be too soon! To think I told the whole tale to Everard-Kipps! Wait till he sees that photo. He'll spread it all over the district—"

She broke off, lost for words. Mopping his eyes, Adam sat down. "Poor old Carrie! And it couldn't have happened to a nicer person. But you're right, of course." His tones were mock-solemn. "This'll go down in Wall history for all time. You'll be a local legend!"

"And don't you start!" she threatened. "It was bad enough babbling the whole thing to you—and then you had to open the paper and show me *that* . . . and you may be sure that phone'll go any minute—Everard-Kipps trying to gloat. There, what did I tell you! I shall let Isa answer it."

Tina's eyes were drawn to Adam's, almost reluctantly. The depths of laughter there attracted her. His welling sense of humor, growing as the situation deepened, marched along with her own. She had to whip her gaze away before disgracing herself by further laughter which could only have hurt Carrie.

"You haven't started your breakfast, Carrie. Have some coffee," she urged.

"Couldn't eat or drink a thing."

Adam gave Tina an approving glance. "Tina's right. Come on, Carrie, it'll only be a nine days' wonder, after all. Worse things happen at sea."

"Yes, but you don't have to live through the nine days. If ever a woman put up—"

Isa poked her head round the door. "It was yon man, Everard-Kipps. I'd my egg on frying, so I told him you were still in bed."

"Good old Isa!" said Carrie.

"No texts this morning?" As Isa disappeared again Adam's mouth twitched. "If Isa only knew what an opportunity she missed for improving the occasion. A little something from the Epistle to the Romans, perhaps?"

He ducked as a bread roll flew violently in his direction.

"I know you're my employer, Adam Copeland," Carrie glared, "but there comes a time—"

"Oh, do please feel perfectly free to cast your bread upon the waters." He grinned again. "Sorry, Carrie, I just couldn't resist it."

Carrie looked about to explode, but suddenly collapsed into hysterical laughter. "It's no use . . . I've just got to see the funny side. S-silver paper helmet and a cardboard spear—but why in heaven's name was he walking the Wall?"

"To keep his f-feet dry!" Tina explained in a smothered voice, and filled in further details. This time all three were overcome again. Isa brought in the post and stood watching them in amazement, almost deafened by Adam's deep diapason of laughter, Carrie's gasping yelps and Tina's uncontrolled giggles.

"The post's come!" Isa shouted. And as no one responded she drew herself up, intoning:

"As the crackling of thorns under a pot, so is the laughter of the fool. Ecclesiastes!" She slammed the door behind her.

This convulsed them all again. But at last Carrie subsided.

"There now, no one can say I can't laugh at myself! But that doesn't mean I've forgiven him. He needn't come round me any more with his pipes and 'Cushie Butterfield'."

"But, Carrie, he *did* ask you to the dance," Adam reminded her. "If you'd gone—"

"Well, I didn't." Something in her tone made Tina straighten her face. Carrie pushed back her plate, showing a lightning change of mood. "It's not being made to look a fool I mind so much—people think I'm pretty odd as it is."

"What do you mind, then?" Adam demanded. He too had sensed Carrie's sudden depression.

Carrie sat staring at the table. "For years now I've wished for three things. One was to make a big find on a dig. . . . Well, that happened with the Mithraeum temple. The second was to have a psychic experience on the Wall—to catch a glimpse of the past. And last night, it seemed I'd got my wish, that the veil of the centuries had been lifted and. . . ." She paused. "Instead I've made an all-time fool of myself, falling for some old tinfoil and a cardboard spear. . . . Well, now I know, don't I? Miracles don't just happen in this day and age. Least of all to me."

She threw down her napkin, snatched a handkerchief from her pocket and blew her nose furiously.

"And the third wish?" Adam asked quietly. But Carrie had gone blindly from the room.

His gaze met Tina's. "And just what was all that about?" He sounded genuinely bewildered.

Tina shook her head. But she thought she knew, for all that. The third wish concerned Lofty. And Carrie might well have reasoned that if the spirit of a long-dead legionary could come to life, there might still be a chance of the third miracle—the return of Lofty.

But she said nothing. "Poor Carrie," Adam said musingly. "We weren't too unkind, were we?" And his look plainly told her that in that shared laughter they had entered into a strange new fellowship of feeling, that for those few hilarious moments she had been one with him in mood and enjoyment.

She shook her head. "I think Carrie knew we were laughing *with* her, not at her."

"Exactly. I felt sure you would have given anything not to have to tell her. But she'd already found out, as it happened." He paused. "We must all make a bit of a fuss of her until she's over it. Heaven knows, she deserves it."

Tina had told herself exactly the same. And as Adam left the room she felt a distinct sense of loss. How near they were to each other in many things, after all. Yet the difference that separated them was as wide and deep as ever. No superficial understanding could really bridge it.

A few days passed in which Carrie was notably quiet and made no further reference to the unfortunate "haunting". That George Everard-Kipps had spread the story was only too evident, for Isa heard it from the travelling butcher, who got it down at the Brown Cow where it was relayed to a fascinated saloon bar by a sales representative from Hexham, who had heard it in the County Hotel.

Whether Carrie had seen Sandy and had it out with him was another matter, but she revealed nothing and Tina respected her silence while at the same time following Adam's injunction to "make a fuss of·her".

Carrie had endured the extra attentions for a day and a half, then rounded on Tina quite fiercely. "Oh, for Pete's sake, girl, I'm not ill. Stop dancing attendance. All right, so I've got things on my mind. It doesn't make me a drooling invalid, does it?"

"Sorry, Carrie."

"I'm the one who should be sorry—just a crotchety stupid woman with middle-aged fancies. That's what they'll be saying, you know. It's her *age*—"

"Why, Carrie, age has never worried you, has it? You always said you were as young as you feel."

"Quite right, so I did. Well now I feel about a hundred. I can't even get excited about the Mithraeum temple right now. And no wonder, when I've upset one of the best men who ever—"

She broke off, conscious of having said more than she intended.

It was a bright spring evening, the colored moor calling to Tina with all its freedom. White-winged peewits wheeled over the undulating distances, and fat lambs grazed peaceably with their mothers beside the unfenced track. She decided to walk to Quarry Farm and find out for herself how Rosie was reacting to the hospital plan.

To her surprise she found the house and farmyard deserted, though the back door was well ajar. Jamey and Francey's absence was understandable at that hour of the evening, and the twins must be out playing. Possibly Matt had gone to round them up.

She called softly up the stairs of the pigeon loft, just in case he was quietly awaiting the return of some of his birds. No answer came, but there was a flash of white wings over her head. A snowy pigeon had just fluttered through the bob-stays into the trap.

Odd, Tina thought, as no bell gave warning. Matt couldn't have been expecting this bird, then. Was it a stray from a previous race, perhaps? So many things could happen to delay a pigeon, she knew.

She ran up the stone stairs and into the loft. Just as she had seen Matt do, she threw a handful of maize to the birds clustered in the trap. As they picked daintily she slipped in her hand and carefully lifted the white pigeon. For without doubt there was a tiny message roll attached to one pink leg.

Tina detached the strip of paper, gently replaced the pigeon and closed the door of the trap. Perhaps the message would solve the mystery of the lone bird. The slip of paper was only one inch wide by three long, and held a very short message. Yet Tina's gaze remained transfixed for some minutes.

"Dear Matt," she read, "I'll watch it, don't worry. Love, Helen."

Her heart seemed to contract. Helen and Matt, after all!

And this was how they kept in touch!

It was fantastic, yet so simple. By this means, centuries old, Matt had continued an effortless communication with Helen despite Adam's policing methods. Matt need only send a basket of pigeons up to the farm with Jamey, whose deliveries would go unremarked, and Helen could launch a bird at any time from the farm buildings.

She remembered that other message Matt had read here, how he had lied over it. Still rigid, her mind racing, she saw again the creamy flutter of wings over the Thornriggs trees. So that was how Matt knew she had been there. Pigeons could fly faster than a car could ride.

Come to that . . . Tina counted the narrow pecking heads of the birds. Yes, three of them were strange to her. Matt would certainly have told her of any new acquisitions, so these could be pigeons from Turret Farm, forming a two-way system. . . .

A shadow fell beside her. With a little cry she spun round. Matt had come silently up the stairs in old canvas shoes. He leaned against the wall just inside the door, his chest heaving as if he had been running.

"I saw the bird from over the moor." He held out his hand. "And I'll thank you for that message, Tina. You'd no right to read it." He took the slip, read it at a glance and twisted it up.

"I know that—now." A chill stole over her at the cold anger in his eyes. She backed clumsily against the trap, causing a rubbery commotion of wings. "I was curious—I just thought it was race news. You once told me—"

"Aye, I did. Well, now you know."

Her chill was now a distinct nausea. "You—and Helen? And you were Bruno's friend, or professed to be."

He eyed her steadily, his gaze still kindled. "Think what you like. Remember I knew her long before you Rutherfords ever set foot on the Wall."

"But she was *engaged* to Bruno!"

"That doesn't mean she has to give up old friends, does it?" There was a certain chosen deliberation about the words.

"I still can't believe it." She found herself trembling. "You both deceived him, all along."

Matt shook his head. "It wasn't really like that, Tina. You don't understand."

"Then *tell* me." She was tearful now. "Matt, you don't mean you're hiding something from me about Bruno?"

He shook his head.

"You lied to me before. How do I know what is the truth now?"

"My first loyalty is to Helen—try to understand that, Tina. And believe me, I hated lying to you—you of all people. But a promise is a promise."

"And you're meeting here—still seeing her?"

He shrugged. "Don't read more into that note than it actually says."

"Perhaps I can read between the lines." She still felt weak and shaken, but struggled to calm herself. "Matt, you know I can't keep quiet about this, don't you—that I've got to tell Adam Copeland. You must realize I've got to notch up one thing on Bruno's side. Adam believes Helen to be blameless. Now I can prove she isn't. Can't you see how important this is to me?"

"I see only one thing." Matt lowered himself to a box and folded his arms about the knees of his faded jeans. "You can tell him about the pigeons and the message, yes. What you can't do is prove I had anything to do with Helen while she was engaged to Bruno. . . . Well, can you?"

"No, I can't." Tina felt her weak knees would scarcely support her any longer. She too pulled up a box and crouched there, still with that clenching chill in her body. "But Adam's no fool. If there's more to learn he'll get it out of you."

Matt made an impatient sound. "*You* might think he always wins. Not with me he doesn't. . . . All right, Tina, you tell him. But I warn you you might send Helen back to square one as far as her health is concerned."

Tina stared. "Why, is she so frightened of her brother?"

"No, it's not that." Matt's head drooped over his bare arms. The sunlight picked out the fine fair hairs running in a groove from wrist to elbow. "Tina, when you were a kid did you ever play that game with the pile of matches—where you had to pull out the bottom one without disturbing the others?"

Wondering, she nodded.

"Well, that's just what you'll be doing if you tell Adam Copeland about that message. And believe me, Tina, the pile won't stand. It'll topple about all our ears."

He stood up. "You'd better go. And I'd advise you to think hard before you say anything. Think hard, Tina. And I'm not asking you for my sake—remember that."

She stumbled to her feet, gave him a long look of doubt and misery, then brushed blindly past him and down the steps.

She scarcely remembered her walk across the moor. In the hall at Hadrian's Edge, still flustered and shocked, she almost blundered into Adam, who had stooped to caress the dog.

"Hallo, you're in a tearing hurry! I don't think supper will be ready yet." He smiled at her. "Isa had an upsetting interview with a gipsy at the back door and has already burned one batch of potatoes."

"Yes, I can smell them." Tina lingered politely, yet longed to escape to her room.

"I've got news for you," he went on. "I've just been on the phone to Helen's doctor. It seems she has made so much improvement she can come home next week."

"Oh!" Tina's heart raced.

"Unless, of course, she happened to have a setback," he finished.

CHAPTER SIX

"So this means," Tina stammered, "you won't want me to stay at Hadrian's Edge after next week?"

Adam straightened, gave her a long direct look. "Whatever put that idea into your head?"

"I thought you didn't wish Helen and me to meet?"

"While she was ill, no. There's no reason now why you

shouldn't. She's made such progress that the risk of upsetting her is over. That is, of course, if you behave as I fully expect you will, making every consideration for her position." It was the old domination in full sway.

"And if I don't?"

His eyebrows lifted, creasing his forehead in a way she found unbearably endearing. "If you don't? But that won't arise. Your sense of a guest's responsibilities has always been acute—with perhaps a few exceptions." Tina knew he meant the two abortive attempts to reach Turret House. "Of course"—he paused—"you may prefer to leave. If so I shall be very sorry, but that's something you must decide for yourself.

Sorry. . . . He would be sorry. She nursed the thought, all others scattering before it.

"Well?" There was something of impatience in his tone.

"I should like to stay, thank you."

"Good!" He walked into his office, leaving her confused and uncertain. Why had he assumed she might want to leave? Because her efforts on Bruno's behalf had failed? Yet something told her she was so near the solution. Perhaps she could persuade Matt to tell her more. Even Helen herself might reveal something of the truth.

She escaped to her room with much food for thought. What exactly was Matt's relationship to Helen? And what did Adam really feel about his sister's return, with all its attendant responsibilities?

With a sinking heart she realized that Hadrian's Edge would never be quite the same again, that Helen's return would destroy the magic which for her had grown about this house. For the girl whom Bruno had loved was still a stranger to her, would seem almost an interloper. It was unreasonable, unfair, but she couldn't help her feelings.

Next day on the dig she sought out Chris and asked if she could lunch with him. "I've brought sandwiches," she explained. "Something's happened, Chris—something I think you ought to know."

Chris, who was abnormally busy at his rough table in

the tarpaulin shelter overlooking the site, looked at her first unseeingly. Before him was a welter of photographs, drawings, unanswered correspondence and labelled objects from the dig.

"You'll be lucky!" he said at last. "I don't know that I'll be having any lunch. I'm up to the eyes with this lot. Then I've got that expert on Mithraeum lore coming at eleven, and another study group from the museums after that. The new is spreading, you know. Everyone wants to be in on it. As it is I've had to leave supervision of that last layer to Carrie—though I'd give anything to be down there using a trowel instead. . . ." He ran a hand through his hair. "Is it really important, Tina?"

"I think so."

"Well, I'll try to spare you ten minutes. I suppose I've got to eat. Now run away, there's a good girl."

Tina was not unduly despondent. She knew that the last week or so had been a crucial point in Chris's career, that on his handling depended the whole success of the excavation. He was doing not only his share of the work but Bruno's too, she reminded herself, and freely forgave him for his impatience with her personal problems in the immediate past. Even he must see the importance of her discovery concerning Matt.

Near lunch-time she kept an eye on Chris, who eventually disentangled himself from a visiting group of archaeologists and waved her over to a group of boulders above the site. It was a dull day, with a hint of rain on the wind. They sat facing the vast saucer of the Tyne Valley, watching the laden clouds drift over the far fells.

"Well, what's all the mystery about?" Chris produced his own sandwiches and a can of light ale.

"I told you, it's something about Bruno—well, Helen, anyway."

His glance was almost exasperated, she thought. "You're not still fretting yourself to a shadow over that business, Tina? I thought you'd had time to get over all that."

She was shocked. "Why, have you?"

He said firmly, "I've already told you it's best to let the

whole scandal die a natural death—and kinder to Bruno in the end.''

"But you wouldn't close your mind to new evidence, surely?"

He frowned. "You're talking like something out of Agatha Christie . . . new evidence?" He gave her closer attention. "Just what have you been up to, young Tina?"

"It's about pigeons," Tina said, hoping by shock treatment to jerk him into awareness.

"*Pigeons!*"

She detailed the events at Quarry Farm. He listened in patient silence, then said:

"But surely Matt's right? What does it prove after all—the existence at one time of a boy and girl affair, which could have flared up again—possibly because Helen was lonely and unhappy. Why should it have any connection with Bruno? Helen certainly wasn't interested in anyone else while he was around. And *I* should know. I saw them together often enough."

"But we don't *know*."

Chris drank some beer, attacked another sandwich. "What can you do about it, anyway? Tell Adam Copeland?"

"I don't see why he shouldn't know. But Helen's coming back next week, and he warned me not to upset her. It's put me in rather a fix . . . oh, and I forgot to tell you, Chris. Matt said such a queer thing. He warned me that if I told Helen Copeland it would be like that old game with the matches—pulling out the bottom one of the pile and having the lot collapse."

Chris lowered his beer-can. "A bit fanciful, isn't it?"

"He was serious, Chris. Now I'm more than ever convinced that Helen has a lot to hide."

"And that's all?"

"All?" She was puzzled.

"All you have to tell me? Is this the end of Revelations, so to speak?" he joked mildly.

"Why, yes. Isn't it enough?" She began to eat her own sandwiches, relieved to have the telling over.

"I'd say it was a very small storm in a teacup—and

that Matt's probably right. Better to leave well alone."

"He doesn't need to be cleared in our eyes, Tina." Chris laid a compelling hand on her arm. "And you say Helen's coming home? You've got to consider *her* feelings."

"I've told you, I've already been warned about that." There was bitterness in her voice.

"You *are* a guest in their house, remember."

"I'm not likely to forget that. It still doesn't mean the truth has to be smothered."

"And what is the truth?" he shrugged. "You'll probably never know. Why not be content to leave things as they are?"

"And you were Bruno's best friend?"

She saw a sadness in his eyes. "Yes, I was. Maybe I'm not living up to your conception of me, Tina. But I never pretended to be perfect. Perhaps you just expected too much. Men are much more inclined to let things alone. We haven't women's curiosity or their urge to keep probing. It seemed much more important to take over Bruno's work here, to see he got due recognition for his investigations. Right?"

"I suppose so." She got up, feeling the chill of the wind matching that of her own heart. "I suppose you think I'm being silly and hysterical—and—well, over-dramatic about all this. But I'd rather be that way than the way you are. It seems so cold-blooded, even if it is sensible."

Chris glanced at his watch, cast a comprehensive glance over the dig. The workers, lunch over, were returning to their sections, the bright anoraks and sweaters vivid dots of color against sable earth and yellow-trodden grass.

"Well, we won't go on about it. Time I was back on the job." He got to his feet. "No hard feelings, Tina?" And he gave her his old patient smile.

"No hard feelings," she said mechanically, and watched his tall figure running in his loose-limbed way down to the dig.

She had achieved nothing, after all. Chris had always been a man who abided by his first decisions. Whether she liked it or not, she was still very much on her own. . . .

A restless, uneasy week followed. Feeling she had better stay away from Quarry Farm for the present, Tina spent some evenings in Carrie's borrowed car, visiting as yet unseen stretches of the western Wall.

She explored the Nine Nicks of Thirlwall, where the craggy ridge carrying the Wall was broken into successive peaks and depressions. Actually she counted only seven, and remembered that Adam had told her two had been destroyed by intensive quarrying.

Another evening she went as far as Gilsland, the pleasant little town on the river Irthing, where the Poltross Burn flowed through a deep gorge to form the boundary between Northumberland and Cumberland. At Willowford she found the beginnings of the turf wall, which from this point had stretched to the Solway coast, only at a later date having been replaced by stone to match the eastern section.

From Birdoswald she climbed to the outpost fort of Bewcastle, a thousand feet high on Gillalees beacon, which had once housed a thousand legionaries. But her greatest thrill was to see the Quarry at Coombe Crag where some excavating legionaries had carved their names in the living rock.

It was a private and exhilarating experience, to have her cardboard Wall come to life in a thousand ways. Yet she knew, even as one evening she drove the whole way to the Wall's western outpost on the Solway Sands, that for her one stretch of the Wall would always have an emotional rather than a historical significance—the section from Chesters to Housesteads, the country of Hadrian's Edge.

Toward the end of the week the weather, which had been kind to her expeditions, changed from brilliant to dull days, with blustery winds and cold lashing rain which cast spring into a mere memory. During a break between showers, feeling she needed fresh air, Tina turned westwards through the woods.

At the little dell before Sandy's cottage she found Rosie crouched by the burn, sailing paper boats. The child looked chilled and disconsolate, she thought, her red knitted hood clashing horribly with her delicate hair and coloring. She reflected that she had never seen the child prettily dressed. Obviously Francey put all her efforts to her own adornment

"Hallo, Rosie. Isn't it cold for you to be playing out?"

Rosie scowled. "I don't care." She stood up, kicking at the mossy bank with a rubber-booted foot. "Where are you off to, Tina?"

"Just for a walk. Like to come?"

She shook her head. "Matt'll get mad if I'm late for supper. He's always chasing me up since yon health visitor came."

"But you'll soon be better now," Tina said gently. "They'll have you right in no time, when you go to hospital."

Rosie's face registered a quick range of emotions. "I've told them, I don't want to go. My throat's better. It's no' aching any more."

Tina felt she had better not pursue the subject. "How's Daring Denise these days?" she asked.

Rosie's face brightened. "Last week she was in the desert, on a camel, an' she found buried treasure an' then she was kidnapped by a desert tribe, on'y she was too smart for them. She wriggled out under the tent an' found an English laddie who was a prisoner too, an' they trekked across the desert wi' on'y one bottle o' water, then they found a lot o' British soldiers in a jeep, an' got to ride with them all the way to their camp. An' the soldiers, they made Denise their *pin-up*!"

"She certainly gets around," Tina smiled. A rough buffet of wind came. Rosie shivered. "I'd best be off home, Tina."

"Yes, I think you should. And, Rosie, you won't worry about the hospital, will you? I had to go into one once, when I was your age. And you know what, I didn't want to come home again."

Rosie looked dubious. "You must have been daft!" was her ungracious reply as she jumped the burn and ran up the opposite slope.

Tina walked on toward Sandy's cottage, feeling she had made little impression. She ached for Rosie, bearing all a child's unreasoning fears without much adult understanding. She had hoped recently that she had made progress, that the little girl trusted her, but today there had been a return to the old defiant sullenness. There didn't seem much she could do until the hospital stay was over. She could only hope that Rosie's attitude would change once she settled into the ward.

As she reached Sandy's cottage she heard a drumming on the window. Next moment his tall figure appeared in the doorway.

"Tina, can you spare a minute?"

She was glad of the distraction, curious too, for she had not seen Sandy since the debacle of the fancy dress dance. He asked her in, offered her a welcome glass of cider, but seemed a little slow in coming to the point.

"Shouldn't your Australian lodger be here?" she asked. "I thought this was his week."

"Oh aye, he's here. Just gone down to the Brown Cow." Sandy drummed his large fingers on the table. "And how's Carrie?"

Tina hesitated. "Haven't you seen her—since—"

"Aye, I saw her. . . . But there, she was angry and fretting. I wouldn't judge her by what she said *then*, on the spur of the moment, you might say. And it did her good to get it off her chest." But he seemed troubled. "Maybe she was right, at that. I should have told her about the fancy dress, not left it as a surprise. The worst surprise she ever had, you might say."

"I shouldn't worry too much," she comforted him. "Carrie isn't the kind to carry a grudge for long."

He nodded, and after what appeared to be some kind of struggle with himself, said: "Does she still go on about yon Air Force bloke she lost in the war?"

"She mentions him sometimes. I don't suppose she'll ever really forget him—unless perhaps something happened to disenchant her."

Sandy set down his mug and asked: "What was his name again—some kind of nickname, wasn't it?"

"Yes—Lofty, because he was tall. But his real name was—wait a minute—oh yes, Laurence Ames."

Sandy's speech now seemed to have deserted him altogether. He sat tracing imaginary patterns on the table with a hefty forefinger.

"I shouldn't worry about Lofty," Tina assured him. "I've always thought that if enough time goes by Carrie will realize she can't live on dreams."

"Aye, but you see, pet, thime's just what we're both short of. We're not young any more. It would be a good thing now, wouldn't it, if she could find out whether he was alive or dead?"

Tina nodded. "But it's not very likely to happen, is it?"

"You never know. But there, I mustn't keep you. You'll be wanting to be away to your supper."

Tina was puzzled. Something seemed to be stirring in Sandy's brain, but she couldn't guess what, unless he was thinking of having inquiries made regarding Lofty. And after such a passage of years, his chances of success must be pretty hopeless.

At supper that evening Adam spoke of Rosie's hospital admission. "I've advised Francey and Matt to keep a close eye on her, just in case she gets second thoughts."

"Think she'll disappear again?" Carrie asked.

"It could happen, knowing Rosie. Though it might turn out to be no more than a token gesture. I can't see her really running away. She's quite a timid child at heart despite her tough ways."

Tina was not so sure. Rosie was also a child of unreasoning fears, which might be strong enough to drive her to reckless acts.

Adam turned to her. "You don't seem to get to Quarry Farm much these days. Got tired of slumming, or is Matt boring you with his pigeons?" His eyes were mild but searching.

His mention of the pigeons was unfortunate, disturbing as it did her confused mass of doubts and perplexities regarding Matt.

"Neither!" She spoke rather shortly. "I've just been doing other things."

"Oh, I thought you might have been—disenchanted?"

This was so near the truth Tina was startled. It had been hurtful to know Matt had deceived her, that their friendship was surely ended and that she was now alone. She was glad when Isa burst in with the pudding and caused a diversion.

"Yon lodger of Sandy Armstrong's has come all the way from Australia," she announced. "Just to have a look at the Wall! My, some folks have queer ways o' spending their money."

She set down the pudding before Carrie, but continued to hover. Adam looked up expectantly, a quirk at his mouth. Sure enough Isa drew herself up and intoned in a pulpit voice: "As a bird who wandereth from her nest, so is a man who wandereth from his place."

Carrie said sharply: "All right, Isa. I don't know that I'm in the mood for texts tonight."

Tina had never heard her sound so bitter. There was disillusion everywhere, she told herself. Carrie's belief in miracles had certainly been shaken by Sandy's blunder. And perhaps Isa's text had conjured up visions of a lost or wandering Lofty, never to be found this side of eternity.

Isa glared at Carrie. "A good text never did a body any harm." She added triumphantly: "I doubt you'll find that pudding's caught on a bit."

"I had noticed," Carrie said drily.

Adam intervened smoothly: "My grandmother used to assure me that the burnt skin was the best part. All right, Isa, thank you."

When Isa had gone, he turned to Carrie. "That wasn't like you."

"No, it wasn't, was it?" Carrie pushed back her chair. "Maybe I'm just disenchanted too."

"What, with a splendid Mithraeum temple only just uncovered? Don't tell me you're tired of archaeology?"

"No, of course not. . . . With life, perhaps." The last words were uttered almost inaudibly. She rose abruptly and left the room. Adam and Tina exchanged glances.

"I think Carrie needs a holiday," he said. "Not only has she spurned the pudding, she's forgotten to serve it."

"I'll do it." Tina took over, strangely moved at being able to do him this humble service.

They finished their meal almost in silence, yet she was intensely aware of his presence at the head of the table. The silence soon held an electric quality that was almost unbearable. At last he broke it.

"We won't be so quiet next week, with Helen home."

"Why, does she make her presence felt?"

He grinned faintly. "You could say so. She's restless, never settles long to one thing. And when she's bored she plays Rimsky-Korsakov records at full belt."

"Oh," said Tina politely.

"Of course she may be more subdued after her illness." She thought his face suddenly shadowed and wondered again just how much of a burden the wilful Helen had been on his life. Possibly the reason he had never married. . . .

He went on, more vigorously: "I hope you two will hit it off. I know *you* are too generous not to try, at least."

Tina felt a little suffocated. Generous—he thought her generous?

"Carrie thinks the world of you," he continued. "It's not every young woman who will bother to understand an older one. And I have a hunch Carrie needs understanding at the present time. But I hope Helen will be deserving of your friendship too."

"Do you?" she said bleakly. The prospect dismayed her. Nothing she had learned of Helen's ways had produced in her much enthusiasm.

Perhaps he sensed something of this, for an awkward silence fell. She was aware of a heaviness of spirit in him, and when she had poured his coffee he excused himself and took it along to the office, his expression forbidding.

She watched him go forlornly. Once more she thought, nothing will ever be the same again when Helen comes. . . .

After a while she roused herself and took the coffee tray along to Carrie's den. As she had hoped, the older woman was quite composed again and welcomed the coffee. She even remarked, rather gruffly, as she changed the position of a gleaming Spitfire: "I hope you didn't take any notice of what I said in there. I'm getting childish, if you ask me."

Composed Carrie might be, but her strange mood had not really passed. Tina longed to do something to help, never guessing that the moment was almost at hand, or of what earth-shaking proportions it was to be.

The following morning Adam dictated his letters as usual. He seemed in a brisk no-nonsense mood, looking more rugged than usual in the thick tweeds and heavy boots he wore in readiness to attend a ploughing demonstration on one of the distant farms. There were none of the usual pleasant comments or snatches of local gossip. Yet Tina felt it was no reflection on her, but rather that he had things on his mind. Helen again, she guessed.

"That's it, then. Oh, and if Sharp calls tell him where I am. And the sawmills might ring about the timber for High Hope. Tell them the farm will be sending their own lorry." He hesitated in the doorway, added on a softer tone: "And have a good day!"

Gray eyes met blue in what seemed a timeless moment, then he was gone. Tina sat motionless until the sound of the Land-Rover had died away. . . . "Have a good day," he had said. And now she knew with a deep dismay that there could be no good days unless they were shared with him.

About mid-morning the bell went at the side door. She slid aside the curtain and opened it, startled to find Sandy there. He looked sweating and cornered. "Are you on your own, Tina? Can I have a word? I don't want Carrie to get wind I'm here."

"Come in. What is it, Sandy? Here, sit down. Carrie never comes in here during the mornings, so you'll be all right."

He looked relieved, but sat twisting his cap between his hands. "It's a right kettle of fish, hinney. I had to take a day off from the quarry."

Tina waited patiently. At last he lifted his head, fixed her with his vivid blue gaze. "I've found him, Tina. I've found Carrie's Lofty. Or I should say that he found me."

Tina felt the blood drain from her face. "*Lofty!*" She groped for a chair. "Sandy, you can't mean it?"

He nodded. "This Aussie bloke, Tina. And he just walked into my cottage, like any other Wall visitor."

"You mean—you didn't know—"

"How could I be sure, until I'd asked you his real name? All I knew was I had a Mr. Ames coming. Then, when he got talking, he gave the show away on all sides. Talking about the old days in the Air Force and courting along the Wall, and a lass he knew in these parts called Carrie. . . . You could have knocked me down with a feather, I can tell you. That's why I asked you about him—though by that time it was a foregone conclusion."

Tina was still struggling against shock. "But where has he been all these years? And he was English, anyway, not Australian—unless—"

"Aye, he was. I got all that out of him. He was taken prisoner, worked on the Railway of Death, as they called it, slaving for the Japs. But he survived, got in with a mob of Australians when the war ended, and decided to start a new life over there."

"And forget all about England?"

"Not deliberately, I'd say. He'd been half dead, beaten up, tortured. Nothing had much meaning any more, even the past. There'd been enough misery to almost blot it out. He said so. . . . Anyhow, he went down under, worked for a sheep-farmer and in the end got a place of his own, I forget how many square miles he said. And he's well lined, I can tell you."

"But why come back now? To look for Carrie?" Tina felt hope rising.

Sandy twisted his cap again. "I can't tell you that, pet. He wanted to see England again, found he had the money, I suppose, and fancied having another look at the Wall."

"Is he married, Sandy?"

"I doubt it, though he didn't say so in as many words."

Sandy fell into silence and Tina divined something was still troubling him. "Shall you tell her?" she asked at last. "Is that what's worrying you?"

"Well now, I'll tell you. When first I found out for sure, when you told me the name, I'd meant to keep it dark. He's got two more days here, that's all. I asked myself why I should speak up, why I shouldn't just let him walk on along the Wall and out of Carrie's life without her being a word the wiser. . . . Oh, I know you'll think it the meanest trick ever, but love makes you mean sometimes—unscrupulous. I told myself I'd never have a chance with Carrie once she knew about Lofty—that would be it! Whereas if I let him walk off there wasn't a chance in a million he'd ever come back. . . . It would have been so easy."

"But you couldn't?" Tina asked softly.

"That's just it. I couldn't, hinney. For it came to me after a sleepless night or two that if I'm as fond of Carrie as I say I am, then what matters is that she should be happy, not that I should grab what's rightly belonged to another man for years. Not but what I think he doesn't deserve her. . . . But that's not the point. I've decided now she's got to know. But how? It's a delicate kind of thing to handle. What would you suggest, now?"

He watched her anxiously. Tina, still struggling against incredulity, deeply touched also by Sandy's confession, found at first she hadn't an idea in her head. Then a brainwave came.

"Can't you ask Carrie to tea—say you've an ex-Air Force man staying with you, and he wants to talk about the old days in the service? You know Carrie—she won't be able to resist it. And then—I don't know—they ought to recognize each other, surely?"

"But you'd come too, pet? I couldn't handle it on my own."

"If you like, yes. Shall I ask her tonight, then?"

Gloom descended again. "What if she says no?"

"Then we'll think of something else."

"Remember I'm not exactly in her good books now."

"Leave it to me, Sandy."

He got up. "You're a canny little lass, Tina. I knew you'd sort it all out for me. And thanks." But there was a resigned sadness in his eyes as he left the house.

When Tina relayed the invitation that evening, Carrie brightened considerably.

"Air Force, eh? I wonder where he was stationed. We had a few Aussie blokes at my last Bomber Command station. Could be we've even met."

"It's a small world," Tina agreed cautiously. Now that the die was cast, she found herself deeply troubled over the whole thing, not really convinced, even now, that this was the right way to deal with such a cataclysmic event. Yet perhaps there *was* no right way. To warn Carrie of Lofty's identity seemed in one sense only fair, yet it would also give her time to get cold feet. Whereas meeting accidentally, her reactions should be much more natural, even if the shock proved tremendous. There was also the fact that meeting Lofty out of the blue could be construed into a miracle, and it was a miracle Carrie needed.

As for Lofty's possible reactions, they were as yet a closed book, and caused Tina considerable unease. Had Lofty any feelings left for his old Wall sweetheart? And if so, why had he not come to England years ago? Would it be to him just a pleasant and nostalgic episode from the fast past?

Even so, she told herself, feelings could be revived, new bonds forged. She was tugged both ways, wanting Carrie's happiness, yet sorrowful for the faithful Sandy, who had resisted a temptation most men would have succumbed to without a conscience.

"What shall you wear?" Tina asked, hoping Carrie wouldn't settle for one of her dull suits.

"What do you think? Mustn't let the side down." Tina knew she meant the Air Force.

"I think you should wear your new peach dress, the one you bought for spring coming. It's spring now, isn't it?"

"You could have fooled me." Carrie glanced out of the window at the wet lashing tree-tops below the house. "And it's got no sleeves. I could always wear that gray cardigan, I suppose."

"No!" Tina cried in despair, for the said gray cardigan did nothing but extinguish Carrie's delicate coloring.

"The cardigan would ruin it. You can wear your best coat, the white tweed, and take it off when you get there. Sandy's cottage is always warm."

And what do *you* know about Sandy's cottage?" Carrie asked sharply.

"He showed me round one day."

"He did, did he?" Carrie seemed suddenly put out. "You've seen more than I have, then. All right, the peach dress, if you insist. It'll be wasted on Sandy, but this other man might appreciate it."

The next day was bright but cold and the white tweed coat very necessary. Tina settled for a sweater and skirt with matching long jacket. They set out in good time along the woodland path; Tina by this time in wild alarm, Carrie mildly resigned.

"If I know Sandy Armstrong, it'll be a pretty rough tea," she remarked. "Slabs of bread and cheese, probably. And I can't think what he's doing away from the quarry at this hour."

They reached the cottage. Sandy met them at the door, displaying a cheerfulness which did not deceive Tina.

"Here you are, then! By, Carrie hinney, you're looking smart!"

"It's not for your benefit," Carrie retorted. "Well, aren't you going to ask us in?" He stood teetering on the doorstep, blocking their way.

"Well now, it's like this. My lodger, he's just gone for a stroll down the path yonder, toward the dig. Why don't you walk down and meet him, Carrie?—tell him tea's ready. It'll give you both the chance of a quiet crack about the Air Force."

"Oh, all right. What does he look like?"

"Tall—he's wearing a raincoat and a slouch hat—looks just like an outback farmer."

"Fair enough." Carrie walked on while Tina followed Sandy indoors. By the redly banked fire they faced each other.

"Isn't it awful?" Tina shivered. "I feel we're throwing her to the lions."

"Well, hardly that. Isn't it the miracle she's always wanted?"

532

"Yes, I know. As long as the miracle doesn't go wrong," Tina was still uneasy.

"Aye. Like yon last one, you mean? Seeing the Roman sentry?" he asked gloomily. "But it's up to them now. There's nowt more we can do, and if we've done wrong—well, she can't think much less of me than she does now."

He gestured toward the tossing branches outside. "Wind's getting into a nasty quarter. I shouldn't be surprised if we don't have a storm tonight. That's why I kept up a good fire. What about the tea-table, pet? Is it all right?"

Tina surveyed the spread table with its thick white crockery, the doorstep slices of bread and butter and bought cakes pathetically waiting on bare platters. But everything was clean, the milk in its jug covered with muslin, the big brown teapot warming at the hearthside. Tina gave her approval, then moved to the fire to warm her hands.

"I feel cold," she confessed. "But it's just panic, I know. They must have met now. I'm trying to imagine what they're thinking and feeling."

Sandy, who seemed too restless to sit down, reached to the mantelshelf to fill his pipe. "I only hope, for her sake, he's saying the right things, even if it means I've to give up hope myself."

"Poor Sandy," Tina said softly. "It's worse for you."

He roved the room while she sat silent, watching the fire. The tick of the clock seemed significantly loud. At times Sandy jerked back the curtain, peering sideways along the path. Tina saw the long plumes of the larches lifted and tossed by the savagely gathering wind. Surely the weather would drive those other two inside soon.

"No sign of them yet," he said on his third trip to the window. "Looks like things are going well, would you say?" His voice was divided between hope and despair.

"It's hard to tell," Tina fretted.

Suddenly Sandy stiffened. "She's coming. . . . On her own, though. Here, she mustn't see us looking!" And he blundered to the armchair and began a furious smoking of his pipe. Tina sat keyed to an unbearable nervous tension.

The door opened. Carrie stood there, her face blank and as white as her coat. For some time she did not move.

"Come in, come in!" Sandy urged her. "But you're on your own. Didn't you see him?" His attempt to be casual was pretty woeful.

She closed the door behind her. "He sent a message." She spoke tonelessly. "He doesn't want any tea. He's gone on walking up the Wall—said to tell you he'd have a sandwich at the pub later."

Tina, with another anxious glance at Carrie's blanched face, began quietly to make the tea, while Sandy hovered in an agony of uncertainty on the hearthrug. "Tea for three, then?" He tried to smile.

Carrie walked to a chair at the table, sat down, and covered her face. "Don't, Sandy—please don't make a joke of *this*."

"I'm sorry. You know me, always put my foot in it." His face was crimson now.

After a moment, she raised her head, looked hard at both of them. "You knew, then? You sent me out there to meet him? But of course you knew—his name and everything. And yet you were both wrong. He's not the Lofty I knew." Tina was shaken by the sorrow in her face.

"Not—" Sandy began.

Carrie dabbed at her eyes with a handkerchief. "Oh, the name's right. And in a sense it's the right man. But that's all."

Tina pushed a cup of tea toward her. "You've had a shock, Carrie. . . . Don't talk just now. Drink some tea."

Carrie looked at her almost without recognition. "Tea? Thanks." She took a sip, set down the cup and remained with her head down, her gaze on the table. At last she spoke again.

"I don't know if I can explain. . . . Oh, we recognized each other. At least I did first—he was a little slower. You can imagine how I felt. I could hardly speak. It was like a miracle. He seemed—just pleased, somehow, not shocked or anything like I was. Long time no see and all that kind of cheery banter—"

She sat dazedly gazing at the tea. "I—I didn't know how to deal with it, you see. He was a stranger. The Lofty I knew—instinct had always told me he was dead. And in a way my instinct had been right. The mistake was mine, thinking that after all those years a man could stay the same, with the same feelings. . . ."

She fell silent again. Tina poured some tea for Sandy, but he shook his head. She noticed his pipe had gone out and that his whole heart was in his eyes as he watched Carrie.

Carrie warmed her hands on the teacup. Tina saw she was shivering. "He told me all about working on the Burma railway, and then his release and going to Australia. That was the part I couldn't understand. It was just as if he'd changed personality during all that horror, so that nothing he'd said or done back here in England meant anything any more. . . . He's never married, either."

She stared in front of her. "But the bit that really shook me, really made me see how changed he was, was his attitude to the Wall. I told him about the Mithraeum temple and he just laughed, said what fanatics we used to be and wondered why we got so hetup about it all. Oh, he'd wanted to see the Wall again, just out of curiosity. But all his interest in archaeology—it's gone. He said—" her voice broke—"He said it was just an old ruin after all. He hardly mentioned it. All he wanted to talk about was Australia—he said he wouldn't come back to England for a fortune."

"Drink your tea, Carrie, please!" Tina pleaded.

"Let me get this off my chest first, there's a good girl. . . . Well, somehow I managed to keep it light. It wasn't really as hard as you might think because as I've told you this wasn't *my* Lofty. He was a brash stranger whose life had been turned upside down since I knew him. He couldn't even remember the names of the R.A.F. stations where he'd served—said the Air Force was a back number now anyway."

Carrie let out a long sighing breath and began to drink her tea. "There, that's about it . . . I suppose I could tell you a lot more, but it's enough to put you in the picture. I suppose you both thought me a fool all along, expecting anything better. And it was kind of you—I do appreciate it—kind of you to arrange it the way you did."

She drank her tea for some time in silence, while Sandy cleared his throat, unnecessarily knocked out his pipe and suggested to Tina that she fill up the teapot.

Suddenly Carrie turned on him. "I just don't understand *you*. After all this asking me to dances, chasing after me—you needn't have said a word. When you found out who he was, why didn't you just let him walk on along the Wall and out of my life?"

Sandy colored and cleared his throat. No words came.

"Well, why?" she insisted. "You took a risk, didn't you?" Tina noticed a return of firmness to her voice, an improvement in the previous chalky color of her face.

Sandy drew up another chair at the table. "It was all I *could* do, Carrie hinney. I'd tried all ways to make you notice me. All yon daft tricks I played, burying things on the dig, playing jokes—why, all I wanted was to give you a laugh. The same with 'Cushie Butterfield' on the pipes. I *meant* well, that was the trouble, yet all I managed to do was put you in a bad fettle."

He hitched his chair nearer hers. "Aye, and that Roman sentry affair. It all went sour on me. Yet that was my first try at being serious. . . . All yon fooling about, playing practical jokes—why, it was the way I'd always gone on with lassies in the past. They'd always seemed to like it. But I'd begun to see, just before the dance, that it wasn't getting me anywhere. So I says to myself: "Sandy," I says, "you've got to stop all this daftness. You've got to show her you can take a serious interest in the things *she* likes." And that's how I came to think up the Roman soldier bit. Only, like I said, it went sour on me."

Carrie was listening intently. Tina felt she ought to leave, yet she too was moved by his words.

"So it came to—to this Lofty," he stammered. "At last I'd found something I could do for you, to prove I—well, cared about you." His face was crimson now. "It was the one thing I could do to make you happy, even if it meant I had to lose out—"

Carrie reached out and touched his hand. "You great soft nitwit! You've behaved like a clot! What you didn't know was—even while you were carrying on with all those jokes—I—" She paused. "I know I tore you off a terrible strip over that Roman sentry. But I know now—why, it was the nicest thing you could have planned—"

She seemed divided between laughter and tears. Tina tiptoed to the door, unnoticed. Time to leave, she decided.

It would be tea for two, after all . . . .

Yet out in the gloom of the woods tears came to her eyes. Sandy and Carrie seemed at last on the brink of a warm understanding, even though it was built on the wreckage of Carrie's dream. While her heart glowed for her two friends, thoughts of Adam overpowered her. Would she and Adam ever sit like that, oblivious of everyone in the spell of their shared emotions?

Her pace dwindled. She had reached the burn where Rosie had sailed her boats. One of the frail craft was even now tossing in a miniature whirlpool under some boulders. She watched it blindly, struggling against a wave of intense feeling.

Adam . . . she knew now, without warning or reason, that she loved him. Mere physical fascination might have passed or been conquered. Now, despite their serious differences, she could no longer deny that her heart too was involved. She knew that she wanted his love, needed his worship, the same worship which Sandy, in his rough-hewn way, had for Carrie. And without it life would be as helpless and storm-tossed as Rosie's paper boat.

She walked home slowly, shaken by her discovery; now elated, now depressed. The rising storm, buffeting her at every step, reminded her of the day of tempest when they first met, suggested again all those elements of conflict they had known. Yet her love soared above and beyond despair. Neither reason nor past resentment could shake its strength and joy.

Carrie, being remote and absorbed on her own account, failed to notice the kindled restlessness of Tina. The next day was the last before Helen's return, and it seemed to Tina that events were sweeping them all along toward inevitable change. This feeling was intensified when she walked into Carrie's den after tea to find her grimly stripping her room of Air Force souvenirs. The Blenheims, the Spitfires, the Short Sunderlands, the Lancasters were wrapped up one by one and entombed in a cardboard carton, bound for the local Air Cadets' Club. The polished wings had already disappeared from above the mantelpiece and the pictures of uniformed groups had been piled into one heap and tied with string.

"Oh, Carrie!" was all she said.

Carrie closed the carton, slung about it and made several fierce knots. "Oh, Carrie, is it?" she said at last. "You know the Air Force motto—*Per ardua ad astra* . . . Through arduous ways to the stars. Well, I've been through the arduous ways, but I didn't find any stars. And my guess is that no one who lives in the past ever does. So don't be sorry for me. Just learn a lesson by it, as I have. And if you ever find you've made a big mistake, do what I'm doing now, cut the threads of it right out of your life and start again. You've got to be ruthless about it, however much it hurts."

She stood winding the rest of the string into a neat hank, her eyes fixed on the distance. "Don't be too sorry for me, Tina," she said softly. "I didn't just discover I'd been chasing an empty dream, I had my eyes opened in another way too. I've learned that a man may be rough and ready, tactless and sometimes infuriating, but still be one of the best men who ever breathed. . . . I've been blind, you know, blind and stupid all along. I've never even begun to get things into proportion."

She walked to the window, stood watching the lashing trees, still storm-tossed. "Maybe I've been too absorbed in history too. But don't worry that I'll ever parcel up the Wall and kick it out of my life. That's different. I began by loving it for one reason but ended by loving it for itself alone, the sheer fascination of it. Lofty hasn't spoiled *that* for me. For how could he, when he didn't care any more? That was the moment of truth, after all."

"I'm glad," said Tina. "I couldn't imagine you giving up archaeology or Wall history. I'm glad about Sandy too." Her voice was so wistful that for a second Carrie eyed her curiously. But the moment passed.

"We're just good friends," Carrie said. "Well, maybe more than that. Sandy knows I've got to have time to find myself again, to shake free of the past. He's a patient man at heart."

At supper Carrie seemed quite composed, though with little to say. Adam, after a shrewd glance or two, directed the conversation toward Tina, but with little more success. Since her cataclysmic discovery that she loved him, she could no longer be natural, could not hold his gaze, or properly concentrate on what he was saying. His nearness, combined with her shattering secret, were too much for her.

Fortunately Isa made a diversion, arriving with the pudding plus dire news of fallen trees and blocked roads farther north. "Aye, and we'll get it worse here yet, they say. Hark at that wind in the chimney! It made me that nervous I wouldn't like to say I'd got the coffee just right, for I was measuring it into the pot and lost count. Storms always get me gey bothered!"

Adam's eyes were alight with laughter. "Ah, but Isa, remember that text about a house built upon a rock—that's Hadrian's Edge. You're safe enough here, never fear."

"Aye, that's right enough. But there's another verse says: 'A house divided against itself cannot stand!' " Isa seemed to look significantly from Tina to Adam.

When she had gone Tina looked at her plate, her heart hurrying in a painful beat. How true it was, and it mattered little how much Isa knew of the conflict between herself and Adam. In many ways it was a house divided and Helen's return could only widen the rift.

What Adam thought she never knew, because at that

moment a gust of violent force hurled itself against the house. Adam said resignedly: "Seventy mile an hour gusts, by the sound of it. We'll be having the telephone lines down next, not to mention the electricity."

As if to prove him wrong the telephone shrilled. He got up to take the call in the alcove off the hall. When he appeared again his face was so grim and concerned both women looked askance.

"I've got to go out—at once," he announced. "Rosie Finch has been missing all day and they're getting alarmed. We'll have to organize a proper search party. She may be lying hurt somewhere, with so many tree branches coming down."

The women both got up. "Can I help?" Tina asked. "And is it because of going into the hospital?"

He shrugged. "That seems the obvious answer. I can't think why they didn't sound the alarm sooner. As it is it'll be like looking for a needle in a haystack. It's nearly dark and blowing the roof off the world. No, there's nothing you can really do—unless one of you can run along to Sandy Armstrong and rope him in. We'll need every man we can get."

"I'll go," Carrie said. "I know the woods better than Tina." And she was gone on the instant, stopping only to unhook an old raincoat from the hall. Adam turned to follow her, then looked back uncertainly at Tina. "Sorry, but there's nothing you can do. If you went out there we'd only have to get up another search party. You'd lose yourself or come to grief in five minutes."

It was not unkindly said, and there was even humor in his expressive glance at her gold kid sandals and cobwebby hose. There might even have been something more, she wasn't sure, an indulgent tenderness, perhaps. But the brief moment had come and gone. She heard him make a few rapped demands on the telephone, then the front door closed behind him and she heard the noise of the Land-Rover rounding the drive.

She stood undecided, quite wretched. Rosie . . . poor little Rosie crouching afraid and helpless in one of her many hidey-holes. It was unthinkable not to do something to help. Yet Adam had clearly counted her help as worth less than nothing. And reason told her why. She was unused to country dark and storm, she knew very little of the surrounding terrain except the woods and fields near the house. On the moor she would be useless, near the quarries even a menace. All hands would be needed to find Rosie and she could imagine Adam's wrath if she ran into difficulties needing rescue.

Yet she ached at her own helplessness. If only she could do something. . . .

It was then the idea came.

The odd thing she remembered was Rosie's precious china. She could hear the child saying: "I don't keep it here. I've got another secret place."

If so, surely it couldn't be so very far from the tree house, where Rosie's tea-parties usually took place? Could it actually be the old quarry, that overgrown chasm quartered and runnelled by fox and rabbit burrows? Would the searchers even think of combing a place so near to Quarry Farm?

The more she thought of it, the more instinct told her this was Rosie's lair. She had seen for herself muddy footmarks at the entrance of one of the ragged tunnels burrowing down into that dark tangle of undergrowth. It could just mean that the twins played there, but on the other hand it was convenient yet lonely, the very kind of secret place Rosie was likely to inhabit.

She could do one of two things, she decided—try to gain on the searchers and pass on her idea, or go herself to the quarry and try to find the child. The first she soon rejected. Why should the men listen to the hunch of a city-bred girl—for a hunch was all it was. And they could be well abroad on the moor by now.

The second also made her pause, hearing the fury of the storm outside and knowing the enveloping darkness that awaited her. Yet the longer she hesitated the more likely was Carrie to return and nip her plan in the bud.

All at once she sprang into action, ran upstairs to change into warm pants and an anorak, zipping herself into her boots. She collected a torch from the office, a flask of brandy from the medicine chest, and considered herself ready.

When she opened the front door, however, she shrank back again, appalled by the violence of the elements, black lashing rain driven on the wings of a mighty wind. She hesitated only for a moment, however, then pulled the front door behind her, took a deep breath and plunged out into the eye of the storm.

CHAPTER SEVEN

TINA dashed for the shelter of the trees, away from the merciless battering of wind and rain in the open drive. But running was impossible. For every two steps she struggled she was driven back one, while the glowing eye of her torch seemed only to accentuate the roaring blackness about her.

Eventually, she never quite knew how, she reached the woodland path leading to the quarry. And immediately her hope of shelter was dashed. The rough ride, tunnelling through the thrashing trees, was a wild funnel of wind. She found the tormented groaning of the trees so terrifying she switched off her torch and crouched against the undergrowth until her eyes became accustomed to the darkness. Better to see, as she could now dimly, the tossing movement of the high boughs against the paler sky, than be trapped within her circle of light, with all kinds of imagined horrors ready to crash down upon her.

It seemed an endless battle to the quarry edge. Though the force of the rain had lessened she was already soaking, her smart boots seeping damp. She was also fighting for breath, almost crying in her frustration and helplessness. Of only one thing could she be certain. Here at the quarry were no lights, no signs of a search party. As she had guessed, they were combing the moor farther afield.

At the quarry brink she flashed her torch on the huge matted mass of undergrowth shelving steeply to the quarry floor. She began to call Rosie's name, but realized the futility of it. The wind flung her words back at her, drowned by its roaring any possible thread of answering sound.

Now her heart sank indeed. Rosie could be there, but the only way to find out was to tunnel into that black sodden mass of bushes, to chance all the horrors of a sudden fall to the quarry floor. To a girl of these moors and woods an inborn instinct would have come to her aid; she would have known every warning sensation of sinking ground or the sudden sharp ring of limestone, would have known where best to follow the burrows and animal tracks into that black maze. But Tina, child of the sunlit Roman streets, of nights made dazzling by artificial lighting, was hampered by fear and ignorance.

It was at this moment, teetering on the edge of a nameless experience, that she thought of Adam, of his disparaging, almost amused glance at her silly sandals, his total acceptance of her uselessness. Why wasn't he here now, to take this weight of terrible responsibility and doubt from her shoulders? He would have been so calm, so capable, so utterly unflappable. . . .

Yet scarcely perhaps as wise as herself. He had viewed Rosie's disappearance as flight, while she with her woman's intuition knew it was much more likely to be a panic cowering in some familiar lair.

She realized that the wind had dropped a little. It was a strange moment's hush as if the storm gathered its forces for a mightier onslaught, but time enough to call Rosie's name again, and to fancy, as the eldritch shriek of the wind rose again, that there had been a faint answering pipe from the depths of the quarry.

It could have been anything, the shriek of some wild creature trapped by another, the cry of a bird even, but Tina knew she could not leave the matter in doubt now. There was a slender chance that it *was* Rosie. Somehow she must get down there and find out.

She flashed her torch to more purpose, saw the large

burrow which seemed the only point of access into the undergrowth, a foot-high tunnel with a muddy floor, dropping steeply through a tangle of brambles. Sure enough there were small footprints in the mud at the entrance, but how new or old she had no way of telling.

The entrance looked sinister. What if some fox or badger lurked down there in the blackness, turning perhaps to clawing savagery if cornered? What if she found, half way down, that the tunnel ended in a precipice and she was plunging to death or injury on the welter of hewn stone below? She knew from daylight walks that the rioting weeds and growth of many summers had successfuly screened the real dangers of the quarry. Only Rosie and her twin could know its secrets.

"If Rosie went down there so can I!" she said aloud, and gave herself no more time to hesitate. She forced herself into the slimy-floored tunnel face downwards, inching her body along, her torch held before her. Down, down, more steeply now, the bramble tendrils ripping her face, clawing her hands. She came to what was almost a clearing in the bushes, where she could feel the rain on her face again and had room to raise her head, seeing by her torch-light other smaller burrows leading off left and right. There was a strong animal stink, a scuttling somewhere ahead. She was sick with panic.

How far had she come? Twenty feet, perhaps? Was she still on the quarry lip, or lucky enough to be on a shallow slope that might take her down all the way? Impossible to tell. She began to fight and tear her way along the tunnel to the left, feeling buried, suffocated for ever in endless undergrowth, clawing aside spearing branches with bleeding hands, gasping and sobbing for breath. There came that scuttling again, a sudden yelp nearby. The quarry must be alive with wild life gone to ground for shelter from the storm.

Only let her escape from this suffocating horror! She knew she was teetering on the verge of hysteria, for she had always been subject to claustrophobia in confined spaces.

And then her thrashing light fell on dark limestone, the

bushes gave way and she found herself on a broad lip or terrace, falling away into more undergrowth and below again what looked like the quarry floor.

She subsided on the wet stone, her breath almost gone, still crouching on all fours like a beaten animal. And it was then she heard it, between two gusts of wind, a tiny lost voice from below.

She gathered her strength, called: "Rosie, is that you? Where are you?"

The faint answering cry sounded like: "In the hut."

"Where is it, Rosie?"

"Down here. . . ."

The voice sounded from the mass of undergrowth below. Then she seemed to hear Rosie shouting something about a hurt foot. Her blood tingled. How long had the child been lying hurt, perhaps in some noisome burrow?

But her torch revealed that the limestone descended in huge jagged steps to the bushes, that with an effort she might get down that way, though she was certain now Rosie's own path must have been much easier. Possibly she should have taken the right hand tunnel instead of the left. . . .

She rested a moment, then let herself over the top. She had to use one hand for her torch, and the descent was a heart-stopping scramble of near falls, of scraped limbs and bleeding hands now cut even more on the sharp edges of shale. The last step of all was five feet deep and here she just had to jump it, turning one ankle painfully as she landed.

Even now she was faced again with another tangle of bushes.

Rosie's voice called again, very near now. "I'm in the hut, Tina—right in the bushes!"

There was another burrow, a little larger this time. She crawled into it, expecting further horrors, but this time it was no suffocating passage of thorns, but widened out almost at once above her head. She was on a rough path standing upright. Blocking the way ahead was a ruined door. Flashing her torch high, Tina saw the shape of the old hut, so buried in countless years of undergrowth that it must be totally invisible by daylight.

She wrenched open the door. The rough interior was dimly lit by a failing torch, and Rosie herself crouched on what looked like an old eiderdown in the corner.

"Rosie darling! Are you all right?" Forgetting her own hurts she propped her torch against the wall, sank down beside her and took the child in her arms.

Rosie sobbed against her shoulder, her thin arms encircling Tina in a frantic grip. "Oh, Tina, I'm so glad it's you." She cried in earnest then, tears of relief and hysteria mingled. Tina wisely let her sob it out while some minutes went by. Her eyes became accustomed to the gloom and she saw worm-eaten rafters, walls of sagging planks and a weedy concrete floor. She guessed that only the huge envelope of tangled bushes was keeping out the rain and wind. Apart from the eiderdown and Rosie's precious cups on a rough shelf, the hut was totally bare and held a clenching chill.

Gradually Rosie was quiet. "It's my foot, Tina. I slipped coming down the quarry. I think it's sprained. I meant to go home when it got dark, after all. I don't care *what* she does to me—I was scared. But I couldn't walk."

Tina did not really take in the incoherent words, but turned her attention to Rosie's foot. She had shed her muddy wellingtons and the left foot was certainly swollen. Rosie winced as she gently prodded it.

"I don't think it's broken, Rosie. You can waggle it a bit, can't you?"

"Aye, I can. But it hurts. And I'm gey cold."

"Here, drink some of this." Tina remembered the brandy.

Rosie drank and grimaced. "It's like fire," she whimpered.

"Yes, but it'll make you feel warmer." Tina decided to take a mouthful herself. A moment ago she had seen Rosie's torch flicker and die. This meant, unless anyone found them, a night in the hut. She couldn't leave Rosie in the dark while she went for help and the child couldn't possibly get up the quarry with that foot.

At first she had been too absorbed in finding Rosie to notice the wind, but now it sounded on a new high note of howling chaos. Even in their sheltered position each gust shook the rough hut, whipped the branches against its roof, swirled dead leaves and twigs under the lintel of the door.

She tried to explain the position to Rosie, as casually as she could. "There are lots of people out looking for you, Rosie, but I was the only one who thought of coming here. We can't move you, so we'll just have to wait until we hear someone calling—" A faint hope, she thought.

Rosie snuggled up to her. "How did you come to think of here? It was my secret."

"Just a guess, Rosie." She questioned her about her own way in to the maze of bushes. Rosie was a little scornful.

"My, you are daft, Tina, coming down the stones. If you'd gone the other way there's a landslide—it come straight through to the hut." She huddled closer. "Listen to the wind—it'll blow all night, likely. We'll get our deaths of cold here."

"No, we won't. We've still got some more brandy. And here, you take my anorak—you've got to remember your sore throat. I've got a thick sweater." But Tina shivered as she removed the layer of padded nylon which had kept out every draught.

"We'll pretend we're camping," she told Rosie. "It'll be quite fun."

Rosie gave her such a look of misery her heart nearly stopped. "We'll be all right, darling. As soon as the wind drops I'll go out and keep calling for help."

Rosie sniffed a little. "I'm not feared—not now you're here."

"What is it, then? Are you worried about Matt being angry? We all know you're not looking forward to going into hospital, Rosie. I'm sure Matt will understand you just panicked."

Rosie stared. "The hospital?"

"Yes, wasn't that the reason you ran away?"

"No, 'course it wasn't!" Rosie's tone was scathing

as she said, "I'm no' feared of the hospital any more."

"How is that, then?"

"'Cos of Daring Denise. *She* was in hospital this week—in my comic."

"Oh!" Tina began to see light.

"Aye, she had a great time." Rosie warmed to the subject. "She was let to take the trays round. An' the doctors, they gave her rides in the wheelchairs. An' when the cross Sister made all the bairns unhappy Denise sorted it all out. . . . An' Denise, she liked Nurse Loveday best, 'cos she was pretty. Nurse Loveday was in love with Doctor Strangeways, but *she* thought he was after the staff nurse. So on the night of the hospital ball Denise pretended she'd had a collapse, to keep Staff on the ward, an' Doctor Strangeways, he danced with Nurse Loveday all night an' they got engaged. So Doctor Strangeways, he bought Denise a brand new bike—just what she'd always wanted!"

"Really?" Tina was divided between amusement and new concern. After Rosie had prattled away at some length about Daring Denise she said quietly, "Rosie, why *did* you run away?" She remembered now those earlier incoherent words—"I don't care what she does to me. "Was it Francey—was she cross with you?" she pressed.

Rosie stared again. "Francey? Why, no, it wasn't Francey."

"Don't you want to tell me, then?"

Rosie was silent. Tina heard a desolate sniff. Then:

"What's it like in prison, Tina?"

"*Prison*! Rosie, what are you talking about?"

"Not prison really, but those homes for naughty girls—re something."

"Remand homes?"

"Aye." Rosie's voice was muffled with tears now. "*She* said she would have me sent there."

"Who? Who said that?" Tina was disturbed. There was no doubting the fear in the child's voice. "Come on, Rosie—you can tell *me*."

The thin arms tightened about her. A new gust of wind, buffeting the front of the hut, sent a swirl of debris under the door. Rosie was shivering. "It was *her*—Helen Copeland. And she's coming back tomorrow. That's why I ran away to hide."

"Helen Copeland! Rosie, do you know what you're saying?"

Rosie hid her face. "She nabbed me, scrumping apples from Hadrian's Edge. She said naughty girls who stole apples got put in homes. But I didn't think she meant it—not then."

Tina was puzzled. "When was this?"

"Oh, before Bruno came. But it was after that I saw—" She broke off. "I wish I'd never seen them," she said passionately. "But I couldn't help it. I was in the tree house, an' I pelted them with acorns, just for fun. But she saw me."

"Wait a minute." Tina's mouth was suddenly dry. "Whom did you see? Helen and—"

But Rosie shook her head. "I'm feared to tell you. She'll find out."

"No, she won't. And even if she did, I wouldn't let her hurt you. Rosie, who was it?"

Rosie said slowly. "It was yon man—Mr. Irwin from the dig. They were kissing when I saw them."

"*Chris—Mr. Irwin from the dig?* Rosie, you're sure?" Tina was stunned.

"Aye, it was him. It wasn't the first time I'd seen them, mind. They kept meeting in the woods. I saw them from some of my other hidey-holes too. Bobby saw them as well. We used to track them."

Tina sat silent, fighting a sick horror. Chris—Bruno's friend. The treachery of it was almost unbelievable.

"But this was when Helen was engaged to Bruno, you mean?" she asked.

"Aye, it was. Bobby and me, we wanted to tell Bruno, but Helen, she waited for me out of school and said if we ever told a mortal soul she'd go to the police about the apples. She said Mr. Copeland would send me to a Home 'cos he's a magistrate and he wouldn't be able to let me off. She—she said they'd shut me up all alone if I was bad."

Tina's anger almost overcame her shock. "And all the time since you've been frightened? Is that why you wouldn't eat?"

"I felt sick a lot, thinking about it. And some nights I couldn't sleep. Bobby said she couldn't do it, but *he* was all right—it wasn't him who was nabbed wi' the apples."

Tina was silent. How simple, how fiendishly simple the whole mystery was becoming. Rosie's behavior, Chris's strange reluctance to dig for the truth concerning Bruno. But even so, this was only the beginning.

"Rosie, is that all? Is there anything else you have to tell me? Anything about Bruno?"

Rosie nodded. "Bruno found me crying in the woods. He made me tell him. I was feared, but he said he wouldn't let anybody hurt me. So I told him and he was right angry, but he said to keep quiet till he'd looked into it. Then—"

The child paused. "Then what, Rosie?" Tina heard her own voice sharpen with anxiety.

Rosie began to sniffle again. "Bruno had yon accident just a few days after. An' when he died I knew I'd no one on my side again, so I was still scared—of *her*. An' even when she went up to Thornriggs to stay, she sent a message to me by Jamey to say not to forget the apples an' that she'd see me when she got home again."

"And that's everything?" Tina asked.

Rosie nodded. "But she's coming home the morn! I'm feared, Tina."

Tina tried to pull herself together. Time enough, if Rosie slept, to mull over the horror of what she had heard. The first thing was to reassure the frightened child at her side.

"Listen, Rosie. She *can't* send you to a Home. And Mr. Copeland would never do such a thing. Why, how could you think so? Hasn't he always tried to help you all? Didn't he get you a council house? Doesn't he worry when you miss school and fall ill? Didn't he pretend not to see your tree house and shut his eyes to all kinds of things? Why, he probably knows all about the scrumping, anyway. Nothing goes on round here that Mr. Copeland doesn't know about."

"Aye, but she might ask him to—make an example of me. That's what she said."

"Rosie, I promise you he won't. She was only trying to frighten you to keep quiet. Now you're to stop worrying and try to get some sleep. The wind's not so strong again. I'm going to stand ouside and call for help. They may be searching the woods very near here. . . . Why, Rosie, don't you know it was Mr. Copeland who organized the search for you? He's out there now, you know, in all the wind and the rain, and he won't give up until he's found you."

"Is that right?" Rosie sounded awed.

"Of course it is. Now lie down, and let me put my anorak over you. Close your eyes and try to sleep. Promise?"

"Promise," Rosie said drowsily, and curled into a ball, hugging herself with her arms for warmth.

Many times that long night Tina stood shivering outside the hut door, often drenched with rain, calling and calling, hearing her voice tossed to silence on the wind. Many times too, she crouched beside Rosie, unable to sleep, hearing the endless creaking of the rotten walls, like a ship at sea, watching the leaves driven in droves under the door.

Chris—and Helen. . . . The one solution she had never guessed, would never have known but for Rosie. When had it begun? she wondered. Possibly even before Bruno had arrived. Hadn't Chris stayed six months at the dig on preliminary arrangements before Bruno came to Hadrian's Edge? And had it ended yet, or was it still going on? Was this why Bruno had taken another girl on that fatal journey? It seemed so, and in her heart he was entirely justified. It could have happened so easily. Bruno's feelings had always run high. Sickened and enraged by Helen's treachery, he was quite likely to do something reckless and unthinking. . . .

And she herself had thought that Matt was the man! Now she knew the meaning of Matt's parable about the matches. He knew, then? But what had been his part in this tangled affair?

Her thoughts roved wildly, her brain was battered and exhausted by thinking, by trying to imagine happenings in which she had no part. She was sickened by treachery, aghast at her own simplicity, angered for Rosie and her long ordeal of fear, saddened most of all for Adam, whose own blindness and resentment had kept him from the truth. . . .

Tina's head nodded, she dozed in a half-conscious state that gave her mental rest but did not entirely blot out the cold and discomfort. She tossed and groaned a little, then was roused by Rosie whimpering with the pain in her foot. A faint light penetrated the dirty hut window. The wind had almost gone and she thought she heard far shouts from high in the woods.

"Hush, Rosie . . . I think someone's calling!"

The voices sounded nearer. She called again outside, waited. There came a crashing in the thickets, then Adam's voice:

"Where the devil are you, Tina?"

Her heart bounded. "In the old hut—with Rosie!"

More crashing, a curse or two, then Adam and Matt burst through the tunnel and stood before her.

"Tina, are you all right?" Adam grabbed her shoulders, looked intently into her face.

"Rosie—" Matt began, but wasted no more words and entered the hut. She heard Rosie's squeal of joy, was aware that Adam had shaken her. "Tina, for God's sake! Were you out of your mind, coming down there in the dark?"

He was dirty and unshaven, his clothes torn, and one eye bruised and blackened. "Oh, Adam—" she faltered. "I'm sorry—I just had to come—I had a hunch about this place—"

He put back her tangled hair with a gentle hand. "You might have been killed—you know that?" His voice was anything but gentle. "I don't know how you did it—*you* of all people. Is Rosie all right?"

She nodded, feeling faintness. How had she done it? She remembered the noisome stink of the burrow, the terrors of the limestone stop. She had come through it somehow, but to think of it now was to see the sky spin. Adam's face swaying strangely. She cried out as his grip tightened. And as darkness came she heard him say:

"I've got you, Tina. You're all right. You've been wonderful . . . I was all wrong about you—"

Her last conscious moment was of strong arms bearing her up, of the dampness of his jacket against her face, of a feeling of absolute safety and joy . . . .

She came to a half-consciousness of swirling mists, in which she was being carried, of a fierce strength bearing her up through the clawing thickets, of voices and lights before an injection bit into her arm and she slept.

She woke to find herself in her own bed, with Carrie's face appearing in her line of vision.

"Ah, you're awake? Feeling better? It was just a faint and exhaustion. Not to worry." Carrie held her hand as the weak tears welled into her eyes.

"Is Rosie—"

"She's fine. They took her straight into hospital for observation before her op. Adam's gone to have a bath and sleep. The doctor gave you a jab. . . . You're quite a heroine, you know."

Tina gave her a tired smile. "Helen—is she back?"

"Not yet. I fancy Adam's bringing her over later, when he's rested. But you don't need to worry about her—"

"But, Carrie—" A rush of memory came. So much to think about, to agonize over. Helen was coming, and Adam didn't know. . . .

"No more talking," Carrie ordered. "You just close your eyes again. Oh, and Matt sent his love and thanks for what you did for Rosie."

Tina closed her eyes, not expecting to sleep again. It was suddenly all too much, her exhaustion, the stinging pain in her hands and arms, Rosie's horrifying disclosures, the knowledge that for Bruno's sake Adam must know, the further conviction that she didn't want to tell him, to increase his burden, the memory of his arms about her, fierce, possessive. . . .

She cried a little, then slept.

Waking again, she knew by the look of the sky that it was late afternoon. The pallid spring sunlight had a sleepy quality. Now she felt physically normal again and quite rested. Her bandaged arms and hands felt comfortable, but her mirror showed her dark-ringed eyes and a scratched face.

She dressed and went downstairs, meeting Carrie at the stairfoot, who exclaimed: "Tina, do you think you should be up?"

"I'm all right. Has Adam brought Helen?"

"Not yet, but he's on his way. Come on, a cup of tea is what you need. I've got it all ready in my den."

Tina was very quiet as she drank her tea, aware that Carrie was watching her anxiously. Her thoughts still revolved in a tight inescapable circle. She knew half, at least, of Bruno's story, enough to partially vindicate him for the girl in the car, but only if she revealed to Adam the sickening truth about his sister's treatment of Rosie Finch.

"Sure you're all right, Tina?"

She smiled and nodded. Carrie went on: "I nearly had a dozen fits when I found you'd gone last night. I rang all round the farms to try to contact Adam—ran the searchers to earth in the end at Moorhope. He nearly hit the roof when he heard you were out. I had to hold the phone a yard away until he stopped shouting. . . . He said"—she hesitated, smiling—"he said: 'She'll be no more use out there than a child—she hasn't a clue when it comes to country dangers . . .' " Carrie cocked her head, listening. "There's the car—they're back."

Tina felt a chill steal over her. "I'll wait here, Carrie. You go and do the honors."

Carrie left. Tina heard Adam's deep voice, a girl's laugh. Bruno's girl, the girl who had broken his heart. She clenched her sore hands. She couldn't meet Helen, she couldn't.

Carrie came back. "Adam asked if you were up. He says will you come and meet Helen? . . . Tina, are you *sure* you feel all right?"

"Yes, thanks." She got up, feeling weak about the

554

knees. Adam had asked for her and so she must go.

She followed Carrie into the living-room. Adam stood near the door, the bruise over his eye now livid. It gave him a curious swashbuckling appearance, she thought. He came forward to take her hands in his. "Tina, are you feeling better?"

She met the stern concern in his eyes, felt the grip of his hands tighten. "I'm fine, Adam," she almost whispered, overcome again by his nearness. Looking down, she saw that his hands were redly and cruelly scored by bramble spines. She remembered how he had carried her through the thickets, in the cold light of dawn. Then she realized she was slipping into a spell. She pulled her hands away, turned to face the girl who stood behind him. "This is Helen, Tina," he said quietly, and stood aside.

So many times she had imagined this meeting, but had never guessed Helen was so lovely. The photograph had done her less than justice. For though Tina saw the same even features, the same dusky shoulder-length hair, Helen's real beauty lay in a strange allure no camera could capture. Her eyes were the same green-flecked gray as Adam's, made huge by make-up and thickly fringed lashes. . . . But no, it wasn't just the eyes either, but a subtle bewitchment to turn all men's heads. Now Tina could understand how Bruno had worshipped this girl, until the cold moment of truth in the woods with Rosie.

"So you're Tina?" Helen smiled, her voice husky and attractive. "Poor Tina, I'm sorry we had to meet this way. It was all going to be so different." Her eyes were guarded.

Yes, so different. But she mustn't think of Bruno now or the tears would come. She struggled to concentrate as Helen spoke of Rosie's rescue. "How brave of you going down there in the dark! I couldn't have done it."

Tina eyed her steadily. "Rosie was badly frightened."

Helen's eyes shifted fractionally. "Oh yes, scared of going into hospital, wasn't it?"

Tina was silent. She turned to Adam. "I think Carrie's gone to see Isa about tea for you both."

"You've had yours?" He seemed disappointed. Then,

eyeing them both, he said: "I hope you'll soon get past the polite conversation stage. Helen hasn't many friends, I'm afraid."

Tina saw a flash of amusement in those dark-fringed eyes. Helen said carelessly: "How is it going on the dig? I believe you're another fanatic. I suppose Chris Irwin's still turning up Roman wonders? What's this I hear about a Mithraeum temple?"

As if you didn't know, Tina thought, and couldn't resist saying: "Why don't you ask him?"

"Ask him?" Helen spoke airily, with a shrug. "My dear, I scarcely know him. He's too dedicated for words—makes me feel quite stupid!"

Her eyes were restless now, almost trapped. Tina detected a trace of that instability which had been such a burden to Adam. Helen might be recovered from her breakdown, but basically she would always have neurotic ways. It was a thing one saw and knew instinctively, rather than from any reasoned facts.

Adam sent a curious glance to each girl in turn, as if he sensed some kind of verbal fencing he did not understand. But at that moment Isa panted in with the tea-trolley, and Tina took the opportunity to excuse herself. "You must have a lot to talk about," she said.

Again she sensed Adam's surprise and disappointment, but knew she must escape. When she reached her room she began to tremble with tension.

How ironic was Adam's hope of friendship between herself and Helen! Little did he know they were all sitting on a keg of gunpowder and that she was in charge of the fuse.

She lay down for a while, feeling a reaction of exhaustion after her meeting with Helen. Snuggled under her eiderdown she was on the verge of sleep when she heard raised voices downstairs.

She sat up, apprehensive. What was happening? One thing was certain, she could no longer rest.

On the upper landing she paused to listen again and could now detect Adam's voice, raised in anger, Helen's low and swift—and another, surely Matt's?

There seemed to be some kind of a showdown going on. If so, perhaps this was a good moment to join in. It could be Matt had already opened Adam's eyes.

She walked into the living-room, saw an arrested tableau of three figures, Adam facing an obviously hysterical Helen, Matt sullen and thunderous by the window.

"Is anything wrong?" Tina asked. "Shall I keep out?"

"No," Adam rapped. "In a way it concerns you, Tina. Sit down—you still look pasty-faced. And you're certainly in for a shock or two. Matt has just been telling me why Rosie ran away."

"A lot of nonsense—child's exaggeration!" Helen flashed. She was leaning against the table, smoking a cigaret with jerky movements.

Tina sat down in an armchair by the fire. "Rosie told you, Matt?"

Adam let out an exclamation. "Tina, you knew?"

"Rosie told me too."

Matt said grimly: "You might say I got it out of Rosie. And she thought, having told you, Tina, it didn't matter much anyway."

Helen spun round to look at Matt. "And you took her word—against mine? You know she's a little liar, always has been!"

Matt said stonily: "She has told lies, yes. All children do to get out of trouble. But she'd no need to lie about this. You threatened her, Helen, you can't deny it. You stole her sleep and made her sick. You frightened her to death. And all to keep your secret about Chris Irwin from your brother here."

Adam came to stand before Tina, magisterial in his anger. "Tina, you knew about Chris Irwin?"

"No. . . . Not until Rosie told me."

"Why didn't you tell me—earlier today?"

"I—don't know." Her own gaze fell before the blazing question in his eyes.

Adam turned again to Matt. "I don't quite see where you come into all this, my lad. There's been something between you and Helen, hasn't there?"

Matt looked distinctly sheepish. "Aye, there has. It started long enough ago, when Helen and I were just kids. We had this secret affair, boy and girl stuff. You remember you'd had that trouble with Jamey hanging about her, and as far as Helen was concerned you gave us both our marching orders. But we kept on meeting in secret. I wasn't like *Jamey*." He paused. "I loved her."

Helen laughed and stubbed out her cigaret. She went to perch on the arm of the chair opposite Tina, her movements graceful and studied. "We sent each other messages by pigeon post," she said. "At the time it seemed terribly exciting. And we used to meet in the woods and think ourselves very romantic, didn't we, Matt?"

Matt didn't return her smile. Adam said brusquely: "I remember—you had a sudden yen to keep a pair of pigeons. And I gave in to you, thought it would keep you happy."

"Oh, it did!"

"So there was this boy and girl affair." Adam took a restless turn down the room. "Then when did Chris Irwin come into the picture?"

Helen examined her pearly nails. "When he first came here."

"It didn't worry you that he was a married man?"

Helen flinched a little at Adam's rough tone. "Separated from his wife. Surely not quite the same thing."

"And you mean to tell me you began another affair with this man, all those months before Bruno came?"

"Yes." Helen met his stare defiantly. "I was serious this time—I knew that what I felt for Matt was kid's stuff. This was real. I also knew that if you found out you'd do all in your power to separate us, so we managed to keep it secret."

"Go on," Adam said. "Then Bruno arrived. And you—had another change of heart?"

The contempt in his voice made Tina wince. Helen colored wildly. "All right, then, I did. Chris and I—it had all gone rather stale by then. We weren't getting anywhere. I wanted him to run away with me, but he refused."

Adam said bitingly: "He showed a little more moral sense than you, then. But we were talking of Bruno. You transferred your attentions to him?"

Helen spoke in a low distressed voice. "Yes—I couldn't help it. To begin with, he fell madly in love with me. And there was this physical attraction—I found him fascinating. He was gay, too . . . Chris had always been on the serious side. I decided I wanted Bruno as much as he wanted me. For once you approved of a man in my life. I know you think I don't know my own mind, that I've been flitting from one man to another like a butterfly. . . . But it wasn't like that. What I felt for Matt—that was one thing. Then my feelings for Chris—they were deep enough at the time. But with Bruno it was love at first sight. And whatever I did afterwards I was crazy about him at the time and longed to be married to him."

Tina slowly raised her head. For the first time she detected a note of genuine emotion and distress in Helen's voice. Could it be true, then, that during that short time of her engagement Helen had given Bruno a taste of true happiness, of rapture even?

"What happened then?" Adam pressed.

"Rosie saw Chris and me in the woods. You've got to understand this, Adam—" She spoke passionately. "Though I'd fallen out of love with Chris—or thought I had—he wouldn't leave me alone. He was jealous, almost out of his mind about Bruno. He threatened to tell you the truth if I didn't keep meeting him. . . . That was how Rosie saw us. That was when I did everything I could to make her keep quiet. All right, so maybe I overdid it. But I was desperate, not only to keep *you* from finding out, but Bruno too. Only he found Rosie crying and got it out of her."

"So you and Bruno had a showdown? What happened?"

Tina held her breath. At last the gap was to be filled, the hiatus of time which had held only mystery for her.

Helen said slowly: "Bruno made a terrible scene. Then

he gave me an ultimatum. He said if I really loved him I had to prove it, to run away with him and get married at once. He said it was that or he wouldn't wait for the wedding. He said he wanted to be sure of me.''

"And you agreed?" Adam said.

"Yes. It was a way out. It would stop Chris eternally pestering me. And I would have Bruno. . . . Only everything went wrong.'' She flung a hand over her eyes.

"Yes," Adam agreed grimly. "He went off without you, didn't he? He took someone else!''

Helen gazed at him in bewilderment. "Went without me? What do you mean, Adam? I went with him.''

The gaze of all three listeners was riveted on her face. She became almost hysterical again.

"Don't you understand? *I* was the girl in the car! I was with him when the accident happened." She covered her face. "It was horrible. Once I knew he was dead I just panicked. I'd seen it coming and as soon as he braked I managed to fling the door open and was thrown out. All I had was bruises—and shock, of course.''

She took her hands from her face, her lovely eyes stony with unbearable memories. "I phoned for the ambulance and began running down the road toward home. I just wanted to blot it all out, to pretend it never happened. . . . I knew I could never face you with the truth, that we were running away—not without Bruno. My one thought was to get back to Hadrian's Edge before you'd found I'd gone. That's where Matt came in—''

Adam swung to look at him. "*You* were in on this?"

Matt nodded. "I was driving across the main road, making for Quarry Farm at the crossroads there. I nearly ran into her in the fog. She was soaked and terrified —nearly out of her mind. She told me everything. . . . Well, I'm not like other people. I'd always been loyal. She knew I'd never give her away, that I still loved her. She threw herself on my care that night. I took her home, helped her to get in the house without anyone knowing. And when the news of the mystery girl came out I advised her to keep quiet. I could see she was on the verge of a breakdown anyway. All I wanted to do was protect her.

Bruno was dead, and the gossip about him seemed to me at the time less important than protecting her. It was only after Tina came"—he turned his head slowly to look at her—"that my conscience began to bother me."

"The pigeons," she said. "That was why you were keeping in touch?"

"Yes. I had to warn her you were looking for the truth."

"Pigeons again!" asked Adam sarcastically. "Not surely at Turret House?"

Helen turned on him passionately. "All right, so it was childish, like spy games. But what else do you expect? You clamped down so hard on me. You read my letters, you vetted my callers, you made me almost a prisoner—"

"For your own good, and acting on the consultant's advice," Adam rasped. "You needed rest and quite. There had to be no risk of you being upset. But knowing you, my dear, it needed constant surveillance."

He turned to Matt. "So you got round all this. Pigeons, eh? Now wait a minute, I begin to get it. Didn't Charlie Phillips keep pigeons at the farm?"

"He does," said Matt. "Jamey didn't know it, but he was the go-between. I couldn't trust him not to talk if I sent letters by him, so I used to ask him to take a few birds up to Charlie when he made his farm deliveries. Then Charlie would give him some to bring back. Charlie knew what was going on, right enough, but doing it that way he had none of the responsibility of it. For it wasn't in his interests to fall out with Miss Coxon, as he only rents the farm from her. So that's how we kept a two-way message system going."

"Oh, so Charlie Phillips knew—and showed a blind eye?"

Matt smiled wryly. "He's sweet on Francey—if that explains it."

Adam's voice held a hint of controlled violence. "And this was how you repaid me for trying to help your family?"

Matt flushed an angry red. "Maybe it was *because* of it. I've always had to touch my cap to you, in a way of speaking. There hasn't been a time since I grew up when I haven't been beholden to you for something. Did it ever occur to you I might resent it? Not to mention the way you treated our Francey."

"Francey?" Adam rasped. "I've never treated Francey badly, whatever you may think. I admit that at one time it may have begun to look that way, but as soon as I realized there was talk I dropped her pretty quickly."

He turned a shoulder on Matt. "We're digressing too much. Helen, I haven't finished with you yet. Where does Chris Irwin come in the picture—now?"

Helen paled a little. "I've been seeing him again. . . . Don't look at me like that, Matt. You surely didn't expect—Oh, but I suppose you did. You thought things were getting back on the old footing, didn't you, back to pigeon post and romantic secrets. You're a fool, Matt! Since Bruno died there's been no one but Chris. He still loves me. He moved heaven and earth to see me, to ask me to marry him. His divorce will be through soon and nothing you can do will stop me, Adam—"

She paused for breath. Adam's jaw was tightly set. "You mean he's been seeing you—at Turret House?"

She gave a defiant smile. "I used to go to bed early, but my bedroom was on the ground floor, remember? It wasn't too easy to give Miss Coxon the slip."

"You mean he drove up there—late at night—and wasn't heard?"

She smiled again. "Charlie Phillips again, I'm afraid. He showed Chris a back way in to the farm through Thornriggs plantation. You see Chris was doing him a favor too. He used to drive Francey up with him sometimes. I'm afraid she's given up hope of you, Adam. It's Charlie Phillips now. And of course it all helped to keep your suspicions off Chris—seeing Francey in his car."

Adam drew a deep breath. "So you were too clever for me—I admit it, my dear. And how long will it take you to tire of Chris Irwin, whether you marry him or not?" The contempt in his voice was scorching.

Helen said sombrely: "I won't tire of him, Adam.

Chris can look after me—better than you can. We've come very close again through Bruno's death. Why not, since we both loved him? Chris loves me and I need him and want to be his wife. Anyway, I shall be twenty-one in a few months, and your guardianship of me will be over. You'll be powerless."

"As you say, I shall be powerless." Adam threw his cigaret end in the fire. "And now perhaps we've had enough of explanations to be going on with." He turned to Matt. "Thank you for coming, Matt. And I appreciate all your kindness to Helen, mistaken though it was. But you showed less than friendship to Tina, deceiving her as you did about her brother's good name. Don't you think you owe her an apology?" And he gave Tina a look that almost stopped her heart.

Matt tore his eyes from Helen. He was pale and Tina knew he had not recovered from the shock of her last disclosure. But he made an effort and said quietly: "I'm sorry, Tina. We were friends and I treated you badly. It was on my conscience all the time, but I suppose I was just weak where Helen was concerned. I don't expect you to understand all that. I just couldn't help myself."

"Don't worry, Matt," she said softly. "I think I do understand." For if Matt's feelings for Helen were anything like her storm of emotion for Adam she could forgive him anything. She was remembering too the pathetic naming of his pigeons. "Dark Joy" and "Hope On". She understood so much more about him now. And she pitied him deeply.

"And thank you again for all you've done for Rosie," Matt said gruffly. "Last night—and all the rest of it. She thinks the world of you and always will."

Now he faced Helen and at the expression in his eyes a dead silence fell on the room. There was guilt and even pity in her eyes, but an underlying defiance too. "I'm still trying to make allowances for you, Helen, for what you did to Rosie."

"How was I to know she would take me so seriously?"

"I think you did know, or you wouldn't have tried it on. As for Chris Irwin—" He broke off as if the name had choked him. A slow flush crept up his fair-skinned face. "You were right, Helen, I did believe we were getting back on the old footing—playing pigeon games again and all that. . . . As you say, I was a fool. Blind and stupid too. You were just using me, weren't you, even having a secret laugh because I was so easy to deceive. But it's over now, Helen. You've cured me. And I can even thank you for it. Otherwise I might have wasted more years of my life on you. You're not the Helen I once thought you were. Perhaps you never were."

He swung to face Adam: "As for you, Mr. Copeland, you meant well, but you tried to do too much. I've always had a deal of pride and I've counted a lot of your ways plain interference, kind though it was. You never did rightly understand us."

"Maybe I understand more than you know," Adam said in a low voice. Again his glance found Tina's. "And all thanks to Tina here. She has bridged a gap between Hadrian's Edge and Quarry Farm. She proved that by Rosie's trust in her. I hope it need never be broken again."

Matt hesitated. "Well, we'll see, Mr. Copeland. There'll be all kinds of changes coming, what with Francey courting and—"

He broke off and made for the door, but he turned to give Helen a long sorrowful look, as if imprinting her face on his memory. Then, suddenly drawing himself up straight, he gave them all a grave "Goodnight" and left the house.

Helen yawned and reached for another cigaret. "Poor old Matt! He was always so faithful. But he'll soon find some willing girl who doesn't mind living at his pace."

Tina, uneasy now there were only three of them and with a queer wild panic that she might be left alone with Adam, now got up. "I think I'd like to go back to my room now, if no one minds. I feel—"

She swayed a little, in a wave of dizziness. Adam made a swift movement to steady her. "Tina, are you all right?" She nodded. "I have so much to say to you." he finished.

Yes, she knew. The proud, the arrogant Adam

Copeland would have to humiliate himself to her, to admit he was wrong, to ask her forgiveness. And she couldn't bear it. It might be all owing to her, but it would be pain indeed to see this man reduced so before her eyes.

"In the morning, Adam, please," she whispered. "I can't take any more tonight. I've so much to think about, too."

He released her, his eyes sombre in the fading light. "In the morning, then. Goodnight, Tina."

The gentleness in his voice almost unnerved her again. Under the watchful eyes of Helen she left the room and escaped upstairs, shaking with nervous exhaustion.

Much later Tina woke from a troubled sleep to hear the sound of a car, then the opening of the front door and Chris's voice. What was happening now? It must have been an hour later that, still awake, she heard the car leave again.

Sheer weariness overcame her again. It was only six-thirty by her watch when she woke next morning. She got up and dressed, knowing she must be alone and out in the air for a while to calm herself. By seven she had passed Sandy's cottage, skirted the deserted dig and climbed up a little way to the mounting ruins of the Wall. Ahead it swung steeply up into the mist toward Sewingshields, holding a strange nebulous quality in the uncertain light.

She sat on a boulder to keep her feet from the soaking turf. Sheep grazed by her undisturbed, their lambs fat and flourishing beside them.

The Wall. . . . Her gaze on the hoary pile of stones, cut with such meticulous exactitude by her own countrymen so many centuries ago, she thought again of the plaster model, the toy of her childhood. How utterly different and vivid had been the reality. She remembered her words to Adam—"It was built to separate the Romans from the barbarians," and his easy laughter; recalled too his kiss in the rain on that fateful journey back from Thornriggs. "That's how we barbarians kiss—" Now she ached and longed for just such another kiss, with all conflict gone between them.

For now that other wall, the invisible barrier between

them, had fallen. Adam knew the truth, that Bruno was blameless if foolish, that all the fault lay at Helen's door. Yet she was still wretched. She had dug for truth and found it as unexpected as the remains of the Mithraeum temple unearthed on the dig.

And it could only mean Adam's humiliation before her. Could any man bear to be proved wrong by a woman? Today, this very morning, it must happen, and her dread rose like a sickness inside her.

The spring sun pearled the mist, the long dawn shadows appeared. She heard a hail from the dig below and saw Chris shading his eyes to look her way. She waved uncertainly. Here was another confrontation she dreaded.

He climbed toward her with a certain deliberation. He met her eyes soberly and without flinching. "Hallo, Chris, you're about early," she said.

"I haven't slept much. I fancy few of us did last night." His eyes were pleading. "You know everything now, don't you, Tina?"

"Yes, I do."

"I hoped you might understand—as you're in love yourself."

She started and crimsoned.

"Oh yes, I know about it—you and Adam." He found a seat on another boulder, folded his arms and stared at the ground. In his thick gray sweater and a blue scarf at his neck he looked almost boyish, she thought. "You see, Tina, being in love makes one sensitive to it in others."

"I suppose so."

He picked up a twig and began prodding at the soft turf. "I was so hopefully in the toils myself, I could spot other people's emotions a mile away. . . . Tina, it seems pretty feeble to say I'm sorry. But I do mean it. I hated leading you up the garden, but by the time Helen fell for Bruno, I was in so deep and was in such uncertainty and misery—"

He paused. "It must be pretty plain to you now that I'm crazy about her, have been since I first set eyes on her. It might be hard for you to understand just what her kind of haunting beauty does to a man. And her *faults*—heaven knows I'm aware of every one—they don't even matter beside my feelings for her."

"You concealed it very well, Chris. I never imagined—"

"I had to conceal it, for her sake at first, then for Bruno's. Bruno was my friend, Tina, and you know how much he meant to me. But I can't tell you the hell of jealousy I went through when she turned to him."

"Didn't you hate her for it?"

"Yes and no. Even then I felt I couldn't give her up. I was possessive and demanding. But Bruno's death—"

His eyes met hers, bleak and sorrowful. "I would never have wanted it *that* way, God alone knows. But she did turn to me again. I'm not going to belittle what she felt for Bruno. It was everything a rapturous love affair can be. Her feelings for me had never been in the same street, but she'd looked up to me, depended on me. I think she knew from the first that I could manage her whims better than anyone, even Adam. So perhaps it was natural for her to turn to me in her grief. . . . And then I got the news that my divorce was going through. That's why I turned up at the house last night, though I didn't know then Rosie had told everything."

"How did Adam take it—last night, I mean?"

"He was cold and sarcastic, but very controlled. And what's more he's given in, Tina. Helen and I are to be married."

"Given in?" It sounded so unlike Adam she could only stare.

Chris got to his feet. "You might put it this way. She's nearly of age, anyway. He probably knew we'd just go ahead then whatever he said. But it was rather more than that. I think he's realized he can't go on protecting her for ever. She has to make her own decisions, her own mistakes. She's not a child any more. He said as much. As if he'd almost washed his hands of her. I think his attitude upset her. After all, she's been under his thumb for so long—"

"But she has used him too, Chris."

"I know. I've told you, I'm not blind to her faults. But I know I can handle them. We're going to be happy, I'm convinced of that. You haven't seen Helen when she's gay and carefree—she's a different person. . . . Oh, I know she behaved badly over Rosie, but I don't honestly think she really considered the hurt she was causing. With Helen it's the moment that counts. She was in a jam, and took the first impulsive way out. And I honestly think she's ashamed now."

Tina looked her doubts. Chris stopped and took her chilled hands in his. "We've all got faults, Tina. We're all human and vulnerable. I hope you'll forgive us both one day."

"I expect I shall. It's just that—it takes time to readjust everything."

"I know." He dropped her hands. "I hope you and Adam will be happy."

She stopped him with a stifled sound. "Don't—we haven't even spoken about it."

They talked a while longer, Chris eager to explain each deception, each reason for his off-hand behavior with her. She could well have done with less of it, for his timing was wrong. Details did not matter at this stage, when realization was so acute and overpowering. At last she stopped him.

"You don't have to explain yourself to me, Chris. I know that, whatever happened, you were still loyal to Bruno, in your own way. And none of it actually matters now, does it?"

"I expect you're right." He stood up. "But you know, don't you, Tina, I hated deceiving you? And if there's anything I can do to help you—"

She shook her head. He regarded her for a moment longer. "It'll be all right, Tina, you take my word for it. You and Adam. It's too right not to happen." His hand closed over her shoulder for a moment, then he had gone, running down the slope with his long-legged stride.

Tina watched him disappear into the trees, her eyes misty.

She had leaned on him in the past in so many ways,

unaware that the man she thought she knew so well had so many secrets from her. How naive she had been! She knew now that love had the power to change all lives beyond recognition.

And now at last Adam's burden was lifted. Chris seemed confident he had the strength and staying power to shoulder all Helen's moods. And it was just possible he would succeed. Marriage was probably the one stability Helen needed.

"You'll get a chill, sitting there!" Adam's voice roused her.

She whipped round to find him standing over her, his broad shoulders huddled in a duffle coat, his face sardonic as ever under the wind-blown thatch of black hair. He had approached her over the moor from the rear, Gyp at his heels. "We're all abroad early this morning. I saw Irwin talking to you." Like Chris he eased himself down to the neighboring boulder. "I imagine he has told you I've consented to their marriage.'

"Yes, he did."

A silence followed. Tina's heart beat an uneasy tattoo. "But that's not what I want to talk about," he said firmly. His gaze, steady and piercing, had gone past her to settle on the outline of the Wall snaking up into the mist.

"Now you see it, now you don't," he mused. "It's something in this light, isn't it?"

Was he playing for time, she wondered, hating the moment when he would have to admit all his past mistakes?

She waited, her gaze on his face.

"I admit I was attracted to Francey, quite fiercely at one time." He hesitated, then looked her full in the face. "It was purely physical, you understand. In other words, even while I was attracted, I was under no illusions about her—her vanity, her selfishness, her neglect of those children." He smiled grimly. "For a time I even persuaded myself that I was a good influence on her, that to please me she was really trying to do better for them. And so she did—for a time."

"And then?"

"Then I began to hear the gossip. I realized that my association with Francey might be wrongly construed. Country people are realists in these things, and in their eyes Francey was no better than she should be. I saw that I was getting in too deeply, that I should either have to leave Francey well alone or else marry her. It was, you might say, a moment of truth and pulled me up pretty sharply. I saw I had done her a wrong by being seen with her at all. And my conscience gave me such a bad time I nearly did decide to marry her."

Tina held her breath. "But you changed your mind?"

"Yes." He eyed her soberly. "Two things happened just then. One, I found Francey had been lying to Matt about our relationship, hoping to force a wedding. And two, you suddenly appeared on the scene."

"But surely—"

He laid a finger on her lips. "You were going to say that wasn't the end of Francey? Too true it wasn't. Remember that at first I felt nothing but resentment toward you, God forgive me for it. I was also trying to shake Francey off without being too brutal about it. The climax came on the night of that supper-party. I don't know if you picked up any of the undercurrents."

Tina smiled faintly. "I certainly did. But you deliberately asked her, as a guest. Wasn't that—"

"Incompatible with trying to shake her off? Not really. I wanted to see *you* in my house, infinitely more beautiful than she was, and with an ease of manner she could never hope to copy. It was cruel, perhaps, but I think you once said that with me honesty and cruelty were the same thing?"

Tina's face flamed, but she kept silent.

He smiled again. "It just so happened Francey was trying the same game, with Chris Irwin. You probably saw I was still capable of jealousy, still not quite cured. But Francey had got the message. And when I did tell her, a day or two later, that I wouldn't be seeing her again, she stormed at me about you like a wildcat. I denied nothing, admitted nothing."

"So that's why she hated me," Tina said quietly.

"Sorry, but that's why. Knowing young Francey, she would have resented you anyway."

"And I thought—I actually suspected that she might be the girl with Bruno."

He shrugged. "Being Francey, she no doubt cast her eyes on him. She could never resist flirting. But you can take it from me Bruno wasn't playing. . . . The rest doesn't take long to tell. Francey retaliated in her own way, by falling back into her old neglect of the house and the twins. But you already know all that."

His tone changed. "That's enough about Francey. I just wanted you to get the record straight. It didn't take me long to change my mind about you, either. Oh, the resentment was still there, but I began to see a girl brave enough and determined enough to stay on in an inhospitable household to clear her brother's name. I was impressed, believe me."

"Not inhospitable—never that! Hadrian's Edge—it's become like home."

He turned her face gently toward him. "You really mean that, don't you?" She saw a deep happiness in his eyes. "Despite my unforgivable behavior."

"Don't talk of forgiving, Adam. I can't bear it. And—well, I said a lot of hard things too. I'm sorry."

"You had a right to say hard things. I deserved every one of them." She felt his hands on her shoulders. He raised her gently to stand facing him. "Tina, you know, don't you, that I love you."

She closed her eyes, unable to meet the brilliance of his gaze.

"Yes, I know now," she said faintly.

"Then look at me."

She obeyed, trembling. "I love you—I've loved you for ages, but I've been fighting it—"

"You won't have to fight it any more." His arms tightened about her, his urgent kisses were rough and possessive.

"No Wall now?" he whispered.

"No Wall. . . . Oh, Adam!" She clung to him again.

It was a long while before he released her, to a dazed

realization of a climbing sun, of an impatient Gyp
barking at their heels. Hand in hand they walked down
the dewy slope, still in an almost stupefied silence. There
was so much more to say, so much to explain. Like all
lovers before them, they would trace every step of their
tempestuous relationship, every misunderstanding, every
stolen happiness. But these first moments of shared
emotion needed no sound but the thrushes belling in the
woods and the cries of the sheep on the moor. . . .

Three weddings followed in quick succession at
Hadrian's Edge.

First of all came Chris's and Helen's, a modest affair at
Hexham register office, as they were to fly to Rome
immediately afterwards. Chris had finished his work at
the dig and was handing over to a local archaeologist who
would supervise the last of the excavation. The
Mithraeum temple had attracted worldwide interest,
ensuring that Bruno's name would be remembered for
ever in archaeological circles. Now Chris and Helen were
to live at his Rome apartment, while he went back to
lecturing.

Helen looked radiant, with a new peace in her eyes,
Chris so gently attentive Tina began to believe at last that
this marriage was inevitable and perhaps in the end, good.
Adam attended throughout in imperturbable calm, but
little enthusiasm. Perhaps, Tina thought, he was
conscious of failure, a little resentful that another man
should succeed with the baffling Helen where he had used
too heavy a hand for too many years.

The second was Carrie's and Sandy's, Sandy having
proved less patient than Carrie predicted. It took place in
the village chapel, decorated with more vigor than
elegance by Isa, who was a great believer in the pictorial
value of masses of bluebells crammed into glass jars.
Carrie, acting on Tina's advice, wore a cream lace suit
and a cartwheel hat of pale turquoise, which she insisted
on ripping off as soon as the reception party began at
Hadrian's Edge. There was a slight hitch over the cutting
of the cake, as the bride had to be almost forcibly
removed from an impassioned argument with a local

farmer about the exact line of the Vallum as it crossed his land. But Sandy had his revenge with a spirited rendering of 'Cushie Butterfield' on his pipes, which made Carrie publicly complain and privately glow. "I suppose I'll have to get used to them" she confessed to Tina. "Anyway, we've made a bargain. I'm going to all his barn dances and he's promised I can start on the Roman bake-oven the minute the honeymoon's over!"

Sandy whispered to Tina: "This was a day worth waiting for, pet! Aye, and thanks to you for most of it. I wish there was something I could do in return."

"There is," Tina dimpled. "You can promise to play the pipes at my wedding, too."

This third wedding took place in the village church, and to Tina's intense joy her father was able to pay a flying visit to attend the ceremony. It was quiet but traditional, Tina in a drift of white chiffon and with an ecstatic Rosie as bridesmaid, now recovered from her operation and pretty as a fairy in pale clover pink. Even Daring Denise, Rosie boasted, had never yet been a bridesmaid!

The wedding itself Tina ever afterwards remembered as a strange confusion of joy; the sound of Adam's responses, made with a ringing confidence, her father's face showing a new serenity, the church crowded with friends and well-wishers, and last but not least Adam's possessive kiss in the vestry, when she had signed her maiden name for the last time.

The reception was again at Hadrian's Edge, where Isa stunned all comers in an outfit of saxe-blue satin, its cape-collar studded with crystal beads. Perhaps stimulated by the champagne, for Isa allowed herself a glass of wine at a wedding, she triumphantly produced text after text suited to the occasion. She did however confess to Carrie that she might find the trifles on the heavy side, as she had been upset by one of the caterer's men the day before, whom she had caught playing 'Blaydon Races' on her precious harmonium.

Matt was there, looking strange and awkward in a formal suit, but there was nothing awkward about his sincere wishes for Tina's happiness.

"It'll be your turn one day, Matt," she said softly. "And don't forget I'm going to keep an eye on Rosie for you. No reason at all why you shouldn't have a girl now."

"I think I'll stick to pigeons for a while," he smiled, but Tina noticed that he spent most of the reception shyly eyeing one of the village girls who had come in to help. She looked strong, pretty and sensible and Tina wished him joy with all her heart.

Her father took her aside at one point. "You've chosen well, darling. And Bruno, he would have approved too. Adam will never let you down, I'm sure of that."

"I'm sure too," she whispered, clutching his hand.

The high spot of the reception was undoubtedly Sandy's surprise rendering of "Arrivederci, Roma" on the Northumbrian pipes, where sincerity and feeling perhaps topped performance. Adam at this point had almost disgraced himself by laughing, and Carrie had confessed to Tina that Sandy had been practising that particular number for weeks. "It did literally drive me up the Wall," she complained. "I had to go up there to escape from it."

At last Adam and Tina left in a shower of confetti and a new car, but once on the Military Road, Tina exclaimed: "Adam, where are you going? We're going the wrong way."

"I know. I want to show you something."

By the rough sloping field which had once been the bustling Roman fort of Carrowbrough he stopped the car, and led her across the grass.

The ground was dry on this occasion, the rough sloping pasture gilded by June sunshine, the sheared sheep dazzling in their whiteness. Before them, the Tyne Valley bloomed in all the tints of summer, the far sapphire line of Cross Fell was clear against an azure sky. And here, at Coventina's Well—

"Oh," gasped Tina. "Wild forget-me-nots!"

And forget-me-nots there were, a wide smother of them under the rough wall, so that even the iron-rusted pool was invisible. Tina gazed at the delicate blue cloud, like specks of fairest sky trapped in a lake of green.

"I promised you, didn't I?" Adam's arm was about her. "I promised you that in June there'd be forget-me-nots at Coventina's Well. Exactly the color of your eyes."

Tina stood radiant, her gaze roving northwards to the many-colored moor, to the dark ridge where the Wall looped and climbed eternally into a lavender haze of distance. "I never knew your country could look like this," she said. "When I came, it was so bleak and cold—and I was so unhappy . . . I wonder what kind of a text Isa would find for this."

"Oh, I can tell you that, but only if you'll stop batting your eyes at me like that, young woman. The text is—" He hesitated, said softly: "For lo, the winter is past, the rain is over and gone—"

Tina smiled up into his face. "And the time of the singing of birds is come," she finished.